THE FIRST PR

Ashapurna Debi was born in 1909. Her conservative family did not send her to school, but encouraged by her mother, she learnt to read and write on her own and published her first poem in the children's magazine *Shishu Saathi*. Married at fifteen to Kalidas Gupta of Krishnanagar, she continued to write with his support. *Pratham Pratisruti* (1964) is the first of a trilogy that includes *Subarnalata* (1966) and *Bakul Katha* (1973). Translated here as *The First Promise*, it won her the Rabindra Puraskar in 1966 and the Bharatiya Jnanpith award in 1977. Ashapurna published 181 novels, 38 anthologies of short stories, and 52 books for children. She died in 1995.

Indira Chowdhury was formerly Professor of English at Jadavpur University, Kolkata. A PhD in History from the School of Oriental and African Studies, London, her book *The Frail Hero and Virile History* (OUP, 1998) was awarded the Tagore Prize (Rabindra Puraskar) in 2001. She also compiled the Supplement of Indian English words published in the *Oxford Advanced Learner's Dictionary* in 1995. In 2006, she was awarded the New India Fellowship for her forthcoming book on the institutional history of Tata Institute of Fundamental Research. Her latest book, (co-authored with Ananya Dasgupta), is titled *Homi Bhabha: A Hundred Years* (Penguin India, 2009). In 2007 she founded Archival Resources for Contemporary History, an archival consultancy service which enables institutions and organisations to set up their archives. Indira Chowdhury lives in Bangalore with her husband and daughter.

THE FIRST PROMISE

REVISED EDITION

Ashapurna Debi

Translated from the Bengali *Pratham Pratisruti* by
Indira Chowdhury

Orient BlackSwan

THE FIRST PROMISE

ORIENT BLACKSWAN PRIVATE LIMITED

Registered Office
3-6-752 Himayatnagar, Hyderabad 500 029 (Telangana), INDIA
e-mail: centraloffice@orientblackswan.com

Other Offices
Bangalore, Bhopal, Bhubaneshwar, Chennai, Ernakulam, Guwahati,
Hyderabad, Jaipur, Kolkata, Lucknow, Mumbai, New Delhi, Noida, Patna

Ashapurna Debi's *Pratham Pratisruti* was first published in 1965.
This translation is from the 33rd reprint published by Mitra and
Ghosh, Calcutta, 1995.

ISBN: 978 81 250 3790 3

Typeset by
InoSoft Systems
NOIDA

Printed in India at
Glorious Printers
Delhi

Published by
Orient Blackswan Private Limited
1/24 Asaf Ali Road,
New Delhi 110 002
e-mail: delhi@orientblackswan.com

TRANSLATOR'S ACKNOWLEDGEMENTS

I started translating *Pratham Pratisruti* in 1996 and completed it in 2000. The rest of the time was spent in looking for a publisher who would publish the text in its entirety. I am very grateful to Hemlata Shankar of Orient Longman for taking up the project with such eager interest. I also thank R. Sivapriya and Vinita Nayar for their editorial suggestions that helped me tighten the translation significantly.

Jashodhara Bagchi's wholehearted keenness about this project has sustained me in more ways than I can say. I have gained much from my consultations with Sibaji Bandyopadhay, Nandinee Bandyopadhyay, Krishna Banerjee, Sutapa Bhattacharya, Bhaswati Chakravorty, Swapan Chakravorty, Amlan Dasgupta and Nabaneeta Dev Sen, who were always willing to discuss the novel and specific translation problems. My discussions with Shivani Banerjee-Chakravorty in the early days of the project have been particularly useful. Abhijit Sen has been extremely helpful in tracing background information, including the cover photograph. Anuradha Roy's comments on an early draft of the translation have been very insightful. I am grateful to them all.

Debts of friendship can hardly be repaid with an acknowledgement. Vivek Dhareshwar read and commented on the draft and delighted me by saying that he had at last grasped the notion of 'abhiman' that most Bengalis claim to be untranslatable! Kaushiki Bose patiently read through the early drafts of the translation and shared with me her invaluable perceptions about the novel. Both, in their different ways, unwaveringly supported me through the years that the translation failed to find a willing publisher. I warmly thank them.

My family has been particularly encouraging about this project. My mother, Pranati Chaudhuri, who was always available to elucidate a tricky turn of phrase, made the process of translating a text that has the status of a classic easier. Indeed, it was her enduring enthusiasm that kept me going through the long years that this translation took. Her memories of the impact of Ashapurna's novel on her generation enabled me to appreciate its significance better. I also had the privilege of discussing the novel with my ninety-year-old grandmother, Induprova Dasgupta, whose response to the novel was tinted by her own struggles to look after three young children when she was widowed at the tender age of twenty-two. My other grandmother, Ashalata Choudhury is no more. She was married at age ten and had her first child when she was eleven. It would have been interesting to know in what ways this novel spoke to her. My daughter, Rohini, who, in a sense, grew up with my never-ending absorption in the life of the eight-year-old and already married Satyabati, was keen that I dedicate this translation to her with the words 'Only because I did not have to marry her off at age eight.' For me, her words reveal the rapid and radical revisions that have so transformed our lives that it often becomes difficult to identify with and understand the experiences of an earlier generation of women. So, it is to her, my mother and my two grandmothers that I dedicate this translation.

INDIRA CHOWDHURY
Bangalore, 2003

FOREWORD

The year was 1993, exactly ten years ago, the place was Costa Rica in Central America. The occasion was an Interdisciplinary Women's Congress. I had just finished presenting a paper on the novel *Pratham Pratisruti (The First Promise)* by a younger colleague who could not get a visa to attend the Congress. The paper was read at the first plenary of the conference of which the theme was 'Search—Participation—Change', as a circular, ever-continuing process.

The response from the women from across the world was electrifying! They swooped on me, asking where could they get this novel. This was especially gratifying as the location meant that the women were mostly from Hispanic societies. Imagine their disappointment when I had to tell them that this wonderful novel only existed in Bengali! Ten years later, Indira Chowdhury has fulfilled the dream of making the book available in English, breathing life into the arduous and ever-continuing search for change that marks the thorny transition to modernity.

The first volume of Ashapurna Debi's intergenerational trilogy is undoubtedly one of the most redoubtable of women's bildungsromans produced in the twentieth century. This genre which characterized the onset of Enlightenment in Europe in the eighteenth century, and Romanticism in die nineteenth, encapsulated the contradictions of modernity. The intense pressures of self-making became highly accentuated under the simultaneity of restrictions and aspirations induced by colonialism, in a multilayered society that was stereotyped as Oriental by the Occidental conquerors. Bengal was the earliest and, possibly, the field of the most intense colonization, and generated a spate of remarkable autobiographies, first of the elite Bhadraloks and then of the Bhadramahilas. The soil was adequately prepared for some of the great bildungsromans of modern India: Saratchandra Chattopadhyay's four-volume *Sreekanta*, Bibhuti Bhushan Bandyopadhyay's *Father Panchali* and *Aparajito*. But it took nearly twenty-five years of hammering of feminist reading and re-canonization of Bengali literature to bring Ashapurna Debi's monumental novels to the fore.

What makes this translation very special is the stout refusal of the translator to reduce the complexity of the text to a bare minimum of a catching and popular storyline about the efficacy of social reform in bring about social transformation and women's empowerment. Ashapurna Debi's narration is as important as the drift of the storyline—the cluster of everyday events are energized by Ashapurna to bring out what it takes to participate in the recalcitrance of gender inequality.

At the centre of the novel stands the figure of the eight-year-old Satyabati, the eternal truth-seeker, whose questioning and uncompromising ways make her a transgressive figure for the orthodox patriarchal society of kulin brahmins.

Social reform of the kind that Vidyasagar had initiated, of course, forms a major backdrop. What I have called elsewhere the three-pronged phalanx of Vidyasagar's programme for the girl child—widow remarriage, restraining child marriage and advocating girl's education—all of these are endorsed in Satyabati's search for and participation in social change. In the novel she faces defeat. Without informing her, Elokeshi, the scheming mother-in-law, with the help of her weakling son gets Subarnalata, the only daughter of Satyabati, married at the age of eight following the brahminical custom of gauri-daana. Satyabati leaves home in protest, decides to visit her father in Kashi, to debate with him why he had given her away in gauri-daana.

A number of women gathered in the International Conference I had referred to, had compared this final act of Satyabati to that of Nora in Doll's House. I would like you to register the differences. The rebellious Satyabati left for Kashi because she wanted one last debate with her own father. The father had rebelled in his youth, ran away from home, and trained as a doctor. He remained straight as a ramrod in performing what he considered to be his duty, but this did not prevent him from being an unflinching patriarch, who had given Satyabati away in marriage at age eight. Satyabati, who had admired her father all her life, must clarify some of her doubts about her father's orthodoxy. What is remarkable is that she sets out with clear plan for earning her living. The distance covered by the eight-year-old Satyabati whose transgressive skill of writing scandalized the female members of her community, to the Satyabati who took advantage of the anonymity of a city like Calcutta to go out to teach destitute girls was great indeed. Getting linked to the world of knowledge was the biggest act of transgression which upper-caste Hindu women (kulin brahmins in this particular case) could commit. She stepped out of the *lakshmanrekha* of the patriarchal Hindu undivided family that the nationalists constructed as the *suraksha chakra* of the inviolate and inviolable social order.

Getting past the social ostracism of the female relatives and growing into a mature woman, confident of earning her own keep in Kashi, makes Satyabati a compelling parable of empowerment. But the stuff of this novel is the complex terrain in which this familiar act of rebellion takes place. It is what Michel Foucault has expressively called the 'micro-technologies of power', within which the larger movements of social change need to be located. It is by capturing this mosaic of oppression and rebellion within the texture of the novel that the translator has earned our singular gratitude.

Writing this foreword in the middle of the fortnight when the Women's movement has taken up cudgels of protest about violence against women, one cannot help noticing the centrality of such a text to this theme. The physical aspect of wife-beating and dowry murder are present at the beginning and towards the end of the novel; but the mental violence of the kulin polygamy seen in the light of the first wife has an extraordinary portrayal in Sharada. Satyabati's own steady decision of going to her marital home prematurely is another instance of abhorrence at the prospect of a co-wife. But it is a great deal more than that. Nor are we allowed to forget the kind of compromises she has to live through.

The rebelliousness of Ramkali, like that of his daughter Satyabati, is fraught with radical conservatism. The firmness of temperament which enables Ramkali is given an endorsement when Satyabati, the girl/woman, assumes the same unflinching approach to truth. Satyabati's husband is a complete weakling, whose only access to power is his knowledge of English that is supposed to be the harbinger of social change in colonial Bengal. The complex husband—wife relationship painted by Ashapurna makes Satyabati's struggle come alive. With all her efforts in making the children literate, and at being a proper helpmeet to her husband, Satyabati remains a steely distant figure, incapable of relaxing into the kind of space she had created as a tomboyish leader of the children in her natal home.

Satyabati's search for a viable alternative to the life of a child-wife, through her participation, turns to a change. But it is a change that makes her start her search all over again. Except that now she has possibilities of self-reliance, an alternative to her tension-ridden family. Elsewhere we have seen Indira Chowdhury's wonderful analysis of the alternative models of maternity etched by Ashapurna Debi that offers a rare and unconventional commentary on the mother-daughter dyad on which the trilogy is premised.[1] While giving birth to her child Satyabati is given the news of her mother's death. The loss of her mother makes Satyabati realize that the mother who had died had been neglected by her while she was alive. Satyabati, in her turn, by leaving home, becomes the absent mother. However, the book remains a tribute to the first promise made by the foremother. Had not Virginia Woolf alerted us that women's creativity has to think through the line of maternity?

By completing the daunting task of translating *Pratham Pratisruti*, Indira Chowdhury has established translation as a grand feminist practice.

JASODHARA BAGCHI
Kolkata
December 2003

---

1. See Indira Chowdhury, 'Redefining the Heroic Mother: Representation and Agency in Ashapurna Debi's *Pratham Pratisruti*, in Supriya Chaudhuri and Sajni Mukherjee, eds. *Literature and Gender: Essays for Jasodhara Bagchi*, New Delhi: Orient Longman, 2002, 216–40.

TRANSLATOR'S INTRODUCTION

Ashapurna Debi: Narrating the Familiar

Ashapurna Debi remained till her death in 1995, the most prolific and popular Bengali writer. Born in 1909, into the conservative Gupta family of north Calcutta that was ruled by a traditional matriarch, neither Ashapurna nor her sisters were sent to school. Although her father, Harendranath Gupta, was an artist and led a relatively unconventional life, the family did not believe in even privately tutoring the girls.[1] Ashapurna learnt to read and write on her own, and encouraged by her mother, Saralasundari, developed a love for literature quite early in life. Her first poem was published in the children's magazine *Shishu Saathi*.

At fifteen, she was married to Kalidas Gupta of Krishnanagar. After spending two years away from the city she loved, she returned to Calcutta to join her husband who worked there. She had three children, of whom two survived. Supported by her husband, she continued to write poems and stories for children. In 1936, she published her first short story for adults, entitled 'Patni O Preyashi' ('The Wife and the Beloved'). Her first novel *Prem O Prayajan* (*Love and Need*) appeared in 1944. Her well-known collections of short stories include *Sagar Sukaye Jai* (*The Ocean Dries Up*, 1947) and *Chhayasurya* (*The Spectre of the Sun*, 1962). Among her early novels, *Mittirbari* (*The House of the Mitras*, 1949) and *Nepathya Nayika* (*The Heroine behind the Scenes*, 1957) were acknowledged as masterpieces. In 1995 she published a collection of essays and autobiographical reminiscences entitled, *Ar ek Ashapurna*, (*Another Ashapurna*). In a writing career that spanned over sixty years, Ashapurna published 181 novels, 38 anthologies of short stories,

---

1. Manasi Dasgupta, 'Ashapurna Debi', in *Bangla Akademi Patrika*, 367–75.

and 52 books for children. At age eighty-two, Ashapurna admitted that she wrote to fulfill the demands of her readers:

> Since I write about what is most familiar to me, day-to-day experiences in middle-class homes, my readers feel that what I write about is very close to their experience, and want to read more and more. So I just keep on writing. I'll probably keep on writing till the day I die.[2]

The domestic world which served as the setting of most of her stories, however, came to be singled out by mainstream critics as the reason for her popularity, and further, provided them with an excuse to discredit the literary value of her work. Ashapurna, however, refused to see this as a reason to discontinue writing. For her, it was important to map the 'dynamics of the domestic space', which was as restless and clamorous as the public world.[3] The way she set out to chart the intricacies of that space came to be recognized by some of her fellow-writers in Bengali quite early. The writer Naren Dev, in particular, was responsible for introducing Ashapurna to literary circles in Calcutta. Ashapurna interacted with her contemporaries, and began to participate in debates and discussions about and around literature. This was an important part of her growth as a writer. Her writing, as scholar and writer, Nabaneeta Dev Sen maintains, paradoxically occupied two separate domains of Bengali literature: the marginalized terrain of women writers like Nirupama Debi, Giribala Debi and Jyotirmoyi Debi, as well as the mainstream realm of male writers like Subodh Ghosh, Narendranath Mitra and Bimal Mitra.[4]

Pratham Pratisruti, translated here as *The First Promise,* is her

---

2. Shivani Banerjee-Chakravorty, interview with Ashapurna Debi, 6 March 1991, published in *Newsletter,* School of Women's Studies, Jadavpur University, Decadal Number, March 2000, 24.

3. See 'Author's Preface', this volume.

4. Speech delivered at Memorial meeting for Ashapurna, at Bangla Akademi, on 9 August 1995, reprinted in *Newsletter,* School of Women's Studies, Jadavpur University, Decadal Number, March 2000, 56.

most widely acclaimed work. It appeared in 1964, and won her the Rabindra Puraskar in 1966, and the Bharatiya Jnanpith award in 1977. The first of a trilogy that includes *Subarnalata* (1966) and *Bakul Katha* (*Bakul's Story*, 1973), *Pratham Pratisruti* attempts to commemorate the struggles and efforts of women of the domestic world so neglected by history. The novel begins with a self-reflexive proclamation about the need to 'repay one's debts to one's grandmothers'. Satyabati's story, we learn right at the outset, is collected from the notebook of Bakul, who is her granddaughter. But the novel is not just the story of a single individual; it captures the story of social and cultural change across four generations. Planned on an epic scale, the novel has forty-eight chapters and more than fifty characters. As internal evidence suggests, the novel begins in eighteenth-century Bengal and ends in the late nineteenth century. The historical markers indicate the passing of the Mughal rule and the institution of British rule—the dwindling of the Nawab's authority; the decline of Persian and the coming of English education; and the gradual displacement of indigenous medical systems with modern, western medicine. Indeed, the novel provides us with extraordinary details of Ramkali's reading of symptoms, and reveals the relationship between a traditional practitioner of Ayurveda and his patients. The novel moves from the village to Calcutta, the capital of colonial India, and simultaneously maps the changes in family structure—the movement from an extended joint family to a nuclearized, smaller unit. It also traces the struggles of reformers to introduce education for girls, the failed project of 'widow remarriage' introduced in 1856, and depicts the agonizing pre-history of the Age of Consent agitation in 1891.[5] Finally, the

---

5. The Age of Consent agitation followed in the wake of the 11-year-old Phulmoni's death after sexual intercourse with her husband. While reformers denounced this brutal act, the orthodox Hindus were in favour of the tradition that permitted cohabitation with a child wife. The colonial penal code that had earlier designated intercourse with a wife under the age of ten as rape, reached a compromise, and by the 1891 Age of (*contd.*)

novel also illustrates the ways in which traditional caste practices came to be impacted by colonialism.

However, despite her obvious engagement with issues of social reform, it would be erroneous to conclude that Ashapurna's sole purpose in this novel is to dramatize social reform. One of the arguments often made by scholars has been that the manner in which the novel emerged in Indian languages in colonial India represents a shift in the very perception of reality, and as a result, the novel form is inevitably linked with social realism.[6] Ashapurna's novel, written as it was in the 1960s, raises questions about the exact nature of that link, and paints a complex and problematic picture, narrating the ways in which social reform fails to provide simple and uncomplicated solutions. The novel also grants a space to the traditional world, presenting it as a cultural resource that can at times contend with ethical dilemmas. I shall analyze some of the themes Ashapurna takes up, in order to draw attention to this particular dynamic of the novel.

Pratham Pratisruti has often been seen as a novel centred on a woman's protest against tradition. Indeed, it is seen as Satyabati's story. However, even though Satyabati remains the main focus, her father, Ramkali, is equally important to the dynamics of the novel. In fact, it is the story of Ramkali's development that is offered as a fairly complete picture. We first meet Ramkali as a defiant child who rejects the family god and leaves home. He returns as a traditional doctor to do socially useful work in his village, and finally, enters the state of *vanprastha* and retires to Kashi. Although he is clearly the hero in many of the early episodes of the novel, Ramkali is certainly not the main protagonist. His presence, however, is hardly accidental, nor is it residual. He clearly epitomizes that part of tradition that Ashapurna finds hard to expunge. Therefore, Ramkali remains an integral part of the narrative.

(*contd.*) Consent Act, the age of sexual intercourse for girls was raised to 12 years. See also Footnote 24.

6. See Meenakshi Mukherjee, *Realism and Reality: The Novel and Society in India*, New Delhi: Oxford University Press, 1985.

The World of Ramkali and the Practice
of Traditional Medicine

The novel begins by telling us that Ramkali was an unusual brahmin—one who practised traditional medicine or Ayurveda. 'At that time,' the narrative informs us about the Chatterji house, 'it was not called the "pulse-reading house".' Ramkali, though initiated into the traditions of a brahmin household, left home as a young boy and trained with a traditional doctor at Murshidabad. The traditional doctor, usually a vaidya by caste, had a 'lower' ritual status because his profession demanded the shedding of blood through surgery and bloodletting. Their social inferiority was equivalent to that of brahmins who embraced the military profession, as Zimmermann tells us.[7] Ashapurna's narrative captures the dilemma of Ramkali's father when he rediscovers the son he had given up for dead:

> The news overwhelmed Jaikali. Its double-edged nature confused him: his son was alive but had lost caste! He hardly knew what to do, shout with joy or howl with grief. His son was dining with a lower caste vaidya person, and living in a vaidya household—that was as good as death within the community.

But Gobinda Gupta, Ramkali's teacher, had strictly observed the prohibition of inter-dining. When the young and defiant Ramkali had argued against such rules, the doctor's wife, who had practically adopted him, had replied sadly,

> 'You mad boy! Can that ever happen?'
> 'You people wear the sacred thread too,' Ramkali had said.
> Gobinda Gupta had laughed, 'That's true. But you know something? Everything has a rank. A cobra is never the same as a water-snake, so your sacred thread and mine are not the same.

---

7. Francis Zimmermann, *The Jungle and the Aroma of Spices: An Ecological Theme in Hindu Medicine*, Domink Wujastyk and Kenneth G. Zysk, eds., *Indian Medical Tradition Series*, New Delhi: Motilal Banarasidas, 1999, 213.

I wish I could adopt you, but I can't. Who knows what boundaries I'd overstep.'

With remarkable economy, Ashapurna captures the world of the traditional practitioner of medicine, alerting us to the fact that it was practically impossible to separate his practices from the world of his social beliefs. In this the Ayurvedic practitioner was similar to the Greek *iatros* for whom the harmony of the social world was as important as the task of diagnosis, prescription, treatment and monitoring of the patient's environment. The Ayurvedic physician too is obliged to follow traditions and customs, as M.S. Valiathan has pointed out in his recent book, *The Legacy of Caraka*.[8] But learning to be a good physician invariably involves much more than knowing tradition and custom, or indeed, Ayurvedic texts. The many virtues of a physician as Caraka enumerated include, 'good heritage, knowledge of the scriptures, practical skills, hygiene, self-control, understanding of the body and its varied responses and the possession of medical equipment.'[9]

Although we are not told about his medical equipment, Ramkali is certainly a physician with extraordinary capabilities. Ashapurna recounts three instances of his diagnostic skills, each serving an important function in the unfolding of events. Ramkali practically 'saves' Jata's wife who had been given up for dead. Through this incident, Ashapurna presents the unusual relationship between father and daughter. Though Ramkali and his daughter occupy separate spheres in their everyday lives, Ramkali is an indulgent father who gives his daughter a fair hearing. In this instance, he is startled by Satya's insight into social practices when she points out:

'But then Baba, if you hadn't felt her pulse and given her the "essence of gold", Jatada's wife would have remained like that—lifeless! And then they'd have put her on a bamboo bier and cremated her!'

---

8. M.S. Valiathan, *The Legacy of Caraka*, Chennai: Orient Longman, 2003, 28.

9. *Ibid.*, 144.

Satya's observations often produce occasions when the traditional Ramkali can reflect on the ways in which atrocities masquerade as social custom and traditional practice.

The second instance of Ramkali's spectacular diagnosis occurs in Chapter Six, when he stops a marriage procession and diagnoses that the young groom is suffering from internal haemorrhage and is about to die.[10] However, in the world of traditional medicine, diagnosis is never separated from social responsibilities. Therefore, Ramkali, the physician, not only takes on the duty of conveying the disastrous news to the hapless family of the bride, but also undertakes the task of finding the unfortunate girl a groom that very night. In this, Ramkali behaves as custom demanded: a girl who remained unwedded after going through the pre-marriage rituals had to spend the rest of her life like a widow. Not only was she treated as a burden to the family, but was also seen as 'inauspicious' and responsible for denying her father the 'merit' of 'gauri-daana'—the ceremonial giving away of a daughter in marriage at age eight. It is this last dishonour that Ramkali sets out to save the bride's father from. There is also another reason why he takes this on as a personal duty: 'Lakshmikanta Banerji studied with my uncle, and I respect him as I would my own father.' Although, Lakshmikanta was not related to him, Ramkali extends the bonds of kinship to include someone who had studied with the same guru as his uncle. We shall return to the consequences of Ramkali's actions in a subsequent section; at this point, it is sufficient to note that the world within which 'doctor' Ramkali practises medicine can hardly be separated from the larger social world in which he functions.

---

10. Vagbhata's *Astangahrdaya* identifies 107 lethal points in the body and describes the pathological process when a duct that belongs one of the lethal point is damaged: 'There is an excessive flow of blood The heat increased by it, creates thirst, dessication, intoxication, and dizziness. The body of such a person sweats heavily and becomes limp. Then death claims him.' Dominik Wujastyk, *The Roots of Ayurveda: Selections from Sanskrit Medical Writings*, New Delhi: Penguin, 1998, 293.

The third instance of Ramkali's diagnostic skills that Ashapurna offers occurs in Chapter Eighteen. In this case, however, the doctor arrives too late and is unable help the child, Raghu, who has already died. He diagnoses the cause of death as snake venom that had been consumed along with the sugarcane that the boy had eaten. His explanation is met with disbelief until the local folk healer uses his skills to 'catch' the snake that had built its nest at the root of the sugarcane clump. Ramkali sees through the folk healer's ploy of planting a cobra and allegedly discovering it only to prove his skills. This event initiates a moment of self-reflection. As the folk healer leaves after getting the reward that he insists on being paid, Ramkali contemplates the helplessness of a doctor in the face of ignorance and irrational beliefs:

> Ramkali stared after him, strangely troubled. There seemed to be no end to the ignorance of these prize specimens of imbeciles, and yet how freely they made a living out of the stupidity of others.
>
> He had had his suspicions about the snake but hadn't expected the folk healer to squirm and confess so easily. Ramkali's heart became heavy with a sad ache. A doctor had the ability to heal the body, but what about the mind? Or the superstitions, ignorance, stupidity and full-fledged shrewdness that went with all that. How astonishing!

Ashapurna places before us the diverse beliefs and practices that make up tradition—at one end of the spectrum stands Ramkali, unflinching in his righteousness and sense of justice, while at the other end appear common cheats like the folk healer and a surfeit of women's rituals that we shall discuss in a separate section. Despite upholding Ramkali as morally superior to all other characters, Ashapurna also exposes his insensitive attitude to women, and comments on his inability to express affection, fondness and friendship. It is his timid wife, Bhubaneswari, whose face floats up before Ramkali as he retires from *samsara*, reminding him that perhaps his life was incomplete after all, because his rigid sense of duty had made him neglect the emotional content of his life.

Apart from his personal inadequacies, Ramkali also embodied the predicament of traditional doctors of his times as their expertise came to be displaced by western medicine introduced by the colonizers. It is this historical dislodgment that Ashapurna captures in the incident where Satya, with help from Bhabatosh-master and Nitai, summons a 'Sahib' doctor to treat the ailing Nabakumar. Recent studies in the history of colonial medicine have demonstrated the ways in which the western medical system impacted and hegemonized the indigenous systems of medicine.[11] The health-care facilities provided by the colonial government in urban centres like Calcutta were one of the reasons for migration to the city. The sense of a crisis in health that was experienced by the rural population was exacerbated by recurrent fevers and epidemics that ravaged Bengal in the late nineteenth century.[12] The indigenous systems of medicine seemed powerless to cope with such calamities. After Nabakumar's fever is cured by the Sahib-doctor Satya reiterates her earlier wish to move to Calcutta—this time for a different reason: to live in a place where 'Sahib-doctors treated illnesses and the nightmare of death did not exist.' Ashapurna uses this occasion as a means of exploring another key theme in the novel—the disparity between the village and the city.

The Village and the City

The nineteenth century saw a rapid decline in the rentier economy in Bengal. Rent income enjoyed by the zamindars since the Permanent Settlement gradually diminished as a consequence of new legislations that granted more power and occupancy rights to

---

11. See Mark Harrison and Biswamoy Pati, eds., *Health, Medicine and Empire: Perspectives on Colonial India*, Hyderabad: Orient Longman, 2001.

12. See Benoy Chowdhury, 'Agrarian Economy and Agrarian Relations in Bengal 1859–1885', in N.K. Sinha, ed., *The History of Bengal: 1757–1905*, Calcutta: University of Calcutta, 1967, 241–43.

the peasants.[13] Nabakumar, a landlord's son, seems happy to ignore these changes when he rejects Satya's suggestion to move to Calcutta, invoking in the same breath the despicable notion of working under a colonial government:[14]

> Nabakumar demanded angrily, 'Why should I be employed by another? Do I lack the means to feed myself? If we are careful, we can take it easy—do you know that? Why should I be a slave?'

This, however, is not the first reference to the city. From the time she was a child in her father's village, the city had always been a source of inspiration for Satya. Given the context of social reform in colonial Calcutta, particularly in the sphere of women's education, it is hardly surprising that the very first mention of the city in the novel brings up this fact. Satya and Neru argue about the conventional belief that women who learn to read and write go blind:

> 'I'd like to know what happens if a woman touches this [palm] leaf. So many women read and write in Calcutta!'

This incident ultimately helps Satya in procuring open support from her traditional father in learning to read and write. We are also told about Satya's literate aunt, Sukumari, who is from Calcutta. However, Sukumari is first described in negative terms by her sister-in-law, Nivanani, because she lacks the skills so essential to everyday life in a village.

> 'She hasn't yet learnt to milk the cows, or winnow the grain. And if you witnessed the farce that happens every time she goes to do the husking, you'd know! She can't move the pedal with her feet, nor can she place grain under it with her hands, I've to beg the neighbours to do the task ...'

---

13. Rajat K. Ray and Ratna Ray, 'Zamindars and jotedars: A study of rural politics in Bengal', *Modern Asian Studies* 1 (1975): 99.

14. For an elaboration of this notion of work see Sumit Sarkar, 'Kaliyuga, Chakri and Bhakti: Ramakrishna and His Times', in Sumit Sarkar, *Writing Social History*, New Delhi: Oxford University Press, 1997, 282–357.

In subtle ways, Ashapurna draws out the contrast between the village and the city through the nature of women's drudgery that each location demands. When Satya finally moves to Calcutta, she recalls the warnings she had been given about the difficulties of organizing her cooking in the mornings:

> A friend of Elokeshi's had enlightened Satya once by narrating within earshot, 'She'll soon know the hassle! Madam will soon know the fun of managing an independent household. She doesn't know what an office-meal means. The other time when I visited my cousins in Kalighat, there were three women struggling to get one man's meal ready!

The city also exerts different pressures on its inhabitants, as decisions have to be taken about drinking water, clothes and ways of child rearing. In fact, the very first discussion between Nabakumar and Satya about the city is an anxiety-ridden one:

> 'If a woman goes to Calcutta, what'll become of caste?'
> Satya replied gravely, 'If your father can keep his caste, if he still has the right to touch the holy stone, I too shall not lose caste if I go to Calcutta.'
> 'Don't go on and on! It's easy for a man to remain pure; it's not the same for a woman. You'll have to drink water that is stored in leather bags.'
> 'I'll drink that if I have to. We'll manage the way other brahmins manage in the city. The second son of the Haldar family has gone to Calcutta, hasn't he?'

Satya answers her husband's apprehensions about violating caste rules by bringing up a counter example of a similar violation— her father-in-law's sexual relationship with a lower caste woman. In one deft stroke, Ashapurna indicates to her readers that there is very little to idealize about the village. In fact, the theme of rural decline touches the village of Satya's childhood that Ashapurna had described with such charm at the beginning of the novel. When Satya visits again, she finds it irrevocably changed.

Perhaps it is Ashapurna's own passion for Calcutta that informs

Satya's eagerness to move to the city.[15] If the availability of doctors was one incentive, better educational opportunity was another. Satya desires to educate her sons and make them into fit human beings. She herself takes the opportunity to learn English from Bhabhatosh-master, shocking her husband and his friend, Nitai.

Despite the opportunities it offers, the city also demands constant alertness and watchfulness from parents. A need Satya is particularly sensitive to. She refuses to let her sons miss school to attend a feast thrown by the landlady. Apart from the issue of discipline, Satya is also concerned about exposing them to wealth. She says, 'No, it's best not to visit the wealthy. The children are immature and naive, they'll start feeling ashamed of themselves after seeing such grandeur.'

At the feast, Satya experiences the arrogance of the urban rich. This becomes an occasion to reflect on the supercilious self-importance of the wealthy in the city:

> The power and predominance of wealth in the world had left Satya's mind dull. What a strange place the city of Calcutta was! The glory of money reigned supreme; it prevailed over talent, learning and any humanitarian efforts. And yet, Satya had looked on the city with such admiration from her childhood!

At times, Satya idealizes nineteenth century Calcutta as the city of Rammohun Roy, Vidyasagar and Debendranath Tagore. It is the city that offers Satya the opportunity to witness the meeting between Keshubchandra Sen, the Brahmo leader, and Ramakrishna Paramahamsa.[16] At other times, she is vigilant about the various

---

15. Writing in an autobiographical mode she said, 'I do not know if the children of today are in love with Calcutta. But we were. At least, I was. And I still am. A first love can never fade away!' Ashapurna Debi, *Ar ek Ashapurna*, Calcutta: Mitra and Ghosh, 1995, 43.

16. Keshubchandra had a brief but intense personal relationship with Ramakrishna from 1875 to 1884. See Amiya P. Sen, 'Hindu-Brahmo Relations (1870–1905): An Enquiry into some Aspects of Community Identity in Late Nineteenth Century Bengal', in *Hindu Revivalism in Bengal, 1872–1905: Some Essays in Interpretation*, New Delhi: Oxford University Press, 1993, 25–79.

forms of enticing entertainment that the city offers. Nabakumar mentions the 1885 performance of the play *Nimai Sanyas* in which the reigning queen of Star theatre, Binodini Dasi, had played.[17] He is also drawn to horse racing. But Satya refuses to expose the children to either. Her firmness in this remains incomprehensible to the weak-willed Nabakumar.

The dynamics of the city and the village plays itself out at other subtle levels. When his teacher, Bhabatosh, converts to the Brahmo faith, Nabakumar disowns him. In fact, he is deeply agitated when he finds out that Satyabati teaches at an informal school Bhabatosh runs. Yet, it is the traditional man from the village, Ramkali, who rebukes Nabakumar for his disrespectful behaviour:

> 'Master-mashai has always helped you, how can you ostracize him? His faith is his business. Look at me—will you take into account if I am a Shakta or a Vaishnav? Or will you regard me simply as father? A guru, or a teacher, is just like a father. Besides he isn't forcing you to accept his faith. How does it harm you?'

The equation between the city and the village, between the traditional and the modern is not fixed and rigid. It is tradition that makes up the deep ethical core of Ramkali's character and offers him ways of accepting the new without surrendering his integrity. Ashapurna constantly plays with the figurative dimensions of the twin spaces, transforming the geographical terms into metaphors of both suppleness and inflexibility.

> The city advances at a rapid pace, the village dozes in the shaded courtyard. By the time a city trend reaches the village, it has already been abandoned by the city which is busy chasing a new one.
>
> But are definitions of city and village dependent just on geographical areas marked out in a map? Isn't it possible for the city and village to reside together? One awake, the other asleep?

---

17. Binodini played the lead role in this play. See Binodini Devi, *My Story and My Life as an Actress*, translated and edited by Rimli Bhattacharya, New Delhi: Kali for Women, 1998, 252.

Aren't human beings as different from one another, especially in their mental make-up?

The authorial voice that intervenes only minimally, points out the ways in which the city moulds and reshapes Satya and Nabakumar. Nabakumar remains rigid and conventional, mindlessly absorbing the pleasures the city offers. Satyabati, on the other hand, finds ways of repaying her debt to the city that has taught her so much, by teaching adult women in a school. The epic dimensions of the novel also take the other characters in its sweep and demonstrate the ways in which the city makes, remakes and unmakes them. Nabakumar's friend, Nitai, falls under its corrupting influence and his wife, Bhabini, who is summoned to 'rescue' him, resists being moulded by the city. Characters like Shankari on the other hand seek out the city for the employment it offers. The effect of the city on her daughter Suhash, whom she protects from the depraved gaze of her employers, is complicated. When Suhash arrives at Satya's she is ill-mannered and dull. Gradually, under Satya's influence she becomes receptive to the education that the city has to offer women. For Ashapurna, the city becomes a space that maps the rapid changes in women's lives. Suhash is married to a member of the Brahmo Samaj and becomes the symbol of the 'new' urban, educated woman when she becomes a teacher in Subarna's school. The novel, finally, is about the rapid social changes that affected women's lives in the nineteenth century, and it is to this theme we shall now turn.

The Mute, Neglected Domestic Space

In her preface to *Pratham Pratisruti*, Ashapurna writes with some irony about the ways in which history has always overlooked the dynamics of the domestic world. It is this domain that she sets out to capture in her novel. This world is hardly a mute one; in fact, it echoes with arguments, ritual chants, jokes and curses. The world of women that Ashapurna portrays is full of what anthropologists like Clifford Geertz have called 'thick descriptions'. It is a world teeming with rituals, festivals and ceremonies, and inevitably, the cooking, cleaning and decorating that accompanies such occasions. But the novel does not simply describe rituals and special occasions; it also offers intricate details of the daily grind of women's lives.[18]

Mokshada, Ramkali's aunt, works hard through all the seasons, preparing spices, sweets and pickles for everyday use, as well as for festivals and rituals, even though as a widow she is prohibited from participating in them.[19] Excluded from rituals because a widow is inauspicious, Mokshada, however, always has the final word on interpretations about tradition as well as the authority to discipline other women in the house. For these reasons, other women fear Mokshada. But the same Mokshada who had thrown a fit on grounds of ritual impurity when the eight-year-old Satya had asked for stale rice, is depicted towards the end of the novel as the senile, ghost-like widow who steals fried fish (prohibited to the widow) by the fistful when nobody is looking. Mokshada who discloses to Satya her uncertain sense of belonging in the Chatterji household because she never had children, is finally, a tragic figure.

> Anybody who had seen Mokshada earlier would never have thought that she didn't belong to this household! That there was nobody here who could ritually mourn for her even for three nights! Whoever did the last rites, would do it out a sense of compassion, and not because they owed it to her.
>
> What then, had been the basis of her authority? Or, was it precisely because she had no such base that Mokshada used to flaunt her vain power? Because she was knew too well that the hollow wall would collapse the moment she let go?

But Mokshada's presence in the narrative is tied up with several events that throw light on the social conditions of women in

---

18. For a historical account of women's lives in the nineteenth century see Usha Chakraborty, *Condition of Bengali Women around the second half of the 19th Century*, Calcutta: Usha Chakraborty, 1963.

19. Widows in most joint families were treated as household drudges. See Uma Chakravarty's essay, 'On Widowhood: The Critique of Cultural Practices in Women's Writings', in *Rewriting History: The Life and Times of Pandita Ramabai*, New Delhi: Kali for Women, 1998, 246–99.

nineteenth-century Bengal. The most significant of these events is Rashu's second marriage to Patli of Patmahal. This marriage, hastily organized by Ramkali after he diagnoses that Patli's groom was fatally ill, upsets several women in the household though Mokshada supportively stands by his decision. The practice of kulin polygamy[20] was acceptable, and the enlightened Ramkali too does not trouble himself with the emotional costs of his gentlemanly intervention to save Patli's father from potential social ostracism. For Ramkali, the first wife ought to accommodate the second wife of her husband because social custom demanded it. It is Satya who confronts her father with questions about such customs:

'If the co-wife is indeed like a sister, why would so many chants be composed? Does any one pray for the misery of their sister? The real reason is that men don't understand the significance of a co-wife, that's why ...' Satya swallowed once, and hesitated because she was not sure if it would be appropriate to utter the sentence hovering at the tip of her tongue, about men.

Ashapurna thus stages a confrontation between what is identified as 'high' brahminical tradition and the world of women's rituals that were part of the socialization process of the girl child in Bengal.[21] She suggests that the tradition Ramkali stands for, despite its deeply ethical core, blinds him to the trials and tribulations of women—a fact that strikes Ramkali later and induces him to make

---

20. A system initiated by King Ballalasena of Bengal (c. AD 1158–79) that granted upper caste brahmins the privilege of marrying several times. In his two tracts on the subject that appeared in 1871 and 1873, the social reformer Ishwar Chandra Vidyasagar records long lists of brahmins, from Hooghly district and the village of Janai, with their age and number of wives. According to his survey, some of them had married as many as eighty times. See Ishwar Chandra Vidyasagar, *Vidyasagar Rachanasamagra, Part Two: Samaj*, Calcutta: Vidyasagar Smarak Jatiya Samiti, 1972, 167–416.

21. Bharati Ray, 'Meyelita o Shishukanyar Shiksha' ('Womanliness and the Education of the Girl Child'), in Kanak Mukherjee, ed., *Eksathe*, Autumn 1990, cited in Jashodhara Bagchi, 'Socializing the Girl Child in Colonial Bengal', *Economic and Political Weekly*, 9 October 1993, 2216.

up his mind about taking Mokshada and Sharada along when he goes on a pilgrimage.

The eight-year-old Satyabati is a child bride whose pranks charm and enthrall us. But trailing behind her, like her double, is the figure of Shankari, the child widow whose deprivations and sufferings occupied a very significant part of the social reform agenda of nineteenth-century Bengal. It was the sexual exploitation of child widows that moved social reformers like Vidyasagar to campaign for the Widow Remarriage Act that was finally passed in 1856. Even though Vidyasagar's efforts were blessed with legislation, the social acceptance of widow remarriage remained a fantasy. Through Shankari's story, Ashapurna effectively captures the harsh reality of a remarried widow who is abandoned by her husband soon after announcing her pregnancy. As a novelist writing in the 1960s, Ashapurna exposes the misplaced hopes of social reformers on legislation alone to solve the problems of the child widow. Instead, she seems to place a greater hope on education of the girl child. Satya educates Shankari's daughter, Suhash and is hopeful of finding a groom for her in the liberal Brahmo Samaj.

The education of the girl child was an important part of social reform in colonial India. The programme for women's education was initiated by European men like John Drinkwater Bethune, who started the Hindu Balika Vidyalaya in Calcutta in 1849, and was taken up enthusiastically by Indian reformers like Keshubchandra Sen and others. From 1863 to 1890, the number of girls' schools went up from 95 to 2,238; and the number of school-going girls from 2,486 to 78,865.[22] Women's education and its content, however, remained a matter of debate for a long time.[23]

---

22. Ghulam Murshid, *Reluctant Debutante: Response of Bengali Women to Modernisation 1849–1905*, Rajshahi: Rajshahi University Press, 1983, 43.

23. See Tanika Sarkar, 'Strishiksha and its Terrors: Re-reading Nineteenth-century Debates on Reform', in Supriya Chaudhuri and Sajni Mukherji, eds., *Literature and Gender: Essays for Jashodhara Bagchi*, New Delhi: Orient Longman, 2002, 153–84; and Himani Bannerji, (*contd.*)

The heroine of Ashapurna's novel enthusiastically embraces education as a means of widening her world, recognizing its potential for bringing about social change. She also places a great deal of hope in the capacity of the colonizer to implement social justice when she protests against the violent murder of Bhabini's ten-year-old sister, Puti, by her husband and mother-in-law. The fact that Puti was murdered for refusing her husband sex echoes the death of another child wife, Phulmoni, caused by forcible intercourse by her twenty-nine-year-old husband, Hari Maiti, in 1889.[24] Satya's letter to the police appealing for justice for Puti fetches a congratulatory response from the British police. But not one to be satisfied by mere words, Satya rages on about inadequate social reform measures:

> 'Just tell me why have you opened your courts of justice? In our country we used to kill our women by burning them on their husband's funeral pyre—you stopped that practice and saved us from that sin. But that's nothing! There are heaps of sins that have collected over centuries. If you can rid us of those, only then would I say that you deserve to be lawmakers. Why have you taken on the guise of ruler in another's land? Why can't you just huddle into your ships and leave?'

It is Bhabatosh-master who reminds her of the nationalist responsibility of social transformation, questioning her naive faith

---

(*contd.*) 'Fashioning a Self: Educational Proposals for and by Women in Popular Magazines in Colonial Bengal', in *Economic and Political Weekly*, 26 October, 1991, WS-50–61. See also Malavika Karlekar, 'Women's Nature and the Access to Education', in Karuna Chanana, ed., *Socialization, Education and Women: Explorations in Gender Identity*, Hyderabad: Orient Longman, 1988, 129–65.

24. For details of this case, see Tanika Sarkar, 'Rhetoric against the Age of Consent and the Death of a Child-Wife', *Economic and Political Weekly*, 4 September 1993, 1869–78. See also, Amiya P. Sen, 'The Hour of Reckoning: Orthodox Hinduism and the Age of Consent Bill Controversy in Bengal (c. 1890–1892)', in *Hindu Revivalism in Bengal*, 363–99.

in colonial justice and reform. But Satya too hopes that times will change. And it is with this hope that she begins educating her daughter, Subarna, with great enthusiasm. Ashapurna's novel, however, does not embrace the social reform agenda in its totality. She ironically places Satya's hopes and aspirations within the limits of Indian modernity, where customs that endorse atrocities like child marriage live on unhampered, and propels the novel towards its traumatic and tragic end.

History, Fiction and Translation

Writing about the literary trends of the 1950s and 1960s, Susie Tharu and K. Lalitha observe that the fervour of building a new nation had created a milieu where the brutality and ruthlessness of the colonial regime were soon forgotten. This period was celebrated as a period of time when the artist was free to pursue enduring and unchanging truths.

> The truths of the nation would seem to have displaced the myths of the empire and to have made the land and its waters available once more as free and neutral ground on which artists who are curiously historyless and universal but at the same time essentially Indian, might once more pursue eternal verities.[25]

Women writers of this period, Tharu and Lalitha remind us, were also engaged in a 'bitter and difficult debate about women and the kind of hospitality gender received within the universalist claims of the post-Independence years.'[26] Perhaps, in our eagerness to read women's writings as expressions of the gendered nature of reality, Indian feminists have been too quick to adopt a preordained model with which to access women's experience.[27] As a result, we have

---

25. Susie Tharu and K. Lalitha, Introduction to *Women Writing in India: 600 B.C. to the Present*, Vol. 2, *The Twentieth Century*, New Delhi: Oxford University Press, 1995, 91.

26. *Ibid.*, 94.

27. Tanika Sarkar, for example, reads Rassundari's *Amar Jiban* as a 'modern' autobiography, taking the liberty of editing the text (*contd.*)

often interpreted women protagonists as replicas of Ibsen's Nora, without pausing to ask what kind of experience Nora's Indian counterpart would have. Would their experience be the same, despite their dissimilar cultural contexts? What roles would tradition and culture play in the way in which they shape her identity? Given the easy, unproblematic way in which the social reform agenda of the nineteenth century is viewed as the precursor of the women's movement in India, there is hardly space within current feminist studies in India to look at the cultural contours of identity critically. As a result, we have frequently produced inflexible and often dogmatic readings of women's lives and their experiences in our attempt to fit the diverse experiences of women in India into a pre-formulated grid. I am not arguing here for a frame of reading that uncritically endorses a static and timeless notion of Indian tradition, which contemporary right-wing political agendas seek out. But neither am I comfortable defending the left-wing vilification of all elements of Indian culture that unwittingly mimic orientalist descriptions of Indian traditions. Instead, I am arguing here for a paradigm shift in the critical domain of Women's Studies that would place women's experiences within the dynamics of their indigenous cultural resources.

In this context, Ashapurna's exploration of women's lives and women's history becomes particularly interesting. The history of Indian feminism has typically been traced back to the social reform movement of the nineteenth century.[28] Ashapurna's version shares several features with this master-narrative of feminism in India; it differs, however, in its subtle details. In mapping women's history through the vehicle of fiction, she refuses to erase completely the role of tradition in women's lives. For her, tradition is a complex

---

(contd.) wherever it does not fit in with Sarkar's notion of 'self'. See *Words to Win: The Making of Amar Jiban, A Modern Autobiography*, New Delhi: Kali for Women, 1999.

28. See for example, Radha Kumar, *The History of Doing: An Illustrated Account of Movements for Women's Rights and Feminism in India 1800–1900*, New Delhi: Kali for Women, 1993.

terrain. It consists of constraining customs and ritual atrocities denigrated by social reformers and the colonial masters alike. At the same time, she also recognizes tradition as a body of knowledge that provides instructions about ways of going about in the world.[29] That is why Ramkali remains so central to the narrative. It is his counsel Satya seeks when she gives shelter to the aberrant widow Shankari, or continues to associate with Bhabatosh-master. When invited to the Datta household, Satya observes all the prescriptions of caste, and towards the end of the novel, a mature Satya, performs her duties as a daughter-in-law when Nilambar lies paralyzed on his death bed. Saudamini, one of the most timid and conservative characters, who had returned to her abusive husband in order to nurse her ailing co-wife, remains Satya's kind-hearted supporter till the very end. By situating her confident and nonconformist heroine within a traditional milieu, Ashapurna invests Satya's final act of turning away with special significance. She offers the ending as a moment of heroic rejection of long-established conventions that perpetuate brutal customs like child marriage. At the same time she signals the beginnings of a quest that will take Satya to the very heart of tradition. Satya will, of course, never find her answer there, as we will discover in the sequel, *Subarnalata*.

It may be argued that unlike novelists who were writing in the nineteenth century with social reform debates raging around them, Ashapurna had the advantage of distance. She could look back with some detachment at the past and render a historically complex, multi-faceted and authentic picture of women's lives that a contemporary nineteenth-century writer would find impossible to produce. But Ashapurna's representation of women's experience

29. I am grateful to the many discussions I have had about tradition and culture with S.N. Balagangadhara and Vivek Dhareshwar. Balagangadhara elaborates on this notion of tradition in his unpublished essay, 'We Shall not Cease from Exploration', 1985. See also, S.N. Balagangadhara, 'Prolegomena to a Comparative Science of Culture', in '*The Heathen in his Blindness': Asia, the West and the Dynamic of Religion*, Leiden: Brill, 1994, 441–500.

rings true, not because of distance alone. Nor on account of her deliberate and self-conscious use of historical facts. Ashapurna succeeds only because she self-consciously seeks to link past with present.

The relationship between fiction and history has always been fraught. Fiction sequences reality into intricate and dynamic forms, while history chronicles facts and events, stacking them in sedimented layers. Ashapurna recognizes that the sediments situated deep underground determine the present lie of the land. Bakul, the putative writer of the trilogy, cannot tell the story of her present without talking about the past. Therefore, Bakul must acquaint herself as intimately as possible with the past.

The act of translating is an equally intimate act. It involves more than a 'surrender to the text'.[30] Given the historical links between colonialism, orientalism and translation, the postcolonial translator has a greater responsibility when translating a literary work from an Indian language into English.[31] What makes the task even more difficult is the almost unshakable analytical framework within which Indian culture is persistently interpreted in terms of western culture.[32] An enduring example being the unproblematic translation of 'dharma' as 'religion', which leaves no space within which to distinguish between the two notions, nor acknowledges the separate conceptual and cultural domains to which each belongs. Recognizing these problems, I have left untranslated all terms that do not have conceptual or material equivalents, relying instead on a glossary. I have also chosen Indian English equivalents over British

---

30. As Gayatri Chakravarty Spivak has urged in 'The Politics of Translation', in *Outside the Teaching Machine*, New York: Routledge, 1993, 178.

31. See Tejaswini Niranjana, *Siting Translation: History, Post-Structuralism and the Colonial Context*, Berkeley: University of California Press, and Hyderabad: Orient Longman, 1992.

32. Vivek Dhareshwar, 'Valorizing the Present: Orientalism, Post-coloniality and the Human Sciences,' *Cultural Dynamics* 10: 2 (July 1998): 211–31.

or American colloquialisms to carry across the flavour of Ashapurna's idiomatic language. Apart from that, I have also chosen not to use terms burdened with colonial valuation. Thus, 'ojha', commonly translated as 'witch doctor' and reminiscent of the colonial vilification of indigenous systems of healing, is translated here as a 'folk healer'. The word 'folk' enables us to contrast this form of therapy with Ayurveda, distinguishing it also from the text-based medical system.

The past, as they say, is a different country. But the historian attempts to visit it through available archival resources. As a historian I have spent many years delving through archives looking at different aspects of the nineteenth century, trying to draw out of brittle and fading records the ideas that shaped the lives of its men and women. Very few historians, however, are fortunate enough to find a text that compresses and condenses the diverse and scattered aspects of a significant part of the eighteenth and nineteenth centuries. The act of re-reading *Pratham Pratisruti* synthesized my archival experience. And the act of translation offered a means of revisiting the past and rediscovering it.

INDIRA CHOWDHURY
Bangalore, 2003

Translator's Preface to the Revised Edition

The publication of *Pratham Praitisruti* in 1964 was a milestone in women's writing in India. This epic novel narrated the history of social transformations in Bengal as mirrored in the domestic space. The dynamics of the lived experience of women who occupied this space was intrinsic to Ashapurna's story. Little wonder then that so many women across generations identified with the struggles she wrote about. During the years I spent translating the novel there were many women I met who recalled ways in which the novel had moved them. After this translation was published in 2004, many more readers have shared with me the emotional impact that this deceptively simple narrative had on them.

When I began translating *Pratham Pratisruti* in 1996, my reasons for choosing the novel were simple enough: I had enjoyed the novel and wished to share the pleasures that the text had offered with a wider audience. Besides, Ashapurna's writing seemed to resonate with the question I had only just begun to explore: how did women in nineteenth century India view tradition? Ashapurna's novel explored this significant question in a manner that was far more complex than my theoretical understanding of the ways in which gender, knowledge and power functioned in a traditional society faced with transition.

Revisiting the novel in the year of Ashapurna's centenary I am fully convinced that Ashapurna felt that the world she wrote about was not lacking in resources for women to use, even if that same world could also be unjust and cruel. It is for this reason that Ashapurna presents us with an abundance of details about the events that shape the lives of the women; when women protest they draw their strength not only from their own inner resources but also from the world they inhabit. Ashapurna's writing emphasised the importance of experience to women's writing.

But unlike modernist writers, she did not lament the lack of a room of her own. She preferred to write, as her daughter-in-law, Dr Nupur Gupta tells me, stretched on her bed, flat on her stomach, balancing her writing pad on a pillow in front of her, every so often raising her head to instruct the cook or the maid. Perhaps she never believed that she needed an exclusive private space in which to write. So she wrote surrounded by the clamour of everyday life, absorbing its aromas and using all the resources that this world held out to her. Maybe she did not want a room of her own because she did not seem to need exclusive space to assert herself as a writer. The cultural space she envisaged for herself was much larger and she seemed content to let life swirl around her as she wrote. Her life, her writing, and indeed, her way of writing, remind us that there is no single way in which to be a feminist writer.

Bangalore
May 2009

INDIRA CHOWDHURY

TRANSLATION AS RECOGNITION

In this essay I shall try to describe what translating the novel Pratham Pratisruti meant for me. The text engrossed me deeply for many years, compelling me to examine many preconceived notions. Finally, it provided me with an understanding of tradition, culture and society in colonial Bengal that went beyond the academic. Therefore, I have deliberately chosen to write about my long engagement with text in personal terms.

I

One cold winter night, the children were summoned early for dinner. No arguments were allowed. We had to finish eating as soon as possible. I was around twelve at the time and the only one privileged enough to be told the reason for haste, though I didn't comprehend the implications of it at the time. My great grandmother who was ninety-two had taken ill and since it was uncertain whether she would survive the night, we children had to be fed before death took over the normal course of or lives. The house had taken on a sombre air. Even the youngest and most boisterous of my cousins was subdued. From my great grandmother's room came the indistinct drone of instructions, *Hari nam*, and gasps. She survived the night. Next morning, before we trudged off to school, we trooped into her room and scolded her roundly: 'What did you think you were trying to do last night? Don't you try anything of this sort before you hit a century! We will all lose face if you die even a day before that!' She did ensure that we didn't 'lose face' for she died at the grand old age of one hundred and one.

My father's grandmother had stayed with us as long as I can remember. She must have joined her stepson, my grandfather who was a doctor in the Gua mines area and later, in the hospital in Burnpur (West Bengal) from the 1930s onwards. She had no children of her own and brought up her husband's two young sons as her own. She survived both sons and till she was ninety enjoyed smoking her hookah and talking to us about the life she had left behind. Unlettered though she was, she would offer us vivid descriptions of the *Jatras* performed at her village – somewhere on the banks of the river Titas. Sometimes she would sing us songs about the fashionable babus of Koilkata (Calcutta) who strutted about with their hair styled with 'pomatam' (pomade). The songs amused us no end.

She was nine when she was married. Nine! Did I wonder about it at that time? I didn't really. Nor did I recognise the difficulties she must have experienced as a child wife. My preconceived notions of childhood did not, at that point, admit of a discomfiting genealogy. I belonged to a generation that took education for granted. Besides, like most fourteen year olds, I was self-assured, unsympathetic and unthinkingly cruel. Lost as I was in a world that accommodated Robert Louis Stevenson, Jules Verne, Dickens, and not unsurprisingly, Enid Blyton alongside Rabindranath Tagore, Sarat Chandra Chattopadhyay, my great grandmother's world seemed strange but unexciting. She belonged I was convinced, to an outmoded and uninteresting world, where she was, at most, an amusing character. Her memories could teach me nothing, so I never did delve into them, nor troubled myself much about how she felt about being married at nine and coming to her husband's village or being dispossessed after Partition.

By contrast to my great grandmother, my grandmother had attended the Faizunissa Girl's School in Comilla, now in Bangladesh. She too narrated amusing stories about her life in Comilla, mainly narratives about her school-going days, which were so different from my own experience of school that they seemed to invoke an alien world. She told us about her difficulties with the school uniform, a saree, which often came off leaving her with no choice but to return home in her chemise, clutching the folded saree in her hands. She stopped going to school when she was married off at eleven, but throughout her life she kept alive her intellectual curiosity that school had stoked only momentarily. She read, no, devoured, whatever she could lay her hands on: magazines, newspapers and my school textbooks. Her addiction to, and absorption in the worlds that books opened up for her, were part of family lore. We all knew about the times she had let the milk boil over because she simply couldn't put down what she was reading. Or we were told about the time she had lost herself in fictional machinations and neglected her howling first born. Family lore hardly focused on the fact that she was being a typical young girl who had just discovered the world of books. For she was twelve when she had had her first child.

II

The worlds that my great grandmother and my grandmother lived in were not identical. But they were similar. By contrast, my world was radically different. Indeed, the world that I thought was mine was different from the world of my mother too. I went to convent school where my mother tongue, Bengali was forbidden and with it, all the practices of that linguistic world. I spoke Bengali at home and English at school and with my friends. I grew up like many others of my generation, in a world I believed to be cosmopolitan, speaking English most of the time. It was also a world that rarely chanced upon the world of the home where my grandparents, parents, aunts and uncles all spoke Bengali. Perhaps that's why reading *Pratham Pratisruti* for the first time as an undergraduate student was a strange experience. The novel spoke of a world that seemed familiar but unrecognisable. As arrogant and generally supercilious students of the English Honours class we misrecognised Ashapurna's use of proverbs, colloquialisms, idioms and maxims in dialogue as failures of style, we argued against the text's repetitiveness, and its huge cast of characters, missing the point entirely. What made matters worse was the fact that the teachers in our Bengali class dismissed the text as echoing the nineteenth century social reform movement too closely. But the impact of the text remained with me. What was Ashapurna Debi trying to do? Why did she insist on telling us about the traditional milieu within which women craved for education? Why was Ramkali's story given so much prominence? And when we moved from the text to the social world, why, I wondered did an enlightened man like Ramkali give his daughter away at the age of eight? It would take me a decade and a half to find those answers.

Meanwhile, English literature kept us busy; opening up a world where we were free to pursue new sports: shadow-boxing with notions of textuality, diving into the depths of Hardy's novels to fathom out the notions of a tragic hero, or engaging in hunts for metaphors, allusions and symbols in Shakespeare, Eliot and Joyce. All these exercises, we were told, were designed to provide a deeper understanding of the world. In the end, I suppose, we did learn how to describe the world of the English literary text. We became skilled in recounting the characteristics of the Renaissance, or elaborating the relationship between Milton and the Puritan politics of his time and repeating the reasons why in 1910, Virginia Woolf felt that 'human nature had changed'. Most of us never stopped to ask, whose world were all these exercises offering us furtive glimpses into? The excitement of discovering this new and unfamiliar world made it seem like mine, even when it wasn't. Even when I argued for the universality of human emotions, emotions alone could not provide the link to that world I believed to be mine because so many things I read about were materially absent from my world. But we were told that the material world mattered little to literary studies, for surely we could imagine the 'host of golden daffodils' or what Yarrow might have looked like. It didn't matter, we were told, that Wordsworth unlike us had grown up seeing the flowers, and had first heard about the river on his tour of Scotland in 1803. Later, when Eng Lit Studies transformed itself into Postcolonial Studies by inventing 'liberating' critical tools with which to read the literature of the coloniser, it still failed to provide a framework with which to understand the complex world embodied in texts written in Indian languages.

III

My training in Eng Lit did not prepare me for the questions that *Pratham Pratisruti* raised both at the level of text and at the level of the social world. Contrary to what we had learnt about the novel form, here was one which had a structure that accommodated more than one main protagonist and a host of other characters equally important to its milieu.

When I finally returned to the novel, it was not through the route of Eng Lit at all. I returned to it only after I had immersed myself in the world of nineteenth century Bengal while doing a PhD in history. When I started re-reading the novel, the framework through which we understand the colonial past seemed inadequate. I realised that some of the richness of the world that Ashapurna had brought alive in the novel would be lost if I attempted to understand this world through Marxist notions of feudalism or through postcolonial notions of hybridity, or even through the feminist category of gender. In fact, these labels were not able to capture the dynamics of Satyabati's world. Let me illustrate through a textual example, what lay at the root of my problem.

In the novel, Ramkali's nephew, Rashu is made to marry a second time, causing a great deal of heartbreak and anxiety to his first wife, Sharada. When, Patli, Rashu's second wife finally comes to live at her in-laws, she finds her husband completely under his first wife's control. Ashapurna captures one moment of the interaction between the two wives with a poignancy that defies easy categorisation.

Sharada called out to her every now and then, 'Notun-bou, come and eat. Notun-bou, which slice of fish do you prefer? Notun-bou do you like mashed-up mango pickle?...Almost as if Sharada had not a clue as to why Notun-bou—the new wife—was called that! As if she was in charge of looking after a relative who was visiting!

At one point, Patli asks Sharada why she looks after her every need. After all, she reasons:

> *'I am your enemy, why don't you get rid of me? You'd be relieved, I would too.'*
> *Sharada made a sad attempt at banter, 'I might be relieved, but why would you be?'*
> *'I wouldn't have to live like a burden—as one to whom everyone has to be kind. It would be such a relief.'*

Patli then begs of Sharada to send her home, because she doesn't want a fight over their husband.

> *'I don't want anything, Didi!' the new bride said passionately.*
> *Sharada laughed, 'Nothing? Not even your husband?'*
> *'No!'*
> *Sharada answered, 'But d'you know something? The ways of the world are such that you get everything when you don't really want it. When you crave something it just slips away! Goodness! Look these fritters have almost lost their crispness, have them quickly. You'll feel better.'*

How can we understand Sharada's retort which is simultaneously philosophical and bantering? Seeing it merely as an echo of her social conditioning somehow does not seem good enough. Ashapurna seems to be signaling at a change in Sharada's mental world. Later in the novel, Sharada will slowly start giving up control over her husband, although she would still retain her jurisdiction over the running of the house. It is through such telling encounters that Ashapurna attempts to capture the complexities of the inner, domestic space.

I suppose what lay at the root of my problem was a reluctance to engage with what I had been taught to identify as a retrograde social order. So completely was I convinced about my generation's break with tradition that I did not stop to examine the ways in which the traditional world lived on around me. Perhaps, I wasn't even prepared to see it as part of my world.

IV

The traditional world of this novel is not fixed and frozen. It is in fact, one that is in the process of change. When the novel opens, the delightful eight-year old Satyabati is already married as was customary, but she has taught herself to write. As she argues with her male cousin about the false superstitions about women touching the palm leaf:

> 'I'd like to know what happens if a woman touches this leaf. So many women read and write in Calcutta!'
> Her cousin, Neru responds: 'Who has told you that? Don't you know they'll all go blind if they did?'
> 'How absurd! You don't know a thing. As if they instantly become blind when they read! Nonsense!...I'm telling you Neru, nothing like that happens. Learning is a good thing. It can never be a sin to learn.'

Women's education occupied a large part of both colonial and social reform agendas in nineteenth century India. Women brought to education an enthusiasm and attentiveness that was unparalleled. In the novel, Satyabati's ability to write a few words is viewed as a transgression by her mother, Bhubaneswari, who reports it to her father. Her father, Ramkali, questions her closely:

> 'What is the use of girls learning? They won't become rent-collectors or cashiers, will they?' Ramkali questioned her with an amused laugh.
> Once more Satya's vehemence returned....
> 'Why should they become cashiers? They will learn to read the Ramayana, Mahabharata and Puranas. Then they'd not have to keep waiting for the Kathak to come around.'

To his wife's utter amazement, instead of disciplining Satya for her transgression, Ramkali promises to teach her every afternoon.

> 'She'll learn!' Bhubaneswari could hardly hold back her words.
> 'Yes, she will read and write....I'll give her a real ink pot and quill too.'
> 'Baba!'
> Just two syllables escaped Satya's lips. And Bhubaneswari's eyes rained tears.

Within two generations of its introduction, women's education had become so successful among the middle classes in Bengal that stories about the earlier struggle for education were forgotten, or at best, identified with a remote past. Since education was perceived as ushering in modernity, whether or not it brought about a complete break with the past, was left unexamined. This novel captured that magical moment in late nineteenth century India, when women were 'permitted' to openly read and write. It brought into focus a moment when the efforts of the autodidact found enlightened male support. But learning to read and write did not dislodge women from their traditional world. The novel also described the ways in which many early women learners remained rooted in tradition, a fact that has remained a source of discomfort to Marxist and feminist theories. Postcolonial critiques of modernity, on the other hand, have been too busy describing the incompleteness and the failures of postcolonial India, to take seriously the resources that the traditional world might have held out to its inhabitants. These interpretative frameworks, in fact, serve as obstacles to fully understanding the world that Ashapurna tried to portray, and I shall return to this later.

V

The novel is set in late eighteenth and early nineteenth century India and maps the many ways in which social transformation was attempted. Ashapurna's masterly narrative tells the story of the limits of such transformations, at times pointing out the failures of the nineteenth century social reform by positioning Satya at the very heart of the despair and the hope that accompanied the social reform movement. Through Shankari's story Ashapurna underscores the failure of the widow remarriage project. Through Puti's death she brings us closer to the brutalities and violence of child marriage that recent critical literature on the social reform movement has focused on.

The Age of Consent debate that raged in Bengal from 1890–1892 was sparked off by the tragic death of Phulmoni Dasi, the child-wife of the twenty nine year old Hari Maiti. The ten-year old girl had bled to death on account of forcible intercourse. In the novel the death of the ten-year old Puti resonates with the death of her historical counterpart, Phulmoni. Satya who appeals to colonial law for justice is reminded by Bhabatosh-master of the limits of colonial justice and reform.

The process of translating the novel made me acutely aware of its historical rootedness. But what came truly as an unexpected discovery was the fact that Ashapurna had not let history become a mere backdrop to her story, she had recognised the way in which the sedimented layers of history control and structure the lay of the land. Her characters therefore lived in a world infused with the beliefs, attitudes and values of their times. I could not evaluate this world as one that is ruled by 'debased' customs and still be appreciative of the text that Ashapurna created. I had to go a step further and ask myself if my own presumptions were getting in the way of understanding the functioning of this world.

In *Pratham Pratisruti*, Ashapurna places before her readers the diverse beliefs and practices that make up tradition, she points out what is corrupt in this world, as well as ways of being ethical within it. Therefore, she places before us the problems of the child widow Shankari who tries to find an escape from oppressive tradition by eloping with her lover. Simultaneously, she tells us of the dilemma of Ramkali, the head of the household, who must reveal the news of her 'social death' to his guests before they sit down for their meal because that's what right conduct would demand. Ashapurna emphasises that a person without Ramkali's strength of character or sincerity, might have found it easier to wait and announce the news after the feast. That would have temporarily saved face and also proved economically viable as revealing the news before the meal carried the risk of ostracism by the village community, who could have refused to touch the food. In deciding to reveal the problem to the village community, Ramkali shows his respect for the community and its beliefs and practices and in turn, keeps intact his own sense of pride.

The second example is a significant part of Satya's rebellion, but it also captures the changes that were surging through nineteenth-century Bengal. When Nabakumar falls seriously ill for a fortnight Ashapurna describes the deluge of home remedies that the village women try out on him with no success. Satya quietly bribes the Barber's wife to take the news to her father, Ramkali. At that point, Ramkali's guru, Vidyaratna had just passed away and the rules of ritual pollution do not permit him to touch medications or books. Therefore, Ramkali sends his nephew Rashu with medications. Satya sends back the medicines out of a sense of hurt that her father, the 'doctor', had not rushed there himself. She then undertakes the unbelievable task of summoning a European doctor from Calcutta, by asking Bhabhatosh master and raising the money required by requesting her husband's friend, Nitai to sell her gold necklace. As the Sahib Doctor examines Nabakumar, Satya watches him from behind a window—she is curious, filled with wonder and also overawed. In her mind she asks forgiveness of her father, whom she had hurt by returning the medicines, she prays to her dead mother for strength. As Ashapurna puts it:

> *Satya didn't seem to value Kali, Durga or Shiva, she prayed fervently again and again to the living gods she knew. So that the Sahib's medicine worked like a miracle.*

In the novel, this moment marks a significant transition in Satya's character; it also captures a transition point in the history of medical practice in colonial India – a move from traditional medical practices to western medicine. But Ashapurna also invests that moment with something else that hints at the nature of Satya's resilience. To understand this moment merely as a consequence of Satya's resistance and rebellion or to comprehend it as a break with the past and a rupture with tradition would be distinctly inadequate. Satya survives at her in-laws and through this crisis and other emergencies because she is able to utilise the resources that are available to her. Satya's traditional world is not without its own resources and she has learnt, better than others perhaps, how to exist within it.

VI

Pratham Pratisruti depicts what was once a familiar world—the experience of its heroine was representative of the experience of millions of young women growing up in colonial Bengal. My grandmother and my mother's generation had no difficulty in relating to that world. Yet, when I first read the novel I found myself entering a world so different that I had trouble calling it my own. Why did that happen? In this last section, I shall attempt a tentative answer.

I lived with the text for four years. At that point, I taught Eng Lit at Jadavpur University, Kolkata. I would teach postcolonial, postmodern and feminist theory all day and return to the text in the evenings. I soon discovered a disjuncture between what I taught as feminist or postcolonial theory and the world of *Pratham Pratisruti*. There seemed to be a wide gap between the experiential world of nineteenth-century Bengali women and the conceptual world of postcolonial and feminist criticism. 'Hybridity' and 'nationalist discourse' did not capture the deep dynamics of the text, invoking 'gendered realities' did not tell us much about Satyabati's world. And at the semantic level, neither did the word 'religion' capture the meaning of '*dharma*'. The gap between the cultural and conceptual worlds of Bengali and English seemed an impossible one at times. Most of all I stumbled against the numerous proverbs and poems that speckled the text. I found myself plowing through dictionaries of proverbs to make sense of them. In the end, it seemed far easier to ask my mother who knew all the proverbs along with a host of stories.

Satyabati's experience was something my mother could connect with easily, having grown up in parts of rural Bengal and old Calcutta as a child. That was barely eighty years ago. The changes that had swept across our lives in that interim period made even my mother's growing up years seem very remote. Furthermore, the theorisations through which we were taught to filter our understanding of the past, presented a grimy picture: the past was 'tainted by tradition' until the winds of progress swept it clean. If traditional practices lived on – they were theorised as part of an unfinished and imperfect modernity. This mode of interpreting the past did not enable us to build relationships with those who touched our lives and were part of that past. Nor did these theories allow us to address a more important question: what was tradition? Was tradition a version of religion? If it was, how then did traditional practices survive in the absence of religious diktat? To find the answer was a struggle that had to go beyond the exhausted theoretical and terminological debates.

Tradition in Satyabati's world is not identified with religious ceremonies; rather, it can be understood as a way of going about the world. Satyabati's protest therefore is not against all of tradition (for she learns from tradition, as does her father), but against certain practices that are brutal. This understanding changed my perception about not just the past but my own world as well. I began to recognise that my world was not only deficient in resources to understand the world my grandmother inhabited, it had also failed to take cognizance of its own deficiency. The 'cosmopolitan', English-speaking world I was so much at ease in had provided me with a list of labels and categories about tradition and modernity. But these labels had in fact obstructed a real understanding of my grandmother's world.

It was only when I understood the foundations of my own disconnection from my grandmother's life that I began to recognise Satya's life as reflecting my grandmother's experience. My grandmother's world was no longer the world of strange stories and practices that I could just amuse myself with. I no longer pitied her and my great grandmother for missing out on being 'modern'. Their world could not have been an entirely debased and corrupt one, where women were just 'victims' or survivors. That world had also offered its resources to its inhabitants and using those resources were part of the life skills of women of my grandmother's generation.

I began this piece by recollecting the lives of my great grandmother and grandmother, both were married off as children. The process of translating *Pratham Pratisruti* brought alive their worlds and made their experience accessible to me. Like Bakul, the putative writer of *Pratham Pratisruti,* who overcomes her scornful laughter and learns to look on the eight-year-old and already-married Satyabati with compassion and admiration, I too learnt through the process of translation to feel for and relate to my grandmother's world.

The novel enabled me to recognise that history was not merely what one found in official archival records; history lived in memories too, embedded in the mental worlds of our grandparents and parents. That's why too I called this piece 'Translation as Recognition'; because the process of translation enabled me to identify the text for what it was: a retelling of our past that reveals the configuration of tradition itself.

Author's Dedication

To all those cherished and unforgettable women.

Who, from within their secluded spaces, left us the etchings of a promise—

AUTHOR'S PREFACE

The history of times past is made up of stories about the rise and fall of the public world. And that restless, clamorous history writ against a backdrop of light and darkness holds out inspiration, ardour and excitement for the future. But is not the mute, domestic space similarly broken and built? From which flows forth the changing colours of a community, an age, and people's mentalities? We would find abundant treasures if only we focussed there. But history has invariably overlooked the dynamics of the domestic world. That domain has always been neglected. This book is about an unknown woman who was among those who carved out the etchings of a promise from within those ignored interior spaces of Bengal.

If this picture, painted as it is on the canvas of insignificant everyday life, can convey the smallest fragment of the past, my efforts would have found fulfilment.

ALPHABETICAL GUIDE

Abhaya	Ramkali's half-brother Kunja's wife; mother of Rashu and Neru
Anna	Khyanta-thakurun's niece; probably a neighbour of Elokeshi's
Bakul	Subarnalata's daughter; Satyabati's granddaughter
Behula	Shyamakanta Banerji's wife; Patli's mother
Bhabatosh Biswas (Master-mashai)	Nabakumar and Nitai's teacher
Bhabini	Nabakumar's friend Nitai's wife
Bhubaneswari	Ramkali's wife; Satyabati's mother
Binde	the folk healer at Nityanandapur
Dinatarini	Ramkali's mother; Satyabati's grandmother; Jaikali's second wife; Satyabati calls her Thakurma
Datta-Ginni	Satyabati and Nabakumar's landlady in Calcutta
Elokeshi	Nilambar Banerji's wife; Nabakumar's mother; Satyabati's mother-in-law
Felu Banerji	Bhubaneswari's father; Ramkali Chatterji's father-in-law
Gobinda Gupta	Ramkali's foster-father; Ayurvedic practitioner at Murshidabad
Jaikali	Ramkali's father; Satyabati's grandfather; Dinatarini's husband
Jashodha	Jaikali's widowed aunt; Ramkali's grandaunt
Jata	Ramkali's cousin's son
Kashiswari	Ramkali's widowed aunt; Satyabati's Pishi-thakurma; Shankari's grandmother-in-law
Khedi	Satyabati's playmate
Kunjakali (Kunja)	Ramkali's elder half-brother; Jaikali's son by his first marriage
Khyanta-thakurun	an elderly, widowed neighbour of Elokeshi

Lakshmikanta Banerji	zamindar of Patmahal; grandfather of Patli, Rashu's second wife
Mokshada	Ramkali's widowed aunt; Satyabati's Pishi-thakurma
Muktakeshi	Elokeshi's friend's daughter
Mukunda Mukherji	Saudamini's husband
Nabakumar Banerji	Nilambar Banerji's son; Satyabati's husband
Nagen	a young man from Katoa; Shankari's aunt's sister's son
Nandarani	Jaikali's cousin; part of the Chatterji household at Nityanandapur; Satyabati calls her Thakurma
Neru	Kunja's young son
Nilambar Banerji	Nabakumar's father; Satyabati's father-in-law
Nitai	Nabakumar's friend; Bhabini's husband
Nivanani	Bhubaneswari's elder brother's wife
Patli	daughter of Shayamakanta Banerji of Patmahal; Rashu's second wife
Punyabati (Punyi)	Satyabati's aunt, also her playmate
Raghu	Tustu the milkman's grandson
Rakhahari Ghoshal	village elder at Patmahal
Rakhali	Satyabati's playmate
Ramkali Chatterji	Jaikali's son; Bhubaneswari's husband; Satyabati's father; Ayurvedic doctor by profession
Rashbehari (Rashu)	Kunja's elder son
Sadhan (Turu)	Nabakumar and Satyabati's oldest son
Saral (Khoka)	Nabakumar and Satyabati's younger son
Satyabati (Satya)	daughter of Ramkali and Bhubaneswari; Nabakumar's wife, mother of Sadhan (Turu), Saral (Khoka) and Subarnalata (Subarna)
Saudamini (Sadu)	Nabakumar's cousin; Nilambar's niece
Shankari (Katoa-bou)	Kashiswari's grandson's wife; mother of Suhashini
Sharada	Rashu's first wife
Shashitara	Jaikali's daughter by his first marriage; Kunja's sister

Shibjaya   cousin of Jaikali; part of the Chatterji household at Nityanandapur; Satyabati calls her Thakurma

Shyamakanta Banerji   son of Lakshmikanta; Patli's father

Subarnalata (Subarna) Nabakumar and Satyabati's daughter; Bakul's mother

Suhashini (Suhash)   Shankari's daughter

Sukumari   Bhubaneswari's younger brother's wife

Tustu   the milkman at Nityanandapur

Ullashi Bagdini   Nilambar Banerji's mistress

Vidyaratna   Ramkali's mentor

ONE

I did not make up Satyabati's story. I took it from Bakul's notebook. Bakul told me, 'You can treat it as fiction, or fact—whatever you wish!'

I have known Bakul from the time she was a child. I meet her even now. I have often told her, 'Bakul, one can write a story about you!' To which Bakul has always smiled. A sceptical, amused smile. Bakul herself does not believe that a story can be written about her. She has no such opinion about herself.

In fact, Bakul hardly attributes any significance to herself. She believes she is nothing—a nobody! Common, and so very ordinary, that anyone who wished to write about her would find nothing at all to say!

Perhaps the fragile foundation of her life has been responsible for letting such a notion take root. Though she has achieved so much now, deep down, she can never forget the rancour of all that she was denied as a child. Such regrets have numbed her mind. And shrivelled her being.

Bakul is one of Subarnalata's many children; among the younger of her many offspring. Bakul's role in Subarnalata's household was always that of an offender. As though fate had decreed that she should always be petrified by some unnamed offence.

In her childhood, Bakul's mind had been shaped by a strange ambience of darkness and light—part comprising fear, distrust and hatred, and part glowing with the mysterious luminescence of a radiant consciousness. And yet, Bakul cannot help loving people. On the contrary, it is because she loves …

But let that be; after all, this is not Bakul's story. Bakul told me, 'Write my story later, if you must. Not now.' Having travelled such a vast expanse of her life, Bakul has learnt that one must repay the debts to one's grandmother and great-grandmother before one begins to talk about oneself.

The shadow-dark waters of a pool in some secluded village overflow in the monsoon to join the river and gush forth in torrents. That same river rushes along, and, one day, joins the ocean. We must never forget that initial flowing forth out of the shadows.

Behind the innumerable Bakuls and Paruls of today's Bengal there is a history of years of struggle. That history is the struggle of their mothers, grandmothers and great-grandmothers. They were few in number, a few individuals among many. And they walked alone. Over ponds and creeks, shattering stones, uprooting bushes. And sometimes while building their road they would sit down, exhausted, on the very path they had cleared. Then, somebody would step forward and lift on to her shoulders the burden of the work that was pledged. That was how the road was built—the road on which the Bakuls and Paruls are striding ahead. Of course, they have had to do their bit too. Because it would not do to have just a track to walk on; it had to be a road fit for chariots!

But who will build that road? And drive those chariots? Perhaps those driving past will laugh when they turn the pages of history in idle curiosity and come across Satyabati.

Nose-ring dangling, heavy anklets round her feet—the eight-year-old Satyabati!

There was a time when Bakul used to laugh too. But she no longer does. Having travelled so far, Bakul has learnt the significance of the road. Therefore, the Satyabati she has never beheld with her eyes, she has seen in her dreams and imaginings, and regarded her with compassion and admiration. Satyabati's portrait is clearly etched in Bakul's notebook.

A ring dangling from her nose, rings on her ears and her chiming anklets! The eight-year-old Satyabati, a printed girl-size sari wrapped around her. Though married for a couple of years now, she still lived at her parents'. And moved about with unabated vigour, just as she pleased, and all the children of the locality followed her. Her mother, her grandmother, or her aunt seemed incapable of controlling her! Perhaps they were not able to, because her father viewed her unfettered conduct with a lenient eye.

Even though he was a brahmin, with a surname like 'Chatterji', Satyabati's father, Ramkali, did not practise a brahmin's traditional occupation. He had chosen Ayurveda above all other shastras and vedas. And in spite of being born a brahmin, he practised traditional medicine. So the village had named him the 'pulse-reading brahmin', and his house, the 'pulse-reading house'.

Ramkali's early life was very different from that of his siblings and cousins. It was a little fantastic too. Or else, why would such an old man have such a young daughter? Satyabati was his first-born. Ramkali had married well past what was regarded as the marriageable age in his time. And Satyabati was a consequence of that delay.

They say that the young Ramkali had left home because he was upset with his father. The matter was trivial, perhaps, but it left a deep mark on his tender mind.

One day, because of some problem or other, his father, Jaikali, had assigned the puja and arati of the family god, Janardhan, to the newly-initiated Ramkali. The boy had taken on the responsibility with great enthusiasm. And the whole household had wailed 'Save us, Janardhan!' on hearing the loud ringing of bells during the arati ceremony. But in the fervour of the moment, he had made one mistake. A grave mistake.

Ramkali's grandaunt had detected it when she had come to mop the puja room. Her close-cropped hair had bristled like the quills of a hedgehog and she had run to her nephew, and flung herself in front of him, 'Jaikali! Something dreadful has happened!'

Jaikali was alarmed, 'What?'

'What else can you expect when a child performs the puja! There's been a terrible oversight! Ramkali has offered Janardhan fruits and sweets without any water!'

That instant Jaikali's blood started boiling. And he let out a terrifying yell.

And his aunt let out a hopeless sigh, and raising her voice to match his pitch, said, 'Now who knows what's in store for whom! This isn't about missing out the flowers or the tulsi leaves, but water that quenches thirst!'

Suddenly, Jaikali picked up his wooden sandal and let out a roar, 'Ramkali!'

At first, Ramkali was not too alarmed by the shout; Jaikali's affection towards progeny or relatives was rarely expressed at a lower pitch. So, wiping his hands clean of the sticky wood-apple he had been eating, he appeared before his father.

But what was this? Here was Jaikali holding a sandal in his hand! Stars flitted before Ramkali's eyes.

'Call the lord, Ramkali!' Jaikali said with a fearsome face. 'You're doomed to die!'

The stars in front of Ramkali's eyes vanished instantly, leaving behind an unperforated darkness. And he groped in that darkness to discover the mistake for which the lord had proclaimed his death. His search proved futile, and he was totally at a loss to detect the flaw. Gradually the darkness took over his entire consciousness. 'Didn't you perform the puja in Janardhan's room today?'

Ramkali kept quiet. It was obvious that he had violated something in the puja room. But what was it? Ramkali had entered the room after washing his hands and feet, then he had covered himself with the silk wrapper he had acquired at his sacred-thread ceremony. What had he done after that? Spread the mat, of course! After that? The ablutions. And after that? The arati ceremony. After that ... a hard thwack landed on his head.

'Did you offer water to the gods?' Jaikali's question was accompanied by a clobbering with the sandal.

A baffled Ramkali, fearing more such blows replied, 'Of course, I did.'

'You did!' Jaikali's aunt, Jashodha, asked cruelly, very unlike the loving foster-mother of Lord Krishna. 'If you did, where did it disappear, you wretch? The tumbler is bone dry!'

The throbbing of his heart subsided somewhat as he faintly pronounced, 'May be the god drank it.'

'What! What did you say?' Another blow, followed by a deeper sensation of descending darkness.

'You useless wretch! You swine! God drank the water! You're more than a ghoul, you are a proper villain! Don't you have any fear? Lying about god?'

Meaning of course, no matter how serious an offence lying was, involving god in the matter had made it the most heinous of crimes. Fear gripped Ramkali, and he lied again, 'Yes, yes ... I am speaking the truth. I had offered water. I swear by god!'

'Really! You scoundrel! You misbegotten brahmin! Swearing by god! You offered water, god drank it up! Do idols really drink water?'

His head was burning inside. And tormented by the burning, Ramkali forgot his fear, 'In that case, why do you offer it?'

'You've also learnt to talk back, have you?' Jaikali used his sandal one last time. 'Out! You brahmin bull! Get out of my sight!'

That was all. Jaikali had not said any more. And there had been nothing unusual about his behaviour. That was how he always behaved with everybody. But what consequences certain actions have! It was as if a curtain had been torn down in Ramkali's mind. He had always been told that Janardhan was compassionate; the whole household would invoke his benevolence at all times. But was there evidence of even an iota of that compassion? Ramkali prayed as if he would burst, 'O god, reveal yourself to these faithless ones! Declare in your divine voice: "O Jaikali! Stop tormenting the boy! It's of no use. I did drink the water. I was so thirsty after eating the sweets."'

But there was not even the hint of a revelation. At that moment, Ramkali discovered that god was a lie. Divinity, rituals, prayers, were all false; the sandal was the only truth! Ramkali had been given a similar pair of wooden sandals during his thread ceremony; who knows when he would be able to put it to similar use! Though that was exactly what he felt like doing at that moment—to the whole world.

At first he pledged, 'I shall not live in this world.' But unable to find a way out of this world, he had finally compromised. Let the world be! One could leave it whenever one wished. There was, in fact, something else that one could leave, a symbol of the world—home.

Ramkali decided to leave home. So that he would never have to perform the puja for Janardhan, ever again.

At that time it was not called the 'pulse-reading house'. It was the plain old 'house of the Chatterjis'. But it commanded respect and awe. For a long time, the news of the missing Chatterji boy shook the whole village. Nets were cast in every pond. Oaths sworn at every village shrine. Ramkali's mother went to the ghat every day to perform the ritual of floating a lamp for his return. Jaikali too began offering Janardhan the sacred tulsi leaf regularly. With no success.

Just when they were all beginning to forget that the Chatterjis once had a boy called Ramkali, a local lad announced that Ramkali was alive. He had gone to Murshidabad and had seen for himself, that Ramkali was living with the nawab's physician, Gobinda Gupta. He was apprenticed to the doctor and was learning the science of Ayurveda.

The news overwhelmed Jaikali. Its double-edged nature confused him: his son was alive but had lost caste! He hardly knew what to do, shout with joy or howl with grief. His son was dining with a lower caste vaidya person, and living in a vaidya household—that was as good as death within the community. But the news of Ramkali being alive had also unbridled something else inside him. Was it joy or affection? Or relief that came with deliverance from repentance?

Jaikali consulted people in the village. And they came to the conclusion that Jaikali should go at once and investigate the matter properly. Apart from that, one had to be sure that it was indeed Ramkali. After all, the young man was not a close relative, and could be mistaken. This suggestion left Jaikali aghast, 'Me? How can I go? It is impossible to abandon my duties to Janardhan.'

On hearing him, Ramkali's mother, Jaikali's second wife, Dinatarini, had wept profusely. She nearly said, 'Is Janardhan so important for you?' But she had not dared. Instead, she wept.

At last, after much discussion, it was decided that one of Jaikali's nephews would go. Jaikali's son by his first wife, Kunjakali, would accompany him. But it was quite difficult to travel to Murshidabad from their primitive village. First, one had to take a bullock cart to the market town and find out about the boat to Murshidabad; then, after stocking up on snacks, travel six miles by bullock cart to the river bank where one would have to wait for the boat. Nor was it inexpensive!

Jaikali mused on the complications of transferring debit to credit! Where was the need for such problems? He felt very annoyed with that young whipper-snapper who had brought this news—the hero who had created this pandemonium! After all, Ramkali had been written off. There would have been no need for all this fuss had that cocky lad not brought the news.

But there was a need as far as Ramkali's mother was concerned So despite the inconvenience, Jaikali had sent his nephew and his son. After some days, they had returned and confirmed that the news was true indeed. Ramkali had practically been adopted by Gobinda-doctor and was living like a prince. It seemed he would go to Patna soon. He had told them that he would return to the village only after he became a court physician and made a lot of money. Not earlier.

On hearing this, the envious declared, 'One should sever ties with such a despicable son! In any case, he has obviously lost caste.' The less resentful murmured, 'But look at his achievements! And why should he lose caste? Kunja told us that Gobinda-doctor has arranged for him to eat at a brahmin's house.'

Such talk went on for a few days in the village. Then, just as the discussion was dying, and people were gradually beginning to forget him, Ramkali himself had appeared unexpectedly, with lots of money.

Gobinda-doctor had advised him, 'Do not become a court physician, my boy. The state of the kingdom is rotten from within.

The nawab's authority too is dwindling. Here, take all my savings, go to your village and reign in your own realm. My wife and I have decided to retire to Kashi.'

So Ramkali had come away. He had arrived from the market town in his own palki. For he had inherited Gobinda Gupta's palki as well and had brought it with him on the boat.

It was a matter of regret that by then Jaikali had died. So Ramkali never saw his father again. The outcaste son had come home a worthy man.

TWO

Like crowds jostling at village fairs to gape at oddities such as 'five-legged cows', the local population flocked to have a look at Ramkali. Though it irritated him, he treated everybody with appropriate respect. He gifted money and clothes to the elderly. And in every household they proclaimed, 'Oh, look how generous he's become!' And many sighed as they gazed at their good-for-nothing sons.

Even so, Ramkali was treated like an outcaste for a brief period. He had to sleep and eat in the outer part of the house. Any child who accidentally touched him had to go and change his clothes. Finally, Ramkali asked the headman of the village to intervene. This was unacceptable; after all he had never had a meal with the lower caste doctor, nor violated any ritual practice. So why should he be treated like an outcaste?

The village worthies had scratched their heads and made unintelligible noises; they were unable to come up with an answer. After all, they reasoned, the lad had brought with him all of Gobinda-doctor's skills and his money. And was blessed with a generous streak as well.

While they were murmuring to themselves, Ramkali proposed, 'My guru's medicines speak for themselves. I have picked up some of his skills and wish to use them to help the village of my birth, my neighbours, and kith and kin. Of course, if you can do without them, I'll be forced to give up my village home and go away.'

This time round, the village worthies protested. This was hardly an offer to fling away! After all, one day, each one of them would reach his end. And pressing his advantage, Ramkali declared, 'Besides, I was planning to dig a pond for the village and throw a feast for everyone. It all appears to be a vain hope now!'

Abandoning their hesitation, the crowd cried out in unison, 'Oh no! Of course not!'

Using that opportunity, Felu Banerji made a smart move. Uttering a Sanskrit shloka he chuckled, 'You know that a girl is seen as undeserving of protection when she isn't married at the right age. Similarly, a man too is looked upon as fallen.'

Ramkali responded with a bowed head, 'I am nearly thirty. Who will offer a daughter in marriage to me?'

To which Felu Banerji said heroically, 'I will! If my brothers here wish to make me an outcaste for that, so be it.'

Cast out Felu Banerji! He who belonged to the crown of all castes! A wave of protest swept through the room. And when they grasped how shrewd his move had been, each one cuffed himself mentally. As if no other households had daughters!

A few days after this, Ramkali was married to Felu Banerji's nine-year-old daughter 'Bhubi' or Bhubaneswari. The village had not witnessed such a grand wedding in a long time. Apparently Ramkali himself had secretly given five hundred rupees to his mother, Dinatarini, for the lavish celebrations. Of course, such shameless behaviour deserved condemnation, though everybody highly commended the feast that was laid out as part of this pomp.

And thus it was that Ramkali came to be reestablished within society. He was given permission to eat and sleep inside the house.

But that was long ago. 'Bhubi' grew up, set up house, and at the age of fifteen or sixteen the little brook became a brimming river! And only after that came Satyabati.

Her father was rather indulgent towards Satyabati, perhaps because she was the first child of his old age.

THREE

Dinatarini was cooking in the vegetarian kitchen, which was a mud hut on stilts, when Satyabati came and stood under the shade of the thatch, her nose barely reaching the edge of the verandah. Balancing her whole body on the tips of her toes, she stretched her neck and called in her characteristically clear tone, 'Thakurma, O Thakurma.'

This kitchen was restricted to those licensed by vegetarianism to enter it; nobody, not even Satyabati, was allowed to climb on to its verandah. The steps of the verandah were hewn out of mud on one side of the structure, and they led to the ghat. Dinatarini, her second sister-in-law Shibjaya, and her two other sisters-in-law, Kashiswari and Mokshada, were the only women who had the right to this pathway. They would take their pots to the pond, bathe, fill the pots, and come back in wet clothes and climb straight up to their 'heaven'. They would hang their clothes to dry inside this kitchen—for after all, there was never any cooking done into the evenings. There was, of course, the job of wiping the room, but no perceivable danger of what was designated as ritually 'impure' could enter. Mokshada kept a strict eye. She was the type who would not even trust god with the handling of 'polluted' items! That was a responsibility she reserved for herself. And being the youngest among them, it was her duty to clean up after they had all eaten.

Dinatarini was in charge of cooking, and Mokshada looked after the ritual purity of the food that entered the kitchen. The other two would help with preparations, by no means trivial. For though they were only four of them, food would be prepared for about ten.

The verandah was totally out of bounds for the children, but no one could control Satyabati. She would come there at all hours and call out from down below, 'Thakurma! Pishi-thakurma!'

Dinatarini peeped out of the door and said, 'Go to hell! Look what a savage she's turning out to be! Why are you here again? Go away, if Mokshada-thakurji sees you, there'll be hell to pay!'

Satyabati made a face, 'Forget about her! Why don't you listen?'

Satyabati was the daughter of Dinatarini's son—and a son who earned well. And because she was already married, nobody yelled too much at her. Dinatarini gave in to her demand and listened.

Satyabati stretched out a large leaf on the hand she had been hiding behind her and whispered, 'Can you give me something?'

'Goodness! What can I give you now? The cooking isn't done yet. And even if it were, if they find out that I gave you food before offering it to the gods, all hell will break loose!'

'That's not what I mean! Keep all your cooked stuff—just give me a fistful of stale rice.'

'Stale rice!'

Dinatarini was hit by a bolt from the blue! And that very moment Mokshada sprouted out of the earth's crust, her white sari sopping wet, with a full pot of water at her hip.

It must have been the third time she had bathed. Whatever the reason, Mokshada took a dip whenever she went to the pond to wash vegetables or rice. Neither Satya nor her grandmother had noticed her come up the steps; now their eyes were riveted on her.

Dinatarini looked embarrassed, Satyabati, irritated. And Mokshada was thrilled, like a detective who had caught a thief red-handed!

'Are you here again?' Mokshada asked in the voice of a wraith.

Satyabati asked hesitantly, 'But look here, I haven't climbed on your verandah, have I?'

'Hah! But haven't you stepped on the courtyard with your dirty feet? And we shall have to climb down there to water the tulsi!'

Satyabati grumbled, 'In any case, you never step down without pouring cauldrons of water first, so what does it matter?'

'Don't you backchat Satya! Control your tongue!' Mokshada said as she put down the water pot noisily on the threshold of the kitchen and wrung the water out of her sari. 'Prancing about without a care! And encouraged by your father too! Don't you have to go to your in-laws? How long can you frolic? At the most two or three more years. And then they'll just drag you there with a rope! As if you can escape that!'

Satya detested such threats of being sent away. Why did they not just beat her instead? She could take that. She loathed this non-stop threat of being sent away. And they used it like their most powerful weapon. Therefore, she asked irritably, 'So what?'

'You'll soon find out! You'll just have to digest your mother-in-law's taunts all the time. Your cheeks will be bruised black and blue like that Patal-kaka's nephew's wife.'

'As if the whole world is like her ferocious sister-in-law!' Satyabati's resounding retort sounded strange for someone her age.

'Just listen to her!' Mokshada said waving her plump hands, 'I knew you'd say that! As if it's always the mother-in-law's fault! What about the daughter-in-law? What do you think they should do with a sharp-tongued daughter-in-law, eh? Worship her with flowers and put her on a pedestal?'

'Hah! As if there's no other way! Why can't they love her a little? Talk to her sweetly!'

'My, my!' Mokshada shrieked with laughter, 'Spoken like a shrewd old hussy! You'll find out how honey-sweet your mother-in-law's words taste! And how fondly she looks at you! But never mind all that—what was that about stale rice?'

Dinatarini had remained silent all this while, now she laughed, 'She came to ask me for some.'

'Stale rice!' Mokshada exploded, 'She asks for this—from our kitchen—and you just laugh about it! How can you indulge your granddaughter like this? You're really the limit! What if she asks for this from the widow's kitchen at her in-laws' house, eh? What'll they say? They'll think that we just eat stale rice by the potful, won't they?'

'Of course not!' Dinatarini tried to ease the situation with a faint smile, 'A child often speaks without thinking.'

'Child! Goodness! Do you realise, she'd have had a child by now had she been sent to her husband?' Mokshada took the gamcha from her shoulder and gave it a vigorous shake. 'Just listen to her! Stop being blind with fondness! And you, Satya, let me warn you! Don't you ever let slip such a thing in front of others! The hags in our neighbourhood keep their ears open all the time; they'll conclude that we don't wash our pots and pans, and eat off them!'

Suddenly, Satya burst out laughing uproariously, 'Let them! Would you get blisters if they talked?'

Because the rules of pollution forbade her to touch Satya, Mokshada slapped her own cheeks instead, and said, 'Just listen to her! The cheek! Let people talk, she says! Custom says "Nothing remains if people condemn!" And she says ...'

'We're done for!' Dinatarini thought to herself; they would have a hard time if Mokshada started now! Mokshada was very sturdy, and had an unmanageable appetite. Yet she would ignore her hunger and thirst and would not touch even a drop of water till late afternoon, nor eat anything till evening. All morning the emptiness would burn inside her. And she would hurl out words which made everybody tremble in fear.

So Dinatarini quickly changed the topic, 'I say, Satya, haven't you had breakfast? Why are you asking for stale rice now?'

'What brains you have!' Satya said disparagingly. 'As if I want to eat it! I want to use it as fishing bait.'

'What do you want to do?' Mokshada's eyes dilated before Dinatarini could react.

'BAIT! For fishing. Can you hear now? Neru had made me a nice fishing rod, and I want to go fishing.'

'Satya!' Mokshada spluttered, 'You'll fish with a rod! Your father has spoilt you silly, but this is the limit! Do girls go fishing?'

Satya tossed her mop of hair, 'Ha! Look how she talks! You think women don't fish? Doesn't Ranga-khurima fish? And all those other aunts there? They all fish!'

'Oh you wretched girl! Do they fish with rods? They sieve up small fish with their gamchas when they're bathing.'

'So what?' Satya rubbed a large leaf against the wall, 'How can you say that sieving up fish is all right and fishing with a rod is all wrong? Or, there's nothing wrong with small fish, and everything wrong with the large ones! Who has made up your customs?'

'Satya!' Dinatarini called out firmly. 'Too many words from a slip of a girl! Thakurji is right, you'll know when you're sent away!'

'My goodness, what a fuss for a bit of stale rice! I'll go and ask at the fish-kitchen instead—but as if I can do that easily! There's

Boro-jethi and her piercing eyes! I should have gone and asked at Khedi's house!'

'Ask for rice at Khedi's? How can you touch rice cooked in a lower caste house?'

'I haven't touched it yet, have I? Goodness! You find fault with everything! All right, I'm off to the other kitchen. And just wait till I catch a huge big fish!'

So saying, Satya flung aside the large leaf, which by now was shredded to pieces with all that rubbing, and left for the other section of the house. There, everyday, things were laid out for a feast. About two hundred and fifty odd people ate there twice a day. The kitchen was on a raised platform too, just like the vegetarian kitchen, but there were no restrictions about entering it. Satya clambered on to the platform brazenly. And after scanning her surroundings, she picked up a coconut shell and let out a fearless shout, 'Boro-jethi!'

FOUR

The whiff of a cool, unexpected breeze started up as the sultry day drew to a close. It cooled the body, but raised a fear too. The season was unpredictable—the end of spring. At the corner of the sky, black clouds veiled half the sky, looking like a rough giant preparing to pounce on the earth.

Those who were out in the fields, on the road or near the pond, started speeding up the work at hand, anxiously looking up at the sky every now and then. And echoing in the wind, from one end of the village to another, arose the dim refrain of a nasal call. The pitch rose and fell in stages. These were the words, 'Come Bundi! Come Sundari! Come Moongli! Lakkhi! Come!' Summoning the dumb animals to come from the pasture to their sheds, out of the storm.

Satyabati was rushing home with news from the Banerji locality.

But hearing the call, she too raised her voice and yelled out, 'Come Shyamali! Come Dhabali!'

Ramkali was walking past the mango grove on his way back from the Ray locality. He had had to leave his palki there. Ray-mashai, one of the village elders, was dying. Ramkali had gone to take a look at him. Judging his condition, Ramkali had advised that they take the old man to the bank of the river—the Ganga; and that was what had landed him in trouble.

Both the sons of the old man had died, and the three grandsons hardly had the means to hire a palki and bearers. And yet, it was unthinkable that such a virtuous old man should die at home! What an unbearable thought! The best place to take him to would be Tribeni, where the three streams meet. But when the three grandsons stood exchanging uncertain looks, Ramkali had been obliged to say, 'Don't worry about the palki, you can take him in mine.'

The grandsons had mumbled a protest, 'You have to go far to visit your patients. How can you do without your palki ...'

And Ramkali had retorted with a dark laugh, 'In that case, carry him on your shoulders! After all, here you are, three strapping young men!'

It would be unthinkable to laugh at the joke of an elder, so they had just scratched their heads.

Finally, taking courage, the eldest had ventured, 'We were thinking of a bullock cart ...'

'Then you were thinking wrong!' Ramkali had responded. 'Do you think this frail ninety-two-year-old body will get there in one piece in a bullock cart? His life will fly out for sure! I am like a son to him, so do not hesitate. And besides, you never know what other quick arrangements you might need to make.'

Tears had rolled down the misty eyes of the old man. He had raised his infirm right hand in blessing.

Outside, Ramkali had instructed his palki-bearers, 'Why carry the palki all the way? Leave it here, and go home and eat. Get back before daybreak. And bring enough food to last the day, okay? And listen, go and ask if there's anything else to be done here. I'm going home.'

He was rushing because he had noticed the clouds on the horizon. It was not as if he was unaccustomed to walking just because he used a palki to visit his patients. Every day he rose at dawn and walked for a mile or so after his morning ablutions—that was the first of his daily duties. But when he visited a patient, it was different; then, it was very much a matter of prestige.

Ramkali had intended taking the short cut through the fruit orchard, but no sooner had he entered the mango grove, a dust storm had started up. Ramkali had quickly come out; and that very instant he had stopped in his tracks, startled. Wasn't that Satya's voice? It did sound like her. It took him a moment, a very wee moment, though, to confirm, because the wind was strong. And the names of the cows were familiar. Though the Chatterjis had a shed full of cows, these two were special and Ramkali was very fond of them. He fed them, stroked them, and, the unmarried girls of the house did their cow-rituals with these two. And the dung they produced was used by Mokshada to preserve ritual purity.

Ramkali strained his ears to determine the direction of that sound, then walking briskly, he caught up with his daughter. By then Satyabati had broken into a run, and was using the corner of her sari to shield her eyes from the dust.

'Where're you off to?' Ramkali asked, his voice booming like thunder.

Satyabati gave a start, removed her sari from her face, and was totally stunned! Everyone called Satyabati her father's darling, which, of course, was true, and her father cherished her too for being his lucky girl. There was, however, no overt display of affection. Naturally, Satyabati panicked on hearing her father's voice.

Ramkali repeated, 'Where had you gone by yourself at this hour?'

Satyabati answered in a faint voice, 'To Sejo-pishi's.'

The person Satyabati called 'Sejo-pishi' was in fact Ramkali's first cousin. She had been married in this village, and lived here.

Ramkali frowned, 'And why did you go so far all by yourself? Why isn't anybody with you?'

This was just the reason why they called her father's darling! Not a slap, nor a box on the ears, merely the command to invent an excuse!

Satyabati regained her courage and said, 'Of course not! Why should I go by myself? Punyi-pishi and Neru had come with me. Then I came running to call you.'

'You came to call me?' Ramkali asked, knitting his brows. 'And why exactly do you need me?'

Salvaging her confidence Satyabati declared excitedly, 'Jatada's wife is dying. Her pulse has stopped! So Sejo-pishi started sobbing and said, "Go and fetch Mejda, Satya, wherever you can find him." So I went to the Ray's and heard you'd just left.'

'So you'd been to that locality too! This is too much! What has happened to Jata's wife that her pulse has gone weak?'

'Not weak, Baba, it's stopped!' Satya said with increased animation, 'Sejo-pishi is weeping and beating her breasts, and is putting away the pillow and mattress.'

'What do you mean? Come, let's have a look,' Ramkali said. 'But there's a storm brewing, it's going to rain. What a bother! Now tell me, what happened?'

'Nothing much! Sejo-pishi said that when Jatada's wife was sitting down to eat, just after she'd finished the cooking, Jatada asked for a paan. His wife said that there wasn't any paan. That was it! His majesty was furious. He gave her a good hard kick on her backside. And she fell on her face in the courtyard—' Satyabati burst into laughter.

'Why're you laughing?' Ramkali scolded irritably. How ill-mannered the girl had become! Was this the time to laugh?

He scolded, 'What's so funny about a person dying? Is this what you've been taught?'

Satyabati had laughed impulsively; she controlled herself somehow after her father's rebuke. Trying to look as sober as she could, she said, 'Sejo-pishi said that as soon as she was kicked she rolled down like a pumpkin on to the courtyard.' And, once again, controlling her laughter, she resumed with great effort, 'Actually, Jatada's wife eats a lot of rice, Baba, so she's really fat!'

Looking annoyed, Ramkali quickened his pace. But Satyabati could walk fast too. And she kept pace with him. No matter how sympathetic he felt towards Jata's wife, Ramkali's mind was enraged by Jata's transgression. The wretch was a misfit in a brahmin's house! Without a scratch of learning! An expert at smoking ganja! And to top it all, the vulgar habit of wife-beating! The creature's father was not like this at all! In fact, it was Ramkali's extraordinary cousin who had dictated to Jata all his life. Who could say how he had hit his wife? If she really was dead, there would be no end of trouble. And quite oblivious of Satyabati, Ramkali quickened his pace. Satyabati broke into a run. She was determined not to lose this race.

Her eyes were transfixed, the froth at the mouth had dried, the hands were stone-cold. There could be no doubt at all—the signs were clear. So she had been moved close to the sacred tulsi in the courtyard soon after she had fallen. In fact, they had been quick to bring her out here. And within minutes the news had spread. The women had gathered, as if swept out of their homes, fearless of the gathering storm. After all, the affair was colourful, and in the dull theatre of their humdrum lives, there were few opportunities to witness such dramatic scenes. First, there came a stifled agitation, 'I believe Jata has finished off his wife?' Then cries of 'Alas!' Finally, comments about Jata were no longer shielded from his mother's ears. How often did one get a chance to speak one's mind, anyway!

'Is she really gone? For shame! What a murderer!' 'What a bitch to bear such a son! And I ask you, why is Jata such a mule? His father was a good man.' 'Why do you think? Don't annoy me so, can't you see what the mother's like! Such virtues!' 'The poor, foolish thing! What a way to die!' And so the discussion went on. One could not expect more compassion for a woman, in any case!

Jata's mother was forced to digest the comments of the neighbours in silence, because today she found herself in a bit of a spot. So she began to wail loudly drowning out all noise, beating her breasts, snivelling and whining.

As he approached the house, Ramkali heard the heart-breaking laments of his cousin. 'Oh our Lakshmi's abandoned us and gone! What shall I do without my golden Lakshmi! Oh my son! Look how the crop's burnt down before the harvest!'

Satyabati exclaimed, 'Gosh! It's all over!'

Ramkali slowed down and frowned. So that was that. There would be no point in going in now! Who knew what other predicaments were in store for Jata? Suddenly a high-pitched scream was heard—perhaps as a 'finishing touch'. 'God! I am ruined! What a pretty wife I had brought my son!'

Ramkali walked up slowly to the door, and turning around said, 'So it's really over. Satya, you go home.'

Satyabati froze, 'By myself?'

'Why, didn't Neru and Punyi come with you?'

Satyabati said anxiously, 'They did, but they aren't going to come back with me.'

'Why won't they? They'll have to! Where are they? I must see to this.'

Satyabati slowly moved to the courtyard of her aunt's house, and failing to spot her friends, Neru or Punyi, returned crestfallen, 'Can't see either of them.'

'Why, where have they disappeared?'

'Who knows?' Slowly, regaining her courage, Satya voiced her innermost thought, 'You can bring back the dead, can't you, Baba?'

'Bring back the dead! Are you mad?'

'But that's what they all say,' Satya said numbly.

'What do they say?' he asked distractedly. And he looked to check if anyone was around. Well, now that he was here he could hardly avoid his duty. He noticed that there were not many bamboo bushes in this house; he would have to order some from his garden for the bier. But there was nobody to be seen. So many diverse pitches could be heard keening inside the house! Outside, it was deserted and calm.

Fortunately the clouds had disappeared unexpectedly, and the clear skies indicated that there was time yet for darkness to descend. And suddenly, Satyabati did something terribly defiant. She clutched her father's hand tightly in both her hands and uttered with great intensity, 'They all say that the doctor can bring the dead back to life! Please Baba, give Jatada's wife some medicine.'

Ramkali faltered in the face of this naive faith and suddenly felt helpless. He shook his head instead of rebuking her. 'There's no truth in what they say, my dear. I can't do a thing! It's just out of vanity that I prescribe herbs, feel the pulse and actually cheat people.'

Satyabati could not catch the irony in his tone, nor was she supposed to. She took it as a sign of his displeasure. But she felt reckless. She would take whatever was in store for her, even a thrashing. What if Jatada's wife should live because of her efforts! So, heedless of her surroundings, she pulled at her father's shawl, 'Baba, I beg of you! For one last time, give her some medicine! Oh! Jatada's wife will die without treatment!'

Ramkali could not explain to his daughter that nobody could treat people once they were dead. He sighed, turned around and said, 'Come, let's see.'

It was as if the trimmings of the stage had fallen off in the middle of a captivating performance. Wasn't that the doctor clearing his throat? Yes, that was right! That tall and handsome man was indeed the doctor. And instantly, Satya's sharp voice rang forth, 'My father says the crowd must move.'

The women of the locality pulled their saris over their heads and were silent. Only Jata's mother wailed, 'Alas Mejda! My wretched Jata's lost his wife!'

'Stop it!' It was like a tiger roaring. 'When wasn't your Jata a wretch? He's completely finished her off, has he?'

The crowd dispersed. The doctor approached the body of his nephew's wife, trying to avoid contact as custom demanded. He bent down and was astonished to find a pulse.

So the farce was finally over! And it is not as if just one scene had been cut, the whole play was ruined! Had anybody seen or heard such a mountain being made out of a molehill? Jata's wife's conduct was unforgivable! The height of wickedness! How shameful for a woman to have a life-span so intact! She was surely doomed to suffer endlessly—there could be no doubts about that, none at all! There she was, stiff as a corpse, lying by the sacred tulsi—and now look at her guzzling milk inside the house! Had anybody heard of such a woman?

'What a shame! A man would never ever open his eyes a second time once his wife was widowed.' 'What a stunt Jata's wife pulled off!' 'Now just wait and see. She'll get it from her mother-in-law —she's been really insulted today.' 'Whatever you say, it wasn't right to take her indoors straightaway, there should have been some rituals for purity. It would only be appropriate.' 'Who knows if she's really alive? What if she's been possessed by a spirit? I really have my doubts.' 'Don't talk like that! I go roaming here and there all by myself—it gives me the creeps! But don't her eyes look at bit strange?' 'Oh that's nothing to worry about, the doctor said the sudden push had made her faint.' 'Come on let's go, there's so much work. What a waste of time!' 'Did you notice what a hypocrite Jata's mother is? Pretended as if her heart was breaking!' 'Didn't I! Couldn't have imagined it! Actually, her heart must have broken when she saw the daughter-in-law wake up! All her hopes were dashed to the ground! She thought her son had got lucky! And she could just get him married again, bring in gold and gifts.' The words flowed non-stop. Words sprouted inside people's homes and outside, on the streets. After losing the golden opportunity of exterminating Jata's wife, people were reluctant to let such a momentous matter cool so quickly. They felt cheated and were annoyed. An aunt-in-law had brought along some sindur and alta, hoping to be the first to adorn the corpse of a married woman. Now she had to throw them into the pond. She was livid. Nobody knew Jata's wife's name. And nobody made the effort to find out. 'Jata's wife'—that was her only name! In time, she would be known as somebody's mother. She had no need for a name. But they all felt the need to talk about her.

The aunt-in-law burst out abruptly, 'In my parents' village they wouldn't have allowed her to live inside the house. She'd have to spend the rest of her life in the cowshed or in the husking room.'

Some people wondered if it was fair to condemn the living. But the aunt-in-law pronounced again, 'After all, she had been brought out to the sacred tulsi, just like a corpse. And then her uncle-in-law touched her. Think of the violation! I was so horrified to see him search for her pulse! I guess he thought she was dead, and purifying rituals would be done before the cremation, anyway. Well, now that she's come alive, surely some rituals are in order …'

After exploring the question in depth, it was decided that Jata's wife would have to perform one ritual to atone for the polluting touch of her uncle-in-law and another one for the transgression of returning to life after dying. Or else, she would be treated like a 'fallen woman'. The poor offender was still unconscious. Jata's mother was out, looking for Jata. Therefore an ex parte decision was arrived at.

Satyabati did not know any of this. She was brimming with happiness from a strange sense of pride. What an untruth her father had uttered about not knowing anything about treatment. It was only because Satya had dared to clasp his hand and ask for medicine that the poor woman was alive now! Suppose Satya's husband (and inadvertently, a smile played on her lips) beat her to death when she was at her in-laws, it would be great! Her father would rush there and give her the 'essence of gold ground with honey', and Satya would open her eyes, and pull her sari over her face in embarrassment when she came to and saw everyone.

What fun! The whole country would celebrate the feats of her eminent father Ramkali. Goodness! As if he was an ordinary man! No other girl in the village had such a father. And she laughed out loud. Satya was very prone to laughing aloud whenever she thought of something funny. Ramkali was taken aback, 'What's the matter? Why're you laughing?'

Satya controlled herself with difficulty, swallowed, and said, 'Just like that!'

'Just stop your just-like-that laughs will you?' Ramkali said, nearly laughing himself. 'Or else you'll be faced with the fate of Jata's wife when you go to your in-laws.'

He felt content. Night was approaching. He would have had to face a few problems but Jata's wife had spared him all that. Even though Satya could not fathom the reason, she could perceive his contentment and taking courage, she declared enthusiastically, 'That was why I laughed. If I die you would always come and save me.'

'Oh, really!' Ramkali responded briefly, being a man of few words. He walked briskly in silence and Satyabati broke into a run to keep up. Suddenly, Ramkali stopped and said, 'Even god can't do a thing if you die, do you understand? Jata's wife hadn't died.'

'Hadn't she?' Satya was perplexed for a moment. 'Then what is dying like?' Suddenly her train of thought changed track; she proclaimed ardently, 'But then Baba, if you hadn't felt her pulse and given her the "essence of gold", Jatada's wife would have remained like that—lifeless! And then they'd have put her on a bamboo bier and cremated her!'

Ramkali was a little startled. Strange! How could such a small girl think so deeply. What a pity she was a girl and it was all in vain. If only Neru had such brains! But it was useless to hope—for he was a full-grown eight-year-old and still tracing the alphabet! Neru was the youngest of Kunja's brood. Ramkali's elder brother, Kunja, and his wife, had become lenient with their youngest after raising thirteen children. This one too would probably turn out to be a misfit in a brahmin's house! But a girl child should not even learn to think so deeply. So Ramkali said in a reproving tone, 'Stop it! Don't talk too much. Walk faster. Can't you see it's dark?'

'Dark?' Satyabati said nonchalantly. 'Huh! As if I fear the dark! Don't I go into the garden when it's very very dark, to count owls by spotting their glistening eyes?'

'What! What is it you do in the dark?' Ramkali was staggered.

Satyabati faltered. 'Not just me—Neru and Punyi-pishi too. We count the eyes of the owls.'

Suddenly, Ramkali started laughing. He laughed for a long while, deep and loud. How could he scold or discipline such a girl! His deep laughter echoed through the silence of the dark road. And the old men, gathered at the courtyard of the temple, heard it too.

'Isn't that the doctor's voice?'

'That's what it sounds like.'

'Why's he laughing by himself at this hour?'

'He's probably not alone. That unruly daughter must be with him. Otherwise ...'

'What a girl he's raised! She's fated to be unhappy!'

'Unhappy! With so much money! I heard that the Raja of Barddhaman sent for him yesterday. Wants him to be the court physician.'

'Is that so? I didn't know anything about it! So is he leaving?'

'No, I hear he isn't going.'

'Really! That's good news. But who told you?'

'Kunja's eldest son.'

'Good! Imagine going and working far away, and at the court too! If only Ramkali cared about etiquette, he wouldn't have let his daughter become so bold. Just look, all the boys are her playmates!'

'Yes! But then she's ten times better than the boys when it comes to swimming, climbing trees and fishing!'

'That's nothing to be proud of. After all, she's a girl and that too a married one. Married into a well-known family too. If they get to know, they'll just refuse to take her.'

'I know! It doesn't take long for a scandal.'

The atmosphere at the temple courtyard grew heavy with discussions about the doctor and his unruly daughter. People respected him publicly, and yet, how would they survive if they could not disparage him in private?

Meanwhile, the prime subject of their discussion was running behind her father and fervently praying, 'Oh god—please make my legs long—like my father's, then I can walk like him and I shall never lose!' Satyabati disapproved of defeat. She would not lose anywhere, at any time. That was her resolve.

⸻

'Hey Punyi! Can you make up a rhyme?'

Satyabati's 'play room' was in the attic. Her chief playmate was Ramkali's cousin's daughter, Punyabati. Even though Satya called her 'Punyi-pishi' in front of others, in her own terrain she called her 'Punyi'.

'Can you find a weaver-bird's nest?' 'Can you catch a blue-beetle?' 'Can you swim across the lake three times?' Satya would often grill Punyi this way. But, 'Can you make up a rhyme?' was an absolutely new query.

Punyi asked, 'Rhyme? What do you mean?'

'A rhyme about Jatada, you know. We'll teach all the children in the village, and they'll clap and chant it whenever they see him!'

They both swayed with laughter, imagining Jata's plight. Finally, Punyabati asked a counter question, 'So you say you'll make up a rhyme. Are girls supposed to do that?'

'Aren't they?' Suddenly, Satya blazed forth, 'Who said that? My foot! As if girls are unnatural and not conceived in their mother's wombs! Do you think girls just come floating with the tide, or what? Don't play with me if you talk like that!'

'Okay, my dear "sir"! But what if your husband talks this way?'

'Which way?'

'In the same way, about girls.'

'Huh! Won't I show him! Do you think I'll be like Jatada's wife? Never! Now just watch how I plague him with a rhyme!'

Punyi asked deferentially, 'How will you do that?'

'How else? The way the Kathak-thakur does—same way! I've made up a bit already. Want to hear?'

'Already! Tell me, please!'

Satya spoke with assurance, almost as if she were slowly savouring sour tamarind:

The elephant-footed Jatadada—there he goes, the blighter!
May a toad kick the back of this stupid wife-beater!

'Goodness Satya!' Punyi suddenly squealed and hugged Satya. 'Look at you! You'll be writing proper poetry next!'

Satya responded airily, as if it would not be too great an achievement if she did, 'I will when I will. Now we have to teach everyone this, understand? And when we see Jatadada ...'

FIVE

Her back had been stinging from the heat for a while now, suddenly it seemed to catch fire! Obviously, the shade of the bakul tree had moved out of the verandah. It was late afternoon. What a bother, thought Mokshada, because both her hands were otherwise occupied to pull back the sari that had slipped off her back, exposing it to direct sunlight. Even if she could not see it for herself, everybody would have noticed how raw and red the glowing skin on her back looked.

She should have had her wet sari draped around her instead of changing into the raw-silk before sitting down to mix pickling spices with the mangoes. The wet sari would have relieved this burning in her body somewhat. Mokshada moved into the shade of the pole in the courtyard, dragging the two heavy stone tureens with raised rims.

But the relief was ever so slight. Besides, the sun was on the run, the shadow would soon flit away. Suddenly, Mokshada hit upon a truth: she really killed herself working in the sun all year long. Here she was preparing the mango in oil; the mango slices in jaggery sauce, or spiced mango would come next, and then it would be time for mango wafers. In short, the mango season was impossible. The rains would follow right after the mango wafers became ready and then there was some respite from the sun. But the chants of the Durga puja came right after the monsoons. And a great din would begin over cleaning and drying everything that was to be stored and stashed away. And the flurry of making sesame balls would start immediately.

The sesame balls of Doctor Chatterji's house were famous. They were so large that one had to hold them in one's hand in order to eat them. The fried sweets and the jaggery-coated puffed rice-balls were well-known too, but everybody helped with those. Except for the sweets that were offered to the goddess, for which pure Ganga water was used, many people worked on the sweets. The sesame balls were Mokshada's department. Nobody in this region had her skills. And it was not for nothing that she had such a reputation —after all, it was because she did everything herself that they turned out so perfect! Sack loads of sesame seeds came in. Mokshada would wash them clean, dry them crisp in the sun and pound them flat before tossing them in a basket with jaggery that she had simmered in a brass pot. After that, she would roll out the balls on her palms. She refused to relinquish the smallest step! Once when Sejo-bou and Boro-bouma had helped flatten the sesame seeds, the sweets had been ruined! They had not even taken the husk off properly! And how black and disgusting they had looked! Ramkali had laughed aloud when he saw them and asked, 'Who made these?'

Since then Mokshada had become very cautious. Except for asking someone to sit by the husking pedal, she would do everything herself. But during the pujas, those were not the only items; Mokshada's duties included going to every home to invite them to the puja, and taking ritual gifts for the family priests. After all, she was a daughter of the family. Kashiswari had done her bit earlier, but of late, she was almost disabled by illness. She could no longer exert herself and walk long distances in the sun. So Mokshada would do it all, and take a dip in the pond fourteen or fifteen times a day!

It would be impossible to figure out why Mokshada thought continually of the sun. She pondered on how she would have to start on the boris soon after the pujas. The household required about fourteen maunds of boris. Both the kitchens used them, but the responsibility rested with the vegetarian kitchen. Like the pickles, these too required ritual purity during preparation. And Mokshada could trust no one except herself in such matters.

Over the years, Mokshada's glowing skin had darkened. But what she made delighted the palate! She had an expert's touch. Besides, she was very careful; she would not let anyone touch the stuff if she could help it. She placed the boris in large covered saucers and stored them away, bringing them out when the need arose. And they tasted so wonderful! They were made from white pumpkin, poppy seeds, sesame seeds, jeera seeds; some were crispy, some spicy. Then there were lentil boris for sour and bitter curries—they had so many uses!

Of course, she always had to remind herself to keep the ones made from radish separate. Because customarily one could not eat them in the month of Magh—it would amount to eating beef!

The shadow had moved and her back began to burn once more. And with that, her mind.

Once the bori chapter got over, the season for plums and tamarind arrived. So when did she ever get a respite from the sun? It would be futile to ask, 'Who had given her such a responsibility?'. Mokshada considered it her duty.

Mixing the mango with oil was a time-consuming task. One had to mash the mango in the oil. Once that was done, a thin layer of mustard powder had to be sprinkled over it and the mixture kept in the sun for a while.

Mokshada stretched and got up. And the movement made her scorched back burn some more. But how strange, why did an emptiness tug at her heart as she entered the kitchen to grind the mustard? Mokshada stood listless for a while. Why did the room suddenly look so huge? It never appeared so large. In fact, it would feel so tiny, whenever they brushed against each other when sitting down for a meal.

There was no sun inside the kitchen, but this cool, shaded room seemed as barren as the empty blazing courtyard outside. And two huge chullahs, scrubbed and clean, stood at one corner of the kitchen as symbols of untold, infinite emptiness. The chullahs would not have to suffer a blazing fire today. Perhaps, they would now have an opportunity to measure the extent of their emptiness. They had a holiday today. Because of ekadashi. Why didn't Mokshada ever have a day off?

A pot of water stood near the kitchen drain, ready for use. Mokshada would fill it and bring it in after her last bath.

Tilting the pot a bit, she poured out water in which she washed her oily hand. And suddenly she began to splash water noisily on her back, to soothe the areas that were burning. What a bother! She should have gone to the pond and taken a dip—she could have wet her whole body. The thirst would lessen a bit if she wet her skin.

It was a sin to even think about thirst on ekadashi. Mokshada knew that well. After all, she was a robust widow, well past her prime. Yet she had no weapon with which to drive away a thought that appeared against her will.

The summer sun made one feel particularly dry and thirsty, but there was no other way. Today was the best day to finish all the extra work. One hardly got such undisrupted leisure!

Looking for mustard seeds, Mokshada brought down a small container painted with flowers that had been stored away on the shelf. The year's spices were cleaned and put away in containers; spices for everyday household use were kept in small bundles of clean cloth. The main stores were raided only for such extraordinary needs.

Just as she was about to sit down to grind the mustard, Shibjaya's voice boomed at the door, 'I ask you, what has this world come to? Mark my words, the end of Kaliyuga is here! Did you hear the latest about our brazen Miss Wayward?'

But much before she heard of that unruly girl's insolence, Mokshada shrieked at her sister-in-law's impertinence, 'How dare you come up here with unclean feet! And that's just where I store the pickle! Now if you too start behaving like one without faith …'

Shibjaya responded a trifle testily, 'I wish you wouldn't go on and on, Thakurji! As if I'd step in here with unclean feet! Look, I've got cow dung on my feet! I brought some with me, flung it below the steps, and trod on it before stepping in here.'

If stepping into the pond and washing one's feet was absolutely impossible, this was the alternative Mokshada prescribed. But she was not easily convinced by her sister-in-law's words. She asked suspiciously, 'I hope the dung is from our cows and not from the neighbour's cows which eat unclean things.'

'Listen to that!' Shibjaya exclaimed in a tone to check further argument. 'How will dung from a neighbour's cow come into our courtyard?'

Well, arguments hardly stop just because one so desires! And nor did Mokshada's queries. She asked with a sarcastic laugh, 'Oh my goodness! Do you really wonder about that? When I listen to you, I feel at times, you were born yesterday!'

Though Shibjaya was scared of her sister-in-law, Mokshada was younger than her, so she answered irritably, 'Come now! It's such a bother approaching you! I was stunned by the accomplishment of our smart madam! I just heard about it on my way back from Gobinda's place. But never mind now ...'

So finally, Mokshada relented. She asked, almost in a tone of truce, 'What is it? Who are you talking about? Satya?'

'Who else?' Shibjaya abandoned her resigned tone and picked up the thread with enthusiasm. 'Who else will have such guts? I believe the cheeky girl has made up a rhyme about Jata and she's taught it to the entire crowd of kids here, and they all break into it as soon as they see Jata or his mother. Jata's mother's livid and swearing like anything!'

Mokshada listened silently till she had finished, then frowned, and asked sharply, 'What do you mean "made up a rhyme"?'

'As if I understood what it meant, when I first heard it! In all my life I've never heard that a girl could make up a rhyme! Then I hear a horde of kids laughing and saying, "The elephant-footed Jatadada—there goes the blighter!" They were making faces and chanting!'

Mokshada's frown deepened, 'Satya has made up a rhyme?'

'That's what I'm telling you!'

'This family will suffer because of that girl,' Mokshada said, as she put down the grinding stone. 'Ramkali ignores it now but he'll know soon enough when they send her back from her in-laws. Is the rhyme for Jata because he beat up his wife?'

'What else? I tell you, find me a man who doesn't beat his wife! And what a delicate wife! Made a mountain out of a molehill and fainted and broadcast it to the world! Jata's mother was saying that Jata can't get out because of the kids.'

Mokshada said as she ground the mustard, 'I'll have a word with her mother once I've finished this. I'll make her see sense. Does a girl become this wild without her mother's indulgence? And where's the need to spend so much time bantering with the boys? If a scandal breaks out how will Ramkali face it? Society won't forgive you just because you have money!'

Shibjaya had achieved her purpose. She had been able to incite Mokshada against her eldest sister-in-law's grand-daughter.

—

Wrapping her raw-silk sari around her, Mokshada crossed the courtyard and walked out of the bamboo door. She would have to take a bath when she got back—and not just once, but many times; however, the problem had to be looked into right away. Mokshada could not stand anybody creating any upheaval in the world. But what was this! Mokshada just froze in her tracks. She halted, as if thunderstruck! She saw Satya, in a sari with a three-striped border, her mass of wild hair flying, knees dusty, walking with a band of boys and girls through the mango grove. They were laughing and chanting something that sounded like a rhyme.

Gritting her teeth, Mokshada followed them. She hid behind a tree trying to listen to their words. It was impossible to hear everything because of their giggles! Still, it was possible to make out from their clear chants and many repetitions. And she heard the rhyme, through the laughter that had entered its every crack and corner:

The elephant-footed Jatadada—there he goes, the blighter!
May a toad kick the back of this stupid wife-beater!
Jata, Jata's really gross, he's an abuser like no other!
Watch the fun, for now he'll run, here comes the wife's father!

They left, chanting. And Mokshada stood there stupefied. No, not because she was moved by the poetic prowess of her grand niece, but because she was stunned by thoughts of her future! Had she come to punish this one? She no longer desired to do that, because it slowly dawned on her that the family would have to suffer this girl forever. Her in-laws would send her back, that was for sure!

———

Satya untied the paper-wrapped pills from the end of her sari, and lowering her clear voice a little, said, 'Take these pills. Baba has said to take one in the morning and one in the evening with betel-leaf juice. It'll make your body stronger.'

A stronger body! When the strength of the mind had sunk to the depths of the ocean and the heart quivered in fear! Jata's wife whispered pathetically, frantically, 'Please, I beg of you, take them back. My mother-in-law will finish me off if she sees that I'm taking medicine!'

Satya put her hand to her cheek and said like a grown-up, 'Good god! Listen to this! You've become weak, and here are medicines for free, and your mother-in-law will kill you if you take them! I am truly surprised!'

'Please, please! Not so loud!' Jata's wife was on the verge on tears. 'I beg of you. If she heard, I'll have no other way than to drown myself in the pond!'

Satya settled herself down and asked in astonishment, 'If she heard what?'

'What I just said about my mother-in-law wanting to finish me off! You know everything, don't you? Can you imagine what would happen if I take the pills your father has sent! Goodness! Look how my heart is thumping inside.'

Satyabati suddenly looked thoughtful as she recognized the hunted look that flickered in the woman's eyes and saw her ashen face. After a brief pause, she began to tie the pills once more onto the end of her sari, 'All right, I'll take them back.'

Take them back! To her father! A different fear froze the blood of Jata's wife. She was no longer on the verge of tears, but actually burst into sobs. 'Please, I'll be your slave forever, don't take them back to your father!'

Not take them back? Suddenly Satya started laughing in her

characteristic manner, 'Great! I think you've lost your mind after your illness. You won't take the pills for fear of your mother-in-law, won't let me take them back either—so should I swallow these pills then? Very well, get me a cup of betel-leaf juice, I'll take the whole lot.'

Jata's wife now opened up her heart. She had neither the guts to take the pills without asking her mother-in-law, nor the nerve to seek her permission to take them, so the only way out was to dump them in the pond.

'Dump them!' Satya's eyes were ablaze. 'Do you know that my father's pills are from Dhanvantari, the god of medicine, himself? If you insult these, you insult god.'

'What shall I do then?' Jata's wife began to sob.

Satya could not help feeling sorry for her. After a moment's thought she said, 'Why don't I do something? Let me hand them over to Pishi. I'll say my father sent them, even though he told me not to give them to her because she'd just throw them away. Let's see if I can plead with her.'

Satya rose and Jata's wife who was clutching on to the end of her sari, tripped and nearly fell at Satya's feet, 'Please, please— why don't you trample me and kill me instead! Bring the kitchen knife and chop me up!'

Satya sat down again. She let out a sigh and said, 'Just tell me, what is it that all of you are so scared of?'

SIX

The palki-bearers hummed as they ran. Crushing the soil under their cracked feet, grinding dust in their mouths, as they sped along an unrelentingly arid road, on a fuming summer afternoon. Part of the way was a vast expanse, bereft of trees and shade. Perhaps they felt most tormented when crossing such fields. Four of them were taking turns at running with the palki, and yet they seemed to be wilting.

However, Ramkali could not afford to be sympathetic to his palki-bearers at the moment. It had been four days since he left the village—there were a couple of patients in serious condition, and he had no idea how they were doing. He had gone to Jiret to see a zamindar patient. After all, Ramkali-doctor's reputation was not confined to his village alone; it had spread to the villages around.

They had taken very good care of him, and had begged him to stay a few more days. But Ramkali had not agreed. He had left saying, 'There's no need. The medicine I've given should make the patient better in about three days. But you must take proper care to prepare the diet I have prescribed.'

They had loaded a basketful of mangoes of a special variety into his palki; his protests had gone unheeded. Now, Ramkali felt irritated every time he stretched and his feet touched the basket. What a bother! They had refused to accept the fact that he never ate anything when he travelled. The zamindar himself had supervised the loading, though Ramkali had intervened when they had brought four green coconuts. He had declared, 'Very well then, let the palki-bearers carry the fruits in the palki. Ray-mashai, looks like I'll have to walk!'

The mangoes were almost ripe, and the warm summer breeze ripened them further and spread their fragrance. And even as Ramkali felt irritated, the bearers tasted the flavour in their minds. And they wished that they could have carried the four green coconuts. What harm would it have done? It would have provided some relief to the beasts of burden. Perhaps the thought had distracted them a bit, and they slackened. They were startled by a shout from their master. Ramkali put his head out of the palki and yelled out, 'All right fellows, hurry and don't fall asleep now!'

But no sooner had he pronounced the words, he changed his tune, 'I say, wait, wait a bit. I can hear another palki approaching from the rear.'

Yes, there was indeed such a sound coming from the rear. And very suddenly too. The humming became clearer. The chief of the bearers, Godai, relieved his shoulders of the handle of the palki and looking back, said enthusiastically, 'That's right, Karta-mashai!

You're absolutely right! There is a palki coming this way—looks like a bridegroom.'

A bridegroom! Ramkali stretched his neck out of the palki and raised his voice, 'Who on earth gave you that news?'

Godai scratched his low-caste head and said, 'I can see the yellow cloth on the door, Karta, and the bearers are wearing red khetos.'

The kheto was a shorter version of the dhoti. Like all labouring people, palki-bearers could not afford to wear a full dhoti. Nor did they possess them. Their 'national costume' was a seven-foot-long kheto, thick as sackcloth. Sometimes they were lucky to get red ones when they worked at a wedding or a sacred-thread ceremony. Those lasted without a wash for nearly three months.

But not just the ceremonial colours, the people gradually became visible too. And Godai made another earnest discovery, 'There's a bullock cart just behind them, Karta! I can hear the bell. This has to be the bridegroom and his party. There's a wedding somewhere this side. They've come from a village on the other side.'

'Stop right here!' Ramkali ordered solemnly.

He wanted to verify if what Godai had assumed was true. And he needed to know too, who in his village had the nerve to get a daughter married without inviting him! And if it was not anyone from his village, then he wanted to find out where they were going; after all, they were passing through his village. Whatever Ramkali's intentions were, the bearers felt relieved. They put the palki down under a tree and stood at a distance, fanning themselves with their gamchas. They dared not fan themselves in front of their master.

After a while, the other palki came closer. Ramkali stepped down and after tidying the tussar chaddar on his shoulder, stood regally and bellowed in a deep, thunderous voice, 'Who goes there?'

The palki stopped. For nobody had the nerve to ignore that voice. Inside the palki, sat the groom and the head of the groom's party. Along with the latter, the young groom too nervously poked his head out to look. Who could keep sitting inside when that tall, elegant man stood down there? So the head of the groom's party descended too. He folded his hands, 'I'm sorry, but you are ...'

By then Ramkali was frowning, his keen eyes were scanning the inside of the palki. He returned the gesture out of habit and said, 'I am Ramkali Chatterji.'

'Ramkali Chatterji!' The gentleman responded in confusion—neither to himself, nor as a question, but rather limply, 'The doctor!'

'That's right! The boy has sandalwood paste smeared on his forehead—is he to be married?'

The man was certainly not younger in age to Ramkali, but he bent down and touched Ramkali's feet, cringing as though he was no more significant than an insect, 'That's right. How fortunate we are to have met you.'

Ramkali's eyes continued to scrutinize, but he smiled slightly and said, 'Do you know of me?'

'Is there anybody so wretched in these parts that he would not know of you? But I hadn't had the good fortune to meet you. Raju, come out and touch his feet.'

'Let him be, he's the groom,' Ramkali said almost mechanically. 'Is he your son?'

'No, he's my nephew. The son of my youngest brother. He is in the bullock cart behind us. There are other relatives as well.'

'I see. Where is the girl from?'

'From Patmahal. The granddaughter of Lakshmikanta Banerji …'

'Lakshmikanta Banerji's granddaughter? Is that right?' Ramkali seemed to wake up suddenly. 'And where are you from? What is your father's name?'

'We are from Balagar. My father was the late Gangadhar Mukherji, my grandfather was Gunadhar Mukherji and I am—'

'That's enough, I don't need to know your name. So, you are a Mukherji-brahmin, a kulin. Why do you behave as if you're a brahmin from the priest class? But let that be. I have to have a few words with you. When did you leave home?'

The man resented being labelled a 'priest', and said solemnly, 'Right after the morning ritual.'

'I know that, but what time was it?'

'About three hours ago.'

'I see. And was the sandalwood paste smeared on his forehead at that time?'

The sandalwood paste? What did that have to do with anything? The groom's uncle was readying himself to answer all kinds of questions but was hardly prepared for such an absurd one about the time of applying the sandalwood paste! So he asked dully, 'What do you mean?'

'I asked if the sandalwood paste on his forehead was applied when you started out.'

'Yes, yes, of course!' The uncle answered enthusiastically, 'The women put it on when we started out, as they usually do. The women of our house are well-known for such skills, you know. People in the locality call them to decorate bridal gifts, or to do the make-up for the bride or the groom ...'

Ramkali was staring, preoccupied. In the mean time the bullock carts had arrived. Spotting the stationary palki, and a conversation taking place with a stranger of the other palki, the father of the groom joined them.

A preoccupied Ramkali let out a sigh and said in a deep voice, 'I am making one request to you, Mukherji-mashai, cancel this trip.'

Cancel the trip! When they had started out for a wedding! The groom's father and uncle stared, mouths agape. Was this a mad man or wicked one? Or, did he nurse a grave grudge against the bride's family?

The palki-bearers were sweating profusely in the unbearable heat. They stood in two groups, at a distance, consulting each other, trying to figure out what was going on. And frequently checking to see if they were going to be summoned soon.

Having figured out that something was wrong, another man jumped off the bullock cart. This was the groom's aunt's husband. The heat inside the bullock cart had unsettled him a bit, and he became absolutely furious when he heard the request to cancel the journey. He said, 'Look here, who the hell do you think you are? A fine place to cancel the wedding! Here we are on our way with the groom and now you stop us!'

Embarrassed by their brother-in-law's outburst, the two Mukherji brothers blurted out, 'Please stop, Ganguly! You have no idea who you're speaking to!'

'I don't care! When a man speaks like a fool ...'

'Shut up!' It was as though a sleeping tiger had woken up. 'Shut up you useless son of a brahmin!'

'I say!' The roar was followed by the jackal's snarl, 'I haven't come to be insulted at this wedding! Is he a relative or what? Take him along for the wedding, I'm leaving.'

'For goodness sake, Ganguly, this is the most eminent doctor in the seven villages around here—Doctor Chatterji! He must have some definite reason ...'

'Doctor Chatterji!' Ganguly cringed in embarrassment, he bit his tongue, cuffed his own ears and forgetting the dignity of age, quickly touched the doctor's feet.

Hardly paying any attention to all this, Ramkali said in a calm and balanced manner, 'Yes, there is a definite and specific reason, Mukherji-mashai. Otherwise, I wouldn't make a dumb request like cancelling your son's wedding. Cancel this journey.'

The elder Mukherji rubbed his hands together, 'Of course not! Is there some defect in Lakshmikanta's family?'

'Please, do not think me to be so vulgar Mukherji! All I am saying is that you'll be in trouble if you try to get your son married. Your son is unwell.'

Was this a trick? It was certainly a bolt from the blue! Totally unexpected! The Mukherjis had thought that the man harboured a grudge against the girl's family and was about to reveal some imperfection. That was perfectly conceivable. But what kind of absurd demand was this?

'My son is ill! How can you say that, doctor? It is impossible! My son is healthy and fine. I suppose the afternoon heat and the fact that he's fasting have made him pale,' the younger Mukherji said pathetically.

'In fact, he's not looking pale at all!' Ramkali said gravely. 'To the contrary! If you look carefully you'll notice he looks puffy. I had noticed it in the beginning and so I stopped you. I can see the symptoms of inflammation in the frontal lobe of the brain. You'll be in serious trouble if you take him to get married. Take him home, send word to the girl's side.'

The groom's uncle flew into a rage, oblivious of earlier civility. 'A wonderful mess you've created now! The wedding is today—tonight! And we're supposed to take the boy home? And send word to the girl's family that he is ill? Is this a game or what? I know now that you bear a grudge against the girl's side!'

Ramkali's face was red from the heat, his face now blazed like fire. But he resisted becoming upset. He contemptuously rolled his eyes at Ganguly, 'You're right, I do bear a grudge! Lakshmikanta Banerji studied with my uncle, and I respect him as I would my own father. I would not wish his granddaughter to be widowed on her wedding night.'

One more bolt from the blue! What a terrible threat! Was this a curse, or the ranting of a fevered brain? Mukherji helplessly twisted his sacred thread in his hand and wailed aloud.

Ramkali remained steady as an unflickering flame. Just as a hard-hearted judge remains unmoved after delivering a death sentence, Ramkali stood motionless, unruffled and calm. Mukherji could not curse him, he took his hand off his sacred thread and cried out, 'What are you saying?'

'What else can I say? I didn't want to say it—you made me spell it out. Listen, if you know what's good for you, take him back to his mother. I can see death waiting to take him. Don't waste time talking. Besides, the boy will get perturbed if you're upset.'

But Mukherji was human after all! And his mind swayed between belief and disbelief. Should he believe a mere mortal who claimed that death awaited his son? This boy who sat inside the palki, peeping out every now and then, his forehead glistening with sandalwood paste, and a sweet-smelling garland around his neck! And placing his faith in this man, should Mukherji return with the groom and hurl a respectable man into the deepest abyss? What about the Banerjis? The fate of a girl abandoned on her wedding night was worse than death!

Impossible! It had to be a plot! May be this man nursed a terrible malice against Lakshmikanta Banerji. May be he was not the doctor at all! Some crazy brahmin, perhaps! A strong personality capable of muddling one's judgement! And cursing a child in this way! The younger Mukherji glanced at the nearby palki and said, his chest tightening, 'I cannot find any sign of illness.'

Ramkali smiled ruefully, 'If you could, there'd be very little difference between you and me! But come here. Do you see the sandalwood paste on his forehead? It looks watery, almost as if it were freshly applied. And yet you just told me that it was applied three hours ago. Normally, it would have dried and become powdery. But it hasn't. That's because the inflammation in his frontal lobe had been concealed so far. But it has increased the fluid in the body—'

'Is that all?' Suddenly the elder Mukherji laughed, 'I think the journey has exhausted you, so you are making a mistake in reading the symptoms. The heavy sweating in summer would hardly let the sandalwood paste dry. All right men! Come, let's start! What a way to stop an auspicious journey!'

A mistake in reading the symptoms! Would Ramkali's nerves snap?

At first, Ramkali made to move towards his own palki, but for some reason he stopped and pronounced grimly, 'Listen, Mukherji, had you dared to say, under any other circumstance, that Ramkali Chatterji had misread the symptoms you'd get an appropriate answer. But you're in deep trouble now, and Banerji too is in danger, so you are forgiven. The Banerji household must be alerted at once. And I shall have to do that. I'll have to leave the palki and hire a horse if necessary. But let me give you one last warning—the boy's vein has ruptured and there's some internal bleeding—if you look carefully at his inflamed eyes and the bulging veins on his forehead you'll be able to make that out as well. I think delirium will set in soon. It was my duty to warn you and that's what I've done. Weren't you accusing me of misreading symptoms? I pray to god that you're right! Let's hope that Ramkali has mistaken normal summer perspiration for the sweat of death! What else can I say?

Namaskar! Godai, let's start. Take me to Basir, fast as you can. I need to find a horse.'

No sooner had his palki started to move than the younger Mukherji came running, howling, 'Doctor, aren't you going to give any medicine after proclaiming such a terrible end?'

Sadly, gravely, Ramkali shook his hand and raising it to his forehead said, 'If there was any medicine, I'd have given it without your asking. But now, even the Sage Dhanvantari can't do a thing.'

Meanwhile, the elder Mukherji had got into the palki and said irritably, 'Goddess save us from such obstacles! Wonder what ill-omened thing we'd looked at when we started out! What a bother! But, hey, hey—Raju—why're you drooping? Are you hot?'

And opening bloodshot eyes, Raju said, 'No. I'm just feeling terribly cold.'

SEVEN

They were playing at 'cooling' the warm waters by 'trapping' the upper layer inside the outstretched ends of their saris and exchanging this with the cooler waters at the bottom. Though the day had cooled somewhat, the pond still seemed to be boiling, and its waters would sooner scald than soothe if one dived in. But it beckoned the young girls of the locality, and they all longed to take a dip before evening fell.

Punyi, Tepi, Puti, Khedi and other young girls were making the waters of the Chatterji's pond curdle with mud. They wondered why Satya had not arrived as yet and, perhaps, to please the absent Satya, they were engaged in this operation of 'cooling' the waters as quickly as possible.

Satya was the darling of their hearts. For she was more than their leader. God alone knew which of her many virtues made Satya the ruler of their hearts! For them playing without Satya was like the tandava dance performed without Lord Shiva. It was Satya who had pioneered this prank of jumping into the pond. So as they 'cooled' the waters they asked each other, 'What do you think happened to Satya?' 'She's not home.' 'She said she'd come here on time.' 'Perhaps she's in the orchard.' 'No! Why would she go there by herself?' 'After all she's a married girl—she wouldn't dare!' 'Satya's very daring! Just wait and see; when she goes to her in-laws she'll be as bold!'

Perhaps her boldness was the reason why Satya had become the goddess of their hearts. It is only human to admire those very virtues which are absent in oneself and so obviously present in another. But Satya had many other qualities too. At games, no one could match her talents, she had both strength and skill—a hundred times more than anybody else. It was not at all impossible for Satya to drag a thick stump of a tree all by herself. And to roll it into the pond and make a raft! She was resourceful enough to do that. And to top it all, she had made up a rhyme! Now all the children of the locality had handed over their souls to her. So it was hardly surprising that they were 'cooling' the waters for Satya. But why was she late? Their time would soon be up. Once the grandmothers and aunts found out, it would all be over.

They had this licence only because it was siesta time for their mothers and aunts. That is right, most housewives took a nap in the late afternoon. Not throughout the year—because there is nothing as wicked as women sleeping during daylight hours—only during the mango season.

The mango made them feel drunk. The women called it mango liquor. And even if you did not gorge on mangoes, your body felt tipsy. Of course, not eating mangoes was simply out of the question! Everybody ate mangoes and jackfruit. Not everyone was like Haru Bhattacharya's mother, who had given up mangoes for the sake of Lord Jagannath when she had visited Puri. Custom demanded that one gave up something after going on this pilgrimage, and she had given up mangoes! Naturally, Haru Bhattacharya was so upset that he had wanted to sell his mango orchard that year, saying, 'What's the point in holding on to this, if my mother can't eat them?' And his mother had held his hand and calmed him down by saying, 'I've had mangoes all my life and yet I always felt it was never enough! That's why I thought it best to give up something I was addicted to. But why get rid of the garden because of that? You have kids.'

Everybody—young and old—was fond of mangoes. In the mango season it was not unusual to eat twenty to forty mangoes in a day. But there are different types of mangoes for different classes of people. That is to say, everyone did not get to taste every variety. Mangoes were classified, just like people in society. The men were offered the varieties known as Jor-kalam, Gulab-khus, Kshirshapati, Nawab-pasand, Badshah-bhog, Dhaush, Fazli, etc. The older women got the Peyaraphuli, Belsubashi, Kashir-chini, Sindure-megh.

And the younger women, girls and children were destined for the common 'Rashi' mango. That was best, especially if one demanded loads of it! The baskets at home, filled to the brim, would always be inadequate for the young. They would smuggle in more whenever the older women were resting after making sweet snacks. And soon they would have finished them and would rush to other gardens in search of inferior varieties that were terribly sour and therefore required plenty of salt. Salt was a common commodity, but because it was kept in the storeroom, children had to work very hard to procure it. The storeroom was guarded jealously by completely merciless older women who were ever-ready to scream. Everyone was aware that they would want to give a stinging slap to anyone who asked for a bit of salt. But the lucky thing was that children were practically treated as untouchable because of the laws of ritual pollution, and so they could not really beat them even if they wanted to! Well, even if the women finally relented, they would only dole out a small quantity of salt—as if it were gold! And with it a scolding, 'It's for gorging on those poisonously sour mangoes, isn't it? Can't get your fill, can you? What large demon tummies you wretches have! Wait till you die of blood dysentery! And catch the pox! You rascals!'

Salt came with curses, always. They could never imagine otherwise.

Earlier, Satya would procure quite an amount from Charan, the grocer, but of late, since she was a little older she felt embarrassed to beg from a grocer's shop. At the most, she would stand at a distance and urge a younger child. Satya was respected in the locality because she was the doctor's daughter. She had to live up to her reputation!

Satya had been part of their mango-grove adventure in the afternoon. Then, at some point she had slipped away home. Khedi was a little imaginative, so she speculated, 'Hope nobody's come from her in-laws.'

'Rubbish! Why should they—for no reason at all? And if they did, how would it affect Satya? They'd wait in the temple courtyard.'

Suddenly Puti yelled out, 'There she comes! Look, she's here!'

'Thank god! I breathe again!'

'Why so late, Satya? We've been "cooling" the waters for so long!'

Satya carefully climbed down the steps of the ghat and entered the water without a word.

'Hey, Satya, why so quiet? Acting high and mighty, eh?'

Satya took a mouthful of water and rinsed her mouth, twisted her face wryly and said, 'High and mighty, my foot! I'm disgusted with the ways of people!'

'Why, what's up? Whom did you meet? Who're you talking about?'

Satya responded fiercely, 'I'm talking about Jatada's wife. Hang her by the neck! A disgrace to womankind!'

Satya was nine, but it would be wrong to think that she was incapable of stringing words together in such a manner because she was young. And not only Satya. In those days, unless they were absolutely dumb, eight- or nine-year-old girls were experts at talking in this manner. And why wouldn't they be? They would be trained from age four onwards to think of being married and leaving for a different home; and so, the realm of grown-ups was seen to be an appropriate enough terrain for them. Language was never ever expunged in their presence because they were children. It was hardly surprising that Satya could label someone 'a disgrace to womankind' because she was annoyed.

Punyi asked promptly, 'What's up?'

'Only Yama knows!' After placing the blame on the god of death for a while, Satya finally elaborated, 'I'll not look at her face again in all my life! Shame! Shame! I went there today. The poor thing couldn't even take the pills for fear of her husband and mother-in-law, so I thought let me go and check on her. I'd heard that aunt was away at Tarakeshwar, so I felt free, you know. And what do I see? God! I'd die of shame! How depraved!'

They all stared in apprehension, who knew what terrible tale Satya was about to reveal. Only Punyi ventured timorously, 'What?'

'You know what I saw? Would you believe it if I told you? I saw Jatada sitting inside and his wife was making him a paan—and they were laughing and joking together!'

Only Jatada?

Khedi, Puti, all of them unanimously exclaimed, 'My god! And this has made you so angry? Her mother-in-law isn't there, so she's feeling very bold, that's all!'

'Just because she's feeling bold, she'll make him a paan, and laugh and joke with him?' Satya fumed.

Punyi said timidly, 'But it isn't another man, it's her own husband ...'

'Her own husband!' Satya quickly rinsed her mouth with water twice. 'Hit such a husband on the face with a broomstick, I say! A husband who beats you and sends you to death's door! Joking and laughing with such a husband! Couldn't she find a rope to hang herself with? And you know what she says to me? "My husband beat me, he didn't beat you, did he? So why're you acting as though it's given you blisters, that you go and insult him with a rhyme?" D'you think I'll ever see her face after this?'

Satya took the end of her sari and beat it against the water forcefully. Her friends were in a spot. They could not blame the sentenced criminal too much, because they found it hard to accept such a harsh, unforgiving attitude that forbade forever the making of paan for a husband who had beaten you black and blue. Nor could they protest against Satya and withdraw their support.

But what was that sound? It was as though god had suddenly saved them from their plight. The galloping of a horse could be heard near the palm trees by the pond. Who had come riding a horse? Punyi dashed up the steps of the ghat, and raced back desperately, 'Hey Satya, it's Mejda!'

Mejda! That was Ramkali!

Satya laughed incredulously and made a face, 'Are you dreaming? Hasn't father gone to Jiret?'

'Has he gone to live there, or what? He must have come back.'

In the meantime, the gallops advanced and slowly receded. Satya peered in that direction, craning her neck, and then said indifferently, 'What brains! Had he gone on horseback to Jiret or did the palki turn into a horse in the middle of the road?'

Palki! That was right! Punyi said hesitantly, 'But I really saw Mejda on the horse just now. He went towards the house.'

Then had the condition of the patient at Jiret worsened? And was an ultimate dose of medicine needed right away? So Ramkali had had to return on horseback, leaving his palki behind?

Khedi suggested, 'Whatever it is, Satya, you go home. Who else but the doctor would ride a horse in this village?'

That was true, too. Nobody else had a horse. Very rarely, the courtiers of the Raja of Barddhaman or officers of the Company came riding on a horse. Nobody else.

Satya's band emerged from the ghat. First, they would all go to Satya's. For who could stay calm until the mystery of the horse was solved?

They started out, their anklets jingling, their wet saris dribbling water. But how strange! This was just like a fairytale! No sooner had they reached Satya's house, they stood gaping at the sight of Ramkali returning on horseback. Only this time, there was another person with him, sitting behind him, clutching his back. Satya's eldest cousin. Rashbihari, the son of Ramkali's stepbrother, Kunjabihari!

So Punyi was right. The rider was indeed Ramkali. But Punyi no longer boasted about that. She just stared at the storm of dust raised by the hooves of the horse for a while, drew in her breath, and said, 'What do you think is the matter?'

'That's what I was wondering too,' Satya exclaimed. 'If my father came back for medicine, why would he take Borda with him?'

'Exactly!'

Though it was terribly hot, the light caress of the breeze through their wet clothes made them shiver. Satya abandoned her puzzled expression and pronounced prudently, 'What's the point in gossiping at the door? We'll know once we go inside. Why don't you change and come. I'll find out what the matter is.'

But what had happened was beyond Satya's reckoning. And not just Satya's, it was beyond everyone's understanding. It was as if Ramkali had come on horseback at lightning speed and tossed a huge boulder on the household before departing. And no one could bear the injury thus inflicted.

When Satya entered the inner courtyard, she saw her eldest aunt standing like a wooden puppet between the two grain bins and her grandmother sitting on the steps, stiff as wood, with her chin on her hands. And the rest of the household swarming on the verandah. Only Pishi-thakurma was missing. That was normal, because she never ever stepped on to this 'polluted' verandah. The children would roam the streets and step in here, as would the men in their sandals. But apart from her, the others were milling around. What could the matter be? And why were they silent? There were faint whispers, and furtive movements behind the covered faces.

Satya came as close as she possibly could, to her grandmother. She was careful not to pollute her by touching, and asked with a gesture, 'What has happened, Thakurma?'

Dinatarini kept silent.

So Satya spoke aloud, 'Thakurma, why did Baba come rushing in and where did he go again?'

Dinatarini remained silent.

'What a bother! Why aren't you answering me? Tell me, why did Baba come panting back from Jiret on the horse and rush back again? Thakurma! Have all of you lost your tongues or what?'

Dinatarini's lips did not move but her sister-in-law Shibjaya's did. And not only her lips, her limbs shook into sudden action and she said, 'If an incident occurs that makes you lose your speech then won't you we be speechless? Your father has done the unthinkable!'

'My goodness! Can't you put it into plain language? Just tell me where did he ride off to, so soon after coming back from Jiret?'

'Oh! So you've seen it all! Then why're you pretending? Your father took Rashu to get him married.'

'To get him married! Nonsense!' Satya forgot the solemnity of the situation and collapsed into hysterical laughter. 'Am I such a fool that you're giving me such a mad explanation? He's already married, and he's a father too.'

'So what?' Suddenly Dinatarini broke her silence to scold her granddaughter, 'Don't act too smart! Can't anyone get married after becoming a father? Would it violate custom if he did?'

Before Satya could respond, Shibjaya flashed her retort to an elder, forgetting the brutish laws of domestic life, 'It isn't a question of violating custom at all! But I will say this—Ramkali didn't let anyone look or see, he snatched at the boy like an eagle. The boy's wife didn't have a glimpse of her husband even from a distance. Was that a good thing?'

Nobody had noticed Mokshada enter through the bamboo-gate at the side. She had heard the last bit of the discussion. Her white sari was tucked up to the knee, a gamcha was thrown over her shoulder, signifying that she was off for a bath. Normally, Mokshada would not have stepped through the inner courtyard on her way to a bath, but today things were different. One could not hold on to such rules rigidly in the middle of such a crisis. Perhaps she would take two to ten dips in the pond and, later, many more in the lake, but now it was necessary for her to join this gathering.

Mokshada had heard the words of her third sister-in-law and guessed the rest. So she took a few steps and craned her neck, 'What was that you said? Say it again, let's hear.'

But Shibjaya did not repeat her words, she pulled her sari over her face and turned away.

Mokshada carried on with a vicious smile, 'You don't have to repeat it. I heard it all! But I wonder since when you've become such a pundit! And I see that you're tormented by the fact that our

Rashu couldn't look into his wife's eyes at the time of departure. All this is a sign of the times! The four yugas have spilled over into the most sinful Kaliyuga! I'd always thought people look at the images of the gods, or respectfully at the feet of their elders before they departed for something auspicious. This is the first time I'm told that a man loses caste if he doesn't look on his wife before departing!'

Though Shibjaya was terrified of Mokshada, she could hardly bear to lose face in front of so many people, so she responded, 'It isn't about Rashu at all! I was thinking of the grand-daughter-in-law. Before she heard or understood anything, the sky fell on her head! And she didn't get to see her husband one last time when he was hers alone. That's all I was saying.'

Mokshada suddenly laughed maliciously, 'Oh dear! Why are you sitting at home? Why don't you start composing scenes for the jatra? Satya's made up a rhyme, why should you be left out? Your aims and actions are clear to me—the domestic air no longer suits you! You old hag, aren't you ashamed to utter such words? Is a husband a piece of candy that the stomach won't fill up if you don't have it whole or all by yourself? Or, do you think the heart will burst if he's shared? For shame! Here is Ramkali rushing to save a gentleman in distress and this is how you interpret his action!'

Satya was staring—mouth agape—at this war of words between adults. As soon as Mokshada finished, she rose up and said, 'But Sejo-thakurma is right! My father has certainly done wrong.'

Father has done wrong! No doubts about it either. No disputes. Certainly!

Had a bolt of thunder hit the courtyard?

Was this the end that was predicted for Kaliyuga?

EIGHT

The ill-tidings brought a wave of weeping that swirled through the house. Grief at the heart of a celebration! Nobody had faced such a disaster! Nobody, in their worst nightmares, could have imagined such a catastrophe.

They had just made the bride take a ritual wash standing on a flat mortar, and had wiped away her unwed status with their rhymes; then they had helped her change into a red-bordered sari for the pre-wedding ritual. And a gaggle of neighbourhood females had begun to fill the inner courtyard with discussions about their hair-styling skills when the news arrived like a sudden heat wave from the men's quarters. It started up an instant forest blaze!

Nobody could disbelieve such an incredible piece of news. For the messenger was Ramkali himself, who could not be distrusted in the least. There were endless numbers of relatives who were always ready to break up a marriage by spreading false rumours. But this was Ramkali! Therefore, no one could nurture the faintest hope that this report was false. None at all! The doctor had seen for himself that death stood waiting for the groom.

The passionate wailing that now encompassed the baffled eight-year-old girl, wrapped in her brand new sari was enough to unsettle her.

The poor thing was hardly able to understand the great calamity that would befall her if the groom who had started out for the wedding had to return because he was dying, and she remained unwed as a result. As far as her understanding went, it would affect her grandfather, not her.

But even then, the swarm of women held her and bawled, 'Oh, Patli! None of us thought you had such a terrible fate! What shall we do with this unlucky girl? Why didn't Yama take you instead—that would've been better!' They rolled on the floor while Patli sat there, frozen. All she could conclude at that moment was that it would have been best had she died of cholera last night.

In their temple courtyard, Lakshmikanta Banerji sat like a stone idol, holding his head with his hand, with the words grinding through his head, 'Why did you do this, god! Why?'

Lakshmikanta had not spoken a word since Ramkali had left, nobody had dared to address him either. His eldest son, Shyamakanta, was sitting in silence at the Shiva temple past the ghat; he did not have the nerve to approach his father. Of course, it was his daughter's wedding, but he was too inexperienced, not yet thirty, and he feared his father like Yama himself.

Patli's mother, Behula, had sought refuge in a corner of the storeroom. She felt like an offender herself. She had to be an unpardonable sinner, or why else should something so inauspicious happen on her daughter's wedding? They were all whispering about her daughter—that she was a demoness who had finished off her husband even before he had stepped into the house. Now Behula was stuck with this hapless, hopeless, baleful girl for the rest of her life. All pride in family, caste and creed had vanished, leaving infernal, eternal suffering in their stead.

Problems centred around the groom were not unusual at weddings. The groom leaving the sacred wedding yagna was quite a familiar sight. But the usual reasons were different, they often arose out of financial arrangements—of the dowry not arriving on time. Or at times, because of rumours circulated by some 'well-wisher' about the 'lack' of something or the other in either family. And at other times, provoked by the fact that the girl's family had substituted the bride with a dark girl they wished to get rid off. And arguments would lead to a brawl and end with the groom leaving with his family in a fit of pique. But such problems also had a way of sorting themselves out.

A girl not wedded at the appointed hour had to live almost like a widow in her father's house. The anguish of such an eventuality usually compelled the neighbours to actively procure another groom for her on that very night, and thus save the honour of her father. But this was a very different situation. Here was a monster-woman! Who would find a man for such a husband-killer?

No, Behula had no hopes of finding a groom for her daughter now. 'I'll try'—was how Ramkali had phrased his assurance; he had left soon after. It was beginning to appear like a false consolation he had been obliged to make to mitigate any remorse he might have felt for bringing such ill-tidings. Behula might be a fool, but even she could see through an empty promise!

Oh Goddess Bhagvati! Why hadn't you ever given a sign that

Patli was such a hapless girl! This blossoming girl—my first-born! Everybody loved her, and she would freely roam the gardens, laughing and playing till now. Just recently, because she had matured somewhat, she had been restricted. But who could imagine such a sunny, pretty girl to be a monster? My mother-in-law had always said that the gods ruled her stars. So how did such a blessed child acquire such a dreadful fate? And it was not a fleeting thing either! If she really had to stay at home this way, the whole household would be ruined in no time! As it is, Manda's aunt had clearly announced the verdict, 'Who'll marry this girl? Nobody would want to wreck their homes! She's done for! Mark my words, she's going to ruin her grandfather's clan, that's for sure!'

Behula sobbed aloud. She called on the gods to carry Patli away, and weeping, she fell on the ground.

Everybody was weeping. From the mistress of the house to the low-caste servant woman. After all, how often did the opportunity to weep for another's sorrow present itself?

The only person not weeping was the leading lady of this drama, Patli. After sitting around stiff with fear for a while, she began to wonder why, if the wedding had been called off, had they left her to fast? Why wasn't somebody saying, 'Now why don't you give Patli some sweets and water to drink?' She felt parched and dry as dust. But nobody seemed to have the time to think about such trivial matters. Instead, they were all mad at her and full of hate.

———

After he had come back from the ghat, Shyamakanta had peeped in a couple of times to check on his father. And each time, the sight of his father sitting listless, not even smoking his tobacco, had shrivelled his heart. Yet he did not have the nerve to bring him a hookah. He waited to see if one of the village elders would call. Perhaps then Lakshmikanta would be obliged to break his silence. For whatever the nature of his afflictions, he was sure to extend courteous treatment to a respected visitor. But most of the local worthies had already visited. They had all put in an appearance one after another.

The evening approached, signalling impending doom. At this point, Shyamakanta's prayers were answered. Rakhahari Ghoshal arrived. He was very old and lived far away and had not managed to come until now. He took his sandals off in silence and sat on the durrie, then taking a pinch of snuff from a mother-of-pearl snuff box, began speaking unhurriedly, 'I've heard it all, Lakshmikanta, but it won't do for you to give up like this.'

Lakshmikanta knew how to show respect to his elders; he could not touch the feet of a brahmin who was lower in the caste hierarchy, so he lowered his head and addressed those within the house in an exhausted voice, 'Will somebody get a hookah for Ghoshal-mashai?'

'Let it be, don't worry,' Rakhahari Ghoshal replied. 'It's nearly evening, what have you decided?'

'What can I decide, Ghoshal-mashai?' Lakshmikanta uttered hopelessly. 'When god himself has chosen to mess things up?'

'Well, you mustn't lose hope, Lakshmikanta! You must prepare yourself. The girl has to be married at the appointed hour. When's that?'

'After midnight.'

'Good. You have all the time you want. I'll tell you what, you come with me at once to Dayal's ...'

'Dayal? Dayal Mukherji?'

'Yes, see if you can plead with him and get him to agree. It's already late.'

Lakshmikanta looked astounded, 'For whom should I plead? I don't understand Ghoshal-mashai!'

'Who else, Lakshmikanta? It seems to me that you are behaving like a child. For Mukherji-mashai himself, of course. Otherwise, how will you find a groom of the same caste?'

Lakshmikanta said pathetically, 'Get Patli married to Mukherji-mashai? Have you seen Patli?'

'Of course, I have!' Rakhahari laughed freely. 'Just one look would be enough to tempt a saint! If my caste matched yours, I'd want to wed her even at my age. It's true that Mukherji is older than you, but he is still a lusty man! The other day, he saw Patli on the street and was saying ...'

Rakhahari paused. Lakshmikanta asked a little irritably, 'What was he saying?'

'Oh nothing wicked, he was only joking! He said, "When I see Banerji's granddaughter, I wish I could abandon my third wife and get married again!"'

Lakshmikanta now responded with extreme irritation, 'Just stop right there, Ghoshal-mashai.'

'Really!' Rakhahari rose instantly. 'I can't understand this. I thought Kaliyuga hadn't ended yet! Well, I've learnt my lesson. Whatever I do, I won't try to help anyone again.'

Lakshmikanta shook with fear, 'Please don't feel unnecessarily provoked, Ghoshal-mashai. Imagine my state! Mukherji-mashai is nearly five years older than me, besides he suffers from asthma.'

'Asthma isn't a killer, Lakshmikanta,' Rakhahari retorted vehemently. 'According to Ayurveda it is an infirmity that prolongs life. And as for age, that's nothing! What does the age of a man matter? Besides, the influence of Mukherji's two wives might prove auspicious for your granddaughter and keep her from being widowed.'

'But ...'

'Let it be. No need for "buts", Lakshmikanta. You may be complacent because you are one of society's worthies but bear in mind that if you fail to get your granddaughter married at the appointed hour, other brahmins will treat you like an outcaste. How can you disregard all social norms at this moment of crisis and worry only about the age of the groom? It's absurd!'

'Ghoshal-mashai, please forgive me. I'd rather go and live in Kashi with Patli.'

'You'll do that, of course,' Rakhahari laughed venomously. 'Is there a more suitable place than Kashi for an unmarried, beautiful, young girl? You can also earn your keep there from her, Lakshmikanta.'

'Ghoshal-mashai!' Lakshmikanta rose quick as lighting. 'You are older than me, which is why you're spared this time. Otherwise …'

'Otherwise what would you have done, Lakshmikanta?' Rakhahari asked with a sneering smile, 'Hit me?'

The time for retaliation had come, and Ghoshal would be avenged. Rakhahari was not unaware of the undercurrent of derision that flowed from the brahmins like Lakshmikanta Banerji towards the Ghoshal-brahmins. No matter how polite Banerji appeared, the difference between high and low was obvious from his demeanour. Today when the time for revenge had arrived, he would not let it pass!

'A suitable groom before the appointed hour!' Rakhahari smirked once more, 'Perhaps god will send the groom down from heaven, huh?'

Lakshmikanta was preparing to make a retort when Shyamakanta rushed in with uncharacteristic excitement and announced, 'Doctor Chatterji is coming on horseback. There is someone sitting behind him!'

'Thank God!' Lakshmikanta fell back even as he tried to stand up.

NINE

There had not been time to formally set up a place for the bridegroom. Everything was so rushed, so the groom was given a shave and a bath and taken directly to the ritual space where the daughter was to be given away. That was where they would hold the ritual of sealing the agreement, and then bless him with durba-grass and a ring.

Rashu had eaten several times already, but nothing could be done about it. In such a hurried affair one was not expected to follow customs like fasting. They say so many girls are married in haste. Just the other day, Lakshmikanta's cousin's daughter had been woken up in the middle of the night and married off! The bridegroom had come to wed a girl of a different family, and the inevitable had happened! Somebody had kicked up a fuss about the girl's family, and insults and arguments had followed, and the family was about to walk away with the groom. Never mind, the main thing was, that one could indeed get married even after a feast.

But what about Rashu? What state was he in? Was he tormented by inner conflict at this moment? Was he torn to bits by a vicious pain, a terrible regret, a repentance? Was there a forceful revolt going on in his mind? Was he not insanely furious with his uncle for swooping down on him like an eagle for a second wedding without solicitation or a 'by your leave'?

It did not appear so from his face. Even though his situation was like that of the sacrificial goat, he did not seem to be shivering like one. He just seemed to be performing his role deadpan, bewildered. Yes, this unexpected blow had affected not just his looks, his mind too was dazed and blank. It no longer ebbed and flowed between happiness and unhappiness, good and evil, or with hesitations and conflicts.

When the rituals of the women began, however, he was jolted back to his senses. He began to experience dreadful anguish. When seven married women approached him with flowers and a lamp on a ritual salver and began to move ceremonially around him, his distress dawned just at that moment! Their faces were covered, of course, but he was struck by a certain resemblance. The woman holding the ritual salver reminded him of Sharada! Although Rashu would never be able to accurately identify Sharada during the day, still, he knew her shape. He had also seen her in a similar aubergine-coloured sari sometimes. Perhaps, at some village wedding or during the annual Durga puja.

He had, however, always seen her from a distance, and lacked the temerity to look openly. There was never any chance of going near her till the house was silent, well past midnight. And by then, Sharada was free from the burden of make-up or ornament. Besides, she would blow out the lamp at the corner as soon as she entered. She would say, 'Suppose somebody sees, somehow.'

Even though there was no way anyone could have seen. The doors and windows of Ramkali Chatterji's house were not made from mango-wood which is so prone to cracks and crevices; they were strong jackfruit-wood doors, fortified with metal. The bolts alone weighed nearly two to five seers. And the windows were more like small ventilators. Small openings were placed higher than a man's head—nobody could have peeped from there. But it was best to be cautious.

However, the men could not sleep in such stuffy rooms during the summer months; so mats were wiped cool with wet rags and spread out for them on the roof top or in the outer courtyard. Bolsters, palm-leaf fans, washing pots and gamchas were carried out for them by the cowherds or the farmhands. The men never had to suffer the heat.

Of course, the souls of newly-married men and women would feel tormented. They would feel restless if they lay outside, and uncomfortable when inside the stuffy inner quarters. However, it was different if one had a wife like Sharada, who would fan Rashu with a wet palm-leaf fan on summer nights.

Rashu's heart twisted in pain. Last night too, Sharada had not neglected this duty. Rashu had lovingly asked her not to, several times, but she had used the excuse of her son's discomfort. And then there had been this horrifying thing, the memory of which now seared Rashu's soul! Sharada had made him promise something dreadful!

When he asked her to stop fanning him, Sharada had smiled and whispered, 'So much of affection! Do you think you'll be able to keep things this way forever?'

Rashu had not caught on exactly, so he had laughed in surprise, 'Why? It's not going to be summer forever, is it?'

'I'm not saying that. I was talking about ...' and Sharada had moved very close to his chest, 'the pain of having a co-wife. Will you be tender towards me then? Will you say, "Oh no, she really fears a co-wife."'

Rashu had laughed as quietly as possible and said, 'Are you daydreaming or what? Who has inflicted a co-wife on you!'

'Not as yet, but it doesn't take long!'

'Very long! I don't like the idea of two or three wives. Besides, there's no need.'

Sharada had not stopped there, 'And when I grow old? Then there'd be a need.'

Rashu had been very amused, he had laughed once more and said, 'This is like arguing with the wind! When you grow old, will I still be young?'

'As if men grow old so easily! Besides, you are the eldest son, and good-looking too. Your family is rich, there will be many good matches. Will you think about me ...'

Sharada had burst into passionate tears. So Rashu had been compelled to hold her close and tight and comfort her with loving caresses. He had consoled her with, 'This is exactly why I call it arguing with the wind. No co-wife in sight and she sits down to cry! Don't be so anxious.'

And after many such exchanges, the devoted Sharada had assured her husband, 'I'm not saying, of course, that you must promise not to marry again once I die. When I'm dead you can marry a hundred times, but not while I'm living.'

'I won't, I won't, I won't! Is that enough? I've promised three times!'

Just last night!

And today the same man was dressed like a bridegroom, and standing in the ritual space fringed with four banana plants, for another wedding. And the woman who was ceremonially blessing him with the ritual salver had begun to recite a wedding rhyme:

Bought you with a cowrie-shell, bound you with a rope,
With a weaver's shuttle in your hand, chappie, you haven't a hope!

How many times could a man be bought? How could something that was bound already, be bound again? Oh god! What pleasure did it give you to hurl Rashu into such a dilemma?

If only Rashu had not been in the village today. If only he had gone away to some other village, perhaps to visit his ailing grandmother, as he often did. If only he had gone today, and if only his grandmother's death had detained him there. If only a cousin or relative had died and the period of ritual impurity had started for Rashu's family. If only Rashu, too, had some fatal disease like that other groom. If something like that happened, then this wedding would never have happened.

The woes of the imperilled father hardly appeared in any corner of Rashu's mind. They could all go to hell! Why had this mishap befallen Rashu? If it had been his father Kunjabihari, instead of his uncle Ramkali, who had ordered, 'The man is in trouble, Rashu, no time to vacillate! Come now, get up!' Rashu would certainly have sat down to think. But it had been his uncle Ramkali, against whose command nothing could be uttered.

And after many such suppositions, Rashu started wishing that he had used the excuse of the heat not to come indoors to sleep at all. At least he would have been spared the oath!

After this, would Sharada ever trust Rashu all her life? Would she believe that Rashu was as helpless as she was? That he had no control over what had happened? Of course not! She would say, 'Oh yes! Tell me another! As if a man's mind is capable of any tenderness! As if a man ever keeps his word!'

But then, would Sharada ever talk to him again? Perhaps she would not say another word to him as long as she lived and, perhaps, out of a sense of hurt she would—and suddenly, Rashu's mind conjured up a picture of the crystal clear waters of the Chatterji's pond. He hoped that Sharada would not do something drastic tonight out of disgust.

He felt as if somebody was digging deep into his heart and rubbing salt into his wounds. He felt that he could no longer manage to hold things in, that he would burst out crying! He did not do that, but the look on his face made somebody from the bride's party pipe out, 'Are you feeling unwell?'

Was this bridegroom indisposed too? Laxmikanta frowned at that foul-mouthed well-wisher and gravely ordered, 'Fetch a palm-leaf fan. Quick!'

The rapid fanning did make Rashu look less pale. And even if it didn't, the wedding was over and after taking the newly-weds to the family puja room, the crowd was now leading them inside the house, ritually pouring water every step of the way.

And he knew that they would torture him once again, just like the last time! Rashu's heart trembled when he thought'of the jokes and the quips of the women inside the basar at Sharada's parent's house. Once again, Rashu was going to have to face that terrifying situation. Helpless and unarmed!

And all of a sudden, Rashu forgot his sufferings and discovered a great philosophical truth. How strange and foolish man was—repeatedly inviting such revolting monstrosities into his life.— Each time, he sold himself for nothing.

———

The next day, they were drawing ritual patterns on the floor. Of course, it was not going to come out as perfect as it would have done in the case of a planned wedding, but one had to stick to the rules. And since it was such a huge courtyard, no less than a seer of rice had to be soaked and ground, even for perfunctorily done designs.

And Ramkali's aunt, Nandarani had soaked the rice. Nandarani was an aunt by marriage, she had been married to his father's elder cousin. All the rituals and ceremonies that had to be followed in this house were done by her and Kunja's wife, Abhaya, because they were both 'flawless child-bearers'. Thanks to Goddess Shashti, Abhaya's seven children were all flourishing. Though Nandarani had just two or three.

Anyway, since Nandarani was in charge of weddings, there was no exception this time too. So, even if she privately disapproved of Rashu's second marriage, she had soaked the rice for making the ritual patterns. After placing a huge stone platter at the centre, filled with milk and red alta, Nandarani had busied herself painting flowers and creepers, conch-shells and lilies around it with a deft hand. It would take a while to complete, but a sweaty cowherd boy came rushing to the courtyard door and said with a wide grin, 'The bride and groom are here. I spotted them on the other side of the lake and came rushing!'

'What shall we do now?' Nandarani looked unsettled, looked around and declared in a loud voice, 'Didi, I hear that the bride and the groom have arrived.'

The bride and groom had arrived!

Dinatarini ran leaving the vegetables she was dicing, 'So soon! Is Ramkali in a hurry about this too?'

'I suppose he wanted to arrive before the inauspicious hour set in.'

Even though he was a nephew by relation, he was more respected, wealthier, and most importantly, he was older, so Nandarani now, as always, referred to him using the honorific.

Dinatarini concentrated on the 'inauspicious hour', and steadying her mind, said, 'That must be the reason. Are you ready with all the rituals?'

Nandarani hastened with the work at hand and replied, 'Almost. Only the milk needs to be boiled. Who'll do that now?'

Milk! Of course! It had to be boiled. If the bride looked on milk boiling over as soon as she stepped in, the household would prosper.

Dinatarini asked with an anxious expression, 'Where is our Boro-bouma?'

'In the kitchen. She has to cook for the whole household quickly. The bride will have to cast her eyes on that too,' Boro-bouma was Rashu's mother. That was what Nandarani called her even though she herself was the same age as Rashu's mother. After all, she was an aunt-in-law by marriage, so Rashu's mother was Bouma.

Kunja's wife was in the kitchen, so someone else would have to boil the milk. And the bride and groom had nearly arrived. Dinatarini ran a check on the people present. The woman had to be the mother of a first-born son, but also one who was the first wife of her husband. Such auspicious rituals could not be performed by someone who was a second or a third wife.

So who else was there? Goodness! No need to think further! There was Sharada, of course. Let her be summoned then. She had been sitting unhappily in a corner; it would do her good to be distracted by putting her mind to some work; besides, where was the time to think about somebody new?

Satya was rushing through the courtyard. Dinatarini called out to her, 'Here, Satya, you, Miss Wayward! Go and call the eldest granddaughter-in-law, quickly! The bride and groom will be here soon, she has to boil the milk!'

'Call her? She's not herself now, is she? She's been crying herself to death from dawn!'

'Crying herself to death!' Dinatarini said irritably, 'Why? What is there to die about? What a bad sign on an auspicious day. Go call her, quick!'

Satya looked around, 'Who will call her? You can say, what is there to cry about? But suppose it had happened to you? Won't a person cry when the co-wife arrives? Are they supposed to raise their hands and prance about in joy? Huh! Here, tell me what needs to be done? I'll boil the milk!'

'You! You're going to boil the milk?'

'What if I do?' Satya asked with enthusiasm. 'Didn't Pishi-thakurma say at Khunti's wedding, "A year has passed for Satya, she can be part of the women's wedding rituals"?'

A year has passed, meaning a year has passed since her marriage. Satya would not put it clearly, of course.

Dinatarini said doubtfully, 'Is it enough if a year's passed? Unless you've started a family—'

'Don't know about that. But just stop doubting everything. Here, let me start!' So saying Satya began to blow on the fire over which sat a small earthenware pot of milk. The dung-cakes glowed faintly, but a little coaxing and a few extra palm leaves would make the flames leap up. The methodical Nandarani had kept a bunch of leaves near by.

Satya was enthusiastic about everything. The force of her breath made the milk boil over much before the arrival of the bride and groom. The milk spilled over, dribbled down and fumes filled the place.

Dinatarini raised a hue and cry, 'Not so fast! The bride has to see it as soon as she enters.'

But before she had finished, conch-shells sounded in the outer courtyard indicating the arrival of the new bride. Mokshada was standing outside with a conch-shell in her hand. Since it was purnima, she would not be cooking, she would eat fruits and sweets at some point. So today was a holiday for her, which was why she was leading the show and standing at the entrance with the conch-shell. Although widows were barred from participating in auspicious rituals, these were a few small acts which neither society nor its pillars had managed to snatch away from them—the conch-shell, and the ululations. Therefore, Mokshada was exercising her rights fully and freely as she looked forward to Rashu's return from his 'second adventure'.

Dinatarini was startled as Satya eagerly rushed out, 'Why're you blowing on your hand like that? Have you scalded it?'

Satya covered up the truth and said quickly, 'Of course not!'

'Then why're you blowing on it?'

'Just like that!'

'Anyway, now blow on the fire, so that the milk swells up. Look! It is swelling, the bride will be lucky. The last time—'

Before she could finish her words, Ramkali's deep voice boomed, 'Finish all your rituals quickly, the inauspicious hour is near!'

The conch-shells sounded repeatedly and drowned out Ramkali's voice. The bride and the groom entered the inner quarters. Behind them, with saris drawn over their faces, swept in the women of the entire locality.

—

Whatever the manner or circumstance of its occurrence, a wedding had to be celebrated with some grandeur. Not so much for fulfilling the need for a jamboree, but rather, out of the necessity of informing society. It was hardly appropriate that the granddaughter of Lakshmikanta Banerji should one day, inadvertently and unexpectedly, be installed within the inner quarters of the Chatterjis without anybody knowing anything about it. There had to be some proper document stating that her entry was legitimate. But what sort of document could that be? Not a written one, not signed or attested, but the testimony of people. And how else could one procure that except by inviting the entire village to a feast?

Besides, the fact that a girl from the Banerji household now belonged to the Chatterji family had to be duly acknowledged. The groom's side could have this fact endorsed by kith and kin, by making the bride serve them rice during the feast.

Therefore, a feast had to be arranged after the wedding. Since there was no prior warning there was a real rush to make arrangements. Ramkali never lacked devoted followers, and he had spread the word. The sandesh would come from Janai, the mihidana from Barddhaman. Tustu, the milkman, was to arrange for the yoghurt, and Bhima, the fisherman, had been asked to arrange for the fish. Ramkali was instructing them about the quantity of fish and in which lake they should cast their nets, when suddenly Mokshada appeared on the scene.

Apart from Mokshada, practically everybody feared Ramkali. She was the only one who dared to tell him things to his face. Even Dinatarini was afraid of her son. One might ask, of course, if and when did the question of telling Ramkali something to his face arise? After all, he was a man who carried out his duties perfectly! But arise, they did. And Mokshada never missed such opportunities. Because Mokshada judged things from her own perspective. What Ramkali regarded as absolute duty, Mokshada viewed as uncalled for excess. And most of the time, the issue would be Satyabati. That was natural! If Ramkali had produced a daughter who was singular in the whole of India, shouldn't Mokshada take the opportunity to tell him things to his face? So Mokshada would often drag that wretched girl to Ramkali and give a proper lashing!

Even now she had not come alone to Ramkali's court, she had brought Satyabati along. Satyabati had come without protest. Perhaps she knew it would be of no use. Or, may be, because she was fearless.

Mokshada waited in silence all the while Bhima, the fisherman, was present. Finally, when Bhima left after doing a pranam to Ramkali, Mokshada sprang into action.

'Here Ramkali, now do something about this gem of yours. And let me warn you, that's what you'll have to do for the rest of your life, for this one will come back from her in-laws—that's for sure!' Mokshada paused for breath.

Ramkali smiled mildly and asked, 'Why, what has happened now?'

'It happens all the time,' Mokshada shook her hand. 'Happens while getting up or sitting down—cuts, bruises, tears. And now, just look at the state of your daughter's hand! She's scalded it and there's a big blister. And she says "No need to tell father, it'll get better." See for yourself.'

Ramkali shuddered as he examined his daughter's hand. 'What's this? How did this happen?'

'Ask her how it happened. I'm forever reciting her talents to you, you never listen! But I'll tell you this, Ramkali, there's grief in store for you because of this girl.'

This outburst was nothing new, it had been repeated all too often. So it was not as if Ramkali was really troubled. But he was trained in the etiquette of showing respect to elders, so he pretended to be perturbed.

'Really, this girl is the limit! Now what did you do? How did you get this huge blister?'

'She was boiling milk. Madam went to boil the milk when Rashu arrived with his bride yesterday. And I say, you over-grown girl, how could you scald your hand doing such a simple task?'

Ramkali examined the state of his daughter's hand and spoke to her seriously, 'Why did you have to go near the fire? Wasn't there anybody else at home?'

Satya inclined her head and replied, 'It's not burning too much.'

'That's not the point, there are medicines to treat it. But tell me, why were you working near a fire?'

Now Satya raised her head and began to speak rapidly in her characteristic manner, 'As if I did that because I was dying to! I did it for the sake of Boro-bou. Poor thing! Here she is suffering from the sting of a co-wife's barb, and over and above that being ordered to boil the milk! She's human after all!'

Satya's clear explanation staggered not just Ramkali, but Mokshada too. What a brash girl! Answering back a father who was so distinguished! Mokshada put her hand to her cheek and fell silent. Ramkali was the one who spoke. He asked in a sharp tone, his brows furrowed, 'And what do you mean by the "sting of a co-wife's barb"?'

'Learn what it means from your daughter, Ramkali!' Mokshada said with utter sarcasm before Satya could answer. 'What we haven't learnt at our age, this slip of a girl has. A regular chatterbox!'

Such bizarre accusations annoyed Satya. Why should people talk any way it suited them? She had just been called 'overgrown girl', and now she had become a 'slip of a girl'. Anything that caught their fancy!

Ramkali looked at his aunt and once more repeated his question in a thunderous voice, 'Why haven't you replied to my question? Why don't you tell me what a co-wife's barb is, and how it can sting?'

As if Satya knew what it was! But she knew, I suppose, from before her birth, that it was a tormenting, painful thing. So, with as anguished an expression as possible, she said, 'Baba, a co-wife is a barb. And when there's a barb, it also stings. This is the sting you've inflicted on her.'

'Stop it!' Ramkali scolded fiercely. He was irked now, and really troubled. And worried for his daughter's future and pained by this confrontation with the squalor of her mind! He had not thought this possible; it was beyond his expectation! What could have caused this? Numerous complaints about Satyabati would reach his ears but so far he had never paid much heed to them because he had perceived her to have a nature that was genuinely spirited. And he thought she was incapable of harbouring hatred or malice. That was what he credited her with in his assessment. So when had she learnt this vocabulary of hate? It was not right to let this grow. It needed correction. So Ramkali roared louder and said, 'Why? Why is the co-wife so terrifying? Has she beaten up your Boro-bou?'

Her father's tiger-like roar almost brought tears to Satyabati's eyes, but she was not one to admit defeat so easily. Lowering her head in fear and pain, and concealing the weakness of tears, she said choking on her words, 'Not physically, no! But she has deprived her, hasn't she? A woman who was the sovereign queen has had her place usurped by this new one ...'

'Stop! For shame!'

Ramkali shuddered and fell silent. The expression on his face indicated that Satyabati had suddenly crumpled and torn to shreds a picture he had painted with great care. And Mokshada took the opportunity to drive home a blow, 'Listen! Just listen to the girl's way of talking! A regular master of words, she is! Speaks like an old hag and prances about like a kid! Stuns you by the minute with the bite of her words!'

Ignoring his aunt's griping, Ramkali said in an extremely irritated tone, 'Where have you learnt to talk so vulgarly? I'm ashamed of you! What do you mean "usurped her place"? Don't two sisters live under the same roof? Can't a co-wife be seen as a sister rather than a "barb"?'

Satya's efforts to control herself failed after that. Countless tears flowed down her cheeks, and from there to the ground, all at once. They flowed unchecked, and Satya made no effort to wipe them away.

Ramkali Chatterji was distressed once again. Tears in Satyabati's eyes looked absurd. He wondered if his expression of abhorrence had been too strong. For Ramkali, it would be a grave violation to administer an unnecessarily high dose of medicine. He reminded himself that the blister on his daughter's hand was painful too. Some remedy had to be found right away. So he relented, 'Don't speak so coarsely again, all right? Don't even think this way. Just as brothers, sisters and in-laws live in a family, so does the co-wife, don't you see? Come, show me your hand.'

Satyabati put out her hand and bit her lips in an attempt to control the turmoil inside her.

Mokshada concluded that the cloud had passed. Ramkali had done with disciplining his daughter. What a shame! She could not bear to stand there a minute longer, 'So the punishing and disciplining is over, huh? Now sit down and hug your girl. Really, you're the limit!'

With that Mokshada exited the scene.

Ramkali applied a salve on his daughter's blister for quick relief and said with a smile, 'Will you remember what I said today? Don't speak like that again. Human beings are not wild animals that they must constantly hate and fight with each other. One should live in peace with everyone in the world.'

The tone of truce was clear in her father's voice, which revived Satyabati's courage somewhat. Otherwise, her father's rebuke had broken her heart. Actually speaking, Satyabati had no idea what her fault was. After all, if it were such a virtue to love everybody why were rituals like the sejuti performed at all? And she voiced the unease she was experiencing, 'If that is so, then why must we do the sejuti ritual, father? Pishi-thakurma has started me, Phentu and Punyi on it from this year.'

Ramkali's irritation was replaced with amazement. He did not know much about this ritual, but it was beyond him how a ritual could be against the principles of humanitarianism. So, washing the salve off his hand with water from an earthen pot, he asked, 'What has a ritual got to do with it?'

'Everything, Baba!' Satya's voice turned crisp even before her tears had dried, 'Because all the chants of this ritual are about protecting oneself from the barb of a co-wife!'

Ramkali was speechless. He began to see a ray of hope somewhere. Yes, some such confusing thing must have entered her head. Otherwise, how could Satya speak like that. There was a lot of work at hand. Still, Ramkali considered it his duty to uproot the notion of the 'co-wife's barb' from his daughter's mind, with the aid of good counsel. So he asked with a frown, 'Really, what is the chant?'

'There isn't just one, Baba!' Satya exclaimed animatedly. 'Lots of them. I can't remember everything. But sit here, I'll remember them and tell you. First, you draw a design with rice paste on the floor—you draw flowers and creepers and fill up the corners and the sides with drawings of ladles, spoons, pots and pans. Then you touch each item and chant. I touch the ladle and say:

Ladle, ladle, I swear on my life!
Off with the head of the stupid co-wife!

'Then I touch the cup,

Cup, cup, cup!
The white police have come
To nab the co-wife's mum!

'And then,

Tongs, tongs, tongs!
The co-wife's face is long!
Knife, knife, knife!
I cook at the funeral of the co-wife!
Pot, pot, pot!
To be wedded is my lot!
Let the harlot co-wife rot!

'Stop it!' Ramkali scolded solemnly, 'Are these your chants?'

Suddenly, that instant, it flashed across Satya's consciousness that these could never be proper chants for a ritual. So she said quietly, without excitement, 'And there's more ...'

'Really! There's more? All right, let's hear them. Let's see how your brains are being ruined. Do you know more?'

Satya inclined her head, 'Yes,

Husking pedal, husk the rice,
The co-wife dies and I feel nice!

'And then,

The tree I chop to make me a shed,
With the co-wife's blood I make my feet red!
Bird, bird that sings!
May he never a co-wife bring!

'Then, you've to pick up a fistful of grass and say,

Fist of grass, fist of green,
May she be blind and ugly as sin.

'Then, ornaments are drawn too and there are chants for each,

Necklace, bracelet, rings and earring,
With a broomstick give her a thrashing!

'Then you've to draw a paan and say,

Paan with cardamom and lots of clove—
The co-wife is hated I am loved!'

'Enough! You don't have to say any more,' Ramkali held up a hand to stop her. 'Do you call such abuses ritual chants?'

'We don't, Baba,' Satya opened her eyes wide in amazement at the ignorance of her learned father. 'The whole world does! If the co-wife were indeed like a sister, why would so many chants be composed? Does any one pray for the misery of their sister? The real reason is that men don't understand the significance of a co-wife, that's why ...' Satya swallowed once, and hesitated because she was not sure if it would be appropriate to utter the sentence hovering at the tip of her tongue, about men.

Ramkali said solemnly, 'Whatever it is, don't perform this ritual any more.'

Don't perform it? Don't perform a ritual! Satya was thunderstruck. What sort of order was this? What should she do? She was torn between her father's command and the violation of a ritual discontinued! A violation which could bring a living hell. And though she had no idea how heinous a crime it was to disobey one's father, she had little doubt that such transgressions also made the sinner suffer in hell! They both fell silent for a while. Then, slowly Satya raised the issue, 'If one discontinues a ritual, one suffers in hell!'

'Not at all, in fact, you'd suffer in hell if you performed such rituals.'

'What shall I tell Pishi-thakurma then?'

'What do you mean?'

'Shall I say you've forbidden me to do it?'

'No, let that be. You don't have to say anything in a hurry. I shall tell her myself. Go now. Take care, don't scrape your hand against anything.'

Satya floundered. Her father had ordered her to leave, yet a sea of questions surged inside her. And the only place those waves could thrash about and seek a solution was before her father.

'Baba ...'

'What is it?'

'If the ritual is unfair, if a co-wife is a good thing, then why is Boro-bou feeling so unhappy?'

'Boro-bouma? Rashu's wife? Unhappy? Has she told you this herself?' Ramkali's tone wore a shade of rebuke.

But Satyabati was hardly the type to give in easily. Taunts might thwart her somewhat, but she always remained undaunted by rebukes. So she spoke animatedly and rapidly, justifying the appellation 'master of words' that Mokshada had given her. 'She doesn't need to tell me that. As if everything has to be put into words! Can't one make out from her expression? Her eyes have sunk into their sockets from so much weeping, her bright complexion has turned dull. And she hasn't touched a drop of water since yesterday. In public, of course, she insists that, "My stomach is aching, I've no appetite and so I'm crying", but we all know the truth. Nobody is as naive as all that! And on top of that, today is the ceremony of untying the ritual thread for the bride—it's like a final blow! Some have been saying, she must be moved out of her room. And others are saying, "Leave the poor thing alone!" And it seems she herself has said to the neighbour, "Where's the need to worry about such things when there's so much space in the Chatterji's pond. That can be my shelter."'

What a calamity that would be! Ramkali attempted to assess the situation. Nothing was impossible for a woman. Who could ensure that the girl would not do something like that? What a trial this was! Such warped thinking, when she could have rejoiced about the fact that a respectable man had been saved humiliation. Didn't other people have co-wives in this whole wide world?

What could be the cause of all this? Nothing but worthless rituals which ruined women's lives from infancy. Women as a race were narrow-minded and orthodox. Of course, they were called 'goddesses of the hearth', out of sheer courtesy, nothing else. In reality, they were 'incarnations of misery'. Each one of them! Or else, how could Rashu's wife—and she was so young too—get such an idea into her head? That she could drown herself? How terribly disgraceful.

'Is that what she said?' Ramkali asked darkly.

'That's what the neighbours tell me.'

Satya felt a little alarmed looking at her father's face. But she could not afford to be scared. It was her responsibility to enlighten her father. Her father was so clever, and yet, he had no idea that a woman's heart broke if her husband married again! And because her heart had broken many years ago, the Queen Kaikeyi had sent her co-wife's son, Rama, off to the forest. Satya had heard the Kathak recite that story. Kaikeyi was a queen with a poisonous mind! And here was her own sister-in-law—a plain, timid creature, who only desired her own death!

There was another reason why Satya was uneasy; since her own father was responsible for her sister-in-law's tragedy she felt she could no longer face her. It was clear from everybody's gestures and movements that they blamed Ramkali. For good reasons too. The mother of a son always occupied a special position. If her sister-in-law was not the mother of a boy, things would have been viewed differently. But now, what if her breasts should dry up from too much weeping? How would the child live?

Meanwhile, Ramkali tried to think out a way of teaching the daughter-in-law a lesson. He had invited the entire village; the feast would start as soon as the night was over. What if she really did something silly? After thinking for a while, he cleared his throat and said, 'Those are childish thoughts. Tell her on my behalf to give them up. Say, "Father has said that you'll feel happier if you tell yourself to be happy." Say that she should get up and start working, eat well—all her misgivings will disappear.'

Once more, Satya was struck by her father's ignorance. But she refused to suffer in silence. She said with a short laugh, 'If they disappeared so easily, there would be paradise on earth, Baba! As a doctor you read symptoms from a patient's appearance and you know exactly what is happening inside his body, Baba, don't you? So can't you guess what's going on inside a person by looking at the face? Come and see for yourself.'

Suddenly, quite inexplicably, Ramkali broke into goose-flesh. He fell silent. Then, after a long interval he signalled his daughter to leave. And what could she do after that? Satya lowered her head and slowly got up to go. But Ramkali called out, 'All right, listen.'

Satyabati turned around.

'Listen, you don't have to say anything to her. Only ... I mean ... I'll give you one task ...'

Ramkali was hesitant, Satyabati, bewildered. Whatever happened she had never seen her father hesitate. But Ramkali had never ever been faced with such a situation before. Had Satyabati really made him see sense? What made him look so embarrassed and perturbed?

'Baba, tell me, what do you want me to do?'

'Oh yes, I was just going to say that you should stay near your sister-in-law, and see to it that she doesn't go near the pond.'

Satyabati was quiet for a split second, trying to absorb the significance of her father's instructions. After absorbing it, she said tenderly, 'I know exactly what you mean. You're asking me to keep a watch on her, police her, right?'

Police her! Ramkali was mortified. Was this the interpretation of his instruction? He said with some irritation, 'What do you mean keep watch? Stay near her, play with her, so that she feels better ...'

Satyabati drew a deep breath, 'It's the same thing, isn't it? As they say, "What's in a name? A grey-haired maid by any other name, is nothing but an old dame!" But even if I do guard her, how long can I carry on? If someone vows to commit suicide then who can prevent her? And not just the pond, there are poisonous fruits, poisonous seeds ...'

'Enough!' Ramkali let out a flaming breath. 'Be quiet! I can see your Sejo-thakurma was right. Where have you learnt so many words from? Go, you don't have to do anything. Go!'

TEN

It is easy enough to get rid of a person by uttering the word 'go', but one cannot rid oneself similarly of worries or conflicts. Ramkali had dismissed Satyabati; but he found it hard to dislodge the unanticipated anxiety and confusion that were beginning to overwhelm him. Had he done something wrong? Had he made a mistake? The upheaval drove him from inside the house to the temple, and from there to the outer courtyard, and then to the orchard. And for some unknown reason he walked right up to the pond and began to pace up and down.

Ramkali's large frame stooped slightly. He walked unhurriedly, hands clasped behind him. This was not an unusual posture, as people would vouch. There had been the odd occasion when Ramkali would pace similarly, worrying about a complicated case. This was how he preferred to think, instead of sitting and leafing through the tomes of his Ayurvedic texts. Perhaps, because he knew them by heart he did not really need to read them again. He could recall them at will. But that too was rare. Doctor Chatterji never needed a great deal of time to select either medication or preventive measures. He would instinctively know both, after one look at his patient. So it was unusual to see him worried.

His straight, large frame was as sturdy as the sal tree; his forehead wide, his nose shaped like a hawk's beak, and his distinctive lips curved slightly as an obvious sign of self-confidence. That was the image everyone was familiar with. But today there was a difference—the lines on his face expressed obvious self-doubt. Had he made a mistake? Had it not been right? Should he have thought a little more? But there had hardly been time for that!

Ramkali mulled over it again and again. Had he lost his mind in taking the prattle of a child so seriously and getting agitated?

What was so disturbing about it anyway? Really! As if a co-wife was such a rare thing! Their numbers were legion! By contrast, one could count on one hand, the number of women who were blessed with husbands who had not married a second time. But the argument collapsed every time. The waves within him seemed to drive away their carefully assembled logic. Ramkali seemed incapable of dismissing the words of that slip of a girl.

Many virtues had merged and shaped Ramkali's ingenious character. But perhaps, this paragon of manhood had one tiny flaw. He knew how to show respect where it was due and to demonstrate deference towards old age, but he had neither of these sentiments when it came to the female sex.

Ramkali had nothing but contempt for this class that had nothing better to do than boil rice, hit the children, roam the locality, gossip, bicker, beat their chests in grief and flood the floors with their tears after hurling the most dreadful abuses! May be, he was unaware of his own bias. And though it never surfaced in his behaviour, it did exist. Of late, however, a tiny girl was beginning to worry and disturb him. And a question was beginning to formulate itself in his mind: Should he have been more considerate towards women?

The sky had not darkened yet, but the shadows of the evening had stretched across the edges of the palm-fringed pond. As he paced this darkening track, Ramkali's gaze suddenly became piercingly sharp, like that of an eagle. Wasn't there somebody sitting on the last step of the ghat? When had she arrived? She had not been there all this while. Why had she come here now, at this hour? It was unusual for women to come here by themselves so late, except for Mokshada, of course. Could it possibly be …?

An unknown fear made him tremble inside. This was an entirely new sensation for Ramkali. He could hardly see in the thickening dark, yet it would not be seemly to go closer for a better view. He could not ignore this either. His suspicions grew stronger. This had to be Rashu's wife.

What was Satya up to? Hadn't she been following his instructions to keep watch?

It appeared that the woman had a large pitcher with her. A pitcher was often an aid to those who knew how to swim. But if that witless woman were to tie that around her neck and ...

His thoughts eddied around this rock of dread. It did not occur to him that this untimely visit might have been warranted by the simple need for water.

It was clear that the woman was not in any hurry to fill the pot. Unless holding on to a pot could be interpreted as a sign of urgency.

No, this could not be someone who had just come to fill a pitcher. It had to be Rashu's wife. She had come with the intention of killing herself. But she could not end it all so quickly since she wished to absorb for one last time the beauty, the sounds, and the touch of the world.

Also, was she not sighing and musing about the person who was responsible for depriving her of such beauty and delight?

Ramkali's eyes began to smart. This feeling was so unfamiliar. Completely new and unexpected.

But he could not just stand and watch, he had to do something about it. She had to be stopped. But how? Ramkali could hardly go down the women's ghat and drag her by the hand! Nor could he deter her from her dangerous intent by offering good counsel. How would he address her? After all, Ramkali was her uncle-in-law.

And yet, he could hardly yield to the impulse of quitting the scene and calling a woman from inside the house. What if something happened meanwhile ...?

The figure was no longer motionless. She was dipping her pot into the water. Ramkali's eyes became razor sharp. He walked towards the ghat almost involuntarily. Codes of right and wrong, appropriate or inappropriate behaviour, could not be held on to during a crisis. A moment's hesitation and that terrible disaster could take place. Ramkali reached the ghat with hasty steps, and almost wailed out, 'Who's that? Who's that in the water at this hour?'

A petrified Ramkali paused to see the effect of his shout. Had that bit of white cloth, visible until now, disappeared suddenly under the impact of his call? Had the last shreds of doubt vanished from her mind? There she was, with her feet in the water, hovering between life and death. Just one dip would put an end to all her pains, like balm on scalded flesh The thought itself was enough to conquer all fears. She had no reason to fear Ramkali's reproach. The white sari was still visible, perhaps it was moving. Ramkali waited with bated breath. Ramkali could only play the role of a mute spectator now. He had no way of rescuing her unless and until she put herself in actual danger. It would be stupid to just pull her out of the water even before she had dived in. Whatever his apprehensions were, he was not insane to drag her away from the ghat just because he suspected that she might drown herself.

What else could he do? The white colour had not disappeared yet, so something could still happen.

Abruptly Ramkali returned to his senses and collected himself. How unnecessarily he had panicked! If he gave a shout, ten or twenty people would come rushing out. That would take care of it. So why was he losing heart?

He shouted again. A shout that would shrivel with fear the heart of the woman who sought death. Ramkali hollered out thunderously, in a commanding tone, 'Whoever you are, get out of the water! I tell you, get out! No need to stay in there at this hour,' he said, emphasizing the 'I'.

His conjecture proved right. The command-laden heavy tone proved effective. The woman filled her pitcher and came out of the water with her sari pulled over her face. Ramkali perceived from the movement of the sari that the woman was walking up the steps of the ghat. He wondered if he should move away and leave, or give the foolish girl some advice.

It was generally unthinkable that a father-in-law should talk directly to a daughter-in-law. But Ramkali was privileged because he was a doctor. Whenever a daughter or a daughter-in-law fell ill, Mokshada or Dinatarini summoned Ramkali and then he spoke to them indirectly, with his aunt or sister as intermediary. Usually, they were instructions about taking care not to catch cold or on the need for a proper diet. But Ramkali was never summoned inside unless the illness was serious; most often he would recommend medication after being described the symptoms. He addressed the women only when it was critical. Even then, he would talk to them from a distance, and with respect, always using the honorific when addressing a daughter-in-law or sister-in-law.

Ramkali did not entirely bypass that code even now—just a little bit. He did not step aside; instead, clearing his throat he said, 'Why have you come by yourself at this hour? Don't do it again. I forbid you.' Once more he emphasized the 'I'.

It was unimaginable that the woman before him should muster enough strength to walk away with stiff, puppet-like movements. So Ramkali concluded, 'There is a happy occasion at home, cheer yourself up. Such things happen, after all.'

Then he quickly walked away.

The puppet stood there for a while, after he had left, stiff as wood, as though she could not comprehend what had happened. How could this be possible? What did the words 'such things happen' mean? Had he come to know everything then? And had he forgiven her? Was he a god, then? Shankari's heart trembled uncontrollably at the thought.

Yes, it was Shankari. Not Rashu's wife, Sharada, but Kashiswari's widowed granddaughter-in-law, Shankari. Kashiswari had lived all her life at her father's house. She had but one daughter who had died an untimely death. So Kashiswari had nurtured her motherless grandson for eighteen years. She had found him a beautiful bride too. But the bride turned out to be a monster, and her grandson had died within a year of marriage. His wife used to live with her parents, but such was her fate that they too died! Only recently had her uncle brought her to the house of the Chatterji's, that was now in the throes of a ceremony. Her uncle was powerless to do anything else. Because it was not merely a matter of feeding or clothing her; there was nobody to watch over her. Here, at her in-laws, she would be under constant surveillance. And for someone as hapless as her, even sweeping the in-laws' courtyard for a fistful of rice was more respectable than living in her parental home. That was what her uncle had said when he had brought her.

And that was that! Nearly a year had passed and he had not come back.

Shankari constantly heard caustic comments about her 'misconduct'. Nobody ever trusted a girl who had spent the prime of her life at her father's. No wonder she had not learnt the proper etiquette for a widow. Otherwise a brahmin widow should have known better than to place the pieces of fruit on a separate plate when eating roasted rice. That way, it was seen to be as good as a fruit-meal! A widow was supposed to chuck fruit pieces one by one into her mouth—that was the only way permissible. And the Beauty had neatly sliced the cucumber and taken it on her plate of roasted rice! It was a good thing that Mokshada had noticed, or custom would have been violated!

Gradually, suspicions about Shankari's character had intensified among the powers that be, mainly because she made such obvious mistakes at every step.

But Ramkali had not a clue about all that. He hardly had the time to keep track of each and every helpless girl sheltered in his house. Therefore, all his thoughts had veered around Rashu's wife. Besides, it was impossible to ascertain from that distance whether that white sari was the traditional widow's garb or had a hint of colour at the border.

It had not been Sharada who had come to die. Satyabati had started her strict vigil following her father's instructions. Besides, dying was hardly easy. Sharada could not simply hand over her husband and son to her newly arrived co-wife and find herself a shelter in the depths of the pool, could she? She would have to live with the barb, and pledge to destroy the co-wife with a sting too!

It was Shankari who had come to die. But she had not managed to.

She had sat down and thought to herself that death had to be the only way out, especially now that she was ruined. But she had wondered too, which would be better—to vanish forever from the face of this sweet world of sight, smell and sound, or to disappear from the social world of superstition, fear and custom? The former had pulled her with the power of all its attraction. But Shankari had recognized that the latter could turn into a living hell. And that was the reason she had come to bid farewell to the tender world that reveals itself in the light at daybreak and in the softness of the evening.

But she could not do that.

Not only because Ramkali had commanded her. The steps of the ghat too had fettered her in a tight bond from which she could not find escape.

Could it be that god did not want her to die? Had he therefore appeared in this form and stopped her? Suddenly, Shankari wondered if indeed that had been Ramkali? Could it have been the prank of a god? The gods appeared in disguise to enlighten humans about right and wrong—she had heard such things. Her doubts would disappear if somehow she could find out where Ramkali was at this moment. The longer she had dwelt on it, the idea that she would hear that he was elsewhere, treating a patient, took firm root in her mind. This had to be the trick of a god! Or else, why would Ramkali of all people be pacing up and down near the women's ghat at nightfall?

And such a booming voice! Could that really be his voice? He would come into the inner quarters sometimes, and talk to the aunts-in-law, but his voice never sounded so loud! It was gentle, deep and heavy. A full voice, its utterances were firm and serious. It was a blessing even to look at him!

He was not like the eldest uncle-in-law. Respect and admiration flew out the window if one looked at Kunjabihari. But the question was, how did one verify this business about god in disguise? The women's quarters were so far away from the men's part of the house. In this huge household of the Chatterjis where wives hardly got to meet their husbands, how would any other woman know about the whereabouts of a man? Of course, women hardly needed to take men's opinions into account, for their lives flowed in an entirely different direction. Just as women had no idea about men's work, men too never had the time to spare even an indifferent glance at women's work. Though they were members of the same household, they were stars of separate skies. Shankari began to wonder about the means of finding out if Ramkali was home, what he was doing at that moment, had he just got back, or had he been sitting at home?

If only she could speak with him. Then perhaps Shankari's desire to see god would be fulfilled. Of course, Shankari thought him to be a god, and why wouldn't she? No other man was capable of such forgiveness, no other heart had so much pity. Could anyone else in this whole wide world speak with so much kindness and such sympathy? Of course not. They would have shaved her head and poured yoghurt over her and expelled her from the village, and they would have clapped their hands and shouted, 'Shame on you! Aren't you a Hindu girl? And a brahmin widow too!'

But ... and suddenly, Shankari got goose-bumps all over—how had Ramkali found out? Who could have told him? Who else had found out? And even if her greatest foe had revealed everything out of fear, how had Ramkali known that Shankari had decided to drown herself that very evening?

Shankari had made up her mind just a moment ago—after spending a lot of time thinking, sighing and drenching the ground with tears. Since everybody was busy with the wedding, nobody would notice what she was up to. It had seemed like the best time. The wedding feast was scheduled for the following day and the house would be swarming with relatives. Supposing one among them should discuss Shankari and gossip about her ways? Everyone would get to know!

If she wanted to die, this was the best time. She had come to the ghat burdened with such thoughts, and was intent on finding relief for herself. Yet—and Shankari felt a tingling at the thought once more—god had intervened! He had brought her back from death's door to the kingdom of life. There was no room for further doubt.

Even though Shankari was a widow, the water she fetched was not used in the vegetarian kitchen, because her body had not been purified by ritual initiation. Shankari placed her pitcher in the middle of the courtyard. This water would be used by the children of the household.

The sound of the pitcher being lowered brought Satya out. She looked around and whispered, 'You're in proper trouble, Katoa-bou! They've been looking for you all over!'

The many women married into the family were distinguished from each other by suffixing the name of their natal villages as 'this-bou' or 'that-bou'. Shankari had joined this household only recently, so she had not been named according to the sequence of kinship—eldest, second, third, etc.

Shankari's heart thumped inside her. Trouble! Had everything been revealed, then? Her face was not visible in the faint light of the earthen lamp, but her voice could be heard—quivering, faint—'Why?'

'Wasn't it your turn to light the lamp for the gods this evening?' Satya's voice was full of panic and pity.

Her turn to light the lamps! Was that all? A stone rolled off Shankari's chest, her heart felt lighter. Let that be the most atrocious offence, the most heinous of crimes! Shankari would accept the harshest punishments. Yet the tenderness in Satya's outburst brought tears to her eyes.

Satya lowered her voice a little and said, 'And I ask you Katoa-bou, where is the need to stay at the ghat till this late? There are snakes and wicked people ...'

Shankari gathered her courage and said, 'Was my grandmother very angry?'

'Angry? That would be telling! The way they went on about you!' Satyabati shook her head and hands, 'Really, Katoa-bou, I must say this, you're too bold! Why spend an age at the ghat in darkness, when it was clearly your turn today? The grandmothers wanted to kill you.'

'I wish they would,' Shankari said intensely. 'Everyone would be relieved and I'd be happy too.'

Satya raised her eyebrows and put her hand on her cheek and said, 'Really! And for what joy, may I ask? The elder sister-in-law's been going on, "Bring me some poison, let me die before they untie the ritual-thread from your brother's hand, then I won't have to witness such things!" '

Shankari had not had the chance to get to know Sharada. Mainly because of the great difference in their ages. Besides, Sharada had become the much cherished wife after the birth of her son; and the widowed Shankari had always been seen as a bit of disposable waste. Their domains were also completely different. Shankari stayed with the widows, catering to all their needs; Sharada, on the other hand, was a blissfully married creature. There was a world of difference in the way they ate, slept, sat—in short, in everything.

But right now, Sharada had suffered a setback, and so, Shankari too could dare to feel sorry for her. She responded compassionately, 'Well, she can say that. Poor thing!'

'I agree! But what happened to *you*? What's aching deep inside you now?'

'It's my fate. It's just messed up,' Shankari sighed.

Satya waggled her fingers, 'Oh, I say, it didn't get messed up this very minute, did it? That's what Thakurma just said. You lost your husband a lifetime ago; why is your mind so restless *now*? What is it you think of all day?'

'Of death,' Shankari sat down, her back against the well. 'There's nothing else I think of.'

'How wonderful!' Satya shook her hands and left, with her anklets chiming out a conclusion, 'All women say the same thing— "I'll die! I'm dying! I wish I was dead!"—what a bother!'

Shankari did not answer her. She sat panting. Let the storm come, let it thunder, she would face anything. But she kept sitting; she lacked the strength to rise and walk to meet it.

And no sooner had she sat down, the gale rushed in. And with it rain and thunder! Hearing of her return, Kashiswari and Mokshada came to question her. Behind them, as an onlooker, Ramkali's wife, Bhubaneswari.

ELEVEN

She had been accused of forgetting to light the lamp in the puja room. Yet the picture that floated up in Shankari's mind and benumbed her senses had no relationship to any item related to a puja. In fact, it had nothing to do with this house or this village. The place of her misdemeanour was a mango grove in her father's village. The time was mid-afternoon when the body tends to go completely slack.

A strong, bracing breeze was blowing in gusts, inciting the trees, heavy with tiny fruit, into a drunken game. Some trees were slow, and had no fruit yet, only bunches of flowers between the leafy spaces. And in that secluded mango grove that afternoon, stood Shankari and Nagen. Shankari's hand was held in Nagen's. And it was not resting there freely—Nagen was holding it in a strong iron grip that she could not prise open. And he would not let go till he had had his say.

So far Nagen had conveyed his messages through gestures and signs, through small insignificant words, tender looks and secret smiles. Today he wanted it out. But had Nagen forced Shankari to come here? Had he gagged her and carried her to the grove? Not at all.

How could an orphan boy like him muster so much courage? His mother's sister had brought him up. Nagen's aunt was Shankari's uncle's wife—her father's brother's wife. She had brought up her motherless nephew along with her own sons. Shankari had grown up in the same house.

The business of her marriage had been an interruption. But not for long. It had ended by the eighth day. Nagen and Shankari had continued to live in the same house. Like siblings. But strange, how their feelings never became sibling-feelings! Or, why was it when Shankari's cousins pulled her hair, or bawled at her for small mistakes, Nagen always tried to comfort her and scold her tormentors?

It was beyond Shankari's comprehension why certain things

happen in the world in certain ways. Her understanding of the world was limited in any case. Or else, an eighteen-year-old girl should have known better than to come in the afternoon to the mango grove to meet a man.

Did Shankari really not have this sense? Hadn't her aunt's way of gnashing her teeth produced that sense in her? Or had she come there free from all worries and fears?

No. Even Shankari could hardly be called naive. She had come there, carrying a nest of fear within her. Ever since that morning, when Nagen had pleaded with her, a husking pedal had been pounding inside her heart. And she had made mistakes all day. But she had come nonetheless.

It was lucky that she had not been in charge of the kitchen that day. The next day, she would be leaving for her in-laws—practically for ever. The thought had induced a tenderness in her aunt and she had released Shankari from her chores. Later, when Shankari had humbly begged, 'Could I visit my friend, Kakima?', her aunt had been unable to refuse.

Nagen had laughed at first when he heard of this contrived excuse, 'So why feel upset because you've lied to an elder? Why can't you think of me as a "friend"?'

But Nagen was no longer laughing. He looked different now. Rough and wild, and a little lost. It was as though he wanted to hold Shankari's hand in his iron fist and drag her to a different world.

'Let's run away to some faraway village where nobody will know us! We'll say we are married—a fire destroyed our house and land—so we left home broken-hearted.'

'If you speak such sinful words, your tongue will fall off, Nagenda. We'll not find a place in hell!' Shankari said. But her words lacked conviction. Was her tongue weighed down with the fear of sin?

'What sin? What kind of marriage was yours anyway? You never even lived with your husband. We have been husband and wife over many lifetimes, don't you see? That's why that freak of a husband they found you didn't last long. Or else, we'd be in different places. Make up your mind, Shankari. Please!'

'Even hearing such words will bring eternal damnation, Nagenda.'

'In that case,' Nagen looked menacing, 'if you go to hell, you don't have to go alone. I'll suffer that for you. Let the whole world go to heaven, you and I shall live in hell. At least we'll have a good life.'

'This isn't just an argument, Nagenda. I beg of you, leave me alone! If someone should see us, I'll be discarded and thrown out.'

'That will be good,' Nagen had tightened his grip instead of letting go, and had pulled her closer too. 'It will be good for me if they drive you out of the house. If there's a scandal, your in-laws will also refuse to take you in. That'll make it easier for us to go away. A blessing in disguise.'

'No, no, Nagendada—let go my hand! If I knew you had so much evil in you, I wouldn't have come. You said you had something to tell me—'

Nagen did what he had never done before. He became livid, and said with utter sarcasm, 'Don't pretend! Wouldn't have come! Would I have discussed the scriptures with you, eh? Come away with me!'

Unconsciously, in a moment of carelessness, the query had spilled out, 'Where?'

Nagen had responded enthusiastically, 'Wherever! Far, far away to some village. Where we will set up a happy home. A small hut, a garden to grow greens, a bit of pond—what else would we need? I'll manage that. After all, I've studied a bit, I could open a small school. Who would it harm, Shankari?'

Had the husking pedal in Shankari's heart stopped pounding for a minute? Had a quiver of bliss swayed her soul? And filled her eyes with tears? Had her body felt numb in the gushing spring air? Had it not struck her, that *really*, who could it harm? She had never set eyes on her in-laws' house, she had not set up house for even a day. They did not know her at all. What would they stand to gain, or lose? What happiness or grief would they experience if they did not

have Shankari! If her uncle sent word that the girl called
Shankari—the doctor's niece-in-law—had suddenly died of cholera,
would anyone in the doctor's house weep for her at all?

And what about her uncle and aunt? Would they escape the
censure of society by spreading rumours about her death? But such
thoughts had not lingered long. The breeze had suddenly dropped
and the place had become stifling, and Shankari had returned to
her senses once more.

She said, 'Aren't you ashamed to make such a filthy suggestion—
asking a Hindu widow to leave home? Aren't you like a brother to
me?'

'No, never!' Nagen roared. 'I've never been like a brother to you.
You know that as well as I do! In my mind, I have always thought
of you as my wife. Why are you trying to be clever when you know
it all? Promise me that you will come here in the afternoon—I'll
be waiting. Then if we can walk quickly out of the village, who
will catch us? My aunt and uncle won't be able to find us. They'd
have no choice but to bear it in silence.'

'Oh Nagenda, there's a tightness in my chest; please let me go.
I can't do it.'

'You'll have to,' Nagen pleaded. 'I won't let go of your hand till
you agree. Let people see, that's what I want.'

'Nagenda, I'll scream and call people,' Shankari had said weakly,
with no conviction at all. 'I shall say you found me alone in the
grove and ...'

Nagen said recklessly, 'Scream then! Call them!'

'Oh Nagenda, why don't you kill me instead!'

'How can I kill you when they've killed you already? It'd be like
beating a corpse! Even in your own home you don't get a fistful of
rice without a beating, and at your in-laws' you'll be battered again.
And here I am, wanting to save you, and care for you, and treasure
you!'

'I don't want your care.' This time Shankari's voice was firm. 'A
battering is good enough for me.'

'Really! A battering is good enough for you?' Nagen suddenly
became aggressive.

Yes, he had held Shankari tight, not in an embrace of love, rather, in a death-like grip. And said, 'All right, I'll see to it that you get an even better battering. Here, see how I brand you; I'll spread rumours in your in-laws' village about what you did with me …'

Shankari could no longer remember how she had freed herself from Nagen's embrace and rushed to the ghat to take a dip, nor how she had returned home to spend the rest of the day in bed. She gave the excuse that she had had to bathe after accidentally touching a lower caste person's pot and so could not go to her friend's house after all, and her head felt heavy from the untimely bath.

She recalled her uncle's kind words when he saw her torrent of tears, 'Why're you crying like this? Every woman has to go to her in-laws' after all. That is her permanent place. Besides, the doctor is a good man. You won't lack anything there, you'll live well and be happy.'

But Shankari had wept passionately. Finally her aunt had consoled her, 'We'll bring you home during festivals. It isn't as if we're turning you out completely.'

A year had passed, but her aunt had not kept her promise. Leave alone coming to fetch her, they had not enquired about her even once. Shankari had not had an iota of news from their village since then. Yet she would stiffen with fear at the thought of someone gossiping, 'Here's a man named Nagen who's saying things about Shankari.'

Outside the house she would shudder with fear when the leaves rustled, and freeze in her tracks at the sound of swishing bamboo.

But was it only fear? Wasn't there a dreadful hope tangled with it? At the back of her mind, did she not believe that should she by any chance meet that dangerous man, by the bamboo bush, or near the pond, she would never ever return home?

Ever since she had heard that her uncle's family was going to come for the feast, Shankari had felt numb. Who knew what her uncle or cousins would come and say! Had Nagen confessed everything? Was he still there? Alive? May be they had found out and killed him.

Why had Shankari gone to the mango grove that day? And why did that man who had enticed her there tug at her heart-strings even now?

Why hadn't Shankari been able to die even when she had wanted to? If a girl called Shankari had ceased to exist, what difference would it have made to the world? She had been worshipping the gods, lighting the lamp before the sacred tulsi with a mind that was tainted. What would be the consequence of such a sin—

Her thoughts were interrupted. Kashiswari called out in a fierce voice, 'Nath-bou!'

TWELVE

A terrifying fear! It was the first time that Satya had experienced such terrible dread.

She had anticipated of course, that Shankari was in for serious trouble. But this was much beyond her expectations. The language of rebuke left her astounded. She had heard many words all her life, and she had learnt many words too, but never words like these! Who was an 'unchaste' woman? What could a 'paramour' be? And how did one darken one's 'kul'? Satya could guess that this word probably did not belong to the same category as the kul-berry which tasted so delicious when rubbed with sugar and salt. But she soon lost her bearings. She stared from a distance at the group— Shankari, Kashiswari and all.

Nobody said a word, they were all silent, including Mokshada. And Kashiswari alone intoned her lines in a sharp, controlled pitch. Their faces looked as though they would not be appeased even if they had skinned Shankari alive and chewed her up.

Mokshada and Kashiswari were very different from one another. Mokshada was robust and strong, and fluent of speech. Kashiswari was not like that. Weakened by miseries, she was ever cautious with words. Only in certain situations would she open her mouth. And the words that flowed were controlled and sharp. But never before had such words escaped from Kashiswari's mouth. Nor had such a hateful expression been seen on her face.

Had someone been to Katoa and gathered something from there? Why did they repeatedly refer to Shankari's natal village? It seemed that her family had refused to come to the wedding feast. They wanted to cut off all ties with Shankari. And had they been her parents, instead of being uncle and aunt, they would have diced her to pieces and thrown her into the river.

Much more was said with matching facial expressions! They suggested that Shankari should go and hang herself. They even recommended that she drown herself. Their indisputable verdict was that Shankari's wicked and sinful ways had brought on the death of Kashiswari's only grandson just within a year of marrying her.

That was what Satya could grasp after listening for a long time. Rakhu and the barber's wife had gone to Katoa with an invitation to the feast. And Shankari's aunt had said utterly horrid things about her.

There was no doubt about the fact that Shankari had done something appalling before coming away. Obviously, it was something far more serious than not lighting the lamp, or sitting at the ghat till dusk.

But what was the link between Shankari's crime and her aunt's sister's son? Why had he disappeared from home because of Shankari?

This was what confused Satya. It was a riddle.

Her blood had been frozen by words which seemed to bear the weight of a different world. They filled her with terror. It was a feeling she had never experienced before and her usual audacity was silenced.

It was the first time that Satya had refrained from disrupting their reprimands with her sharp retorts. Otherwise, it was a habit with her to defend the accused, even if she was a subordinate.

Once the low-caste Bagdi woman, who did the washing up, had

lost a bowl at the ghat. It had probably fallen in, but Dinatarini and Shibjaya had accused her of stealing it and had raged on and on. Mokshada had ordered, 'Well, if you haven't stolen it, go and look for it in the pond—all night if it comes to that, and find it!'

The more she sobbed, the more aggressively they charged her. They insinuated that she had deliberately come back late from the ghat so that she could steal the bowl. Finally, it was Satya who had saved the woman.

She had intervened, 'Come here, you and I shall look for the bowl together. I can swim well. We'll both dive in and look for the bowl.'

'What do you mean you'll look for it?' Everyone had scolded.

Astounding everyone, Satya had replied unhappily, 'Well, I shall have to do it. Since god has sent me as a daughter to this house, I have to atone for the sins of this household. If people who're so rich and don't lack a thing want to finish off a person for just a small bowl that's gone missing, someone will have to make amends.'

Everyone had been struck speechless. And they had recognized for the first time the extent of their own pettiness.

'All right then, since you have plenty, just give it away as you please! Your father has money after all,' they had remarked limply and admitted defeat.

The Bagdi woman had pulled her sari around her neck, and touched Satya's feet that day.

In this way, Satya had saved many a person from danger. So why was she silent now? It was as though the trembling induced by some mysterious, dark forest had robbed Satya of speech.

Satya could hardly keep track of when the castigation chapter ended, and the older women left the scene to return to work. Nor had she any idea about the whereabouts of Shankari. After a while, she had slowly come into Sharada's room. Spreading out the end of her shimmering sari, she stretched herself out on the floor. Sharada too was similarly stretched out with her baby beside her.

Sharada had asked, 'Why're you lying down?'

'Just like that,' Satya had evaded an answer.

Sharada had sighed once more and asked, 'Why were they cursing Katoa-bou?'

'I don't know,' Satya had replied.

This sort of abbreviated, brief communication, was rare for Satya, but Sharada herself was so miserable that she did not press further. At one point, she fell asleep with her son.

But sleep eluded Satya. The feeling of dread refused to go away. Her heart felt cold and empty. Even if she were to ignore those unfamiliar words, she could hardly overlook the new fear that was taking root inside her. Suppose Katoa-bou should ...

Satya did not know the method nor the consequences of hanging oneself, but apprehension about the other possibility was sending a chill down her spine. Suppose it were to really happen? And the fishermen hauled up something else with the fish when they cast their nets for tomorrow's feast? And after dragging it in with great enthusiasm, suppose they noticed that it was not a fish at all! A husking pedal started pounding inside Satya's chest. How many people could she keep an eye on?

Satya hardly had a relationship with Katoa-bou. She had arrived just a year ago, practically a stranger. Besides, she belonged to the vegetarian part of the house. They never ate together. They would speak whenever they met. But Shankari seemed distracted most of the time, and she would not socialize much.

That evening when Satya had secretly come to warn her, she had not felt any more compassion for Shankari than for a pet animal. But now her heart filled with pity. She must be sobbing away—the poor thing! She had nobody in the world to console her. How pathetic it was to be a widow!

Satya was married. To a man who was her 'husband'. If he suddenly died, would Satya become a widow too? Then would all the others scream at her like that?

Pishi-thakurma was a widow too. There were others too; everyone seemed in awe of them. They had the absolute authority to chastise you. What could be the reason for that? Could it be their age? That could hardly be the reason. Besides, how could elderly people behave so abominably? Satya could not comprehend it.

Age could not be everything either. Everybody respected her father, and feared him. But they did not have the same feelings of awe for his elder brother. To the contrary! Her father's elder brother was scared to death of Ramkali. So were his uncles. Everybody was! Not only the women. It probably had nothing to do with age.

Where did fear reside? Satya felt completely out of her depth. Even so, she kept trying to figure out this riddle. God alone knew who had assigned her this task.

Late at night, Bhubaneswari came to call her.

'Here, Satya! How can you fall asleep without eating? Get up!'

First Satya turned the other way, feigning sleep, and then claimed she had no appetite.

Bhubaneswari scolded, 'Why is that? Go on, you mustn't fast at night. They say fasting at night weakens even an elephant! And Boro-bou, you get up too! You've not eaten all day. You mustn't do this. It'll have dire consequences for your husband and son.'

Sharada hurriedly sat up on hearing Bhubaneswari's voice. Although she had been lying on the floor with a fierce desire to bid the world adieu, it was unthinkable that she would neglect to show respect to her aunt-in-law. She had got up hurriedly, her heart fluttering at the mention of dire consequences for her husband and son.

Bhubaneswari repeated, 'Let me look after your son. Go now. And take Satya too. Your mother-in-law's managing the kitchen. A huge fish was caught this afternoon, just in case people dropped by. She's cooked a lovely sour curry with thick pieces of fish and mango—just go and taste it.'

Bhubaneswari's words hardly reached Satya's ears. As soon as she had she heard that a net had been cast, the image of another creature trapped in the waters floated up in her mind. The creature landed on the bank with a thud. Thousands of bystanders looked on that face, which was forbidden by custom to look at the sun or the moon. But were the eyes embedded in that face able to see anything at all? Would they look at anything ever again?

She sat up suddenly and asked, 'Ma! Were is Katoa-bou?'

'Where else should she be?' Bhubaneswari burst out, 'She's sleeping with the quilt over her head. Why do you need to know where she is? Go and eat!'

'I won't! I'm not hungry.' Satya lay herself down again.

Meanwhile, 'the thick pieces of fish and mango' had begun their work elsewhere. The nursing of her baby all day long, and the fierce vigour of her sixteen-year body had left Sharada utterly exhausted. Besides, the co-wife's 'sting' had begun to dwindle a little. Nevertheless, she found herself faced with a hurdle. She had been starving herself since morning, and had not seen her husband yet. Nor was she certain that she would see him tonight. But the 'new' bride had to observe the ritual of sleeping separately tonight, and the first wife just might get priority. How could she express her sense of hurt authentically if she had dinner now? That was why Sharada whimpered, 'I had a stomach-ache all this while. It's just stopped ...'

'Let that be. It'll go as soon as you eat,' Bhubaneswari said gently. 'Satya might eat a bit if you took her along.'

Custom did not permit Sharada to speak to her own mother-in-law with her face uncovered. But she felt quite free with this particular aunt-in-law. In fact, Bhubaneswari's gentle tone brought tears to Sharada's eyes. She found it hard to hold on to her resolve to present a starving image to her husband. She tried to shake Satya awake, 'Come on! Eat whatever you can manage.'

Satya sat up, yawned and said irritably, 'Goodness, if only one could be left alone for two seconds! Come, let's go.'

As soon as Sharada left, Bhubaneswari did something exceptionally bold. She picked up the sleeping child and came out of the room quietly and instructed the maid, 'Go and call the eldest son inside. Say it is urgent.'

Rashu was the eldest son. The maid looked around and whispered, 'I saw him sleeping in the courtyard.'

'Doesn't matter, tell him that I'm calling him.'

Why call Satya away with this urgent whisper? There could be only one reason that Sharada could figure out, even if Satya could not. That is why her heart froze one minute, and soared with hope and desire the next. Sharada knew what this meant. Because she had a memory: as an innocent child, she would demand to sleep next to her newly wedded aunt and her mother always called her away with a similar whisper. It amused her to think about it now.

—

On hearing Bhubaneswari's voice, Satyabati stopped. Alarm and anticipation transformed Sharada's heart into a still, cold pond in winter.

Bhubaneswari had not called out in her usual manner. She had called furtively, urgently, 'Here, come this way!'

She had addressed Satya, who stopped in her tracks and asked, 'Is Boro-bou going to sleep by herself, then? How absurd!'

Bhubaneswari suppressed a giggle and reprimanded, 'Stop it! Don't you try telling me what's absurd and what isn't. Why should she sleep alone? She has a son, is he to be scoffed at?'

'I just don't understand this. All of you seem to change your minds all the time. He's still wet behind the ears—as if he can look after his mother!'

'Will you listen to me?'

'All right then. You're forever in a hurry! If you think that it's best to leave a distressed person by herself in a dark room, then so be it. I can't understand at all, how all of you go on and on about right conduct and custom. Really!'

Twisting more than half of her sari around her waist, Satyabati followed her mother reluctantly. She had really wanted to sleep next to Sharada tonight, chiefly because she felt sympathetic, but also because she had hoped to find out the meaning of those dreadful words as they chatted at night. They were wicked words, that was for sure, and if she asked the grown-ups she would never get a straight answer. They would inevitably combine reprimand and suggestive misinformation.

A severe and uncontrollable curiosity took hold of her. She was certain that many a mysterious room would open up if she could only procure the meaning of those words. Perhaps they would reveal the reason why Shankari had said that she wished to die all the time, and also why nobody treated her with any kindness.

But it was just like her mother to spoil it. Well, there was nothing new about it. This was something Satyabati had observed from the time she was born: grown-ups had just a single occupation —to spoil things for children!

—

All the girls who had come of age would sleep in Dinatarini's room. Obviously because the room was very large, but also because custom dictated that grown girls could not sleep in any old room. Among them Satyabati was the oldest, and she was married too; therefore, she was the leader. Punyi, Raju, Neri, Tepi, Puti, Rakhali— everyone looked up to her.

They had waited up for Satya before falling asleep. Satya now gazed on a kingdom in slumber! Everyone was sleeping, limbs stretched out any which way. There was hardly any place, so she had to push and shove to make place for herself. She said irritably, 'Only the goddess knows what harm it would do to sleep elsewhere for one night! Come now—move a bit—hey Puti, move your leg a little.'

Needless to say, this request hardly pierced the depths of Puti's sleep. Satya had to abandon the power of words and resort to brute force. She moved Puti's leg and Rakhali's leg and made space for herself, and finally stretched herself out on the bed. Dinatarini had not entered the room yet, she always came in late. It took her a while to chew the hard roasted rice and sesame sweets—the nightly victuals of widows.

Satyabati checked to see if her grandmother's bed was made. It was, so there was a bit of space. But this could hardly be called a bed—basically, it was a huge rug spread out on the floor with some thick quilts on it and a row of long pillows at the head. The unique length of the pillows ensured that the maximum number of heads fitted on each row. Each pillow, therefore, was more than a yard long and very heavy; those who slept on them could hardly move an inch. They did not know the pleasure of placing a pillow under their heads just the way they liked.

The pillows were not only large and heavy, they were stuffed with old cotton. No matter how cheap or how abundant it was, wasting anything was out of the question. New bolsters with new covers would be made with fresh cotton whenever the large bolsters of the men of the house split open. The rejected cotton and covers would be used for the children. Every house followed the same practice. Children had to make do with things that were considered worthless.

The doctor was quite well-off. A washerman was fixed at an annual rate to wash everything regularly. Which hardly meant that he washed, dried and folded each item. He would do his washing at the ghat that was meant for 'washing', and leave the clothes in a heap on the steps leading to the pond by the back-door. Then Mokshada would take over. She was responsible for purging the wet pile of clothes by washing them with water from the 'clean' pond. Then she would hang them out in the sun. The next part of the duty was carried out by Shibjaya's daughters-in-law, Kunja's wife and Bhubaneswari.

It was quite a bother changing the bed linen every day, so Ramkali had strictly instructed the washerman to wash everything twice a month. May be today was one such day, that is why everything had an earthy smell. Satyabati detested that smell and covered her nose. She wondered why clothes could not be washed without giving them such an awful smell. Thinking of one thing, her mind wandered to another.

The eldest sister-in-law was sleeping all by herself. What if she should get up at night and attempt to kill herself by drowning? She would die, and how would Satya face her father? From daybreak the house would be full of relatives and there would be total chaos about a missing daughter-in-law. A real predicament this was!

She could no longer afford to be complacent. Later, when the house became silent, she would get up and check. It would be best to lock Sharada in her room. Otherwise she would have to get up several times to check. And in the meanwhile, suppose she took a chance and did the worst! Satyabati was not tall enough to reach the latch that was high up on the door, so she started thinking of ways to reach it.

—

Sharada entered the room, her heart drumming. She had not even managed to ask Bhubaneswari whether her son had cried or bothered her. Bhubaneswari had volunteered, 'Come! Quietly now! Just go to sleep. The boy has just fallen asleep, don't wake him. I've just left him sleeping, and I placed the kajal-container under his pillow.'

Bhubaneswari fretted till she had managed to summon Rashu, and pushed him into his room. Supposing Sharada was unable to recognize him in the dark, and started to scream? She could hardly warn Rashu about this, because propriety demanded that a woman did not speak to a man, who was like a son to her, inside his bedroom. Rashu was her nephew. She could not be too explicit with Sharada either. It was hardly proper that she should blurt out, 'Look! I found you a treasure!' That would be very improper, hence she had used the child as a pretext.

But there was a different reason too—her longing for amusement. She might be an elder, but she was a woman, after all. Though she was the wife of the awe-inspiring Ramkali, Bhubaneswari was, in many ways still young and green.

The metaphor of 'treasure' had occurred to her because she could well imagine how precious the familiar man had suddenly become to Sharada. It was uncertain yet, how successfully she would manage to hold on to her husband. The chances were slim because it was a man's heart. By the time the 'new' bride turned into a nubile girl, Sharada would be a mother of three, and Rashu would be hard put to resist the nectar of a new flower ...

Bhubaneswari was startled by her own thoughts. She cuffed herself mentally. Rashu was like a son to her. How could she think about him like that? Decorum had to be preserved in relationships…

Wiping away such thoughts, Bhubaneswari went into the kitchen. It was now time for the women of her age-group to eat. But tonight they couldn't sleep afterwards. They would have to stay up and chop vegetables for tomorrow's feast. Despite the fact that she was a rich man's wife, Bhubaneswari was never granted any opportunity to be lazy. A daughter-in-law had to be kept busy all the time, it would be unforgivable if she forgot her obligations! But of course, nobody would say a thing if Rashu's mother neglected her duties.

Had all the sisters-in-law been allowed to work together in a group, nobody would have complained. Because they could always chat as they worked. But that was never allowed to happen—there would always be an older woman keeping watch. They had to keep watch, in case any of the wives were plotting to break the family up! The burden of this particular responsibility had kept Shibjaya awake many a night, her ears straining against the ventilators of her son's room.

— ·

Sharada's room had no such ventilator, but a proper window. The room nearest the inner courtyard belonged to Sharada. When Ramkali had summoned a workman from Barddhaman to have this room built on the southern part of the courtyard, everyone had thought he was getting it built for himself. When the workman finished, even Dinatarini had said, 'Look up the almanac and enter the room on an auspicious day.'

Ramkali had said with a laugh, 'Don't count your chickens before they've hatched, Ma! Wait for the person whose room it is to arrive.'

Dinatarini was astonished, 'Who could that be? Who are you talking about?'

'About the Lakshmi of the house, Ma.' Having guessed his mother's thoughts, Ramkali had axed them at the root, and had calmly concluded, 'Haven't you heard? There's talk of Rashu's marriage.'

So, would Rashu's wife occupy that room? The grand-daughter-in-law of Dinatarini's co-wife! Unable to contain herself, Dinatarini said irritably, 'Don't talk like a fool, Ramkali. How can you give up the best room to Rashu?'

Ramkali had stopped laughing. He had replied rather seriously, 'It isn't a question of giving up, everyone gets what is rightfully theirs.'

Though she feared her son's temper, Dinatarini was unable to control her annoyance and had burst out, 'You sweat out your guts to make money, you put together every bit and piece to build a room fit for a king. And Kunja's daughter-in-law gets to live in it! What is the logic here, Ramkali?'

Ramkali had not scolded his mother publicly, instead, he had said even more calmly, 'The logic by which humans cover their nakedness instead of moving about unclothed like forest animals. Never mind that, you do know the custom of offering the best to the eldest. Rashu is the eldest son in this household.'

A sense of woe and humiliation had brought Dinatarini close to tears. So she made a last ditch attempt at arguing, 'You ought to think about your own wife too. She is still young, and ever since the building began she might have harboured some hope ...'

Ramkali had smiled some more, 'If your daughter-in-law had fanned such a base hope then it ought to be put out.'

'It ought to be put out!'

Dinatarini had wiped her eyes with the end of her sari. Not so much at the thought of her daughter-in-law's disappointment, as at her own. How could one bear to see Kunja, who hardly took any responsibility, getting the best portion all the time? Dinatarini had hoped that at least when it came to this room, Kunja and his wife would be made to feel small. But that hope had been crushed. So she had started weeping, 'It ought to be put out!'

'Of course! So that such brazen hopes can never take birth in the future.'

After that Dinatarini had watched the carpenter from

Chandannagore enter that room. Yes, those days, if a double bed had to be made, it had to be made inside the room. The custom of bringing in a readymade bed was not yet known.

And a very ornate bed it was. The carpenters from Chandannagore had to be paid for a month and a half to make it. They were fed and paid, and gifted with clothes; then they had left. After that Rashu had got married, and spent his wedding night on that bed.

Today, Sharada had abandoned that very bed and spent all day on the floor. Even now, after she had latched the door as her aunt-in-law asked her, she lay herself down on the floor.

As she entered, Sharada had sensed, even without looking, that her desire and anticipation had not been not in vain. Her thoughts, her heartbeats, and her sense of smell had collectively conveyed to her, 'Your treasure is right here in this room, waiting for you.'

Almost as if he were still her 'new' groom! She recalled how her friends had pushed her into the room and locked her in, once when she had visited her parents after her wedding. Sharada's heart had drummed inside her just like this. She had been only twelve then. Now, she was sixteen. The storm inside a sixteen-year-old heart was far more intense.

The condition of the offender was not any better. A hammer was beating inside his heart too. He had never hoped to face Sharada again in his life. All day he had thought that his joys and delights had ended.

He had not even grasped fully why his aunt had called him indoors. He had thought he would be asked once again to enter into the maze of some ritual or other. But what he heard was extraordinary. Apparently Sharada was busy in the kitchen and his aunt too was rushing off to the storeroom, so Rashu had to watch over his sleeping son. No big deal, he had to just wait in the room for a while.

The obtuse Rashu had not suspected anything at that time. Of course, he had been baffled by the suggestion. Anybody else could have watched over the boy, why Rashu? What a strange idea! The maid who had been sent to call him could well have done the job. She had done it often too. But he had not been able to protest.

Nor ask any question. He was as embarrassed about his newborn son as he was about his 'new' bride.

So Rashu had entered the room noiselessly. Immediately, a hammer of doubt had started to beat inside his chest. Was this one of his aunt's tricks? Rashu was fond of his aunt, but at this moment, he felt like worshipping her. He blew out the lamp, sat down uneasily, and began to think.

As he thought, he suddenly realized that the latch had turned and the still stuffiness of the room was being pounded by a sobbing. A few drops of tears spilled out of Rashu's eyes too. He might be a man, but he was human too.

Sharada sat up with a start. She tried hard to free herself from the strong embrace that held her, and choked on her words, 'What's the use, what's the use now?'

She could not say more. Her eyes betrayed her. All day she had resolved that if she ever met that brute, she would not weep, nor look pale. She would be as distant as a stranger. But this situation had thrown everything into confusion.

And not just a few drops! A monsoon downpour! How could she stop this? With what could she build a dam that could stem the flow?

'Boro-bou!' So much of pleading and supplication packed into one word!

But nobody answered that piteous plea.

'Boro-bou, what have I done? Why are you cross with me? Don't you see that my heart is ground to dust too?'

The downpour became a deluge.

'Come, come, there's no need to lure me with lies. As if a man's heart is capable of tenderness!'

'Here, do what you want, Boro-bou. Believe me, I too am hurting as much as you. If you think I have betrayed you, I won't be able to cope with that!'

'Where's the need to cope with it?' Sharada tried to control her tears and appear tough. 'Tomorrow is your night with the "new" bride! A night of new joys! Why moan and lament tonight?'

'Boro-bou, tell me, how can I convince you?'

The strength of the embrace seemed to want to crush Sharada; how could she resist? Still, she made one last attempt, 'What does it matter to you if I am convinced or not? You reject the old mother of your son for the tender kernel—'

'Boro-bou, if you treat me this way, I'll have no other choice than to take my own life …'

Rashu knew how to be tough too, so he continued, 'I'm going to my uncle's medicine chest. There is snake poison there. I know where it is. After that don't blame me if you're widowed!'

A widow!

Sharada's heart trembled. She would rather share the house with a hundred co-wives. Was there a curse worse than that of being widowed? Yet what could anyone say at such a moment?

'All right, I'm going. This is our last meeting while I'm alive.' Rashu moved towards the door hoping that Sharada would stop him. But Sharada made no such move.

'I thought I would abandon her forever, and you would remain the empress of my heart as you always have been …' Rashu soliloquized his regret with his hand on the latch. 'Instead, you turned husband-killer and ruined your chances!' Rashu moved the latch.

Now Sharada spoke, but what words were these? Was this the language of a dumb woman, helpless and madly in love?

She uttered in a choked voice, 'Why are you wailing out your lines to your own wife in the style of a jatra? You think it's very manly to open the door and go out? If you have snake's poison, don't I have the pot and rope?'

'Your heart is made of stone, Boro-bou! When uncle forcibly dragged me away, couldn't you go and tell him, "I have the pot and rope too!" Wait, I'll show everyone what the harmless Rashu is capable of doing!'

Having played out this heroic role, Rashu gave the door a quick push, but it did not take him long to comprehend the situation. The door was locked from outside. Who could have done it? His aunt? Was she capable of such a flippant jest? Who else could it be? Nobody had seen Rashu enter the house. Bhubaneswari must have scripted tonight's drama.

'It's locked from outside!' Slowly, a tenor of helplessness filled the room.

'Locked!' Sharada broke her silence with wonder and fear.

'That's what I see—' Rashu sounded perplexed, 'What to do now? Suppose it's locked till morning. What will happen, Boro-bou?'

All of a sudden a curious thing happened. Totally unforeseen, unexpected. Perhaps Sharada herself could not have imagined it even a moment ago. She had no idea that a voice choking with tears could burst into amused laughter. And though it was muted, her laughter was bursting with disbelief.

That was Sharada's nature, she could laugh at a joke even during times of grief. However today it was different. Today it had been a matter of life and death for her. Her voice was clogged with tears. But Rashu's voice and its sense of crisis gave her some cause for mirth and she burst out in amazed laughter. She said with a chuckle, 'What else? Mister will be forced to spend the night with another woman!'

Rashu gave a start; he was stunned. Was Sharada pretending? Having a co-wife could not have hurt her that much then. Her laughter and her words sounded so indulgent.

One could deal with the door later; it was best to tackle what was at hand first. The latch was fastened once more. And the unused bed was once again made warm with caresses.

But Sharada was not one to give in so easily. She was determined to extract a promise from her husband.

'No, don't touch me—first swear on the Goddess Durga that you will not touch the younger one while I am alive.'

Rashu's heart trembled. What a terrible oath! He said fearfully, 'Is it a good thing to swear on the goddess, Boro-bou?'

'It is, unless your heart is sinful. If you have the integrity of heart and mind, why should you fear?'

'Still, it involves a goddess after all!'

'All right then! I'm not forcing you. Don't you touch me.'

Oh, Goddess Durga! Had anyone in the village faced such a dilemma before? On the one hand, a guilt-burdened, restless heart swaying with hope, and on the other, an unbending woman of

stone! Was her laughter a trick then? Or else why was she getting
ready to sleep next to the boy?

'Boro-bou!'

'Why are you bothering me?'

Rashu would not be able to leave in a flash of anger, Sharada
could depend on the locked door for that. God! Who was the
goddess who had imprisoned Rashu this way? Was she Durga
herself?

'Then you won't take pity on me?'

'You are my husband, an elder—why raise the question of pity?
A wife is a bonded slave, after all.'

'All right, I swear. Happy?'

'Well, I can't hear you saying it.'

'I am. In my mind.'

'In your mind! Huh! Words in the mind can travel far! Say it
aloud.'

'All right, all right! As the goddess is my witness, I won't touch
anybody else except you.'

'Not "except me" but "until I die".' That was all that Sharada
requested.

'It's all the same. Who can say who will go first.'

'My horoscope says that I shall die a married woman,' Sharada
smiled contentedly. 'Remember the goddess is your witness.'

'I will! I will!'

But had he really managed to remember that? Had Rashu finally
been able to honour the goddess? Could any man ever do such a
thing? Especially a spineless man like Rashu?

But it is a woman's fate to build her home on the quicksand of
such false vows.

THIRTEEN

They were frying chanabora for the feast. The confectioners had
started work at dawn, kindling firewood in a chullah they had built

under a shack. They had already finished frying the bonde sweets and had piled them in mounds on wooden platters. It would not do to make these in small quantities—each guest would eat more than his fill and take away sweets packed in a chyada too. Besides, the guests were going to be offered just these two types of sweets. A greater variety was hardly possible at such short notice. But that was not the real reason either. Had Ramkali Chatterji thought it right, it would not have been impossible for him to get master confectioners from Katoa or Guptipara to make several types of sweets. But he had not thought it necessary.

Rashu's first wedding had been celebrated with pomp and splendour. Tales about it still circulated. Confectioners had come from Natore, Keshtonagar and Murogacha. There were about twelve or thirteen types of sweets, all perfectly made. And the fish— one could not stop talking about it! Each guest had a tureen of fish curry set before him and was served several helpings. Apart from that there had been fifty-two items on the menu. What was pomp without fifty-two items? There had been baskets full of large earthenware pots that had been specially made by potters and filled to the brim with sweets.

But that was different. There could be no comparison between that wedding and this. Any other house would not have bothered with a feast; all these arrangements were made only because it was Ramkali Chatterji's house. Food was cooked in enormous quantities, but there were just about two types of sweets, and about sixteen or twenty items on the menu. The cooking had not begun as yet, although preparations were on in a nearby hut. The confectioner had gone for his bath.

In this village, Ramkali was the first to start this custom of bringing in a cook from outside to cater for a feast—an arrangement he had seen in Murshidabad. Or else, the daughters of brahmins cooked for festivals—that was the usual practice. And a matter of prestige too. The women who were reputed cooks were coaxed and cajoled and invited to undertake the task. They had to be offered a ritual welcome into the kitchen with a potful of oil, a pair of saris, and, if they were married, with alta and sindur. But such occasions often turned into a scuffle or fight. There were always people looking for an excuse to turn a banquet into a battlefield. Misunderstandings, harsh words and hurt pride were intrinsic to a feast. But Ramkali disliked such hassles. He wanted to hire a person to do the work and avoid such troubles. Those who disapproved of eating what a hired cook prepared could eat whatever the widows of the house cooked. Naturally, they would have to do without fish.

Except for a couple of very orthodox old men, most people ate whatever was served at a feast thrown by Ramkali Chatterji. The three things that drew them there were—the cook's expertise, Ramkali's generosity, and the awe in which they held Ramkali. He was not the only wealthy person in this region, but nobody else was as large-hearted as Ramkali.

By now, the fragrance of sweets fried in pure ghee was beginning to pour out and fill the entire village, and adults struggled to keep the children indoors. Ramkali dressed in a short kurta and a fine white dhoti, with silver-topped wooden sandals on his feet, was busy, attentively supervising everything. The only responsibility he had delegated to his elder brother, Kunja, was to sit rooted to the spot where the sweets were being fried. One could hardly trust Kunja with more than that.

The milkmen had brought in pots of curds and Ramkali was calculating the number of pots they had managed to supply, when Neru came and stood near him. Ramkali would not have paid him any attention, but Neru stood very close as if he had something to say. With his eyes on the milkmen, Ramkali patted Neru's head and said, 'What is it, Neru?'

Neru looked around anxiously and said, 'They've asked you to go inside.'

'Oh! Whom have they asked to go inside?'

'You.'

Ramkali frowned, 'They've asked me to go in now? Has somebody gone mad or what?' Ignoring Neru, he once again focussed on the milkmen, 'What is this, Tustu, can't you supply enough curds? What should I do now? You'd promised me ...'

Tustu scratched his head, 'Well, I did, but the goddess dashed my hopes. Didn't sleep a wink last night, went to every milkman possible but this is all that I managed.'

'Yes, I can see that. But what'll happen to me now? People are sure to insult me!'

'Insult you!' Tustu said heroically, 'A man would need more than a single head on his shoulders to do that, Thakur.'

'Each person in this village has a hundred heads, do you understand?' Ramkali smiled, and just at that moment Neru called again softly, 'Mejo-khuro.'

'Gosh! This lad is a real bother! Who's sent you, eh?'

'Pishi-thakurma.'

Ramkali said irritably, 'I can well imagine that, or else who would—' I suppose, he would have said 'have the guts', but he checked himself. He was really annoyed by this near-careless act of expressing contempt about an elder in front of a child. And yet, it was difficult to maintain the rules of deference about a witless elder such as Mokshada. He checked his indiscretion and said, 'Go and say that I have a lot of work now, she can talk to me when I go inside.'

'Pishi-thakurma knew you're going to say that, so she told me,' Neru swallowed, 'that the elder Pishi-thakurma has cholera, she might die this minute.'

Ramkali's frown deepened. Not because of the anxiety caused by his aunt's cholera but on account of the unashamed thoughtlessness of women. Clearly, Kashiswari was not ill, the summons were designed to annoy him. Perhaps there was some problem with the relatives who had arrived and Ramkali was being summoned to arbitrate. But this was hardly the appropriate time.

Mokshada was one person Ramkali could not cope with. He could have ignored her, had he not had so much reverence for elders. Mokshada always managed to subdue Ramkali only because she was older.

But was Ramkali overpowered only by elders? Wasn't there another person to whom Ramkali would occasionally have to submit? That person was extremely young. Ramkali would have to admit to himself that sometimes he gave in to Satyabati and lost to her. But that hardly irritated him.

'Mejo-khuro!' The boy was adamant. He did not flee from Ramkali's frown, and repeated, 'Pishi-thakurma says that I must call you quietly. The situation is serious.'

What a predicament!

'Looks like my situation is serious.' So saying, Ramkali called out, 'Tustu, put the curds inside and see if you can find more somewhere else.'

'If it were available, Thakur-mashai, I myself would ...' Tustu scratched his head and became impertinent, 'And besides, this isn't a small amount! After all, this isn't his first wedding ...'

Ramkali frowned a little and then smiled gently. 'Spoken like a milkman's son. Tustu! Should I have the guests half-fed because it isn't a first wedding? Go, put those away, I'm coming.'

Ramkali crossed the huge inner courtyard and entered the inner part of the house with Neru. This courtyard had the grain bins and a loft for the year's supply of firewood, underneath which there was a drum full of seeds.

Neru came and stood at Kashiswari's door like a conqueror, because nobody else had wanted to take on the responsibility of calling Ramkali. Even Satya had been quite clear on that, saying, 'I just saw Pishi-thakurma come in after a bath. What could have happened this minute that my father has to be called away from all his responsibilities? As if he's in a state to think now! Let her take digestive pills if she has to.'

'Get lost, you wicked shrew!' Mokshada had dismissed her and grabbed hold of Neru.

But Neru was not allowed to enter the quarters of the older women, and so he stood outside with a 'Here, Thakurma!'

Ramkali took his sandals off and lowered his head as he entered through the low doorway. Forgetting his help, Mokshada shooed Neru away with a 'Off with you now, you useless boy!'

Ramkali saw Kashiswari lying on the floor, her face covered with her white sari. What was this? Must be a tiff. He was irritated, but asked calmly, 'What is the matter?'

'The matter is truly stupefying!' Mokshada enlightened him in a hushed voice and then whispered, 'To hear it you'll have to shut the door.'

Ramkali looked out for a moment. Except for this area, the rest of the house was bustling with people. To hold a secret conclave in the midst of such activity! He had not gone mad! So he said gravely, 'Let the door be. Tell me what you want to say.'

But what could one say? After such a loss of face, how could one even utter a word? And yet, what else could these two illiterate women do except tell Ramkali? They could no longer make sense of good and evil—both Mokshada and Kashiswari. For Shankari was Kashiswari's granddaughter-in-law.

The terrible news had not spread yet because the household was still plunged in activity. But how long would people be distracted? How much longer could the news be kept from their ears? And soon it would spread from one ear to five, and in less than a second, reach five hundred ears! The scandal about a widow spreads from mouth to mouth as fast as fire on straw roofs. And that wretch of a woman could find no other day to disappear!

If she was really lost in the watery depths, it was at least better than going and ruining herself.

Those were Kashiswari's fears. And so she was lying down with her face covered. Only now it was plain to her why the wretched woman's uncle had refused to keep her and sent her to Kashiswari. God! Kashiswari had guessed from what the barber's wife reported yesterday. If only she had locked that misbegotten girl indoors! Then she could have covered up in front of the relatives by saying that Shankari had suddenly gone mad and Kashiswari did not dare leave her unguarded in a busy household.

Mokshada, of course, brought up the topic of drowning. 'Who knows when she got up and did it. Neither of us realized, Ramkali. In the morning I thought she might have gone for a bath or something, then later, I was absolutely flabbergasted. I really think the wretched thing has drowned herself in the big pond. If you get them to cast a net—'

'No!' Ramkali said in a thunderous voice, 'No nets will be cast.'

'No nets will be cast!' Mokshada repeated mechanically.

'No. I will not spoil the feast for so many people.'

Mokshada said with uncharacteristic mildness, 'Does a feast matter more to you than a living human being?'

'Not just to me, but to any thinking person,' Ramkali said as he paced up and down. 'You say you couldn't find her from morning—so it follows that the deed was probably done at night. Do you think a net will catch a living person now?'

Mokshada was silent for lack of a suitable answer. Kashiswari began to weep noisily.

'Stop it! Don't make a noise about it before people have eaten. If she's drowned then let her stay underwater till the body floats up. The body would have to float up—it isn't a river that she'll float away. But ...' Ramkali stopped pacing and came very close to Kashiswari, and said in a low, serious tone, 'But if she has not drowned herself, can you imagine the reaction in the community if we cast a net in vain? When you don't have the power to control your women, then learn to control your tongue at least!'

Suddenly Kashiswari howled, 'Oh Ramkali, give me some poison, son, for I can't show my face to anyone!'

'Don't be childish,' Ramkali scolded mildly. 'Keep quiet now. Give me time to think. What amazes me is that you say she slept in your room. How come both of you didn't notice?'

'We were dead to the world,' Kashiswari sobbed again.

'Pishi-ma, I beg of you, don't make a noise. May be you could tell everyone that she has gone to see her uncle who has taken ill.'

'Well, people don't get gulled so easily,' Mokshada reverted to her own style of talking, 'She'd chopped vegetables with everyone till late last night, the wretched woman!'

'Strange!' Ramkali again paced up and down. 'Can you guess the reason why this happened?'

Kashiswari drew the cover over her mouth tighter and said, 'I can, Ramkali. Her ways were bad. She'd stayed with her aunt till she was quite old and had no parents to guide her. And devilish thoughts just grew inside her. I know that she hasn't drowned herself, she has disgraced us.'

The room had a low ceiling and was sort of dark. But even if there was no window, Mokshada could guess how flushed Ramkali's fair face had become. One would think it was fuming. It scared even the dauntless Mokshada.

And just at that moment the bell tolled. A sharp, clear pealing. 'Hey you, Thakurma! Where on earth is that Katoa-bou? Everyone is calling her for making the paans. What are you two sisters up to in the afternoon—chatting in there, are you? How come you've crept in there after a bath? You want to take another bath again, eh? Then go and do what you want, but send that woman.'

Not having the permission to enter the room, Satya poured out her stream of words from outside. She could hardly imagine the possibility of her father being inside.

Mokshada came out in silence, demonstrating that she was indeed inside. Satya said impatiently, 'What is this? Struck speechless are you? Just tell me, where is that Katoa-bou? I've looked for her everywhere—'

Suddenly Mokshada moved aside to reveal the figure of Ramkali.

Baba! Satya was thunderstruck. Her father was here! And Satya had been talking so brazenly! But why was he here? It must mean that the Katoa-bou was ill and the grandmothers were struggling with her fever. For shame—so much had happened and here was Satya trying to bulldoze her about the paan. What would her father think? It just went to show that Satya did not know the goings-on of the house.

Mentally she bit her tongue, embarrassed. And stood in silence like a poor thing! Today there was no chance of biting the end of her sari in her accustomed way, because she was dressed for the occasion in a brocade sari, one she had been given at her own wedding.

Ramkali turned and addressed the two sisters mildly, 'Go and do what you'd normally do, no need to stay indoors.' Then he came out and teased his daughter casually, 'You're all decked up today, eh!'

That was not far from the truth, for Bhubaneswari had dressed Satya not just in a brocade sari, but covered her with ornaments from head to toe. Satya had been given a lot of jewellery at her wedding and she hardly ever had the chance to wear them. At her father's words she bowed her head and smiled shyly. Now Ramkali returned to the earlier issue, 'Who was calling her?'

He obviously meant Shankari. Satya was unnerved, not so much by her father's question but by his manner of asking it, so she replied helplessly, 'The women making paan.'

'Go and tell them she can't come today.' It was as though Ramkali suddenly felt defenceless. He quickly added, 'No, leave it. No need to go that side now. Let them be.'

Intentionally, Ramkali moved towards the husking room at the back, as he talked. The crestfallen Satya hardly noticed that, 'Is she seriously ill, Baba?'

'Ill! I didn't say that!' Ramkali gave a start. Then pulling himself together, he said gravely, 'Well, don't call out for her uselessly. She's not ill, she has disappeared suddenly.'

How strange! Why did Ramkali reveal that? Hadn't he decided just a moment ago that he would not disclose this news to anyone? Perhaps, with other people he would have done that. He would have stopped Bhubaneswari with a 'Don't call her.' But Satya's large, bright, trusting eyes would hardly let him do that.

Ramkali looked distressed, as though he had been craving for the relief of sharing his problem and had found refuge in this nine-year-old.

Satya was flabbergasted. Disappeared! How could a person disappear? And a woman too! She was not a man who could just walk away somewhere. If a woman was lost, it was clear as crystal that the pond had something to do with it! Satya had recently acquired this kind of knowledge on account of Sharada. So she said agitatedly, 'Disappeared! That's what I feared for the eldest sister-in-law. So I'd locked her inside all night. And now Katoa-bou had to go and do it! God! I wish I'd locked them both in!'

'Is that what you did?' Ramkali was astounded.

'Well, if I hadn't,' Satya countered spiritedly, 'I would not have managed to sleep a wink. I had to place small stools, one of top of the other, to reach the latch. And I begged Ma to open it this morning. I should've done the same for Katoa-bou—' Satya's tone changed suddenly. And she replaced misery with bravado, 'Well, thank goodness the poor thing found relief in death. Just because she was late from the ghat one day and had forgotten to light the lamp—what a scolding she got! And what curses! Ten people coming and torturing one! As if the elder Pishi-thakurma is innocent! No end to her cursing! Even a stone would jump into the pond hearing such harsh words.'

Ramkali slowly started fitting pieces of the puzzle together. 'When did this happen?'

'Just last night. Not that she was innocent either. Why couldn't she just fetch water and come home? Why sit at the ghat till so late? But these elders! Such a heavy punishment for a small offence. She's a widow after all, with no pleasures at all! Why scream at her like that for being a little late? And everybody knows that kul-berries don't grow in summer; you won't find a single one if you searched high and low—but they kept blaming her for going to the ghat and finishing off the kul! And they said so many other things ...' Satya gave a resigned sigh, 'I don't know the meaning of those words!'

The mystery was beginning to unravel. The woman Ramkali saw at the ghat last evening was not Sharada at all, but Kashiswari's granddaughter-in-law. She had been trying to drown herself. And because she had been thwarted once, she must have taken a second chance. But he had a small niggling doubt—the scolding had happened *after* she had returned. Nevertheless, Satyabati's classification of kul, or lineage, as the kul-fruit, brought a smile to Ramkali's lips even in the midst of this crisis.

Kashiswari had expressed similar fears. Could such an affair be possible in the house of Ramkali Chatterji? Ramkali experienced a deep ache inside. Not at the thought of Shankari's suicide, nor at the besmirching of family honour, but at his own mistake. He should have been careful—far more careful. It was as though an insignificant woman had suddenly scoffed at

Ramkali's powers and diminished them. Her insolence seemed unforgivable.

Ramkali realized that Satya had fallen behind. He turned to look and froze. Satyabati had stopped and was sobbing silently. Ramkali retraced his steps and said solemnly, 'There's no need for you to cry.'

'Baba!' Satyabati burst out sobbing, 'It's all my fault. Katoa-bou used to say, "I wish I could die!" Had I reported it to you, we could have done something about it. But I used to think those were empty words, that all women speak like that! And now she's gone and done it. She had not a soul to call her own! Look how helplessly she died. If you'd known ...' Satya's tears flowed freely.

Had Ramkali become stock-still because he had been struck by lightning? What could be the reason behind that peculiar expression on his face? He had been scowling at this woman's audacity a moment ago. What made his frown disappear suddenly? As though an unexpected blow had stemmed his flow of thought.

'Stop crying,' he consoled softly, and walked out to the outer quarters where he found Kunja absorbed in tasting the sweets the confectioners were frying.

'I shall have to go out urgently. See that the guests are treated well.'

'Me!' Kunja choked on a sweet.

'Yes. Why not? You are an elder.'

Yes, Ramkali had decided that he would go out. And that he would order the fishermen to cast their nets again. It was unlikely that anybody would suspect anything because there was a feast on at home; most people would conclude that they had run short of fish.

Ramkali also knew that it would be a futile exercise. Kashiswari's granddaughter-in-law had not drowned herself at all, she had obviously plunged the family name in a swamp.

Would Ramkali seek solace from tradition because he had lost faith in himself? How had his views about that insignificant creature, whose insolence had aroused his irritation earlier, altered so suddenly? And so drastically that he thought that she probably deserved better from life! Was that the reason why Ramkali sensed the need for a mentor?

FOURTEEN

'Faster men, a little faster! I'm in a hurry!' Ramkali urged the men from inside his palki. If he did not manage to reach before noon, he would not meet Vidyaratna-mashai. After completing his morning rituals, Vidyaratna usually went for a dip in the Ganga which was six miles away. After covering twelve miles back and forth for his daily bath, he would make his offerings at the family shrine. Then he would take some prasad and rest. He would not meet anybody after that. So, the best time to see him was right after his bath, or in the evening.

But Ramkali could not afford to wait till then. This was urgent. Throughout his life, Ramkali had turned up at Vidyaratna's tribunal whenever he was faced with the crucial need of solving a problem. But such occasions had been rare.

At this point, it was crucial to get there quickly. Vidyaratna's village, Debipur, was just one village away now. Ramkali peeked out once more to urge the bearers and then checked himself. There was no need to get agitated, they would get him there for sure. Ramkali hated getting perturbed. But he could not really deny that he was disturbed today. He felt defeated, his mind seemed to be smarting from the intensity of such a sharp insult. But what made him feel so weary with failure? If a foolish girl had brought about misfortune, what did it have to do with Ramkali?

A horse would have been faster. But Ramkali disliked riding a horse in front of someone who was older, or like a guru to him; not if he could help it. So he had started out in the palki. He had left a little surreptitiously, after instructing the fishermen. If they caught more fish, well and good. Food in excess was always welcome. They could all carry on with their work. It would be best if they did not notice that Ramkali was missing. For then their pace would slacken.

There was no one he could depend on anyway. Well, there was his uncle—the third one—Sejo-kaka. But what a problem he would have created! Because he believed that the primary virtue of a man was to shout and scold everyone without reason. Though he had gotten on in years, he was always ready to demonstrate his manliness. Letting him take charge would mean asking for trouble.

And Kunja? There was no point in speaking about him! The image of Kunja's sweet-crammed, syrup-streaked face floated up before Ramkali's eyes. He had been annoyed then, but now the memory brought compassion and pity. What else could anyone feel for a man who furtively ate sweets at his own son's wedding! There was no point wasting one's anger on people like him.

How strange that Rashu too was turning out to be as unreliable as his father. There was no hope for the future. But that was not the reason why he despaired. His faith in himself remained firm and unwavering. Such people hardly occupied any space in his thoughts. Only Satya had him worried at times. He would worry because of the terribly complex questions she asked, in her guileless voice. What of her future? Would the world understand Satyabati?

Ramkali stopped the palki and got off at some distance from Vidyaratna's hut. Courtesy and respect demanded that. Customarily, emerging from a palki, or any vehicle, in front of an elder was perceived to be immodest.

The mud hut had a courtyard, a verandah and a small picturesque garden around it. The garden, as also the fence around it, were both constructed by Vidyaratna himself. Flowers of many hues bloomed there through the year. There was a bush of the sacred tulsi by the fence. After his bath and before his puja, Vidyaratna usually tended his plants. Vidyaratna was watering his plants with a brass watering-can, wearing a cotton dhoti which he himself had spun. His upper body was covered with a cotton cloth and he had wooden sandals on his feet. He looked up when he noticed Ramkali's shadow.

Vidyaratna refrained from greeting him loudly. Nor did he express surprise at his sudden appearance. After Ramkali had touched his feet, he placed his hands on his head and blessed him, 'May you live long.'

He was a calm, serene, small-built man with dark skin and completely white hair. Vidyaratna's face had not the hint of a wrinkle. Nobody would believe that he was nearly eighty. His gleaming teeth frustrated any such calculation.

There were two or three small stools on the verandah, a small pot of water on the steps. Ramkali washed his feet and sat on a stool, and said with a diffident smile, 'It is time for your anhik ritual ...'

'Yes, it is,' Vidyaratna smiled indulgently. 'Is there anything you wanted to ask?'

Of course, there was! Or why had he rushed here at this hour? Ramkali now abandoned his preamble. Raising his face, he asked in a clear voice, 'Tell me, is human life worth more than family pride?'

At that very moment a little girl too was asking a similar question, not aimed at anyone in particular, 'Of course, you're annoyed—but tell me, aren't you concerned about the missing person even one bit?'

How strange! How very strange! Here was a living person who had gone missing, and the women were threatening Satya, 'Not one word out of you! If anyone gets to know, we'll just dice you to bits.'

Very well then, she thought to herself, go and throw a fit! Savour your temper as long as you like!

Elsewhere, Vidyaratna-mashai was saying to Ramkali, 'What is a man's misery or joy, his life or death in the great ocean of time, Ramkali? A mere bubble. There is no need to enquire after the whereabouts of the fallen woman.'

'But society will demand an answer.'

'Say whatever is true with courage. One should speak the truth clearly. That is what dharma is about. You are not about to reinstate the adventuress in your house. Think of her as dead.'

'But Pundit-mashai, I hate to think that others will discuss my family.'

'Ramkali, if your body had contracted some malignant disease, what would you have done? Perhaps this had become necessary. May be you had become arrogant ...'

'Arrogant! Pundit-mashai, is it wrong for a man to have self-respect?'

'This is a confusing area, Ramkali—self-respect and arrogance resemble each other, just as twins do. You can tell them apart only with refined inner judgement. You are a brahmin! Passion is not for you. But today your mind is disturbed; you're busy too. So it's best that you leave now. Let us not discuss this further.'

Ramkali lowered his head and focussing his gaze on the ground, thought for a while. Then raising his head suddenly, he said firmly, 'All right, I shall take your advice.'

Touching Vidyaratna's feet once more, Ramkali sat inside the palki. This time he forgot to urge the bearers to hurry. Vidyaratna's admonition had given him a jolt, 'You're a brahmin; passion is not for you.'

But could that be true? Should a brahmin have no passion at all? Should he only possess a motionless calm, bereft of fervour?

He returned to a house teeming with people. Nearly all the guests had arrived. The cooking was done. But they could not begin serving in Ramkali's absence, so the guests were sitting around chatting. In the midst of such animation, the familiar sing-song chant of the palki-bearers became audible. Everyone was restless with expectation and the crowd hummed, 'He's here! He's here!' Of course, everyone had surmised that Ramkali had been compelled to go and attend to a patient who had taken ill suddenly. That was what he had told Kunja.

In the inner quarters rumours about Shankari had begun; those outside remained totally ignorant.

As soon as Ramkali arrived, the guests milled around him, 'Who is ill, Ramkali? In which village? Somebody saw your palki near Debipur, is it someone there ...'

'No, I did not go because of anyone's illness,' Ramkali ran his eyes over the gathering, and added after a pause, 'I had gone out for something else, and I shall now tell you about it. I know you have not eaten yet and you must be hungry. But I cannot make out what your reaction will be to what I have to say. So, I think it is appropriate for me to announce this before you eat. Please allow me.'

Ramkali's voice reverberated in that silent gathering; many hearts trembled with an unknown terror. Kunja moved back and sat on the ground suddenly. Rashu, who was standing right behind him, stared at his uncle's flushed face. The throng could hardly guess what the matter was.

Had the food been spoilt by someone's polluting touch? But how could that be? Whatever it was it had to be related to Ramkali's sudden departure. Had some distant relative died suddenly and was it now obligatory to throw away all the cooked food as custom demanded? Had Ramkali left because of that? But then, surely Ramkali would not do something as foolish as revealing that news right away? The period of ritual pollution after a death was customarily computed from the time the news was received. If he avoided announcing the news right away, the rice would not be polluted for the others. At such moments, it was not uncommon to even hide the corpse! So what could it be?

They all forgot that Ramkali had asked for permission to speak; he had to remind them once more.

'So you grant me leave to speak?'

'Yes, of course, say what you have to.'

'Then let me say—last night, one of the widowed women sheltered in my house deserted us.'

'Uh-oh!'

Suddenly a terrible storm started up. Not an aimless nor-wester, but a deep growling forest storm, crazed with the collective sound of hurt and shock. Was this the thunderbolt Ramkali had prepared to fling at his guests? The intense storm had muffled the last bit of Ramkali's statement, but once again his voice resounded thunderously. 'Now you must decide if you wish to cast me out for my sin.' Ramkali spoke as if he was making a formal speech, his manner was calm, collected and righteous.

Cast *him* out! How could that be possible? Of course, it was about social rules, after all. Bipin Lahiri, Nibaran Chaudhuri's uncle drew up a small stool to stand on and gnashed out, 'It isn't a matter of casting you out. That can be judged later. But at the moment, we cannot possibly dine here, Ramkali.'

Ramkali folded his hands and said quietly, gravely, 'I do not wish to torment anyone with pleading, but I just wish to state that I consider that depraved woman as good as dead. To human society, she is indeed dead. I feel infinitely unhappy at having to mention this before serving food, but I saw it as a duty to my conscience to do so.'

And in his mind, Bipin Lahiri sneered, 'Thought it a duty to my conscience! Truthful as Yuddhisthira, are we? Now the feast is ruined. Just you wait, you'll be made to pay for this.' In actual fact, he was close to tears. Even so, he spoke up, 'I think you ought to have kept it a secret at this moment.'

'I did consider that.' Ramkali spoke once more facing them all, 'But later I made up my mind to speak. If you do not declare me an outcast after such a scandal I shall consider myself fortunate. But if you do, I shall accept it humbly.'

The storm subsided and was replaced by a hum. The sound of which gradually became clear, 'Why should we hold you responsible?'

'But of course! I'm guilty for failing to protect my domestic space. It's my crime. But I won't ask you to pardon me. For there can be no forgiveness. But I appeal to the affection and love that you have for me and request you to punish me later. I shall accept it humbly. But just for today, please do dine here.'

A storm started up once more. Of dissatisfaction? Or cheer? The latter, perhaps, but the voice of Bipin Lahiri was heard, 'All right. Just for today, we have decided to heed your plea.'

Ramkali slowly moved away. His head still high.

FIFTEEN

Every morning Neru would sit down to practise handwriting. The orders were that he should carry on with this trying task until the sunbeam lengthened from the courtyard and reached the foot of the guava tree. The span would change from season to season, but at the moment, it stopped at the foot of the guava tree.

He had been given one more instruction. He had to offer his pranams to Goddess Saraswati when he sat down with his bunch of dried leaves, ink pot and quill. And add a mantra that accompanied the pranam after the prayer. But Neru preferred the prayer to gain the blessings of the goddess. And therefore, with his primer shut, he would very often spend most of the time praying. He would raise the leaves to his forehead, and skilfully observe the foot of the guava tree through one eye that he would keep crookedly open.

O goddess whose skin is the hue of pearl,
With jewels gracing the ears' whorl,
Whose swan-neck a long necklace adorns,
Goddess Saraswati grant me this boon!
Let words touch my voice with their magical art!
And there let them dwell till life and I part—
Let thoughts of the mischievous one depart.
Let me ever be under the teacher's spell.
And let the universe my glory tell.

But even as he prayed to the goddess, Neru thought constantly of a god—the sun god. How strange! Even though Neru sincerely addressed the sun god as his 'uncle', he did not seem inclined to show any mercy! He appeared in no hurry to drive his beams in the direction of the guava tree. Had he been merciful, Neru's pains for the day would have ended. How long could he pray? Still, Neru continued to hold up the leaves or the quill to his forehead, as though he had only just started.

'Goodness! So much learning! I'll die from watching his devotion,' Satya's sharp voice rang out. Neru's heart quivered.

Gosh, that girl! And her questions! But he continued to mutter with his eyes shut, with no sign of acknowledgement.

Satyabati chuckled loudly and gave him a push, 'Shutting your eyes now are you? What were you up to all this while? Peeping out at the guava tree, weren't you?'

'Really Satya!' Neru put down his leaves and quill carefully on the low stool and said irritably, 'Stop disturbing me when I'm praying!'

'You've been praying from morning. And you've prayed away more than a quarter of the morning! Do you think I haven't noticed?'

'What nonsense!' Neru glanced in the direction of the courtyard. It looked like 'uncle' sun had softened a bit and was about to turn his gaze to the foot of the guava tree. Therefore, he took courage and declared superciliously, 'Have you seen how much I've written since morning?'

'Let's have a look.' Satya wiped her hands on her hair, did a quick pranam to the Goddess Saraswati and snatched up his bunch of leaves.

'Hey! hey! What's this?' Neru shuddered, terrified, 'Satya! How could you touch the leaves?'

'So what?' Satya retorted fearlessly, 'I touched them only after pranam.'

'As if that's enough! Aren't you a woman? Do you know what happens when a woman touches these leaves?'

Meanwhile, Satya had started scrutinizing the results of Neru's efforts since morning. Needless to say, only a single leaf was stained with ink, the rest were unblemished, untarnished. Therefore, another round of laughter followed.

'And here you were telling me you'd written so much. Where's it? Had you filled the ink pot with water or what? Is that why I can't see?'

Satya's gibes were sharp. She narrowed her eyes till her pupils were barely visible under her lashes. As she threw out her heated words, her face glowed with obvious enjoyment.

This was unbearable! Neru snatched away his property and choked on his words, 'All right, let that be! It's none of your business! Do what you like. I'll tell everyone that you touched the leaves.'

Such a threat would have crushed anyone else and made them intone a conciliatory 'All right' and they would have attempted to mollify the opponent. But Satya remained unrelenting. No matter what her inner feelings were, she betrayed no outward signs of disturbance, and said fiercely, 'Do that if you want to! What will happen, eh? Will they impale me on a stake?'

'I'm sure they will. This isn't a joke!'

'I'd like to know what happens if a woman touches this leaf. So many women read and write in Calcutta!'

'Who has told you that? Don't you know they'd all go blind if they did?'

'How absurd! You don't know a thing. As if they instantly become blind when they read! Nonsense!'

Neru had heard the name of the big city off and on, but he had no idea if, in that unseen place called Calcutta, women who could read and write actually existed, and whether they had gone blind as a consequence. But he continued to argue, 'Not now perhaps, but they'll certainly go blind in their next life. Huh!'

'In their next life! And you've gone and seen them in their lives to come! I'm telling you, Neru, nothing like that happens. Learning is a good thing. It can never be a sin to learn.'

Neru might not be dazzlingly brilliant at studies but he was the master of useless arguments. So he presented an irrefutable point, 'Women do a good thing by worshipping Narayana don't they? But they aren't supposed to touch the idol. God decreed that work that was worthy had to be done by men, and the trashy bits had to be done by girls.'

'Right! And he came and muttered that in your ear!' Satya's voice rang out, 'God isn't so partial. Men have made all that up.'

Their voices were raised and Punyi showed up drawn by the sound of the exchange and asked loudly, 'What have men made up, hey?'

Satya's tone instantly lost its enthusiasm, 'Nothing. We were just talking about custom.'

Custom! The topic threw Punyi completely. She wondered what could have prompted this sudden discussion. Meanwhile, Neru pronounced in his 'I'll tell on you' style, 'You want to hear how bold Satya is, Punyi-pishi? She touched the palm leaves we write on and she said "It doesn't matter"!'

Touched those leaves! This was yet another shock. Punyi was confounded. 'What's that?' she asked looking at Satya.

Satya giggled and brought down a hand fan made of the same leaves, from a hook on the wall, and stunned Punyi some more, 'Here! Look, I've touched this! Did anything happen to my hands?'

'Satya!' Neru glared at her, 'Don't you mock the goddess of learning.'

Whatever the topic of argument, Neru always lost to Satya. And deep down Neru's male ego felt terribly hurt. Now he was thrilled by this opportunity to defeat her. So he remained calm; he could afford to deal with the challenge bit by bit.

Satya stopped smiling, and showed her annoyance with a characteristic frown, 'Don't talk like a fool, Neru! I'm not mocking the goddess—it's you I'm mocking! Look at the way you're fussing just because I touched the leaves. As if heaven has moved to hell! But do you know that I can write too?'

'What?' the boy and the girl exclaimed in unison, as if they had been knocked out with snake venom. They looked stiff with fear. But the cruel Satya flung one more injury on their wounded spirits, 'Course I can—here, look!'

She seized the much discussed palm leaf and dipping the quill in the ink pot neatly wrote, 'DO, BAD, POT'. Then aiming one more pranam towards the invisible supreme being, said, 'And I can write more.'

It took a while for that stupefying daze to pass. Neru was more astonished than Punyi. How could Satya accomplish with such ease what Neru sweated over? Had the goddess suddenly put a spell on her? As she had done to the poet Kalidasa—everyone knew that!

Neru stared numbly at the words. Punyi bent over the palm leaf and taking care not to touch it, said with wide-eyed wonder, 'Where did you learn, Satya? Who taught you?'

'Who'll waste time teaching me? I've learnt by myself. Just by looking at it carefully.'

'Learnt by yourself! Just by looking carefully!'

'How else?'

'Where did you get leaves and quill?'

'Who'll give me ink and quill?' On an impulse Satya gave away her secret, 'I made a holder out of bat leaves and filled it with plant juice for ink.'

The two flabbergasted creatures asked faintly, 'And the quill?'

'Don't ask such naive questions. As if all the palm leaves of the world have been locked up! Any wretch will find a reed if they looked for one!' Satya exclaimed like a matron.

It took Punyi a while to figure out. Now she too held her cheek in her hand like an old woman and said, 'My god, you've been hiding this! How is it that nobody's found out? When do you practise?'

Satya replied enigmatically, 'When you are not there.'

'But then Satya,' Punyi continued anxiously, 'I'm glad you've been careful. Isn't it a sin, since you're a girl?'

'Why should it be a sin?' Satya blazed forth spiritedly, 'If it isn't a sin when women fight and argue all day and curse away, how can it be a sin to learn? And isn't the goddess herself a woman? Doesn't she hold the four Vedas in her hands?'

Neru was dumbfounded. As though this irrefutable fact had opened up the gateway to a larger vision. True! Saraswati herself was a women! How had such a clear fact eluded him all these days? How had Satya perceived this unmistakable truth which everyone had overlooked?

'Come, Punyi, let's go to the ghat,' Satya concluded the discussion and stood up. 'If we waste more time, the oldies will start yelling for us to eat, and we won't be able to take a proper bath.'

It was true that they were not easily satisfied when they entered the pool. They were not happy until the swimming made them pant. Punyi left with her, but not before she had signalled to Neru. Not with any mischievous intent, or to 'tell on' Satya. But they did want to publicize her talent and stun everybody. Satya was one of them, they had some stake in her achievements!

But all good intentions do not yield fruits that are sweet. That was what Neru's disclosure validated. There was a furore in the house. Everyone freely criticized Ramkali for turning his daughter into a brat and openly condemned Satya's daring! Had Ramkali forgotten that she would have to go and live with her in-laws?

'Well, now she won't have to!' Shibjaya declared sharply, 'When her father-in-law finds out, he'll disown her right away!'

Mokshada added, 'I'd suspected as much when the wretched girl had made that rhyme about Jata. Now I'm certain.'

Rashu's mother never ever entered such discussions; she usually buried herself in a pile of chores, but today she felt compelled to speak, perhaps because her son had unearthed the crime. She said softly, 'One of the women in this family has done the unthinkable and disgraced us before our worst foes! And now if the girls too begin to do as they please ...'

Rashu's mother trailed off hinting that both transgressions belonged to the same category. Bhubaneswari just looked on nervously. Kashiswari was the only one who was silent. She had nothing to say.

After the burst of criticism had slackened a bit, Dinatarini pleaded, 'Never mind, no need to talk too much about this. As they say, "words walk on ears". Who knows from which source it will travel to the in-laws and what chaos will follow. As it is ...'

Dinatarini too left unsaid an unimaginable possibility. She did not bring up the topic of Shankari directly in front of Kashiswari. But that hardly deterred Mokshada from predicting, 'You can be as careful as you please, but let me tell you, this girl is fated to suffer. You and I might keep quiet today, but won't they find out soon enough when she goes to live with them? It had to happen—her father has spoilt her.'

Clutching at that last straw, Dinatarini urged gently, 'Why don't you explain this to Ramkali?'

'Spare me, please! I don't want to be mocked again. I'll go and tell him, and instead of scolding his daughter he'll just spoil her some more!'

So a perplexed Dinatarini turned to Bhubaneswari, 'Well, you can explain to him when you find him in a good mood, can't you? Your daughter is really becoming too headstrong. You have to send her away, after all.'

Bhubaneswari kept silent. It would not be seemly to answer. Although she had a married daughter, it was indecorous to refer to one's husband in the presence of elders. Why did her mother-in-law have to mention the disconcerting fact of Bhubaneswari talking to Ramkali in front of everybody! Bhubaneswari was mortified and finding no other way of facing the situation, she lowered her face and drew her sari to cover her face some more. In any case, Bhubaneswari never ever raised her head. She was terribly scared of her husband. But now, she too was worried about her daughter's future. Everyone kept saying all the time, 'That girl won't last at her in-laws!'

The judge and the criminal were the same, only the plaintiff had changed, and so had the witness stand. Bhubaneswari had threatened the culprit and made her wait before presenting her. Then, very craftily, and with much daring, she set up a meeting with her husband during the day. She walked in when Ramkali was preparing for his afternoon siesta, her sari drawn over her face.

Ramkali asked with some surprise, 'Do you wish to say something?'

The kindness of his tone nearly brought tears to Bhubaneswari's eyes, and she could not reply. Instead, she lifted her veil a bit.

'What is it?' Ramkali asked with slight amusement, 'Do you feel like visiting your parents?'

'No,' Bhubaneswari said in a tear-choked voice. 'I wanted to talk about Satya.'

'Satya! Why?' Ramkali smiled some more. 'What great crime has she done now?'

'She's doing it all the time!' A sense of hurt lent her voice a certain intensity, 'You laugh everything away. But I have to face the music.'

'You shouldn't listen to useless words!'

'Useless! If only you heard what she's done ...'

'What?'

'She's been writing!'

'Writing! What has she written?'

'I don't know. She's written from books or something on Neru's palm leaves. And it seems she's boldly declared that she can write more. And just look at her guts! It seems she taught herself with leaves she's picked up from the garden and a reed and plant juice!'

Ramkali was truly amazed. He said, 'Really? Who is her teacher? Neru?'

'Neru! He says he cannot write like that if he tried for seven lifetimes!'

'Really! Just call her in here.'

The culprit had been waiting in the next room, Bhubaneswari had scolded her and installed her there.

But Bhubaneswari hardly believed that she had managed to adequately perturb her husband. What degree of severity would the punishment have? A light sentence would have no effect, because Satya would be obstinate as usual. And hoping to incite her husband, she suggested, 'I'm calling her in. Please give her a proper scolding. As if it isn't enough that she's been so bold, she's also arguing that women in Calcutta are learning to read and write nowadays, and they aren't going blind, and that Saraswati herself is a woman—so much chatter! You will give her a proper scolding, won't you?'

Ending her speech on this note of supplication, she moved to the adjacent room and summoned her daughter. She could hardly raise her voice in front of her husband.

Satya came and stood with her head bowed. This was her way of standing in the dock. She raised her head to answer.

Bhubaneswari had hoped that Ramkali would begin with a scolding, but he disappointed her. He asked Satya in an unperturbed and easy voice, 'I believe you've learnt to write?'

Satya's face turned a little pale.

'Show me what you've written.'

The gist of Satya's indistinct answer was that after the crime she was no longer in possession of its evidence. Neru was.

'That's all right. Can you write again?'

Satya looked up. There was no sign of displeasure on her father's face. Perhaps he was not *that* angry. So she nodded in the affirmative.

'Come on, write something.'

Ramkali pulled a piece of coarse-textured paper, ink pot and quill from the stool near the bed. 'Write here. Whatever you've learnt.'

This was contrary to all expectations. Leave alone a scolding, Ramkali was actually handing over ink and paper to his daughter! Was this the last act of the drama? Or did he want to verify Neru's allegation? To check if Neru had made it up? But was that really the case? The wretched girl was not even denying anything.

By then, Satya had bent over the paper and written two or three words. Of course, she had pierced the paper in places with too much pressure—a result of her habit of writing on palm leaves. But she had written all the same.

Ramkali inspected the paper from several angles with no comments and asked calmly, 'Who told you that many women in Calcutta are learning to read and write?'

'Choto-mami.'

'Is that so? How did she ... well, she's from Calcutta, isn't she?'

The last bit was addressed to Bhubaneswari. But Bhubaneswari was not supposed to talk to her husband in front of a grown daughter, so she nodded.

'So, does she know how to read and write, your Choto-mami?'

'A bit. She was hardly given a chance, poor thing! She was saying that a Memsahib has opened an Indian school and a Sahib has opened an English one—the girls of Calcutta won't be illiterate anymore.'

'What is the use of girls learning? They won't become rent-collectors or cashiers, will they?' Ramkali questioned her with an amused laugh.

Once more, Satya's vehemence returned. She could suffer anything except taunts. 'Why should they become cashiers? They'll learn to read the *Ramayana*, *Mahabharata* and Puranas. Then they'd not have to keep waiting for the Kathak to come around.'

Had her indignant face and proud repartee become the cause of Ramkali's amusement? Was that why he wanted to provoke her further?

'But then, why do women need to know the Puranas at all?'

Now Satyabati revealed her true colours, forgetting time, place and occasion, 'All this talk of need! Well, just tell me, Baba, where is the need for women to be born at all?'

Bhubaneswari's heart fluttered at her child's audacity, talking back to such a man! Such a girl would not last at her in-laws! Never! But Ramkali startled Bhubaneswari by laughing out loud. Then he looked at his daughter, 'Do you want to learn to read and write?'

'Of course. But there's no chance.'

'Supposing you got the chance.'

'Then I'll read and write all day.'

'You don't have to do that. It would be enough if you study regularly for a while. From tomorrow afternoon, at this time, you'll learn with me.'

'She'll learn!' Bhubaneswari could hardly hold back her words.

'Yes, she'll read and write. Not with plant juice, I'll give her a real ink pot and a quill too.'

'Baba!'

Just two syllables escaped Satya's lips. And Bhubaneswari's eyes rained tears.

SIXTEEN

A poetry-reading session. A poem about the seasons. Goddess Nature had completed the 'Monsoon Canto' and had just opened the pages of 'Autumn'. She had not begun reading yet. The kaash flowers had not yet started their ceremonial dance with their white whisking fans.

The breeze carried the cadence of an unaccountable joy. The blue of the sky was clear as a mirror, and bird-calls had a piercing ecstasy. The goddess had been reciting the same poem for ages, going back to the beginning every time she came to the end, and yet the poem had not become obsolete. It never would. Through the ages, it always brought words of hope, dreams of desires, and enraptured music to all humans.

A tide of excitement swept through the villages of Bengal. The joy of anticipation. 'The goddess was coming!' 'She was coming to her father's house. Coming from heaven to earth.' This was no idle fantasy but the true story of Bengal's deeply cherished belief. For how could one not believe that at the end of each year the goddess descended to the lap of Mother Earth and spoke to her of her joys and sorrows and shed tears when it was time to leave? The Bengali household functioned by establishing bonds of kinship with the gods, turning them into family members. And so they married off Shiva with Parvati, performed the shaadh ceremony before Itu and Manasha gave birth, expressed their fondness for Bhadu and drenched their hearts with tears when they sent the goddess back to her husband. The rest were gods and goddesses, but Uma was a special daughter. She may have a thousand glorious names, but her real name was Uma. That was what the Baishnab with his begging bowl reminded everyone when he sang to the beat of his tambourine:

Come dear Uma, let me see your face,
I've been waiting for you day and night.

Somewhere, in a village, in one family perhaps, the daughter-goddess would indeed appear, but songs of welcome played in every heart.

This year, the pujas were at the beginning of Ashwin, so preparations had to begin as soon as Bhadra ended. Except for everyday meals, all other items took a month to prepare. After all, during the puja month, everybody would be too busy to roast puffed rice, make parched rice, and other varieties of dry snacks, or swab the mud walls with dung. Everything had to be completed before that auspicious fortnight—the lamp-wicks had to be made, the betel-nuts sliced, the coconut palm trimmed. After the full moon, such chores could be taken up again. And then, once more, they would turn to stitching quilts even as they churned in their minds memories of the festival that had just passed.

Bhadra was not merely the month of preparation, there were many tasks for the women right after the rains. They would sun the damp mattresses and the warm clothes that were stashed away in trunks, and the spices, the pickles, the dal, and the utensils.

Bhubaneswari's mother was no more. Her sisters-in-law were in charge of the house and for the last few days they were staggering under the strain of such tasks. Right now they were busy with the sweets. If they could store up sweets made of dal and of coconut by the pot-full, it would take care of snacks for a month at least. And besides, during the festival, one had to hand out treats to the children as well. Bhubaneswari's elder sister-in-law, Nivanani, was grating coconut with both hands, and the younger, Sukumari, was grinding the dal, when the latch of the courtyard door rattled.

'I wonder who's there? As they say, "Interruption always rules over toil!" ' Nivanani said in a low voice, 'Who's come now to put an end to our work? Go and open the door.'

Sukumari's feelings, however, did not exactly echo her sister-in-law's; she liked such intrusions while doing monotonous work. If only Nivanani knew how to chat a little! She just worked away wordlessly. Sukumari made delighted noises on opening the door, 'Goodness! Has the sun risen in the west today, or did I look on someone lucky when I woke up?'

This kind of chatter softened even the indifferent Nivanani and she looked up with curiosity, 'Who's that? Who're you greeting with such cheer?'

'You've become rare as a blue moon, haven't you?' Sukumari ran to fetch water for her husband's sister to wash her feet. Bhubaneswari uncovered her face and sat on the raised platform of the courtyard, swinging her dusty feet. Her face was red from the harsh sun and sweat was trickling down from her head and neck.

It was really unthinkable that Bhubaneswari had walked all this way in the sun. She rarely visited; if she ever had expressed such a desire, Ramkali would send the palki. Despite the fact that people at home teased her and the neighbouring women called her the 'badshah's wife', she could not disobey Ramkali. So, what could have happened today?

After giving her water to wash her feet, and handing her a gamcha, Sukumari fanned her with a palm-leaf fan trimmed with an ornate border. She was an elder and besides, the wife of a wealthy man.

'Whom did you come with?' Nivanani asked.

But Bhubaneswari spoke without replying to that, 'Who has made this trimming?'

'Who else—the younger one!' Nivanani pursed her lips in disdain. 'She's forever decorating some household item or other!'

Sukumari's face fell, Bhubaneswari said quickly, 'But that's nice, see how pretty it looks.'

'Never mind!' Nivanani made a face once more, 'She hasn't yet learnt to milk the cows or winnow the grain. And if you witnessed the farce that happens every time she goes to do the husking, you'd know! She can't move the pedal with her feet, nor can she place grain under it with her hands, I've to beg the neighbours to do the task. Painting the pots, decorating the cords that hold them with shells and adding a red trimming to a palm fan—I tell you! As if all this will open up stairs to heaven!'

Bhubaneswari realized that her praise had had an undesirable effect, and Nivanani might just drag the issue too far. The real purpose would then be lost. Because she needed help from her younger sister-in-law. Despite knowing that, Bhubaneswari had made a wrong move. Perhaps, because she had never mastered the art of pleasing those in power by condemning the subordinate. This same fear would never let her speak her mind in her own house. She had concluded that covering her face and keeping silent would protect her from many risks there. But this was Bhubaneswari's parental home, so she ventured boldly, 'Why, look how she roasts the dal! She can make puffed rice too. What more do you expect of a city-girl?'

'Yes, of course!' Nivanani let out a scalding breath, 'I haven't set eyes on the city and I don't understand what it means. I only know the home, and I know that a woman must hang her head in shame if she fails here. But do sit down, I'll get a jaggery drink for you.'

When there was nothing available at home, it was the custom in these parts to add a few drops of lemon to jaggery and water and make a drink, especially during the summer months. This was what Nivanani had in mind. But Sukumari could not stand that concoction, so she did the audacious thing of speaking before an elder, out of consideration for Bhubaneswari. She said diffidently, 'Why, didi, there are sweet green coconuts at home.'

Nivanani had forgotten about that, but the reminder tormented her. What if Bhubaneswari thought that she had deliberately forgotten? This younger sister-in-law may look innocent but she was really cunning. But Nivanani had to conceal her annoyance and smile. And she had to say with a smile, 'Oh look at that! Thank god you reminded me. I've really become forgetful these days, you know. I have to ask brother-in-law for medicine for my memory. Choto-bou, why don't you get one?'

'Don't bother.' Bhubaneswari lowered her voice unnecessarily, 'I've come on a specific mission, I have to go back immediately.'

'God, listen to that! What do you mean you have to go immediately? What is the special mission? Who have you come with, who will you leave with? By yourself, eh?'

'By myself?' Bhubaneswari laughed, 'That won't happen in the present set-up. I've come with my aunt-in-law. She dropped me here, and says she'll pick me up on her way back. I've slipped away quietly, nobody knows at home.'

'Your husband?' Nivanani smiled enigmatically.

At the mention of her husband, Bhubaneswari pulled her sari tightly over her face, 'He has gone to look at a patient in another village, I wouldn't have dared were he around! Had to come because of a problem. My aunt-in-law was coming to her friend's house, so I begged her saying, "It will be on your way." She's a good person at heart. Anyone who seeks refuge, she takes under her wing.'

'And what work is this?'

Now Bhubaneswari faltered, for it just dawned on her that it may not be appropriate to mention the work in front of Nivanani. Actually, she had come to Sukumari with a piece of paper, the scribbling on which had been glowering at her for the past couple of days.

A piece of paper on which Satyabati had written—it had made Bhubaneswari uneasy. Satyabati had been in one corner of the room, writing with her head bent. Suddenly, hearing that the image-makers had arrived near the temple yard she had tucked the paper under the mat and rushed off with Punyi, Neru and the children. A curious Bhubaneswari had raised the mat slightly to have a look at Satya's handwriting, but what she saw had amazed her. What Satya had been writing in a clear hand looked just like a poem! Had she been copying it? If that was the case, there would have been an open book before her. Had the wretched girl been making up another rhyme? Bhubaneswari's blood had frozen with fear. There was nobody to whom she could show this in order to solve the riddle.

She was very scared of Ramkali. It was possible that a rumour would start up if she asked Rashu. The other literate people at home were elders, so poor Bhubaneswari was completely confounded. And suddenly she had remembered Sukumari. She knew how to read!

She had hidden her loot and had been on the look out for an opportunity to visit Sukumari. Out of the corner of her eye she had noticed Satya searching frantically under the mat, and sitting down with a fresh piece of paper after giving up her search in frustration. Satya would get livid if she was questioned about the mysterious things she scrawled on paper. She would promptly proclaim that she never had a moment to herself, and everybody bothered her all the time.

So, all hopes rested on this single piece of paper! Her mother worried for many reasons and wanted to know what it was that she had been writing. She fretted out of curiosity, and anxiety. Because Satya had to be sent to her in-laws! If only Satya was Bhubaneswari's son, and not her daughter. A worthy child of her worthy father. But Bhubaneswari was, as they say, fated to taste 'a single dish spoilt with too much salt'. She had just a single child, that too a daughter.

'I say, why don't you say something?' Nivanani was surprised. Why was she hesitating? After all, she was not a poor sister-in-law who had come to ask for a loan and would mention it only after dawdling a while.

Bhubaneswari could not conceal it any longer, she swallowed, 'I've come to Choto-bou. I wanted her to read a piece of paper.'

'Paper!' Nivanani was astounded, 'Is it some deed or document or what?'

'No, no, of course not. Where would I get such stuff from? Somewhat like a letter.'

'Like a letter—what sort of thing is that? In your entire household, couldn't you find a man to read it? Where's the need to come all the way and get it read by a woman? Is it something confidential?'

Sukumari had gone inside to fetch the green coconut. Bhubaneswari looked around helplessly, then suddenly, shaking off her hesitation, she said, 'Look how you talk! Nothing like that. It's something written by Satya. I just wanted to see what she writes away all day. If anyone at home found out they'd just curse the girl to hell.'

Nivanani had heard, of course, that Satya was learning to read and write, but she feigned ignorance, 'What? Is Satya learning to read and write like her Choto-mami? What has the world come to? Just tell me, will you dress your daughter and send her to office?

All men aren't as meek as your brothers who'd tolerate anything. What if her in-laws found out?'

'What can I do? You know how stubborn your brother-in-law is. The girl wants to read—let her! He'd get her the moon if she asked for it. That's the kind of man he is. So I thought let's see what she writes. She's a child after all!'

Sukumari brought in the coconut water in a large stone bowl.

'Goodness! So much! I can't drink all of it. Here, let me give you some,' Bhubaneswari protested.

'Have it. You've been walking in this heat.'

'Even so, not so much.'

So Sukumari had to do some pouring in and out. Meanwhile Bhubaneswari had devised a plan to deal with the whole matter lightly, and so, taking a sip of the coconut water, she quickly displayed the piece of paper she had been holding in her left fist, 'Take a look, our learned Bou! Read this for us. For I'm blind inspite of having eyes.'

'May I remain blind in lives to come!' Nivanani said viciously, 'Where's the need for those who have so little to sprout eyes and ears, eh?' So saying she fell on the piece of paper—it looked as though she would devour it whole with her eyes and ears! Whatever Bhubaneswari might have said, this looked really suspicious.

Sukumari turned the paper in her hand and asked, 'What's this?'

Bhubaneswari laughed, 'How do I know? You tell me.'

'This looks like a tribute to the goddess written in the three-foot metre.'

Even if she did not understand what the 'three-foot metre' was, Bhubaneswari understood 'tribute to the goddess' and a stone rolled off her chest—so it was not anything sacrilegious.

'Let's hear it.'

Sukumari looked uneasily at her elder sister-in-law. Read in front of Nivanani! Would she take it as a disrespectful gesture? But Nivanani reassured her, 'Go on, let's hear it. Enlighten the stupid, the blind and the deaf.'

Therefore, Sukumari cleared her throat and read hesitantly,

Dear Mother arise,   Goddess of three eyes,
Welcome! Wife of Almighty Lord,
To the abode of your child,   Bring a heart that is kind,
Great Goddess of the whole wide world.
To see you at last,   With heart full of trust,
I've been waiting with fervour, so long,
Descend Mother Immortal,   To the home of the mortals,
And bring your children along.
For one full year,   The house has lain bare,
I am struck with inconsolable grief,
Through night and day,   Time flits away,
When will you grant me—

'Goodness, it doesn't have an ending ...' Sukumari said in amazement. 'Where did you get this stotra?'

'Don't even talk about it,' Bhubaneswari controlled her mortification by fanning herself vigorously. 'It's Satya's doing! She was writing. When she heard that the image-makers had arrived, she ran off. And I picked it up—'

'From where could she have copied it?' Sukumari asked inquisitively.

'I don't think she's copied it,' Bhubaneswari said uncertainly. 'I think that the wretched girl has made it up herself.'

'Really!' Sukumari sounded sceptical. 'How could a little girl like her know the meanings of these words?'

'Well, I'm not so sure. The naughty girl sometimes attempts to read your brother-in-law's books on Ayurveda too!'

'That's different. She might read them, but it isn't easy to sit down and rhyme words and make up a stotra.'

Bhubaneswari was a bit shaken by her younger sister-in-law's incredulity, but Nivanani dispelled the cloud. She had been looking darkly at her younger sister-law's effortless reading all this while. As soon as Sukumari had finished, Nivanani shook her head, 'What is so surprising about this, I ask? Let's not try to cushion the blow for our sister-in-law here. Is her daughter as innocent as all that? Hadn't she made up a rhyme earlier? Now here's another one about the goddess. But it's disturbing all the same. After all, our lips are sealed because our brother-in-law is wealthy. But the in-laws won't keep quiet, will they? If they get to know—'

She could hardly finish before the figure of Mokshada appeared in a flurry at the doorway. 'Come quickly now, Mejo-bou! You can't imagine what's happened!'

What could it be? Bhubaneswari was speechless, she stared with her mouth open. Sukumari covered her head with her sari. But Nivanani's case was different, she was the mistress of the house after all, so she walked up and asked, 'What is the matter?'

'Don't talk about it, my dear. I had hardly sat down at my friend's when the cowherd boy comes rushing on stilts as it were. What's up, I asked. Come quickly, he says to me, somebody has arrived from Satya's in-laws' place. Thank goodness I had told them where I was—'

Mokshada had hardly finished when Bhubaneswari suddenly began to sob aloud.

'What's this? Why're you crying like this? Come let's go! There's not a moment to lose!'

But how could she? Bhubaneswari's feet refused to move; in fact, every pore of her body felt immobilized. Somebody from Satya's in-laws' place! There could be no doubt that everyone had found out. What other reason could there be for someone to come from her in-laws' without a warning? May be some enemy from within the house itself had gone and reported about Satya's terrible misdeed and her father's daring.

What would happen now? Bhubaneswari could think no further. She sobbed louder, 'Why don't you kill me this minute? I can't go home!'

'Stop acting so distressed,' Mokshada turned around and bustled about. 'This isn't the time for it! Get a hold on yourself and come later with your sister-in-law, I'm off. My feet are trembling too, who knows what news has come. But I can't forget my duty, can I? All right then!'

And Mokshada departed with the swiftness of someone on stilts. When Bhubaneswari finally returned home with Nivanani, the atmosphere was still and lifeless. As though someone had brought the news of a death.

Nivanani whispered, 'Why is the house so still? Doesn't look good to me—that's what the mind is like—thinking the worst all the time. Hope there's no bad news about brother-in-law.' Thus, striking a half-dead person three-quarters dead, Nivanani stepped into the courtyard and looked around.

A group of people were huddled together on the courtyard, their faces covered. May be Sharada would be around. But not a child was in sight.

'Come on up. You'll have to bear whatever fate has in store for you. Let's go and see what's up.'

Even if Nivanani was not really conscious of it, a certain expectation would have revealed itself if anyone had taken a photograph of her unconscious mind. A hope that would find fulfilment if something had happened to her brother-in-law. Such an eventuality would have quenched that ever-blazing fire that his wealth ignited in her.

Bhubaneswari could hardly gather the strength to step inside the courtyard and cross the threshold. She sat on the steps, 'I can't move my limbs, you go and see.'

'Listen to that. It won't do if you sit here like this. You'll have to bear it no matter how hard it is.' Nivanani's voice softened with compassion, 'Here, I'll come with you.'

But the intense anxiety held out a fierce attraction too. So Bhubaneswari stood up. She moved slowly across the verandah and peeped through a window. By then Nivanani had reached the door.

What could the matter be? It hardly looked grim. At least, not from the point of view of the robust woman who had come from Satya's in-laws. May be, she was a servant or the barber's wife. Usually these were the people sent for such jobs. Whoever she was, at the moment, she was being treated like a queen, plied with snacks. And in a circle around her sat Dinatarini, Kashiswari, Mokshada, Shibjaya and a whole horde of women who lived in the house.

The faces around wore an expression of **mild devotion and awe**.

And the face at the centre looked exultant and glowing. In front of her was arranged a plate piled high with a small mound of parched rice, a bowl of curds, a piece of banana leaf with four bananas and a huge assortment of homemade sweets. The last item attested the fact that all the sweets available at home had been brought out in an effort to satisfy this woman from the in-laws.

Well, it was obvious from the way Dinatarini addressed her that she was indeed the barber's wife. For she pleaded, 'Shall I give you a little more, Napit-beyan? But why am I calling you that, I shall call you meye—daughter! Have some more, it gets shrunk to nothing once you mix in the curds. You must have started out very early. Your face looks pale and drawn.'

Perhaps Bhubaneswari's state of bewilderment rooted her to the spot outside the window. She stood there and stared unblinkingly at that goddess-figure plied with offerings. And she started at the soft voice that spoke just behind her. She looked around and discovered Sharada.

'Why're you standing here?'

'Just like that. My feet don't want to move. Why has she come?'

'Why else?' Sharada said with muted melancholy, 'She's come with a great purpose. They say they want their bride. In Ashwin.'

'In Ashwin! There are just a few days left!'

'That's what they say. And this time they've got the priest to look up the almanac for an auspicious time.'

After a few moments of silence, a question tore itself out of Bhubaneswari's heart, 'Does Satya know?'

'I think so.'

'What's she doing?'

'Don't know. She must have gone indoors in a panic, probably.'

'Did anyone find out that I wasn't home?'

This time Sharada concealed the truth, 'I don't really know. Perhaps not. Everyone's been busy.'

How could the truth be revealed? Recounting the discussion that went on about an absent person would amount to complaining or tattling.

'What a relief!' Bhubaneswari let out another sigh, 'But what's this unexpected trouble we've been landed with?'

Before Sharada could answer her, the clear voice of the barber's wife rang out, 'Don't give me the excuse that her father isn't home! I haven't come to take her right away, have I? They've told me to stay here for the rest of this month and take her finally on the third of Ashwin.'

SEVENTEEN

Can a single question ever contain all the amazement in the world, and also mock at the most intolerable audacity? Nobody, to my knowledge, has ever managed to ask it. Except Banerji-Ginni of Baruipur, whose tiny question reverberated with immeasurable shock and derision.

'They wouldn't send her?'

'No.'

With that, the travel-weary barber's wife sat down stretching out her legs before her.

A small ripple followed the breaker.

'And you had to beat a retreat, eh?'

Now it was the barber's wife's turn to express surprise and disdain, 'Now listen to that! She's their daughter, isn't she? If they decide not to send her, could I just grab her and bring her here?'

Banerji-Ginni sat down with her feet outstretched, brows knitted together, 'And what was their excuse?'

'No excuse at all! They didn't mince their words. They told me to my face—they're not going to send the girl now.'

The barber's wife unwrapped the paan container that was tied to the end of her sari.

'Don't you go and stuff a paan in your mouth now! You'll interrupt your tale a dozen times with all that spitting. Answer me first. Didn't they offer an excuse or an explanation? They just told you that they're not going to send the girl?'

'Well, they said that they weren't going to send her now.'

'Then when will they send her? When I am dead and gone or what? I'm really shocked. What cheek! What has the world come to? Didn't her father think that we could just disown his daughter? Didn't his heart flutter with fear?'

The barber's wife disobeyed directives and popped a paan with chewing tobacco into her mouth, 'Why should it? He can well afford to feed and clothe a hundred such girls! They're really rich.'

'I see! They've looked after you well, I can see.' Banerji-Ginni cloaked her ire with mockery, 'And that's what has dazzled your eyes! I tell you, just because they're rich they can't afford to shake off all relations with the in-laws, can they? Wait and see, I'm not going to send for their daughter after such cheekiness.'

'Don't you scoff at me! By your grace, and god's, I get enough. But yes, they are refined. After all, it isn't enough to have money, one needs to be large-hearted too.'

The insinuation pierced Banerji-Ginni's innermost core, but she controlled herself and asked, 'And how did they demonstrate that? Did they gift you a heavy gold necklace, or a heavier girdle, eh?'

'Spare me your quips! But I'm not one to understate things either. After all, whoever gives such generous gifts? Two pieces of fine white cloth, and a dhoti, and full five rupees! So much to somebody who'd come from the in-laws place!'

'Well, I'm not surprised. They wish to hang on to their daughter, naturally, they'll want to bribe the in-laws into silence. That's why you've been heaping praise on them instead of cursing them. And I had so much faith in you! Nobody here has as sharp a tongue, and look how you've let me down. The tigress returned changed to a lamb, eh?'

'Look how you talk! The girl's father stood at a distance and said to his mother, "Mother, tell the woman that we'd agreed at the time of marriage that the girl will not be sent to her in-laws' till she reaches puberty. They might have forgotten that, I haven't. She will go, of course, when it is time."'

Banerji-Ginni leapt up at the mention of a marital contract, 'What did you say? An agreement at the time of marriage. Really!

That was mere talk. A marriage, after all, takes place after a lot of talk! But when did anybody sign a contract? How does it matter if I want to bring home my daughter-in-law? All right, let's check this out. Let's see how far they take it. If it were simply a question of feeding and clothing their daughters, why would anyone bother to marry them off? I'll get my son married again next month. Mark my words!'

The barber's wife had been regaled with gifts and food, so she could not be ungrateful, she was a bit crestfallen, 'That's entirely up to you. Her father's written a letter to Bamun-dada—here keep it.'

'How shocking! What kind of spell have they put on you? Betraying your own people! And you keep defending them! Come, give me the letter.'

'Here you are.' The barber's wife opened her bundle.

And Banerji-Ginni's ever-alert hawk-eyes instantly inspected the bundle, 'Let's see your gifts.'

Untying her ragged bundle, the barber's wife took out a squashed-up letter and put it on the floor and started displaying her bounty.

'Here's the dhoti, the than-cloth, this gamcha, and—'

'My goodness! A bell-metal pot and plate too!' Banerji-Ginni said, 'That's why I said that they've bribed you. You're back after reaping a real profit! This plate's heavy as a stone!'

'Yes, isn't it?' And they're well-spoken too. The women of the house just doted on me. Your son married into a good family. Don't cheat yourself by mistreating them. But to be honest with you, your daughter in-law has a real gift of the gab.'

The gift of the gab! Banerji-Ginni instantly turned into stone.

'Now she tells me! Not surprising at all! I could guess from her father's manners. Thinks no end of himself just because he's Mr. Money Bags! Must have spoilt his daughter silly. Wait till I cure her of her chatter, or my name isn't Elokeshi!'

'I've no doubt that you will,' the barber's wife said bluntly. 'Look at the state you've driven the other girl to. Everybody knows that.

But weren't you talking about getting your son married a second time? When will you cure his first wife then?'

Now Elokeshi felt uneasy. The barber's wife was such a gossip. She was sure to spread it all over and let the cat out of the bag. If people gossiped about how she had sent for her daughter-in-law but the rich father had not agreed to send her, she would really have to hang her head in shame. So it would not be right to annoy the barber's wife. Nobody irritated her, nobody dared to. She knew everyone's secrets, visited everyone, and there wasn't a soul who did not seek her help in times of trouble. She was a proper shrew, but trustworthy and spunky too. And as hardy as any strapping young man. The whole village depended on her to visit the families their children had married into. Recognizing that, Banerji-Ginni smiled broadly. 'Then go tell the world that I'm getting my son married again. But you tell me, doesn't it make you mad? Anyway, give me all the details, what did they say, and what did the girl—'

'I've no time to recite the epics now! I've been on my feet for two days, and my body's aching. I want to go home.'

'Why go home?' Banerji-Ginni said half-heartedly, 'You could have a bite here …'

'Don't want to. They say "to dine at my brother's is to eat with his wife". I'll go home and rest for a while. Then I'll see if I can come.'

So Banerji-Ginni had to mollify her further, fuss some more. After all, the world always bows to the implacable.

'Look here, relieve me from the poison you've pierced me with. What did the girl say? You'd gone from her in-laws, hadn't you? What gifts could she display in your presence?'

'Well, she didn't climb a tree or something, if that's what you want to know. But there she was emphatically holding forth to her grandmother. The women were generally saying how it wasn't right to annoy the in-laws, and they were criticizing her father. And then I saw her giving vent to her passion. "Speaking against my father!" she says, "Do you think you have better brains than him? If it was agreed at the time of marriage that they won't send for the bride until she's twelve, by what rights have they sent for her now"—some such thing.'

But by then, Banerji-Ginni had lost her power of speech. The account of her daughter-in-law's language and phraseology seemed to deprive her of her own. Holding her chin in her hand for a while in silence, she responded with a sigh, 'And there you were mocking me for wanting to get my son married again! Tell me, honestly, how can any house run if there's such a daughter-in-law? Who's ever heard of a daughter-in-law talking about going to her in-laws? And with such disdain too!'

'She's an only child, her father really adores her. Why blame her? Such faults will disappear soon. As they say, "A grinding stone crushes turmeric, a beating cures a thief, and a naughty girl is truly tamed when she becomes a wife."'

'Well, I don't know about that. My hands and feet are cold with fear. Who knows what kind of beating I'll have to take from my son's wife in my old age. And I can't even get him married again. Your Bamun-dada has an eye on the father-in-law's property. He says she's an only child—once he's gone it'll all belong to his daughter and her husband.'

'Listen to that!' Now it was the barber's wife's turn to express amazement, 'It's a large family and the nephews are handsome as princes. And it's an undivided family.'

'I don't know all that. I just heard my husband mention it. He says, "Let the father shut his eyes ..."'

'Who can tell whose eyes will shut first, and who will inherit whose property? The man looked fit and fine to me—one could marry him off even now. But never mind, you know what you're talking about. Let me go. Give Bamun-dada the letter.'

Just as the barber's wife rose to leave, the click of wooden sandals announced the arrival of Nilambar Banerji. 'What's this? How come you're back?' He stepped into the inner courtyard with the question.

'What else could I do? Couldn't just sit and polish off meals at their place, could I? Although they did ask me to stay for ten more days ...'

'But you went there with a purpose, didn't you? Where's the daughter-in-law?'

'They wouldn't send her,' his wife thundered.

'They wouldn't send her?'

It was once more confirmed that it was indeed possible for a single question to contain all the amazement in the world.

———

Elokeshi broached the subject soon after serving her son his meal. The flame ignited by the barber's wife had been swirling inside her and her face had turned purple. Nabakumar trembled as he looked at her fearsome face. She sat herself down in front of him, and raised the wick of the lamp a bit.

Though Nabakumar was nearly eighteen or nineteen, his mother treated him like a milk-fed infant. And for Nabakumar, his mother and the awesome Lord Yama were synonymous. And his hands and feet turned cold the moment his mother let fly. It hardly mattered whom she addressed those words to, Nabakumar would always shudder in fear.

Today's torrent of abuse was aimed at Nabakumar's in-laws, so the poor fellow hardly managed to eat. He lowered his head in fear and shame till it almost touched the plate. Ever since the barber's wife had left for his in-laws', a murmur of joy had been wafting inside him, for he had gathered from bits and pieces of what Elokeshi let on, that she had been sent to fetch his wife. His wife! What was her name? What did she look like? Nabakumar had been unable to drive away such disconcerting queries from his mind. In his dreams, and in sleep, a dim, hazy face flitted about the house, near Elokeshi, with her veil drawn.

And what about the bedroom? Was her veil drawn there as well? Oh no! Nabakumar did not have the temerity to have such impertinent imaginings. His heart trembled in fear if it so much as approached such thoughts. Because whenever he stood before his mother, he always felt that she could look right into his heart, as though it were a transparent pool. Therefore, Nabakumar never envisaged his wife near the bedroom or even near him; he imagined her standing beside his mother.

Even in his dreams he had not imagined such an impossible accident. That the barber's wife's campaign would come to nought! For every evening when he returned home from his English lessons with Bhabatosh-master, he would strain his ears in the hope of catching the soft tinkling of anklets. But in vain. Nabakumar did not know the terms on which the barber's wife was sent, still he had hoped that she would come before the pujas. In his heart he had mingled the season's festivities with yet another celebration and was continually overwhelmed. The pujas were coming! His wife was coming! The first was known, but who knew what the other would be like.

He had married soon after he had turned fifteen, not too innocent an age. But the timid Nabakumar had not even tried to steal a glance at his bride during the wedding ceremony. Now, if anyone sent some other girl, Nabakumar would have been incapable of telling the difference. So much so, that for the last couple of days, no matter how hard he tried, he had been unable to recall her name. Earlier he had not given it a thought. But the moment the barber's wife started out on her journey, Nabakumar had moved a step further, from adolescence to youth. He remembered the name being uttered a couple of times during the ceremony, but he had hardly surmised at that point that it would be his responsibility to remember it. Nabakumar had been sweating away. Even now, he could recall the sweating but not the name. Besides, his father-in-law looked so arrogant and unbending, with a solemn voice and such an imposing demeanour. That had also contributed to the escalation of Nabakumar's awe.

Apart from all that, there had followed a different set of apprehensions inside the basar. A bit of that dread still remained.

But the word 'bride' sounded rather sweet. Awakening romance in the heart of fear!

Look up my bride and speak to me,
Open your eyes and look at me!

The words and the tune kept ringing through his mind. But Nabakumar was incapable of discussing the imminent arrival of his wife with his friends. Whenever friends in his locality tried to tease him about it, an embarrassed 'shut up' would be his only response. And yet, when returning from his lessons, while passing the desolate banks of the Kach lake, he would repeatedly sing the words to himself:

I've brought you a garland that shall brighten
Your tresses, so soft, and glistening with oil!
…
How pretty those teeth which flash in a smile,
And her face, so lovely to behold!

And after that? He could not remember the next line at all, nor where he had learnt it. But the wondrous hum of that incomplete song would fill the path he took home.

His expectations had built up over the past few days, and his heart skipped a beat at the news Elokeshi supplied. And he started sweating just as he did on his wedding day.

'Have you heard that the barber's wife has come back?' Elokeshi began.

She was sitting like a tigress in the verandah. She could not wait for her son to finish washing his hands and feet, to give him the news. She announced it in the dark without even bothering to get a lamp.

This news conveyed a very different message to Nabakumar and he was overcome. He could hardly fathom his mother's state of mind. Nor could he understand the fury in her voice. Instead, he shivered with a strange delight. But that did not last long. The next minute, the devastating truth came out.

Attaching appellations such as 'cheap', 'misbegotten', 'cocky' to his respectable father-in-law, Elokeshi declared, 'They didn't send the girl.'

Did not send her! What a bizarre message! The possibility that the girl would not be sent had not entered the remotest corner of

Nabakumar's mind. He had no answer to that. But Elokeshi did not expect a reply.

After she had gone on for quite a while about the wealthy father-in-law and his attempts at bribing the barber's wife, Elokeshi noticed her son standing all stiff in the courtyard. Instantly, her motherly emotions welled up.

'You don't need to stand around, go have a wash.' Then raising her voice she shouted, 'Sadu, is the rice done?'

A voice had answered from the kitchen. 'It's done, Mami.'

'Come here, let me serve you.' Elokeshi went towards the kitchen. Nabakumar slowly hung up his coat on the nail on the wall and made his way to the pond at the back. His mind suddenly felt slack and empty. Was it possible to feel the loss of something he had never possessed, or enjoyed, and experience such a vacuum?

But matters did not end there. Elokeshi brought up the real issue after she had served her son, when she had stretched her legs and sat down after raising the wick of the lamp. Her face was a sight that froze Nabakumar's heart.

'I tell you Naba, I'll make your father send an ultimatum to that "misbegotten wretch"! And if he doesn't relent, I shall marry you off again—very soon.'

Another marriage! Did his mother want him to die from an overwrought heart! Another marriage would be like one more useless game they would play with his life. The same rituals in another house and the sweating all over again.

Nabakumar bent low over his plate. No words escaped him, and not a morsel entered his mouth. At one point, Elokeshi stopped her barrage of insults, 'Why aren't you eating?'

'Of course I am,' Nabakumar spoke indistinctly, and to demonstrate the truth of his statement, shoved a bit of rice into his mouth.

Sadu or Saudamini entered the stage. Carrying steaming hot rice on an earthenware platter, she remarked with some surprise, 'What's this? He's not touched the rice at all. Haven't you been eating all this while, Naba?'

'Of course!' Nabakumar repeated the words and action.

'Have some more?'

'No, no more.' His mouth full, Nabakumar shook his head and hand in protest.

'Aren't you hungry?'

Nabakumar repeated, once more, 'Of course.' He was close to tears.

Elokeshi commented, 'His appetite's gone, because I'm carping away about his wife's father. Boys of his generation can't stomach that. But you mark my words, Naba, I'll rub his pompous nose in the mud. If he knows what's good for him, he'll come yelping with his daughter here. I'll make him pay for his sins! If he doesn't, you'll just go through one more ceremony. And this time, I'll find a girl from a poor family, and not a grand princess.'

'My goodness!' Sadu burst out laughing, 'Stop sulking, Naba! You have hope yet. Now finish your meal. Have you noticed, Mami, he hasn't touched the sour fish curry just because his wife hasn't come!'

'Stop your wisecracks.' Elokeshi looked disgusted, 'Joking and cackling twenty-four hours a day! I just can't see how there's so much mirth inside you.'

That was true. Nobody expected Sadu to be jolly. And yet, the mirth in her always seemed to surface. Sadu laughed at wisecracks and jokes. She herself could hardly understand why her laughter came bubbling out. Perhaps, because in all the world, that was the only thing she could control. So she chuckled at misfortune to roll the stone off her chest. Otherwise, could she have worked like a horse if she had to carry such a weight around?

Everyone in the village pitied Sadu; they all knew that she had been rejected by her husband. Just like that! For no proper reason, Sadu's husband had sent her packing. It was not uncommon for men to be depraved, but it was exceptional to reject a wife!

Sadu was an orphan; her uncle had brought her up from the time she was an infant. Her uncle had attempted several times to get her to settle down at her in-laws', but the unfortunate girl never did manage to find her place there. Every time, she had run away from the threat of being battered. Finally, she had stayed on at her uncle's. There was no other way. She stayed there and had taken charge of the daily meals at the kitchen, and each and every chore, and digested her aunt's curses.

In spite of all that she smiled. How simply amazing!

'How astonishing!' her aunt would remark, and the neighbours would agree. Since he was accustomed to hearing this, Nabakumar too was of the opinion that Sadu was forbidden to laugh, and he would never join her. But of course, today there was a slight difference. After all, he himself, was the butt of the joke.

'Are you going to get the milk or will you stand around bantering?' Elokeshi scolded.

Elokeshi would not lift a finger after she had served her son. She would call for Sadu to serve any second helping. It was a big advantage that Sadu was not a widow who had sought shelter in this house. It would have been such a hassle had she been one; a widow could not be given charge of cooking fish at night. But in Sadu's case, there could be no question of hesitating or feeling obliged. Since Sadu would eat some of the fish curry, she could jolly well cut, slice and cook the fish!

The master of the house, Nilambar Banerji, was not that old, but he had stopped eating rice at night for quite some time now. Unadulterated milk, that came from the cow they kept, was boiled to a creamy thickness and Nilambar would mix it with homemade lightly puffed rice, eight sandesh sweets and polish off the lot right after his evening prayers, long before Nabakumar came back from his tuitions. By the time he came back from his evening jaunts, his son would be fast asleep; as a result, father and son hardly ever met. His son had had this violent desire to learn English. Although he was uncertain about any glorious standing being gained from learning the mlechcha's language, the fond father had not stopped him. He had just said, 'Let him learn if he wants to.'

It was Bhabatosh Biswas who started this plague. The babu had come back from Calcutta after learning English and had opened a school in the village. Classes were held twice a day—mornings and evenings. And the village youth had gone berserk because of his tutoring. He would whisper the magic words—English for progress!

Learn it, and go off to Calcutta, and a well-paid job at the Sahib's office was assured. So everyone had been rushing to his school. A proper monarch of cunning, he was too! He had brought the First and Second Books and other such tough ones from Calcutta and had been attempting to enlighten the masses. And the sons of brahmins were being taught by a sudra! The end of Kaliyuga was near!

Nevertheless, Nilambar had not stopped his son from learning, he had moved with the times. The only constraint was that he could not walk into the house with clothes polluted by the mlechcha language, nor touch anything while he had them on. He had to take them off, and wash his hands and feet with holy Ganga water. That was all.

Elokeshi and her niece usually sat down for their meal after Nabakumar finished eating. They would not serve themselves on plates, they would just squat on the floor and eat out of the tureens and bowls, and chat for a while. Although Elokeshi constantly scolded her niece, she could not really do without her. There was no other soul she could talk to.

After they finished, it was Sadu's responsibility to wash the kitchen. She would wash and clean, keep the wood and flintstones ready for the next day, wash the sari she was wearing and then go to bed. Of course, she had a bedroom to her name and a bed too, but she hardly spent much time there. Until Nilambar came back, she had to keep her aunt company because Elokeshi feared ghosts.

When Nilambar came back, Sadu had to tend to his needs— giving him water, tobacco, whatever he required, after which she would be free. By then, half the night was over.

Of course, nobody would ever ask who would look after Sadu the rest of the night. Sadu was Sadu! If one pointed out this thoughtlessness to her she would say with a laugh, 'The ghosts look after me! I'm a female ghoul after all!'

Even then, Sadu loved her aunt, revered her uncle and treated Nabakumar like the treasure of her life.

For in the thirty-two years that she had lived, she had found no other person to bestow her love, reverence and affection on.

Nabakumar had woken up very early the next morning. And he could not remember the reason why his heart felt so heavy, as though somebody had placed a stone on it. Or, perhaps, a mountain. He had also had a horrible dream.

He remembered it all after he sat at the open window for a while. He recalled his mother's vow. And his limbs went limp.

Slowly he rose and came out, covering his upper body with the end of his dhoti. The mornings were quite chilly. The breeze that made the body shiver often carried the mind far far away.

He saw Saudamini sweeping the courtyard. He walked up to her and asked, 'Hasn't Ma got up, Sadudi?'

'Mami!' Sadu collapsed with laughter early in the morning. 'When does she ever get up at this hour, eh? She's at loggerheads with the goddess of dawn, isn't she!'

Sadu added as she moved the broom noisily, 'Move aside, Naba—there's dirt flying.'

'Never mind.' So saying, Naba moved closer, and uttered with the desperation of someone diving into cold water in winter, 'Sadudi, just tell my mother that I can't do it.'

Saudamini stopped sweeping. Her eyes opened wide, 'What should I tell her? What do you mean?'

'All those things!' Nabakumar blurted out, 'You heard it yesterday—why ask me?'

'I'm totally at sea, Naba. I heard so many things yesterday, how do I know what has got stuck in your head?'

'Really! What a bother! Don't you remember what my mother said when she got annoyed with the barber's wife?'

'Oh, I see! That she'll make you marry again, right?' Once more Sadu started giggling, 'So, did you lose sleep over that? Or is this a case of the offender betraying himself, eh? You're trying to remind your mother about her vow, in case she forgets it?'

'Don't say that, Sadudi! I'm telling you, I really don't want it. I won't be able to take it all over again.'

Sadu busied herself one more, 'What's the point in telling me? Go tell your mother.'

'How can I?'

Sadu said with a smile, 'Why not? You're old enough, don't you have the guts now?'

'I just wouldn't dare! I'm telling you and that's enough for me. You do what you can.'

Saudamini stopped once again, 'All right then. I shall tell her that your son just loves his first wife terribly, he refuses to give her up and marry somebody else.'

'Sadudi, please! I tell you—where's the need for one more farce. Suppose they don't send her, what difference does it make?'

'No difference at all!' Sadu said forcefully. 'If it made no difference, people wouldn't have bothered with farces of this sort. One day, that girl will become the person closest to you, don't you see?'

'Nonsense!' And it spilled out of Nabakumar, 'That didn't happen for your husband, did it?'

Sadu's ebullience abated a bit, she said gravely, 'Well, forget about that. I wouldn't curse even an enemy with my fate.'

Sadu's transformation made Nabakumar falter a bit, 'I didn't really mean that, Sadudi. But you must protect me.

'All right. I shall tell her. I can see that I'm in for trouble.'

And Sadu was right. Trouble was exactly what Elokeshi created.

Except that it had no shape. Words, after all, are invisible. But when Elokeshi let fly, it appeared as though a jet of fire emanated from her mouth.

Saudamini brought it up while chopping the greens, 'I say Mami, here you are thinking of getting your son married again, but the boy won't hear of it.'

'What do you mean?' A blaze started up that instant.

Finally, after an intense bout of cursing Sadu, Elokeshi announced, 'Let me warn you, Sadu, I'll beat the daylights out of anyone who eats my food and sleeps under my roof and thinks nothing of breaking up my family. Don't you go putting such spiteful ideas into my son's head. Let your uncle finish his prayers—I'll show you.'

Sadu did not protest; she neither defended herself nor raised questions about apportionment of blame. Her face remained so expressionless and passive that one would have thought that those vicious utterances were not addressed to her at all.

As soon as Nilambar had completed his ritual offerings to the sun god, and finished his puja, Elokeshi quoted to him the proverb about the uselessness of offering victuals to a viper.

'I swear that my life will end if you don't write a letter this minute.'

Nilambar said, 'Oh-oh, no need to swear. I shall write it. But who will deliver it? The barber's wife—'

'Isn't there any other person in the whole village? The other time, Rakhal had gone.'

'Rakhal? How can he go so far all by himself?'

'Then send Govinda Acharya's son, Gopen. He'll agree if you pay him enough for his ganja.'

'Send Gopen to the in-laws'! Who knows what he'll go and say!'

'Let him!' Elokeshi was undaunted. 'The wicked words of an addict may make the man see sense. Let's see how long he can hold on to his beloved daughter. Also tell Gopen to enquire about other kulin girls in the vicinity. It will be good to find somebody right under their noses.'

Nilambar took the discussion no further, he sat down with pen and paper. And putting to use his drafting skills he wrote the letter. The letter explained in detail that Ramkali would have to bear a lot of suffering if he insisted on doggedly holding on to his earlier position. They would, of course, get their son married again, and as to their other intentions, they would reveal them later. It was, in fact, a threat. Elokeshi approved of its tone and language. Nilambar got busy with arrangements to send it. But he felt troubled—Satyabati was Ramkali's only daughter. What if the rope broke with too hard a tug!

———

Nabakumar had no clue about all this because he was at school. When he got back in the afternoon, he first approached Sadu, 'Here, Sadudi, give me some oil.'

Sadu poured some out for him in a ladle, 'I'd warned you that it won't work and I'd be the one to face a drubbing. And that's what happened. The arrow has been poisoned for your father-in-law. They've probably sent off the letter. It might have waited a couple of days, but Mami got so excited when she heard you were unwilling.'

Poor Nabakumar just stared at her helplessly, the oil dribbling through the gaps between his fingers.

Perhaps Sadu was moved by the expression on his face, so she consoled him, 'Never mind, don't you get upset now. What does it matter if you have to be a groom again! Not to worry, so long as you get a wife. But I personally feel that your father-in-law will relent—he's a girl's father, after all.'

Suddenly Nabakumar blurted out something improper and unrelated, 'The Sahibs marry only once—they never marry many times.'

That did it! A peal of laughter broke out from Sadu. 'Really! Now I get it, you've got all this from the Sahib's books you've been reading. But tell me, if the White man marries just once, what happens to all the other White women? When god created the world he made thirty women to one man—d'you know that? Then tell me, what happens to the rest if they marry just once—'

'What utter nonsense!' Nabakumar's voice was loud because his mother was not there. 'If all the men in the world married thirty—'

He had hardly uttered the words when Elokeshi entered the arena, 'I say, Naba, don't you have to take a bath? It's always time to joke when you two are together. And I ask you, Sadu, do you think you're the same age as him? Just stop egging him on. Wait till I bring a daughter-in-law home. Then there'll be someone to deal with you. And I can just drive you out!'

Nabakumar always looked guilty as a thief when his mother was around. Therefore, though he was agitated by the insults heaped on Sadu, not a word came out of his mouth. But the strange thing was that Sadu's expression remained totally unchanged. She winked at Naba as before, meaning to say, 'Go take a bath, your mother is cross.'

All the oil in his palm had trickled out, so Nabakumar rubbed his oily hands on his head as he walked towards Kach lake. The pond at the back was not good enough today. As he walked, Naba felt annoyed with the father-in-law he had seen but once—there would have been no need for such hassles had he sent the girl, or whatever!

His heart was weighed down with a stone, and now it had been pricked by a thorn too. Damn!

EIGHTEEN

Tustu, the milkman and his whole family were beating their breasts and wailing. They rolled on the ground berserk with grief. A whole horde of people were lamenting loudly and discussing similar incidents they had witnessed. Although Ashwin is not a month when one catches a fever, the days were scorching hot. Especially the afternoons. But the boys would just gulp down their lunch and roam about. Their mothers could hardly stop them.

The boy in question was Tustu's grandson, Raghu. He was a part of Neru's gang since he was of the same age. As this was the sugarcane season, their afternoon game included stealing sugarcane. A sharp piece of metal was the only instrument they required. Once they got the sugarcane, they had their teeth.

They had stripped off the hard skin with their teeth and had been sucking in the juice when something had happened to Raghu. They had been squatting under the old banyan tree, when they saw Raghu suddenly drop down drunkenly. They had hardly paid attention at first, as they had been busy with plans for the next day's expedition. They noticed him only as they were getting up to leave.

'Hey, Raghu! Look how you're sleeping.' One of them had laughed and given him a playful push. But his laughter had frozen the next minute. Raghu's body appeared stiff to touch, and he was foaming at the mouth.

'Come, look! What's the matter with Raghu?'

'Nothing!'

At first the wild boys had given Raghu a shove and laughed aloud, 'Look how cunning he is! Just pretending! We'll let loose some ants on you, Raghu, if you don't get up now.'

Not just ants, when their pinches or the water they had poured into his ears, failed to wake him, they had been terrified. They were convinced that Raghu would not wake up again—this was the sleep of death. Why else would his bright skin be taking on the colour of aubergines?

'Let's run,' someone had said.

'Run?' Neru had dug in his heels.

'Or d'you think we should all die with him? You think the elders will let us off easily when they get to know?'

'Exactly, Tustu-thakurda will break our heads with the bamboo pole on which he carries milk-pots!'

'I say! It wasn't our fault! Did we kill him or what?'

'Who'll listen to that? They'll say that he was playing with you and you've done something. Let's run away, somebody might see us!'

Neru said in a huff, 'Wonderful, I say! Isn't Raghu our friend? How can we leave him to the jackals and run away ourselves?'

Actually, the fact that Raghu was their friend had been influencing each one of them, and yet, they were scared to death. Finally, one pragmatic and god-fearing boy among them had said resignedly, 'Whatever fate god has designed for him will happen. We're powerless to undo that.'

'And when Raghu's mother asks, "Raghu had gone to play with you boys, why hasn't he come home?" what'll you say?'

'We'll say Raghu didn't come with us.'

'You'll lie?'

'Why not? Even the gods lie when they're in trouble.'

'Of course, the gods themselves came down and told you that!' Neru retorted vehemently, 'Now, watch over him. I'll go and see if Mejo-kaka is around.'

'As if Mejo-kaka can help now! Yama has taken him away.'

'Mejo-kaka doesn't fear that. Remember, Jatada's wife had died and he saved her, didn't he? He saves so many people. I'll just go and get him. But if I'm unlucky and don't find him, there's no hope for Raghu.'

Raghu's pragmatic friends had to agree to sit and guard his corpse, and abandon their plan of running away. They themselves were feeling terribly dejected, but there was little else they could do.

In a little while, the news had spread in a flash like fire from one house to another, and had soon turned into a blaze that had brought the entire village to the foot of the banyan tree. Since then there had been no end to the speculations and discussions. Could it be a sudden summer fever? Could that be possible in this season?

'Of course! The sun can be a real killer. Last time, the son of oil-seller Ganesh's sister-in-law died just this way ...'

'Yes, and so did the nephew of the ornament-maker!'

'Remember Nepal's niece?'

'You don't say! I thought that was something different!'

'I believe at my uncle-in-law's village somebody's father was coming back from the ghat and ...'

The surging waves stopped abruptly. The doctor had arrived. He had not been home, but he had come on his palki as soon as he had heard the news on his return.

Ramkali got a shock when he saw the supine body. He asked with a start, 'When did this happen?'

He addressed Neru. Neru described the events a little apprehensively. Ramkali bent down and took the boy's hand in his and examined the pulse. He asked quietly with a little sigh, 'Whose cane fields did you go to?'

All the other boys were out of reach, so Neru, the sole 'approver' confessed their secret a little helplessly, 'The Basak's.'

'Did he scream that something had bitten him?'

'No!' Neru was flabbergasted. The whole assembly stood motionless, like painted figures, looking at one man. Even Tustu and his family were silent, staring with mouth agape, nursing perhaps a faint hope.

'It wasn't summer fever,' Ramkali pronounced like merciless fate personified, 'but snake venom!'

'Snake venom!' A collective outcry was heard, 'Where did it bite him?'

'It did not bite him, as his friends are saying.' Ramkali gave a sigh, 'The venom entered his body with whatever he ate. Had I found him earlier, I'd have tried. But now, there's nothing to be done.'

'Thakur!' Tustu wailed and flung himself at his feet, 'You give everyone life, Thakur! Please don't give up on my grandson.'

Ramkali raised his right hand to his forehead, 'It's my bad luck.'

'I beg of you, Thakur, give him some medicine!' Now it was Tustu's wife, the old woman, who fell to the ground.

Ramkali made no reply but stared blankly at the crowd.

But what did he mean by saying it was snake venom? How could snake venom surface in food? What kind of bolt from the blue was this! Was it possible that a harmless man like Tustu could have such a vicious enemy who would want to pluck out the last of his clan and injure him like this? A murmur arose.

'But doctor, if you insist that it's snake venom, who could Tustu's enemy be?'

'God, of course!' Ramkali concluded with sharp sarcasm, 'Do men have a greater enemy than god, Tustu?'

Nobody could make sense of this abbreviated lecture. And why should people let go of the opportunity to listen to all the details? Naturally, they would writhe in agony with the poison of questions if one maintained a cruel silence after ruling that it had been snake venom! Ramkali would have to tell them where the snake venom came from if there had been no snakebite. But Ramkali's answer left everyone speechless. It was truly incredible!

A snake must have made its home in the sugarcane field. Not unusual at all. And it had rubbed its venom on the roots of the very sugarcane that the wretched boy had consumed.

'How can you say that, doctor?'

'Well, that's the truth.' Ramkali wiped the sweat off his forehead with the back of his hand. He said gravely, 'Nobody can win against fate. Nor can you add anything to the number of years you're fated to live. I could have tried to rid his body of the venom, had I got to know earlier. But that didn't happen. Fate is invisible, but infallible, and cruel.'

Infallible fate!

Even so, one of them had run to the low-caste quarters in the village and summoned Binde-Ojha, the folk healer, as soon as they had heard about the snake venom. Binde arrived and slowly shook his head. Meaning to say, that he felt the same way—there was nothing to be done. But even if Binde could not bring the dead to life, he could, at least, kill the thing that was still alive. With his spells, he could destroy that which engineered this devastation. Public pressure heightened. And hidden within that intense desire was, perhaps, another purpose. There could be no doubt that Doctor Ramkali was like a god and that he had been correct in his interpretation. But it would be worth checking out such a curious explanation. So they had all started pleading with Binde.

Ramkali asked with a rueful smile, 'So you wish to check it out, do you?'

'Oh no! Don't say that, Thakur!'

'But I'm right about that. Never mind, there is no reason to take anything on trust. But you must do something about his poor, wretched body ...'

Binde shook his head and said, 'I suppose, since the snake didn't bite him, you'll have to treat it like a "normal" death and make arrangements accordingly.'

'But see how the venom has made his body blue.'

'That's right. As if a King Cobra had bitten him. But according to custom ...'

'Well, there's no need to crowd around here. Get down to work,' Ramkali said limply. He could no longer bear to look at Raghu.

But nobody would get down to work now. The excitement had made everyone restless. Everyone was yelling at Binde, 'Go on! Read your mantras! The bastard is sure to come out and get lured into your basket. After that take out your poison-stone. And you can beat it to death later.'

'Why are all of you being so childish? You don't even know if you'll find the snake.'

'Why not? You yourself told us ...'

'Yes, I did say it was poison. But I am only guessing that it is from the sugarcane field—since they say he hadn't had water to drink. But now, if all of you busy yourselves with Binde ...'

However much everyone feared and respected Ramkali, at that moment they were all too carried away by excitement. They had to check if the snake that had finished off Tustu's grandson in a flash had indeed built its nest at the root of the sugarcane clump. They would not stir till they had found it. So, the scene refused to alter. Not one of them bothered about Raghu, and Binde-Ojha began to loudly chant his snake-catching mantras.

Ramkali stood there in silence. Perhaps he would have continued standing there in silence, had his elder brother not come and called him in an undertone, 'Ramkali!'

A little while ago, his elder brother had come to check out the scene. Why had he come back? He refused to divulge the reason. But he claimed that it was urgent, Ramkali would have to go home.

Slowly, Ramkali walked away without further questions. And an useless set of people busied themselves in a mad hullabaloo around Binde.

Ramkali regretted revealing the cause of death to them. A death was a death, after all. Would Tustu get his grandson back if they could check out the cause of death? Or even after they had destroyed the killer? That was impossible. Even then, people do fret over the cause of death. And in the case of a murder, they fight tooth and nail to get the killer hanged.

———

From the high heavens into the inferno; from the mountains into the depths of the ocean! From one environment to a totally different one!

Whatever its cause, there was a scene of mourning within the inner quarters of Ramkali's house. Dinatarini was wiping her eyes, so was Kashiswari, and Bhubaneswari lay in a corner as though in a swoon. Mokshada and Sejo-khuri seemed to be bustling about; and in a low voice, Kunja's wife was disparaging Ramkali's bullheadedness and lack of foresight to the other women. Sharada was the only one absent, she was cooking for the person who had come from the in-laws.

The whole village was upset about Tustu's grandson's death, but the women of this household did not have the right to peep out at outside affairs. Except, of course, Mokshada. She had gone there to have a look. After that she had taken a bath, and she would not go a second time. It would serve no useful purpose anyway!

A sorrowful hurricane had started blowing through the house from the moment Kunjabihari read out the letter from Satya's father-in-law. It would almost be like the death of their daughter, if they were serious about marrying off their son a second time! It was easy enough to advise other girls about generosity, and so very simple to criticize the resentment towards a co-wife. But it was a different matter where one's own daughter was concerned.

An exhausted Ramkali entered the house, dejected by the fate of Tustu's grandson, and heard the news too. His eyes flared. It looked as though he would explode, that he would lose control of himself and scream. But, he asked in an awesome, solemn voice, 'Who has brought the letter?'

No one except Mokshada had the nerve to face him at such times. So she came forward and said, 'The son of one of their Acharyas. Called Gopen or something.'

'Where is he? In the courtyard?'

'No, he's eating.'

'All right. When he's done, send him to me. I'll be in the courtyard.'

'But you haven't eaten or bathed today,' Mokshada ventured.

'Never mind, it is nearly afternoon, I'll eat something after my evening prayers.'

'The man is ill-tempered. Be careful how you speak to him.'

Ramkali frowned and asked, 'What was that about the man?'

'I mean, he's hot-headed.'

Ramkali surprised Mokshada by suddenly laughing aloud, 'So what? I'm not hot-headed, am I?'

Ramkali was right. He kept his composure, perhaps to a fault. He summoned Gopen Acharya, and after enquiring about the health of the in-laws, asked with a smile, 'I believe that their son is getting married again? Tell them that I am very pleased to hear that. When I'm invited, I shall send an appropriate present.'

Gopen Acharya, the opium addict, forgot his curse, and his speech too—he stared, his mouth wide open.

'Have you eaten?'

'Yes, sir.'

'So you're not going back tonight.'

'No, sir.'

'All right. You could leave after you've eaten something in the morning.'

'So you're not going to send the girl.'

'Girl! What girl are you talking about? Where should I send her?'

Now Gopen declared boldly, 'Your girl, of course. Who else will I talk about? So you won't send her?'

'But where can I send her? A girl from a respectable home can only go to a similar home—not to any old place!'

Gopen's gaunt face twisted, 'All right. Write that in the letter then.'

'Do I have to? Won't you be able to say these simple words?'

'No, sir. I'm a ganja addict. Nobody will believe me. Now that I'm here, I'll go back with a written document.'

'Right.' Ramkali stood frowning for a while. 'All right. I'll write a letter, take it before you leave tomorrow.'

⟶

Evening had set in. Ramkali stepped out slowly. No, he did not walk towards the ghat to wash up before his evening prayers, instead, he moved towards the old banyan tree. To see what arrangements they had made. Once again, Raghu's face flashed before his eyes. How heartless fate was!

Soon after he stepped out of the house, Ramkali stopped in his tracks. Who was that in the dark, walking in quick steps? Wasn't that Satya?

'Why're you by yourself here?'

'Not by myself—Neru was with me—but he doesn't want to come home now.'

'Why had you come here?'

'Why ask me that, Baba?' Satya said despondently. 'I wanted to see Raghu for one last time.'

'It wasn't right to come by yourself. You could have come with Sejo-thakurma.'

'She's bathed eight times already, she wouldn't have come.'

'All right, go home now.'

'Yes ... Baba—'

'What is it?'

'Well ...'

'Tell me.'

'Isn't there a man who has come with a letter?'

Ramkali was staggered on hearing Satyabati raise the subject. He reasoned then that she had always been a little rash. Perhaps she wanted to appeal against going to her in-laws. So he said affectionately, 'Yes. From your in-laws. What about it?'

'I was thinking ...' It was astonishing to hear Satyabati admitting to thinking before speaking!

Ramkali laughed to himself; what a weight the word 'in-laws' carried for girls!

'Tell me what's on your mind.'

'No, let it be now. You come back. I have to say it properly. Ever since I saw Raghu's dead body, I'm sobbing inside. Let me go home and rest a little.'

'All right then.' Ramkali left with that.

How could such an innocent child be sent off to her in-laws right now? It was preposterous!

'We found it! We found it!'

A wild, collective exultation reached the house of the doctor, 'Look! Doctor!'

What had they found? What was the jubilation in aid of? Which wondrous recovery had driven the men to such distraction? Ramkali came down to the temple courtyard. Had Tustu miraculously got back his grandson because of some good he had done in his past life? Do the gods listen to prayers even in Kaliyuga? Could it be that Raghu had merely fainted and descended into that deep coma that is so near death? Just like Jata's wife? Had Ramkali made a mistake? Let it be a mistake! Oh god! Just this once, smash Ramkali's arrogance! And prove his diagnosis wrong!

But the god of Kaliyuga was deaf, mute and crippled. Nor was he particularly interested in smashing Ramkali's arrogance. They had not come back with Raghu, but with his killer. The spell of the folk healer's mantras had brought it out of its hole, foaming at the mouth. It was an amazing sight.

The folk healer had wanted to keep the snake. He had pleaded, 'It's rare to find a King Cobra.' But he could not protect the king of snakes from the rage of the crowd. Its glistening rotund shape had been beaten flat with sticks and bamboo poles by the horde.

'Mother Nature forgive us!' They had recited as they cudgelled it.

Now they had come to Ramkali triumphant, the snake hanging on a pole. Even the old, short and knotty-bodied folk healer had come running in the hope of a tip. After all, Ramkali would give him nothing less than a hefty baksheesh. His success was Ramkali's victory too.

The screaming crowd and its wild jubilation seemed to signify barbarism. And Ramkali's heart was tainted with hatred and disgust. He raised his hands and silenced them and then asked with a frown, 'What is it? What is this ecstasy in aid of? Has Raghu come back to life?'

'Impossible!' Somebody quipped enthusiastically, 'Even god couldn't have brought him back to life. The venom of a King Cobra after all! We all admire your learning, doctor. It's just that he wasn't bitten ...'

Suddenly, a surge of emotion choked Ramkali Chatterji's voice. An occurrence that was rare. Raghu's tragic death had affected him deeply. He kept thinking that he could have saved the boy if he had come to know about it on time. And all his attempts to convince himself that fate was infallible and that every human being had a limited life-span seemed to be in vain. All the anti-venom medications seemed to be mocking him.

'Well, Thakur, who can save him if the mother of poisons strikes him! You showed us up!' The old folk healer exclaimed, 'But I had to literally sweat blood. As if the blighter would come out easily! I had to chant the most forceful mantras ...'

'All right, I'm glad to hear that. Well, now go and dispose of it properly.'

According to the shastric customs, when a snake was killed, it had to be cremated. Ramkali added solemnly, 'Go and do something about that wretch as well. Don't leave it all to Tustu.'

The enthusiasm of the crowd stemmed slightly. What kind of reaction was this? It was not what they had expected at all. They had thought that the discovery of the snake would definitely thrill Ramkali, because it would be like a victory flag for him. After all, many people had been sceptical despite his confidence, because he had said something completely incredible. But the snake had proved beyond doubt that even the incredible could be possible. Yet, Ramkali seemed indifferent.

They were offended. And hurt.

'It isn't as though we aren't making arrangements!' They said, 'By now the bamboo must have been trimmed for the bier. But he's died of snake venom, we should let the corpse float away.'

'No,' said Ramkali solemnly, 'there was no snakebite. Make arrangements for a cremation. Don't create an unnecessary din here.'

They left with the snake on the pole, and in their wake, surged all the children of the village, irrespective of rank. Looking at their departing figures, it struck Ramkali—were these his kinsmen? His neighbours? How could they be considered any more civilized than the savage Santhals when they relished every opportunity to indulge in such savage acts? They had not learnt that death deserved respect; and silence was just a token of that respect.

'Thakur, what about my baksheesh?'

'Baksheesh?' Ramkali asked with a frown, 'For what?'

'What do you mean?'

'I just asked—what do you want a baksheesh for? Did you bring the boy back to life?'

'Who can save him after he's dead.'

'Right, I know that. What I can't understand is how can you claim a baksheesh.'

'All right, if not a baksheesh at least pay me my charges,' the folk healer was defiant.

'Those who had called you shall pay,' Ramkali said calmly, gravely. 'I didn't call you.'

'Who can I get hold of in that crowd?' Binde said sulkily, 'I'll go away if you don't pay me. After all, I'm a poor man ...'

'Wait!' Ramkali took out two rupees from the pocket of his kurta and said even more gravely, 'This will pay your charges and for the snake too. After all, you lost an expensive snake.'

The old man looked perplexed and stunned, 'What do you mean, Thakur?'

'You know what I mean. Now go.'

'Thakur!'

'How many snakes did you have in your basket?' Ramkali asked softly while looking at his face unblinkingly.

The old man shuddered before that gaze, and nearly broke down, 'Thakur, You know everything.'

'So, now are you convinced? Go in peace.'

The man left before Ramkali changed his mind, for he had got his money as well as reassurance. After all, Ramkali was a brahmin —almost a god who could spit fire!

Ramkali stared after him, strangely troubled. There seemed to be no end to the ignorance of these prize specimens of imbeciles, and yet how freely they made a living out of the stupidity of others.

He had had his suspicions about the snake but he had not

expected the folk healer to squirm and confess so easily. Ramkali's heart became heavy with a sad ache. A doctor had the ability to heal the body, but what about the mind? Or the superstitions, ignorance, stupidity and full-fledged shrewdness that went with it?

Darkness had descended. It was nearly time for his evening prayers, yet Ramkali continued to sit on a stool in the courtyard. His bare feet rested lightly on top of his wooden sandals. The silver clasps on his sandals were shining in the dark.

'Baba.'

He started at this unexpected call.

'Satya, what are you doing here? Oh, have you come to tell me that it is time for my evening anhik? All right, dear, go inside.'

'I didn't come to tell you that, Baba.'

'You didn't come for that! What is it then?'

'I was saying—' Satya said almost desperately, 'Why don't you say "yes" to that man from Baruipur, Baba.'

The man from Baruipur! Ramkali repeated with surprise, 'I'll say "yes"? What will I say "yes" to?'

'You know what I mean, Baba,' Satya said dismally, 'What can I say?'

Though Ramkali could hardly see his daughter's face in the dark, he heard her clearly, but he could not really grasp what she meant. Did she want him to say 'yes' to sending the man away? Well, Ramkali had done that already. What else could she mean? Perhaps the women of the house were still going on and on. So he consoled her, 'Have no fear, you don't have to go to your in-laws just now.'

Satya understood that her father had not caught on, nor was he supposed to. No girl in Satya's position would ever want to sacrifice her own life. But Satya had thought things through clearly before deciding to do precisely that. She had readied her neck for slaughter. The grandmothers had declared vehemently, 'Pride has made Ramkali slight the world and there's no future for his daughter now. It isn't as though the in-laws are unfeeling stones—you think they'll stomach insult? They'll certainly get their son married again and Ramkali will have to keep his daughter forever. And such girls are nothing but burdens.'

So Satya had thought it out—it was not a good thing to become a burden to one's parents. Best to make her father see sense. And here was her father not comprehending what she meant!

She had to cast aside her veil of embarrassment. She shut her eyes and ears, almost as though she were swallowing a bitter pill, and said, 'I'm not thinking about that fear, Baba. I'm saying the opposite thing—just make up your mind to send me there. I'll suffer whatever fate has in store for me.'

Ramkali was astounded. Until now he had seen many instances of his daughter's spunk and had digested them too—because he had always understood the reason. But what was this? She wanted to go to her in-laws herself! Of course, if she were a young woman he could have interpreted her desire differently. But what was this?

His tone was solemn, perhaps slightly curt as well, 'You yourself want to go to your in-laws?'

'Not out of any great desire!' The firmness of her father's voice had nearly brought tears to Satya's eyes, 'But because I've thought a lot about this. Where's the need to annoy them and invite a disaster?'

Ramkali guessed that such discussions were being propagated inside the house. An innocent child would naturally pick it up. But was she so naive that she could not understand that such things should not be mentioned in front of her father?

He responded firmly, 'Let me take care of that, Satya. You're a child, there's no need for you to get mixed up in this. All this is too much!'

But Satya was not one to be suppressed. It was not written in her stars to turn away. She said firmly but faintly, 'I know that, it's too much! And shameless too! But what else can I do? It is a serious problem. If you have to suffer after this because of me, you'll not find peace even when you die. They've threatened to get their son married again. That's an insult! Why should you suffer humiliation for an insignificant girl child, Baba?'

Ramkali thought of silencing his daughter with a frightful scolding, but a different feeling struck him. What did the girl have on her mind? Why was this little girl thinking so much? From where had she gathered such unyielding courage? Had any girl in the whole of India ever discussed going to her in-laws with her father? And with a father as imposing as Ramkali! Even his mother, Dinatarini spoke to him with deference. Besides, the word 'in-laws' generated more fear than 'snakes', 'tigers', 'bears', 'ghosts', or 'thieves'. What magical dauntlessness had helped her conquer such a fear?

Ramkali decided not to rebuke her into silence, but to hear her out. He wanted to observe the strange dynamics of her mind. An amazed curiosity had been stirred up in him.

He said quietly, 'You have never said before that a girl child is "insignificant".'

'I am not saying that, Baba—it's the situation that's saying it. If she weren't insignificant, why would there be such a sick hurry to give her away? What's the point in being deluded into further attachment, Baba? When you have given me away to another, there are no rights anymore. You will have to send me away—today, or tomorrow. You can't insist then, "She's my girl, I won't hand her over." Can you?'

'There is a time for sending away girls, there are rules too. You won't understand all that now. Don't fret about that. Go in.'

'Yes, I shall go in. But my mind is disturbed, Baba. Raghu's death has opened my eyes. If in god's world there are no rules about time, and no laws either, then how can there be any such rule in man's world? Today it hurts you to send me away, but if death should come and ask for me, you'd have to hand me over.' Satya wiped her eyes with the corner of her sari, then added in a heavy voice, 'Will you be able to say then that "It is not time yet. This isn't the rule"? When going to the in-laws is like going to the kingdom of death, don't regret it! Send me off and think that Satya has died.'

Satya could no longer check herself; she sobbed aloud, grieving that imagined death. A silent Ramkali stared at the weeping girl. Had she just repeated what she had been taught, or did she think that way? Breaking the silence after a while he said, 'I'm not thinking about heartbreaks Satya. I'm telling you this because you have learnt to talk like a grown-up. I will be humiliated if I send you.'

Satya was deeply dejected and crestfallen. 'I do understand it all, Baba. But this isn't merely about saving your dignity and not being insulted further. You lost your dignity the day you humbled yourself and gave me away. If they disown your daughter now, you'll be insulted in front of everybody! Consider both sides, Baba.'

'All right, you go now. Let me think.'

'Think, but think it out by tonight. That wretch will leave as soon as the night passes.'

'For shame, dear—must you talk that way?'

'I know I mustn't, but he looks so disreputable. Couldn't they find anyone better to send?'

Ramkali said lightly, 'You keep fearing for my humiliation, but won't your in-laws be compelled to disown you? They'll just send you back after two days. Who will share a house with you, Satya? Nobody can stomach so much talk!'

Satya raised her head with pride, 'Rest assured, Baba. Satya will never let you down.'

Ramkali placed his hand on her shoulder with great affection. He could never quite understand her. From time to time, she appeared before him like an acute question. The words she uttered could never be dismissed as words learnt by rote, they worried him and perhaps scared him too. Even so, Ramkali could sympathize with her, but would the world be able to do that?

Why hadn't she turned out to be ordinary? Like Punyi, like the other girls of the family? Then Ramkali would not be so anxious about her. He would have been happy.

But was that really true? Would he have been positively contented if Satya had been ordinary, silly and obtuse? Would he have considered her precious, as he did now? Would affection alone increase her worth?

'Go inside now, I have my evening anhik.'

'I'm going,' and Ramkali's extraordinary daughter made a ridiculously ordinary request, 'Will you walk me to the inner courtyard, Baba?'

'Walk with you? Why?'

'Ever since I saw Raghu, I've been feeling so uneasy. It is so dark there.'

'All right. I'm coming with you. Why did you go there? It wasn't right.'

Was Ramkali relieved to find his intrepid daughter expressing fear? After walking through the dark, Satya stood still, then she said suddenly, 'Don't forget to think, Baba.'

'Think? Of what? Oh, I see!' Consciousness returned to the preoccupied Ramkali, 'I've thought about it already. I shall send you.'

Suddenly, Satya's tears brimmed over, 'Are you angry with me, Baba?'

'No, I'm not angry.'

'Will you bring me home again?' The tears became uncontrollable.

'If they send you,' Ramkali said calmly.

'Aha! As if they won't send me!' Satya stopped crying that instant and said enthusiastically, 'You have kept their request, won't they keep yours? I shall go even though my heart is breaking—just to avoid any ugly scene that will cut off all relations. They should understand that.'

Once more, Ramkali was stunned. How did that little mind think so deeply? Then he let out a sigh of resignation—if only everyone could understand the obvious. When getting a daughter married, one could take into consideration the looks of the groom, one could judge the family and estimate their wealth, but nobody could examine the temperament of each member of the family.

Ramkali had performed the gauri-daana. When they had been hunting for a groom, Dinatarini had said, 'You have just one daughter, why send her away? Find a good-looking kulin boy who'll move in here as a son-in-law.'

Bhubaneswari was just behind her mother-in-law and waited eagerly, her heart aflutter. But Ramkali had poured cold water on their hopes. 'How could you ever think that? Shame on you!'

'Why?' Dinatarini had suppressed her fears and said with some stubbornness, 'People do it all the time.'

'We don't have to follow them, Ma.'

'Well, I don't think my daughter-in-law will have more children, even her horoscope says there'll just be one child. In that case, your son-in-law will inherit everything. If he isn't trained from a young age ...'

Ramkali's vehement protest had silenced his mother, 'How can you say that the son-in-law will inherit everything when Rashu and his brothers are there? For shame! Why should Satya have to live off her father? I'll find her a husband who won't need to covet his father-in-law's property.'

Ramkali had kept his word. The family he had married his daughter into had no need to lust after his property. They were wealthy, the groom was an only child. One heard that the father was a miser. But one could not have everything!

His son-in-law was very handsome. Besides, they were a highly revered kulin family. What else could one check out?

But greed is rarely driven by want. Ramkali would never have guessed that his daughter's kulin father-in-law kept a sharp watch over his property. He was also clueless about the intense greed that drove Nilambar to muse constantly on Ramkali's death. Though he was almost ten years older than Ramkali, he hoped to live forever!

Ramkali had no idea about all this. He knew that his son-in-law was studying and he was pleased about that. Ramkali was not so irrational that he would discredit that learning for being mlechcha. Learning was a good thing. And after all, the mlechchas were the rulers now.

NINETEEN

Lakshmikanta Banerji passed away. He had lived a virtuous and healthy life, he did not suffer too much, and did not let others suffer either. He was in full control of his senses just before he died. That morning too he had bathed, plucked flowers and offered his puja according to routine. And after he had finished, he had called his eldest son and said, 'Eat early today. I don't feel too well, I think my time is up.'

The eldest son stared stupefied; he failed to see the link between Lakshmikanta feeling unwell and everyone eating early. And what did his father mean by saying that his 'time was up'?

Lakshmikanta smiled at his son's astonishment. He said, 'After you have eaten, I want you two brothers to come and sit by me, I want to give you some advice. But of course, I really don't have a right to—how much of life have I seen? Still, there's the experience of age. Tell the daughters-in-law that they shouldn't delay by cooking too many items for the meal.'

His father kept mentioning their meal—but what about his own? The eldest asked in a choked voice, 'Aren't you going to have some rice?'

'Silly boy, don't be so distressed! I don't eat rice when there's a full moon. I'll have some fruits and prasad. It will purify my body and soul.'

The son had burst into tears in front of his younger brother. And the women had got to know. Within a short while a pall of gloom cast itself over the entire household. No one was sceptical, none amused; they saw it as infallible and inevitable, and were shattered.

The news spread from within the house to outside. Could fire be confined to one place? In a minute it circulated everywhere: 'Banerji is going.'

As if Banerji was going abroad on a journey, as if the boat had been booked already, as if his friends were ready and waiting somewhere!

Lakshmikanta's bed was moved into the courtyard, at the foot of the sacred tulsi, and he lay straight, head on the pillow and his two hands folded over his chest.

On his forehead the name of Hari had been painted with sandalwood paste, and leaves of the tulsi dipped in sandalwood paste had been placed over his eyes and on his ears. On his chest, a tiny hand-written scroll on which Lakshmikanta himself had written a few shlokas from the *Gita*. He used to read it everyday, and he was taking that with him.

Nobody should touch him as he set out on his journey; those

were his instructions. His sons sat at a distance from the bed, their heads bowed, and with them, the village elders. The women of the house were weeping silently, their heads and faces completely buried under their saris.

Till the moment of death arrived, none could wail aloud; that was forbidden too. The sound of weeping could hinder the progress of the spirit in its ascent.

Abiding by that rule, Lakshmikanta's wife was sobbing silently.

Ghosal arrived and said in a trembling voice, 'So, you're leaving us Banerji, as regally as King Janaka?'

Lakshmikanta replied with a smile, 'Leaving these foreign shores for my homeland. Going to my mother's, leaving my stepmother behind.'

Then he looked at his sons and said, 'Repeat the holy name.'

Meaning to say, there was no point wasting time in useless words.

'Namo Narayana namo Narayana, Harenamaiva kevalam.'

Gently, Lakshmikanta shut his eyes. The tulsi leaves covered both his lids.

And with each breath he recited the holy name in silence, as long as his chest rose and fell.

At one point it stopped.

Well, Lakshmikanta was an old man, he did not suffer much, he just passed away, it was not tragic at all. At least, there was nothing to lament about it. Men come to earth to die, and there is nothing more fortunate, if they can do that perfectly and flawlessly. No, there was nothing deplorable about his death. But it did leave the near and dear ones sad.

But someone who was neither near nor dear also plunged herself into that flood of grief, and that was Sharada. The sons of Lakshmikanta had invited their 'new' kinsmen for the funeral and had especially requested that Rashu stay till after the funeral. And metaphorically speaking, they had placed a brick on Sharada's head.

They wanted him to leave the next day. All day the discussion had gone on.

Ramkali had gone as soon as he had heard the news; he had also sent provisions as was appropriate for such an occasion. He had sent many items. Now Rashu would go with some of the menfolk, carrying money and clothes for the family to wear for the funeral ritual. The day after the funeral, they would send freshly caught fish, and sindur-alta and betel-nuts for Rashu's mother-in-law and his aunts-in-law.

All day they had discussed this. It all seemed a bit too much for Sharada. No such fuss had taken place when her father's aunt had died. Never mind! Since they had the money, let them gift it away! But let us hope Sharada's most precious possession was not going to be doled out as well. There was no way of talking to him except at night, so Sharada carried out her chores with a throbbing heart and counted the hours. Thank goodness they had not called him during the day—she had, at least, one night in hand.

The work in this household got over well past midnight. At long last, that craved-for hour arrived—when the door could be locked, and finally, the two of them could sit by themselves. Sharada was not one to start talking immediately. She raised the wick of the lamp, warmed the milk for her son on its flame, fed the child and only after patting him to sleep, did she go to his side, where she sat swinging her legs from the bed.

She let out a sigh, 'So you're going?'

Rashu, of course, was prepared for this question, so he replied, unruffled, 'I don't see any other way out.'

'But were you looking for a way out?' A tone of sharp sarcasm.

'How can I? I know there's no escape.'

'There's escape only with some effort.' Sharada's stings became sharper.

'How?' Rashu asked, a trifle annoyed.

'Could anyone pull you there if you said you were ill?'

Rashu said irritably, 'How will I use that excuse when there's nothing wrong with me physically?'

Sharada did not fear this irritation, and she did not give up either. She said coolly, 'Anything can be achieved with effort. You know that unboiled milk does not suit your nature, if you drank a couple of litres, you'd have to run to the field with an upset stomach twenty times. Everyone would think that you were ill. There'd be no need to lie to the elders.'

The logical Rashu stated emphatically, 'As if that wouldn't be a lie—not in speech but in act, it'd be false anyway!'

'Stop it!' Sharada protested vehemently, 'As if Mr. Truthful doesn't ever do such things! What about the times when you come back late after playing cards—why do you enter from the backdoor then? Do you ever tell Mejokaka-mashai that you don't attend the Sanskrit classes he's fixed for you? Don't you go here and there just like that? Don't you preach to me!'

'I don't wish to do that!' the fearless Rashu said. 'But I have to follow the instructions of elders, that's all.'

'Of course you will follow instructions—there's nectar there after all! Fresh blossoms in a new garden! The queen of the palace!'

'Don't talk rubbish!'

'As if it's rubbish!' Sharada took a deep breath and said, 'Do you recall what you'd sworn to me?'

'Why won't I recall that? I'm not going for a special feast, I'm going to attend the funeral of a respectable man.'

'I know for sure that my funeral is also being planned. Now there'll be talk about sending their girl.'

Rashu pretended to charge, 'Look how you talk! Does the girl's side ever mention such things on their own?'

'Of course they do. Depending on the circumstances. They always talk about her replacing the first wife!'

'But she must come of age, no? You're forever mistaking a rope for a snake.'

'Age!' Sharada's voice rang forth, 'How long does it take a girl to come of age? Soon as she's ten! And Mejokaka-mashai's stubbornness is gone now that he's sending his own daughter before it's time.'

'Don't you comment on what the elders do. There must have been a reason.'

But Sharada would not be checked, she was unstoppable. She retorted with equal passion, 'So, there'll also be a reason invented for fetching your second wife here. But remember this, if she comes, she'll enter through one door and I'll exit through the other, a rope in one hand and a pot in the other.'

An unfailing weapon, that. And finally, Rashu yielded. He said in a tone of truce, 'Why do you invite sorrow with so much effort? I'm just going for a funeral. I'll eat and come back. I'm not going to fetch anybody!'

'As long as you remember that.'

Sharada suddenly pulled Rashu's hand and placed it on the forehead of her sleeping child, 'Then swear on him.'

'For shame! Look how you talk! Swear on the child ...'

Sharada was fearless, 'Why fear that? Ask me to swear on the baby that I'll never ever look on another man—I'll swear it a hundred times.'

'Wonderful! Is that the same thing?'

'Why not? If you think of all women except me as "other" women, there's no problem at all.'

'But then, I married her before the sacred fire—'

'I see!' Sharada stood up quickly. She opened the latch and standing with her hand on the door said in a muted but fearsome voice, 'Really! Finally the truth is out! You could have told me that without making me suffer for so long. All right then—'

Rashu was scared now, he got off the bed, 'Why're you opening the door? Where are you going?'

'I'll go where there is no betrayal, no suffering.' With that Sharada disappeared into the darkness.

What could he do now? After staring at the darkness in helpless resentment, Rashu quietly shut the door, but left it unbolted. He was sweating profusely. Not from the heat but from fear. But what could be done now? He could not go out and look for her, nor could he wake up his mother and aunt to give them this terrible news. There was only one thing he could do now—slap himself.

TWENTY

Elokeshi sat on a mat in the courtyard and was busy tying Satya's hair. She had been at it for a while now. She had started in the afternoon and it was nearing dusk. It was as if she had vowed to display her most creative feat today. She sat on her haunches behind her daughter-in-law, her expression stern and severe.

The veins on Satyabati's temples bulged from all that pulling, the roots of her hair appeared to almost separate from her scalp; her shoulders had been aching for a while, and now the discomfort spread to her spine.

But there was little hope that Elokeshi would easily give up the attempt at creating a great work of art with Satyabati's hair. It would be wrong to blame it on Elokeshi's incompetence, it was all the other one's fault. Satyabati's hair was like a refractory horse that refused to be tamed.

No matter how beautiful her curly hair looked when left loose, it was most frustrating to braid the heavy and short mass and shape it into a bun. It came apart if one tried to tie it up, and even if one managed to divide it into three clusters, it was impossible to further divide it into five or seven or nine clusters.

But Elokeshi was determined to twist her daughter-in-law's hair into an S-shaped knot. Therefore, after a couple of failed attempts, she had managed to gather all the hair to the top of the head and after using all her strength to tie it up tightly with a thick cord, she was now dividing it into seven bunches.

This long-drawn out attempt had left Satyabati in the state described earlier. After sitting cross-legged for a long time, she had drawn up her knees and folded them against her chest in order to relieve the pins and needles in her feet. Her face looked skywards and over it she held the end of her turquoise-blue sari.

She had to hold her sari over her face because she could not cover her head when her hair was being done. And yet, it was unthinkable that her face should be in full view of the world! Never mind that nobody else was present, and never mind that she was not facing her mother-in-law—she was a 'new bride' after all. So Satyabati had covered her face. In fact, she had been forced to. Much before she had uncovered her head, Elokeshi had instructed her, 'Cover your face with the end of your sari, please. You don't seem to have any sense anyway, I have to spell out everything clearly!'

Was this Satyabati's first day at her in-laws? Not really, she had arrived about a month ago, but until now Satyabati's hair had never yielded to her mother-in-law's hands. Saudamini would take care of her toilet: braiding her hair, scrubbing her face, putting alta on her feet. But suddenly, just today, Elokeshi happened to notice that her daughter-in-law's hair was braided into two intertwining plaits which were pinned up. Elokeshi had flared up. She had frowned and called out, just to make sure, 'Just come here, Bouma.'

The sari was drawn over her head. With a tug, Elokeshi had raised the end of the sari covering her back, and taken a look at the hairstyle. It confirmed her suspicion. And she yelled in a frenzy, 'Sadu! Sadu!'

Saudamini had come running helter-skelter. And she saw Satya standing with her head bent low, and her aunt standing with the end of the sari raised—eyes smouldering, forehead furrowed. She did not pronounce her query, but stood there looking alarmed. Was there something on her back? Some birthmark or skin disease, or an old wound that had not healed? Was she blemished, then? Had her aunt's hawk-like eyes just found that out?

But Saudamini did not have to hold on to her mistaken notion for long. Elokeshi said fiercely, 'I ask you Sadu, why do you work so carelessly?'

A stone rolled off Saudamini's chest. What a relief! Nothing new. The same old and unfailing strategy of fault-finding! So she said with courage, 'Why, what's the matter?'

'What's the matter, she asks! Aren't you ashamed? Here you are polishing off loads of rice twice a day like a sacred cow and you don't have any qualms! It isn't as if you have ten or twenty sisters-in-law—just the one, and look how you've braided her hair? Why? How brazen can you get, eh?'

'Why don't you tell me what has happened?'

Saudamini spoke calmly, and Satyabati looked at her from under the sari that covered her face and trembled in amazement. No, not on account of Elokeshi's insulting oration; during her neighbourhood rambles back home, Satya had become accustomed to hearing older women use such abuses. Inside Ramkali Chatterji's house, the conversation was slightly more courteous, but then Satya's aunts constantly spouted such words. No, it was not because of Elokeshi's words; she was amazed at Saudamini's forbearance. How could she talk so calmly after being insulted so crudely! This was something Satyabati had never seen before. Insult was usually traded with insult, or tears—that was what she was used to. And here was Saudamini calmly asking, 'Why don't you tell me what has happened!'

Elokeshi, of course, was not amazed, she was used to Saudamini's self-restraint. But far from brimming over with appreciation she raged at what she perceived to be an expression of indifference. She said, 'Do I have to explain it? Don't you realize it yourself? What style of braiding is this? Such plaits on a daughter-in-law! Shame on you! I haven't seen a girl wearing such braids at her in-laws' ever in my life! You should go and hang yourself, Sadu! There's just one head of hair and you can't even do a fancy hairstyle!'

Sadu began to laugh, 'Well, her hair is too fancy to style it any other way. It's so unmanageable.'

'Unmanageable!' Elokeshi blasted out, 'Let me see if it can be managed or not. There's nothing on earth that's unmanageable for Banerji-Ginni. The only person I haven't managed to control is you.'

'All right then, Mami, why don't you do her hair—she's the wife of your only son after all!' Saudamini retorted.

Instantly Elokeshi pounced on her, 'What was that, Sadu? How dare you! Talking back, eh? Too much pride! Your fall is near! Wait till cats and dogs howl at your funeral! I'll curse the life out of you, I swear, if you touch my daughter-in-law's hair again.'

'Nothing happens when an elder curses, so I don't mind,' Sadu said unperturbed. 'You are a person of moods, some days you will do her hair, other days, you'll forget ...'

'What was that? You wretched girl! You think I'll forget my only son's wife?'

'Nothing surprising in that, is there?' Sadu answered amicably, 'You're blessed with that virtue. People eat when they're hungry, but you forget that too—I have to call you to eat.'

Elokeshi was dumbfounded. She could not fathom if this was a complaint or commendation. So she said grimly, 'Oh yes, I forget and you have to feed me with your own hands!'

'All right, may be I don't do that. But you do forget.'

'So what? From now on I shall braid her hair, I'll have you know. Keep her pins, ribbons and everything in my room. And don't forget the bird-clips.'

'Of course, I won't. Besides, her father's given a gold comb, a snake-pin, gold flowers and a whole lot of ornaments for her hair—why have you locked those away? Take them out and make the fanciest style.'

'I'll do what I think best, I don't need your advice. So much of smart talk! I don't know why god doesn't give you some illness that'll strike you dumb. I swear if you ever lost your speech, I'd send a special offering to the gods at Nisinghatala.'

'Please, Mami, don't swear before the gods. The gods often hear things differently. If they should make me a cripple instead of a mute, you'll die from the running around you'll have to do.'

'How dare you! You think if you're crippled, my house won't run? Not for nothing do I say that you're vain. D'you think I can't run the house? I can do it with the little finger of my left hand. But why should I, when I've reared you, fed and clothed you.'

'That's exactly what I'm saying. You'll have to feed and clothe me even if I'm crippled.'

'As if I will! I'll drag you by the legs and throw you in the ditch!'

'Goodness, Mami! Don't even dream of that! The neighbours will throw mud at you from that very ditch.' Saudamini left laughing, leaving Satyabati astounded.

Satyabati came from a large family; in her brief life she had seen many characters, but nobody like this.

Anyway, the aftermath of the morning's incident was this afternoon's wrestling match.

Satya's hair was really heavy at the roots and short in length. Even if Elokeshi managed to elongate the plaits by adding numerous tassles to the hair and tying it tight with a cord, the whole thing would come loose as soon as she tried to twist it into a butterfly style. And it was Satyabati's bad luck that just at that moment, she had moved just a little to stretch her back and relieve the tingling in her feet.

It was a chicken and egg situation. One could not make out if Satyabati wriggled with the pleasure of freedom because the cord had slackened, or the cord had loosened because she had moved. According to Elokeshi, her daughter-in-law moved and consequently the hair come loose. She was not a stone idol after all, she was a flesh-and-blood human being. It would be madness to hope that she would sit calmly and at ease after that. Such crazy hopes never get fulfilled, ever.

All her time and effort had come to nought, and her hopes of showing up Saudamini had been frustrated. So Elokeshi lost her mind and did something unimaginable. She pitched a full-fisted punch on that stretched-to-ease back—'Just look! What a waste of time this is! Can't you sit still for a second?'

But Elokeshi could hardly complete her sentence before a different cataclysm occurred. Satyabati stood up, freed her hair from her mother-in-law's grip with a violent tug, and completely overlooking the custom of not talking back to a mother-in-law, she demanded adamantly, 'Why did you hit me?'

For a tiny, fleeting moment, Elokeshi might have even regretted the thump, but such an unexpected flash of lightning turned Elokeshi into stone long before that contrition could crystallize. Elokeshi had had no opportunity of finding out what her daughter-in-law's voice sounded like, for she had not spoken with her, or in front of her. It was not the done thing at all. Satya would nod a 'yes' or a 'no' in response to questions. She spoke only with

Sadu, in private. She would sleep beside Saudamini at night, because until she had reached puberty, the question of sleeping with her husband did not arise.

Elokeshi had never heard her speak, and today, out of the blue, the voice exploded like thunder against her ears. What a loud voice for a daughter-in-law! And from such a little person! The vapours of remorse vanished like fizz. Elokeshi stood up and yelled as she charged, 'So what? What can you do about it, eh? Do you want to beat me up?'

Satya thrust her fingers through her plaits and had started pulling them open vigorously. The end of her sari had fallen away from her head, and exposed her blazing face. Turning that fiery face towards Elokeshi, Satya uttered scornfully, 'I'm not so vulgar. But don't you ever—'

'What was that? Don't I ever, what? You slip of a girl, still wet behind the ears and speaking like this! I can beat the daylight out of you, do you hear? Just let me get a piece of firewood, I'll show the world how to discipline a daughter-in-law! When it lands on your back it'll douse your fire.'

'Go ahead, then! Bring all the wood you have.' Satyabati stood arrogantly before her mother-in-law with fearless, unblinking eyes.

In her whole life Elokeshi had been blinded with rage several times, she had beaten her breasts and cursed and yelled, but never before had she been confronted by such a situation. This was beyond her imagination, beyond her dreams. She suddenly froze, looking at that incarnation of fearlessness with a cold, snake-like gaze.

Who knows what might have happened had she remained in that state, but the pranks of fate brought about another disaster. At that dramatic moment, Nabakumar pushed open the courtyard fencing and entered the inner house.

He was thunderstruck as soon as he entered. What a situation! Who was that girl standing in front of Elokeshi, her face uncovered, and framed by hair that stood out like the hoods of a million snakes? Could that be his wife? But how could that be possible? How could his wife stand like that before his mother without the earth cracking open or a terrible storm starting up? Why didn't she pay any attention to the fact that Nabakumar was standing there and gaping? Impossible! This had to be someone else! Some neighbour's girl whom Nabakumar did not know. Perhaps there had been some terrible fight.

Nabakumar forgot to clear his throat, forgot to move away; he only stared, stunned and stupefied. He was faced with a serious dilemma. He could hardly dismiss the suspicion that this was his wife with any conviction.

Though he had not really seen his wife's face, over this last month he had glanced at her least twenty or twenty-five times. Fleeting glimpses that hardly lasted for a split second for fear that somebody should notice him staring at her! But the lens of a camera can capture an image forever. He knew her shape even though he had not seen her face. And he had seen that blue sari. There was no point in deceiving himself. It was as ridiculous as shutting one's eyes and claiming that the sun did not exist! She was not a neighbour at all—that dauntless creature was none other than Nabakumar's wife! The wife to whom Nabakumar had been singing, and still sang to, silently in his waking moments and in his dreams—'Look up, my bride, and speak to me, open your eyes and look at me!' But were those her eyes?

Perhaps, if Nabakumar had left the scene as silently as he had entered it, the climax of this drama would never have reached such a pitch. Perhaps, Satyabati would have moved away fearlessly, and Elokeshi would have uttered every single profanity that she had learnt. And later, when her husband and son came home, she would have presented an elaborate description of her daughter-in-law's dreadful insolence and terrible rudeness. The whole thing would have blown over.

But the witless Nabakumar just stood there and stared. And at some point Elokeshi's eyes chanced on him. She on the verandah, her son down below on the courtyard. For a moment, she too gaped at his staring face. Then a fierce scream arose out of that wide-open mouth that had been frozen until now, 'You wretched, pathetic sissy! Don't you wear shoes? Can't you pick your shoes and grind her face to pulp? I'd say you're some son then.'

But Nabakumar just stood motionless.

Elokeshi changed her tune the very next minute, 'Oh my mother! Come and see how my son and his wife are abusing me! Oh Naba—cow of a brahmin—how lowly you've become after marrying this girl from that lowly family! How can you just stand and watch your mother being insulted? Come and hit me with the broom! That's what I deserve. Or why would I let her stand here still? I should have shaved her head and dismissed her. My god, my god—the daughter-in-law beats me and my son just watches.'

Nabakumar came back to his senses finally, but as soon as he did, he ran out through the open door.

Saudamini had been washing the utensils at the pond in the backyard. She stood up with her ash-smeared hands and called out to Nabakumar who was running breathlessly, 'Naba, what's up? Why're you running like that?'

At first, Nabakumar had thought nothing of ignoring her call and going straight to Nitai's house and asking for a full jug of water; because Nitai was his closest friend, one he could rush to in times of distress. But for some reason, he stopped, turned and slowly came and sat on the stub of a palm tree by the ghat, and choked on his words, 'I'm not going back home ever, Sadudi.'

'Listen to the boy! What has happened, tell me.'

'A disaster, Sadudi!'

'Oh god, must you say that!'

'Yes, if that is what has happened I must say it.'

Sadu was used to his ways, so she ventured boldly, 'Has your mother kicked the bucket, or what?'

'Not my mother, Sadudi, but may be I have. I can't believe that I am really alive.'

'Pinch yourself then.' Sadu dipped her hand in the water and washed off the mud and ash, 'Did Mami come rushing at you like the wrathful goddess, or what?'

'Can't say.'

'Can't say! Stop being silly, tell me what happened or go where you're going. Are you a man or a girl?'

'Sadudi, the bravest of men will go cold with fear if they saw what I saw.'

'Gosh! What an endless preface! Just tell me if you want to, otherwise let it be. I can't make out if you saw a ghost or if dacoits have attacked the house.'

Nabakumar regained his courage, coaxed the words from his throat and hastily said, 'My mother and my wife are beating each other up!'

'What do you mean?' Saudamini asked with a start.

'I just told you. They're beating each other up.'

Saudamini was silent for a moment and then said, 'Why put it like that? Say that Mami is beating up your wife. And witnessing that scene—great man that you are—you fled as fast as you could. Don't know why you weren't born a woman, Naba! Let me go and see what's happened. When I left with these utensils a while ago, Mami was braiding her hair. What could have happened?'

'I have no idea. I'd only just stepped into the house. Go quickly, Sadudi.'

'I will. God! A disaster a minute—an instant mountain out of a molehill! What could the matter be?'

'I'll stay the night at Nitai's, Sadudi. I'm off.'

Saudamini frowned, 'How long will you stay away?'

'As long as I can.'

'I see. You'll save your own skin while that girl from another home—that slip of a girl—gets a beating from your mother!'

The girl from another home—a slip of a girl. The words tugged at Nabakumar's heart, tears came to his eyes. He hid his pain and said, 'What can I do?'

Saudamini stole a glance at his face and said placidly, 'You could have stayed on, and perhaps, if she saw you, Mami would have controlled herself, wouldn't have gone to this extent. Let me go and see if the girl is dead or alive.'

Nabakumar abandoned his shyness and said suddenly, 'But whatever you say, Sadudi, from what I saw, the girl isn't one to take a beating lying down.'

'I think so too.' Sadu smiled an amused smile, 'She may not raise her hands, but she won't take a beating lying down. But you haven't told me what happened.'

'How do I know how it started? When I walked in I saw those two facing each other. One hissing like a snake and the other growling like a tigress.'

Saudamini said with a laugh, 'Wonderful! You've become quite eloquent, I can see. You'll find some use for it in the future. You wife is quite learned.'

Nabakumar felt like filling his ears with stories about his wife; he forgot that he had just compared her to a tigress. But how could he ask about those stories? He considered the phrase in the future'. Which future? How far away was it? Now and again the tigress's face gave him a jolt. Terrifying, but beautiful! What large eyes! What a splendid pair of eyebrows! But who knows, suppose his wife should turn out to be as ill-tempered as his mother! She could not remain the timid and bashful bride forever. Did such an image match the one in Nabakumar's imagination?

Nabakumar's heart ached with a loss. What harm would it have done to give Nabakumar a clay doll for a wife! So many people have such wives. But that face framed by hair puffed up like the hoods of a million snakes—it held the attraction of fire. Nabakumar was a mere moth.

Saudamini said, 'If you wish to give up the life of a householder, go. But don't you make me wait too long with your dinner.'

Dinner! Nabakumar could not believe it! He said timidly, 'I'll wait here. Why don't you go check and let me know? Then I can go off to play cards with a lighter mind.'

'Oh I see, he'll wait like a babu and I must bring him news.' Saudamini lifted the stack of utensils over her shoulder. She carried the smaller pots tied in a cloth in her hand. She reassured her cousin once more as she was leaving, 'Don't get upset worrying about your wife. If Mami doesn't get hanged for murdering her, she'll be taught a lesson by your wife. Your wife is not an ordinary girl.'

If his mother did not murder her! The 'if' stabbed at his heart. But he could not ask anything; he just sat there glumly.

'It's getting dark. Don't sit around here. Go where you want to.'

Sadu took large strides and almost crossed the bamboo bush. But Nabakumar followed her. His face troubled, his eyes tearful.

'Sadudi, can I come with you?'

Sadu smiled slightly and said as she walked, 'But didn't you just say that you were never going to return home?'

'I'm feeling so upset, Sadudi.' He followed her and changed his tone suddenly, 'If my wife has insulted my mother, she must be punished too.'

'Rest assured, she isn't the kind of person who will needlessly insult anyone. But if anyone wishes to invite insults that's a different matter. Actually, you know what? She is a high-born girl, educated too, reads huge books, makes up poems—'

'What!' Nabakumar yelled out, oblivious of his surroundings or the situation, 'Are you joking?'

'Why should I? Why should I make it up? And what do I understand of such things anyway! She confided in me, so I've come to know.'

She confided in Sadu! God! When would such coveted heavenly pleasures come to Nabakumar—when his wife could confide in him! Sadu continued, 'It wasn't right for her to be married into your family. Let me say this clearly, even if it makes you cross, this family is not worthy of her. Mami has money of course, but is she large-hearted? And your wife isn't used to mean ways. The other day, she just went pale when she heard that villagers pawn their jewellery to your mother, and she charges a high interest on the money she lends.'

Nabakumar said irritably, 'There was no need to tell her all that.'

'Well, I didn't drag her by the ears to make her hear. The Ghosh-woman pawned a pair of armlets and began to bargain. She says one paisa per rupee and Mami says one and a half—a real tussle over half a paisa! In the end—'

Nabakumar did not get to hear what happened in the end. Abruptly a howl floated out of the house.

'A disaster.' Nabakumar said, oblivious of the fact that Sadu had forbidden him to use that word, 'Something must have happened.'

By then Sadu had gone inside. And Nabakumar? He had lost all powers of locomotion and stood there staring at his own house. Whose sharp high-pitched nasal voice was that? It sounded like Elokeshi. What had happened to them? But whatever had happened, one realization overwhelmed Nabakumar and filled his heart with grief. He was certainly not fated to set up house with his extraordinary wife. His mother would either send her to the cremation ground or send her packing to her father's.

By degrees, the pitch of his mother's screams touched the sky. And hordes of neighbours began to flock towards Nabakumar's house. And Nabakumar watched, frozen stiff, like a spectator at a performance.

TWENTY ONE

Ramkali had come to Tribeni, where the three rivers meet. Not to see a patient, but to take a dip because it was considered auspicious. He had hired a boat for himself. Ramkali disliked the idea of huddling in a boat packed with strangers. He preferred to hire a boat for himself when the need arose. Earlier, it would be difficult to get away on his own. Because when Satya got to know about his boat trips, whether to Tribeni, Katoa or Nabadwip, she would insist on accompanying him. Ramkali would find it hard to escape from his daughter who constantly pursued him with her pleas. He would give in and bring her along with Neru and Punyi. It was unimaginable for Ramkali to ignore propriety and take only his daughter to the exclusion of other children. So they would come along too.

Ramkali would to caution them about the tide. After they had bathed, he would take them to the temples and turn back. All the way, the river, the boat and the temple would echo with the words that flowed from that talkative girl.

But today only the sound of the oars on the water could be heard. Ramkali gazed at the river stretching before him, and let out a small sigh. He wondered how a bird accustomed to the skies felt inside a cage.

Punyi's wedding had been fixed. The famine of the past couple of months had prevented it from taking place. Now, Punyi was a different type of girl. She would get into mischief only as Satya's 'follower'; left to herself, she was a typical homebody. Punyi and girls like her were birds bred in captivity. But had Ramkali ever seen another girl like Satya, who would ask 'what' or 'why' at every step?

The boatman asked, 'Is your girl at her in-laws?'

Ramkali replied, 'Yes.'

Two more thrashes of the oar, and the man asked again, 'Will she stay there now?'

Ramkali ended the discussion with a brief, 'Let's see.'

Because the wedding was approaching, there was a faint ray of hope. Otherwise, of course, she would stay there. She would have to, all her life! And that was really desirable. No one chose a fate like Mokshada who, despite her beauty and intelligence, ended up staying at her parents all her life. Only unlucky girls stayed at their natal homes. Would it have been different if it were a son? A son would never go away after he married, and could be commanded. But that was as far as it went. It was all the same when a son grew up. Perhaps that was why human beings repeatedly invited new children into their lives, to fill it up and enjoy it. And afterwards, sought consolation in calculating material gain.

Nityanandapur was only a short distance from Tribeni. The boatman stopped the boat. The first person Ramkali encountered as he stepped off was the 'runner' Gokul Das. Seeing Ramkali alight, he ran towards him. Gokul stretched himself out on the mud in obeisance and said with a humble smile, 'How fortunate I am, Karta!'

Ramkali gave a slight smile, 'Why praise fortune early in the morning, Gokul?'

Gokul answered, 'Why shouldn't I? It's good that I met you, or I'd have to run all the way to Nityanandapur. Here, there's a letter for you.'

A letter from Calcutta. How unexpected! Even though Ramkali was astonished, he did not express it. Placing the envelope on his bundle of used clothes, he said, 'All right. All well?'

'By your blessings, yes.' After some hesitation, Gokul said, 'Uh … a letter from Calcutta?'

'That's what I noticed.' With that response, Ramkali went down into the water with his gamcha; the first rays of the sun gleamed on his imposing golden body. Gokul stared and thought to himself, 'Just like a god from the skies. What presence!'

Pushing away all thoughts of the letter from his mind, Ramkali finished his rituals, then tying the letter to the end of his chaddar, he proceeded to the temple. Gokul stretched his body out once more in farewell. His curiosity about the letter from Calcutta remained unsatisfied.

Ramkali opened the letter inside the boat. He was stunned. It was as though the morning light had suddenly lost its brightness and the darkness of evening had descended. As though Ramkali, who had just purified himself with a dip in the holy river, had been polluted by contact with something impure.

The letter was not from anyone he knew, but from a stranger. It bore no name or signature. Yet this anonymous letter addressed him with an exaggerated flourish. And not just that, the content was outrageous!

Ramkali held the letter up in front of him once more, even though he had read it several times. A stylish hand, neat lines, perfect spelling.

Undoubtedly written by an 'educated' person; with an invocation to Saraswati at the top of the page:

For the respectful attention of the esteemed and honourable
Ramkali Chattopadhyay,

   With due respect, I wish to submit, sir, that your daughter's
life is in severe danger. It is as a woman tortured, abused and
insulted beyond measure that she expends her time at her
in-laws'. Despite my quaking soul and trembling body, I write
to inform that your daughter is being battered by her respected
mother-in-law. There is nobody in that cruel fortress to protect
the docile girl. Witnessing the persecution of his wedded wife,
your son-in-law has been weeping incessantly. What can he say
to his elders? Under the circumstances, it would be beneficial if
your honour took his daughter home. Or else, my head spins at
the thought of the consequences. I draw this to your attention
on account of my duty as a human being. Please forgive my
audacity.

With regards—

There was no signature.

Ramkali was not in a state to be amused by the verbosity or
rhetoric of the letter-writer. He slowly folded the letter and put it
away in his pocket, and stared out at the sun-lit landscape. So much
light on earth, and yet men remained in such darkness.

   Who could have written this letter? Some enemy of Satya's
in-laws who wanted to tarnish their name? But how did the letter
come from Calcutta? Ramkali concluded that the writer must have
some connection with Calcutta and had posted the letter there in
order to preserve his anonymity. But there was the other problem
too. Was this terrible piece of news true, or fabricated? Should
Ramkali try to find that out or should he send someone? But could
an outsider possibly unearth real facts from inside? Well, if he sent
a woman—one of the many who lived a life of domestic toil in
Ramkali's house. If one such woman were paid for the journey, she
would manage to bring news. Usually they did such work in
villages. But the fact that anything they found out would be
broadcast to the world at large disgusted Ramkali. God alone knew

what kind of news they would bring, which the entire village would discuss.

If only Satya herself had written. She knew enough to be able to write. However, could she gather enough courage or competence to write home with her news? But then, if she could not, no other girl could. The reserved Ramkali felt something tug at his heart. The image of Satya's lively face floated up before him. Was that same girl being battered? It was hard to believe that.

The letter had to be a lie! The work of an enemy! What other reason could there be? Why would they want to torture Satya? How could any human be needlessly cruel? Besides, apart from her mother-in-law, she had a father-in-law too. He was a respectable man, surely *he* would never let such a thing happen. And if the men of the house were not aware of such abuse, how could the neighbours know?

Ramkali turned it over in his mind once more. Satyabati was their one and only daughter-in-law. Ramkali had sent her to her in-laws without a murmur, with plenty of gifts to mollify her mother-in-law. How could they torture Satya after all that? Could it be possible?

Although it would be wrong to speak his mind, Ramkali could not help thinking about it—he had chosen this son-in-law out of a horde of others simply because he belonged to a small family. He knew his daughter was stubborn, impetuous and unbendable from childhood. It would not be easy for her to adjust to a large household, therefore, he had surmised that this would be best. So what if he was the only child of his parents? Satya too was an only child!

Ramkali had avoided looking for a son-in-law who would move in with the family. He had hoped that the boy would not turn out to be useless. And would have some learning. Ramkali's wish had been granted so far. His son-in-law had passed middle school, and was learning Sanskrit at a tol. He had also heard rumours about his son-in-law's English lessons. Ramkali was pleased. Even though he had no direct contact, he had made enquiries and had been relieved to learn that his son-in-law did not keep bad company, or have bad habits.

Everything seemed fine. And yet, here was a bolt from the blue. Once again, he thought that this had to be the work of an enemy. Finally, unable to ignore the storm in his mind, Ramkali decided to visit Satya's in-laws. Would it be demeaning if he went uninvited? But then, his dignity had been diminished the day he had ritually placed his hands on his son-in-law's knees and gifted his daughter away. Unlike in the olden days, he had not let his daughter choose her own husband! Besides, he would not really have to suffer the discourtesy of visiting his son-in-law without a cause. He could go with a request that they send Satya with him for Punyi's wedding. And he would invite the in-laws too. What could be more appropriate than going in person to invite them?

On his return from Tribeni, Ramkali briefly announced to Dinatarini, 'I think I will go to Baruipur.'

Baruipur? To visit Satya's in-laws? Dinatarini gave a start, 'Why suddenly? Is Satya ill?'

'How absurd! Why should she be ill? I was thinking that after Punyi gets married who knows when they'll meet. They are such good friends. Let them spend some time together before the wedding.'

Dinatarini stared at her son. She found it hard to believe Ramkali could speak so plainly, and use such simple words. After all, she had dubbed her son the 'God of Stone'!

The words were simple enough. But nobody could take them at face value because they had been uttered by Ramkali.

Mokshada rasped, 'Of course, it isn't just like that! She's a girl who knows to read and write—I'm sure she's written him a letter secretly, "Bring me home, I'm tired of all the restrictions."'

Shibjaya rolled her eyes at Bhubaneswari's bowed face and pronounced plaintively, 'I don't believe that. I feel there's some bad news, which Ramkali is hiding from us.'

Needless to say, after this, Bhubaneswari burst into tears, as was expected.

The only person Bhubaneswari was close to was younger than

her in age and relationship—that was her niece-in-law, Sharada. But such was her luck that Sharada had left for her parents' four months ago. She was expecting her second child and hence was staying at her parents'.

No, Sharada had not drowned herself the night she had fought with Rashu. She had gone into her sister-in-law's room and slept there. But just for that one night. She could not have carried on doing that night after night!

After all, for a woman the night was like an oasis in the desert of her in-laws' house. A breath of life in the kingdom of death. No matter how much hurt pride they nursed, women had no other way except to swallow it.

That was true of everybody. That night, Bhubaneswari's sobs became uncontrollable. Ramkali could guess that from the other bed. Though he overlooked it at first and pretended to sleep, it soon became impossible to ignore. He quietly asked, 'Why are you crying like that?'

Needless to say, the expected response followed. The sobbing intensified.

Ramkali said, 'Don't act childish. Come here. Tell me why you're crying.'

Wiping her eyes, Bhubaneswari rose. And she came and sat on the edge of her husband's bed, rubbing her eyes with the end of her sari.

Ramkali asked uneasily, 'Now stop behaving like other women, please! It was my mistake to say that I shall bring Satya a few days before Punyi's wedding. If I go myself, they can't say no. Instead of understanding that, here you are acting as though something terrible has happened. How strange!'

'It isn't that.' Bhubaneswari said sadly, 'I miss the girl ...'

'Of course, that's natural,' Ramkali said tenderly. 'She's your only child. But it doesn't help to cry, does it? A mother feels sad all right, but isn't a father supposed to feel anything?' Ramkali smiled uneasily.

Bhubaneswari had no answer to that. The poor thing just sat there embarrassed.

After a while Ramkali said, 'Go, say your prayers and go to sleep. Let's see if I can bring her.'

Bhubaneswari broke down once again, 'I feel it in my bones—they're not going to send her.'

Ramkali said nothing in response; he uttered the name of the goddess and turned the other way. After weeping for a long time, Bhubaneswari finally went to bed.

The next day, Ramkali started out for his daughter's house.

English lessons were suspended at the moment since Bhabatosh-master was away. He had gone to Calcutta for copies of the Second Book for his students. Therefore, Nabakumar was sort of free now. But Nabakumar, alas, had not the good fortune to dream away his leisure. There was no way he could enjoy the pleasure of resting at home, or eating, or sleeping. At home, throughout his waking hours, his heart would throb violently. Nor would he manage long stretches of sleep. Nabakumar could no longer sleep the undisturbed sleep of a beast. He would lie awake, then get up, sit, walk about, then, he would drink water, and lie down again. This was how he passed most of his time. During the day, however, he would busy himself with the occupation of the unemployed—fishing. He and his friend Nitai would fish all afternoon. And that was what they were doing when Nitai raised his eyes from the fishing rod and spotted the palki.

He asked, 'Who d'you think is coming in that fancy palki?'

Nabakumar turned to look and said, 'Really! That's neat! Don't think anyone's coming though, probably just passing through.'

But neither of them could turn away from the sight. With trembling hearts and fearful eyes they noted that the palki was coming towards them.

Nabakumar announced, 'Come let's run away!'

Nitai asked in amazement, 'Why?'

'Something tells me this is from Nityanandapur.'

'Really? Are you sure?'

'No. Just guessing. They must have sent it for their daughter. Nitai, I must run away.'

'What d'you mean? You can't leave now!'

The palki came towards them and stopped at the command of the occupant. The occupant beckoned them without getting off. They both got up from the ghat, trying hard to cover their bodies with the ends of their dhotis. 'Are you from this village?'

Their hearts quivered at the deep, solemn tone. Nabakumar did not really know his father-in-law, because he had not really looked at him at the time of his wedding, and after that he had been too scared to accept the two invitations he had received. Yet, something told him that 'this was he.'

It was indeed Ramkali. He asked once more in response to their nods, 'Are you from here, or are you visiting?'

Nitai stepped forward and said, 'I am visiting; Krishnadhan Datta is my uncle. I am Nitaichandra Ghosh. And he is the son of the Banerjis—Nabakumar Banerji—my friend.'

Nabakumar Banerji! A spark of lightning played in Ramkali's eyes, he felt confident for having guessed right. He inspected the boy once more. And noted his almost feminine fairness, his pink lips and sun-scorched red face. Then he got off his palki. And announced even more solemnly, 'I am Ramkali Chatterji.'

The boys quickly took the opportunity of bending and touching his feet, because they craved the relief of sitting down. Ramkali touched both their heads with a 'let it be'. He looked at Nitai and addressed Nabakumar, 'Since he is your friend, there's no harm in talking in front of him. Let me ask you, do you fish all day?'

Nabakumar's chin touched his chest. But the kayastha boy Nitai was cannier and quicker to respond. And bolder too. He quickly replied, 'No, we don't. Most days we go to Bhabatosh-master's house to study. Today he is—'

'What do you study?'

Nabakumar tried to pinch his friend and warn him not to mention that they study English. Who knew if the news of learning the language of the mlechchas would enrage this fearsome man. Fearsome? Yes, Nabakumar found him fearsome.

But Nitai hardly paid attention to the warning. Instead he veiled his pride with humility, 'Well, English.'

'English! That's good! How far have you read?'

'We've completed the First and Second Books. Now—'

'Good. I'm pleased to know that. But why haven't you gone for lessons today?'

The question was for Nabakumar, but Nitai answered, 'Our teacher has gone to Calcutta to get some books.'

'To Calcutta! Oh, I see. Well, I had something to say to you. I want to know, do you have any enemies in the village?'

'Enemies?' Nabakumar repeated in confusion. Well, if his mother were to be believed, everybody in the village was their enemy.

'Yes, enemy. Someone who wishes you ill. Who spreads false stories about you to harm you. Do you think there is any one like that?'

Nabakumar slowly shook his head to indicate a negative answer. But Nitai had already said something to the contrary, 'Well, in the village everyone is everyone's enemy. All the friendliness is superficial. And because of Naba's mother's temper—'

'Let that be,' Ramkali reproved mildly, and said in a thunder-deep voice, 'Can you recognize this handwriting? Can you tell me who wrote this?'

Ramkali took out the letter from his pocket and opened it just a little. But there was no need to open it. They knew whose writing it was—Bhabatosh-master's! And Nitai himself had provided the motivation. He had described in detail the painful life-story of the wife of the wretched Nabakumar to Bhabatosh-master, and the teacher had declared, 'All right. I shall try to remedy the situation. Nobody tolerates abuse of the fair sex in the White man's land.'

'So, do you know the hand?'

They both shook their heads vigorously. Meaning 'no'. Who would want to place his head inside the lion's mouth and say 'yes'?

'All right. I am going to your place. I hope your father is home.'

Leaving instructions for his palki-bearers, Ramkali said, 'Come, I shall walk the distance with you.'

'I think I will run and tell them at home.' Nitai broke into a run, abandoning his friend Nabakumar to deep waters.

Ramkali took a few steps forward, and suddenly questioned in a tone that was not normal, 'Has my daughter caused any problems at home?'

'I—I—what?' Nabakumar stuttered, 'No—no.' He began to sweat profusely and wiped his forehead with the end of his dhoti.

Ramkali added with a slight smile, 'No need to get agitated, I was merely asking out of curiosity. Anyway, let me tell you why I am here, since you're my son-in-law. There is a celebration coming up, and I'd like to take my daughter home. At the time of the wedding, you will be invited too, and you and your father can visit then. The women may want you to stay on for a couple of days, I shall speak to your parents about that. Be prepared to stay for a while.'

What could Nabakumar say in reply? He shivered and sweated and was tingling with fear and joy, hope and anxiety—all at the same time. As soon as he reached the door of the house, Nabakumar asked pathetically, 'May I leave now?'

'How strange, why should you leave?'

'Well, there's Nitai ...' He looked around and quickly dived to touch his father-in-law's feet.

Ramkali looked in his direction and sighed. He was studying all right, but would he grow up into a man?

At that moment, Nitai emerged from Nabakumar's house and Nilambar Banerji greeted Ramkali with a sly smile, 'Behai-mashai? Is anything the matter?'

TWENTY TWO

It was much before sundown, but Ramkali's palki was on its way back, with only Ramkali. The glow of the setting sun peeped in, and a late spring breeze naughtily raced in and out, like a boy at play. A dazzling joy permeated the sky, the breeze, the trees and the leaves. But Ramkali was not in a state to pay attention to all this. An intense sorrow was wailing inside him. He felt as though he had suffered a tremendous loss.

Had Ramkali been insulted by the uncultured Nilambar Banerji? Did it have to do with Ramkali not being able to bring his daughter with him? In actual fact, it had not been like that at all. Nilambar had been most cordial.

No sooner had he proposed 'taking his daughter with him', Nilambar had smiled amicably, 'Of course, that's excellent. She's your daughter, you can keep her as long as you wish—what can I say to that? I say, will somebody bring the almanac.'

Ramkali had said, 'I have already looked up the almanac. Tomorrow is trayadashi. It is auspicious. I shall take her tomorrow. It would be necessary to stay the night. Please arrange for me to pass the night at a brahmin's house. But kindly do not arrange for food. The palki-bearers are carrying their food with them.'

Nilambar had placed a palm against his chin in an effeminate way, and exclaimed, 'How can you say that! I have such a large house, how can you go elsewhere?'

Ramkali had stopped him with a grave smile, 'Behai-mashai, you are probably forgetting the ways of a Hindu Bengali. Does custom allow one to spend the night at the son-in-law's?'

Nilambar had laughed in agreement, 'That's true. But you can't be so unyielding when your daughter has a child.'

Ramkali had said even more gravely, 'Not just a child—a son! But why waste time talking about the distant future? Please arrange for me to meet my daughter.'

'Of course! That's simple enough! Hey Sadu, bring the daughter-in-law to the middle room, Behai-mashai wants to see her.'

So Nilambar's behaviour was not at fault. He could not have been more civil. In so many households the father or brother of the daughter-in-law were given food and water outside and sent off, they were not allowed to meet the girl. Besides, in some houses, even if one was permitted to meet the daughter after much pleading, someone always stood guard. Ramkali should have been gratified that he had been granted the wish as soon as he had asked.

But the human mind is really strange! Nilambar's manner of summoning Sadu seemed to Ramkali to be full of disdain. As though the words that better suited his tone were: 'Will somebody please give this beggar a handful of something. Just to stop him wailing!'

Ramkali had felt depleted, the whole ambience seemed desecrated. But there was nothing he could have done. He wondered if this 'Sadu' was a girl or a boy. He had heard that the man did not have a daughter. His swarming thoughts were interrupted by the rattling bolt.

Ramkali had gone inside. And inside that darkened room, he had noticed a girl-shape near the bed, her sari drawn over her face. The sari was a heavy brocade, probably draped around her for the occasion. A young woman with her face covered, stood outside. The woman quickly touched his feet as he entered and said in a whisper, 'Here, speak to her.' Then lowered her voice some more, 'Make sure you take her with you!' And she had disappeared through the door.

Even before he could figure out her indistinct words, a harsh muttering had reached his ears: 'Who asked you to leave her alone?'

And he had caught her response as well. 'How could I stand around like a puppet? It's so embarrassing!'

The harsh voice had responded, 'I see! A proper blushing rosebud we have here! Now she'll spill the beans to her father!'

The rejoinder to this had not reached Ramkali's ears, but his already embittered mind had turned numb and dull. The joy of seeing his daughter had gone limp. Satya, her sari drawn over her face, had silently touched her father's feet. And she had not omitted the custom of brushing her hand over her head after that.

But why had Ramkali suddenly felt unsettled? Why had Satya's action induced this wailing inside him? A lament that this level-headed man failed to control even now? Had he hoped that Satya would remain unchanged? That she would come running as soon as she saw him, perfunctorily touch his feet, and exclaim pertly, 'Now at last, he spares a thought for his daughter! What a heartless father! Hadn't come once to ask if his girl was dead or alive! Isn't it lucky that Punyi's getting married ...'

Or, had he thought that Satya had changed, that she had become totally different? That she would plunge on his chest and burst into silent tears? Tears that would soothe Ramkali's scorching heart.

But Ramkali was incapable of having such desires. Emotional indulgence of any kind went completely against his nature. He frowned on a wife who cried on account of absence or because she was meeting her husband after ages. He would probably have been disappointed had his daughter expressed her emotions in so cheap a manner.

But the human mind is fashioned out of an excess of desires that are hard to fathom. Often it knows not what it wants, but pronounces with great anguish, 'What is this? This isn't what I wanted at all!' That was exactly what the ever-unruffled Ramkali felt when he saw his daughter incarnated as a calm, poised married woman. At a loss for words, his low, solemn voice had uttered just a single question about Satya's well-being, 'Are you well?'

She had answered, her head lowered, 'Yes, I am. Is all well at home?'

How amazing! Was this the way all girls unremembered the shelter of their lives after they married? Smashed it up like a doll's house? Completely wiping it out of their minds. Was that the reason why Shakuntala disappeared from Rishi Kanva's ashram, and Sita was never seen again in her father Janaka's palace? The quill of our great poets had probably accepted this as the infallible truth and moved on with cruel indifference, without a backward look.

Such waves of thought eddied around in Ramkali's mind; this was totally unprecedented. He wondered if Satya merited the esteem he had credited her with all these days. Could it be that she was just an ordinary girl, vulnerable to change? He wondered if the rumour about her being battered was true, and if Satya was merely frightened. Girls who suffer a beating are petrified and lack the nerve to express themselves.

Ramkali's agitation had stemmed from a sense of disappointment in Satya. But he had controlled it and answered, 'Yes, all is well. Punyi is getting married on the sixteenth of Baisakh, so I wish to take you home.'

No sooner had he pronounced the words than a hammer had started up inside his chest.

Satya had not cried out, 'How wonderful you are, father!' Instead she had said, 'The wedding is in the middle of Baisakh—there is almost a month and a half between—they might object, Baba.'

Ramkali had concealed a deep sigh and said, 'Well, they haven't said "no".'

'They're just being civil. But we need to be considerate too, don't we? I wouldn't like to place them in trouble ...'

'So, you don't wish to go?'

Ramkali had had to conceal another sigh.

This time, Satya had raised her eyes and looked her father straight in the face. The end of her dazzling sari had slipped down to her shoulder, and her face framed by her unmanageable hair had become clearly visible. She had held her father's face in that gaze for a moment, and then, lowering her eyes, she had covered her head again, 'In actual fact it is as good as saying I don't wish to go. My mother-in-law isn't well, to leave all the responsibility with my sister-in-law ...'

Ramkali had asked with some surprise, 'Sister-in-law! Does Nabakumar have a sister?'

'Not his own, but she means much more than that. A cousin—the one who brought you in here.'

'I see.' Ramkali had terminated the discussion. 'If there's no way you can come, then there's nothing to be done. Therefore, I don't see the need to pass the night in the village. I shall leave right away. But before that, let me ask you one thing—you had learnt to read and write a little. I think you can read letters, can you make out what this letter means?' He had taken out the letter from his pocket.

Satya had seemed in no hurry to take the letter. But she had quietly asked, 'Whose letter?'

'That's what I don't know. May be you do.'

So Satya had taken the letter and read a few lines. God knows what her face looked like under the sari, but her voice had remained steady. She had said calmly, 'Couldn't a wise and learned man like you see that this is the work of an enemy.'

'Do you have such an enemy?'

'Who knows? Enemies always disguise themselves as friends.'

Satya had returned the letter without reading it through. Ramkali had put it back in his pocket and without concealing his sigh, had said, 'So there is no reason for you to feel unhappy here. God is good. I can console your mother with that.'

'Ma!' Satya had given a slight start, 'Does Ma know about this?'

'No. She knows nothing.' Ramkali had said in a slightly bantering tone, 'Just that she's been moping about her girl. Anyway, it is good to know that you are not treated badly. And I trust you are speaking the truth.'

Satya had looked up once more. A sad, reproachful look in her eyes. Then dropping her eyes she had said in a quiet, firm voice, 'When brass pots and pans are kept together they do clash and clang. These are human beings, after all. How can one guarantee that there'll be no clashes. But trust your daughter this much, Baba, she won't be unjust, nor will she suffer injustice.'

Ramkali had left. Satya had touched his feet once again.

But that was not the end.

'Leaving without your daughter, Behai-mashai?'

Ramkali had had to answer the question. Due to his inability at inventing a lie, he had had to face sneers and stunned queries.

Satya's father-in-law had said in his effeminate manner, a palm on his cheek, 'What! Your daughter doesn't want to visit you? How astonishing!'

Strange! They had been civil enough. So, why had Ramkali come away with the feeling that they were base and uncivilized? His son-in-law was a bit of a simpleton, he had disappeared after a fleeting appearance. He had seen the friend again, but not his son-in-law. It was clear that the friend felt no respect for Satya's parents-in-law, perhaps they were undeserving of respect.

Still, Ramkali had got a jolt. Because it looked as though Satya had got absorbed into this family. So much so that she had found the excuse of her mother-in-law's ailment and had refused to give in to the temptation of visiting her parents. In his whole, long life, Ramkali had never seen such a girl! And yet, it was hard to figure her out. Perhaps she could never be understood. Ramkali's daughter had moved far away from him, perhaps, she would move even farther and be lost to him forever! The gleaming star in Ramkali's sky, the little companion of the ever-lonely Ramkali already seemed to have disappeared forever.

His thoughts were suddenly interrupted. He noticed a figure running alongside his palki-bearers. When had he appeared? Where did he come from? Did he want to say anything? Ramkali commanded the bearers to stop. And then realized that it was Nitai, his son-in-law's friend.

'What's up?' Ramkali's face had glowed with expectation.

What had he expected? That Satya had sent for her father? And that this time, she would sob out, 'How could you listen to your daughter's words and ignore her sense of hurt? Did you have to leave in a huff just because I'd said "no" once?' So many thoughts had rushed about in his mind, but he had asked calmly, 'What's the matter?'

Nitai was panting. After getting his breath back, he said, 'Forgive my audacity, please! But I came to ask—why did you do this? Why are you leaving without your daughter? How could you lose out to Banerji-mashai?'

Ramkali turned crimson. Controlling himself with difficulty he replied, 'It's hard to forgive your audacity.'

'I know. But I had hoped that you'd take your daughter home—and you're not doing that! After this, you may not see her alive. She might commit suicide! Your daughter, after all, would rather break than bend.'

Ramkali suddenly reproached him sharply, in a low fierce tone,

'You appear to be from a respectable family, how is it you're so vulgar?'

Vulgar! Nitai stared uncomprehending.

Ramkali explained in his characteristic grave tone, 'To discuss another man's wife is another name for vulgarity.'

'All right!' Nitai had lowered his hurt face and touched his feet, 'There's nothing else I can say. But I wasn't the only impertinent person. Your son-in-law ...' Here, Nitai swallowed, 'He'd said he couldn't silently stand by and watch the killing of his wife. So I ...'

Nitai had slowly turned away. Ramkali had silently stared after him. Should he dismiss his pride and call him back? And question him about the incident and rush to his son-in-law's place? And after that tell them once more, 'I had made a mistake. My daughter is a child, her whims are of no importance. I shall take her with me.' But could Ramkali do that after what Satya had said? Could he tell her, 'You foolish girl! Stop being so silly, your mother is crying for you!' And add, 'If I go back without you, my heart will burst!' To what extent could Ramkali cast out pride?

'Let's go!' Ramkali ordered the palki-bearers. They began to move towards his village. With Ramkali inside, alone and dazed.

Slowly the shock had faded, giving way to the real cause—Ramkali had not lost to Nilambar Banerji, he had lost to his own flesh and blood! Satya had defeated him in a battle of wits. She had shown her father how happy and contented she was at her in-laws'. For that reason it had not been difficult for her to cast aside the sweetest attractions of her father's home in favour of duties to her in-laws. Satya could barter her life for her father's peace of mind.

And Ramkali? Ramkali was disturbed by Satya's strategy, he was blind with hurt. But his pride forced him to return to his village. There was no way he could go back now.

<hr>

Well, it was hardly untrue that the letter was the 'work of an enemy'. For it would be unfair to say that Elokeshi abused her daughter-in-law with daily beatings. Just that one day—while braiding her hair. Of course, she had picked up a small log of firewood hoping to quench her anger, but she never did have the pleasure of breaking it on her daughter-in-law's back. The odious wretch of a daughter-in-law had snatched the wood from her hand and forcefully declared, 'Look, you are an elder, behave like one. Or you shall suffer a lot of pain. You don't know me, so you think you can do anything. Just give up such thoughts.'

Before she could finish, Elokeshi had let out a wail and gathered the neighbours around. A commotion had started. By then Satya had exited the stage. Sadu had checked the curiosity of the shocked neighbours with something about her aunt being affected by the 'warm spring air'. She had softly whispered it to them, individually.

Then, she had quietly told her aunt, 'Don't step on a serpent's tail, aunt. Your daughter-in-law is far from ordinary.' Elokeshi had almost cursed the life out of Sadu and shouted that the villagers would witness the way in which she would drive her son's wife out after shaving her head and dousing her with yoghurt.

In actuality, she never managed to do all that. In response to this, her son's wife had clearly informed Sadu, 'If that will earn her any glory, tell your aunt to do it. But let her also figure out whom the villagers will aim their insults at.'

Elokeshi had rushed up screaming, 'Come here, let me slaughter you! Let the blood flow! I can get hanged afterwards. Who has seen a married woman with such a sharp tongue!'

Satya had silently brought the large cleaver from the kitchen and held it out to Elokeshi saying, 'Go on, then. I, at least, won't be around to see who is disgraced.'

It was strange indeed, that after that incident Elokeshi had turned cold. No further words escaped her lips. After staring at the shining blade of the cleaver, she had slowly moved away. Since then Elokeshi had stopped shouting and screaming and had resorted to silence. At the same time, she would exhort Nilambar to seize Satya's jewellery and send her back to her parents' on some excuse or other. If only she could send her off once, she would never ever bring this shrew back. But the days passed trying to find an excuse. And then, out of the blue, Ramkali had arrived.

It was as if Elokeshi had been handed the moon! She had made up her mind that she would get rid of the girl for ever. For in the mean time, Elokeshi had seen another girl, about seven or eight years old, a harmless type whose father had promised to wrap his daughter in Chinese gold. Elokeshi had been repeating this mantra to her husband continually.

Nilambar had readily consented. He had not thought in his wildest dreams that the daughter-in-law herself would refuse to go! Elokeshi had glared at her husband as soon as Ramkali left, 'Did you see that? What a cunning shrew! Didn't I tell you, she's a trickster, that girl.'

Nilambar agreed, 'Yes, I can see that.'

'Then tell me, why must I live with her? As it is, Sadu wears me down to the bones, and on top of that a daughter-in-law like this! How similar they are! All the more reason why I want to drive her out. The thing is ...' Elokeshi lowered her voice, 'I haven't yet allowed her to share a bed with my son. When this impudent hussy sleeps with her husband she'll just take over. My Naba will no longer remain mine. At least, my friend's niece is slightly dim-witted.'

Nevertheless, Nilambar had been powerless to scream at the departing Ramkali, 'Here! If you know what's best for you, take your daughter, or we'll have to drive her out of here!'

Nilambar had one flaw: no matter how brave he appeared, he was incapable of speaking with authority.

Elokeshi had slapped her own face and said, 'What can I say—Behai is a man after all, it doesn't look good if I talked with him. Or I'd have given it to the cunning father and his detestable daughter!'

Elokeshi, however, had failed in her resolve of not talking to her daughter-in-law. She had rushed to Satya who was making paan, 'So why didn't you go with your father?'

Satya had raised her face once, and lowered it again.

'Answer me! Why didn't you go for your aunt's wedding?'

Satya had replied with a quiet seriousness, 'There's lots of time before the wedding.'

'Oh, but your doting father had come nevertheless!'

'Don't speak about my father in such a disrespectful tone.' So saying, Satya had covered the paans with a wet cloth in the holder and put them away.

Elokeshi was struck speechless with blinding rage; not finding any other response, she had said, 'You wretched, loathsome creature! What is it you're scheming, eh? Why won't you go to your father's? Why do you want to sit around and torture me?'

Satya had turned, and fixing an intense gaze on her mother-in-law, she had said, 'Since this wretched creature was given a bride's welcome into this house with proper rituals, you will have to carry this millstone around your neck all your life.'

———

Nabakumar had received the news from a shattered messenger. Nitai told him, 'Your father-in-law all but reduced me to dust.'

Nabakumar had stopped listening. He himself had embarked on this exceedingly courageous mission to rescue his battered wife! But he was surprised by his own reaction on hearing about Ramkali's departure. How utterly surprising that a wave of joy should be welling up inside him because his wife had not left. Nabakumar could hardly fathom this mystery. He had no idea that yet another surprise awaited him.

It was not very late, a little after dusk. Elokeshi had already found refuge in her bed, as was her wont, and Nilambar was out on his nightly prowl, as was his habit. Sadu was in the kitchen cooking by the light of a lamp she had placed on a piece of wood to give it some height. Nabakumar was cautiously crossing the courtyard when a muted but firm voice called out from near a door, 'Please wait here.'

This voice did not belong to either of his parents, or to Sadu. Who else could it be? Except for the one who dwelt in Nabakumar's dreams? They could hardly see each other clearly in the dark. Only the voice could be heard, 'Who sent the letter to Nityanandapur describing my tragic fate?'

Needless to say, Nabakumar had turned into a statue. A figure that can never possess the faculty of speech.

'Why isn't there an answer?'

Nabakumar replied in a muffled voice, 'What can I say?'

'You can give a clear answer. Who wrote to my father?'

It was beyond Nabakumar's capacity to remain silent before this tone. He somehow managed, 'You're speaking to me. Who knows who will see us.'

'That's for me to worry about. Give me a true answer instead of dodging my question.'

Nabakumar swallowed hard, scratched his neck and broke into a sweat, 'How should I know about the letter? What letter?'

'Look, don't you lie to me! Even hell won't have a place for you!' Satyabati hissed, 'I am certain that you did this.'

At once, Nabakumar's self-image as a man, and as a husband felt affronted. He retorted fiercely, 'What if I did? You were suffering, weren't you?'

Out of the darkness the sharp low-pitched voice answered, 'My suffering is not something to announce to the beat of drums to all relatives. How can anyone who tars his own mother's reputation call himself educated? The whole world spurns those who betray their own. Keep that in mind in future.'

The faint image by the door disappeared into the darkness of the room. The echo of her voice faded away too, but Nabakumar stood transfixed. It was as though somebody had upturned a pot of ink over the sweet, romantic and fervent imaginings that Nabakumar's shy mind had harboured for so long about his first conversation with his wife.

In fact, Nabakumar's very first communication with his wife was over.

TWENTY THREE

Everybody in the entire locality came to know about Satya's shameless behaviour. She had refused to go with her father when he had come to take her home, even though her parents-in-law had given permission—this incredible piece of news spread like fire on straw roofs from this locality to that. The married women of the village had heard many tales of Satya's notoriety, but now they thought that she had to be a complete lunatic. Poor Nabakumar! His father had burdened him with a mad wife because he lusted after the father's property.

But this sort of discussion about Satya had taken place earlier, in her father's village. When word had spread that Doctor Ramkali had been reluctant to send her, but his daughter had insisted on going, it had been a real scandal.

Bhubaneswari had wet the floor with her tears; Satya's friends had frozen in amazement but Satya had remained unshaken. But she had responded when Sharada had told her, 'It's like taking an axe and chopping off your own feet, Thakurji!'

She had replied, 'Well, my father placed the axe on my neck when he married me off at eight, didn't he? So what's new?'

'But you could have stayed another year.'

'What difference would that make? They've threatened with another marriage or something, in which case I'd have to suffer a co-wife for the rest of my life.'

Sharada had sighed and fallen silent.

When a whimpering Bhubaneswari had held her daughter's hand and begged, 'Don't you have any feelings for us, Satya?'

Satya had responded, 'I don't need to announce my feelings to the whole wide world, do I?'

'Then why did you offer to go?'

'No point asking that. Isn't there a proverb that says, "Oh my mother, how foolishly you weep; just stop and think once, whose house you keep!" That's exactly how it is.'

But Bhubaneswari had not grasped that, she had said, 'My parent's place is nearby, but your in-laws' place is many miles away!'

She had not managed to complete her sentence.

Suddenly, Satya had floundered and burst into tears, 'Why hadn't you thought of that earlier? I am your only daughter. If you had any feelings, would you have sent me so far away, out of sight, away from the village to some strange land? Here's Punyi, just a year younger to me, and she's happily prancing about! And you gave me away ages ago!' She had stopped to clear her throat, 'If you hadn't given me away, could they have dragged me away like this? My father hardly cared for his daughter, he earned merit by performing the gauri-daana. I'm the hard-hearted daughter of a heartless father, that's all!' And she had flung herself on the floor and sobbed for a long time.

But that had not stopped anything. Ramkali and his daughter were similar in nature. Once they had given their word, the matter could not be raised a second time. A hurricane of criticism had raged in Satya's presence and behind her father's back.

This time, it was different. Most of the discussions took place behind Satya's back. Only Sadu had told her, 'You're really something! I don't know if I should jeer at you or fall at your feet out of admiration.'

In reply, Satya had bent down and touched Sadu's feet, 'Goddess save us! You're an elder, why should you fall at my feet? Better for you to curse me—I've faced that all my life!'

Would Satya reveal the raging seas within her? Because inside her, there was indeed a sea rocked by a storm. Even so, she had not broken down after her father had left. She had busied herself with the wicks and the oil for the lamps. Then, after a wash at the ghat where she had also washed her clothes, she had filled a huge pot and brought it in. After that, she had watered the tulsi plant, lit the lamp in the puja room and blown on the conch-shell. Finally, changing into dry clothes, she had started work in the kitchen.

Nowadays, Satya cooked the evening meal. A prerogative she had earned after persuading Sadu. But there was no one to witness the tears that flowed as she cooked. No matter how many times she counted, the number of days to the middle of Baisakh seemed incorrect every time.

Did the 'middle of Baisakh' finally surface in Satya's life resplendent and joyous? No. Satya had no such pleasure. She could not go to Punyi's wedding. Because around that time her mother-in-law had a serious bout of blood dysentry that nearly killed her. That bed-ridden figure, with a quilt wrapped around her, had screeched at Sadu, 'What did you say, Sadu? Is the wretched girl doing a jig to go to her father's? She refused when the loving father had come, hadn't she? Does she want to go now, when I'm dying? Just tell her that she can't. And get rid of the person who's come to fetch her.'

But Sadu was not one to let past a repartee just because her aunt was dying. She retorted 'They had fed and showered your messenger with gifts, and you're just going to get rid of their's? Wonderful! It will certainly earn you honour! I suggest you send her for a few days at least. She's young—besides, I've heard that this aunt is her childhood friend …'

Elokeshi had said feebly, 'Then let her go. No need for you to stay either! And before you leave, you might as well bring a knife and slit my throat!'

Sadu did not bring a knife, nor did she leave herself. She began to arrange for Satya's departure. This time, Nabakumar proved to be the stumbling block. He suddenly took on the role of the 'master of the house' and declared in no uncertain terms, 'Nobody's going anywhere. My mother's dying here and people want to go to an aunt's wedding. No need to fan false hopes. Nobody's going.'

The elder couple were delighted with Nabakumar's announcement and said dispassionately, 'What can we say? if Naba refuses …'

But Sadu had persisted. She had said, 'But you don't dance to Naba's tune all the time, do you?'

It had not worked. Elokeshi's curses were enough to chase even ghosts away.

Satyabati had said, 'I had promised my father that I'd go ...'

Nabakumar had responded indirectly; he had told Sadu, 'If anyone wants to humiliate us, let them go.'

Sadu had looked at his face for a minute and burst out laughing, 'Speaking like a wise man, are we? Just tell me the truth. You don't share a bed with your wife yet, but you don't want to part with her, eh?'

Sadu's words had wiped out Nabakumar's authority. He had moved away in embarrassment. I suppose he had wondered how Sadudi could guess everything!

Finally, however, it was Satyabati who declined when Sadu had nearly resolved it. Nabakumar would go for the sake of courtesy, and his wife would accompany him for three days, they would return as soon as the new bride had left for her in-law's. But Satyabati had suddenly said, 'I don't want alms! In three days I won't manage to meet everyone at home properly, leave alone the people in the locality. What's the use? People will think that I just arrived and left—how awful!'

'Listen to that! This is like the naked wishing for jewels! You weren't even getting these alms. At least, you'll get to see the wedding.'

'Best not to see it this way. Whoever wishes to go for the sake of being civil can go.'

'Of course, he won't go by himself!' Sadu said and rightly too. For Nabakumar begged with folded hands, 'Spare me!'

So, Nilambar had had to keep up appearances. He had handed over a letter to Ramkali's man, 'Nabakumar's mother is on her deathbed, so it is not possible for anyone to go. I am sending a gift of two rupees with the bearer of this letter for the occasion.'

On receiving the letter, Ramkali had been silent for a long time. Then he had said quietly, 'Keep the money for a cup of tea. And ... just let everyone inside know that Satya's mother-in-law's dying, so it wasn't possible for her to come.'

TWENTY FOUR

Nilambar Banerji finished his evening prayers, and after popping some prasad into his mouth with some water, he gave a shout, 'Sadu! Don't bother with the snack, I don't feel too well.'

Sadu was mixing salt and oil with roasted rice for her uncle. There were also various homemade sweets, which would do nicely. Nilambar had become a light eater these days.

His yell brought her out, 'What's the matter, Mama?'

'Can't really tell, I just don't feel hungry.' And Nilambar slipped on his kurta, threw a shawl over his shoulder, and went out as usual.

Satyabati also came out and remarked, 'If he's feeling unwell, why did he go out on a chilly night like this?'

Sadu suppressed a smile, 'You could have asked him!'

'Listen to that! As if I'd open my mouth!'

'Of course, you wouldn't.' Sadu smirked.

Quite abruptly, Satya grasped Sadu's hand and voiced her suspicions, 'Why do you smile like that whenever he goes out? Where does he go?'

Sadu replied pleasantly, 'Listen to that, as if I smile! Perhaps he goes to play cards or something.'

'When he's not well? Can't he stay away on a stormy day? Why can't you stop him?'

'Stop him! Goodness! From such a demonic attraction?' Once more Sadu concealed a smile.

'If I could talk to him, I would have got him out of this deadly addiction.'

'Why don't you try then? And if you can't say it yourself—speak to your husband. He's a good son—may be he'll cure his father of his craving!' Sadu no longer attempted to hide her smile, she laughed aloud.

Satya did not really take it to heart, but she did spot an obvious amusement in Sadu's tone. The possibility that her father-in-law's addiction had little to do with cards took firm root in her. And that was the first question she raised when she went into her room at night, 'Tell me, where does your father go every night?'

For quite some time now, Satya had earned her right to the night. Mainly because Sadu had worked on her aunt, driven by the tenderness she felt for her cousin. Otherwise, Satya was not one to bring it up.

Steeped as he was in dreams of his new bride, Nabakumar was hardly prepared for such a question. So he fumbled, 'Where else? Didn't you know?'

'I wouldn't have asked if I did.'

Nabakumar turned solemn, 'Well, he's an elder. It is best not to discuss him.'

Satya frowned, 'It's wrong, of course, to spread slander about an elder, but it can't be wrong to just talk about him.'

Nabakumar's gravity deepened, 'But isn't it slander—when a brahmin visits a low-caste locality, and accepts food and drink from them? Hardly does one proud, does it?'

He visits a low-caste locality! Eats and drinks with them! It was as if Satya's husband had taken her and dashed her against the floor. So Satya stumbled too.

'What do you mean?'

Without sparing any thought for her tender age, Nabakumar answered her; because he believed that infinite wisdom resided in a wife. He remarked resignedly, 'What can I do if you can't understand? I can't speak too plainly about my father! After all, they say, "Father is heaven itself." Otherwise, my whole body flares up when I see that Ullashi Bagdini on the streets! But there's nothing I can do. I have to calm myself down because she's like a mother to me, after all.'

Disclosing everything about his much respected father, even as he claimed otherwise, Nabakumar sighed in relief and tried to pull his wife close. But what was this? Why had that charming doll become so stiff? Satya's entire body seemed frozen. Deep inside, her heart too had hardened with some unknown fear. A fear similar to the one that had paralyzed her a long time ago with dark tidings about that woman of Katoa—Shankari. But that day, there was fear mingled with darkness. Now, a fierce, blinding light flashed in that darkness. Satya was no longer an innocent girl; she was wiser about the world. Flashes of disgust kept pulsating through that darkness of fear.

After several vain attempts, Nabakumar despaired, 'What's wrong with you? Here I am waiting the whole day to talk to you! How I look forward to the joy and laughter!'

Satya said huffily, 'As though joy and laughter are pots and pans you can order and buy from the potter's! What if I'm not in the mood?'

Still, the foolish Nabakumar vainly attempted to joke, 'But why get so upset about it? It isn't as though I've fallen for a low-caste woman.'

'Stop it!' The harsh rebuke resonated against the walls of the closed room. The silent winter's night permitted one to raise one's voice higher than usual. But to tell the truth, Satya was not too coy, and often her voice would carry.

After that, Satya pulled the cover over herself and turned her back to him, 'Aren't you ashamed to joke about a filthy thing like this? Let me tell you clearly, don't you blame me if I don't feel respect for your father after this.'

All Nabakumar's attempts to talk were futile after that. And he cursed himself in silence. What an ass he was! He should have said, 'I don't know where my father goes.' After all, he knew his wife. She could be as placid as the Ganga when in a good mood; when provoked, she was like a house in a blaze. Such a headstrong girl!

Once when she had caught Nabakumar lying, she had stopped talking to him for five days! Finally, Nabakumar had consulted his friend, Nitai, and recited a shloka from the scriptures to prove that it was not a sin to lie to one's wife. Only then had his wife unlocked her mouth—not to accept the holy texts, but to volubly protest against them. She had said passionately, 'Don't you go quoting the scriptures to me! I've no appetite for sacred texts which say it isn't a sin to lie. Isn't a wife a human being in whom god's spirit resides? As if I'll ever believe a word you say after this!' But at least the argument had forced the doors to open. Who knew what would happen this time?

And now, Satya kept thinking, 'For shame! Is this what my father-in-law is like!' The person she was supposed to address respectfully? She had noticed his various flaws—his pettiness, his meanness, his selfishness—which equally matched his wife Elokeshi's qualities. Until now, Satya had accepted all that, and had thought to herself that there were not very many people like her father in this world. But now, her blood shuddered with revulsion. What a base craving, at his age too! The most astonishing thing was that everybody knew about it! Only Satya had been stupid and obtuse, that was why she had not fathomed the meaning of her father-in-law's nightly outings. She had noticed that he always came back long after they had all gone to bed. She had not understood the implication. No, she could not treat such a father-in-law with respect, no matter what.

Suddenly a wave of tears wracked her whole body, and finally, an intense ache of accusation against her father welled up inside her. Satya had seen a lot of narrowness and pettiness after coming into this household. She had suffered it all, explaining it away as manifestations of their ignorance. But today, the depravity of the old man seemed to shake her completely. So Satya, who would never cry when she was harassed, wet her pillow with tears saying, 'Baba! You had just one daughter! Not ten, or five, just the one! How could you choose such a house to marry her into? With all your wisdom, was this the way you judged?'

After crying for a long time, at some point Satya fell asleep.

But a daughter-in-law never has the privilege of sleeping till late just because she has not slept well at night. The next morning, a cheerless Satya, pristine after a bath, entered the room, as was her routine. As she began to make the sandal paste, in her accustomed way, a question flashed through her like lightning: were all her rituals of making sandal paste, picking flowers and filling the room with incense worth anything at all? It would be Nilambar Banerji who would perform the puja with these ingredients. Since he was prone to colds he would not even bathe in the mornings, he would just wrap the silk cloth around himself and sit for his rituals. But even if he had taken a bath, would it have purified the body, the mind and the soul that were all tainted? Satya stopped working and sat silently, resting her face on her knees and ignoring the flowers and the leaves.

After a while, Saudamini came in for some work, 'What is this, why are you sitting like this?'

Satya kept silent. Sadu anxiously came up to the threshold and asked, 'Are you unwell?'

Satya shook her head.

'Then, are you missing home? Really, it has been a long time—'

Satya suddenly stood up, 'Have you ever seen me feel homesick?' Sadu was her elder sister-in-law, so with her she had the licence to say this.

Sadu chuckled, 'Well, I must admit, I haven't. Have you had a fight with your husband, or something?'

'What nonsense! As if I'd lose heart over such trivial things! I don't feel happy—I shall not work in the puja room from now on.'

Sadu was taken aback by this unexpected declaration, 'What do you mean?'

'Just what I said. I don't want to speak about an elder, but I no longer wish to put the puja things together for my father-in-law.'

Sadu's hand went up to her gaping mouth in awe, 'Do you think she'll leave you in one piece when she gets to know?'

Satya turned her face and said drily, 'I no longer wish to remain in one piece—not in this household, anyway!'

Sadu tried to the assess what was wrong. What kind of talk was this? She was sure that her question last night about her father-in-law lay at the root of it all. Perhaps she now knew the answer. But Sadu could not figure out how the two were connected. Nor was she expected to. Sadu had grown up with such things and they meant little to her. She had witnessed so much of it around her that she was fed up. It was beyond her ken that anybody could get agitated because of the debauchery of a man who was not even her husband! But Sadu was quick-witted, so instead of taking the discussion further she said, 'All right then, I'll take a quick bath and come and work here—let's change places.'

'Don't be angry, please, I cannot accept it in my mind. Show me what you were doing, I'll do that.' With that, Satya actually stepped out of the room.

But even if Sadu could manage the chores, there was one particular duty that the daughter-in-law had to perform every morning. Nobody else could undertake that on her behalf. Touching the feet of her parents-in-law first thing in the morning was one of Satya's daily duties. Such were the instructions Elokeshi had conveyed through Sadu. Satya, of course, had accepted it so far. But today, Satya was dauntless and resolved. There was no way she was going to touch the feet of that 'polluted' man. Let them do what they liked! He may be an elder, but what could she do when an elder behaved disgracefully.

Usually, Elokeshi went into her room after her bath. She had no household responsibilities as such. There was Sadu, and Satya, to take those on. And Elokeshi was deeply devoted to the gods and the brahmins. Nilambar too practically stayed in that room all day reading the *Chandi*, and reciting shlokas about Shiva. All their intimate conversation too, took place in that room. After all, Elokeshi had no control over the crucial time for such conversations. The prospect of talking inside the mosquito-net had never been hers to enjoy.

This was the room Satya entered every day in order to touch their feet. But today she was not to be seen. After a while, Elokeshi called Sadu and asked irritably, 'The princess is not to be seen today. Where's her highness?'

It did not take Sadu long to figure it out. She began to feel a little annoyed by Satya's unseemly mulishness; restraining herself she said, 'Where else? She's somewhere that side ...' Sadu gazed at that imagined other side.

Elokeshi said, 'Am I to understand that the daily ritual of showing respect is going to be dropped from now on?'

Nilambar pricked up his ears in the middle of his reading. By then Sadu had vanished. She rushed out and said, 'What is this? Haven't you gone and touched their feet as yet?'

Satya had finished the work at hand and was sitting dejectedly. She replied without turning her head, 'No.'

'Your mother-in-law's just noticed it. Go and get it over with.'

As though Satya had forgotten and Sadu was just reminding her.

Satya replied solemnly, 'If they're sitting together, it doesn't look good if I don't touch one person's feet, does it? Let her come this way, I'll touch her feet then.'

Sadu could no longer conceal her irritation. She burst out, 'You do carry things too far! Show me a man who doesn't have bad habits? Is everyone as god-like as your father? Will the father-in-law not get the respect that's due to him because of a flaw in his character?'

'No point in bringing up my father. I can't do what my mind refuses to accept. He is fallen. He shouldn't be performing puja at all!' Satya was breathless with agitation.

Sadu was speechless for a while. After standing bewildered for a minute, she said slowly, 'I haven't learnt to read and write like you, so I don't understand everything. I only know that no matter what others do, I should not fail in my duties.'

'Surely, duty isn't about displaying respect even when one is feeling deeply disrespectful inside!'

Sadu was at a loss for a quick repartee; she attempted to say something, but the tigress had come out and was standing right behind her. Elokeshi was suspicious. She had sensed that something was wrong. So she entered the battlefield with a roar, 'What was that about duty and all, Sadu?'

Sadu fell silent. So did Satya.

Elokeshi spoke again, 'Why are both of you silent? What were you two conspiring about? You, Sadu, ungrateful wretch? You gobble my food and turn my daughter-in-law against me, eh? When will you leave my household in peace?'

This was nothing new. This was the pitch at which Elokeshi

usually spoke. Sadu never ever protested, but today, all of a sudden, she became incensed, 'I have never conspired with your daughter-in-law, I always give her good advice. Let her tell you herself.'

Satya, of course, was not supposed to speak before her mother-in-law. But Satya often broke rules, so she burst out, 'That's right! And I shall say that a thousand times! She has always given me good advice. But what if my heart cannot accept that advice as just? It's good that you've come here,' so saying Satya bent down to touch her feet. 'After all, you're a virtuous woman.'

The 'virtuous' woman, of course, was completely taken aback, and she asked, 'What's the meaning of all this, Sadu?'

'As if I know,' Sadu answered sulkily. 'Let her explain if she can.'

She was really peeved today. What was this! Making a mountain out of a molehill! Just asking for trouble! How could that slip of a girl even think of things that nobody on earth had heard, spoken, or thought of? And such guts too! Satya's daring would make Sadu faint in fear, but nothing matched today's act. But Sadu heard as she stepped out, 'It's terribly shameful for me to mention it, but I must say that I no longer wish to touch his feet. I did, until I heard …'

Sadu did not dare hear the conclusion. She picked up a pot and quite purposelessly started out towards the ghat.

She returned quietly, after a long while. It was absolutely still, not a sound could be heard. Had somebody died? It was like the silence of a cremation ground!

Sadu entered the courtyard and was in for another shock. She saw a couple of bundles near the door of the central room, and noticed her aunt and uncle tying up a basket with cloth. The basket was full, of course, though it was not quite obvious with what. This was completely unexpected. Sadu's blood froze. Had they packed so much in so little time! What could be the reason? Were they leaving because they could no longer cope with their daughter-in-law?

That was the exact reason. Yet another of Elokeshi's whims. As soon as she caught Sadu's eye, she said, 'You and your sister-in-law can keep the house running perfectly, the sinners are leaving.'

Sadu put down the pot, and said, 'Have you lost your mind?'

'Nobody can scold people who've lost their minds! But you can ask anyone you know, if this wouldn't make them lose their heads.'

'She's just crazy. Don't pay her any attention!' Sadu lowered her voice.

'Crazy, my foot! She's nothing but a vile, venomous snake! Don't you try to plead on her behalf. A respectable man like him was ready to kill himself after hearing her taunts. I begged and implored, and now we are going off to our guru. We'll accept whatever fate has in store!' Elokeshi tightened the rope round the bundle.

Sadu felt the urge to rush to Satya and plead, 'Quickly beg forgiveness if you know what's good for you!' But she knew it would be useless. Satya would not bend even if god himself descended from heaven and implored. Satya had so many good qualities, but had this one terrible flaw of being obstinate. Too wilful for a woman! Sadu found today's incident indefensible. So she decided to try a different tack.

'But why should you be the ones to leave? The house doesn't belong to your son and his wife, does it?'

'We don't want to stay where we have to see their faces, that's all!' At last Nilambar opened his mouth to speak, and this was what came out.

'But you can't leave just like that! I've put on the rice. You'll have to have your meal.'

But it really was a hollow strategy, a bit like building a dam of sand across the ocean. For though Sadu had put on the rice, she no longer knew what state the kitchen was in. The wood might have burnt itself out, and the fire could have died by now.

Nilambar let out a fierce shout and stamped his feet, 'Rice! D'you think I'll accept water in this house?'

Sadu's heart trembled. She could have talked some more with her aunt, but not with her uncle! Though she knew enough about his affair with Ullashi, the terror with which she regarded her uncle had not waned one bit. It was as though Satya had chanced upon some magic chant with which to overcome fear, and had found the strength to say that he had violated custom and should not be performing puja!

Sadu did not have the capacity to think too deeply about anything; soon she began to wonder why Naba was taking so long at the market. And why was market-day on so foul a day. What should Sadu do? Should she go and plead with Satya? Or, should she shut the kitchen and just rest somewhere? After all, why should she be scared—it was not her fault that Nabakumar's parents were leaving.

But does courage breed courage? And daring give rise to daring? For Sadu suddenly took on a different tone, 'Very well then, I'll go and pour water on the fire.' So saying, she left.

But what a strange thing! She found Satya in the kitchen cleaning the spinach, as if nothing had happened. Sadu could not bear it any longer, 'What's the point of doing this infernal work? Who'll eat all this, eh? They're getting ready to leave.'

Satya's reply truly astounded Sadu, 'It isn't so easy to leave. Nobody packs all their belongings in bundles if they truly want to renounce the world. Don't worry uselessly. Nobody's going anywhere. I've taken care of the fire—now just watch.'

And Satya was right.

In the end, the old couple gave up their plans of departure and stayed on. Sadu, of course, had to undertake excessive pleading to get them to eat. But basically they stayed because Nabakumar repented. He said he wanted to dash his head at their feet and let a river of blood spurt forth. Apart from which, he placed his hands on his mother's feet and vowed to castigate his wife. Powerless before their son's distress, they shelved their plans of leaving, at least for the present.

Naba did what he had never done till now—he spoke to his wife during the day! But did he finally get to control his wife with scolding, flattery or supplication? He never did manage to make her say, 'What I did was wrong.' When he threatened suicide, Satya had finally said, 'I'm disgusted with everything. God alone knows why you weren't born a woman! All right, if you want me to touch his feet without feeling any respect for him, I'll start that charade from tomorrow.'

At night, though, Nabakumar became a different man. He could hardly endure the terrible pain of not talking with his beautiful young wife. So he admitted to her, 'I had to scold you just to show my parents, or they'd say, "the boy is henpecked!"'

'I don't feel like talking tonight, please excuse me.' Satya had turned away. Then after some time, she had sat up all of a sudden, 'I want to go to Calcutta.'

Nabakumar was taken aback, 'Calcutta! Go to Calcutta? I can see you've gone mad!'

'Why, do only mad people go to Calcutta? Is your teacher mad?'

'Comparing yourself with my teacher! He is a man, goes and comes on his own, stays with a friend. Which of these things can you do?'

Satya had retorted with passion, 'I'm not a man, but you are! Can't you go? I'll go with you. We'll take up a house.'

Nabakumar answered in a daze, 'I haven't gone mad like you! How can I leave my parent's home and go and live in Calcutta? And why should I?'

'I'll tell you why. To see that there is another world beyond Baruipur!'

'And why do I need to see that?'

Satya had said with biting contempt, 'Need! Staying in this hole you'll never have the courage to understand that need!'

Nabakumar could not make sense of that, so he had repeated a major argument forcefully, 'If a woman goes to Calcutta, what'll become of caste?'

Satya replied gravely, 'If your father can keep his caste, if he still has the right to touch the holy stone, I too shall not lose caste if I go to Calcutta.'

'Don't go on and on! It's easy for a man to remain pure, it's not the same for a woman. You'll have to drink water that is stored in leather bags.'

'I'll drink that if I have to. We'll manage the way other brahmins manage in the city. The second son of the Haldar family has gone to Calcutta, hasn't he?'

'He hasn't taken his wife.'

'His wife's dead, how could he have taken her?'

'Well, he's gone with a job.'

Satya said resolutely, 'And so will you.'

'Me?' Nabakumar laughed scornfully in reply, 'You think I can work in Calcutta?'

'Why not? Has anyone in this village learnt as much English as you?'

On any other day, Naba would have melted at this endorsement from his wife, but today he had lost the joy and the music. So he said, 'That is not enough ...'

Satya asked with a frown, 'Well, what else does one need?'

At that critical moment, the truth spurted out of Naba, 'One needs courage, of course.'

After a moment of silence, Satya said, as she lay herself down, 'All right, I'll provide that.'

But this immense assurance also failed to work. Nabakumar demanded angrily, 'Why should I be employed by another? Do I lack the means to feed myself? If we are careful, we can take it easy—d'you know that? Why should I be a slave?'

Satya answered solemnly, 'Perhaps to unlearn this desire to take it easy.'

The argument had continued for a while. In the end Nabakumar had revealed, 'It just isn't my cup of tea, let me tell you clearly!'

To which Satya responded spiritedly, 'And let me tell you clearly too—I will, will, will go to Calcutta! Just to check out for myself if a woman is struck down by thunder when she steps into the city!'

Had Satya managed to find that out for herself? Soon? No, she had to wait for a long time to see all that. After all, a damp wick takes a long time to dry and crackle into a flame. By then Satya had become a mother of two boys.

TWENTY FIVE

The world courses ahead fettered to the ceaseless sequence of the four seasons. Though they are governed by this rule-driven world, men possess neither the certainty of rules nor the guarantee of sequences. Neither god, nor nature, can ever provide them with the assurance of definite rules. Therefore, a man who is hale and hearty, can never confidently declare before going to bed that he will see the light of dawn the next day. For he can never be sure that he will not be struck down by lightning on a perfect spring day, or that an unrelenting downpour will not wipe out the dazzling autumn light. Man can never take anything for granted. He can never know when the claws of fearsome death will tear apart the home he had built with so much hope. Or when a sudden accident or some incurable disease will render that home worthless. Nobody can guess where the god of lawlessness dwells with his infallible laws. Even so, the chain of accidents at Ramkali's house astounded the whole village.

People were not really baffled when the large thatch outside was burnt to cinders. Though the raging flames could be seen as a cruel blow of fate, it was fairly clear that human carelessness, or conspiracy, had played some sort of role. This was how it had happened—

Most of the neighbours lit their chullahs with fire from the Chatterji's house. Most often, they would come at a time that suited them and take a burning log of wood from the Chatterji's kitchen. Their chullahs would be ready, filled with dried palm leaves, and crispy dung-cakes, bits of kindling and timber; they just needed to touch the pile with the flaming log, that was all.

At least three or four chullahs were lit in Ramkali's house. So there was no reason why the neighbours should go through the hassle of keeping a fire burning in their houses. It was too much trouble. One needed to keep tinder and rub together flintstones—a waste of time! This was more convenient. And that day, as usual, around mid-morning, the widowed daughter of the Ghosal's, Toru, was carrying a flaming piece of firewood home when a crow cawed just above her head.

Everybody knows that the cawing of a crow is ominous! The Ghosal girl, Toru knew it too. Besides, she had heard it said that the day she was widowed, a crow had cawed continuously. And on top of that today was chaturdashi! Toru's heart trembled. She quickened her pace.

But she was thwarted even as she tried to walk faster. The crow dipped low and circled over Toru's head and cawed again. Toru's heart froze to ice, and she lost hold of her senses. With no regard for the consequences of her actions, she threw the flaming firewood at the crow.

Needless to say, the fire did not touch even a feather, instead, it fell on the large thatch that was at the outer part of the Chatterji house. Ramkali had had the temple yard and the sitting room done in concrete, but he had built two huge thatched structures to accommodate the crowds that thronged there for festivals and ceremonies. These became twin offerings to the fire god.

Toru was not just careless, she was absent-minded too. Without stopping to see where the log fell and the result of the fall, Toru went back into the Chatterji house, picked up another stick of flaming firewood, and went home. She realized what she had done when she noticed the leaping gigantic flames, the heavy smoke-filled skies, and heard the screams of the neighbours mounting upwards.

The naive Toru had almost started beating her breasts with a 'Look at the damage I've done!' but her uncle had motioned her to stop.

But the fire could not be stopped. There was no way of stopping it. Unless one brought water in by the pot-full all the way from the pond. There was no point in attempting that.

Ramkali pronounced grimly, 'No need to pour water on the fire, that will make it worse. Pour water on the walls of the temple and on the walls of the houses nearby.'

It was evening when everyone finally went home lamenting. There was no end to the speculations as to why a fire should destroy the thatch of a fiery, spirited man like Ramkali, who was as innocent as he was virtuous.

Besides, that was the first blow.

A few days later, Dinatarini came back after her bath and took to her bed with palsy. Dinatarini knew that no one survived palsy. So she appealed to her son with tearful eyes to spare her the pain. Ramkali touched his forehead with his hand on the pretext of wiping off sweat. And in three days, Dinatarini passed away.

Satya was very disturbed on hearing of her grandmother's death. But the fact that Rashu had come to fetch her had pleased her no end. It was a good thing that her father had not sent the weaver's wife for such an occasion. This was the first time in three and a half years that she would go home. But was Satya unaware of the fact that deep inside her body another 'first' had begun to declare its presence? Had she not grasped that yet?

Well, even if she had not, Sadu had. But she had not dared report it to her ferocious aunt. She had thought that after a few days the old woman herself would read the signs. When the news of Dinatarini's death came, Sadu fretted a bit about the timing. Should she tell her aunt or not? It was not as if she did not dare to. Her compassion came in the way. What if Elokeshi should prevent Satya's going when she heard? The poor thing had stayed at her in-laws for so long. Even if she herself was to blame for that! Here was a chance for her to go. Let god take care of the rest.

So Sadu had warned her at the time of departure, 'You're going on a visit to your parents' after so long! But mind you, take good care, don't jump around like a calf let loose! I suspect ...'

Satya had looked anxious and asked in a muffled tone, 'What?'

'Look at that! Do I have to spell out everything? And to a married woman too! Look here, I think there's a baby inside. You must take care.'

Was it fear, or pleasure? It had to be fear—plain and simple! Though it was strange! Because the thought that an unknown mystery had built its nest inside her, began to send a strange thrill through Satya's body.

———

Inside the bullock cart, with her sari drawn over her head, Satya peeped out at Nabakumar again and again. How unfamiliar the man suddenly seemed in some ways! How would he greet this piece of news? She could hardly imagine the situation! The cart jerked along. And she asked in a whisper, 'Why didn't you get the palki?'

Her question flustered Rashu, 'Feeling very uncomfortable, aren't you? I'd mentioned it, but uncle said ...' Rashu added after a bit of hesitation, 'He said, so many relatives have to come, he can't send the palki for everyone! Of course, I'd told him that everyone isn't the same as your son-in-law. To that he said, "Is there just one son-in-law, Rashu?" So what could I say?'

Satya forgot to whisper and burst out, 'What's wrong with that? After all, all the sons-in-law of the house are equal. You can't treat your own son-in-law as special! Besides, Punyi's newly married—' She awoke to Nabakumar's presence and bit her tongue.

But how long can a dam of sand hold back the sea? Soon she was talking again. So many questions, so much excitement! For so much had happened in these three and a half years, so many births and deaths, children had grown up, girls had been married. These were significant facts—didn't she have to know them all?

'You haven't changed at all!' Satya said with a smile.

Nabakumar stared at that radiant smiling face in amazement. Amazement? Yes! Because he had not seen Satya's face like this before. Nabakumar had never previously known that Satya's face could look so charming when she smiled.

Rashu laughed aloud at Satya's declaration, 'How could you expect me to change so soon?'

Soon! For Satya aeons had passed. So she said, all wide-eyed, 'How can you say that? It's been three and a half years!'

'Really!' Rashu laughed once more, 'Three and a half years already? It does sound long, but how time flies!'

'Of course, it flies for you! Men have a free and easy life! But we women feel as if we've crossed a lifetime!'

That was exactly what she felt when she entered her father's house. As though she had been transported across a lifetime.

But what was this shore she had arrived at? Was it the same as the place from which she had left? Did it still have a room for her—vacant and unoccupied? Unclaimed till now? If it did, would she who had traversed a lifetime to arrive here, fit in once more into her old niche? Had any girl ever managed that? For wasn't a girl overcome by a massive transformation the moment she changed her family name? She who was scolded at every step and ignored, instantly became a cherished guest—a kinswoman, who invoked deference! Where could such a person find her home?

The whole house was busy, but they would not stop following Satya around—Sharada, Bhubaneswari, Shibjaya's granddaughters, even Mokshada. What would Satya eat, where would she sit, or sleep; was there anything she had asked for that she had not been given. They were concerned about everything! Especially, Bhubaneswari. Her mother-in-law had died, so she was forbidden by the laws of ritual pollution to handle things herself, but she would give instructions anyway.

It was hardly a comfortable situation; it constantly reminded her 'You're our guest, our kinswoman!' So, at one point, Satya reacted harshly to her mother.

'Do you want me to leave immediately for my in-laws? I can't stand such an excess of attention! Aren't there other girls who have come visiting from their in-laws—why don't you go and fuss over them?'

There was some truth in what she said. Several married girls had come—Punyi, Kunja's two girls, Shibjaya's daughter, the three daughters of Ramkali's dead aunt. But they were treated like fish in a shoal. Satya was the only one being fussed over.

Bhubaneswari was taken aback by her outburst, 'But they all visit off and on. No one's like you—going off to her in-laws and returning only after three-four years ...' Bhubaneswari could not finish her sentence.

Satya noticed her mother's hurt face and softened, 'Well, I can understand. But I'm here for a while. I'm not going to run away soon as the sraddha is over—all that's been settled. Then you can fuss over your daughter as much as you like. Now it is your mother-in-law's funeral, it doesn't look good, does it?'

Bhubaneswari said tearfully, 'Who knows how long you will stay!'

'Of course, I'll stay for at least two months, that's been decided. Come, Punyi, let's go and see our play room under the banyan tree.' She had literally pulled Punyi by the hand and run out of the main door.

Their play room was a really charming place. They certainly deserved praise for selecting such a location. This shaded hideaway was created by a huge banyan tree that had lowered a number of aerial roots; those who sought its shelter would not be touched by the rains, nor by the sun, which had been forbidden entry. This was the play room of Satya's childhood. She had played here almost till the day she had left for her in-laws. Now it lay abandoned. Because the children played elsewhere.

Though the place was no longer swept clean as it used to be, the row of small chullahs still seemed to hold old memories in their cracked bodies. They had been set up with so much care!

For a while, Satya sat at the foot of the tree in silence. As if she did not have the strength to speak immediately. So Punyi kept silent too. After a long time, Satya sighed, 'Strange isn't it Punyi? Everything has changed; only these small things remain the same.'

Punyi sighed too, 'Yes, exactly.'

Satya slowly pointed, 'Look, that was Puti's, that was Khedi's, Giribala's, Sushila's. And this one here was yours, wasn't it?' She did not mention her own.

But Punyi did, 'And that was yours. And look, the broken pots and pans are still in the garbage dump!'

Yes, the play room had a 'garbage dump' too. It was essential to have every item—garbage dump, a pond, a cow shed, a husking room—it was a flawless set-up! After all, they mimicked perfectly the 'play room' which kept the grown-ups busy! Their clay and wooden dolls had also washed clothes and pots and pans at the pond, husked paddy, chopped vegetables, ground spices and rocked their babies to sleep. In fact, they had not overlooked any duty! The space under the tree would ring with the noise of their daily toil. Satya suddenly stood up, 'Let's go, Punyi. I can't stand this any more, it's as though my heart's being wrenched.'

Punyi's heart had been tugging at her too, she said, 'Let's! No need to deceive ourselves with nostalgia. It was all over that very day they married us and sent us off. A girl's life is worthless!'

Satya let out a deep sigh, 'No, it isn't a girl's life that's worthless, Punyi. It's the rule-makers who are worthless. God hadn't ordered anyone to marry and send the girls off for life. Here you are, my childhood friend, and I couldn't come for your wedding. Won't I regret it till I die? Even so, I couldn't come. Could god have ordered that?'

Even though she sighed, Satya had not given up her cheeriness, or stopped chatting or roaming around. It would be wrong to think that. Everything continued—the mountain of chatter, the sea of stories. The tide flowed unabated—finding out which girl of the locality had gone to her in-laws, which one was at her father's, and all their stories! The sigh remained undisclosed. Hidden deep inside. As though in the midst of such abundance, Satya had stepped into an emptiness and could no longer find the ground beneath her feet.

This emptiness told her that she no longer belonged to them. That this was not Satya's place.

It was a busy house and nobody knew who had been accommodated where. The women slept in the inner quarters, the men in the outer part of the house. The sons-in-law and closer relatives slept inside rooms in the outer part of the house, and all the distant cousins were accommodated under the newly constructed thatched structure. Satya had no idea where Nabakumar was, and she occasionally thought about him. He was such a timid creature—who knew how he was coping! She had not seen him ever since they had arrived. Her father was too busy organizing things to bother with his son-in-law. She hoped people were looking after him. Or what would he think of Satya!

Satya missed him and yet felt haughtily mischievous too. She felt like calling the man and telling him, 'Do you see all this? No matter how much your mother spurns me, my family isn't one to be scoffed at.'

But where was the opportunity to say all that?

It was not a wedding that they could joke and laugh. The last rites for a mother was a serious affair. Though she had been one among many, Dinatarini had occupied the main role in this house, no matter how scared she had been of her younger sister-in-law or how much she had dreaded her son—everybody knew her to be the mistress of the house. Since the space occupied by the mistress had been vacated, everyone experienced the emptiness. And they were all slaving away, nobody had the leisure to think up an excuse so that Satya could meet her husband. Besides, nobody thought Satya was longing to see him. After all, she had lived with him without a break all these years. Therefore, it did not strike anybody that Satya would want to meet her husband.

Except Bhubaneswari.

But she was restricted on every side. Firstly, she had to obey all the ritual prohibitions because her mother-in-law had died, and over and above that, she was scared stiff of her daughter. Who would reassure Bhubaneswari that her daughter would not get annoyed if she tried to bring about a meeting?

But had Satya's mother fathomed everything? Of course not! For how could she have guessed that Satya herself was on the lookout for an opportunity? And finally, they managed to meet. The ritual feast after the funeral lasted almost till dusk. After the meal, Satya washed her hands at the ghat and went with her aunts to visit her uncle. As she hurried back from there, she bumped into Neru. Neru stopped her.

His face was exuberant with a secret, 'Hey Satya, you're scared of ghosts, aren't you?'

'What do you mean?'

'You know what I mean? Ghosts that live on trees. I'm certain they scare you!'

'*I'm certain they scare you!*' Satya had mimicked. 'So says the prophet!'

'But are you sure you're not afraid? Can you walk up to the banyan tree at this twilight hour? I'm sure you can't—no humans step in there!'

'Oh, I see! No humans step in there, eh? Speak for yourself! You played there too, but you've no memories. Punyi and I would go there, wouldn't we?'

'You would?'

'Of course! Stop pretending, Neru! We used to count the eyes of the owls, remember?'

'Oh that! All that belongs to the past. Now your in-laws must have snatched away whatever courage you had.'

'As if it's so simple! Come, I'll show you. Do you know, I can keep sitting there till well into the night?'

So saying, Satya had walked resolutely into what appeared like deep darkness in that fading twilight. But who was that? Who stood there? Satya had almost screamed, but controlled herself when she thought of Neru. If he heard her, that would be the end! He would tell everyone about how she had panicked. But the man seemed to be coming her way. Should she flee? It had to be Neru's doing, or else ...

That instance, one possibility flashed through her body like lightning, and the next moment, that possibility took concrete shape.

'You! What are you doing here?' Satya pretended to be surprised.

Nabakumar replied miserably, 'What could I do? I was hoping to see you! God! You've really become a rare sight after coming to your father's place! Don't you feel the need to find out if the man is dead or alive?'

Satya made a futile attempt to conceal her delight and burst out laughing, 'Listen to that! As if I'm supposed to do that!'

'But you could meet me at least! Poor me, I had to really work out a plan—'

'Yes, I can see that. Does anybody else know of this, apart from Neru?'

'No, only Neru.'

'That's all right then. Neru isn't a traitor. So what's the matter, then?'

'Matter!' Nabakumar's misery deepened, 'Can't one wish to see one's wife without something being the matter? Not everyone is as stone-hearted as you!'

'Stone-hearted! But of course!' Satya chuckled quietly. Then she asked, 'How do you like it here?'

'Very much!' Nabakumar said in all sincerity. 'I swear, I'd never thought in my dreams that my in-laws' place was like this! So opulent—really flourishing! And the countryside is beautiful too. The sight of the river just soothes the soul.'

Satya let out a sigh, 'Then you can understand what sacrifices a woman has to make.'

'That's true.'

Nabakumar made another candid confession, 'Ever since I arrived, that's what I've been thinking. You're like a princess. And compared to that, I am—'

Satya restrained him before emotions swayed him to speak further, 'Goddess save us! What a thing to say! You are my husband, an elder. I don't have to be a princess to miss it all intensely, do I?'

'But it's true! A hundred times! A thousand times!' Taking supreme courage, Nabakumar placed a hand on Satya's shoulder.

Of course, Satya was thrilled by this loving contact. Even so, she whispered with girlish caution, 'Don't stand so close. Who knows who will see us like this? And we won't be able show our faces in public after that! We'll have to die of shame!'

This threat hardly scared Nabakumar. Instead, he placed his

other hand on her other shoulder and tried to draw her closer, 'Why? Am I a stranger?'

'Even so. It's shameful to meet in public!'

'Yes, I suppose so; it would be something if people saw us meeting like this secretively. But your cousin said that nobody comes here.'

'That's true,' Satya softened slightly, 'which is why we'd chosen this place, and not the fruit orchards. A banyan tree is so useless—doesn't have flowers, or fruit, or use for the leaves or the wood. So nobody ever comes this way. And it provides such lovely shade.'

The evening darkened. Nabakumar suddenly began to speak poetically, 'But really, I think of a banyan tree when I think of your father—I mean, my father-in-law. He's like a huge tree.'

Satya was staggered. She was overwhelmed. And compelled by that passion, forgot all about being seen in public with her husband and clasped both his hands in hers, 'Really! Did you like my father?'

'I'm not talking about liking him. I'm talking about respecting him, of being in awe of him! Just the way one feels when facing a mighty banyan—'

'Have you talked to him?'

'Talk to him! Goodness! I can hardly dare to! Besides, he's a busy man, I've seen him only from a distance ...'

Satya was overwhelmed and said faintly, 'Everyone sees Baba from a distance. Everyone. Even my mother. Only this wretched Satya ...'

Once more, oblivious of the 'public', Satya rested her head on his thirsting chest. Nabakumar took advantage of that sweetness for a while, then whispered, 'I'm a "new" son-in-law, and this is the first time I've come; it's a sad occasion, besides. If we'd come for a wedding, I'm sure they'd give us a room to ourselves.'

Satya laughed at such an effeminate confession, 'As if we'd take it if it were offered!'

'Why not?'

'Are you mad? As if we wouldn't feel embarrassed! Don't you see, it is best to have a husband in one's in-laws' house!'

Nabakumar sounded hurt, 'I see. That is why you'll stay on for two whole months after this wretch goes away!'

A bolt of lightning flashed inside Satya. Two months or more, who knows! Pishi-thakurma had already voiced her suspicions about that fateful thing with which Sadu had alarmed her when she started out. Little by little, Satya too had come to recognize the uneasiness that was nesting inside her. The main discomfort seemed to be inside her throat. It was as if something wanted to push itself out, making it difficult for her to swallow her meals—anything she ate wanted to come out. That was how Pishi-thakurma had caught on. And she had immediately restrained Satya with numerous warnings. She had been particularly cautioned against going into the bushes, or under the trees after dark. Clearly, Satya, was paying no heed to such advice! But suddenly, she grew restless, 'Let me go, they'll scold me.'

'As if anyone will scold you here!' Nabakumar said confidently, 'You are a queen here. Neru told me everything! What a treasured child you were, and look how you're persecuted now—'

Satya recovered her characteristic firmness, 'Don't you talk like that! Each to her own fate. Every girl gets scolded at her in-laws'! Don't even mention it. I must go!'

'Must you? What can I say? When will I see you again?'

'I can't say!'

'I'm leaving next Wednesday. Before that?'

'Let's see.'

Nabakumar said slowly, 'I feel like staying on here. What a household, bustling with activity. And our house is like—'

'Doesn't matter. What one has is good enough,' Satya was firm again. 'When you become important in your own right, your house will look like this too.'

'That's impossible! But never mind. When will you come back to this poor man's hut?'

Satya abruptly blurted out, 'Can't say—in six months, may be one year.'

'Six months! A year!' Nabakumar was bewildered, 'What does that mean?'

'Well, it does mean something!' Satya fled at lightning speed.

—

Although everyone had been commenting on how 'grown-up' Satya looked, and how beautiful she had become, how her body had filled out—Satya's running about had not ceased one bit. Though it was beginning to look as though she would have to stop running about in front of Pishi-thakurma.

Satya rushed about the locality gleefully, turning a blind eye to the suspicion Sadu had articulated just before she came here. If the uneasy turbulence inside had cast its shadow of some unknown fear, the excitement outside had wiped all that out. Nobody had caught on immediately. In any case, Satya hardly spent too much time with any one person. Everyone was busy with the massive arrangements for the occasion. But it had suddenly struck Bhubaneswari—the person whose gaze was ever focussed on Satya, though she was busy with countless chores. She had murmured her hunch to Sharada, who had confirmed it after watching her target carefully. And that did it—in a moment, the news travelled from this mouth to that ear. Within half a day, the women of the entire village knew. And from the women, the men came to know too.

But the news took a while to reach Ramkali's ears, though. Ramkali had stopped sleeping inside the house after his mother's death. It was written in invisible ink that this was the rule he would follow for a year after her death. So there was no way in which Bhubaneswari could have communicated this news to him. Though she lacked the means to communicate it, she found it unbearable to keep this deeply delightful news all to herself. And two days seemed as long as two years to Bhubaneswari. But she did not want somebody else to convey the news to him either. She quivered with desire to reveal this wondrous, sweet, delectable piece of news, and slowly hold it out like a gift to her husband.

Finally, she never got the opportunity to present it herself.

Mokshada suddenly appeared when Ramkali had sat down to eat and declared, 'I don't know if it makes sense to say it now, but it's my duty to let you know. You're going to become a grandfather!' Ramkali gave a start. He did not get it right away. And Mokshada did not like this. So she spelt it out clearly, 'I'm not speaking in Urdu or Persian am I? I just said that Satya's going to have a baby.'

Ramkali choked on his food. He took a sip of water and lowered his head as if to look for meaning in the food on his plate. He was not supposed to speak now. He had said his prayers before his meal. And he wanted to follow all such rituals of mourning for the rest of the year. Never before had he believed in such things. But his accurate observance of custom since his mother's death demonstrated once again how peculiar man's mind was. He was not supposed to speak, so there was no question of a response. And there was no other time when he would be available. So it was best to pour into his ear all that he needed to know at this particular moment.

After Ramkali had settled somewhat, Mokshada reiterated, 'Now that I've told you, you'll have to decide how best to convey this news to her extraordinary in-laws. The woman is so hard to please! You'll have to send a basket of sweets, a cauldron of oil and other gifts with somebody.'

Ramkali continued to eat in silence, and tears sprang up in Bhubaneswari's eyes. What a time to choose to give him news that would gladden his heart and make it brim over! He could not talk now! Couldn't it have waited? Besides, Bhubaneswari's hopes and desires, her anxieties and joys had hardly had a chance to unfurl their petals and bloom! Bhubaneswari of course, had never been able to formulate things in so organized a manner. So her tears flowed ceaselessly, propelled by the force of so many emotions and untold hurts.

Mokshada had then brandished her final weapon, 'There's one more thing I can't help saying. Your daughter hasn't changed a bit, even after being sent to her in-laws. She's still the tomboy she was! She keeps wandering around anywhere, and doesn't care if it's dark, she just steps on anything without care. I've become something of a joke for constantly deterring her. Now it's up to you to discipline her.'

Had the food stopped moving down Ramkali's gullet? Was that the reason he was taking so long over his meal today? But Mokshada had no time to stand around, so she instructed Sharada, 'See if he needs anything else.'

With that she left. She was really annoyed today. True he had lost his mother, but couldn't he look happy at least! This was a bit much! She would have to see to it that the news reached Satya's in-laws. Women had to take care of such things.

Sharada was sitting at a distance holding a palm-leaf fan; she had been instructed to serve Ramkali. Yes, it was Sharada, though her face was concealed under her sari. This was her chief duty. Even if Kashiswari and Shibjaya were present, Sharada would sit at a distance and fan him.

There was nobody else who could undertake this. Bhubaneswari could hardly be expected to come forth brazenly and serve her husband heedless of all the elders.

Ramkali got up as\soon as Mokshada left. A well-polished vessel for water and his gamcha awaited him neatly by the verandah. But ignoring all that, for some reason he headed for the pond. In the period of mourning that followed the death, he was supposed to wash there, but now, it was no longer necessary.

Bhubaneswari did something extraordinarily daring. She rushed out through the back door and walked up to the pond, and hid behind the trees and waited. Ramkali gave a start when he noticed her on his way back. 'What's this? How come you're here?'

Her face was covered with her sari, but her voice sounded breathless, 'What else can I do? I know it's not done! But when it's urgent ...'

Ramkali was rather annoyed, 'How can we talk here?'

Although her face was covered, it was quite clear that tears were raining down Bhubaneswari's eyes. Her voice floated out from behind that downpour, 'But I never get to see you!'

Ramkali responded quietly, 'What is it? Tell me quickly! There are people everywhere—'

'It's about Satya—'

Ramkali's voice took on a note of displeasure, 'Yes, I've heard that. Do look after her. See that she doesn't jump about. Now just go inside, please!'

Bhubaneswari's entire body trembled with a mute sense of hurt. She turned away without another word. Staring after her, Ramkali wondered if he should have spoken a little gently. The foolish woman was so anxious about her daughter. But what could Ramkali do—this was not the place to talk to his wife! He had thought of telling her that there was no need to fear. But what would be an appropriate time to say that? As if Ramkali knew! He hardly knew what it meant to chat with a wife. He only knew that fondness, affection and love should never be expressed. Who would be the right person to send to Satya's in-laws? Pondering on this, Ramkali sat down at the temple courtyard.

Mokshada had come away. And busied herself trying to supervise how the news would be sent to Satya's in-laws. Giri, the weaver's wife, would go with the news. And Rakhu would follow in a bullock cart. A raw-silk sari was purchased for Giri, a dhoti and chaddar were dyed yellow for Rakhu. A huge bell-metal cauldron was filled with freshly pressed oil, and a large earthenware pot was filled with candied milk sweets. Satya's mother-in-law would get the picture immediately, they would not have to open their mouths at all!

Just as they were starting out, Ramkali came in suddenly. He handed over a pouch of cash to Mokshada saying, 'Ask them to hand this out to those who help there, let them be happy; and give this to Giri.'

The whole family was overjoyed; a joy that triumphed over the grieving for Dinatarini's death. Only Ramkali seemed to have suffered a defeat, no matter how hard he tried he could not feel that delight.

Ramkali felt that he had suffered a loss! Satya was growing up. No, that was not true, she had grown up already! But he had harboured a hope. When he saw Satya rushing about, chatting away during the ceremony, he had wondered if what he had been thinking could possibly be true. It must have been the various pressures at her in-laws …

He had meant to ask Satya to come to him once his work was lighter so that he could talk to her. But before he could do that, Mokshada had brought this staggering message! And now Ramkali could no longer summon her. She had moved beyond his reach. Ramkali would no longer get her to sit next to him.

Sucked into the whirlpool of a different machination, Satya was now governed by the laws of another kingdom. A whirlpool designed by the creator, a kingdom ruled by women!

TWENTY SIX

After Nabakumar left for his village, Satya rushed around freely, much like an untethered calf; the strictures that operated when he was around disappeared. But suddenly, Mokshada's hawk-eyes discovered the truth with such a finality that her freedom was pruned down quite drastically.

A barrage of instructions at every step! And she was unable to revolt. 'Don't you go and sit on the threshold; don't walk between two people; don't step into the courtyard after dusk; don't go out on Tuesdays and Saturdays; don't go to the pond by yourself.' A veritable surfeit of 'don'ts'! Apart from that, there were also rules to be followed: Wear silver toe-rings. Tie a knot at the end of your sari and at the ends of your hair at all times. Stay away from hostile women, and if you sense that a woman has cast an evil eye on you, heat a piece of iron and give yourself a small scalding on any part of your body. Stick a toothpick in your hair when you go to bed. Satya was expected to follow many such instructions!

Satya felt fettered. Yet every so often, she would do the forbidden or inauspicious thing. She would walk across the water in which the paan had been washed, skip over the water in which the fish had been washed, spread out the end of her sari and sit by the sweepings on the courtyard and carry out a hundred other inauspicious acts! Bhubaneswari would plead, 'Satya! Who knows what trouble you'll bring upon yourself—come and sit with me for a while!'

Yes, there would be times when she would sit down. More from the exhaustion she felt inside. Yet she would feel too self-conscious to linger for long near her mother. Actually, her restless spirit had taken on a calm and collected role at her in-laws for too long a time. Now it just refused to yield to easy exhaustion, or be tamed by affection. And as was inevitable, one day, Ramkali was asked to control his daughter.

But had Ramkali scolded her? Or issued a warning like a physician? He had done neither. For some reason he too was suffering inside, and feeling rather listless. Almost as if even after exhausting all his resources, he had been left with a dispassionate emptiness inside. He had summoned his daughter and instructed her, 'Listen to the elders. They know best. Something might go wrong if you don't.'

Then Satya had taken to her bed for three days out of a deep sense of hurt. She had retorted when Bhubaneswari pleaded with her, 'Wasn't this exactly what you wanted? I'm just carrying out your wish!'

Quite unexpectedly, Satya had become silent. But that had hardly staved off the damage. For the planets were against Ramkali. So his first granddaughter was lost to the kingdom of darkness long before she could sparkle in the light of this world. There could be no other explanation! After all, lately, Satya had been observing all the restrictions. Mokshada, of course, had her own explanation, 'It's all because she pranced about during the early months.' But Ramkali, the physician, had not confirmed that. It had struck him suddenly that perhaps he had been negligent. May be, in this case, he had duties, not as a father, but as a physician.

They had sent her in-laws the news of her pregnancy just a couple of days ago, along with gifts of oil and sweets. Even the tight-fisted Elokeshi had rewarded the bearer of the news with a new sari. She had also granted her daughter-in-law the permission to stay for a long time at her father's. And now, she would have to be given this news!

The feast of the shaadh that Satya's wealthy father had thrown just before the baby was due, was a grand affair. But what a waste it turned out to be! Well, even if it were a girl child, this was a first-born, after all. Henceforth, Satya would be looked on as 'imperfect'; she could no longer claim the glory of being a 'flawless' child-bearer. As a result, she would also lose the privilege of participating in a number of rites and rituals.

Elokeshi responded with strict instructions that they should take good care of Satya and send her back as soon as she was feeling better. She had no doubts that this had happened because the darling girl was spoilt rotten at her father's! Ramkali had to digest this verdict, and comply with the instructions. Once more, Rashu had to accompany a tearful, red-eyed Satya to Baruipur.

But did that appease the fury of fate? Ramkali's guru passed away; a year went by, yet one disaster followed another in Ramkali's household. Without warning, or cause, the innocent Neru left home. Just the way Ramkali himself had disappeared many years ago. But nobody had beaten Neru with a slipper! Ramkali searched high and low, Kunja wept like a woman, but there was no news at all. A few months after that, Kashiswari died, and some months later, Shibjaya's eldest daughter was widowed and returned with a swarm of children. Everybody was convinced that all these events had to do with Ramkali's stars.

Ramkali had to bear the consequences. The strange thing was, that no matter how difficult the circumstances were, Ramkali could never bring himself to grumble about its unfairness! He would never complain that he could not cope. So he had duly sent for a match-maker and a goldsmith to prepare for the weddings of the two marriageable daughters of his widowed cousin. Grooms had to be found, ornaments had to be made! He did not neglect her four sons either. He got them admitted to a tol or a patshala, whatever was suitable. Ramkali had never neglected his duties, or disregarded custom. In spite of that, the fell blow of fate struck again and again.

They say that the skill of an expert manifests itself in the final event. Who could be a greater expert than 'Fate' himself? And so it happened that in that half-light just before dawn, fate demonstrated his supreme mastery yet again. Bhubaneswari died after a brief attack of cholera.

Had Ramkali's excellent and celebrated medications failed? Perhaps they had; after all nobody can stop what is fated! Nor stall the inevitable. But then Ramkali had hardly got a chance to use them. He would have had fewer regrets if he had. But the timid and foolish Bhubaneswari had not given him the opportunity at all. She had got up late at night and had gone to the ghat and collapsed nearby, and she had not called anybody. Perhaps because she had not been able to. A low-caste woman had chanced upon that terrible scene in the wee hours of the morning. She had screamed and fainted. It had taken a while for people around to figure out what had happened. Not that it would have helped if they had found out a couple of minutes earlier, because it really was the end. Her face looked drained, her pulse was faint.

Ramkali examined her pulse, and slowly lowered that nearly motionless hand. Bending over her, he said in a choked voice, 'How can you do this?'

Rashu brought the lamp closer to the face of the patient. Bhubaneswari opened her eyes once with great difficulty. She tried to say something, but could not move her lips. Two tear-drops rolled down.

This disease usually left the patient conscious till the end, it never affected the senses. But the faint lamp light quivering in the wind had made visible the inner struggle of the dying to articulate words. Ramkali spoke again in that same voice, trembling with emotion, 'Why're you punishing me so harshly?'

For a fraction of a second the patient triumphed over the struggle. The lips moved. And pronounced, 'Chhi!'

'And will you leave without meeting Satya?'

Suddenly that almost rigid body had quivered like lightning and a stream of tears had spilled out of the sunken eyes. And a sudden gust of breeze had snuffed out the lamp in Rashu's hand.

The night before, a fit and fine Bhubaneswari had discharged her various household duties: she had diced three banana flowers for the next day's meal, soaked a huge bowl full of dal, and gone to bed. But her eyes did not see the light of the next day. The first rays of the dawn fell on her closed eyes, futile and useless. Rashu sobbed loudly like a woman. Mokshada's howls tore to shreds the pure serenity of the dawn. Custom prevented Kunja, an elder brother-in-law, from coming closer. He beat his chest and wailed, 'You've saved so many people, Ramkali! How could you not save our own Lakshmi? You lost out to death!'

Ramkali took one look at the scene of lamentation. He did not protest about not being given a chance. She, who had known no enemies all her life, had dealt her lord and master the most malicious blow of all.

Kunja started invoking Lord Narayana, 'It's the final moment, Ramkali. The spirit hasn't departed yet. Call the lord!'

'You do that!' With that Ramkali left the place.

A death as sudden as this hardly gives neighbours a chance to be present, leave alone people from another village. Naturally, nobody expected Satyabati to be present when her mother was dying, but she could not come for her mother's sraddha either.

Bhubaneswari's sraddha ritual was observed with appropriate ceremony. Ramkali was not one to place checks on expenditure just because older women, who were still living, would find it indecorous. The large-scale ritual upset Mokshada and she said, 'Even if you leave us old women out, your uncle is still living. Doesn't it look unseemly to have such a grand ritual for someone so young?'

Ramkali avoided looking his aunt in the face and answered, 'I'm not being inconsiderate to anybody. It's only proper to do it this way.'

Mokshada sighed enviously and said, 'It's so unfair to have such a grand ritual performed before our very eyes. We're such old hags, after all!'

Once again Ramkali avoided her eyes and said, 'The soul never ages.'

'But it's so hard to accept!'

Ramkali replied mildly, 'There's so much that's hard to accept in this world, but one has to accept them all the same. No point discussing it.'

Mokshada fell silent. True, if one could accept the death of a younger person, and consign to the flames of the pyre that cherished body and resume life all over again, how could one not accept the funeral rites!

So had they considered Satya not to be old enough to bear the tragedy of performing her mother's last rites? Was that why they had not brought her? No, Satya was not in a position to come. She was with her two-day-old son inside the birthing room when the news of her mother's death reached her. The day Bhubaneswari died, that very morning, Satya had given birth to her second child. A boy. Two messengers had arrived at the two households, each with his news.

But why hadn't Satya come to her father's for the birth? After all, her father was a such a renowned doctor. There was a reason for that too. A woman's reason actually. In such instances, women's customs and superstitions always won. There had been no exception in Satya's case. Satya's first miscarriage had been the result of not following regulations. After that untoward incident at her father's, it was best to do something different this time. They had mutually agreed that the child would be born at the in-laws'. Therefore, Satya was here. She had kept well and had just given birth to a boy. A self-satisfied Elokeshi had instructed the messenger she had sent to the wealthy in-laws, 'Don't accept it if they give you a bell-metal tureen, insist on a large pitcher.'

However, given the circumstances, the messenger had not managed to ask for anything.

An elated and expectant Satyabati was waiting with pride and hope for the messenger to return with the pitcher. She did not have to wait long. The messenger from her father's house arrived soon.

Elokeshi came up to the threshold of the birthing room and announced in a tone that blended brutality with concern, 'I should warn you before I tell you the news. It's inauspicious to weep inside the birthing room, don't you forget that! That mother of yours has died of cholera. It isn't a piece of news I could just hang on to without telling you. Of course, there's no question of you doing the fourth-day ritual. But no fish or rice for the next couple of days. I had to tell you, see? I'll send someone to ask the priest what rituals we should have in this case.'

Callously driving a knife into the unsuspecting heart of a young girl who had just had a baby, Elokeshi walked off indifferently. Without a backward glance at the effect of that thrust. However, she doled out this curious piece of information to her friends in the locality, 'You can't imagine how stone-hearted she is! She didn't cry at all—just gaped at me!'

True, Satya had not wailed out loud. Dazed and shocked, she had stared unblinkingly for a long time. Then at one point, the newborn had let out a loud scream, quite at odds with his tiny size. And she had slowly lifted the child and held him against her shoulder. Ever since, she had been sitting in silence staring at the wall.

If there was even a chink of a window, then Satya's soul would have traversed that open trail in her mind's eye and set sail till she had dashed her boat against the nest of her childhood home. There, where a chubby, fair-faced, petite person called Mejo-bou moved about diffidently, looking after everyone's needs. And near her with utter indifference and great confidence moved a robust girl child, sari tucked around her waist.

But there were no windows in this birthing room. All three sides had solid mud walls. Thwarting vision and arresting it.

Satya used to be annoyed by her mother's timidity. She would say, 'You're so scared! Your fear won't let you go even to heaven!'

Had Satyabati's mother not gone to heaven, then? Or else why was Satya's heart wailing as it wandered in that unseen vast emptiness called 'Heaven'? Satya seemed oblivious to the fact that her mother was dead, that she would never see her ever again. It seemed to her that her ever-compassionate mother was playing some kind of cruel game. She had raced away to some faraway place from where she was mocking Satya with a laugh. And teasing her, 'Always busy with your own games, weren't you? Had you ever noticed that there was a person called "mother" at home? Had you ever acknowledged that you were her only child? That she had nobody but you to call her own?'

'Mother was dead'—at this moment, for Satya, worse than the spasm of that realization was the anguish of her childhood insensitivity towards her mother. Why hadn't she been attentive, and sat close to her quietly even for a minute? Why had she not slept with her arms locked round her mother's neck instead of sleeping with five other girls in her grandmother's room? And yet, how often had that self-effacing woman pleaded softly, her timid face alight with a smile, 'Come, sleep in my bed here! I'll tell you a fairytale.'

But the child with whom she pleaded would never oblige. Instead, she would retort scornfully, 'As if you know so many stories! Here are my friends waiting for me—and I'll sleep with you! What a thought!'

What a stone-hearted girl! How hard-hearted! Satya felt like banging her head on the solid mud walls and splitting to smithereens that brutal gadget inside her head. God, could you not bring back that time just for one day? So that Satya could atone for the sins of that girl! So that she could embrace that tiny body and bury her face in her breasts and say, 'She wasn't a cruel child, Ma, she was just foolish!'

Satya could hardly recall the mother she had seen when she had recently visited; in her imagination, her mother, who walked about in the doctor's house, was a youthful woman. If Satya were to die right now, would she meet her mother in that place called 'Heaven'? And would Satya then fling herself on her breast and cry out, 'Ma, how could you be so stone-hearted!'

Had Satya forgotten where she was? Had she thought that she

had already reached heaven and had flung herself onto her mother's breast? That the echoes of her sobs could now be heard on earth? For that was what brought Elokeshi rushing and shrieking.

'Just what do you think you're doing? Isn't it enough that you sacrificed one? Do you want to lose this one as well? How can you howl with a newborn on your lap? You have no fears at all, do you? No parent lives forever. And it has to be said, it's a blessing in disguise that it's your mother and not your father! She went like a lucky woman too—before she was widowed. You can rejoice about that, can't you? Instead, here you are, screeching aloud for that mother of yours! I tell you, she'd have been miserable had she lived longer! She'd be widowed, and she'd have to wear white and eat in a separate kitchen. I'm warning you—I'll curse that entire clan of yours if a single teardrop falls on the child! I'll make you stop this silly whining for good! I'm warning you!'

A teardrop on the child! Satya dried her eyes with the end of her sari and checked anxiously for a teardrop on her boy. There, right there! There was a drop! Satya shivered. Shashti, goddess of infants, protect him! Satya would never behave so foolishly again.

Satya wiped that imagined teardrop and held her baby close. And turning her back on death, sat face to face with life.

TWENTY SEVEN

They say that fortune favours the brave. Rashu's wife, Sharada, hardly considered herself fortunate; in fact, at every opportunity she would declare how unfortunate she was. Even so, one could say that in a way fortune had favoured her—by cleverly creating a particular constellation of planets and stars.

Or else, Lakshmikanta Banerji's granddaughter would not have remained at Patmahal for so long. But there she stayed, giving Sharada the opportunity to enjoy her husband all by herself.

Lakshmikanta had died, but his son Shyamakanta took after his father. He would follow each and every rule and ritual with care.

He never moved without consulting the almanac, and obtained advice from Kashi-returned astrologer-pundits about the influence of complex constellations. And after studying Patli's horoscope at length, the astrologers had pronounced certain restrictions about sending her to her husband's house. They declared that it would be dangerous for Patli to see her husband before she turned eighteen. Because, until then, the planets were not favourable at all towards her wedded life.

Of course, nobody was surprised by the declaration of the astrologers, they would have been surprised if the verdict said anything to the contrary. After all, one did not need an astrologer to point out that Patli's bad luck as far as her husband was concerned! Everyone had found that out on the day of her wedding!

They said that it was the merits of her father's last life that had made Ramkali chance upon the groom. Or Patli would have been widowed on her wedding night! Or spent the rest of her life almost like a widow. It was the doctor who had saved her—just like a god. Otherwise, who could have prevented what was fated? And the planets had warned Patli: 'Don't you dare look your husband in the face! Not till you turn eighteen in any case.'

Shyamakanta had invited his son-in-law for his father Lakshmikanta's sraddha. But he had left strict instructions that his daughter and her husband should not meet. But then his son-in-law had not been able to come. He had taken ill with blood dysentery that very day. Of course, nobody would know if that was induced by consuming unboiled milk! But never mind, all that was past history.

Shyamakanta had informed his daughter's father-in-law about this danger. Therefore, their side had not raised the issue so far. In fact, she had not even come for Dinatarini's funeral. When all the relatives had turned up for ritual offerings at Dinatarini's funeral, Patli was the only significant person who was absent.

But now the time had come. Patli had turned eighteen. And Kunja's wife, Abhaya, was very keen to send for her. Of course, she maintained a facade by saying 'It doesn't look decent to leave her at her parents',' but she actually had a deeper purpose. Her aim was to shatter her elder daughter-in-law's pride. Sharada was as fiery as she was proud. And her confidence swelled with every passing day. Nobody knew how she had slowly come to occupy the space that Bhubaneswari had left behind. Without Sharada nothing functioned, just as it used to be with Bhubaneswari. But Sharada did not have Bhubaneswari's quiet docility, Sharada was sharp and impetuous. It was her deepest desire to outdo her mother-in-law.

Abhaya had not gained the status of mistress of the house after Dinatarini's death as she had expected. Her duties had not extended beyond working in the kitchen, they had only become more complicated. Kashiswari hardly lifted a finger, and Mokshada had become weak after suddenly breaking her arm in a fall. So right after her bath, Abhaya had to help in the vegetarian kitchen too. She had to fetch water and grind the spices. Although, strictly speaking, she was not supposed to handle things in that kitchen, she now helped there. Since Mokshada was reduced to a state of helplessness—like a trapped elephant—she could not protest.

Because of that, the fish-kitchen stayed in Sharada's control for most of the morning. Of course, Shibjaya and other relatives also worked there, but Abhaya felt they were all privileged. And that she was just a piece of trash.

Abhaya hated her daughter-in-law's stamina and strength. She wished she could teach her a lesson. And now she had a weapon in her hand. Shyamakanta had sent word that Patli had turned eighteen.

The news made Abhaya feel stronger. She thought to herself, 'Wait till the elder daughter-in-law loses some of her power!' Nothing like the arrival of a co-wife to teach a woman a lesson!

There was a great flurry of activity at Patmahal. The inauspicious period was over, and at long last Patli would go to her husband's house. Her mother, Behula, wanted to saturate the in-laws with gifts. So she spent all her time packing things, and at every step, she would give Patli advice about how to cultivate a sense of belonging with her husband's family. Behula was especially anxious because her daughter was such a nitwit.

On the other hand, Behula was also reassured by something.

Every so often, she would steal a glance at her daughter and beam with satisfaction. The glow on her face would grow more intense every time she calculated the age of her daughter's co-wife. Nobody could compete with Patli! First of all, she was in the full bloom of youth, and the long period of secure nurture at her parents' had filled out her body. And her looks? She was gorgeous to look at from the time she was that high! So much so that people used to scoff at her beauty. They would say, 'Here's a ravishing beauty that never found a groom! Patli, you've proved that proverb true! Our dark and ugly daughters have better luck! At your age they've had three kids!'

People uttered many a word of caution even now. 'Let's hope your co-wife steps aside. After all, she's been the sole queen all these days. Your mother better give you a couple of amulets. Who knows what awaits you there! And don't you accept water or paan from your co-wife!'

The days passed, swaying between hope and desire, dreams and fears. Finally, that wonderful day arrived, and Patli left for her husband's house.

She did have faint memories of the house. Bits of it—the enormous courtyard where she had stood for the ceremony, the huge verandah where they had made her sit, the ghat where they had taken her for a bath, the room where she had stayed for eight days. But nothing more than that.

Among all the women, Patli had not been able to make out which one was her co-wife. Not that the girl had tried too hard, particularly because her eyes had been berry-red from weeping. Her tears had not been only about coming to her in-laws, but also because she saw herself as a terrible offender. Was there anybody in this whole wide world as hapless as her? Had anybody heard of a groom who died on the way to his wedding? And a woman from this house had disappeared on the day of the wedding feast, even as the house was teeming with people! It had amazed Patli.

A man could go missing when he went out—he could be bitten by a snake, or eaten by a tiger, or carried off by dacoits—but a woman! That too, one who lived at her in-laws? How could such a woman go missing from the house? Unless a ghost should have flown her away, there could be no other explanation. Having settled on that explanation, Patli had cried out of fear and guilt. That was when Satya had given her a piece of her mind.

Yes—that was another thing Patli could recall—Satya! Eyes flashing like mirrors under thick brows that joined over her nose! Patli remembered her clearly. Satya had frowned after listening to Patli's reasons for weeping, 'Why shed tears and blame yourself for being unlucky? Whatever was fated by god has to happen. No point thinking that you're the cause of each and every disaster! As if the world would come to a standstill if you weren't born!'

Patli had been astounded by these words from a sister-in-law who was about her age. Never in her life, had she heard such things, and from such a young girl too! Until now, all the elders had been blaming Patli for the calamity. They said it was all because of her! That girl must have left for her in-laws by now. No other girl stayed on at her parents' because the planets were hostile!

Preparations were on at this end too. Abhaya was carrying things too far. Not so much out of affection, but because she wanted people to know, especially Sharada and her friends, that the expected bride was not in need of anyone's charity at all. She had certain inalienable rights!

She had not yet managed to raise the subject of the bedroom with Sharada, though. But she had dropped broad hints that Sharada should henceforth move out to a separate room with her children. Her son had grown up, and she should stop holding on to her room.

But Sharada had hardly paid any heed to these hints. Ever since her son had grown, she had sent him off to be supervised by his uncles. In this way, she had kept her own territory intact.

Her eldest boy, Bonu or Banabihari, was devoted to his youngest uncle, Neru. And ever since Neru had left home, the others had indulged him. Everybody was very fond of him, but Abhaya could not stand him. Not only because he was Sharada's son, but also because he was so utterly devoted to his mother. Abhaya would take every opportunity to screech at him, 'Why do you stick to Neru, your youngest uncle, eh? What'll happen when he gets married?'

The boy would never question her as to why his youngest uncle should get married before the second one had, or if he did, how that would create a conflict with his nephew; instead he would protest loudly, 'As if I'll let him marry!'

And Abhaya would retort vehemently, 'I know you won't! You think just like your mother, that nobody should come or demand a share—you just want sole access!'

Well, Neru had not married, he had disappeared instead. And Abhaya blamed that on the words of that hapless boy! Words he had picked up from his mother.

Because she had no hold over Sharada, Abhaya looked forward to having a doll under her thumb! Abhaya would dress her, feed her, and make her dance to her tune at the snap of her fingers.

'I wish the second son would marry.'

But Ramkali refused to allow that possibility to raise its head. In fact, he had clearly told Kunja to his face, 'What's the point in getting that good-for-nothing married?'

Whoever's heard that a man could not marry because he was good-for-nothing—how bizarre! And as always, Kunja had been too scared of his younger brother to raise any questions. But he had criticized him behind his back. All such comments were uttered in private. Though he had not attempted to make any arrangements himself.

Now, at long last, Abhaya could hope to get an object that was hers to command!

But where in this world could one ever find unfailing bliss? She felt uncomfortable thinking of the 'new' bride's youth. Would the experienced one abdicate? Would the unbendable bend?

Was Patli going to spell the elder one's ruin? Nobody knew!

Nobody ever knows what a woman is until she stands on the testing ground of self-interest! And in such cases, labels such as 'good girl' and 'lovely girl' are known to fail miserably.

Though she had no idea what kind of woman Patli was, ever since she had found out about her arrival, Sharada's heart felt as though it was being pounded by a bamboo pole. And somebody seemed to be ceaselessly prising her heart apart with the pole.

And Rashu? His suffering seemed endless! His mind was tormented by fear mingled with an intense, tremulous joy. He wondered what that seven-year-old girl looked like now that she had turned eighteen? The messenger-woman had announced, 'The bride is as pretty as a lotus!'

Ever since he had heard that, an indescribable, pleasurable pain had been shredding Rashu's heart to bits. Would Sharada allow that lotus to be part of Rashu's puja? Or would she deprive him and remind him of the oath taken ages ago?

Sharada had never been a lotus. Nor a chameli or mallika. If at all one had to compare her to a flower, she was more like that blue creeper—the aparajita. Her complexion was dark, yet her sharp features and her pleasing face had granted her the privilege of becoming the eldest daughter-in-law of this family. And she had risen to take charge of the house because of her forceful personality. Compared to her, Rashu was an inexperienced youth, still chasing after pleasures. Nowadays, he feared Sharada.

But Sharada had kept him under her thumb by attending to his needs impeccably. Even now, on summer nights, she would fan him with a wet palm-leaf fan. On winter nights when his hands and feet tingled with cold, she would warm them with her touch, heating her hands on the lamp. No matter how tired she felt after working in the kitchen all day, at night she would never forget to use scented oil on her hair and wear a fresh sari of a fine weave. But could scented oil compete with a freshly bloomed lotus?

The house reverberated with cheers when the bride stepped in. Not only was she beautiful, the items she had brought as dowry were exquisite too.

Ramkali's house overflowed with things. He hardly needed an excuse to get extra household items. If one enumerated there would be at least a dozen stone-mills, sixteen grinding stones, and at least forty to fifty water vessels. Even so, the women were always delighted with the smallest household item—grinding stones, stone-mills, pots and pans etc.

Everyone admitted at once that Patli's family was generous. The grandmother Nandarani joked, 'I see that the only item missing is a husking pedal! That would complete it! Why did he leave that out?'

No, Patli's father had not sent a husking pedal. But he had sent Patli. And like a husking pedal, Patli was thrashing away, deep inside someone else's heart. But despite the thumping, Sharada pulled herself together. And she plotted how not to let this co-wife near her husband, ever! She was going to take the fullest advantage of that Goddess Durga oath. There was no other way! After all, Sharada knew Rashu well! If he were allowed to come near this beauty, Rashu would pledge his soul at her feet!

The first day, Abhaya made Patli sleep beside her and gave her a lot of advice late into the night. Mainly about who could be trusted in this household, and who could not. Who must be respected, and who was dependable.

But what about the next day? And the day after? And, forevermore? Sharada kept thinking about that. Today was over, but what would happen tomorrow? After that, every other day? The Goddess Durga oath was applicable to Rashu but what about the others in the house? What would her answer be, especially when their questions started piercing her like poisoned arrows?

The lamp had been blown off, even though Rashu had not yet come inside the house. An unruly summer breeze was blowing, laden with the intoxicating scent of the champa; it wafted in through the smallest window, filling the whole room with its fragrance.

The night, the alluring breeze, and a heart throbbing with pain! In the midst of all this, how could it be possible for her to remember that her son was now twelve? And that Sharada had had a long spell with her husband. How could Sharada imagine it unseemly to stretch her hands out to grab at the pleasures of life? Or think it only appropriate that she should sacrifice her husband and find fulfillment among the pots and pans in the kitchen?

Amazing! Sharada found it impossible to believe that she had enjoyed this room for so long! Through a blinding mist of tears, she kept thinking how brief it had been! Sometimes, very rarely, she had visited her parents. Those visits now appeared like long drawn-out periods. Sharada's poor father had hardly managed to take his daughter home that often! In the sixteen-seventeen years that she had been married, if one counted each month, each day and every hour, she had been away for four or five years at most. That still left her with more than a whole decade! But how had that slipped away so quickly?

Rashu entered the room stealthily, as he always did. Like a thief, as Sharada had once described wryly. And his manner, which resembled a new groom, had not changed in all these years. Did that also imply that he hardly grasped how he had grown from eighteen to thirty-four? That those years had just slipped through his fingers? Was that why he still felt embarrassed to enter his bedroom?

Rashu had spent the whole day in anguish. Though he could hardly pinpoint the cause of that mute suffering, it had left his heart heavy. Of course, there was a reason for his anguish. But it wasn't just about not seeing his pretty wife. The conflict of duty tortured him no end! What was he supposed to do? Be faithful to the oath and not look at her at all? And keep his word to Sharada? Or should he just dismiss the oath?

This was where it hurt. What if Sharada did something terrible? The thought that Sharada would be hurt, that she would taunt him, hate him, was also breaking his heart. And yet, if he kept his vow of being devoted to Sharada, he would be unfair to a simple, innocent girl! Wouldn't her husband's cruel indifference make her want to die—of shame, grief and hurt? How could anyone dream of tormenting her! He had heard it said that she was more like a 'radiant lotus' than a bride!

Through the day, this dilemma had torn Rashu in two. But he feigned indifference when he entered the room, 'God! How dark it is!'

In those days, to believe that all the darkness of a large room could be chased away by a single lamp was not considered a ridiculous idea. So, the absence of that one lamp made Rashu exclaim, 'God! How dark it is!'

But nobody responded to that. Rashu latched the door and asked, 'Why didn't you light the lamp?'

Now Sharada spoke. And strangely, her lament took on a tone of harsh sarcasm. May be, that is why they say that habits live on even after death. Sharada said sharply, 'Where's the need to light a lamp when there is a full moon?'

'A full moon?' Stupid Rashu, naive Rashu, as though he had just landed from the moon! 'What do you mean?'

'Don't you understand?' Sharada's jeers tore her husband to bits, 'The whole house is singing her praises—how come *you* haven't heard yet? The beauty of your second wife lights up the world! So I didn't want to waste oil and light a lamp!'

Rashu gathered his courage and said, 'Women are such jealous creatures!'

'What was that?' It was as though Sharada had entered a shrillness contest, 'Women are jealous?'

'Yes, what else?'

'Yes, of course, and esteemed men are like the gods themselves!' Sharada bitterly raged on, 'What can I say, it is the gravest sin to compare, still I'll say it. Why don't you compare your position with that of a woman? If a wife just looks at another man, then the noblest of husbands turn into murderers!'

Rashu scoffed, 'What a comparison! Don't you feel ashamed to mention another man? As if a second wife is another woman!'

Sharada was not unsettled by such scorn, 'Where's the need for another woman if one can get a second, a third, a fourth—any number of wives! A woman has no such privileges!'

Rashu sighed hopelessly, 'Jealousy has blurred your judgment, Boro-bou, so you're saying anything at all! I didn't go and fetch the new bride, the elders did what they thought best. Otherwise, she lived at her parents all these days.'

'Oh, I see! Your sympathy's brimming over! She was drowning there, was she? How painful!' Sharada sharpened each word she flung out, 'Let me tell you clearly, I am not one to go into the filthy practice of sharing. If you want me, you cannot touch her, and if you want her—'

At this point Sharada's voice choked. And this was the voice that Rashu feared. So he said with greater despair, 'Then tell me what you want to me to do. Should I obey the elders, or scream at them in protest?'

'You will do what you think best. You are not a little boy. If the elders asked you to consume poison, would you? Khuro-thakur has done his duty, he has done right and saved another bhadralok at my expense! If his sense of justice was so strong why didn't he himself—'

'Boro-bou!' Rashu hollered out suddenly, 'What are you saying? Have you lost your mind?'

Sharada suddenly lay down on the bed and said seriously, 'Is it so unusual for a person to lose her mind when something maddening happens? Khuro-thakur would have been a happier man today had he not split up my marriage!'

'Boro-bou! Who are you comparing yourself with? Do you know it is a sin to say such things?'

'But it can't be a sin to think it? Nobody can browbeat the mind! But never mind, I won't say anything. I have said what I had to say.'

Rashu tried to compromise, 'Why are you feeling so upset? You are the main wife, the mother of a big boy! Nobody can snatch away your position! A facade has to be maintained for the public, isn't it? I can't just abandon her.'

Sharada replied solemnly, 'I suppose you have forgotten all about the oath?'

'Why should I forget?' Rashu said irritably, 'But one has to think about what people will say.'

Sharada sat up suddenly, 'Why? Aren't there ways of explaining to people? There are so many ways! Can't you tell them that some sadhu or fakir has read your palm and predicted that years would be deducted from your life-span if you touched your second wife?'

TWENTY EIGHT

Everybody had hoped that Sharada herself would bring up the matter. For surely she could not be so base, or dense? But Sharada whiled away a lot time by being obtuse. Nor did she show any signs of embarrassment. Therefore, there was no other way but to point it out to her. But who would dare raise her finger? Sharada was sharp-tongued, and given a chance, would not spare even an elder. Even when she had her sari drawn over her face, her victim's whole body would smart from the sharpness of her sting!

Thus, furtive, and concealed, the discussion grew. Until the situation became something like this—whenever Sharada moved from one place to another carrying out her duties, she would notice two or three heads whispering together, which would separate as soon as they spotted her; they would stop murmuring instantly and start a loud discussion about some chore or other.

It was not as if Sharada was unable to guess the subject of their discussion. She knew exactly what it was, and it made her whole body shudder with disgust, but she just pretended not to understand. Otherwise, it would all come out in the open, and they would stop caring for seemliness and accost her openly. As long as she could avoid such a confrontation!

Sharada was quite circumspect, she never volunteered to say anything to anybody. Finally, they decided to talk to her directly. That is to say, Sharada's mother-in-law and her aunt-in-law, Shashitara. Sharada had only recently become acquainted with this aunt-in-law. Because she had come to visit after a good thirty years. The reason for this long absence was a family quarrel. Jaikali, the father of Ramkali, Kunja and Shashitara, the head of one of the feuding families, had expired long ago. The head of the other, that is Shashitara's father-in-law, had been alive until recently, and had been the main impediment who prevented his daughter-in-law from visiting her parental family. Anyway, his sraddha ceremony had just got over, and Shashitara had come to her father's house after all these years. Now she would stay for a while.

It had taken her a day or two to figure out the goings-on in the household. At last, she had got down to work. She was tormented by her stepbrother Ramkali's predominance and her brother Kunja's lack of authority. And the shameless behaviour of Rashu's first wife had amazed her no end! So she voiced her view with stupefaction, 'I say, will that hag hold on to her man with all her might and leave the nubile thing to count the rafters in her mother-in-law's bedroom? Are you just going to sit around and do nothing? Shouldn't you think of the boy? Why torture him with dry and stale food and hide the fresh stuff at the bottom of the basket, eh? Never heard of such a thing all my life!'

Sharada's mother-in-law treated this sister-in-law, whom she had not met for many years, like her closest relative and oozed sweetness in response, 'Yes, just look at that! The longer you stay, the more you shall see! In the first place, your brother's timid nature has given me no powers at all—I've just run the kitchen all my life! And to top it all, I've a shrew for a daughter-in-law! She looks innocent, but is very proud. Try ordering her about and see if she listens! And she acts so high and mighty, who'd have the guts to summon her?'

'None of you perhaps, but I do!' Shashitara pronounced her stubborn verdict, 'I shall fix this piece of nastiness!'

So Shashitara accompanied by her sister-in-law, summoned the culprit to court. Sharada arrived, and covering her head with her sari, asked in a clear voice, 'What is it?'

Shashitara sat up and said, as she fanned herself, 'I just want to say what is fair. Don't mind. When people don't have any sense it becomes a duty to bluntly point out what is sensible. Don't blame me if it hurts you.'

A laugh could be heard in Sharada's repartee, 'Blame you! As if I'd dare!'

'As if you wouldn't!' Shashitara fanned herself briskly, 'I see no such signs. But neither do I see the tiniest bit of sense! Don't you think of the "new" Bouma at all!'

Almost immediately, astounding both women, Sharada's voice was heard low and clear, 'May be I don't, but you all do!'

'We do! All of us do! You simply amaze me! Tell me, how are we to help her with our concern? You have threatened your husband with suicide and he is frozen stiff—what can we do? The other night I dragged him here, I said, "Rashu come here. There are so many rooms. If this one lacks a huge bed, a small bed is regal enough for a woman when she gets her husband." But did I manage to convince him? He was petrified and ran away! He said, "My elder wife will commit suicide." I'd heard it said that your father was a gentleman—what sort of coarseness is this?'

Even before Shashitara had finished, a streak of lightning flashed across the room. It came from the fire in Sharada's eyes. She raised her head to speak and her face became uncovered. She pulled her sari over her head again, leaving her face uncovered, and said, 'Even a god can fall into a trap, so how can a mere human hope to be an exception! Does it surprise you that family intrigues can make a gentleman's daughter coarse?'

She had dared to open her mouth, and that too with such words! Her mother-in-law suddenly became aware of her own position. So she shook her head, dangling her huge nose-ring, 'Fighting with an in-law with your face uncovered, are you? Really, I can't imagine how you can behave this way! Do you know I can drive you away to your father's place forever?'

This court was something Sharada had pictured before, and she was prepared for the questions. So she said with a bitter laugh, 'If it's a question of leaving forever, why should I go to my father's? Nobody has snatched away the shelter of death from me!'

Now Shashitara swivelled her hoop-like nose-ring and bellowed, 'Don't you dare think that we are like Rashu, to be crushed with such threats! I tell you, she is a rich man's daughter, her father's filled the house with things. Are you going to leave her deprived? Will you deny your husband such a beautiful lotus-like girl? You won't find a place in hell for your sins!'

Suddenly Sharada laughed, and said clearly, 'That'll be wonderful then! If I don't find a place in hell, I'll go to heaven! After all, there are only two choices!' And leaving the two women utterly stunned, Sharada stood up, 'The youngest brother-in-law wants palm fritters—I must go and mash the palm.' Meaning to say: 'Here I go, fleeing from your witness-box!'

Shashitara could well see that it was not as she had expected. Taunts alone would not do the trick. So she launched a different kind of attack, 'I can see that you haven't learnt etiquette at all! I haven't ever seen any woman leave the presence of her elders without their permission. Speaking for our generation, whenever any elder called us we'd come and speak humbly, and sit till they asked us to go!'

This did not unsettle Sharada either; she replied with a slight smile, 'It's such a pleasure to sit when one has the leisure!'

'Well, I see you're infected with quick answers. And a witless mother-in-law has brought things to this. Anyway, I was talking about making a compromise. You're the mother of a son, and you have enjoyed your husband for long. She can't be cast away like this, can she? After all, she too was married with the fire god as witness. Why not take turns?'

Shashitara laughed to herself. If only one could get Rashu started on this new addiction, we will see how devoted he is to you! We will see what becomes of this fire! Once he gets a taste of the new one, it won't matter to him if you drown or hang yourself! Shashitara congratulated herself for thinking of 'turns'.

But Sharada did not let that pleasure last too long. She retorted sharply, 'I shall leave without your permission now. I'm appalled and embarrassed by such coarseness.'

'What did you say? You find this coarse? You daughter of a savage! Why doesn't your tongue fall off!' Shashitara hollered, 'You're very refined, are you? Very respectable is it—to enjoy everything without sharing! Taking "turns" sounds coarse, eh? Especially when that would save face for both!'

Sharada had thought of a harsher retort, but controlled herself, 'No need to save both—why don't all of you save just one of them?'

It was not possible to stand there any longer. It would be hard to keep one's dignity. Her own eyes would betray Sharada. And transforming both her elders into stone, Sharada sauntered off.

At such moments of humiliation, Sharada thought of

Bhubaneswari. Sharada must be really unlucky, or how could she lose her sole refuge of affection? What an age to die!

It was true that Sharada was shameless and discourteous, and she was selfish. But when had fate ever given her the opportunity to be generous to others? In fact, fate had betrayed her! And that betrayal had come from an elder. How could she respect elders after that? After all, would any one think of reaching out for a cup of poison when ambrosia was available?

Shashitara addressed Abhaya, her hand on her cheek, 'You are an elder, so it's only appropriate that I touch your feet. But I feel like rolling at your feet out of respect! How could you survive with such a serpent?'

Kunja's wife touched her forehead, 'Such is my fate!'

Actually, such a realization had dawned on her only recently. Under the influence of her sister-in-law's insights! So she wanted to make up for all the foolish things she had done until then.

'I know of an antidote that will take Rashu's mind off that viper,' Shashitara said in a low fierce voice. 'It's an unfailing charm. It will bring Rashu writhing to the feet of his younger wife. He'll just begin to adore her and detest the first one like poison.'

Her sister-in-law was amazed, 'Really, you know of such a medicine?'

A strange smile lit up Shashitara's face, 'If I didn't, how could I have made my husband my slave, eh? He was quite impulsive in his youth! He wouldn't care for kinship or anything, he'd just go crazy if he saw a pretty face. An old Bagdi woman taught me the charm, after that he became such a simpleton—utterly devoted to me! He now stands, sits, eats and sleeps according to my wish. He looks dazed all the time. I tell you, that's fine with me, never mind that he doesn't earn or say much, but there's no dearth of food at home. And he's tied to the end of my sari forever!'

Rashu's mother hesitated, 'Is it some herb or what? I hope it won't harm Rashu.'

'Listen to that! Why should I suggest such a thing? This is nothing but turning his affections from one to the other. So, listen to me. It's your good luck that two nights later it's a new moon.

Late at night, the "new" Bou should remove all her clothes, leave her hair loose and stick a needle at one go into a banana plant, then ...'

But before Shashitara could finish, Sharada's son came running in, 'Come quickly all of you! Mejo-thakurda has fallen unconscious.'

Mejo-thakurda! That was Ramkali! He, who was the ocean of consciousness, had 'fallen unconscious'—what an expression! Everyone ran. Would Ramkali also depart without prior notice like his wife? The news had spread because he had fallen in the inner quarters. If he had fallen outside, the women would not have had the chance to crowd around and lament this way. The ones who had the right to touch, poured a stream of water on his head, they brought out all the palm-leaf fans. Not out of concern but for the thrill of it! The man they had not dared look in the eye, was lying helpless with his eyes shut; one could even pity him, fan him, pour water on his head. This was almost close to pleasure.

Sharada too had brought a fan and was fanning him from a distance. And she thought it strange that all these days she did not know what the man looked like! Perhaps, this complexion was what the classical texts described as 'the hue of gleaming gold' ...

A torrent of emotion made Sharada's eyes brim over. This was the kind of husband Bhubaneswari had to sacrifice! Perhaps, she was not satisfied in heaven and was beckoning him? A cherished husband was such a wonderful thing! Then, wiping her eyes, she thought, Mejo-khuro is leaving us.

But Sharada's fears proved baseless. The ever-placid, ever-amiable, timid Bhubaneswari's invitation failed to overpower the force of gravity. Ramkali opened his eyes. He frowned on seeing so many faces around, and shut his eyes once more. And after a long time he said, 'Make my bed outside, by the temple courtyard.'

Yes, Ramkali would sleep outside, he could not stand the laments of women. He was ashamed of himself. Such weakness was unforgivable. He had fainted, people fanned him and poured water on him—could anything be more detestable? Why had it happened?

For a long time, he had been feeling drained inside, as if he could hear the footsteps of ruin. His body had been wasting away ever since.

A tumult of emotions had awakened in Ramkali too. He had never imagined that the tiny person, whom he had not even considered full-grown, could take away so much strength from the stout-hearted Ramkali. He used to feel an affection, akin to the tenderness one bears a child, for Bhubaneswari. He had never asked her to share his ideals, his thoughts, or his joys and sorrows. Now he felt he had been unfair to her. Perhaps, she had not been that tiny or insignificant after all. Had Ramkali blended respect with affection and transformed her into his companion, he would not have had to live such a lonely life. It was as if the glory of death had transformed Bhubaneswari.

Lying in bed, Ramkali resolved to go on a pilgrimage. A change of air was necessary. Or, it would not be possible to recover. Ramkali announced his decision.

Everyone was anxious about Ramkali for the next couple of days. Rashu spent two nights in the temple courtyard, quietly looking after his uncle, even though Ramkali had forbidden him. Slowly, things had returned to normal. Of course, they all worried about the pilgrimage—but it would take him a while to start out. After all, a pilgrimage required a lot of preparation.

Shashitara once again summoned Rashu, 'Look, if you have a man's pride, don't let your wife's tears dampen your spirit. It's not so simple to commit suicide! Tonight you shall sleep here.'

Rashu had spent three nights outside and was quite distressed. This proposal agitated him further. But he had no way of agreeing to it. He was like a starving person who finds a great feast laid out in front of him and finds his mouth gagged! Besides, Rashu was not like Sharada, that he would find an immediate answer. He bowed his head in dismay. Shashitara understood the silence to mean assent. So she said, satisfied, 'You don't have to worry. Just come to my room after dinner. We'll chat till late and then ... I tell you, shouldn't you think of the "new" wife? She must be feeling awful!'

Tears filled Rashu's eyes, and he moved away. Think of his 'new' wife! Of course he did! All the time!

———

And what about her—on whose account Shashitara was so anxious? Patli, the granddaughter of Lakshmikanta Banerji of Patmahal? She was frozen stiff with fear. By now she knew who her co-wife was. She had no idea that a co-wife could be so awesome. She could hardly look her in the eye, leave alone talk to her.

Yet, Sharada constantly came and talked to her. After all, Sharada was the one who was in charge of feeding everybody in the house, so Patli was under her thumb. Her mother-in-law had tried keeping an eye on Patli, but being incompetent she had given up after a while.

Sharada called out to her every now and then, 'Notun-bou, come and eat. Notun-bou, which slice of fish do you prefer? Notun-bou, do you like mashed-up mango pickle? Have you ever had wood-apple chutney—should I make some, Notun-bou?'

Almost as if Sharada had not a clue as to why Notun-bou—the new wife—was called that! As if she was in charge of looking after a relative who was visiting!

Today she had come with freshly fried fritters in a bowl, 'Want some?'

Patli refused, shaking her head. Sharada was surprised because Patli never refused anything. And that amused Sharada. She would think that she could feed her and keep her happy. Sharada had not grasped that Patli could not refuse out of fear. Perhaps she was not supposed to grasp that, so she asked, 'Why, why won't you eat, no appetite, eh?'

Patli shook her head again. Sharada said with a smile, 'Anything the matter, Notun-bou? I haven't seen you like this!'

The 'new wife' made no answer, her head drooped some more.

Sharada said as she turned to go, 'Then let me send some sweets, drink some water after you have them.'

Suddenly Notun-bou spoke, 'Why do you look after me like this?'

Sharada was unprepared for such a question, so she was flustered for a minute. But she collected herself and gave a laugh the next moment, 'Why shouldn't I? After all, the relationship demands it!'

So long her head had been drooping, now almost unconsciously Patli raised her head, and two teardrops rolled down from under her black lashes. Her eyes expressed a helpless rebuke. Fixing those eyes on Sharada's face, she asked, 'Are you teasing me?'

Suddenly the talkative Sharada was speechless. She could not bear to look at those tears, and for some mysterious reason of the heart that god alone would understand, her eyes too brimmed over. But she controlled herself, 'What if I should tease you a little? Shouldn't I?'

Patli suddenly realized that her eyes had done more than shed tears, so she lowered her gaze. Clearing her throat with some difficulty, said, 'I am your enemy, why don't you get rid of me? You'd be relieved, I would too!'

Sharada made a sad attempt at banter, 'I might be relieved, but why would you be?'

'I wouldn't have to live like a burden—as one to whom everyone has to be kind. It would be such a relief!'

Sharada was dumbstruck once again. She saw the tears spill on to the plump fair hands of the 'new bride' from her lowered head. She stared in silence for a while and quickly regained her composure, and said calmly, 'Wipe your tears. Don't cry.'

'I beg you, Didi, send me back home.'

'Listen to that! Who am I to send you back?' Sharada laughed, 'I'm the one who's been ordered to leave forever! But never mind, are you going to weep and lose the fight, with all your good looks? Don't you want to snatch away your husband from your co-wife?'

'I don't want a fight, Didi!'

'Don't want a fight? Then charity becomes the only way!' Sharada again sadly attempted banter, 'You've ruined the pleasure of winning. When one fights there is a test of strength; when one has to give away, then nothing short of handing everything over will do!'

'I don't want anything, Didi!' the new bride said passionately.

Sharada laughed, 'Nothing! Not even your husband?'

'No!'

Sharada answered, 'But d'you know something? The ways of the world are such that you get everything when you don't really want it! When you crave something it just slips away! Goodness! Look these fritters have almost lost their crispness, have them quickly. You'll feel better.'

—

'Mejo-thakurda!'

Ramkali was bent over a notebook calculating the costs of the imminent pilgrimage, when the voice of Rashu's youngest son startled him. He responded with tender affection, 'What is it, Dada?'

'Ma says she wants to beg you for something.'

What an extraordinary thing to say! Ramkali looked bewildered. He could make out the presence of Rashu's wife on the other side of the door. He asked in a perplexed tone, 'What do you mean, Dada? I can't quite understand.'

At this point, the go-between lost its significance. Reducing his role literally to a 'go-between', Sharada said quietly, 'Khoka tell him: My mother is the eldest daughter-in-law here, she has never asked for anything, now she is begging for something.'

Ramkali assumed that this had to do with the drama around Rashu's second wife. The jealous and intolerant girl must have come with the request to send the other wife home.

Feeling displeased, he said with a grave laugh, 'Unless I know what it is, I can't sign on a blank sheet, can I? What if it isn't something I can grant?'

'Khoka, tell him he can if he wants to.'

If Ramkali was appalled by her boldness, he was also amazed by it. He suddenly remembered another fearless girl and relented,

'Dada, tell your mother that if it is within my power I shall grant her wish.'

'Khoka tell him that your mother wants to accompany him on the pilgrimage.'

What kind of request was this! This was beyond Ramkali's imagination or his dreams! Was this what she had come to say? Was she mad? Was this a joke or just empty words? So he replied playfully, 'How can I dare to do that? You shall take her when you grow up!'

'Mejo-thakurda, my mother says you must not dismiss this as a joke. My mother is pleading with you.'

Ramkali could no longer heed the go-between, he said, 'But this is impossible! I am a man, I don't know where I will stay, how I will travel—'

'Mejo-thakurda, my mother says she does not fear hardship. She will cook and wash for you—you would need someone to do all that. My mother will take care of all that.'

'Dada-bhai, your mother is young, so she can't understand. If it were possible, she wouldn't have to ask twice. Tell your mother that she is the eldest daughter-in-law and it pains me to refuse her request. Instead of that I shall give her twenty bighas of khas farmland. She can do what she wants with the revenue. And when you're older—'

'Khoka, tell him that your mother doesn't need property.'

Twenty bighas of khas farmland! The girl was not tempted by that? Strange! To tell the truth it was not as if Ramkali had thought it up this minute. He had been thinking of settling something like this on her for a while now. Even if he thought of her as a jealous woman, somewhere at the back of his mind he was tormented by guilt whenever he thought about her. That was why he had thought he should somehow make it up to her.

But here was the girl saying that she did not need property! Ramkali was silent for a while, then said, 'But what can I do, Dada-bhai? I can't do something to make tongues wag!'

'Mejo-thakurda, you don't fear wagging tongues, do you?'

It was as though Ramkali had arrived at the gateway of a

mysterious city. What did these people think of Ramkali? There was a world of opinion about Ramkali about which he had no idea! With amused curiosity, Ramkali, the man of few words spoke more than he usually did, 'Who says that I don't fear wagging tongues? Of course, I do. Suppose I did something wrong ...' Ramkali reflected as he completed his sentence and paused.

During this lull, the hushed voice almost rang loud, 'Khoka, say, if you had a poor daughter, would tongues have wagged if you took her with you on a pilgrimage?'

Ramkali was dumbstruck. After a long silence, he said, 'All right Dada, both of you go inside. Let me think.'

Yes, Ramkali would have to think. About so many things. He would have to fathom that mental state which makes it possible for a young girl to resist the temptation of property and want to go on a pilgrimage. He would have to consider taking Mokshada along in order to fulfil Sharada's request. Mokshada had fractured her arm but she could walk. Besides, she had not had much of a life. Ramkali had a duty towards her. All his life, Ramkali had never thought so deeply about the creatures of the kitchen.

There used to be a girl who used to worry him from time to time. But she was long separated from him. And Ramkali was amazed that he had not spared her a thought all these days. They had not informed her about his recent illness because she would worry. But how could the news about his pilgrimage be kept from her?

TWENTY NINE

Raging fever for a full fortnight! The temperature just spiralled up with no signs of abating. And slowly delirium had set in. The patient would clench his fists and move violently about in bed, and lunge about wildly. Two persons sat by him to hold him down. Another kept pouring pots of cold water from the pond on his head. The Kaviraj was treating him, but the way he slowly shook his head, it was clear that the medicines were having no effect.

The house was crowded as though it were a festival. The neighbours waited sleeplessly, fearful for the climax; none wanted to miss the last act of the drama. Of course, they all loved the naive Nabakumar. A few of them had sworn oaths to the gods asking them to cure him, some had started the ritual of dropping five cowrie-shells into a pot of Ganga water to bring down his fever, still others had started bringing holy water for him from the temple of the cholera goddess. People were concerned and anxious about the one and only precious darling of Banerji-Ginni. Even if there was nothing to hope for, why should they give up on moments of high drama? So they had shortened their mealtimes in order to turn up here. And each one was an experienced 'doctor'! Now that they had a chance, they were going to apply their skills! For the moment, Ayurveda had been abandoned, and the women of the locality were carrying out their experiments. Under the supervision of goldsmith Nutu's mother, last night the patient's abdomen had been coated with rotten moss from the pond. It appeared that this medicine had worked miracles when Nutu's nephew was suffering similarly.

But it was Nutu's mother's bad luck that the miracle-cure had not had any effect. The patient had started rubbing his head on the bed. So today, Hari Ghosal's wife's prescription was being tried out. Because his body seemed hot enough to puff up unhusked paddy, she had ordered that the patient be wrapped up in sopping wet cloth and fanned. And doused with water as soon as the cloth dried.

Well, it was not as though there was no one who was sensible and outspoken in the entire locality. But Elokeshi had bickered with them all. Nevertheless they had come, when they had heard about Nabakumar's critical state. They had suggested reasonable things too. Bhaju's aunt had asked, 'Have you sent word to your daughter-in-law's family?'

Elokeshi had pooh-poohed, 'What good would that do?'

'But he is their son-in-law! I didn't want to mention it, but who knows what blow fate has in store! If anything untoward should happen, you'll have to answer for it!'

'Answer for it, my foot!' Elokeshi had turned furious, and had forgotten her misery for a moment, 'Do I live in their courtyard or what? Am I their vassal? Or do I depend on them? Tell me, am I the guilty party that I have to answer for it? This is a bad time for me, or I would have given you a proper answer, that's all!'

One day, Sanat's aunt had mentioned, 'I believe Naba's father-in-law is a great doctor. Why don't you inform him about the illness?'

Elokeshi had gravely replied, 'I don't have ten or twenty messengers at my disposal, have I, that I can send word instantly? And I've had such a hard time with my son's illness! Why don't you inform him? Ask him to come here and treat his son-in-law.'

Nobody had dared to say anything after that. But then, was Elokeshi so vicious that she was blind to what was good for her son? Not quite that. Actually, Elokeshi did not believe that her daughter-in-law's father could work miracles. Besides, she could not have withstood the humiliation of having him cure her son.

But to which act of this drama did Satya belong? Had she not earned the privilege of nursing her husband even once? That service had not been hers to claim! For she could hardly walk into a room full of elders and sit by her husband and stroke his feet. It would be immodest to enter the room! Even at night? That's when her in-laws sat there clutching their son to their bosom! And Sadu kept vigil. Satya did not belong there. Apart from that, she had a baby to care for. Less than six months old. And the entire burden of running the house too.

There was, however, one part of the nursing that she was in charge of. She brewed the medicines. She spent a lot of time grinding, mixing and boiling. Since the medicines did not seem to be working, the Kaviraj had started blaming it on faulty brewing. The spirited girl would stare dry-eyed. She would work quietly in a corner of the kitchen, with her head bowed. And at night, when her son fell asleep, she would unleash an ocean of tears.

What if Nabakumar should really die? It was as though a sudden storm had ripped through the earth, sky and underworld. It struck Satya, now, as he lay dying, that the person she had regarded as an innocent, inexperienced youth was in fact her main refuge.

Why had Satya always scolded him? Why hadn't she been loving always? And spoken to him with a smile? Oh God! Let him live this once and Satya would be loving, always. Even if he acted foolish, timid or childish—Satya would never notice his flaws! But would he live? Satya had neglected her mother, her mother had died. Would she get away with neglecting her husband? Well, she had been a silly girl then, she had not realized what it meant to have a mother. But now? What answer did she have now?

Satya would stay up all night, alert. What if that terrible clamour started suddenly at night? She would walk restlessly from one window to another. But with no success. Who would leave the window of the patient's room open at night? A breeze could prove fatal for enteric fever. Besides, wouldn't evil spirits peep in if the windows were left open? Even if the heart trembled at the thought, the thought was inevitable—what if the god of death should come in? Would Elokeshi leave the window open for him?

So Satya had tuned her hearing to its finest mode. But her duties hardly ended there. She would have to do much more than that for her husband. They might be his parents. But if they were ignorant, what could be done? Nabakumar had had this fever for nearly a month now, and there was no sign of remission. There had been no appropriate treatment either. And Satya had done nothing about it! Would god ever forgive her for this?

The women consoled Elokeshi after her bout of weeping, 'You've never done anything wrong to anybody, why should god punish you by killing your son?'

The next minute they gave her good advice, 'But who knows, if something untoward should happen, then bid him adieu through one door and kick out that bitch through the other! A daughter-in-law who speaks like that to her mother-in-law—'

'But I tell you, Batashi's mother, that's not all she said. I was just going to go out at night, when I suddenly saw something move away from the door. I screamed out in fear. And I saw it was my very own girl in the flesh! I was annoyed, naturally bad words came out—What were you doing here, you bitch? Casting a spell? You know what she said? "Your tongue doesn't lose it's sharpness even when your son is dying! What sort of mother are you?"'

One of the women listening immediately slapped her own

cheeks, 'My goodness, just imagine! Why didn't you give her a kick in the face, Naba's mother?'

Who knows what the response of Naba's 'generous' mother would have been to this mode of disciplining for suddenly another storm arose. The barber's wife was seen entering through the cow shed and stealing her way to the kitchen. Obviously in search of Satya. What scheme could they be hatching together? A stupefied Elokeshi yelled out, 'Where're you off to?'

The clever barber's wife realized she had been caught. So instead of lying, she walked over and whispered, 'She'd sent me to her father's with the news—'

She had hardly finished when Elokeshi gasped, 'To whom had she sent you?'

'To her father, you know. He is a well-known doctor, see? She had written the details in a letter she sent with me. Asking him to come and treat—'

'And you left on your own accord, without so much as asking me?'

The barber's wife did not succumb easily. The moment she caught on to the tone of rebuke, she said heatedly, 'What does that matter? She was worried sick about her husband and I felt bad—'

'Bad! You felt bad, was it? Don't you tell tales! As if you do anything for anybody for free—felt bad indeed!'

'I didn't say for free, did I?' The barber's wife said sulkily, 'I can't afford to do that! She offered a fair price and I went ...'

'Offered a fair price! She did?' Elokeshi fumed, 'Where would she get that, eh? That means she's learnt to steal from me! And you advised her—'

There was a sudden burst of thunder behind her.

Heedless of so many elders, Satya pronounced, 'Don't speak so vulgarly. I paid for her journey with my anklets.'

With her anklets! The elders were stunned. Giving away ornaments without telling her mother-in-law! The impact of this massive blow could not be absorbed even if one swooned every second. Nobody could imagine such audacity!

Elokeshi beat her breast, 'Just look at this! And tell me if you want to beat me for vilifying her! What shall I do—'

Satya paid no attention to her and asked the barber's wife calmly, 'Was father at the temple courtyard?'

'I say, listen to that!' The barber's wife responded in astonishment, 'Is he around now? Someone is dying, so he couldn't come and see for himself. So he sent some stuff. Your elder brother has come with it—there's a letter for you also. Hey, she's collapsed! What is this?'

A tremendous commotion surrounded the stream that had lost track of its embankment and had suddenly flowed out.

'She's passed out! It's all a pretence! She did something awful and has now got caught!'

Many a ripple surrounded the stream.

—

Technically, according to the shastras, one must observe three days of ritual pollution after the death of one's guru. Vidyaratna was not Ramkali's guru in the strict sense of the term. Nor was Ramkali the type who would follow the shastras word for word. Even so, Ramkali was sitting quietly in the outer courtyard the day after Vidyaratna's death. He had decided not to touch medications, or his books. Nor would he eat cooked food.

He had returned from the patient's house after losing the battle with death. His face had darkened with signs of that defeat. He saw no sense in going to visit his son-in-law in such a state. Especially if he had to refrain from practising his trade and not touch medications either. Perhaps, day after tomorrow, after the ritual bath….

His thoughts were suddenly interrupted. He saw his palki returning. With Rashu perhaps, or with some news from him. He had told Rashu that even though Satya had conveyed the news with so much anxiety, Rashu should assess the seriousness of the ailment and either come back himself or send back the palki and apprise him of the gravity of the situation. Ramkali was a little anxious till he could determine if the palki was empty or not.

It was not empty. Rashu was getting off. God had been good!

Ramkali stepped back as Rashu attempted to touch his feet, 'Touching of feet is forbidden during mourning. How did you find him?'

Rashu shook his head slowly, 'Quite serious.'

Serious! Suddenly, an image floated up in Ramkali's mind. A plain image in white. Ramkali shuddered and said feebly, 'The medicine didn't work then.'

'The medicine was not used—' Rashu said gravely, 'Satya has sent it back.'

'She sent it back?'

Satya had sent back her father's medicine! Rashu put down the bundle and avoided looking at that helpless face, 'Yes. Nor did she take your letter and read it.'

Ramkali uttered with some distress, 'Did they not let you meet her?'

'No, they did let me meet her. Satya wasn't well either. I believe she had fainted just as I'd arrived. Later, when she felt bette she met me and said, "Since it wasn't possible for Baba to come himself, let the letter be. What's the point in reading it. And take back the medicine too. Whatever is fated will happen. If I am a true daughter of Sati—that virtue shall keep me from being widowed." '

Perhaps this was the first time Ramkali stared in stupefaction. He was at a loss for words. How could he start out after his ritual bath, thinking of Satya, his ingenuous girl? What if his candid daughter should tell him to his face, 'Why did you bother to come, Baba—when we're not using your medicines?'

THIRTY

In the annals of this place this was a first! This incident of calling a Sahib-doctor. This historical event was made possible by the astrological confluence of three bodies—Bhabatosh-master, Nitai, and she who brought disgrace upon the Banerji family! The news made people stand rooted to their spots, and time stood still.

Everyone knew of the 'virtues' of the shameless, ill-tempered daughter-in-law. What they could not understand was why they had tolerated her for so long. Why could they not just drive her away? They had all tried to puzzle out the reason. She was her father's only daughter. And a well-to-do father at that! He must have set some conditions at the time of marriage. May be Naba would not inherit the property of this brahmin doctor if he threw out his wife. Or else, why would Banerji-Ginni seek to avenge herself indirectly by cursing and beating her breasts? They were all vexed by the recurring anticlimax that came just when they thought that the drama of getting rid of the daughter-in-law had neared its denouement. They had now almost begun to regard Satya with some fondness because she was the one responsible for a new twist in the tale.

It was certainly a blessing to have her as a topic of discussion or as a negative example to hold up before young wives. But when Naba fell ill, nobody could find a language adequate enough to criticize his wife. Such a prototype of a shrew could not be found in the Vedas or the Puranas, nor the Jatras! They had no language in which to describe her. But none of them could have imagined it even in a nightmare that the woman had actually met Naba's friend, Nitai, and given him her heavy gold necklace to sell, and arranged for Bhabatosh-master to fetch a Sahib-doctor from Calcutta! And she had spoken with Bhabatosh-master too!

Whether Naba would live or die because of the Sahib-doctor's medications was not significant. Far weightier was the task of dealing with his father.

The affair was no longer restricted to the women; it had upset the men—who comprised the crown of society! They had heard from their wives how Naba's wife quarrelled with her mother-in-law, spoke in front of her father-in-law, or did similar wicked acts. But apart from feeling annoyed they had not been able to do anything about it.

But they could no longer dismiss this as just the misdemeanour of one woman! It was a question of caste now. Banerji may occupy the highest place in the community, but he had no right to demand that everyone tolerate such shameless conduct! So far the question of his 'lower-caste' mistress had become sort of acceptable through numerous jokes. It was not really perceived as unnatural. But here was a Sahib entering the inner quarters, a married woman who spoke to other men! Society had not lost its claws or teeth that it would accept such aberrations!

A meeting was called in the temple yard and the group decided to pressurize Nilambar Banerji into disowning his daughter-in-law, and to make him an outcaste if he did not comply.

Living in society was not a matter to joke about. If that dying invalid really recovered because of the White doctor's treatment (not entirely impossible, because rumours had it that their medicines were miraculous—may god save him!) then they would have to make him undergo the purifying rituals.

And Bhabatosh-master? That man's body ought to be rubbed with nettles and then they should just cast him out from the village! But the devil had actually left in the coach for Calcutta to fetch the doctor! And he had arrived with the doctor too!

Well, one could hardly talk of banishing him because he had already set up home in Calcutta. He visited sometimes because his aunt was still living.

The only culprit who could be captured was Nitai. But he was not to be found either. Like the legendary Hanuman with fire on his tail, he had brought in the Sahib, and he had disappeared after setting Lanka on fire. And now the fire had spread.

Nobody had a clue! God knows when Satya had set it all up! Like a magic trick with the entire village looking on! They saw a horse-drawn coach coming up the village road. Nilambar saw the coach stop at his door. And a hardy English man emerged. Nilambar's blood turned into ice. This had to be either the collector or the magistrate! May be someone had pressed charges against him and they had come to handcuff him! Nilambar lost the ability to think through the causes, and he forgot to note that another figure had also descended. He started wailing and flung himself at the Sahib's feet.

Meanwhile the news of the Sahib's arrival in Nilambar's house had spread through the village. Nothing apart from legal and court matters had occurred to anybody. They had all peeped out of their windows and murmured, 'Like they say, it never rains but it pours! The son is dying, and now this!'

And they had peeped into Nilambar's house too. Suddenly somebody had noticed the stethoscope around the Sahib's neck 'A doctor—look at that!' A muted sense of excitement had spread.

A Sahib-doctor for Naba! Nilambar had pulled a fast trick! And he had not even thought of consulting anybody. It was like giving the neighbours a sharp slap in the face. Now he was pretending to weep at the Sahib's feet!

For indeed, that was what Nilambar was doing, clutching the Sahib's feet, 'Sahib, I don't know anything about it! I've done nothing wrong. My son is dying inside—'

And the Sahib's reassurance, 'Don't worry. The patient will get better—' hardly entered his ears.

But Bhabatosh's words did.

'Stop behaving like this! This is a doctor from Calcutta, he's come to treat Nabakumar.'

Nilambar looked up. And he noticed Nitai too. In a flash, he sensed a plot at work. Immediately it had occurred to him that the heroine of this plot could be none other than Satya. But how had it come about? Whatever it was, not a word could be said now. Trembling like a goat readied for sacrifice, Nilambar followed Bhabatosh-master into his own house.

Satya was standing by the window that faced the garden, still as a statue. The window was close to the patient's head and she had fixed the shutter in such a way that she could see the people in the room, while remaining out of their range of vision. When a massive red-faced man, almost a foot taller than Bhabatosh-master, entered the room, for some unknown reason Satya's heart trembled. Suddenly her eyes brimmed over with tears. Though she did not literally fold her hands, she prayed in her mind, 'Forgive your brazen and disobedient daughter, Baba. Bless me so that my husband lives. I know I have hurt you deeply but I am *your* daughter, after all. I've got this boldness and pride from you.'

Then she had tried to remember her mother's face, 'Ma, I'd sworn in your name, to make him well again when I'd returned the medicines. Don't let that be a vain oath!'

Satya didn't seem to value Kali, Durga or Shiva, she prayed fervently again and again to the living gods she knew. So that the Sahib's medicines worked like a miracle!

But even at such a grave moment, her ever-curious mind had filled with wonder like a child's. She had looked wide-eyed as the doctor placed one end of his stethoscope on the patient's chest and back, and put the other to his ear and listened solemnly. After a while, she had heard a sombre voice, 'No fear. He will get better.'

Was it contemptible to think of a mlechcha as a god?

After that, the coach had cleared. Those who had brought the doctor disappeared with him.

Two persons sat motionless, fuming, ready to explode—Banerji and his wife. They sat like wooden puppets, unable to figure out what they should do, what would be the wisest path to take. They themselves looked thunderstruck! They had forgotten all about their son.

Sadu appeared relatively sensible. She had summoned Nitai just before he left and asked him to clarify the doctor's instructions. And had taken the opportunity to quickly ask, 'Who paid for all this? The master?'

Nitai scratched his head, 'Not really, I mean, you know what Sadudi, it's because Bou-than started crying after she called me near the ghat the other day—'

Sadu stopped him sternly, 'She isn't the type to cry in front of any old person! Stop lying, and tell me the truth quickly.'

So Nitai had told her the facts. Satya had handed him her necklace on the way to the ghat, 'He's my husband and your friend. Act accordingly. Sell this and get a Sahib-doctor.'

She had wanted to give a pair of amulets too but Nitai had stopped her.

There was nobody else present in the sickroom. Satya had slowly come in and was standing near the bed. Sadu had almost entered but had changed her mind. In her mind she had said, 'If he lives, it'll be because of you! Behula had followed her dead husband to heaven and Savitri had pursued Lord Yama himself! And they are worshipped even today!'

After a while, as she was passing, she had heard Satya speaking softly to her mother-in-law, 'You wouldn't want to touch the medicine given by the Sahib-doctor, why don't you let me look after the patient, you can look after the cooking—'

Elokeshi had stirred a bit and responded drily, 'We'll have to obey whatever you say from now on. You occupy a place right next to Queen Victoria! So your slave here will be in charge of the kitchen, but what about your sons?'

Satya had said even more gently, 'They usually stay with Sadudi.'

'Just because the kids stay with her, you shouldn't impose.'

Everything was possible in this world! Here was Elokeshi speaking up for Sadu! Sadu had waited to listen to the next bit. And she had heard Satya say even more mildly, 'Sadudi loves them with all her heart. Why should it be an imposition?'

But Satya's gentle tone had brought tears to Sadu's eyes. This tone hardly suited Satya. Her firm voice was better. Much better.

THIRTY ONE

Perhaps it was the Sahib-doctor's skill, or Satya's good fortune, or Nabakumar's own luck that had held in the end—he survived. But deep within himself, who knows why, he now came to look upon Satya as the one who had given him life. So Satya could do what she liked with his life! Therefore when she sought to establish Nabakumar in that part of the country where Sahib-doctors treated illnesses, where the nightmare of death did not exist, Nabakumar had not laughed and dismissed it as useless. And Satya's work had become easier. May be that was the reason they said that whatever god wills ultimately benefits us. The illness that had nearly killed Nabakumar had finally brought some good into Satya's life, at least that was what she thought. Satya wanted to bring up her sons as fit human beings. And for that they needed to see the world. But she had had to work hard in spite of everything. Quite hard. Finally, little by little, the clouds had moved and the rays of light had become visible.

Thanks to the efforts of Bhabatosh-master, both Nitai and Nabakumar had got jobs in Calcutta. Nitai at Raleigh Brothers, and Nabakumar at a government office. So they were both, literally, 'moving up'. Of course, Nabakumar could not tell his parents himself, Satya had to do that. And they stopped speaking to their son and his wife. Elokeshi hardly stayed at home nowadays, she returned home only to eat and sleep. And Nilambar had started going on his evening jaunts again.

A while ago, Sadu had been annoyed with Satya. But after Satya had done the impossible by calling in the Sahib-doctor, Sadu had been totally enthralled.

Of late, Sadu had started turning the pages of her own life. If only she had had the same courage! Her life would not have been such a waste then. Perhaps she could have wrenched her errant husband on to the right path and led a happy life. But Sadu lacked Satya's skill with words. She did not know how to say, 'Why should I fear disgrace when I don't perceive something to be wrong, or if I don't believe it to be a sin? To refrain from doing something because of disgrace or praise is a type of selfishness. If I only worried about how people will praise or blame me, and don't think of what would be best for my husband and my sons, it would be very self-centered.'

Sadu could have tried really hard to make her husband mend his ways. Sadu had not, she had been afraid. Sadu had come to her uncle's and had been afraid of her uncle and aunt for no reason at all. She could never articulate what was right or wrong. Sadu was cowardly.

But Satya had courage. Which is why she had ventured to free herself from this stagnant pond and set sail on the sea. She had created a ripple among the young women of the neighbourhood too. And had come to occupy so much of their everyday thoughts.

Strange! Astonishing! Miraculous! A woman just like them was going to live in Calcutta with only her husband and sons! Escaping the clutches of a fierce woman like Elokeshi! Nowadays, their husbands were a little deprived of nuptial joys. Because, at every intimate moment, the women kept referring to Nabakumar's exemplary courage and love. The wretched husbands could hardly escape by calling him 'hen-pecked' or 'a wife's slave'!

To their disadvantage, these women had no opportunity of meeting Satya secretly and learning the spell with which to make their own husbands 'hen-pecked'. There were strict instructions against interacting with the daughter-in-law of the Banerjis, and whenever they came to the ghat, they were accompanied by their mother-in-law or aunt-in-law or at least a younger sister-in-law. Hence they could not learn the spell.

Of course, they always made it a point to curse Satya in front of elders. After all, shouldn't other women taunt the one who was ready to abandon her sacred duty of caring for her aging in-laws just to educate her sons in a 'good school'?

Let them! Such things never entered Satya's ears. If they did, they hardly affected her. Because she was busy preparing to leave.

Around this time, Satya had raised the matter. Perhaps because she saw it as part of her preparation. Or perhaps because she intensely desired to see the village of her birth for one last time before stepping out into the unknown. Whatever her reason, Satya broached the subject, 'I shall go there before leaving.'

She had not phrased it as 'it would be a good thing to go there', or 'it is my duty to go there'. But as 'I shall go'! Meaning to say that the matter belonged to the category of a firm decision. One that no incarnation of the lord himself could revoke!

Elokeshi said sullenly, 'That's good. But why're you telling me? Are you asking for my suggestion or my permission?'

Yes, Elokeshi was once more on speaking terms with her daughter-in-law. Because talking was a disease with her. It was not written in her stars to shut her mouth for two seconds. Even when she thought of stopping, she would involuntarily start speaking!

Satya turned her large eyes on her for a moment, 'I don't see the need for that kind of farce. When I have made up my mind, I'll have to make the preparations. I'm just informing you. Please ask Thakur to look up the almanac.'

Elokesh returned to her habitual style. She had mocked, 'Your father doesn't seem bothered! How is it appropriate to visit him?'

'I'll go to ask for his blessings.' Satya had looked ruefully at the sky, 'Children have their duties too, just as parents do.'

'All right then, go and do your duty. Go and ask his blessings. But let me tell you, my son won't go without an invitation.'

Satya stood up, 'You really say absurd things at times! If you stop your son, shall I travel with a stranger?'

'As if you need to be accompanied!' Elokeshi spat out the betel-juice, 'Even thugs would fear you!'

'I hope they do.' Satya had drawn the conversation to an end, 'But there should be a man with me, just to keep up appearances. Besides, it is also your son's duty to ask for my father's blessings.'

'Oh, tell me another! What kind of game is this! When did a father-in-law become one's guru, eh?'

'If women can have so many, I don't see why a man can't have one! Both parents are elders after all.' With that Satya had left. She knew what would follow, which was why she had not ridiculously attempted to seek permission.

But victory inevitably blesses the strong. An auspicious day from the almanac was fixed for travelling, and Satya set out on the palki with her husband and sons. There were no further obstacles. They had given up.

Once the palki passed out of her in-laws' village, Satya peered out.

Nabakumar cautioned, 'Why is your face uncovered? Who knows who will see you!'

Satya's voice quivered with delight, 'As if it matters! I'm no longer at my in-laws'!'

'That's not what I said!'

'Then just keep quiet! Is it written on my face that I am a

daughter-in-law? I'll show you how I tuck up my sari and tramp around there!'

The elder boy, Turu, was old enough to understand such discussions, 'Tui! Ha! As if you can!'

Satya scolded him vehemently, 'Stop that! Haven't I told you not to use "tui" when you speak to your mother. Show some respect!'

'Enough!' Nabakumar interrupted her with a laugh, 'Teaching big things to such a tiny person! I used to address my mother that way till I was quite old.'

Satya's face hardened, 'Please point out examples from your childhood some other time. Don't argue with me when I'm teaching him something!'

'My goodness! What is this! I can't understand your reaction at all!'

Nabakumar failed to comprehend how he had bungled. The exhilarated, graceful face of a moment ago, had eclipsed behind hardness. So he tried making amends.

Such liveliness, such grace! In fact, when Satya's face lit up with pleasure it looked so lovely. But how briefly it lasted! Covered by clouds in an instant. And all because of Nabakumar's stupidity! He could never understand which thing would lead to what, or where. Would he ever be able to fathom Satya?

But Nabakumar's child successfully dispelled the clouds. He crept up to his mother, 'One must be good when visiting one's grandfather, isn't it? Of course not! One must be good when one visits anybody! Only you must be very good when you visit your grandfather. I know all that, but baby doesn't, does he? He's really stupid. Doesn't know a thing! He'll just cry "wah" when we get there.'

Satya laughed at his imitation of his little brother.

Nabakumar had no need to be apprehensive for the rest of the journey, the clouds were not going to stay. Perhaps the movement of the palki had the flavour of joy. Satya seemed to be bursting with exultation just like an adolescent!

'Oh, just look at that black cow! As if it's made of black stone! Turu, look at the lotus in that pond. I used to pluck loads of them when I was a child. I'll show you the pond when we get there. Tell me, what is that tree? I can't make out. The leaves look different. My, what a wild smell! It's just like our part of the world!'

In her delight, Satya started talking to herself. Her sons and her husband were mere pretexts.

Nabakumar stared at that face. He had been married for so long, he had become the father of two sons, and yet, he had never seen her graceful face so clearly before! His fear of moving to Calcutta had receded, and in its place, there was a sense of excitement and romance. There, he need not fear the disapproval of his elders any longer, nor the displeasure of neighbours. There would just be Nabakumar and Satya!

He had his apprehensions about his job, of course. But Bhabatosh-master had assured him. He had said many people were working in government offices with less than a fraction of the English Nabakumar knew. The Sahib would certainly take to Nabakumar immediately. And living off the land was an outdated aspiration nowadays.

He would have to get a couple of shirts stitched in Calcutta and get himself a pair of shoes. Or else how could he go to office?

Bhabatosh had fixed up a place for them as well. He himself stayed in a shared accommodation—in what was called a 'mess', but that would not suit Nabakumar. After all, he was taking his family. Nitai was really unlucky! He would not be able to bring his wife along. For if she moved to Calcutta, his uncle had threatened to stop accepting food from them. Nitai's wife did not have the nerve to ignore such a punishment and live with her husband.

So they would have to look after poor Nitai. If only Nitai could have persuaded his wife—the two women could have given each other company. Of course, the rules of caste would not allow them to cook rice together; still, they could sit and chat, braid their hair, make paan and while away their time. But that was not to be. Nabakumar would have to look after Nitai. Bhabatosh said that the house was nice. Three or four rooms, a large hall, kitchen, storeroom, courtyard and a well. There was tap water too. Not inside, but right outside. But even if that were the case, it would be best not to drink that water and lose caste. Especially when there was a well.

Anyway, what would be would be. The main thing was the rent. It was really going to pinch. After all, Nabakumar was not going to ask his father to help him out. But Bhabatosh had said that nobody got to rent such a place even at ten rupees; only because it belonged to his friend had he got it for eight. Never mind. Nabakumar was going to get quite a good salary—fifty-eight rupees. It was not right for a well-paid man to get disheartened by such things. No point thinking about it.

But he was not going to listen to what Nitai had proposed. Nitai had said he would share the rent. That would be awful! Nitai was such a good friend—how could one take money from him?

But who knew how Satya would react! Here she was blithe one moment and irritable the next, what would happen there? Nitai was not a relative after all. What if Satya lost her temper in front of him? But perhaps, she would not do that. She would know how to behave.

When would that day arrive! When the two friends would sit down in that unknown house and eat their meal before going to office! Satya, her hair swaying, the end of her sari tucked at the waist, would rush about preparing the food. And serve them. It was Satya's strength that would make it all happen! Nabakumar gazed at her, his eyes brimming with love.

But Satya's eyes had turned piercing sharp, her nose flared, and she seemed to be concentrating hard. Quite unexpectedly, she cried out, 'There it is, right there! There's the attic of Jatada's house, there's the courtyard of Ganguly-kaka, and the palm tree that was struck by thunder! Take a left turn, a left turn here ...'

She had taken on the responsibility of showing them the way.

A thrill ran through the house when the palki stopped, followed by a collective gasp of astonishment. Why had the girl arrived this way, without informing them? This was not how it was supposed to be! What was the state she had come in? Had somebody come to discard her?

Not at all! She stepped off the palki like a magnificent queen, almost like the mother-goddess herself, holding her Ganesha and Kartika by the hand, and with her Shiva in tow. She had come because she had been missing her father and her family. She had come to see the land of her birth.

When the commotion outside subsided, Satya entered the inner quarters, her perplexed eyes darting about. And a slow, subdued wailing arose as soon as she entered. Weeping mixed with sounds of lamentation. There was no way of telling apart the individual voices. It was an unified choir. And a number of women from the locality had joined the women of the house.

Who were they mourning afresh? Bhubaneswari had passed away a long while ago. But this was not a grieving for anyone in particular, it had nothing to do with any recent loss. These were tears of joy for Satya's arrival, mingled with a lamentation that inventoried all the bereavements that had happened in her absence.

In the midst of this crying, Satya stood nonplussed, holding on to her sons, and Nabakumar sat outside in the outer courtyard, with an ear tuned to the inner quarters. His father-in-law sat across, but Nabakumar hadn't the nerve to ask him anything. He had touched his feet and sat down with head bowed, and he carried on sitting that way.

Besides, the man looked totally unperturbed. If this wailing inside the house did not disturb him, surely it could not be important. Nabakumar was a village lad. He knew full well that it was not unusual for a family to weep when the daughter came back from her in-laws.

At long last, the sound of the wailing faded.

Ramkali stirred slightly and asked, 'When did you start out?'

'Pardon me ...' Nabakumar gave a start.

Ramkali looked at him. He had the body of a handsome, robust man with the shy face of a youngster! A pleasant face, not an intelligent one though. He smiled regretfully to himself. It was possible to be fond of him, but one could hardly depend on him. Perhaps, that was why god had made Satya so strong, so she could provide support like a tree instead of being a creeper in need of support herself. He sighed. He feared Satya was condemned to suffer. She had inherited her father's misfortunes. How unfortunate Ramkali had been! Bhubaneswari was fortunate! Ramkali had never thought of it this way before. Never had he counted himself among the unfortunate!

Hearing Nabakumar's stiff 'pardon me', Ramkali smiled and repeated, 'When did you start out?'

'Quite early, after a small meal of stewed rice ...'

Nabakumar realized his foolishness as soon as he spoke. He should not have mentioned the 'stewed rice'. It would have done to just say 'morning'. The words seemed to hint at something!

Ramkali was flustered, 'Goodness! Has it taken that long! No, don't sit around any longer. Have a wash quickly—'

Nabakumar said a little more confidently, 'No, please don't trouble yourself. We ate on the way. We brought food with us.'

'Even so. It is late. I say, will somebody come this way ...'

A gang of boys appeared. They had been peering from a distance till now, lacking the courage to come closer.

Ramkali said, 'Go inside and tell them to arrange for him to have a wash.'

'Having a wash' was a signal that meant 'arrange for him to eat something'. A couple of boys left briskly, some stood around. And somebody said abruptly, 'What fun! You'll be living in Calcutta soon!'

Ramkali was startled. What a strange thing to say! Satya had disappeared indoors after touching his feet. She would not have spoken to her father in her husband's presence, with the neighbours clamouring around.

Nabakumar sat like a shy girl. Ramkali asked in an amused tone, 'What is this about living in Calcutta?'

The question was for Nabakumar. He could not ignore it. So he replied slowly, 'Yes. That is what's been decided.'

'I'm happy to hear that. Many opportunities for self-improvement are available in Calcutta. Have you attempted to find employment as well?'

'Yes, indeed. My teacher has arranged for a job.'

He was Ramkali's son-in-law. So it was Ramkali's duty to ask, 'Where?'

'In a government office.'

'That is good to know. And where will you stay? In a "mess"?'

'No, in a rented place. My teacher has also arranged that.'

Ramkali did not ask about the salary, but enquired anxiously, 'Then you'll have to arrange for a cook. If you take up a place—'

Nabakumar could no longer remain coy, for his face glowed in an attempt to hide his pleasure, 'No need for that! Turu's mother, I mean, your daughter, is coming along.'

'My daughter! Satya! She is going to Calcutta too?'

Nabakumar fumbled and fell silent. He could not fathom Ramkali's tone. Was he a little perturbed? Yes, Ramkali felt unsettled. He recalled a day in the far distant past. The image of Satya as a girl floated up in his mind, and along with it an ever-fearful face. Raising a finger before that face, Satya was saying, 'I really can't understand what you're afraid of, Ma! I will, I will, I will go to Calcutta! See if I don't!'

Satya was going to keep her promise, but where was she who would have been dazed with pride, pleasure, disbelief and delight?

He concealed a sigh and said, 'I feel happy that you have the courage to do this. But what about your parents?'

'My cousin's there. And the neigbours.'

'I see. Didn't they object?'

It was impossible for Nabakumar to contain himself any longer. He nearly grinned, 'As if they didn't! But it didn't hold. She said we must send our boys to good schools. She's the 'champion of reason' after all!'

Ramkali felt a sudden tenderness looking at his glowing face. He sent him inside.

The inner quarters were ringing with laughter. The grand-mothers were joking with Satya's sons. The rest were sitting in a circle around Satya—Rashu's second wife, Shibjaya's grown granddaughters, Rashu's brothers' wives, two nieces and a host of neighbours, young and old. Mokshada could no longer talk much, even so she sat in one corner, resting against the wall. The only person missing was Sharada. Sharada was so busy that she did not have the time to die! Her apathy mocked at the unfamiliar singularity of Satya's circumstance.

But not everyone was like Sharada; therefore the endless questions Satya was faced with blocked her from asking questions of her own. And yet, she had not come to show herself, she had come to see them. But their curiosity was endless. Two boys, and they had grown so big, and they had all been out of touch for so long! They had been invited to the rice ceremony of both the boys, but Ramkali had been away on his pilgrimage at that time. And after he had got back, they had not made an attempt …

But the question as to why she had not come earlier, and her arrival at this point, lay buried for now. The focus shifted to the place in Calcutta. Numerous prying queries. Who had encouraged Satya? Who would look after her there? How could she think of living separately with her husband when his parents were still alive? How did she get permission? By which magic spell?

And so much more.

Would she lose caste if she went there? Would they have to drink water provided by the mlechcha? And irrelevant questions like: would she have to ride in a phaeton to the Maidan in Calcutta?

After many such questions, an exhausted Satya said, 'My goodness! Here I am reciting my own tale! Let's hear your news.'

Mokshada groaned wearily, 'As if we have any! Those that haven't died continue to eat and drink whatever god makes available—that's all!'

'What a way to talk!'

'It's true, Satya. All my life I have lashed out at you. I used to think you'd have a hard time. Now I see that you're the winner. You have shown us! It's really good that you hatched this plan. Nowadays everyone praises English education. If you can educate your sons in an English school—'

Shibjaya had been widowed recently. And just a moment ago, she had informed Satya in deafening wails about how virtuous her mother had been, and how death had transformed her into virtue incarnate; and how all fortunate women who had not lost their husbands should die to preserve the glory of their married state! After that she had lain herself down covering her star-crossed face which she wished to hide from the world. But her resolve had broken as soon as she had heard Mokshada, her long-standing rival. So she uncovered her face and said, 'That's a new one! How very surprising! Like they say, "I spent a lifetime eating kids, now you say that I'm a witch!" I tell you, all this while it was Bengali and Sanskrit, and Persian for the learned, and now you're telling me that one has to learn the mlechcha's language—'

'Persian is mlechcha too!'

'Just listen to that! All my life I have heard Persian spoken, I never knew it was mlechcha!'

Now Satya responded, 'Let that be, Pishi-thakurma, they're all stories about losing or not losing caste! Whatever you have to lose you'll lose anyway. Who can stop that? Let's not get into that. Tell me, how come you look so weak? After the pilgrimage and the change, your health should have improved.'

'Improved!' Mokshada clicked her tongue, 'That'll happen when Yama comes for me. I've never set eyes on a husband, so I shall go like Yama's bride! But there's been a general decline these days. The village that you saw the last time, is no longer the same. People don't fear god or brahmins anymore, they've no sense of right or wrong. They've just stopped being humane. I suppose you'll want to look around. It won't make you happy, I can tell you that!'

On her way back, after a week, that was exactly what Satya thought to herself, 'I saw what you meant, Pishi-thakurma. I wasn't happy at all! The village is not the same. It no longer holds the pleasures and the joys of the past.'

This time too Satya had visited all her childhood haunts, she had sat down and tried to tune herself to the past, but had not been able to. It had become ridiculous in the end. She wanted to demonstrate to her boys that she could climb a tree, but they had protested so loudly that she had had to stop. She had gone swimming in the lake that she had been so fervent about, but had found no pleasure in it. She felt foolish when she went looking for wild berries, but she had brought them back nevertheless. Later, she had abandoned the chutney she had made. She knew that it would give her no pleasure.

Pleasure, after all, involved the whole. But where was that whole? Where were her friends? Would Satya ever find happiness in any other place? Where would she find that naughty girl who roamed the fields? That girl, in whose pursuit, she had come all the way.

And what about that girl's mother? There was not even a shadow left. Everything was wiped clean. Everything had changed.

Satya's familiar world had disappeared. Her particular space had been wiped out completely. Satya had become a stranger and an outsider in the land of her birth. She could hardly intervene if she noticed something unjust, she had to keep quiet and tell herself, 'Let it be!' One can hardly be rash and bold when visiting for a short while and proclaim, 'Let me tell you, you're being so unfair!'

Or else, there was so much she had noticed during her short visit. So many unfair things happened nowadays. All because her father had stopped taking an interest. Earlier, even the boys in the locality would not dare to step out of line because they feared Ramkali; now even the boys within the Chatterji household only kept up a facade of respecting him, and did just as they liked behind his back.

She had seen that in her locality too. Jatada's wife now quarrelled loudly with her mother-in-law. Apparently these days Jatada was totally devoted to his wife. The joint-family on Satya's mother's side had split into two. She was invited on two separate occasions. Tustu, the milkman, was paralyzed in bed. His wife had been literally begging from door to door to sell her wares but nobody wanted to buy ghee or milk from her. They would make excuses and buy from someone else. They would say, 'Curds made by Tustu's wife! When did that woman learn to make ghee?'

Even if the taste was not right, shouldn't one care for people when hard times befell them? Otherwise, in what ways were human beings different from animals?

Satya had secretly given two rupees to Tustu. Tears had streamed down the man's face. 'You heart is like your father's. It's because of him that I am alive.'

The village potter, the blacksmith, the washerwoman—Satya had met each one of them. But nobody had greeted her with a gleeful 'So! Here you are at last! Come and sit!'—as they used to.

Instead, they had spread out a rug and said, 'Please be seated.'

Strange! How had all of them changed all together?

Only the village had not changed. The trees, the fields, the woods, the ponds and lakes were the same. They had greeted her with tumultuous elation, swaying their heads. And at the time of parting, they had gazed sorrowfully, mute with suffering.

Those were the only things that had not changed.

But what security could she expect from them? A refuge can only be sought from the spirit, from the warmth of the heart. Where was that warmth? Everyone had taken care of her and said, 'My goodness, what a brief visit!' Nobody had said, 'You'll always belong to us!'

Wouldn't it have been different had her mother been alive? Wouldn't her mother have saved up her childhood and carefully preserved it in a golden case? When Satya arrived, wouldn't she have opened it with a smile and said, 'Look! You haven't lost anything. It's all here. I have saved it all for you.'

Then perhaps Satya would have seen her box of dolls. Her mother would have said, 'Look, here are the dolls you'd dressed. They're all just as you left them.'

Satya had dressed her dolls when she had come the last time for her grandmother's sraddha. Soon after that there had been the incident of a broken doll in her own life. Ever since, she had not had the time to think about clay dolls!

Perhaps, Satya would have laughed at her mother's foolishness. Still, it would have made her happy. 'There's no joy in coming back to one's father's house when one's mother's gone!' Satya thought with a sigh. In this huge family her mother had been but one among many—she had not thought about her in any other way. Today, she suddenly grasped that in the absence of that one person, everyone else became insignificant.

Among them, only in Mokshada's company had she found some comfort. But it had broken her heart to see how shattered that once fearsome person now appeared.

Satya had said, 'Too much hard work has ruined your health, Pishi-thakurma. In just a few years you've begun to look so fragile!'

Mokshada had scoffed, 'What else could I have done with this barren body, eh? The ghoul inside would drive me to work day and night.'

'And that ghoul drove your health to ruin too!'

'Forget it. I shall live as long as I am destined to. After that, somebody or other will light my funeral pyre—and if they care, they'll do the last rites. What use is it to live or die when there's no one to observe ritual mourning?'

Satya had said with anguish, 'Baba will do everything for you, Pishi-thakurma.'

Mokshada had said with despair, 'That he will. He's wonderful that way. And perhaps he will observe his aunt's sraddha just as he did his mother's. But in his mind, he'd probably see it as something extra, like charity.'

How strange! Anybody who had seen Mokshada earlier, would never have thought that she did not belong to this household. That there was nobody here who could ritually mourn for her even for three nights! Whoever did the last rites would do it out of a sense of compassion, and not because they owed it to her.

What then, had been the basis of her authority? Or was it precisely because she had no such right that Mokshada used to flaunt her vain power? Because she knew too well that the hollow wall would collapse the moment she let go? Lost in thought, Satya drew her sons close. They were her strength, the cornerstones of her edifice.

Satya had not been able to figure out Sharada either. Not one bit! Of course, Sharada had fed her, and looked after her too. She had especially cooked all the things Satya loved to eat, and she had joked, 'D'you know Turu, in your grandfather's grand house, where there was always a feast, your mother preferred to eat fried greens, fritters made of cucumber leaves and bitter-sour fish curry!'

When Satya had said, 'But I must say, you've been very noble. The "new" wife was telling me how like a goddess you are ...' Sharada had turned harsh. She had said with a bitter laugh, 'You're a sharp woman, aren't you? So why are you listening to what others say?'

And Rashu? Satya had not felt like talking to him at all. He seemed totally oblivious to the fact that he had a wife as old as Sharada and that he had fathered two boys! He behaved like the newly married groom of the 'new bride'. And he even tried telling Satya about their jokes and flirtations. How disgusting!

It was as if she had got no pleasure from talking to anybody.

Of course, they had all expressed their grief, shed tears and moaned about when they would see her again. Some had even wailed aloud. But it was as if deep inside, Satya's roots had been snipped off. Therefore, though she herself had shed tears, she was not going back with the feelings she had come with.

Ramkali had always been inaccessible to everybody, and only the fearless Satya could break through his armour of distance. But this time, she too had not managed to articulate her intrepid demand. She had not got an opportunity either. Ramkali had kept Nabakumar by his side most of the time. And the women's quarters had drawn Satya away. Still, the fact that Ramkali had been affectionate to Nabakumar had been deeply satisfying to her.

When coming away she had touched his feet and oblivious of the presence of her husband, had uttered in a choked voice, 'I take courage because you have forgiven your insolent, unruly girl, Baba! I am your only child, I hope I shall have the privilege of attending on you when it's time.'

Had Ramkali's voice quivered slightly? Something Satya failed to catch in that atmosphere of lamentation? She heard only the words. He had ruffled her hair, 'She's always like a grandmother! And what a wonderful arrangement for your father! Why should I need attending to, eh?'

Satya had not found any answer to that. But that deeply tender touch had provoked a surge of tears from deep within. Trying hard to control her sobs, her tears flowing, Satya had climbed on to the palki.

And she had been unable to speak for quite a while after that.

Suddenly, at some point Nabakumar had burst out, 'Your father does not belong to our ordinary everyday world!' Satya had looked at him with a start.

The tears on her cheeks had dried in the breeze, and her dry eyes looked dismal, parched.

Nabakumar had repeated, 'His spirit is like the kings of old. You can fear and respect him! It's a blessing to have a father like him!'

Satya nearly said, 'But here's a faded idol, and the festival's long over. If only you'd seen him earlier! Now he's broken in mind and spirit.' But she did not feel like saying much, because her heart was filled with sorrow. She said quietly, 'You never saw him when my mother was living. Nor have you met my mother. That's what I regret!' In her mind she said, 'Do you now see why I'm so proud of him?'

And yet, she was only a girl child. She could only hoard that glory within her. She had no right to that honour, nor the privilege of making claims. She had had to give up his shelter, and that was how she would have to remain. There was no way she could find fulfilment, shield herself with that glory, or use it to structure her life. God, why did you create such a social system? When it came to social matters, Satya blamed god!

Then she had looked out at the silent world of nature, and said in her mind, 'I am leaving you. Perhaps, forever. And I am about to take a step towards the limitless unknown. Let's see if I win or lose. Ramkali's daughter will never give up, even when defeat threatens her!'

After their return to Baruipur, they busied themselves with preparations to leave. At the time of their actual departure, neither parent had spoken to them; in fact, they had both left the house and stayed out. Sadu had done whatever was needed to be done.

But how amazing! Nabakumar no longer looked at this as his greatest loss. Ever since he had seen Ramkali, an exalted notion of 'father' had taken shape inside him, and by comparison, Nilambar's effeminate parochialism had begun to appear gross. He had thought of discussing his parents' boorish behaviour with Satya, that is, he had thought he would vilify them somewhat, but refrained because he was really scared of her. He moved on towards his new life.

THIRTY TWO

It was a wondrous morning! As though joy and fear and many a mystery waited motionless beneath the surface of the dawn. A mystery that would reveal itself slowly, a joy that would spread into a contented smile even as fear gripped one's whole existence. Therefore, it would not be easy to feel enthusiastic, or elated. And it would be difficult to accept all that was available.

This amazing new day, that hinted at the unknown, looked Satyabati straight in the eye. She thought, 'How different the sky looks!'

Yet, it was not as if Satya had only just stepped into the city and looked at the sky. They had arrived the previous evening at this single-storey house at Pathuriaghata.

Satya had woken early and had come to the verandah. And there she stood in a daze. She stood there oblivious of the chores that needed to get done. In the life she was previously accustomed to, the daily tasks would take on a life of their own and confront her; but all the chores of that familiar realm seemed to have faded away. Satya's raft would no longer sail in the waters of Elokeshi's creek. Satya would now have to create her own channel.

Somewhere early birds twittered, and Satya wondered if they had come from Nityanandapur in search of Satya or if they were calling out from the branch of some unknown tree in Baruipur! Saying, 'Satya, you're making a mistake! Think again, there's still time to return.'

Had Satya really made a mistake? Or else, why was her heart so full of fear? Why did she feel so helpless? Satya felt she no longer had the strength to remain standing, and she abruptly sat down. May be her head felt light after waking up. She would sit for a while before going for a bath. Today they could do as they pleased, Nabakumar would start work only from tomorrow.

It was not any old job at some village cutcherry, but a job at an office in Calcutta! The meal could not be served a minute late. A friend of Elokeshi's had enlightened Satya once by narrating within earshot, 'She'll soon know the hassle! Madam will soon know the fun of managing an independent household. She doesn't know what an office-meal means! The other time when I visited my cousins in Kalighat, there were three women struggling to get one man's meal ready! Your daughter-in-law is efficient but here she gets a lot of help from her mother-in-law and Sadu. It's very different trying to manage the entire expedition on your own.'

Elokeshi had said, 'She'll manage. She's got guts. It's my son who'll be miserable. The poor darling knows nothing of the world, and she's about to make him pull her cart for her! Anyway, god is watching it all.'

The friend had said, 'That is true. God will judge the ones who seek pleasure through wrongful means. Running a house isn't just about having a good meal, there are so many hassles. So the saying goes: "It's fun to feast without the clan and there are just two of you, but you can't protest when the beatings come, there's nothing you can do!" '

After that they had predicted, 'Once she realizes the hassles, Naba's wife won't have a place to run to!'

That day Satya had laughed scornfully to herself. But now she felt panicky. She wondered if this city would understand her. And accept her. Would it draw her close? Or would she live here like an outsider, as someone to be pitied? Satya did not fear the 'office-meal', nor the fact that she was on her own. It was the unfamiliar that she feared.

'Ma!'

Her older boy, Turu, had woken up and was standing right behind her. Nilambar had nicknamed him Turu after the Turk horsemen! He had been named Sadhan. After she lost her first child, this one was a treasure procured after many austerities; that was what his name signified. Turu's sleep-puffed eyes were full of wonder.

Satya turned quickly and asked, 'So, you're up? Isn't your brother awake yet?'

'No!'

'And your father?'

'No!'

'Well, of course, he won't get up now! He's the indolent nawab, isn't he? He'll know tomorrow!'

Satya abandoned her own lethargy and stood up. How foolishly she had been sitting around! And thinking up so much of nonsense! It would take her a while to get things organized in this new place. She had not cooked the previous evening.

After showing them around, Bhabatosh-master had taken Nabakumar aside and said, 'So, Nabakumar, help them settle. Ask your wife to light the lamp well before it gets dark, it's a new place. I'll get you something to eat. No need to cook now—'

Satya had jangled the chain of the door-latch.

Nabakumar had turned and come to her and had gone back wringing his hands, 'Why should you take the trouble? I mean—we could just boil something.'

Bhabatosh-master had looked at the door and directly addressed the occupant within, 'Even that can be quite a hassle, Bouma. Start everything from tomorrow morning. Tomorrow I shall arrange for a maid who will do the washing up. For tonight, I'll get puris, vegetable curry and sweets from the shops ...'

Nabakumar had suddenly said, 'Food from the shop! Should I lose caste as soon as I step into the city?'

Bhabatosh had laughed aloud.

'Really! You're as old-fashioned as ever, Nabakumar! Why should you lose caste? Am I trying to bring you food from a mlechcha shop? Don't you buy and eat sweets and fritters in the village? This is a similar shop.'

Nabakumar had scratched his head. 'Well, you mentioned the vegetable curry, that's why. Why bother?'

Bhabatosh-master said firmly, 'Why not? It is possible here. After all, Bouma is by herself. She can fall ill. And what if she cannot cook then? Shouldn't the children taste the range of food available here? I'm not asking you to eat rice, after all. But of course, if Bouma has any objections ...'

The latch had jangled once more.

Nabakumar had gone inside once again and returned to say, 'Well, there aren't any objections at all! She says we'll obey whatever you say. You are our well-wisher as well as our guru. You're—'

'Enough of that! No need to spend so many nice words, Nabakumar! Once all of you have eaten and rested I shall go home.'

Bhabatosh had bought a large quantity of food. Puris, vegetable curry, rabri and cham-cham, and paan too. The children were astounded. What a wonderful place they had come to!

The arrangement was to share the place with Nitai, but Nitai had not been able to join them yet. He would come after a few days. So Bhabatosh had asked, 'Will you be scared at night, Nabakumar? It's a new place, after all. I could come and stay with you till Nitai arrives.'

Nabakumar had been ready to snatch at the opportunity. But Satya had prevented that. She had jangled the latch again and informed him that Bhabatosh-master need not take the trouble, they would bolt the doors and be quite safe. Bhabatosh had left.

And soon after that Nabakumar had given it to Satya. He had said what he always said, 'Always ready to take a risk! I wonder why god made you a woman instead of a man!'

But Satya's face had not hardened. Instead, she had laughed. Spontaneously. Her unrestrained laughter had sounded unfamiliar to her own ears.

She had said in that easy manner, 'Where's the need to wonder about that? God has made you a man. Why depend on another? He won't be around all the time. One must gather the confidence to stand on one's own feet from the very beginning.'

After finding courage in the dim light of the evening lamp, would Satya grow infirm in the dazzling daylight? No, she would not! So wrapping her sari around her waist she got down to work, and embarked on this new expedition.

This household was her very own. She could mould it as she pleased, with her spirit and her dreams. Bhabatosh had had the place washed and cleaned. A clay chullah had been readied too. He had also stocked cow-dung cakes for fuel. He had also taught Satya the method of lighting the chullah, by instructing Nabakumar. Satya felt overwhelmed when she lit the chullah that way. She could work any way she chose, there would be nobody watching over her, nobody to find gaps and flaws. What an extraordinary feeling! What exquisite bliss!

But she had not fought only for the joys. She had wanted to move to a place where there would be a doctor to treat illnesses, where the boys could go to a good school, where men could work. She had not thought about the good things that would be there for her. She had known that there would be slander and disgrace. But now she was beginning to recognize that there would be a lot more than that. The joy of freedom! An open sparkling sky above, instead of a sword dangling over her head!

Satya was beginning to understand why city women were learned and smart. When they had so many benefits, it was only natural that they should want to repay something. Suddenly Satya paused. She would receive a lot too, would she have something to give in return?

Satya stepped out and returned to the kitchen in utter confusion, for Bhabatosh was standing in the courtyard. This courtyard was not a structure familiar to Satya. This was a four-sided space with a concrete floor. They would have called it by a different name in the village.

Whatever it was called, Bhabatosh was standing there and he cleared his throat, 'Are you there, Nabakumar?'

'Baba is asleep,' said his son.

Bhabatosh raised his voice, 'Still asleep! He'll have to go to work at ten from tomorrow! I've fixed up a woman to help. Khoka, ask your mother to have a word with her. I've sort of talked to her—she'll wash up, mop, wash clothes, break coal, light the chullah and grind spices. She must be paid twelve annas a month; four annas for her snack. That apart, she'll need a bit of oil for her hair before she bathes. She can't grind spices otherwise.'

Still not a sound from Nabakumar. A bewildered Satya began to sweat inside the kitchen. If the woman did everything, what would be left for Satya to do? It would have been enough if the woman had just washed up.

Bhabatosh addressed the woman saying, 'Come here. Go have a word with the mistress. Start right away then. Last night's dishes are still unwashed.'

It became impossible for Satya to limit herself to a bashful role. She pulled her sari over her head and standing near the door uttered softly, 'There was no need to ask her to do so much. I can manage ...'

Bhabatosh was a bit taken aback at first, because he had not expected Satya to come up and speak to him. But regaining his composure, he said, 'What's the point? If you're going to employ her, let her do it all. Even if she only washes up she won't agree to less than eight annas. You can pay little more and ...'

'It isn't the money,' Satya said clearly. 'It will ruin *my* habits. If a maid does all the work I will tend to take it easy. Besides, how shall I pass time?'

For a minute or two, Bhabatosh stared, totally baffled. He needed time to assimilate her words. It struck him as unique that a girl should not want to take it easy at her own place after having worked her fingers to the bone at her in-laws'. He had always felt a little wary of his student Nabakumar's wife, but today he felt at a loss for words. Perhaps a little overwhelmed too.

Then he said calmly, 'There are numerous good things for women to do. That's how you can pass time. Besides, you can read in your spare time.'

Before he could finish, Nabakumar came out of the room rubbing his eyes. He said quite formally, 'Master-mashai! You really didn't have to trouble yourself so early ...'

'No trouble! I just fixed this maid. Tell her what to do. Now if a milkman is fixed, everything will be in place.'

'How much more trouble will you take?' Satya asked.

Nabakumar was startled. When had the chapter of jangling

the door-latch ended? Speaking directly in this manner! How strange!

Bhabatosh said, 'You will feel uncomfortable as long as you think of me as an outsider. I don't think of myself as one.'

'Of course not! Why should we think that?' Nabakumar trailed off. And perhaps to demonstrate his familiarity, quickly added, 'In fact, I was thinking that I should go to the market with you. When is it market-day here?'

Bhabatosh laughed, 'Everyday is market-day in Calcutta.'

'Really!'

'And there's not just one market, there are several. But you don't have to go today. I have arranged for it. Why don't you see to the house?'

'There won't be problems on that front,' Satya intervened in a calm and serious voice. Then she brought out a basket and placed it in front of Nabakumar.

And this was how Satya set up her home in the city. Her own home. Nitai joined them in a couple of days. Nabakumar had told her, 'You mustn't feel shy. We're going to stay together. Treat him like a brother. There isn't another woman in the house. You'll have to serve him food—'

Satya had smiled lightly, 'No need to tell me. Do I strike you as shy and retiring?'

'Not at all! There's no question of shyness—you seem to carry on conversations with Master-mashai. D'you know Nitai, I was totally baffled the first day! Thank goodness, my mother isn't here. Your sister-in-law is really bold, you know. Or else, even we shiver in front of Master-mashai ...'

Nitai looked at Satya for a second and said, 'You don't see her for what she is! She isn't made of the same material as you or me. It is your good fortune that—'

Suddenly Satya startled them by laughing aloud, 'Busying yourself in a discussion of fortune are you? And you've forgotten all about the food! But just tell me Thakur-po, a master is a guru, isn't he? How can I be shy in front of the guru? I can respect him, esteem him and honour him, why should I fear him or feel shy in his presence? I have decided to learn English from him.'

'What?'

Nabakumar fluttered like a bow that had come unstrung, 'What will you learn?'

'I just told you.'

'Don't be mad! This is too much! It's best not to cross the limit. You have come to Calcutta, set up a separate house. That's one thing, but it's quite another ...'

'I just said I'll learn English. Does that mean that I shall wear a gown and go and dine in a hotel?' Satya's eyebrows danced in amusement, her happy face glowed. She faced Nitai directly and said, 'Your friend fears everything. What's wrong with reading a few books at home? Or will I lose caste if I look upon the mlechcha alphabet?'

Nabakumar said, 'It's all very well for you to say that. But after all, you are a Hindu woman.'

'And aren't you a Hindu man?'

'It's different for men.'

'Nothing like that. Everything is equal before god. And as for losing caste,' Satya's face shone with amusement, 'I've lost that a while ago.'

'What!'

The two friends gaped and remained that way as though they had forgotten to shut their mouths.

Satya continued to smile.

Nabakumar recovered his senses and asked, 'So you've started learning English?'

'Just a little bit. Whatever I can manage by myself. There were two of your books at home.'

'Amazing!' Nitai's voice was able to articulate only this one word.

'So, Thakur-po, do you think I can serve you your meal? Or perhaps you wouldn't want someone who has lost caste to do that?'

Without words, or warning, Nitai did something outrageous.

Instead of answering Satya, he stretched himself out on the floor and touched her feet. Satya was hardly prepared for this. She moved back a couple of steps. Then said calmly. 'Well, at last you've acknowledged me as an elder! All right, now listen to me. You have two days of leave now, so take your nephews and get them admitted to a school. They're prancing about ever since they came. That's the main reason why we're here.'

THIRTY THREE

A few more pages of the Book of Time flipped from right to left, and the days rolled past. Nabakumar had almost got used to this unfamiliar rhythm of life. The pace had quickened somewhat, he had learnt to come home and talk about his office, and had acquired the habit of carrying a container full of paan and chewing-tobacco with him to office.

The boys, meanwhile, had progressed to new classes at school, and they had moved house once. There was, of course, a delicate and private history to their move, but that knowledge was confined to Satyabati and Bhabatosh. Life went on smoothly.

Satya would rush about cooking the office-meal for her husband and his friend, and making them their paan. As soon as they left, she would busy herself with readying the children for school and after she had sent them off, she would finish the rest of the household work. Only then could she sit with her lessons in Bengali and English.

Bhabatosh, who brought her the books, would teach her too. Not regularly, but off and on—whenever Satya found something difficult. The teacher usually sat on the cot, and in front of him, on a mat on the floor, sat the two boys with their books. And Satya sat at a distance, her sari drawn over her face.

Satya always spoke clearly. So, despite the distance, Bhabatosh never had any problems understanding her questions.

One day, in the middle of the lessons, Satya had suddenly said,

'You have done so much for us. But we'll have to bother you once more.'

Bhabatosh had appeared troubled, 'Why should it be a bother?'

'Of course, it's a bother. You have really taken a lot of trouble. Whatever it is, you are like a father to me, I am like your daughter, so I shall not hesitate.'

Satya's elder boy had noticed that the teacher's face changed. He looked distressed. Satya's head was lowered, her face, covered.

Bhabatosh had said something indistinctly and in response Satya had said, 'Yes, that's what I mean and I am saying it plainly. Please do something for Kayet-thakur-po. I hear that men pay to live in shared rooms and work in offices—something called a "mess".'

Kayet-thakur-po was Nitai. Even though she called him Thakur-po to his face, she would refer to him as Kayet-thakur-po to clarify it for others. The caste-term was only used as an explanation. He lived like a brother here with Nabakumar. There was, of course, the matter of violating rules of ritual pollution—that happened when she served him rice. But apart from that, the distinction between brahmin and kayastha did not really matter to Satya. In fact, there was always great affability. Had something happened, then?

Bhabatosh had mused, 'Yes, there are such places.'

'That's the kind of place I meant. You must fix up such a place for him.'

Bhabatosh had scratched his head, 'I'll do that. But what has happened? Has he said something about not wanting to stay?'

'No, he hasn't said anything like that,' Satya had been firm. 'But I am saying it. You will have to do something.'

Bhabatosh had been silent for a while and then said, 'Because it's you, there must be a good reason. I am confused because I can't understand it yet.'

This time there had been no response from Satya. Bhabatosh had risen, and said, 'I trust Nabakumar is of the same opinion?'

Satya had replied, 'The opinion of a man doesn't matter in the day-to-day functioning of a home. He will be told once it's fixed.'

Bhabatosh had guessed that something had happened. But what could a boy like Nitai have done? How could he just announce to Nitai that he had found him a place, out of the blue? So he mentioned that.

'Without sounding Nitai out ...'

'That is a worry. But what to do? Since somebody has to tell him, I shall.'

After that, Bhabatosh had left.

The elder boy had asked, 'Why will Uncle not stay here, Ma?'

Satya had responded gravely, 'A child shouldn't get involved in everything. You'll see when it happens. No need to think about "why" or "what".'

And that is exactly what they saw. They saw that their father avoided the scene, while their mother stood silently by the door as Nitai packed his trunk and bedding and loaded them on to the hired horse-coach. It was such a tense situation that they had not dared to ask anything.

Neither had Nabakumar. That was why he had disappeared since morning. Later, when he had entered the house, tip-toeing, like a thief, he had checked out Nitai's room and seen that it had been latched shut. Nabakumar's heart had thumped in his chest. It was as if the door to his heart had been grimly latched shut. Never to be reopened, with so many of his joys and pleasures locked inside.

God alone knows why Satya had suddenly decided this! It had not appeared as if she had been annoyed with Nitai's conduct. Just yesterday, Nabakumar had noticed Satya weeping silently as she served Nitai his meal. He had also noticed that she had been cooking all the things Nitai loved. What could it be then? Something did not seem to fit. Had Satya begun to worry about the cost? But that could not be right either. Nitai had been paying his share. Nabakumar found himself in a maze.

Neither had he got a satisfactory answer when he had questioned Satya about it. She had said, 'This is too good an arrangement. If he gets to eat well twice a day he won't put in any effort into getting his wife here.'

Nabakumar had responded heatedly, 'Let him figure out what he'll do about his wife. He isn't compelled to make an effort to bring her. As though all the wives in the village are waiting to come to the city like you!'

On hearing this Satya had not been upset or stopped talking, as she used to earlier. From their early days Nabakumar had had this habit of scoffing at her desire to come to the city. Though he now enjoyed its comforts and pleasures, and actually admired Satya in his mind, his taunts had become more of a habit with him than anything else.

There used to be a time when Satya would become numb with hurt. And when Nabakumar could no longer stand her frostiness, he would be compelled to make peace. He used to beg her pardon a hundred times and declare that it had been a joke. He had got her used to it by repeating that it was a joke. So it no longer affected Satya. Nor did it trouble her now. She had frowned and said, 'Till such time you become a god you won't know if they're waiting to come here or not. But there is something called right and wrong for human beings. After all, people marry in order to set up a home.'

Nabakumar had expended a few more words. In a monologue. He had hoped that in the end, talk of Nitai's departure would vanish into thin air. But gradually, he saw it taking concrete shape. Nobody spoke a word, yet something was afoot. It was not as though the two friends had stopped chatting while they ate. But it all seemed a bit dry, as though it no longer held together. And yet, he had not dared question Nitai directly. Or, for that matter, Satya.

But his gush of grief made him bold now. He turned away from the latched door and asked fiercely, 'Didn't it break your heart to drive out an innocent man like that? What a woman you are!'

Satya had been sitting with her head bent over a book, by the lamp. She had raised her head once on hearing this, and had then lowered it again.

A turmoil had been churning inside Nabakumar which made him unpleasant. He had been provoked even more by the turning of the page. He had said, 'What my mother says is true. A woman's learning is the origin of all destruction.'

Satya had quickly shut the book and stood up, 'Mother's words are straight out of the Vedas themselves! Naturally I'm the one who's destroyed your life. Well, there's nothing to be done about it. Learning isn't like a pot or a pan that you can pack it away whenever it's in the way! But I wouldn't say he is innocent. In any case, how do you know for sure that it hasn't broken my heart?'

'Heart! Even a stone has a heart, you don't!'

Satya knew how much Nabakumar loved his friend, therefore, even such a tremendous accusation did not perturb her. She understood that he had said it out of anger and hurt. That was Nabakumar's nature. He said harsh words whenever he lost his temper and grovelled whenever he got over it.

Therefore, Satya's response had been placid, 'If I am such a stone, why ask if I'm heartbroken? But what is the reason to count him innocent? I don't consider a man who maligns his guru innocent.'

His guru! Nabakumar had been astounded, 'What do you mean?'

'I can't tell you what that means. You are worse than a woman when it comes to keeping secrets, you'll let the whole world know. But have faith in me, I'm never unjust. Nor inconsiderate.'

Nabakumar had not gathered anything beyond this. Nor was he expected to. But he did not possess the mental capacity to grasp what was wrong. Satya had implored him with folded hands, 'Please don't ask me more. I cannot bring myself to utter it.'

She really would not have been able to. She was not supposed to either. But Nitai had spoken the unspeakable. He had said one day, soon after Bhabatosh had left, 'What a nice relationship our teacher has created! Teacher and student! But he just feasts on the student with his eyes all the while he teaches.'

Satya had said fiercely, 'Thakur-po!'

'What's the point in getting angry. I'm only saying what is true. I don't like his conduct these days. He finds any excuse to come into the house, can't you make out from that? Not with good intentions. There must be another reason. I am warning you, if you don't watch out now, one day he'll be the source of trouble.'

Satya had asked harshly, 'Since you've raised the topic—how do I know for sure that the same trouble won't come from you?'

'From me! What do you mean?'

Nitai had turned red in the face. But Satya had remained unbending.

'Go into your room and figure out what I mean. Ask yourself. And let me ask you too—how do you know who is feasting his eyes on whom?'

'Why shouldn't I?' Nitai had retorted in anger, 'Anyone except a blind man like Naba would have noticed it.'

'One sees only what one wants to see. If such a wicked notion can enter your mind, Thakur-po, then I feel it isn't right to live in the same house any longer.'

'Isn't right!' Nitai had repeated in astonishment, 'To stay in the same house?'

'No, it isn't.'

Nitai had hissed, 'Will the danger vanish if you get rid of me?'

'Danger!' Satya had started laughing, 'Why should I be in danger? When one touches fire, is the fire in danger or the hand that touches it? Haven't you read in the *Ramayana* and *Mahabharata* about the powerful Sati-women? I am asking you to go away for your own good.'

At a loss for words, Nitai had said, 'Wonderful! What a verdict!'

Satya had said, 'There are several reasons why you are blind now, Thakur-po, so you are not wise. You'll understand later. There's no need for further talk. Bad words spawn like maggots. It's best to root them out!'

The request to Bhabatosh to search for a 'mess' had followed.

But was Nitai's accusation completely baseless? It would not be right to say that. Was Satyabati not aware of the way Bhabatosh looked at her lowered face—his gaze full of respect, awe, fondness and delight? She was. Even a stone idol can sense the offerings of a devotee! But she did not worry about it. She knew there was no reason to fear. That gaze would not hurt her one bit. Just as Nitai's suspicious, resentful gaze would not harm her. She had ignored both. But she had to rethink all that after Nitai had openly expressed his rancour. What if the foolish Nitai should mention his base suspicions to Nabakumar!

And what if Bhabatosh had got to know? How shameful! He was affectionate. He was the guru. He was not a pervert. That was why no harm had come to him. But it was a different matter with Nitai, who did not have pure admiration. He could bring harm to himself. Something had to be done about him.

So Satyabati could tell Nabakumar firmly, 'I shall never do something inconsiderate, nor something petty. Trust me.'

Soon after Nitai had left, Nabakumar had begun to complain, 'The house is large enough to swallow us up!' Or, 'Why do we need four rooms?'

Satya could guess that the latched room was an eyesore for him. One day she had suggested gently, 'Why don't we look for another place?'

'Why do we need to do that?' Nabakumar had been upset.

'There's no need, of course. But it would be a change. Besides, the rent is quite high here. And things are getting more and more expensive. The school fees and books cost so much.'

'That suits you, doesn't it? After all, there was a person who was paying a lot for his two meals ...'

Satya had gone away without another word. She had vowed in her mind that she would not ask Nabakumar, nor request Bhabatosh-master, but take charge herself. She would get the maid to find her a place. After all, the maid worked in so many houses and kept track of many things. And she had not been mistaken.

It was her maid, Panchu's mother, who had found her this place in Muktarambabu Street. The landlord was very wealthy, the family, aristocratic. Earlier, when times were flourishing, they had built small quarters for their administrators and clerks. Now that they had fewer employees, they had rented out a few of these places.

Panchu's mother brought news about one such place.

Nabakumar could not help expressing his satisfaction when he saw the place. For though it was small, it was neat. Bhabatosh-master had felt hurt, 'If you needed to change house, why didn't you ask me, Nabakumar?'

Nabakumar had repeated the lesson he had learnt at home, 'How much more can we burden you with? There's no end to the support you provide us. When the maid could help us with this …'

'Well, it is a little far from my place.' Bhabatosh had sighed.

But they had moved. And Satya had become a little more self-sufficient. She had slowly begun to get over the habit of depending on Bhabatosh for everything.

But this place had one disadvantage. The landlord was wealthy, but belonged to a lower caste. Therefore, he was very devoted to brahmins. Whenever there was a festival, he would send gifts to the brahmins, and present the women with red-bordered saris, and sweets, and paan with betel-nuts. It was embarrassing to receive such gifts, especially because they could not be returned.

Nabakumar of course, hardly saw this as embarrassing. He would say, 'Why do you hesitate so much? As they say, you can never give enough to a brahmin! And on top of that they are a sonar-bene family, they're reaping merit by giving gifts to brahmins.'

'So what?' Satya had protested, 'We aren't able to give anything in return, are we? I feel mortified!'

'What contrary logic! Aren't you giving them your blessings?'

'Blessings!' Satya had laughed openly. 'As if they were waiting for my blessings! As if their power and prosperity are products of my blessings! Whatever you say, this is a real problem.'

'Whatever other people wish for appear like problems to you! Whatever other people fear, you feel pleased about—that's what I've seen all my life. I wonder which of the gods made you!'

This sort of conversation took place quite frequently.

One day, Panchu's mother had said, 'The Boro-Ginni often says to me, "I say, everyone comes to meet me, how come the Ginni at house number seven hasn't visited yet?" So I say to her, "Rani-ma, she's hardly a Ginni, she's quite young." But whatever you may think, I guess it's your duty to go there sometimes. All their subordinates go to pay their respects to her.'

A subordinate! Satya had been outraged, 'I'm not their subordinate! I pay them rent to live here.'

'The same difference!' Panchu's mother had tried to mollify her, 'Whether you pay land revenue or rent, it's the same thing. The Ginni looked displeased, so I thought I'd mention it. She's a wealthy woman after all. She's fawned on day and night, so she's really snobbish. She must be wondering why you're not forthcoming. If you just visited her once, she'd be pleased.'

'Where do I have the time?' Satya had asked gravely.

'Listen to that!' Panchu's mother had hardly managed to contain her amazement, 'It's just across the gully, and you don't have the time for a visit? Let me tell you, Bou-didi, you are no less haughty.'

'So, now you know!' Satya had burst into laughter.

'Yes. But I always knew it! I was telling you for your own good. When you live in the marshes, it's best to be on good terms with the crocodiles, eh?'

'Look, I'm just not the type to go and dote on her. If I have to get bitten by the crocodile, so be it!'

'I never said that, did I? You belong to the highest caste. Your glory can hardly be equated to the pomp of wealth. But it is Kaliyuga, after all! Money brings salvation. Or else why would Chakraborty-Ginni grovel in front of Datta-Ginni?'

'Let that be. It makes me mad to hear such things. To tell you plainly, it doesn't suit me to visit the wealthy. Even if it means giving up this place.'

But Panchu's mother was nice. Not the type to gossip. And I guess she was in awe of Satya's spirited nature. Which was the reason why she did not mention the matter to Datta-Ginni. Even though she was constantly dropping in at the Datta house.

Although she worked as a maid, in actuality, Panchu's mother was a gardener's daughter. Her niece was in charge of the flowers at the Datta house, and she was quite a figure there. Panchu's mother would therefore take the liberty of having her evening snack at the Datta's on a regular basis. After all, Datta-Ginni spent all her time in the company of the weaver's wife and gardener's daughter. Panchu's mother had thought it would please Datta-Ginni if Satya managed to visit her one day. But Satya just dismissed it by saying, 'Step into the parlour of the rich! Impossible!'

But a day came when Satya had to cross the threshold of that wealthy household. The cook and the chief maid had come and invited her to the grandson's rice ceremony. They had brought a bell-metal bowl with eight sandesh-sweets and a brass pot full of oil and said, 'You're invited to the grandson's rice ceremony. Everybody must come. Don't bother cooking at all that day!'

Satya had asked solemnly, 'When is the ceremony?'

'Day after tomorrow.'

Satya had said even more seriously, 'So? It isn't a holiday, is it? Babu has to go to office at ten. It won't do if I don't bother with cooking. He won't be able to eat there that early.'

'Don't know about that,' the cook had rasped. 'If the Ginni sees smoke coming from anyone's house, there'll be a lot to answer for—and that's the truth!'

'I suppose Babu shall have to make do with stale rice that day,' Satya had said without expression.

The chief maid had been astounded. Then her grating voice had sounded again, 'Goodness! She's dangerous. That's why Rani-ma says, "To all other houses it'd be enough to send just any maid, I'll send you to number seven because you're a brahmin. She's really high and mighty, what if she refuses an invitation because the messenger is a sudra?"'

'Good for her! She seems to know people even before she's met them. Your Rani-ma is really great!'

Not grasping the implication of the remark, the cook had responded, 'That she is! A hundred times. You'll know when you visit how kind she is, and she's as beautiful as she's kind. Just like the Goddess Jagatdhatri!'

She knew full well, with the chief maid present, that such adulation would not go waste.

Satya had said, 'Just wait, let me return the pot and the bowl.'

Hearing this, both maids had burst into laughter, 'My goodness! Why should you return those? They come with the invitation. They've had about a thousand such items made to order. Haven't you seen such things before?'

And without another word, Satya had put away the bowl and the pot. Their laughter had wounded her. Of course, she had seen such things! The daughter of Ramkali Chatterji had seen plenty! She had seen utensils being gifted as well, but she had not known, until now, the disdain with which they were given away! And she had mulled over this burning sting that had come with this nice house she had rented for five rupees! Now it would no longer be possible to avoid a visit, as she had done so far. It was a social event after all.

———

It was customary to go in a palki, even though the place was close by. Panchu's mother had said, 'I shall finish the washing up and come back in fresh clothes. Meanwhile, you can get ready and get the boys dressed ...'

'The boys? They're off to school now!' Satya had said.

'What? Won't they go for the feast?'

'And miss school?'

Panchu's mother had said in amazement, 'Would it matter if they missed school for a day? All the boys in the locality are bunking school today. They've been counting the days for more than a week now. A feast at a rich man's house, it will really be grand—full of things nobody sees everyday!'

Satya had said a trifle harshly, 'How does it help to see them just for a day then? You come back, I shall go with you.'

'I don't understand your ways at all! I say, if the boys don't go, then you'd lose out on the individual chyada they're gifting.'

'I don't want to discuss profit and loss with you. Finish your work and come back here.'

But Panchu's mother had not given up. 'Well, the boys can go after they come back from school. The festivities will go on till evening.'

'Will you stop?' Satya had moved away with the reprimand.

———

Putting his paan-container into his pocket, Nabakumar had said, 'You could have taken the boys!'

'Why?'

'Just like that. It's a feast.'

'No, it's best not to visit the wealthy. The children are immature and naive, they'll start feeling ashamed of themselves after seeing such grandeur.'

'You really say such strange things. Only you can think them up! Anyway, take a rupee to give with your blessing.'

Satya's eyebrows had danced in amusement, and her face had glowed, 'Just a rupee! Now that I've got a chance to return something for all their gifts, why should I take just a rupee?'

'Then what'll you give? A garland of guineas?' Nabakumar had quipped.

'I can't be so extravagant. But I'll give this.'

Satya had taken something out from the trunk, and held out her closed fist, 'Just guess what this is?'

'Can't guess. I'm getting late. Show me, if you want to.'

Satya had unclenched her fist and held it out. The gold sparkled. A heavy gold chain, of at least five bhori weight.

Nabakumar had teased, 'Won't it break your heart to give this away?'

'Of course not! My heart doesn't break that easily.'

'Are you serious?'

'Of course, I am.'

'You'll give away such a heavy chain? Trying to keep up with the rich, are you?'

'It isn't about "keeping up",' Satya had answered gravely. 'I'm just trying to reclaim my pride—they think we're their subordinates.'

'What is your pride before their's, eh? They're millionaires!'

'So what?'

Nabakumar had understood that she had not been joking, she had been serious. And he had exploded. He had said nobody in their right minds would want to do such a dangerous thing. Where was the need to give away such a heavy gold chain when just a rupee would suffice? Besides, who had given Satya the right to squander gold in such a wayward manner? What would happen should Elokeshi get to know?

Satya had said solemnly, 'This doesn't belong to your mother.'

'What d'you mean? Your father has given you away along with your gold jewellery.'

'This isn't something I got for my wedding. And nor has your mother handed over those to me. The last time I went to Nityanandapur, Pishi-thakurma gave it to me for the younger boy.'

'And you have to give it away, just because she gave it to you?'

'I cannot go otherwise.'

'Extraordinary! I tell you, if you really want to keep up with them, go find yourself a heavy brocade and diamonds and pearls.'

'Why should I do that?' Satya had been firm, 'A brahmin woman looks grand enough in a red-bordered white sari and conch bangles.'

Finally, decked out in the self-same grand attire she had arrived at the ceremony, accompanied by Panchu's mother. She had with her a new bell-metal thali on which she had placed the gold chain and some durba-grass as blessing. The magnitude of the ceremonial offering had amazed even Panchu's mother. With a hand on her cheek, she had said, 'I say, even relatives give one or two rupees. Tenants like you give less than a rupee. And here you are ...'

'Never mind. Come with me!'

———

'Where is the child?' Satya had asked someone.

She must have been one of the maids, because Panchu's mother had greeted her with a grin, 'Here you are! Just brought our Bou-didi. From number seven, you know ...'

'I see!'

Indicating direction by a lift of her eyebrows, the woman had said, 'Make her sit that side.'

'Of course, she'll sit. But let her bless the boy first.'

On noticing the item that Satya was holding, the maid had responded in a tone that combined surprise and awe, 'Take her upstairs, then. The boy is with Mokshada.'

Mokshada was the most important maid. Her place was after the mistress herself! The rest of the women of this household were scared stiff of her. And she ruled over all the other maidservants. She was in charge of the boy, because the boy had been decked in jewellery from head to toe. His head had been shaven, and he wore ornaments on every limb, but the boy was irritated with the sequinned velvet jacket he was dressed in, and was shrieking away. And Mokshada, dark and huge as a buffalo had been sitting with the boy on her lap. In front of her was placed a thali for the gifts. As soon as she had spotted Panchu's mother, she had bellowed out, 'Is that your mistress, hey? Thank goodness, she's blessed us by coming!'

Satya had frowned. Even so, she had walked up calmly and after blessing the boy with the durba-grass, she had placed her thali with the chain by their thali for gifts. It was filled with small change rather than rupee coins.

Instantly, Mokshada had frowned.

'What's this Pancha's mum?'

Panchu's mother replied agitatedly, 'Blessings for the boy, Mokshada-di. Boudi was saying what's the use of just a rupee. It's a wealthy household, they have so much money, so ...'

'Don't you talk nonsense!' Satyabati had reprimanded her fiercely.

Mokshada had given Satya a once-over, and then she had picked up the chain and inspected it. Then, she had said drily, 'Take this chain back, d'you hear? Children of this house don't wear fake trinkets.'

Fake! Panchu's mother's heart had shrivelled to the core. In her mind, she had been snickering at her callow mistress's witlessness. May be she had no experience of wealthy families of the city, so she was being so extravagant. Let her be! Panchu's mother's renown would increase—after all, her niece worked here.

But what was this? Such a disgrace! How foolish of her! How could you come to the Datta household and gift a trinket that was fake? She had stared, appalled.

By then Satya had responded. Her voice was sharp but low, 'Have you just started work here, my dear?'

'Just started! Me?' Mokshada had flared up, 'I say, who do you think you are, eh? Just because it's the first time you've stepped in here, you think I'm a new maid, eh? My hair has turned grey working for them, understand? Anyway, why such a question, eh?'

'Well, you yourself begged the question, my dear! If you've worked here for that long, how come you can't recognize gold when you see it?'

Mokshada's dark face had darkened further, 'You really talk smart, I can see. Pancha's mum, take her to the elder Rani-ma. Let me tell you, lady, keep a hold on your tongue in front of her. Don't you mistake it for a gathering of maidservants or something!'

Panchu's mother had whispered, 'Mokshada is very powerful, you see, one must humour her a little. Let me go and look for my niece. I'd feel better then. She's the maid in charge of the flowers and garlands here. There are so many women in this house and she makes the garlands they wear on their hair. And ornaments for their hair too, stars of silver paper, flowers of gold paper—she makes them all. I say, hey Saila! Where are you?' So saying Panchu's mother had moved away. Satyabati had stood by a pillar and observed the splendour of the house, the decorations and the trimmings.

The ceiling was really high. As though it had not been able to figure out where to stop and had climbed higher and higher. Huge chandeliers hung from the ceiling, Satya had counted them quickly, four at the four corners and one each in the middle of each side—a total of eight. The entire house was made of marble, bordered with black granite. Between each pillar, from the dome, hung numerous cages of birds. How amazing! Why were there so many birds? What was the use of keeping so many birds as pets?

At each corner of the house, there was a marble figure of a nude woman. Satya had quickly averted her eyes. Goodness, they were so life-like! Smiling to herself, she thought that perhaps the poor things were once flesh and blood women who had turned to stone because they had had to stand in that state before thousands of people.

One could hardly guess at the magnificence of the house from outside. But one would be awestruck once one entered. In her childhood Satya had heard stories about the nawab's palace from her father. Driven by her sharp questions, Ramkali would have to elaborate so many things in order to satisfy her endless curiosity. As soon as she had stepped into the Datta household, Satya recalled the stories of the nawab's household from her childhood.

Blending those stories with the colours of her imagination, in her mind, Satya had painted a picture somewhat similar. So, on entering, she thought the place to be like a nawab's palace!

'Come this way, Bou-didi.' Panchu's mother had rushed to her, 'Come quickly, and sit down to eat, it's less crowded now.'

Satya had asked softly, 'There's a festival going on, but I can't see a soul. Where are the women of the house anyway?'

'Listen to that!' Panchu's mother had placed a hand on her cheek in amazement.

'What happened? Does that make you faint?'

'Well, it could! D'you think this an ordinary household like yours or mine, that the grandmother will slave away at her grandson's rice ceremony? The women of this house don't come downstairs at all.'

'Why's that?' Satya had giggled, 'Do they have gout, or something?'

'Don't joke, Bou-didi! They don't need to. They have hundreds of servants. Besides, there are so many poor widows sheltered here—they run the house. And there's a Sarkar-mashai to look after the purchases. Well, it's not as though they never come down. They come downstairs during festivals and pujas. There is a separate stairway for that. This side is between the inner quarters and the outer part of the house. Less people can be seen this side. If you want to see a crowd, you have go to the inner quarters. In this house there's no system of setting up a tent for the confectioners, there are huge rooms for the purpose. Downstairs there's place for the fisherwomen to scale and slice fish. God knows how many maunds of fish they've bought—and one look at their cleavers is enough to make your head spin! The young boys lop off the head and the tail and pass on the fish, then the fisherwomen do the rest. I'll show it all to you. Nobody says a thing to me because I'm Saila's aunt, you see. And why should they, anyway? I'll say you're my mistress. She's from the village, she's never seen the style of the Sahibs, doesn't know the ways of the city, so ...'

The conversation was taking place as they were walking from one end of the house to the other. They had just reached the stairs when Satya had stopped and said sharp and furious, 'Stop it!'

'What happened?' Panchu's mother had been flabbergasted.

'Don't talk so much if you're so stupid and don't know how to speak!'

'What's wrong with what I said?'

'You'd know if you had the brains! Let me warn you, don't speak too much about me. Finish what you've come here for.'

'My goodness! What a temper! You behave like royalty itself when you're annoyed! One hears that the luxury of this household was so well-known in Calcutta that the Sahibs themselves would come here. And here you're saying ...'

'Yes, that's what I'm like!'

As they climbed the stairs, Panchu's mother had whispered, 'I know you won't listen, but let me tell you and do my duty. Even if you are a brahmin woman, please show some respect to Datta-Ginni. They're used to seeing folded hands, any exception to that rule will upset her.'

Once more, Satya had stopped abruptly and had said sharply, 'Then show me how I should fold my hands? Should I also wrap my sari round my neck? Really! The glory of money is so amazing! And let me ask you, even after singing their praises high and low, has it in any way improved your lot, eh? You earn your keep doing the washing up. Fold your hands before god, in front of a virtuous human being with qualities, why're you dying to pay homage to wealth?'

Satya was intelligent, but naive. The 'dying' she had mentioned had not been something Panchu's mother alone desired—so many were dying to do that! So many were ready to drown themselves in the ocean of that particular death. Or else, why would Chakraborty-Ginni prostrate herself before Datta-Ginni? Was Chakraborty-Ginni ignorant of the fact that it was forbidden to accept water from a sonar-bene like Datta-Ginni?

When Satya had climbed up to Datta-Ginni's room, Chakraborty-Ginni, was cringing and saying with docile humility, 'That's what I'm telling you, Ma, there's nobody as generous as you. That's what we say at home, what a large heart Datta-Ginni has!'

The discourse had ceased when Satya had arrived. Everyone inside had turned to look at Satya. I do not know the feminine of 'flunkies' but that's what Datta-Ginni's companions were. And at the start of day, from the moment Datta-Ginni held court, they would sit around her and compete against each other in flattering her.

Whenever there was a ceremony, Datta-Ginni or any other wealthy woman would sit in this way, surrounded by adulation. Those invited would arrive in twos and threes to talk to her. Wealthy women like her knew how to weigh the words they spoke according to the worth of the visitors. That was exactly the scene that was being enacted when Satya had arrived with her particular offering.

Satya had no idea that the senior Datta-Ginni was a widow. But what kind of a widow was she? The question had crystallized within her. Why was she dressed like that? Datta-Ginni was wearing a near-transparent Chandrakona dhoti that assaulted the viewer's sight, and a pouch for keys was tied to the end of her sari. Her hair was parted and peaked in front, and twisted into a small round bun at the nape of her neck. Her lower arms were bare, but she wore solid gold amulets on her upper arms. Around her neck she wore a thick chain of solid gold. A silver paan-container packed with paan lay nearby.

A maid, or perhaps a woman who was sheltered in the house, stood by the bed and fanned her with an ornate fan. Under the bed, close to her feet, was placed a big brass spittoon that glittered like gold. Gathered around her sat her sycophants. Corresponding to position, relationship and prestige, a few sat close to her on the bed, some sat at a distance, and some stood around the bed. Among them were married women, widows, old women and young ladies.

The bare lower arms and the thick amulets on the upper arms had appeared unbecoming to Satya. So had the picture of a widow sitting on a bed with a paan-container. Never before had she seen a widow sit on a bed this way.

She had felt disgusted. Of course, she had tried to tell herself that these were the ways of the city, she should not bother herself with them. But it had been in vain. Her eyes had fixed themselves on the thick amulets and the bare, podgy forearms that were so like child-size bolsters.

Datta-Ginni had given a sign and in an instant somebody had raised the spittoon from the footstool to her mouth. After spitting into it she had asked, 'Who's that standing there? Can't seem to recognize her.'

Panchu's mother had come forward, 'She lives in your number seven house.'

'I see! That's why I wondered why I couldn't identify her. She's never come here. Come this way and bless me with dust from your feet.'

Satya had never heard in her whole life that the 'dust' of one's feet could be voluntarily given. All she knew was that whoever desired it had to bend their heads and procure it. Not knowing what she should do under the circumstances, she had stood there in silence.

'Come on!' One of the 'flunkies' had said with some intensity, 'Take a bit of dust from under your feet and put it on her head.'

Satya had responded solemnly, 'My feet aren't dusty.'

What an answer! But Datta-Ginni wanted it! And besides, she

had not asked for gold or anything precious, just a trifle. It was unimaginable that a plea for such a simple thing could be ignored this way!

' With a hand on her cheek, Datta-Ginni had somehow managed to drive away her expression of shock and irreverence and had smirked, 'Like they say, even the sea evaporates when the hapless desire water! That's my fate! Even a bit of dust from the feet is hard to come by!'

Satya had stared in amazement at that shapeless, bloated blob of a face. It was hard to guess her age from that lumpiness, but a woman celebrating the rice ceremony of her grandson could hardly be young herself, she could well be Satya's grandmother's age! What kind of joke was she cracking with Satya?

A thin-skinned woman had announced, 'Learn to temper your speech, my dear! One must open the eyes wide and take proper note of the person one speaks to.'

Needless to say, Satya had remained silent. Only her jaws had clenched characteristically.

'You've done us the courtesy of gifting a gold chain, haven't you?'

Satya had responded to that. She had said mildly, 'Why put it that way? It's just something to accompany my blessings for the child.'

'Whatever it is,' Datta-Ginni had said with displeasure, 'you'll have to take it back.'

Take it back! Satya had been stunned, 'How can I do that?'

'That's for you to figure out. We don't accept gold gifted by subordinates.'

Subordinates! Again!

A ribbon of lightning had streaked through Satya's whole body, but she had controlled herself, 'In that case, you shouldn't have invited your subordinates! Tell me, whoever goes to a ceremony without taking a gift? And besides, a brahmin can never take back a gift.'

A brahmin! Datta-Ginni had turned a shade pale.

'My goodness, such razor-sharp words!' Datta-Ginni had

exclaimed, 'That hag, Mokshada, was right! All right, you win! A guest is like a god they say, so we'll have to listen to whatever you say. But it was wrong of you to do it. You're a brahmin woman, the dust of your feet is sacred for me, so I don't say anything to you. But just let me say one thing—can a big fish ever match a small fry, tell me that? But never mind, I've said already that a guest is like a god! I say Subas, take her to the room where the brahmins are being served.'

Indicating the end of the interaction.

Slowly, Satya had turned to leave and all of a sudden it had dawned on her, that somehow she had suffered a defeat. What should she do? Leave without eating? Should she claim that she was not well?

But before she could say anything, Datta-Ginni had spoken again, 'Haven't you brought your boys?'

'No.'

'Why? Hadn't we invited your whole family?'

Satya's eyebrows had knitted themselves into a familiar frown, and her low firm tone had returned, 'There was nothing wrong with your invitation. But what can be done if the whole family doesn't have the time? Never mind! I've come: As they say, water poured on the head trickles down to the whole body.'

Those present were dazed beyond words at the insolence of the woman from number seven, and the expressionless blob of fat had stiffened somewhat. But she was the head Ginni of the Datta household. And so she had controlled herself and said, 'My, my, she does have a way with words! You must know to read and write. That's good. I haven't met anyone like this before, it's been a delight to meet you. Never mind, enjoy your meal. And take the chyada for your sons.'

Satya was leaving with the woman called Subas, when she had suddenly turned and said with a mocking smile, 'I'm a village girl, I don't know the ways of the city. But is it a custom here to invite people and insult them?'

'Listen to that!'

Datta-Ginni's milk-white face had darkened suddenly, she had faltered, 'You belong to the highest kulin family, the best among brahmins—like the cobra among snakes. Who would dare to insult you, tell me? If I have made any mistake, please do forgive me out of the generosity of your heart and bless our grandson.'

Satya had said calmly, 'I shall always bless him. But you'll have to let me go quickly, I'm in a hurry.'

She was a brahmin dining at a sudra's! There were coarse puris, a pumpkin curry and fried aubergines—all salt-free. Of course, there were several types of sweets, and curds. None of this attracted Satya. She finished her meal quickly and went looking for Panchu's mother. But the maid was nowhere to be found. She had settled down to listen to the 'dhop-kirtan'. The soiree was being held in a huge hall on the second floor. Datta-Ginni had organized this in aid of her grandson's rice ceremony.

They had called the famous Manada Dhopi. And she had started the prelude to her song in a high-pitched nasal tone. Satya's queries about Panchu's mother brought out her niece Saila.

Saila was dark and wore a white sari with a black ribbon-border, her hair was parted neatly at the centre and the parting was bare. She wore not a single piece of jewellery and yet she looked so grand! Perhaps because her body was scrubbed and glowing, or perhaps because her lips were reddened with paan.

Saila was amazed by what Satya said, 'What do you mean, you'll leave? Won't you listen to the singing?'

'No.'

'How strange! People are spellbound by her—how can you pretend to be indifferent? Are you thinking you have to pay her something? Well, it won't matter if you don't.'

'Will you please call Panchu's mother?'

'My goodness! I'll just get her. It's just as she'd told me ...'

'Listen, could you ask her to fetch a palki for me, as well.'

'A palki, goodness!' Saila pursed her lips in a peculiar way and walked off.

The sharp, shrill voice could be heard from her house as well. It could probably be heard in the whole neighbourhood. Manada Dhopi was famous, not so much for her tunes, but for her voice!

It was a piercing sharp voice; the strains erupted against the wind long after she had stopped singing. Satya had never heard dhop-kirtan in her life.

As a child she had listened to kirtans when she went to a few gatherings with her father's uncle. But those were different. The loud beats of the accompanying clappers drowned out the song. She faintly recalled accompanying her father to Halishahar or some such place by boat to listen to kirtans about the Goddess Kali when she was very young. That must have been the last time. Baruipur had no such culture, except agriculture; they cultivated paan! If her mood had not soured, she could have left after listening to a couple of songs. But she had left in a pique, her mood completely marred.

The power and predominance of wealth in the world had left Satya's mind dull. What a strange place the city of Calcutta was! The glory of money reigned supreme, it prevailed over talent, learning and any humanitarian efforts. And yet, Satya had looked on the city with such admiration from her childhood!

Satya had sat listlessly for a while, then had asked herself how the attitude of a single person could make her feel so dejected. There were so many people, and so much of activity in this huge city. This was the city of Raja Rammohan Roy, a city which had people like Vidyasagar, Bankimchandra and Maharshi Debendranath Tagore of the Pirali Thakur family. Bhabatosh-master had spoken to her about their lives and deeds. Completely disregarding all that, here she was judging this city by looking at Datta-Ginni! Brushing aside her thoughts, Satya stood up. Panchu's mother would not come in today, so she would have to finish all the chores by herself. Before she was done, her sons had come back from school and raised a hue and cry.

'Ma! So, you gorged at the feast, didn't you!' They had asked in a chorus.

Satya had burst into laughter, 'Yes, of course! Gorged and glutted there. Now don't you go rampaging about in your school clothes! Go and have a wash!'

'What shall we eat? Manda-mithai, khaja-gaja, chana-bora?

We've been fantasizing about all that ...' They were fired with impatience.

Satya had looked at them fondly. Had they thought about sweets all day instead of their school work? But this was not the time to indulge in tenderness. So she had pretended to be surprised and had said, 'What are you two dreaming about? Where would I get such things?'

They had hardly paid any attention to her surprise, they had tugged at her hands and exclaimed, 'As if we believe you! Haven't you brought a chyada for us?'

A chyada!

Satya's tender face had hardened and she had asked sharply, 'Who mentioned the chyada to you?'

'Baba did when he was going to office.'

'He must have made a mistake or he was joking,' Satya had answered.

But Turu was overwhelmed with disappointment. He had said, 'There was no need to send us to school today! Nobody else from this locality went today. All the boys around had a real feast and brought back their individual chyadas. Except for us! They'd made sixteen varieties of sweets ...'

Satya had asked solemnly, 'Who told you that? Your father?'

'How would Baba know all that? Panchu's mother told us.'

'Oh! That's why you couldn't stop thinking about it! Come on, you know it looks very greedy to bring back a chyada. Come eat whatever we have at home.'

Although Turu was older, compared to Khoka, he was obtuse. So he had started crying, 'I don't want to eat muri-murki and other stuff at home. Panchu's mother was right ...'

He had suddenly shuddered at his own words and had fallen silent.

But Satya was not a woman to let him get away with it. She had grilled him fiercely in order to find out what it was that the woman had said. Although Turu had frozen with fear, Khoka had been forthcoming, 'She said, as if the world would turn topsy-turvy if you're absent for a day! What a monster of a mother, depriving her children of a feast!'

'What was that? Say it again!' Satya had lost her bearings. She could hardly believe her own ears. So this was how her own sons were turning out! Had she come away from her village with so much fanfare for this?

She had only had one desire—that her sons would be civilized and well-bred. Were they turning out to be ill-bred and coarse instead? Would she hit them? But finally, Satya had not raised her hand. She had fallen silent after that one fierce question. She had kept sitting, lost in thought. She had forgotten to feed her boys. They were surrounded by danger, how much could she protect them from?

Nabakumar had arrived after a while. He had taken one peek at Satya's grim face and had summoned his sons outside and found out what the matter was. That was how he always found out whenever the situation looked critical. Usually he would ask Khoka, for he knew Turu was somewhat dense and could never explain clearly.

After hearing the cause, Nabakumar could hardly figure out why such an irrelevant thing had upset Satya. After all, the boys had not called her a monster, Panchu's mother had. So he had entered the room and smiled stupidly, 'Now what's the matter?'

Satya had continued to sit in silence.

Nabakumar had said, 'It's the same thing always! Panchu's mother must have observed how hard-headed you are. Why punish the boys so severely for such a small thing? They've pranced back from school thinking about the treats that are waiting, and here you are making them fast. Really!'

Had she really left them hungry? Of course! She had not served them food. Her heart had relented instantly and she deeply regretted it. How could she be sitting without feeding her sons? In her fury, she had not given it any thought. Panchu's mother must have been right. They were mere infants, how much did they grasp? Especially when their full-grown father had painted such an attractive picture of a rich man's feast? Even though her raging had abated and been replaced by a lament, Satya could not admit defeat. She had said sternly, 'What's the point in serving them ordinary home-made sweets, go and talk to them about manda-mithai, khaja-gaja—it will fill their stomachs for sure!'

What a relief! She had spoken! Nabakumar had felt relieved. If Satya had opened her mouth, the situation could never be that serious. Nabakumar would really become tense whenever she sat silently with her jaws clenched. At his office, Nabakumar was acclaimed for his intelligence and skill, his subordinates treated him with so much deference that he usually felt like somebody important. But something invariably befell him whenever he stepped into his house—his same old helplessness!

But today Satya had spoken. So Nabakumar took courage, 'They look weak with hunger. I can understand how famished one feels when one comes back from school or from office.'

Nabakumar had taken the opportunity to include himself.

After this, it had not been possible for her to keep sitting. Satya had got up. Surmising that he would not get another opportune moment, Nabakumar had hastily blurted out, 'I know you're upset. But tell me what is so despicable about the chyada? Everybody accepts it! Wasn't there such a custom at your father's village, eh? As a small boy, I'd look forward to the chyada whenever I went for a feast. How much could a small boy eat anyway? The next day, I'd open up the chyada at home and ...'

'Enough! Stop your stories. Go and have a wash.' And Satya had got up. Satya's mind had mellowed. Really, why had she lost her temper? Even in her childhood, she would ...

Well, of course, they had the same custom at her father's village. She had seen pots and trays being decorated and filled with foodstuff, and people taking them home after they had eaten. Ramkali himself would supervise the distribution. Nobody could be left out—the maidservant, the cowherd, the farmhand—whoever came would get one. People would give Satya and the children such gifts too whenever they went for a feast with Pishi-thakurma. It was not as if the custom had not existed.

And there was another charming festival, called the At-kaure. On the eighth day after a child's birth, all the little children of the locality would be called to pound on winnowing trays. Of course, only the boys were allowed to do that. Though the girls were not denied the sweets and eight types of roasted snacks that were distributed on the occasion. Satya suddenly saw herself dressed in a striped sari with its end tied round her waist, intertwining plaits braided together and the chimes of her anklets alerting the whole locality.

She would cleverly wrap the end of her sari around her waist converting it into a pocket which she would fill with loads of sweets and snacks. There would be some loose change mixed with the snacks too—and they would eagerly look for the coins when they got home. Never had she thought herself as greedy! But why hadn't she? Why was it different today?

Earlier she had never seen the act of receiving as demeaning the recipient. Why had she felt that way today? Satya attempted to find a reason as she readied their snack, and she had discovered one too. And she had elaborated on it while serving them.

'Weren't you asking me if we had the custom of distributing the chyada at Nityanandapur? Of course, we had. But the difference was that the arrogance of the host would never reveal itself in the act of giving. Those accepting it would never be made to feel small. Whatever you say, the Datta household is too haughty for words. They put fifty-two types of sweets in a brass pot near me, they themselves should have got someone to put it inside the palki, shouldn't they? But there was not a person to be seen around, it would be useless to look for anyone. And just as I was leaving a maid came and screeched out, "I say, you there, why're you leaving your chyada behind?" How uncivil! As if I could I pick it up myself.'

What effect the 'fifty-two varieties' had on her husband and sons was not apparent, but Nabakumar was forced to agree with his wife. After that, he had brought up the other matter himself, 'Did you actually give away the chain?'

'Of course! I'd made up my mind to gift it.'

Concealing his anguish, Nabakumar had said casually, 'Well, it was yours, you have every right to give it away. But I was asking around in the locality, nobody gave more than a rupee.'

Satya had drawn the topic to a close by saying, 'Anyway, let's not waste words on what's been gifted to an infant. Let that be. Now, I want you to take on a task like a man—find another house.'

'Another house? Shall we move out of here?'

'That's what I've settled on.'

She had not been pondering on it, or wishing for it, she had just decided!

Nabakumar plunged into a quarrel, knowing full well that he would lose, 'Of course, you'll settle on that, it's because your own mind is unsettled, that's why! And you change your mind everyday! I ask you, where will you find a house at this rent, eh? I believe the Dattas don't care for money, so they've let out these houses so cheap. Anybody else would have demanded one and half times what we pay. Forget it!'

Suddenly those dark eyes under Satya's brows had danced in amusement, 'When have I ever forgotten something I proposed!'

Nabakumar had stared at that face. Was it because it was so rare, that her smile appeared so beautiful? Well, Nabakumar could hardly accuse her of forgetting whatever she proposed. But Nabakumar could not understand the joy Satya got out of needless hassles. He had shut his gaping mouth at once and had said sullkily, 'What's wrong with this house?'

'You wouldn't understand it if I told you.'

'Of course, I don't ever understand anything! You're the master of all understanding! We're not going to move. It's always the same chant! Are we birds that we need to change our nests every other day? I'm telling you, we won't move. That's final!'

'All right then. It will be as the boss says.'

With that Satya had got up.

Satya did not really wish to move from here. The place was very convenient. But she could no longer stand being a subordinate. Moreover, it was such a pain not to be able to live freely, the maidservants gossiped all the time. It would help to sack the maid, of course, but that would go against Satya's principles. The maid was honest. And helpful too. Her only fault was that she was a bit dumb. Which was why she talked too much. And her words had been responsible for misguiding the boys.

Well, that's what she would tell Panchu's mother before dismissing her. She would say, 'If you teach my sons that their mother is a monster, how can I have you working here? Find another place to work from next month.'

That was what she decided. She would not stoop to mentioning the gossip. But let her come tomorrow morning.

Satya did not have to wait that long, Panchu's mother arrived that very evening with a completely unexpected piece of news. What was this! What disaster was this that stared Satya in the face?

But before talking about the evening, it is best to present the events of the afternoon.

Datta-Ginni spat out the betel-juice from her mouth and asked, 'I say Pancha's mum, Your mistress is such a young thing—why's she so snobbish, tell me that?'

Her niece-in-law, who was her ever-faithful flunkey, cackled aloud, 'It's the arrogance of youth, Mami! I can't see any other reason at all!'

'I don't think so, it looks like it's a habit with her,' said Datta-Ginni glumly. 'Who else lives with her, hey Pancha's mum?'

Panchu's mother was always called 'Pancha's mum' in this house, so she had got used to the insulting tone. Melting with humility, she said, 'Nobody else. Her husband and their two sons—seven and eight years old.'

'Oh! That's why! As they say, "The sun that shines after the rains is quick to burn one's skin, and a hussy handed charge too soon; self-importance is her sin!" Has her mother-in-law died, or what?'

Panchu's mother said cheerfully, 'God forbid! Why should she die? The parents-in-law live in the village. She has come with her husband and her sons. The husband works at the Sahib's office.'

'Really? That's why she's bursting with pride! Where's their village?'

'Who knows?' Although Panchu's mother liked Satya and admired her, she had disparaged her to placate Datta-Ginni, 'As if she ever has the time to chat! Soon as she finishes the housework, she buries her face in her books.'

Books! A titter of derision pervaded the room.

'Really, Pancha's mum, what a household you've found yourself! Watch out or under her influence, you might become a pundit too!'

Panchu's mother said with a smile, 'She would make me read if she could! Goodness, the way she drives her sons to study! The boys chat with me. I've heard from them that they're from Baruipur, their grandparents and an aunt live there. Their mother's village is near Tribeni—Nityanandapur or something. Their mum's father is a doctor, really wealthy ...'

And instantly, in the corner of that room, by a low brass stool, a certain face began to look agitated, and busy hands stopped their activity of paan-making. She stared at Panchu's mother, oblivious of Datta-Ginni's comments.

Datta-Ginni surmised that the woman from number seven was arrogant because she was a rich man's daughter.

Panchu's mother concluded, 'Of course!'

'I heard she didn't take the chyada.' The niece-in-law stoked the dying fire.

'That's what I kept saying ...' Panchu's mother lamented, 'So many people find the time to visit, how come you never have the time? And all the boys around stayed home, do you have to send your sons to school? My heart really breaks for the boys ...'

'Why don't you take the pot of sweets? Give it to the boys,' another woman advised.

But the paan-maker widow seemed not to hear even one whit of that discussion. She kept on staring at Panchu's mother with the hope of hearing what else she would say. But Panchu's mother did not say more. Her conscience would never have permitted her to say anything against Satya, just that the wind here was against her. One had to curry favour with the rich. Besides, she was really annoyed with Satya.

She had thought that she would show Satya the grandeur of this house, and demonstrate to her how loved and respected her niece,

Saila, was in this house. And how proud she was to have such a niece!

Of course she was proud! Saila's close relationship with Datta-Ginni's second son was an open secret. Everyone knew Saila's hold over Mejo-babu. Datta-Ginni would add fuel to this fire, in order to keep her daughter-in-law in her place. She herself would supply Saila with perfumed oil and soap. She would pay for the masala stuffing of Saila's paans. Mejo-babu himself bought Saila her ribbon-bordered Santipuri half-saris. But if she noticed the slightest tear or dirt, Datta-Ginni would say within earshot of her dour-faced daughter-in-law, 'I say, why is your sari so dirty, Saila? Don't you have another? Haven't you told your Mejo-dadababu?'

Of course, it always remained unsaid why she should ask Mejo-babu of all people.

Though Panchu's mother would never have dared to recount such anecdotes to her mistress, she could have shown off Saila's standing here. But it had not been possible.

Never mind. To each her own wit. It did not always help to have brains. Her mistress was so clever, and yet she had lost out, hadn't she? She hardly ate anything herself, and did not let her husband and sons enjoy the feast either! What did she get out of it?

The disheartened Panchu's mother approached the paan-maker woman, 'Here, give me a couple of crisp paans.'

Making her a couple of paans hastily, the woman handed them to her, hands trembling, and said in a low whisper, 'You never showed me who your mistress is.'

'How could I? She hardly stayed. She just came in and rushed off!'

'I'm so curious after hearing you speak. I believe she's really haughty. I wish I could see her!'

'Show you! As if she'll come this way again. But if you came with me ...'

The paan-maker had whispered really softly, 'Then let's go and see her.'

'What has she done to get into your good books, eh?'

'Hush! If the mistress hears she'll stop me from going.'

344 | ASHAPURNA DEBI

'All right then, I shall take you in the evening.'

When they were ready, the paan-maker seemed to falter, her eagerness had stemmed a bit. She said, 'Let it be, Pancha's mum, let's forget it.'

'Goodness! Whatever for? You were so keen!'

'True, I'd said that on the spur of the moment, but what if it annoys the mistress?'

'Why should it? In any case, who's going to let on to her? She can hardly be bothered with small fry like us! With the chaos of the ceremony and so many servants busy working, we can get away. This is the best time to do a bunk!'

'I was thinking, what's the point in going. I hear she's very conceited—supposing she refuses to talk to a paan-maker?'

'Goodness! Don't think that way at all,' Panchu's mother reassured her. 'If people don't pester her, she leaves them alone. She is very nice to guests, and it won't bother her that you're a servant. The other day, the weaver's wife had dropped in, she made her sit, gave her a paan and some water to drink. She didn't buy a sari from her, but she didn't throw her out either.'

After many arguments, in favour of going and against it, the former won. Wrapping her frayed, threadbare silk shawl around her, the paan-maker woman stepped out through the back door along with Panchu's mother.

The woman had once come to the Datta household in search of a job. Since she was a brahmin, she could not be given the work of a maid, so she had been given the task of making paan. Although paan-making sounds like a light task, in this house it was not. She had to make about three thousand odd paans every day. And had to slice a proportionate quantity of betel-nuts as well. Besides, all the paans could not be made in the same way, there were different categories of paan. Some wanted the sweet-leaved paan, some wanted the grand mixture of mace, cinnamon, cubeb and camphor, and those who chewed tobacco preferred it plain with catechu and betel-nut. And the betel-nut had to be sliced fine in several lots. She had to take her tray of assorted paan to each room and place them in the containers, covering them with a cloth soaked in rose water.

Besides, the coarse-leaved Bangla paan had to be made for the administrative staff, the stewards, the visiting fakirs and numerous people who lived in the house or passed through it. It was part of the paan-maker's job. She nearly passed out from making so many paans all day. Over and above that, things became worse when there was a ceremony at home. And those happened frequently enough. Weddings, shaadh ceremonies and rice ceremonies apart, there were numerous bratas the women observed round the year. There were feasts every other day. The younger sister-in-law of Datta-Ginni had just observed the anantachaturdashi—three hundred odd guests were invited. It made no difference that she was a widow without a son. The large-hearted Datta-Ginni had said, 'So what? What does it matter that she has no one to call her own. I'm there for her. Her life has passed in vain, let her do things for the next life.'

Her younger sister-in-law was a real traitor though. She would crib behind her back, 'Don't I have a share in this property? Do they think I came floating in with the tide, or what? I didn't come drifting in on some scrap of wood! One of their men had brought me here as his wife.'

But she said all that behind her back. In front of Datta-Ginni everyone was quiet.

But never mind that.

As they walked, Panchu's mother had the following conversation with the paan-maker.

'Whatever it is, you're of the same caste. She'll treat you with respect.'

Meaning, of course, Satyabati—because she was a brahmin too.

But this assurance hardly thrilled the paan-maker. She said gloomily, 'As if a brahmin remains a brahmin when she works for a sonar-bene! Don't be stupid! You people call me "Bamun-didi" but I feel so ashamed to say I am a brahmin. I presented myself as a brahmin so that I wouldn't have to press anyone's feet, or do the washing up, or wash clothes in a sudra household.'

'Not just that, Bamun-didi, you behave like a brahmin woman too. I know the way the other brahmin maids behave! Ghecha's mother had got a fish-bone stuck in her hand so she was caught redhanded trying to steal fried fish. And she wasn't flustered at all! Actually, you know, Bamun-didi, only those who are sinful give up customs. Once they've given that up, you'll know that they've transgressed. Morality and customs are like dams, that keep a river in check ...'

The concluding part of Panchu's mother's sermon had to be deferred. They had arrived at Satyabati's door. Panchu's mother called out in her shrill voice, 'Where are you Bou-didi? Come out for a second. There's someone here to see you.'

THIRTY FOUR

Since he had not seen Nitai in a long while, Nabakumar had taken his umbrella and sauntered out. It was a holiday, Nitai was sure to be home. After Nitai had left, Nabakumar had felt embarrassed to speak to him. He would feel very guilty. But with time, one gets accustomed to everything. So the unease had diminished slowly. Satyabati would send him often to invite Nitai home. Strangely she herself would speak quite freely to Nitai, cook what he liked to eat and urge him to eat.

It was amazing how Satya managed to behave in such a self-assured way! Anyway, today Nabakumar himself was going to pay him a visit. He had been feeling restless at home. Something seemed to have happened to Satya ever since the maid had brought home a widowed woman with her just two days ago. They had chatted for a while and since then, Satya had stopped talking to the children, she had stopped laughing too. She seemed to be living in a different world.

That was true. Satya had been living in a world full of questions ever since. Who had the maid brought with her? Wasn't she the paan-maker woman employed in the Datta household? Why had she come? Why had she felt such a strong urge to see Satya? And in that case, why had she not felt free to speak? It looked as though she had held back her words, and had stopped to sigh. As though there was so much happening inside her!

Had Satya seen her somewhere before? Did she resemble someone Satya knew well? But that person had not been so dark! Had the flames of fate charred her like this? Turbulent waves had thrashed inside both women, yet neither had hastened to hold the other by the hand and exclaim, 'So, it's you!'

The maid had said bluntly, 'So, why were you so eager to come? Now has the cat got your tongue or what?'

The woman had replied, 'I hadn't come to talk, I just wanted to see.'

Had Satya recognized that voice? Had she heard it ages ago, in a land beyond the seas? Even then, it had not been possible to exclaim, 'You can't fool me! I've caught you out!'

There were so many obstacles. Obstacles that eddied around the question—'was she or wasn't she'—and around social protocol and economic differences. Above all, the complication of the maid's presence had been the toughest to overcome. Perhaps many of these barriers would have fallen away had they suddenly found each other face to face, just the two of them. Then it would have been possible to say without hesitation, 'Look at the state you're in! And for what joy, may I ask?' She could have said that earlier, ages ago, when she was the young girl she no longer was.

Nothing like that had happened. After a while, the maid had yawned and said, 'Come let's go. I'll walk you back and go home. I've worked hard the whole day, I'm sleepy.'

'Let's go,' the woman had said and got up. She had not said, 'Just let me stay for a while!'

Nor had Satya said, 'Sit for a while.'

Since then, Satya had been distracted. Nabakumar had asked, 'Who was that hussy who came with the maid? And why did she come ...'

Before he could finish his words, she had stopped him fiercely, 'Why do you speak so vulgarly in front of the children?'

Ever since, she had been totally self-absorbed.

On a holiday morning, it felt so good to sit by the kitchen door and chat. Satya was wonderful when she was in a good mood. But to be honest, even when she was not in a good mood it was such an attraction! As if she had bound Nabakumar with a rope. Except for going to office, he never felt like stepping out. Nowadays he had to supervise the children's lessons because the tutor was not coming regularly. But it was not a duty he enjoyed. He liked doing the shopping. Apart from that he just wanted to sit with her. But there was no way that could happen. Really, where was the need to make heavy weather of family life? One could laugh, chat, play and sleep, and it was done! No, instead one must try to become 'exemplary', 'raise your children to be righteous', worry one's head silly whether you had lost your honour or not—what on earth for? What was the good of leaving the village to come to the city then? After all, one just expected to live in comfort and enjoy oneself!

Just the other day, he had heard that his colleague Ramratan-babu had gone with his wife to see the play 'Nimai-Sanyas'. Ramratan's wife had wept while watching it and had cried for three days afterwards. Nabakumar had begged Satya to go with him to see the play.

She had said, 'It's the end of the month—there's so little money. It costs a lot to go to the theatre. Besides, who will look after the boys till so late?'

She had dismissed his suggestion to take them along. Nabakumar had wanted to take the boys to see the races, but that was forbidden too. Why was Satya like this? Nabakumar had been asking himself that for ages now

Today clearly was not his day! He never got to meet Nitai either. Where was he? A gentleman living in the same mess said, 'I have no idea. Nitai-babu hardly wants to mix with anybody. We don't like his ways. One shouldn't speak unless one sees for himself, but one of his colleagues was saying that Nitai-babu's morals are rather loose.'

'What?'

Nabakumar almost sat down on the floor. What a terrible bit of news this was!

The gentleman continued, 'Is he a close friend of yours? Then I'm sorry I told you this. But it may turn out to be a good thing. You might be able to draw him back to the right path. But, of course, it's hard to give up bad ways.'

Nabakumar had rushed to Bhabatosh with a terrible ache inside. For once he had done something without consulting Satya.

The teacher was bent over a book and had been copying things into a notebook. Nabakumar had sat himself down near his feet, and had burst out without preamble, 'I'm in a real fix and so I'm here!'

Bhabatosh had been flabbergasted. What could have happened? Was someone ill? Had Satyabati scalded her hand while cooking the rice? Or had she had a fall?

He had given a start and said, 'Sit here and calm down. What is the matter?'

'The matter is serious. Nitai has gone to the dogs!'

'What has happened to Nitai?'

Nabakumar had felt embarrassed after having said the words instinctively. So he had scratched his head and whispered, 'I had gone to visit him today, I couldn't meet him. Someone there said that Nitai goes to all kinds of bad places and that his morals are loose.'

After a moment's silence, Bhabatosh had said, 'He wasn't someone who hates Nitai, was he?'

'I don't think so.'

'Then it is really serious.' Bhabatosh had murmured to himself, 'This is what I feared ...'

Nabakumar had asked, 'What are you saying?'

'Nothing.'

'Please meet him and talk to him, Master-mashai.'

'Talk to him?' Bhabatosh had smiled, 'In such cases a talking to from a teacher can have no effect.'

'But something has to be done.'

Bhabatosh was moved by the intensity of the timid Nabakumar.
He had said tenderly, 'All right, I shall try. But you know what ...'
'What?'

'I mean, I was saying, it would be much more effective if Bouma
spoke.'

Bouma!

Nabakumar had sounded stupefied and stupid, 'D'you mean
Turu's mother?'

'That's right. If she makes him swear he'll stop, it might work.'

Nabakumar had asked in that same tone, 'It won't work if you
tell him, and it will work if she does?'

A hint of a smile had appeared on Bhabatosh's enigmatic face,
'Her words will work. Otherwise ...'

'Then we'll have to tell her.' So saying, a bewildered Nabakumar
had stood up. But he had not been able to accept the proposal fully.
And to tell the truth, he did not like it either. This idea of bringing
Nitai and Satya face to face. No matter how good a friend Nitai
was, if he had fallen into bad ways, how could one trust him? Who
knew if he had taken to drink as well? A drunken debauch! Women
had to be kept a hundred yards away from such characters.

That his own father, Nilambar Banerji, had committed the same
crime and yet enjoyed an exalted social position never struck
Nabakumar.

He had returned home, trying to work out how to present the
news of Nitai's degradation to Satya, and he had been wondering
how she would react.

It had been quite late. Satya must have been waiting with his
lunch. Nabakumar had walked up quickly to the door but even
before he could knock, the door had opened at his slight push.
Which meant that it had not been latched. What a thing to do!
Leaving the door open in the middle of the afternoon! He had
rushed in to tell her off, and had had to step back immediately.

Satya was standing by the pillar of the kitchen holding someone's
hand.

THIRTY FIVE

Nobody could lose caste for holding hands, neither men, nor women. And this was a widow who looked bewildered, and was frail and dark. Nabakumar was aghast, and had looked as dazed on hearing Satya utter in her usual unfaltering manner, 'Now that I've found you, do you think I'll let you go? Bring your daughter and come here. If I get two meals a day, you will get a meal too. If my sons can be fed and clothed so can your daughter.'

Nabakumar's blood had frozen to ice. What kind of talk was this? Who was this woman? How was she related to Satya? Then, all of a sudden, his frozen blood had started to boil. It was a man's blood, after all! How could Satya presume to offer food and shelter to two people without even consulting Nabakumar! How could a woman be so bold? She had overstepped limits just because Nabakumar never ever protested.

Nabakumar's dear friend Nitai had been asked to leave for no fault óf his. And out of a sense of hurt, disgust and heartache, the man had gone and ruined himself! It would not have happened had he stayed on with Nabakumar. He had fallen into bad company at the mess.

Nabakumar's eyes had filled with tears. Where had this hussy come from, he wondered. She was someone Nabakumar had never set eyes on and there was already conspiracy afoot to install her in his house. How very clever! It would not do! It would not do at all! Nabakumar would declare plainly that such things just would not do in his house.

She had to be someone from Satya's father's village. That was why there was so much love! Frankly speaking, Nabakumar had also felt somewhat jealous that Satya was giving a completely unknown person a place in her heart. The very thought was unbearable. Even if it was a woman.

But only the mind can know what thoughts it has. This is the one fact that saves the world. Or else, the world with all its pride in society, civilization, education and culture would have long disappeared into some deep abyss. Nobody outside can ever know what goes on in the mind. Not even the person closest to the heart. This is why man can afford the luxury of doing just as he pleases, and he can vaunt about the glory of love, affection and devotion. But the odd thing is that man himself seems unaware of this paradox.

Nabakumar too did not reflect on this gift he had been granted by providence. Therefore, in his mind he cursed not just Satya but also the creator of the universe. Why had the creator made Nabakumar a man and Satya a woman? He could not stand this. He could not stand this hand-holding!

Nabakumar had cleared his throat. Till now Satya had been in her own world, she had not noticed another person standing against the wall. Now they both woke up. The widow moved away. Satya let go of her hand and pulled her sari over her head.

Of course, Satya being prudent, had not immediately offered her husband information about the woman. Besides, it was not seemly to speak with your husband in front of an elder. So she had drawn her sari over her head and said quietly, 'Come Bou, let us sit in that room.'

Nabakumar had thought of raising his voice and speaking aloud so that the woman could hear. So she would know who the real boss was. She would realize that it would not do to entertain false hopes. Satya was young, she may have made an offer without thinking, but in reality, it was not possible. That was what Nabakumar had hoped to convey. But his voice had refused to rise. And not just that. Words had failed him too. Shaking with fury he had gone for a bath and had come back and sat down to eat.

While serving him lunch, Satya had asked, 'Where were you till so late?'

Nabakumar had upturned the bowl of dal over his mound of rice in a huff, and said as he mixed the dal with rice, 'Do I have to offer you an explanation for that?'

'Listen to that! What an answer! Who wants an explanation? I'm asking because you got back so late for lunch.'

'You don't have to ask,' Nabakumar had responded in the same harsh tone. 'You don't have any right to ask. Why should you ask? Do you listen to me, that I should listen to you?'

Satya had been amazed, 'It must be the sun that has made you so hot-headed! Why are you talking such nonsense?'

'Nonsense! Am I talking nonsense? And when you say without any warning—'

In a futile attempt to raise his voice, Nabakumar had choked on his food. So, Satya had had to tend to her tough husband. She had to fan him, offer water, blow it away! It had taken a while for him to settle down. As soon as he had, Satya had announced in a low voice, 'I just wanted to let you know that there will be two more mouths to feed in this house. Or else, you'd be perfectly capable of asking suddenly, who they are, where they came from!'

Nabakumar could have said, 'Of course, that is what I *should* ask you. Really, who are these people? Where did they come from? And why on earth should I let them stay here?' But he had not been able to say that. Instead he had said in his choked voice, 'Where's the need to let me know. Whatever you think best—'

Was that Nabakumar's voice? Why did Nabakumar say that? These were certainly not the words he had been rehearsing in his mind all this while!

———

Ever since she had seen Satya, the paan-maker woman had been feeling like beating her head on the wall. God alone knew the reason. He was her sole witness. The maid had been surprised when she had asked to go there again. She had said, 'But you didn't speak to her at all that day. What d'you mean you want to go again?'

'I don't know why, my heart draws me there. I had a sister who looked a bit like her.'

The maid had been relieved to be offered a reason. But she had asked her how they would manage to keep it a secret in broad daylight. The paan-maker had found a way out. They could say that they were going to go to the Kali temple at Thanthane—the idol was so life-like that people went to worship there at all hours.

In a certain sense, the paan-maker had indeed come to worship a goddess. And she had been blessed!

It was then Nabakumar had entered.

Shankari had said, 'I can't presume to address you as Thakurji, but I feel like calling you that, so I shall say, "Don't be ridiculous, Satya Thakurji, what you're suggesting can never happen."'

'Can never happen?' Satya had responded with vehemence, 'But why ever not, tell me that, Katoa-bou? Human beings make mistakes. Aren't they allowed to make amends?'

'It isn't so simple! Society never listens to that.' Shankari had sighed, 'A woman is like an earthen pot, Thakurji, once she's polluted by a touch, nothing can be done.'

'Did god brand women as earthen pots when he sent them to earth?' Satya had responded sharply. 'And put a stamp on men that they are made of gold? That they had to be praised no matter what they did? It's true you did something immoral; really, really immoral. You are older than I am, so I ought not say it, but what you did was extremely sinful. I was immature then, so I didn't grasp it fully. I understood only later. And I won't lie to you. In my mind, I would crush you to pulp with a grinding stone. Not only because you'd sinned, but because you had made my father's high head droop low with shame. I'd cursed you a hundred times for that! But even the greatest of sinners are allowed to atone for their sins. And you have done that. You have burnt slowly and long, like husk on fire.'

'Satya Thakurji!' Shankari said in a voice trembling with emotion, 'Just that you're half my age, or I'd have touched your feet! How could you know that I've been burning like that?'

'Listen to that! I can see that for myself, can't I? I'm not blind! Your charred appearance bears witness to that. I haven't forgotten how glowing and soft your skin was! Never mind, a good thing that the curse of being pretty is gone now—what would you have done with it anyway? It proved as fatal as a viper's bite for you. Now you must look after yourself. Since you didn't hang yourself and put an end to the widow's one-meal ritual!'

Shankari said pathetically, 'Do you think I didn't feel like doing that, Thakurji? I was driven by that thought day and night, but the trash in my stomach became the shackle round my feet. I was the sinner, what harm had she done? She had nobody in the world to call her own, how could I die and abandon her?'

Satya had burst out, 'At least you had that much sense! That would be the sin of suicide over and above the burden of mortal sin—you wouldn't find a place in hell! Never mind, it's pointless lamenting the past. Now the simple fact is—you've done what you've done and since I've found out, you'll now stop slaving away at that sudra household.'

Shankari had smiled sadly, 'You are older now, a mother too, and still as bold as you used to be! But you don't know the world. If you took me in, you'd be thrown out yourself.'

Suddenly Satya's face had brightened. She had smiled a little, 'Who would throw me out—your brother-in-law?'

'That's not what I'm saying. May he always treasure you like a queen, like the jewel in his crown! I'm talking about society. If people get to know.'

'What do you mean Katoa-bou? Am I about to hide anything? I have decided to write to my father right away. I'll say this is what I wish to do, if you want to beat me, do that, cut me to pieces or keep me—do whatever you want!'

When Satya mentioned her father, Shankari brought her hands together and lifted them respectfully to her forehead. Was this intended for the man or for god? God, perhaps. She did not have the courage to ask about the people of that house, especially about that awe-inspiring, god-like person. In addition to her fear, and the shame and guilt she was feeling, there was another anxiety. What if she were told that the man was no more? That would be terrifying!

But Satya said she would write her father a letter. And Shankari had raised her palms to her head. Now that the anxiety was ousted, fear, shame and guilt had moved aside too. As if out of pity. So Shankari had asked hesitantly, 'Is your father keeping well?'

Satya sighed, 'Not too good. You know the man, he'll break but not bend. But he is broken inside after Ma died. I met him before we came to Calcutta.'

Ma dead! Shankari thought this referred to Ramkali's mother, Dinatarini. She wondered in what way her death had been surprising or tragic. May be because Ramkali was a compassionate man, he had become heartbroken by his mother's passing away. So Shankari said, 'Has he been so dejected despite his wisdom? When did Boro-didima die?'

'Boro-didima!' Satya had frowned, 'Are you asking about Thakurma? She died some years ago. I was talking about my mother. My mother has passed away.'

Satya had fallen silent. She had felt embarrassed to disclose the tremor in her voice.

Shankari had looked stunned, 'Really!'

Satya had remained silent. She had looked down.

After a long while, Shankari had given out a mournful sigh, 'How long has it been?'

'When my elder son was born.'

Then slowly, their frenzied breathing had calmed. They had hardly noticed when they had gradually moved a step ahead—from sighing to exchanging stories. And they had engrossed themselves in the churning of memories. Shankari had asked, Satya had answered. It was as though Shankari had been trying to delve deep into an ocean in search of lost treasure, and her search was bringing up Satya's vanished childhood.

Hadn't the inner quarters of Ramkali's house at Nityanandapur appeared to Shankari like a dark prison surrounded by guards? Then why did it now appear like a bright heaven? A heaven she had willingly forsaken. And exchanged for the mirage of a paradise that the devil had beguiled her with; so much so that she had tossed it aside carelessly as one discards a broken earthen pot.

So many words, so many sighs. The air had become heavy. Yet, Satya had let out one more heavy sigh, 'You're making paan at the Dattas' now, Katoa-bou, but it would have been far more respectable to sweep the doctor's courtyard.'

'I'd lost my mind. I must have been a terrible sinner in my last birth. What else can I say?'

'Anyway, don't hesitate any more. You and your girl just come here right away. You cannot purge yourself in a day, but you'd have to leave behind the polluted clothes, or you won't manage a fresh start. Never mind that, how big is your girl?'

'How big? Are you asking how old she is?' There had been a dismal emptiness in Shankari's eyes. An emptiness that had touched her voice, 'I won't hide anything from you, Thakurji—let me say frankly, she completed fourteen in Magh.'

'In Magh! So she's fifteen. Running on fifteen.' Satya had said with alarm, 'What of her marriage?'

'Marriage!' Shankari's smile combined pain with scorn. Pain at the question, scorn at her fate.

Satya had said after a moment's silence, 'Don't the people you work for ask? What do you tell them?'

Shankari had smiled a little, 'I had thought of an answer long ago. I've said that she was married at five and widowed at seven. Hasn't set eyes on her in-laws ...'

Satya had shuddered. 'How could you? What kind of mother are you to say that your unmarried daughter is a widow! Has anyone heard of such a thing? And because of you the poor thing must suffer, and eat rice and boiled plantain all her life.'

'Yes, she's having to do that. It's the same for both of us. It isn't as if we'd get more than this anywhere else, Thakurji.'

Satya had said heatedly, 'Even if that were true, how will you ever get her married after this?'

Shankari had sighed, 'How could I have got her married in any case? Who would've taken a girl with no father or grandfather to speak of as a wife?'

Satya had frowned for a while, 'But that Nagen—the one you had got married to—'

'A hoax. It was all a hoax! That vermin from hell, that sinful devil actually deceived me ...' Shankari had continued after clearing her throat, 'What can I say, Thakurji? If I hadn't been cheated, I wouldn't have been so foolish. He said that there's a new trend of widow remarriage in Calcutta. So many young widows are leading happy married lives. I believed him and stepped into hell.'

Satya had asked glumly, 'So he didn't marry you?'

'No, I won't lie, he did. He had summoned a brahmin priest who assented to widow marriage. There was a show of a wedding before the sacred fire. But if he really thought of that as marriage, why would he discard me like a rag as soon as he heard that I was carrying his child?'

'Never mind that,' Satya had sighed uneasily. 'He's not acted out of character. But you abandoned your duties. Well, one can't really call your daughter illegitimate. Even though I don't really approve of widow remarriage, it's better than nothing. And one cannot reject the prescriptions that learned pundits have given after reading the shastras. I'm not more learned than them. But I'll say this, Katoa-bou, you've not done right by giving your girl a fake identity. You shall be answerable to her as well! When she's older and she sees others getting married, decking up, how do you think she'll feel? Won't she accuse you one day—"How could you do this to me being my mother?" '

Shankari had interrupted in a deep dismal tone, 'I've dealt with that too, Thakurji. I have explained to her that she has no memories of that event, for it happened when she was only five.'

'Bou!' Satya's quavering voice had managed to pronounce just that monosyllable.

Shankari had looked at Satya's hurt and shocked expression, 'You can thrash me a hundred times, Thakurji, but I couldn't see any other way out. You can say I'm no mother but a monster! But still, I couldn't go and drown myself in the Ganga when I was carrying her! It was for her sake that I roamed from door to door, suffered a thousand kicks and blows, and sacrificed my sense of shame. Even now I'm slaving away in a low-caste household. It's not a nice place. One mustn't speak ill of the provider, but I must say living with a grown-up daughter in that house terrifies me. If you could take the girl …' Shankari had fallen silent.

After a long period of silence, Satya had asked softly, 'What have you named her?'

'Her name!' Shankari voice had resonated with guilt, 'Her smile was so winsome from the time she was just two that I named her Suhashini!'

It was understandable that she should feel guilty about the name. Names like 'Malina'—the tarnished one, or 'Asrumati'—the one full of tears, or at best, 'Chaya'—the shadow, or 'Dasi'—the enslaved, would have suited her better!

But Satya had not taunted her with that. She had said, 'Not bad. Anyway, when you say the place is like that then it isn't right for you to stay there. Bring your daughter and come here right away.'

— ⁓ —

'Yes, that's what their house is like!' Satya had recounted in suppressed fury to Nabakumar, 'It is a sin for a respectable woman to speak like this, but you wouldn't understand unless I explained the situation clearly. With a beautiful daughter like that, think how terrified she is all the time! She says there's a small room next to the kitchen where they store the coal and dung-cakes, they've cleaned that room and live in it. Just so that nobody notices. She lets her daughter step out once a day to bathe and to eat, that too when she's around. She's told everyone that her unmarried daughter is a widow. Poor thing!'

Nabakumar was hardly perturbed, he had said sulkily, 'Let her deal with her own situation, why do you need to take on so much? It would be one thing if she is only a poor, miserable, helpless, widowed sister-in-law—but what's all this? No, you can't bring in such slander into my house! Just because we have a separate place, I haven't become a pariah, have I? Do you think my mother won't disown me after this? Do you think she'll accept water from your hands?'

Satya had said calmly, 'I could say a lot, but I won't. But what if I can get your parents to agree?'

'Get them to agree!' Nabakumar had exclaimed, 'As if they're like the easygoing Nabakumar Banerji who is always ordered about! They are very firm.'

Satya had raised her eyebrows, 'No need for self-praise. Is it enough if they give their consent?'

'There's no trusting you! You're so bold that you might even physically force them. But why bother with all this? I'm telling you this won't do in my house—'

Satya had suddenly stopped smiling and had said indifferently, 'That's fine then. I shall tell my sister-in-law that. I'll say there's no place for you in this house. I'd made a mistake because I'd thought that this was my house too! My blunder's been hammered into me. My eyes have opened. A good thing too. I've learnt my lesson.'

Nabakumar had fallen back. He had begun to see stars. And he had abandoned all pretensions to boldness, and repeated the words he had learnt by rote, 'There, you're angry now! Have I said anything to annoy you? I've only said why take on trouble when we are comfortable?'

Satya's face had lost some of its hardness. She had said firmly, 'I have answered that once before. But I shall repeat it again. Do you know why we take on trouble? Because we are human beings, and not birds or beasts.'

'But then, she also has a daughter.'

'She has. And we have already talked about that.'

'But what if she turns out to be like her mother?'

'We'll have to see to it that she doesn't.'

—

Suhashini! Suhash for short. Yes, she was really growing into a beauty. As if the young girl from Shankari's refugee days had once more taken refuge in her. Her body seemed to be growing into a fullness in total defiance of the sorrows and troubles, insults and humiliations, and the austere discipline. One more phase, and it would be a full moon!

Shankari's heart would fill with gladness whenever she looked at her. But it would also shrivel in fear. She would clutch her daughter to her bosom and weep, sometimes she would grind her teeth. Not at her daughter. But at herself, as though she were crushing herself in a grinding mill. She felt hemmed in, there was nothing she could do.

The day Shankari had held Satya's hand, that same night she had given her daughter hell. She had said, 'Then go, go and get poison—let's both take it! Let's end our suffering and all our troubles!'

Suhash had made clear her extreme unwillingness. She was not ready to enter into such a strange arrangement. After so many miseries, and so much wandering, they had found shelter in what appeared to be a palace. Where was the need to take another leap into the sea of uncertainty?

Their own people! There was nobody on earth to call their own. Why, nobody had ever come up with even charred food for them! And now their 'own people' had suddenly sprouted from the earth, had they? They might have come from the same village—but so what? Why were they suddenly brimming over with compassion? So that they would get a cook and a maid for free? They thought they could just say a few kind words and cram them into their house! Shankari could not see through the ploy because she was foolish. They would lose everything this way.

That was what Suhash had said in the beginning. That was how much she could talk! Not with anyone else though, only with her mother. She would boss over her mother no end. All her life she had punished her mother for all the miseries and deprivations that she had had to suffer.

But she had not heard the complete story. The real history. She only knew that everyone had cursed Shankari for being pregnant when her husband had died. And Shankari had left home in anger and anguish. That was exactly what Suhash criticized. She had no doubts that her mother's rash behaviour was responsible for their misery.

Anyway, all that was the past. But what was this now? Mother and daughter had quarrelled. Shankari had given her daughter hell.

And Suhash had retorted passionately, 'All right, then. I know I'm a burden, let me lighten your load forever!'

THIRTY SIX

The earth is dumb, they say. But the soil of Calcutta has a tongue! For nature has blessed this city with all the sprightliness and loquacity of a young girl. May be, to make up in some ways for the lack of a million layers of civilization. The blast of her effusiveness has the power to induce the mute to chatter. Therefore, the inhabitants of Calcutta are learned without learning, knowledgeable without knowing.

According to Satya, it was not just Calcutta's soil but also its tap water that should be credited with this singular property. Perhaps there was some truth in that. From the beginning of time, people have quenched their thirst drinking with cupped hands, the water that bubbled forth from the depths of the earth, and used it in their daily lives. Where there was no stream, they had dug the earth and created one, filling their pots to store water for hard times. Who could have learnt to devise a machine that would draw up water from under the ground and command it at will? Nobody! Except Calcutta—a city that had made available such a rare commodity at the turn of a tap. Amazing! The special quality of the water probably does have some effect on the body. If nothing else, it produces courage.

Or, how else could Nabakumar have mustered up the courage to tell Bhabatosh-master to his face, 'From now on I shall not associate with you, Master-mashai. Please don't come here in future.'

Nabakumar had told Nitai himself. He had said, 'I didn't beat about the bush, you know, I gave it to him good! I'd honoured him when he was worthy of it, but if he was going to give up respectability and disgrace himself, it wasn't my responsibility to show him respect. If he was going to abandon faith in his old age, of course, people would stop respecting him too. I can't figure out at all how he could be so foolish. He was like a guardian to me in this alien place—but all that's over now!'

Nitai had smiled contentedly, 'So, you'll stop seeing him today, eh?'

'Are you mad? He is a "fallen" man—an "outcaste". Of course, one can't mix with the likes of him!'

No, Nabakumar had not cut off his ties with Nitai because he had fallen into bad company. He would call on him every day and plead with him; finally, he had even succeeded in bringing him back to the straight and narrow path by getting Satya to talk to him, as Bhabatosh had advised.

That had happened a long time ago. At that time Nabakumar's elder son, Sadhan, had been studying in the fourth class. Now he was on the verge of his entrance exam. Satya had demanded that he try the qualifying test for the scholarship. Or else all her efforts would be in vain! After all, if village boys could be successful after walking five miles to the district school, and Satya's son failed after getting so many facilities, all this struggle would be in vain. All this energy would be wasted.

Of course, the scholarship was not her sole aim. Satya wanted her sons to become good human beings too. But the first step was to do well in school. It was quite apparent that the boy would live up to such expectations. At least, that was what his tutor said. Nabakumar had been spending ten rupees a month on a tutor.

But Nabakumar had never ever imagined that his own tutor would disgrace him this way. How hard it is to find satisfaction!

A long while had passed since Nitai had fallen into disgraceful ways. Nabakumar would walk to his mess to plead with him. Every so often Nitai used to snigger at him bitterly, caustically. He would argue, 'No use worrying about a good-for-nothing! Who would care in this whole wide world if I went to the dogs? I'm fine as I am. I eat, drink and my days pass in a colourful haze. You're a "good boy". Very very precious! The world needs you—you be good!'

But Nabakumar had refused to give up, he had been firm. He had resolved to reform Nitai. In the end, he had dragged him to

Satya just as Bhabatosh had advised. He had said, 'Now, make him see sense. Explain to him what he is worth.'

Satya was upset about Shankari, so she had asked dismally, 'Am I the one who's supposed to tell him that?'

Nabakumar had scratched his head, 'Well, that's what he said. He says it won't make any difference to anybody if he ruins or squanders his life.'

For a minute Satya had looked Nitai straight in the eye, 'How do you know that? Do you know everything?'

Nitai had cowered before her.

Satya had said passionately, 'Would you believe me if I told you that it would matter a lot to me?'

Nabakumar was befuddled by this tone and he could not fathom it. He had imagined that Satya would implore him, advice him. But there was none of that. Was it a scolding, then? It did not look like that, and yet the words were undoubtedly forceful. Once more Satya had said in that same tone, 'Let me tell you, you'll have to mend your ways, become a respectable man. You must remember that men are not beasts. Take leave from your office, go home and bring your wife. I shall look for a place for you.'

Wife! Place! Nitai had shaken his head, 'That is impossible.'

'Why is it impossible?'

'They won't agree at home.'

'Who won't agree? Your wife?'

'In a manner of speaking, yes.' Nitai said dully, 'My uncle and aunt won't agree, so she wouldn't either.'

'She wouldn't either! How can she be so self-centred?'

Self-centred! Nitai had been stumped. How could the model of selfless service be called self-centred?

'I don't quite understand you, Bou-than.'

Nabakumar had added, 'Really! You're speaking complete nonsense!'

'If you wrack your brains a little, you'll know it isn't nonsense. I ask you, does your wife serve your uncle and aunt out of respect or love? Explain to me. Does she love them more than her husband?

Is she getting more satisfaction out of cooking for them than she would if she cooked for her husband? Surely that can't be true!'

The question had been directed at Nitai, but Nabakumar had answered. 'As if there is any logic to this! Won't people speak ill of her if she wanted to come here? Everyone isn't like you ...'

'Yes, who else is as daring as me? But that's stale news now. I ask you, just because people will speak ill of me, should I let go of my husband? Let him eat out, let him ruin his health? Isn't that self-centred? Will I get blisters if people consider me a disgrace? Won't I be clear in my mind that I haven't done anything wrong? I believe she doesn't have children. So what is she busy with? Spending her time uselessly from dawn to dusk, and getting praised for it too! Is that a life? If you know what's good for you, bring your wife here. I shall find you a place.'

Suddenly, Nitai had repeated an earlier action. He had touched Satya's feet. 'I don't know what is good for me, Bou-than. But if that's your command, then ...'

'Yes, it is,' Satya had said firmly. 'I command you to live like a man and not waste time on empty dreams!'

Nitai had left. Satya had gone back to work. Nabakumar had stood staring in bafflement. As if he could not comprehend what exactly had happened. But he had realized that something extraordinary had taken place before his own eyes. It seemed as though Nitai and Satya had been speaking in Urdu or Persian.

Yet, he could hardly ask Satya about it. She was depressed about Shankari.

Really, Satya had never imagined in her dreams that Shankari would betray her this way. As if she had paid back what she owed to an enemy from her last life. Or else, why would a lost person who had not occupied any space in her thoughts, suddenly come back and re-acquaint herself?

Satya's days were passing happily enough; suddenly Shankari had to inflict an injury at the heart of that happiness. As in stories where the dead rose from their graves to torture the living—Shankari had acted exactly like that!

What had Satya done, that she chose to wound her in this way?

She had written to her father, informing him about Shankari in order to find out his reaction. But Shankari had created news even before the reply to that letter could arrive. Couldn't she have waited for a couple of days? It was as though she had caught Satya and plunged a sharp knife into her heart. After digesting heaps of insult and abuse and staying alive, it was as though she had not been able to stomach Satya's affection and so, had thrown her life away. What could be more cruel?

Satya had sat down in a daze when she had heard the news. 'I knew it, I knew it! Always stone-hearted. How heartless women are!' Then she had howled aloud, 'Bou, I regret the day I met you again! I regret telling you that I'd look after your girl! Why did I say that? If I hadn't, you wouldn't have felt free to die!'

That was not untrue, it was because of Suhash that Shankari had tolerated her disgraceful existence. It was because she was now relieved from that responsibility that she had ...

Or was it the result of a momentary turmoil? When the girl had squabbled with her, had Shankari's face flared up with a cruel, vengeful smile? Had she thought, 'Really! Will you always beat me at everything? Can nothing make up for my sins? I've been cringing ever since your birth—now *you* want to crush me by dying? All right, let's see who wins!'

Had Shankari thought it through calmly and done what she had planned over a long period of time, or had a moment's carelessness led her to sink her boat just as she neared the shore?

Nobody knew the truth. Nobody knew what had really happened. Shankari had not had a clue that one should write a note to the effect that, 'Nobody is responsible for my death.' Or, may be, in those days, that was not the usual practice. Perhaps because they did not know how to write. But because it was not usual, early that morning there was commotion in the house. The paan-maker woman had hanged herself from the rafters of her room by the kitchen. Why? Why had she done it? How sad!

Just the day before, she had been floating on a sea of bliss because she had found someone from her village, who had fed her with so much love. She had, of course, declared that she would give up her job and leave. She had said, 'She's from my village. I've known her all my life. She keeps insisting, and says she'll take in my daughter too. I can't pass over such a chance! I've been a servant for so long.'

She said that they met near the Kali temple. And the woman she meant was none other than that haughty tenant at number seven! That same woman had reassured her. She would have gone right away. But she had brought up the excuse of finding an auspicious day to leave, 'Nobody lets even a cat or a dog leave during the months of Chaitra, Paush or Bhadra—it brings bad luck to the family. You've fed me for so long. I won't harm you. I won't leave this month.'

So what could have shattered her sense of good and evil? What was it that had made her suddenly forget what she owed them?

There was great commotion. But after all, it was the life of an upper-class household against the death of one miserable widow. The hubbub had sputtered and faded. Let alone the law, even the men of the house did not get any whiff of the matter. Or, if they had, they did not let on.

Perhaps, for just a tiny moment, the rhythmic dragging on the hookah was disrupted, and a growl had erupted, nothing more than that.

Shankari's body was taken out through the backdoor. A petrified Satya stood by her door and watched. When the corpse disappeared out of sight, she raised her hands to her forehead and said to herself, 'I realize now how proud you were despite your fall. That is why you didn't want to stay on with a younger sister-in-law. Everyone's seeking the "cause", but I'm the cause—I can feel it in my bones. That's the role god had chosen for me.'

At that moment a maidservant of the Datta family had come to summon Satya, 'The Boro-Ginni is calling you.'

Satya did not protest. Perhaps she had been waiting for this.

Of course, there was no reason for her to think that Datta-Ginni had called her to give her a treat! But Satya had not expected this kind of encounter either. She had not thought in her wildest dreams that any woman could curse a tenant's wife so violently. She had even threatened to call the police, saying she could get witnesses to prove that the innocent woman had been acting strangely on account of Satya's interventions.

'You're the cause of her death. She was fine until she met you,' Datta-Ginni had said.

Satya listened to all the charges with a bowed head and said, 'It's all over now, let me have her daughter.'

'Let you have her!'

Datta-Ginni was not a fool to give away a nubile and beautiful girl just like that! The girl could turn out to be a powerful weapon. So many deeds could be achieved through her. She could be so useful. Therefore, she had frowned and said, 'What do you mean let you have her? Are you related to her? She'll stay in my household. Just like her mother did.'

Satya had raised her face to ask, 'As a servant who makes paans?'

Datta-Ginni had said harshly, her face dark, 'Of course! Will a servant's daughter become a queen or what? But of course, our men are rather kind-hearted. If she caught someone's eye—she might become a queen too!'

There could be no doubt that Datta-Ginni had deliberately attempted to pierce her with that poisonous sting. In fact, she blamed Satya totally for Shankari's death—it had to be her doing—or could her maid who had been alive and kicking till now, vanish like camphor? And here she had come to claim the daughter! She thought, 'I say, who the hell d'you think you are? I can teach you a lesson or two! I know what you're made of! If Suhash's mother was from your village, I know exactly where you come from. You can't fool me with your high and mighty airs!'

Satyabati had guessed from the woman's expression what must have been on her mind. So vowing to herself that she would not be perturbed, she had declared, 'That would be wonderful! When the men in your house are so kind, she'll be well taken care of.'

Datta-Ginni had frowned, 'What do you mean?'

'What I just said.'

'What did you mean by "being taken care of"?'

'Exactly what I said. If you haven't got it, I can't explain, you can find out later. Permit me to leave.'

Datta-Ginni had reverted to her usual style, 'Do you know I can get you arrested? I can say that you conspired and my maid died.'

Satya had given a slight smile, 'Why don't you go ahead? But right now, do ask a maid or a young boy to show me where the sitting room is.'

'Show you the sitting room? You'll go in there? What are you scheming now?'

'I'll beg something from the kind-hearted men! There's no harm in a brahmin girl doing that.'

'You shrewd hussy!' Datta-Ginni charged out of the bed, 'I don't like your manners! Want to con the men, do you? Aren't you ashamed?'

The sari had slipped off Satya's head and her face was red. Taking control, she said, 'What is there to feel ashamed of? Every sudra is like a son to a brahmin. Should a mother feel ashamed before her son?'

After that Datta-Ginni could not figure out what happened and how. But she had had to let Suhash go to Satya's household. Mejo-karta, her husband's second brother, had flip-flopped into the house and ordered, 'Send the brahmin-hussy's girl to the number seven house. She's from their village.'

This brother-in-law of hers was a widower, so Datta-Ginni usually behaved as if she owned him. So she had responded with a frown, 'How do you get to know who comes from which village?'

'How do I get to know? Won't I know when it is poured into my ears? That wife of Banerji came and said so herself—'

'She did! She talked to you herself?'

'Not directly. She spoke via a maid—'

'And one look at that pretty face, you melted! How wonderful! You don't need to involve yourself in the affairs of the inner-quarters. I know how to break women who seduce men!'

Mejo-karta had looked baffled. 'What are you talking about? She's from a respectable family and is almost my daughter's age. What kind of nonsense are you talking!'

Datta-Ginni had said with suppressed rage, 'Look at our guru here! Don't you try to fool me. As if I haven't seen a young woman before! Go back to where you belong. I shan't send Suhash anywhere, that's final!'

Mejo-karta had said helplessly, 'But I promised. My words carry some weight, don't they?'

'I see! And mine don't?'

'How strange! Did I say that?' Mejo-karta had changed tactics, 'If the problem goes away without any effort on our part, why worry? You know that there's no forgiveness in heaven for hanging oneself. The spirit returns to the one it loved. That girl is her only daughter, of course, she loved her a lot.'

Datta-Ginni had shuddered and invoked Lord Rama. Of course, she had loved her daughter! It would be an understatement to say the least. Datta-Ginni had never ever seen such devotion towards one's child. Anyway, no further effort had been necessary, that one missile had secured Mejo-karta's victory. And so Suhashini had come into Satya's household with great reluctance.

But then everyone had been reluctant. Nabakumar had been against it. Satya too, had no longer felt the joy of carrying out a pleasant duty. She had brought the girl home out of a sense of duty. As she had promised Shankari.

But all that had happened about four years ago. Now Suhashini had completed three years in Bethune School.

Perhaps to make it easier for her to go to school, or perhaps because she wanted to free herself from the grip of the Dattas, Satya had given up the house at Muktarambabu Street and moved to Baghbazar. The rent here was higher, and it was far more inconvenient, but the Ganga was close by. One could secure the virtue of bathing in it everyday.

And?

There was another attraction which Nabakumar knew nothing about. Unbeknown to him, Satya had started to visit another place every afternoon.

But never mind that, Nabakumar had felt neither happy nor sad, because he knew nothing about it. He was supposed to be contented; after all, just as the rent had gone up, so had his salary. The two boys had been topping their class every year—one had finished school. The house looked picture-perfect thanks to Satya's stamina and phenomenal skills. Back at the village, his parents too were fine. Nitai had mended his ways. What else could one ask for?

Nothing else!

And yet, suddenly, he had suffered a tremendous loss. Yes, it was very abrupt. There had been nothing to compensate for the loss. It had come like a bolt from the blue—misery in the midst of plenty!

Bhabatosh-master had become a Brahmo. He had lost caste!

THIRTY SEVEN

Back in the village, Bhabini used to be a different creature. She worked like a beast of burden, and slept like one too. And she suffered every abuse in silence. She was scared to death of each and every creature in her uncle-in-law's house.

Even after she had come of age, Nitai could count on his fingers the number of words his wife had exchanged with him before they had come to Calcutta. Only once, many days ago, when he had mentioned moving to Calcutta, had she spoken quite clearly.

She had said, 'I'd rather hang myself! Should I be so shameless as to ignore what people say and go and live with you?'

Perhaps she had raised her voice only because she was acutely aware of other people listening. Nitai's ashen face had turned a shade paler.

The next day, his aunt had asked, 'So, are you going to take your wife to Calcutta, like your bosom pal?'

Nitai had dismissed it with, 'What! Have you gone out of your mind?'

His aunt had said, 'Don't blame me later. I did tell your wife that there was no need to suppress her desires and stay here with us. That she could go if she wanted. But the wretched girl said, "I'd rather lie at your feet. Let's see who takes me away!"'

His aunt's voice had dripped with contentment. Nitai had left, satisfied that his wife was very conscientious about her duties. And so, he had installed himself at Nabakumar's house.

But all that was a long while ago. Since then a lot of water had flowed under the bridge, and had been muddied as well. Nitai's life had taken a toss. Finally, on the advice of his friend's wife, he had gone back to his village with the same proposal.

He had thought he would have to fight a bit. But the strange thing was that he seemed to have won the kingdom without a battle. God alone knew who had pulled the strings, but his aunt proposed, much before Nitai could bring it up himself, 'How long will you eat at the "mess", Nitai? Take your wife with you.'

His uncle said the same thing too. Without a word, his wife had followed in his footsteps. And from her behaviour it had not appeared as if she was feeling ashamed of it either.

What had actually happened was this:

The story of Nitai's fall had reached the village. Because bad news and slander always travel on wings. Wings that have high horsepower!

After hearing the news, his wife had lain herself down on the floor in mourning, and his worried relatives decided that it was necessary to send a lieutenant to guard the territory. Besides, in recent years, a number of the village wives had gone with their husbands. From his aunt's father's village too, four women had left to join their husbands in Jamalpur. Another woman from this very village, had gone to Kachrapara, and another to Sahibgunj. Most of the village boys had become extremely audacious and shameless after finding jobs with the Railways, and they had started taking their wives with them. Therefore, there would be no danger of losing caste, if Nitai took his wife to Calcutta. Besides, the city was blessed with the holy Ganga, and the living presence of the goddess, Kali, at the Kalighat temple. So the ground had already been prepared.

But Nitai had not a clue about it. He was astonished that he got permission so easily. But that could hardly compare with the astonishment he felt now! Bhabini amazed him by the minute! As though she had taken on a different role. Nitai had not imagined in his wildest dreams that Bhabini had such a sharp tongue!

But one could hardly blame Bhabini. She had come to guard her territory, and had vowed to teach her husband a lesson. Throughout her married life, Bhabini had forced her tongue into silence, sometimes out of fear, sometimes to buy praise. A backlash was sure to follow! But most of all, she no longer needed to control her tongue. Naturally, waters dammed up for so long would want to break free and expand into loud, splashing waves!

These days, Nitai would be pierced with sharp words every waking moment. But he did not have the nerve to protest. It was as though he had lost out. It would be hard to understand exactly how this had happened, but a certain sense of shame would prevent him from holding his head high.

But the heart-rending thing was that most of Bhabini's malice seemed to be directed towards that high altar where Nitai would pour the offerings of his heart. Bhabini flared up at any mention of Satyabati's name. Nitai could hardly figure out the cause of such eruptions. Was it because humans are innately ungrateful?

On his own, Nitai would muse, 'Who was it that helped you come here? Who fixed up the house for you? And wrenched your husband away from the path of vice? Without Satyabati's intervention, could you have ever had this free and fancy lifestyle? You'd have been boiling paddy, washing clothes and husking grain all your life! Don't you have any gratitude at all?'

But did Bhabini really not grasp that? Nitai himself had told her as soon as they had stepped into their home in Calcutta, 'It's because of one person's efforts that you've got the freedom to run your own house! Had Bou-than not ordered it, this bastard would never have bothered!'

That very day, Nitai had a taste of Bhabini's tongue. She had exclaimed, 'Does this civilized city make everybody's speech so vulgar?'

Nitai's speech had become unmannerly of late, as a fallout of the company he had kept. The 'friend' who had steered the path of his fall had similar manners, obviously, it left its mark on his speech and other habits. Nitai had felt slightly embarrassed on having used the word 'bastard', but he had felt chastened by Bhabini, 'Look how you talk! You've started to boss me around as soon as you've come home!'

It had gone no further than that.

But like the moon which increases in size with every passing day, Bhabini had bloomed to her utmost limit.

This morning there had been yet another fracas. Nitai had complained of fever and headache the previous night. He had declared that he would not eat or go out to work either. Bhabini had been quite pleased about this. She was childless and spent the day all alone, at least the man would be around today, she had thought.

Besides, it was not a Sunday, a thought that had pleased Bhabini. Her mind had become lazy and inactive by the lack of work in the city, and so she thought there was no need to cook. If Nitai took some puffed rice, she could do the same. But the day was not very auspicious, since it was dashami, and tradition demanded that, as a married woman she would have to eat some fish. She could do that in the evening, anyway. There were a few live fish kept in a pot of water.

That was the frame of mind in which she had sat down to embroider her unfinished quilt, late that morning. Nitai was lying awake in bed. Suddenly, he had come out and enquired, 'Are you stitching now? What about the cooking?'

Bhabini frowned, 'I thought I needn't bother, especially since you're not going to eat.'

Nitai was taken aback, 'What do you mean? Just because I'm not going to eat, you won't either? Whoever's heard of such a thing! What will you eat?'

Bhabini had put on a superior philosophical air, 'What good is food for a woman? I can eat some puffed rice with you. That'll do nicely.'

'What nonsense! Aren't you going to light the chullah?'

'I don't see why I should.'

Then Nitai mentioned the matter a bit hesitantly, 'All right, then. But I was wondering ...'

'What is it?'

'Doesn't matter!'

Bhabini lay her sewing aside, 'Of course not! Just tell me.'

Nitai said, 'Well, I was thinking, since the fever is not very high, it would be nice to have rotis with potato curry.'

Rotis! The sky had fallen on Bhabini's head as soon as she heard the word! She had heard of rotis but had never made them herself. Nobody did, at their village. There was always rice, or puffed rice, sweets and a range of fried and boiled snacks—one could eat whatever suited one's constitution. Rotis never appeared on the horizon!

This was a fad Nitai had picked up in Calcutta. A few days ago, he had come home in the evening and said, 'I don't feel too well. Why don't you make me some rotis. I have brought the flour.'

That day, Bhabini had made up an excuse. Cuffing herself mentally, she had said, 'My God! I wish I'd known! I've put the rice on the fire already!'

Of course, Nitai had not checked to see if the rice was indeed cooking. 'Let it be,' he had said and had put the packet of flour down. That packet was still around. Nitai obviously knew about it, and now he made his demand without feeling any unease.

A mountain of anxiety now appeared, and sat on Bhabini's shoulders. It was as difficult for her to say, 'I can't make them,' as it was to admit 'I don't know how to.' But she took one last chance.

She said, 'Why eat dry rotis in the afternoon. Let me make some khichri instead, you can have it hot—'

'No, not khichri,' Nitai had axed the root of Bhabini's hope, 'No rice. It isn't good for the body. Don't make the roti dry, smear it with a bit of ghee. Don't make too many—just twelve or fourteen. A small meal is medicine enough.'

Therefore, cursing her fate, Bhabini had entered the kitchen with the packet of flour. She had hoped not to get tied to the kitchen and to finish the quilt today, and the sky had fallen on her head instead!

Needless to say, her efforts had not met with success. First, she had managed to make the dough into a paste. And then she had struggled to roll out the rotis—but those shapeless things had got charred as soon as she had put them on the fire. Moreover, at places the shapes appeared visibly uncooked.

Since it was well past noon, Nitai had assumed that Bhabini was making rotis for herself as well. Estimating the number of rotis that were being made, he had waited patiently. But there had to be a limit to patience! Besides, his stomach had begun to growl. And repeated growling had made Nitai restless, so finally he had come up to the kitchen door, 'Are you cooking nine hundred and fifty items? I only asked for a few rotis and potato curry …'

Once again, Bhabini had cuffed herself mentally, 'As if anyone can eat like that! I'll make a dal too.'

'Look at that! That's too much! No wonder it's taking so long. No need for all that. Give me whatever is ready.'

But if she had to serve him now, there was no potato curry! The potatoes were still inside the basket. So Bhabini had had to let the cat out of the bag. Not fully out though. She was compelled to say, 'Wait a bit. It'll take a while longer.'

Nitai had become fidgety and said, 'Forget all that. Rotis and jaggery will do fine.'

So in the end, that was what Bhabini had to serve him. Nitai was famished, and one look at the jaggery pieces with the lumpy half-cooked dough had made every molecule of his blood boil. He had exploded.

After serving him, Bhabini had disappeared into the kitchen with some excuse or other. Suddenly, she had heard the plate crashing to the floor. She had come out, and stood motionless. She had not quite expected this. But she saw that he had tossed the plate away.

Squashing the half-done rotis in his hands, Nitai was bellowing, 'What are these? Offerings you've made for my funeral or what? Why didn't you tell me that you didn't know how to make rotis? No stupid bastard would've wanted them then! What a fool I've been! I should've bought puris and curry from the shops for two annas. Instead, I went and asked my hardworking wife! I should have known better. Such work is only for those who're capable. As we say, "If you've never ploughed the land, paddy looks like grass!" Same difference! I tell you, now that you're here in this city, you have to learn a few civilized things. All that chaffing and husking are useless here. Go and learn a few things from Bou-than.'

Perhaps Nitai's hunger and extreme disappointment were responsible for this outburst. But there was a limit to what could be tolerated. Perhaps, till that point, Bhabini had listened in silence because she had been embarrassed to say the least. Because he was famished, she had figured that it was best not to retort. She intended to offer him some puffed rice and milk after he had calmed down. But there had been no such happy conclusion.

Suddenly, that last tug seemed hard to withstand. It looked as though a string from an instrument had broken and fallen with a clatter. That was inevitable. After all, just because I had accidentally stepped on you, should I tolerate a kick from you in return? And if a spark from my hookah fell on your cow-shed, should I let you set fire to my house? Because my goat had just nibbled a bit at your plants, should you let your cows loose into my garden, while I look on helplessly? As if it was all a joke! A human being was not a stone, after all!

So there could be no happy conclusion. Much before Nitai completed his sentence, Bhabini had charged at him angrily.

'What was that again? Just repeat it! Are you suggesting that I go and learn to cook from your beloved Bou-than? What other insults have you stored up for me? Bring them all out! After that I'll go and drown myself in the Ganga! Why don't you just take me back to Baruipur? Let me tell you clearly—I can't live here after such an insult. Oh god! Was this the happiness you brought me to the city for? Damn it! And just as I was thinking, I'd apologize for my mistake and it'd end there without sprouting branches! But there's no end in sight! Really, you're a classic example of those who flatter the strong and tyrannize the weak! It's all "Bou-than" this and "Bou-than" that—every waking moment! I tell you, if she's cast such a spell on you, why did you bring me here? Just to keep up a facade, or what? So that you can conceal your sins? Your ...'

The arrow had hit home! Words had hammered themselves on words!

Nitai stood up and screamed at the top of his voice, 'Tui! How dare you say that!'

'Don't you use "tui" while talking to me! Talking like a low-caste man! Is this part of your city-bred culture?' Bhabini had charged, 'I don't respect you at all! D'you hear? Not the slightest bit! An immoral husband isn't a husband at all. You think I'll go to that witch to learn anything? I'd rather hang myself! You can go and drink the water in which she washes her feet!'

Nitai had suddenly become grave. He paced about in silence for a while, folding his hands over his chest, and then said, 'Well, I'd not only drink it, but I'd pour it over my head. And women like you should do that too. If you just did that twice a day and learnt from her for twenty years, even then, may be, you'd measure up to her little toe.'

Nitai's heightened proclamation may have been an expression of deference, but to Bhabini, his admiration for another woman had positively felt like salt on her wounds. Therefore, one could hardly blame Bhabini when, tying her sari round her waist, she had jumped into the fray.

'Really! Measure up only to her little toe, is it? Spoken like a fallen man—the type that adores other men's wives! Let me ask you—are you aware of what that "darling" of your heart is up to? I've avoided mentioning it because I didn't want to talk about it. In any case, a man like you would've rushed to her defence had I mentioned it. So I'd thought I'd let you find out for yourself. For I've known it for a long time now. I'll tell you now. Where do you think she goes all decked-up every afternoon, eh? Without telling her husband too! You don't know that, do you?'

'What do you mean "without telling her husband"?'

Nitai had become the weaker party. His mighty opponent had said with a crooked smile, 'It means what it means! Her maid spoke to my maid about it. She's even trained her boys to keep mum!'

Nitai could hardly believe that Satyabati could be capable of doing anything secretly. So he had bellowed, 'I don't believe it!'

'Oh really? But this is nothing! Wonder what you'll say when you hear the whole story. I say, do you know that she secretly hobnobs with that casteless Master too? I believe she even went to the Brahmo Samaj office with him. I didn't mention it because I couldn't bear to speak about that man with you. But let me warn you, one day that dame is ...'

'Don't you dare!' Nitai had charged at her, screaming, 'You liar! Don't you make things up—your tongue will fall off! Shut up, just shut up!'

Nitai had looked utterly helpless. Both the accusations were serious ones, and yet he had dared not dismiss them totally because they seemed to bear the whiff of some dangerous truth. And to top it all, this thing about Bhabatosh-master! Nitai had been so relieved when the man had become a Brahmo. He had thought that at least the Master would stop coming to Nabakumar's house. But what a piece of treacherous news this was! Nitai began to feel unwell.

Bhabini had taken the opportunity to tighten the sari around her waist a little more.

'You can't change the truth into a lie just by making me shut up! Let me warn you, that darling Bou-than of yours is going to become a Brahmo. Just you wait! And that grown girl she's taken in—claiming that she's a niece—who knows if she's a widow or unmarried? You can't tell her age—you can't pass that one into a Hindu family! So she'll become a Brahmo and get her married.'

'Will you shut up?'

Bhabini had mockingly put a finger on her lips, 'All right, I will. But the world won't shut up, even if I do! Everyone will get to know.'

With that Bhabini had actually stopped. I suppose, mainly because her husband who had neither bathed nor eaten had begun to look like a battered opponent. Yet Nitai was at that time insane with restlessness. How could Bou-than be capable of such things— lying, going on a tryst, visiting the Brahmo Samaj, and meeting

Bhabatosh on the sly? If such allegations were true, why then, god, dharma and everything else in the world had to be false! His agitation had been exacerbated by illness, hunger and the want of a bath.

Finally, Bhabini had approached him and begged to be forgiven. She had offered water and sweets to appease him, but they would not go down his throat. And he had turned away with a 'later'. Rubbing his face on his pillow, he had finally fallen asleep.

All that had happened in the afternoon.

Around dusk, Nitai woke to Nabakumar's shout. Nabakumar was trying to shake him awake, 'Nitai, Nitai, has your Bou-than come here?'

Nitai sat up with a start. He was feeling weak from the fasting, his head reeled, and so it took him a while to understand the question. Instead of an answer, he asked a question, 'Who are you talking about?'

'Who else, but your Bou-than! Who else would I look for? Just go inside and ask, she might have come to visit your wife.'

A stupefied Nitai slowly shook his head.

'Look, don't just sit here and guess! You were asleep after all, you fool! She might have come then.'

Finally, after deep thought, Nitai asked seriously, 'Why? Isn't she home?'

'I say, if she were home, would I have come all the way just to bother you? Just get up!'

So Nitai was forced to get up. All of a sudden, for the first time in his life, he realized the disadvantage of not having a third person in the house. He would have to speak to Bhabini to enquire about Satyabati. And he knew already what her response would be. On the other hand, he could not ignore Nabakumar. Was it possible for him to have missed Satyabati's visit? It was unlikely, after all, he had been sleeping; he had not died!

Nabakumar lived just two houses away. And there was constant coming and going. When Bhabini had first arrived, Satya used to come and help her very often. She had stopped because Bhabini did not seem to encourage it. And she used to come often when

Nitai was out. She rarely came when he was home. Could today have been an exception?

Nitai went inside in response to Nabakumar's restlessness. He looked inside and returned shaking his head. He had not been able to swallow his pride and ask Bhabini. He noticed that she was sewing, totally oblivious of the approaching dark. Almost as if she had forgotten the custom of not touching needle and thread in the evenings.

'What shall we do, Nitai?' Nabakumar was close to tears.

Nitai responded in a hollow voice, 'Perhaps she has gone to some other place.'

'Where else can she go? All by herself?' Nabakumar asked plaintively. 'Just my luck that the boys are away at the village now, visiting their grandparents.'

'Have they gone by themselves?' Nitai had been startled.

'No, our Abani was going back to the village, I thought I'd send them because they had holidays. They've hardly spent any time at the village. How was I to know that this would happen?'

Nitai's hollow voice sounded worse, 'Did you have a fight? She hasn't gone towards the river ...'

'No! No! It's nothing like that, Nitai. But she doesn't go anywhere without telling me.'

Nitai almost said impulsively, 'That she does. I know about it.'

But he stopped himself and mentioned something else, 'That girl—Suhash, isn't she home?'

'She's been worried ever since she got back from school. The maid doesn't know anything either. What shall we do now, Nitai?'

Nitai was totally confounded. A thousand wasps were buzzing inside his head. His shoulders felt too weak and unwilling to bear the weight of his head. So he abruptly put his head on the pillow and said brokenly, 'I don't understand it at all!'

But someone else had figured it all out! Ever since she had noticed Nitai go inside and come out again, Bhabini had abandoned her sewing. She had come up to the door and had been eavesdropping. She had immediately figured it all out. And she found it intolerable that a pair of full-grown men should be reduced to helpless flies because of a wicked hag! What an eyesore! Bhabini could not tolerate it any further, she jangled the door-latch loudly. The loud clanging presaged mysterious tidings.

——

No matter what one's daughter-in-law was like, grandsons were always significantly different. After all, they would be the successors, the masters of everything; they appeared to be bonded to one's nerve fibres! Ever since the two boys had arrived Elokeshi had spared no efforts in pampering them. Simultaneously, she had kept unabated the stream of insults about her daughter-in-law. After declaring that the 'low-born' woman responsible for depriving her of these treasures could never ever come to any good, Elokeshi had busied herself in tending to her grandsons. This time they had come without their parents. On other occasions they would come with their father during the pujas and stay for just a couple of days. She hardly had enough time with them, then.

Satya had never visited after she had left. Elokeshi, of course, had announced loud and clear that she never wished to see her face again. Nabakumar had come by himself to the village for the sacred-thread ceremonies of the boys. The boys had had their heads shaven as was the custom. The household of the close-fisted Nilambar had hardly known lavish ceremonies. So Nabakumar was quite clueless about such things. But what about Satya? Well, even if she craved for a large celebration, she had deferred to Elokeshi. She would have to consult Elokeshi if she desired anything elaborate. Therefore, she had preferred to stay in the Calcutta house, calling the maid to stay the nights so that she would not be alone.

Sadhan and Saral were still called 'Turu' and 'Khoka' respectively, they had not yet graduated to their formal names. They were both small eaters. But nets were cast for fresh fish every day, puffed rice was prepared, and all kinds of sweets were made. In short, Elokeshi made every dish that she knew. Rather, to put it correctly, every dish that Sadu knew! Naturally, Sadu was up to her eyes in work.

Frequently, Nilambar would sound a warning, 'Hope you're both well. How's your stomach? It's a bad season. But let's hope your mother doesn't say that you fell ill because your grandmother stuffed you too much.'

But Elokeshi had hardly paid any attention to such warnings. Nor did she appear scared of what their mother might say. Instead she would snap, 'You stop it! Why should they fall ill? Bless them! Do you think I feed them rice that's rotten and stale? In any case, nobody but their mother's to blame if they fall ill. She's picked up the ways of the city and has been starving them. And their stomachs have shrunk. She feeds them rice just once a day. And I'd give Naba rice three times a day! What do these boys eat in the morning—fried sweets, jalebis, sesame sweets! All bought from the shops. As if such food fills the stomach. Would her hands get bruised if she boiled some rice for them in the mornings? And what does she give them when they get back from school? Parathas! Flour for the famished—I tell you! Of course, they'll feel like crying! When Naba came back from school he'd throw a tantrum and fling the food away if he wasn't served his fish curry and rice.'

Sadu had tried intervening a couple of times, 'But have Naba's sons told you that they feel like crying?'

Elokeshi had dismissed that too. 'You think they'd dare? With that monster of a mother! Do you think they'd ever speak against her? Whatever words I manage to squeeze out are from the older one, the younger one is really shrewd. He knows full well that his mother will never send him here if he lets on anything, so ...'

'But what is there to "let on"? It isn't as if she's involved with some theft or robbery in Calcutta?'

'But there are many things she's done, hasn't she? She's taken in some girl—who knows from where—and she's been spending money on her education, buying her books and all! But leave that aside, I hear that she goes to some place every afternoon—to teach. The learned witch! How's it any better than stealing? Whoever's heard of such a thing? When did the wife of a respectable man ever become a teacher?'

Nilambar too was thrown by this piece of news. He had cursed Nabakumar and warned him that his death was imminent. At any rate, he claimed that he would give the couple a thrashing and bring them back to the village.

Later, he had abandoned that scheme, saying, 'No need to do that! They've lost caste, in any case. Why needlessly bring them here when we're not about to accept rice cooked by her? Let them stay far away—her people will get to know. She's hardly the type that draws her sari over her face and stays quietly in a corner. It's best that she stays out of sight. See if you can influence the sons. There has to be somebody to look after us in our old age.'

Elokeshi had lowered her voice and said with a smile, 'Do you think I'm sparing any effort? I've been narrating every quirk of their mother's so that they begin to hate her. But she's really bewitched them! They simply adore her. If it wasn't for her spell would my own son turn away from me?'

Sadhan and Saral were totally oblivious to these discussions, busy as they were enjoying their holiday. Of course, as much they relished this break from their routine in Calcutta and rediscovered their childhood, they felt miffed with their mother. Because every waking moment they would hear vilifying details about their mother's mulishness that had brought about their move to Calcutta.

Though never in front of her aunt, for she really feared Elokeshi's belligerence, Sadu would be fair. Elokeshi would go to bed quite early, and Sadu would have her nephews to herself during the evening meal. She would serve them and sit around chatting.

She would tell them, 'Don't blame your mother on the basis of what your grandmother says! Had your mother not dragged you there, you wouldn't have learnt so much, and you wouldn't have done well in school either. Would it have happened had you stayed on here? Have you seen boys of your age in the village? Some fish all day, or take to smoking, and some struggle in the same class for three or four years. They don't know how to behave; no manners at all. You can't tell if they're brahmins or peasants!'

Sadhan however would duplicate his grandmother's logic, 'But people stayed in the village for a long time—years and years! As if they were all brutes! And my mother's father grew up in the village too.'

'Your grandfather? Don't mention him in the same breath! He is one in a million! And he's hardly as limited as your father's father. He's free-flowing like a river. He hasn't grown up just in the village. He'd spent a lot of time in small towns. But don't you go to visit him ever?'

'No.'

'Really? I thought, now that your mother is free, perhaps ...'

Suddenly Saral had blurted out, 'As if Ma can become free all by herself. Nobody in our country is free. India is not independent.'

It had taken Sadu a while to grasp his meaning, 'What was that you said about India?'

'That it isn't independent! The White Sahibs rule here, don't they?'

Sadu had said in utter astonishment, 'Listen to that! It is their kingdom, after all, so they will rule, won't they?'

'How can it be their kingdom? They don't belong to our race.'

'But they are rulers! And besides, they've come from across the seas and done us so much good.'

'Good! My foot! They're doing us a lot of harm. Our mother says it is essential that each country should be ruled by its own people. Those who have come from another place and grown their roots here should be ...'

Sadu had been amazed, 'Your mother says all this? Then I can well believe Mami! She's lost her mind! Don't you repeat such things Khoka! The White Sahibs have employed your father.'

Perhaps because he had not quite understood what Sadu meant, Saral's answer had taken a different line of argument, 'Well, Ma doesn't criticize the White Sahibs. She only says all children should grow up with such thoughts so that they can hold their heads high in the world. But how can those who belong to a country that isn't free hold their heads high?'

Sadu had sighed dejectedly, 'Well, I can't understand all that. Your mother always had a sharp tongue, and had the weirdest thoughts. And of all people in the world, she bothers her head about Bengalis and White men—debating about who should be subject and who should be king! I've not had freedom from the moment of my birth. How am I supposed to understand all that? I recognize that men can be independent or dependent, but is it the same with a country? But never mind. I hear your mother goes to teach, tell me about it.'

The two brothers had exchanged a look. All of a sudden Saral had said vehemently, 'Let's just tell her, no point feeling scared. After all, Ma says that doing things on the sly and being secretive are the worst of sins. But we'd only have to be careful with our father—because he can stop her from going. And that would be awful! But Master-mashai says ...'

Sadu had frowned, 'Who's this?'

'Don't you know? Bhabatosh-babu. The one who got father ...

'I know. But hasn't he become a Brahmo?'

Sadhan had nodded apprehensively.

'And your mother speaks with him?'

Sadhan had nodded with greater apprehension.

'Does he visit you even after he's become a Brahmo?'

'No, he doesn't,' Saral had answered gravely. 'Our father doesn't respect him anymore, he has asked him not to come home. So our mother said, "All right, in that case, I shall visit him. After all, Master-mashai has helped us so much ..."'

Sadu had put a hand on her cheek in astonishment, 'I'm truly stupefied! I wish I could go and check for myself if your mother's grown extra pairs of hands or legs! She seems to be doing things nobody in the whole wide world has ever heard of. I know Bhabatosh-master did a lot for them, but even so, where's the need to visit him after he's lost caste?'

A sinful thought had jabbed at Sadu. Which had prompted her

to ask the question. But then, Sadhan's explanation was feasible enough.

'Well, Master-mashai is the one who's opened the school. And grown-up married women come there to learn the alphabet. The Master says, otherwise they spend all their time gossiping, playing cards, quarrelling or just sleeping. It's best that they learn to read and write instead. So he has opened a school at Sarbamanagalatala in the afternoons. Even women as old as you come there.'

Sadu had let out a sigh, 'When I die, I wish I could be reborn in your city and learn to read at your mother's school.'

'But you can learn now, can't you?'

'Of course, I can. After I've been placed on my funeral pyre! Go on now, eat up!'

'I can't. I feel stuffed.'

'Let it be then. Don't force yourself.'

Sadu's face had suddenly turned dull, and after a glance at her face, Sadhan had said, 'Pishi, why don't you come with us to Calcutta?'

'Me!' Sadu had given a start, 'And let the old man and woman perish here without food?'

'Well, not forever. Just for a few days?'

'Let it be. I'm happy enough that you thought of asking me! I'm not going anywhere as long as I live. When I do, I shall go forever into death's kingdom. But now that you're grown up, could you quietly do something for me? And you mustn't breathe a word of this to anybody. Or you'll find me dead.'

'Just tell us what it is.'

'I'll tell you. Because the locality's the same as yours—Baghbazar. I'll send a letter for someone who lives there. You'd have to deliver the letter. Will you manage that?'

Sadhan had said enthusiastically, 'Of course! What's the number of the house?'

'I have it written down. I'll give it to you. But listen, nobody must know.'

'Why?'

'I'll tell you later.'

THIRTY-EIGHT

It was almost evening when the 'missing' Satya reached home. She got out of a hired horse-coach accompanied by a matronly widow.

'Just wait a while, will you? Let me pay the driver first.' With that Satya had stepped inside.

Suhash had been anxiously peeping out from one window and then another; Nabakumar was still at Nitai's. Suhash nearly shrieked when she saw Satya. 'Pishi-ma!' she had cried, her tone full of reproach.

Satya replied briskly, 'Yes, I shall explain everything. But first, go wash your hands with some Ganga water and give me four annas from the change-box—I don't want to touch it without changing these clothes.'

Untying her bunch of keys from the end of her sari, Satya had dropped them in front of Suhash. Suhash was a person of few words, she had shrieked out of anxiety. Now, she obeyed without another word. But unbeknown to Satya she was looking at her in a new light—Satya seemed a mystery woman to her!

As soon as she had paid the fare, Satya said to the woman, 'Come and sit. Wash your hands and have some sweets. You can't leave otherwise.'

The woman replied happily, 'No need for all that. I now know where you live. That's enough! Your words are so sweet that they calm the soul.'

'But I can't let you go without feeding you. Especially, after all that you did for me.' So saying Satya removed her silk shawl and had a quick wash in the bathroom. After that she returned, clothes still wet, with coconut sweets and water for the woman.

After the woman left, Satya changed into dry clothes and came inside. She asked Suhash, 'Well then, has a police circular been issued for me by now?'

Suhash looked away, 'It isn't like that at all. Uncle left the house in great anxiety, that's all.'

'Goodness! All my misdeeds shall be revealed!' Satya replied. 'I'd kept the school a secret until now.'

And Suhash aired the doubts she had nursed within. She raised her face and abruptly asked, 'Is it good to keep such secrets? Especially from your husband, when you yourself claim that a woman should worship her husband.'

Satya nearly joked, 'Are you already worshipping the husband you don't have?' but checked herself. Nobody could tell for sure if Suhash would ever have a husband. Her foolish, helpless mother had ruined her chances by proclaiming that she was a widow. And such a beautiful girl too! Polite, gentle, she worked hard at school— any man would be proud to be her husband. May be the wretched girl was doomed to unhappiness. But Satya had made up her mind to put up a fight till the end.

That was the reason why she had been so eager to get acquainted with the Brahmos. Brahmos were believed to be broad-minded. They did not regard marrying a child-widow as disgraceful.

Satya had contemplated telling Suhash the truth, and getting her admitted to school as an unmarried girl. But finally, after much thought, she had desisted. Firstly, before all else, one stood in danger of losing caste if a girl was not married at the right time. But in such a case, Satya could have fairly argued, 'How can society have the power to seize her caste if it failed to find her a husband?' And she would have argued like that, had there not been another hurdle.

If the brutal truth came out, in what light would Suhash view her dead mother? Would she ever forgive her when she found out that it was her own mother who had branded her a wretched widow and deprived her from eating or dressing because it suited her? Wouldn't that reduce her mother to a woman who was petty and mean? Selfish and cruel? It would be like rubbing salt on her wounds.

Conversely, if Suhash really adored her mother, and nothing could affect her steady devotion, she would just not believe Satya. She would conclude that Satya was looking for an excuse to marry her off.

That was how Satya had figured it out. And she had decided to let the matter wait till Suhash was older and could differentiate truth from untruth. She would deal with it then.

So, Satya checked herself, and said appealingly, 'I'm not alone—the whole wide world says that the husband is like a god, he is to be worshipped. But it isn't right to displease a god, is it? If your uncle heard that I've started tutoring students in a school, he'll become the personification of wrath, won't he? Why annoy him needlessly? It would be such a problem if he refused to understand and asked me to stop!'

After a moment's silence, Suhash said softly, 'Perhaps you shouldn't do anything that uncle wouldn't approve of.'

Satya was pleased to note that Suhash had become very prudent, but she could not help smiling to herself as she said in her mind, 'In that case, where would you have been, my dear? Where would you have found this wisdom? The battles I fought for your sake! And not just for keeping you here, but for sending you to school too!' For Nabakumar had tried to dissuade her by saying that if the girl went to a Sahib's school her touch would become polluting. Satya had made it work despite the odds.

Such thoughts churned up in her mind because of Suhash's remark. She almost spoke out aloud, but stopped herself. Instead she said with a smile, 'You seem to have learnt a lot! You're right, I shouldn't have done it. But look, it doesn't always work that way. There are so many husbands who detest prayers, but does that mean that the wife shouldn't pray? At the same time, would it do any good to chant them aloud in his ears? Actually, what's important is to see if the work one wants to do is good or bad. One has to give a lot of thought and then organize and get it done with, without raising anyone's hackles. That way you can work without offending those who disapprove.'

Had Satya started regarding Suhash as an adult, then? Was that the reason she felt obliged to explain at length? Or was Suhash merely a pretext for clarifying things to herself? Or, were all these excuses actually being offered to those subtle pricks of conscience she experienced for deceiving her husband?

Suhash, of course, thought of herself as an adult and a full-grown woman and had felt bold enough to respond to that explanation. Apart from which she always felt free to express herself with Satya. So she said softly, 'In such a case, I think, it would be best to explain that praying is a good thing.'

Satya laughed, 'I used to think just like you when I was young, Suhash. I used to fight, argue and try to convince everyone. But as I grew older I realized that constant fighting wears you out. If I spend most of my energy in arguments, then there'd be no energy left to work with. So I try to work without causing too much friction. But, as I said, this works only in certain cases. As I've so often argued, "Aren't women human?" But it's so futile! You know, it's so agonizing to be a woman in our country! You'll be prevented from doing an honest piece of work at every step! Master-mashai says the virtue in imparting knowledge is greater than feeding the needy. Only through knowledge do we know the difference between humans and animals. Or else, all living creatures eat, sleep and breed, be they insects or humans! But humans who have a bit of knowledge can pass it on to another. And sharing increases it. But how many people want to understand that? They don't! Earlier, I used to think I'll explain to everybody what I think is right. I'll straighten them out. But now I've learnt that it's as hard as trying to measure an elephant with your hands or attempting to count the stars! I'd rather do what I understand to be right with my heart and soul. And some day, people will learn to distinguish right from wrong. Those who dislike what's right, and have always opposed it, will come around finally.'

Satya had spoken without a break, she now paused for breath. Suhash took the opportunity to fetch her a sweet drink. Satya had probably been thirsting for a cool drink. After all, she had been out for a long time. She gulped down the drink without a word and smiled gently, 'Now that you've learnt to guess when someone's thirsty, there's little I've left to teach you! To possess this wisdom is enough for this world.'

Suhash had lowered her face embarrassed. Satya looked at her. The girl lit up the place! And she was as winsome as she was wise! But then, she did not have these qualities to begin with. Suhash had been moody. Satya had to really suffer because of her. Satya would control herself only because the girl was motherless, and because her mother's death had been so tragic and sudden.

Gradually, Suhash had softened. She had mellowed and become refined. Little by little, all the habits she had picked up from the Datta household, which used to irritate Satya, disappeared altogether. And Suhash became an exemplary girl!

But her nature was reserved, reticent. She rarely expressed her inner feelings. It was hard to judge her joys and sorrows, her likes and dislikes, or her gratitude, admiration and affection. That was especially why this assertion of feelings had pleased Satya. She studied Suhash's bashful face and said, 'But why didn't you ask me why I'm so late?'

Suhash replied with a slight smile, 'Because you'll tell me if you think it fit.'

'If I think it fit! Listen to that!' Satya had said. 'Do you think you aunt would do things that couldn't be talked about?'

'That's not what I meant. I meant—'

But before Suhash could complete her sentence, the two avatars had pushed open the courtyard door and entered. And they both addressed the same person in unison.

'Bou-than!'

'Boro-bou!'

Satya pulled her sari over her face and stood up. Nabakumar came inside and sat down, and shouted, 'What's the matter with you? Where is it you go every afternoon? I don't like your ways!'

Satya took one look at Nabakumar's frustrated face and suppressed a smile, 'Really? You've stopped liking my ways, have you?'

A smile! Satya was smiling! It could mean one of two things: either that she was not guilty or that she was extremely artful. But Nitai could hardly remember that as he gaped at that sari-framed face brightened by a smile, and *that* was not seemly either!

Nabakumar was not charmed by this. All the agony of a long drawn-out period of anxiety, fear and worry exploded in an angry flash. And Satya's smile was fuel to the fire. So he stood up and charged, 'Of course, I don't! I think you've ruined your reputation!'

Who knows if Satya would have flared up if Nabakumar were alone? But Nitai was present too. One could not lose face by fuming in front of him! Therefore, Satya replied in the same vein,

THE FIRST PROMISE | 393

'If that's the way you feel, you must have a reason. After all, you're a wise and observant man. Tell me then, what'll you subject your disobedient wife to? A test by fire? Or will you slaughter her and throw her in the river?'

What intolerable cheek! Nabakumar was speechless! At last, Nitai spoke.

'Well, you might be enjoying these riddles you're putting to us, but we need an answer as well. What a plight this wretch has been in since evening! And as for me—I hadn't eaten all day and on top of that, I've been slighted by the wife ...'

'Listen to that! You're the one putting riddles now! How am I responsible if you've not eaten all day? Or if your wife slights you! Really, I can't figure it out at all! But you're looking weak too.'

Poor Nitai! He could not bear to miss a meal and he had been fasting all day, and to top it all, this sort of talk, and tenderness! Tears nearly spurted out! And to cover up, he lowered the face he had lost in front of his wife.

'Well, I must say, you two are behaving like boys!' Satya replaced her sarcasm with kindness, 'It's your foolish attitude that made me play hide and seek. Thakur-po, I can guess that you've had a fight with your wife and not eaten much. Suhash, why don't you bring your uncle something to eat.'

'No, I don't need anything,' Nitai protested.

Satya smiled slightly, 'As if I believe you!'

Suhash had brought out food for the two men—whatever was available at home—coconut fudge-balls, sweet fritters and a bowl of puffed rice.

Nabakumar protested glumly, 'I don't want anything.'

Satya responded gravely, 'Eat it for my sake, not for your own! Why don't you start while I justify my ways.'

And so the two felt obliged to eat. Satya started by saying, 'Suhash and the boys know where I go everyday, you're the only one who doesn't. I'll tell you, but you must promise that you'll not stop me.'

'Oh! Asking me to sign on a blank piece of paper!' Nabakumar responded, 'I must first know if its good or bad.'

Satya was silent for a minute and then said calmly and steadily,

'Look at me. I am asking you both—just look straight at me and tell me if you really think that I'm capable of doing something bad? Tell me, and I'll answer you.' Needless to say, neither raised his eyes, instead they both lowered their gaze.

Satya waited awhile and said, 'All right. Now listen to me. I go to teach in a school every afternoon.'

Nabakumar raised his face. He was startled, and scared. And so was Nitai. He exclaimed, 'To teach!'

'Yes, to teach. There is a women's gathering at Sarba-mangalatala temple every afternoon—housewives, middle-aged women—a couple of them are just married. One among them used to arrange flowers for the goddess, one would recite from the Puranas, the *Mahabharata* and the *Ramayana*—others would listen. And they'd gossip too. Seeing this Master-mashai decided ...'

Master-mashai! Nabakumar made a face. Satya pretended not to notice and carried on, '... that it would be a good idea to open a school for these women. And he started one calling it "Sarbamangala Vidyapith". He asked me to teach saying I could pay my guru dakshina this way. I thought it was a good idea and so I agreed.'

'Agreed!' Nabakumar was distraught, 'You didn't think it necessary to ask me?'

'I must admit that it was wrong—I'd repeat it a hundred times. But suppose you'd said "no" and sworn an oath or something? I couldn't have done it then, could I? So I said a prayer to the goddess, and started. Master-mashai pays for the books, slates and paper.'

'Are you so learned that you can teach now?'

Satya had smiled at his sarcasm, 'Teaching is in my blood—I've taught all my life! I could start out because that's how I was made. And my education? That will progress as I read. I do what I can.'

Nitai asked softly, 'So, are the women responding?'

'Very well! Except for one or two, they're learning fast. If you saw them you'd realize how eager they are to read the Puranas and the epics. It's so satisfying to see that.'

But Nabakumar could not take it lightly. He said, 'Do the

women know that Master-mashai has thrown his faith away and become a Brahmo?'

'Of course, they do. But everyone isn't conservative like you. Besides, it's not as though they're eating food cooked by him. And why put it that way? Brahmos are Hindus. Don't you listen to anything? Today Paramahamsa himself came to visit the great Brahmo leader, Keshub Sen ...'

'What? Who are you talking about? And where did you go?' Nabakumar stood up in a huff.

'Paramahamsa—don't tell me you haven't even heard of him?'

'Of course, I've heard of him,' Nabakumar uttered sullenly. 'I had even gone to Dakshineswar with my colleagues. But he ...'

'Yes, he himself had come to Keshub Sen's house. That's why I was late today. And now I've been caught!'

Nabakumar stared in amazement for a while, 'I have nothing to tell you, you're really beyond my reach. But how did you go to Keshub Sen's house?'

'How else? As if I went alone! So many women went. We went in a group—hired a horse-coach and shared the cost—the greater the number, the more the strength! What wonderful singing, so soothing!'

'Weren't you scared?'

'Why should I be?' Satya asked in surprise, 'When women go on a pilgrimage, or for a dip in the holy Ganga, or for a mela near some temple, or to see sadhus—is there ever a question of being scared? You should go to such places some time, it'll open your eyes.'

'As if we can!' Nabakumar made a face, 'We're small creatures, where will we find the courage?'

Satya stood up, 'If you call yourself "small" twenty-four hours a day, the mind just shrivels up. Why should I think of myself as small? You accept that god resides in every human being, don't you? That itself is a source of strength. In that case, everybody is great.'

Nitai sighed softly. He had instructed his wife to come and see Satya. But would his wife ever have the capacity to think this way? Nabakumar was right, Satya had really gone beyond their reach.

Nabakumar tried to pull her down a peg, 'Anyway, I hope you've changed your clothes after coming back from that Brahmo house. And have you purified yourself with holy water from the Ganga?'

Satya answered with a smile, 'I did that not because of the house but because of the horse-coach. In any case, I always change my clothes when I get back. Was this the only thing that struck you after all this while? But never mind! When will the boys come back? It feels so empty without them.'

Nabakumar answered glumly, 'As if you ever feel the emptiness! Your mind is so full of theories, where's the space for your husband and children? I can see that you're becoming as hard-hearted as your father.'

Satya replied calmly, 'My father! I'd be proud if I was worth his little toe. But why are you saying all this now? You yourself had said that my father wasn't a man but a god.'

'Oh, I'd say that again. But a god is best worshipped from a distance; living with a god doesn't come to any good.'

Satya burst out laughing, 'Mark your friend's progress, Thakur-po! Look how he's learnt to use his words!'

Nitai found his bearings at last and responded, 'The shastras would be proved wrong, otherwise. Virtue fosters virtue ...'

But before he finished, Suhash suddenly rushed in and announced, 'I think somebody's coming.'

The windows in the adjacent room faced the street, perhaps that was where Suhash had been standing. They were startled and asked, 'Who is that?'

'I don't know him. He looks old, but is very tall and straight and fair ...'

Tall! Fair and straight! Satya's heart gave a leap. And froze the very next minute when a deep, awe-inspiring heavy voice resonated with the question, 'Is there anybody home?'

'Baba!'

Satya swept out at lightning speed. Nitai had come out even before her, followed by Nabakumar. By then, that heavy voice had asked another question, 'Is this the house of Nabakumar Bandopadhyay?'

'Baba! Baba! It's really you!' Satya exclaimed even before she had touched his feet, 'I can't believe this is real ...'

'Then think of it as a dream.' So saying Ramkali stepped into the courtyard with a smile.

Nitai and Nabakumar both touched his feet. In their minds they believed that he would live long, since they had just been talking about him and he had arrived out of the blue.

It took a while for the elation to subside and a while longer for the exchange of news. Only then had Ramkali revealed the reason for his visit. He had decided to retire to Kashi. Therefore, he had come to see Satya.

On one side, there was unanticipated joy, and on the other, a hidden anxiety—would her father accept water here? It was tap water, after all! If he refused, then she would have to arrange for water from the Ganga. But how could one nullify the 'polluting' effect of a rented place? Satya knew the ceremony with which a guru was received into a household, but she was not sure whether her father would accept similar formality. And along with these worries, the unstated pain of separation welled up inside her. The fact that Satya never saw her father everyday was fine with her, in her mind she knew he was at the village—in a place she could visualize, and in his own familiar surroundings.

But to live in Kashi! That was like eternal separation. A kind of death! To decide to live in Kashi was to retire from the life of a householder. These thoughts had wrought Satya's voice with a particular intensity. Ramkali could guess that, and he had been able to look upon it with some indulgence.

He replied to his daughter with a smile, 'Even if you didn't come, I came to see you. It's the same thing!'

Nitai had left after touching Ramkali's feet. And Nabakumar had moved away in order to make it easier for Satya to speak. Satya had responded ruefully, 'It isn't the same thing, Baba! If I went to my father's house, I'd be the child I used to be. I'd say whatever I pleased. But now you've come as a guest, and I'm a housewife here. My feet are shackled at every step. What can I say!'

Although Nabakumar was sitting at a distance, he was well

within earshot. And all of a sudden, he pronounced loudly, to no one in particular, 'My god! Her feet are shackled at every step! Who knows what would've happened if they were really unfettered.'

Ramkali gave a start, 'What was that?'

Nabakumar replied gravely, 'Nothing. But your daughter seems to regret the shackles at every step. It's best to ask her which girl in Nityanandapur, or which housewife of Baruipur is as free as she is.'

Ramkali sensed that it was a form of complaint. So he smiled, 'If that's the case, it's a good thing. I knew my daughter wasn't born to be ordinary. I knew that from the time she was an infant.'

Satya gave up all pretence of the modesty that was called for in the presence of her husband, and drawing her sari a little more tightly around her face, she remarked, 'Really, Baba! Here you are totally scorched in the sun—is it fair to start complaining now? You'll be here for a few days, let a few days pass, then ...'

'Goodness! A few days! I've come just for a day. I shall leave tomorrow.'

'Just a day! Baba, how could you come for just a day!' With that Satya burst into tears, 'I have so much to tell you ...'

That was true, Satya did have an awful lot to tell her father. Many a time she had thought of writing him a letter—a letter with questions about what was right and what was wrong. But she had soon discovered that the content would probably turn out to be too vast. How could anyone write so much in a letter? Besides, one could clarify the issues in a conversation, a letter was so one-sided, like submitting a catalogue. What if her father had responded by asking why she needed to ask him so much?

And yet, there were questions regarding the nature of the Brahmo faith, and whether it was justified to ostracize an elder who had always been helpful. If the offence of being a housewife should deprive a woman from undertaking different work in the world, or whether it was a rule that a woman should blindly follow her husband, even if he lacked discernment. But most important, was her question about Shankari's daughter. When she had written to him about Shankari, her father had responded, 'No matter how heinous the crime anyone is guilty of, if the person repents, it is one's duty to forgive. Besides, I trust your judgement.'

Satya had particularly wanted to ask her father what decision she should take about Suhash. But her father had announced that he would stay for just a day! That meant he would not eat a cooked meal in Satya's rented place. He would perhaps eat fruits and drink water brought from the Ganga. Satya would not earn the merit of serving her father. With all these emotions churning inside her, her tears had flowed freely.

Ramkali gently touched her head, 'One day isn't too brief. Tell me what you want to say.'

'Tell you! But I only feel like sobbing, Baba!'

The sobbing took a long time to subside. Later, they started talking. And Satya spoke to her ever-constant pole star of the things she had on her mind.

Ramkali rebuked Nabakumar mildly, 'Goodness! Master-mashai has always helped you, how can you ostracize him? His faith is his business. Look at me—will you take into account if I am a Shakta or a Vaishnav? Or will you regard me simply as a father? A guru, or a teacher, is just like a father. Besides he isn't forcing you to accept his faith. How does it harm you?'

Ramkali fell silent for a while when he heard that Satya was teaching in a school. Finally, he said with a sigh, 'Satya, do you remember your mother?'

'Don't I remember Ma! How can you ask that, Baba?' Satya's eyes brimmed over.

'That's what I was thinking. If she were around, she'd feel scared, wouldn't she? I'm sure she'd be scared! But she'd secretly admit to herself, "I always knew my daughter was extraordinary!" '

And Satya found the answer to her question. She began to comprehend the justification for her action. They discussed Suhash for a long time. Argued too. Until that point, Satya had not introduced Suhash to her father. Ramkali had argued that there was no need to get her married. It was fine that she was studying. It would be a good thing if she earned her own living. After all, this was beginning to happen in Calcutta—educated women were taking up tutoring at home or teaching in girl's schools and earning their living.

'But Baba,' Satya intervened, 'her mother was an unhappy soul and died unhappy. Shouldn't the daughter have a better life? Shouldn't she get married and settle down?'

'A child has to pay for the sins of her parents, Satya.'

'And suppose someone wants to marry her?'

Ramkali shook his head, 'Who'd want to do that? First of all, her birth itself was a mistake, and besides it's been very long since she came of age. And nobody knows her status—if she is unmarried or a widow.'

It was then that Satya expressed her secret wish. If the girl could be converted to the Brahmo faith, she could then get married to some benevolent young man involved in social welfare. It might be possible to find a Brahmo boy whose age was compatible with Suhash.

Ramkali was resistant to the idea. To his thinking, there was no need to undertake so much because of a girl. He suddenly became serious and asked, 'If you ask me, what is to be gained in propagating a defective family?'

'But she would gain a family, Baba. How can she be treated as insignificant just because she's a girl? She's a human being, after all!'

'A human being needn't fulfil herself through enjoyment alone; sacrifice can bring its own rewards. She knows that she's a widow, let her live the way a child-widow does.'

'And how do they live, Baba?' Satya gave a sigh of despair, 'They're eternally unhappy. There aren't too many people like Pishi-thakurma. Even she transformed her unhappiness into an obsession with "pollution" and made others miserable.'

Ramkali fell silent abruptly. As though in his mind's eye, he suddenly saw Mokshada. He could see the fair and bright woman of the past and behind her—like a ghost, like a shadow, like the eclipsed sun—the ailing Mokshada as she now looked. Mokshada, who had gone completely senile and would do anything she liked. She craved to eat all the time and stole food, she even stole fried fish by the fistful when nobody was looking. Sharada had to drag her to the pond for a dip, even as she cursed away ...

But Satya knew nothing about this. She knew only about her obsession with 'pollution'.

After a while, Ramkali said, 'Well, see if you can find such a man.'

'If you didn't bless me, I'd feel daunted by the enormity of it. If you welcome and approve with an open mind ...'

Ramkali laughed slightly, 'Does the mind have doors or windows which you can force open, Satya? But I give you my blessings— may god give you strength.'

It was just as Satya had feared. Ramkali dined on some fruit and announced that he would have to fast because the next day was the full moon.

'Was this why you came, Baba?' Satya was close to tears. 'I am such a worthless daughter that I didn't even have the opportunity to cook you a meal!'

Ramkali sighed deeply, 'Well, we can hardly expect to complete the conversation of a whole lifetime in one brief instant, can we? After all, life ends in the darkness of the cave ...'

And then, he asked, 'We talked at length about her, but I haven't seen the girl yet.'

'I don't know, Baba. I think she's feeling self-conscious, she's been crying.'

Crying! Ramkali was surprised. But he had made no further comment.

The next day, soon after Ramkali finished his morning ablutions, Suhash, her head bowed, came in and touched his feet. From the east window, the morning light had suffused her face with a mild, youthful loveliness. There was a glow of confidence in the firm lines of her gentle face. And a steadfast assurance also seemed evident in the tall, slim structure of her body.

Perhaps Ramkali had not quite expected this. He was troubled. In a flash, he remembered an incident from the past. He recalled the figure of a widow sitting at the ghat. Had Ramkali seen that figure properly? Ramkali reached out and touched her head and blessed her. And then remarked, gravely, calmly, 'She's like Uma, the goddess when she was doing penance!'

Satya smiled indulgently at Suhash. This praise was for her, actually. After all, Suhash was the goddess she had shaped and moulded with her own hands. She was not a glass doll, and no infant either. Satya had taken her in as a fifteen-year-old, badly brought up with numerous offensive habits and flaws. In a few years she had managed to refashion the girl completely. Of course, a stupendous remoulding had been naturally happening already. Her mother's sudden death and her becoming aware of her mother's history had brought about that change.

Only then had Suhash started living her new life. There had been a sea of difference between the filthy, impure and decadent environment of the Datta household and Satya's exemplary firmness. Apart from which there had been school—that had seemed like heaven! Suhash had changed mentally and physically too. The garrulous girl had become circumspect. And the plump girl had shot up and became tall and slender as a bamboo shoot, almost thin. It was her slimness that had reminded Ramkali of Uma—the goddess when she was doing penance.

Satya said with a smile, 'She's stood first twice in a row.'

'Really!' Ramkali responded.

Suhash was probably feeling very embarrassed. She smiled diffidently and said, 'The news of the grandsons coming first in class seems to be shelved ...'

But that was not the case. Ramkali had heard about that too. Nabakumar had told him. Ramkali had expressed his regret at not meeting them, 'It's true, I've not seen them in a long while. I'm happy to hear about their success.'

But that had happened the previous night. Suhash knew it too. But she mentioned it in order to camouflage her own embarrassment.

Ramkali smiled mildly, 'It's a pleasure to hear about a grandson doing well, but it isn't anything new. It's novel to hear of a granddaughter coming first! May you be successful and happy.'

With that he turned to Satya, 'I bless her with an open mind.'

Once more, Satya's eyes filled with tears. Her father's way of speaking had changed. An air of intimacy had replaced the earlier reserve, where one had to measure one's words when speaking to him. Had this sudden advent of softness towards the world happened to Ramkali because he had decided to turn his back to the world? Or had the actions of his whimsical daughter perturbed him?

Satya's voice grew heavier as the moment of departure drew near. There had been no way of requesting him to stay on. There was no way of requesting him to accept cooked food in this house. She would have to let him go.

Small words and small sighs.

'Will you give up treating patients, Baba?'

'Give it up? Why should I, Satya? That is the only knowledge that helps others, but I'll give up doing it professionally.' Meaning he would no longer accept 'fees' for his services.

'I hope you won't have a hard time there.'

'You mad girl! How can I have a hard time in Kashi, where Lord Shiva himself resides!'

'Will you send word to your disobedient daughter in case you fall ill?'

'I can't promise that now!'

'I knew you'd say that!'

Nabakumar touched his feet and asked, 'When will you be starting out for Kashi?'

'The boat leaves on the coming ashtami.'

'Boat!' Nabakumar risked exclaiming. 'But there are trains now.'

'There are. But there are boats too!' Ramkali laughed in reply. 'Boats haven't become redundant, you know.'

'But a train would take you there in a day.' Satya pleaded.

Ramkali smiled, 'Where's the hurry? It isn't as though I'm going to see a dying patient! The pilgrim's journey is part of his pilgrimage. What's the point in speeding by with one's eyes shut? In a boat, I can ride on the lap of the Ganga and get there.'

'Baba, what about your address?'

'Address? It isn't fixed yet.'

'Will you write as soon as you get there?'

'Look at that! This girl wants to trap me into committing myself to the truth!'

'And why not? After all, my name is derived from truth!'

Just as he was leaving, Ramkali abruptly took out two folded pieces of paper from his pocket and said, 'Here, keep these two things.'

'What's this?' Satya didn't reach out to take them, but looked startled.

Ramkali said, 'One is your horoscope. It was with me all this while ...'

'What will I do with it, Baba?'

'Keep it. It's useful. And this ...' Ramkali paused. 'The land and property at the village will remain with the boys of the family. I had some freehold land at Tribeni, that's for you ....'

'No, Baba!' Satya sobbed, 'I don't want it. I am a girl child, I can claim only your love!'

'Then accept this as a token of love.'

'Baba! Why should I know your love through a token? I don't need it!'

Satya did not put out her hand, nor uncover her eyes that were covered with the end of her sari. Satya had never cried like this in her whole life. Not even when her mother had died.

Ramkali turned his face and collected himself, then he passed the paper to Nabakumar, 'Keep it.'

Nabakumar was upset by Satya's extreme reaction. To his thinking, in the absence of a son, a daughter should inherit everything. That was how Empress Victoria had got her kingdom. And what was being offered was just a pittance, just a gift of alms—and the daughter refused to accept it! Therefore, Nabakumar was quick to reach out for it.

Ramkali climbed onto his palki. He would go by palki now. He would see some specific temples in Calcutta and then get on his boat. Ramkali never particularly cared for the train. He always said, 'If there's no hurry, where's the need?'

Satya stood at the door and watched the palki till it disappeared into the distance. Then she went inside and sat down. After a long time, she wiped her eyes and sighed, 'If I could, I would definitely have gone with Baba.'

Nabakumar responded, 'Why didn't you? Suhash would have

managed and you could have gone. You could have stayed there till he left for Kashi. Why didn't you tell me?'

And blending regret and coyness Satya sighed again, 'It isn't a question of running the house. It's a different matter. I don't think I am well. Who knows what's in store for me at this age!'

Nabakumar stared for a moment at Satya's bashful, hurt and helpless face. It had taken him a while to grasp her meaning. Then suddenly, he had been thrilled to the core with a sudden rush of delight. Oh god!

At last, Satya's feet would be fettered. That was the first thing that struck Nabakumar.

And that made him brim over with joy. He clutched her hand at once, 'Really? Is it true?'

Slowly, Satya took her hand away, 'No need to jump about for joy!'

THIRTY NINE

It was mid-afternoon. The boat was midstream. Except for the sound of the oar on the water, it was silent. And from time to time, the boatman's unintelligible shout would startle the placid landscape. The water rippled in circles where the oar struck, and at a distance, a breeze trembled gently on the smooth, silken surface of the water. On that almost white, billowing veil, shone a cluster of glistening sun spots like bits of diamond.

Ramkali sat in silence contemplating that cluster. It was mid-afternoon, the Ganga was calm, the boat was sailing smoothly, there was no disturbance. But what about his mind? The mind that was buried inside the fortress of the body? There was no disturbance there either. Ramkali had unfettered his buried mind. He had released it to roam freely as it pleased. The mind he had suddenly set free whirled through the sixty-eight long years that Ramkali had travelled. Never before had Ramkali indulged in reminiscences. But he did so today. Perhaps, unconsciously.

Ramkali had retired from the world, he had turned his back on it. But so many arrangements, enumerations and instructions, and so much organization had preceded this moment.

He had had to arrange for the upkeep of the few needy students at the village school he had established, because he had felt responsible for them. He had had to find a doctor for the charitable dispensary he had started and also had to ensure the continued functioning of the huts that served water during the summer months by donating an appropriate measure of tax-free land for the purpose. He had had to make land arrangements for the poor pundits who had been getting an allowance. Apart from those, Ramkali had always provided support to fathers burdened with the cost of a daughter's wedding, and helpless, unprotected widows, sick and disabled men and orphans. People from faraway places used to approach him too. He had set aside the revenue from a largish taluka so that such people were not entirely deprived or driven away, Rashu had been given appropriate instructions. Of course, if Rashu did not heed them and if he used up the revenue for his own needs, there was nothing one could do about it. It had been, after all, an unusual arrangement.

But he had had to hand over charge to Rashu. Nobody else had seemed fit enough. There had been no trace of Neru. He had written a couple of letters without revealing his address. So they had come to know that he had not died; that he was alive. Rashu's other brothers had turned out to be useless. Sejo-kaka's sons were masters at scheming. And Rashu's elder boy had become a dandified 'babu'. Sharada was partly responsible for that. She had turned her son into a babu just to spite her husband. At every step she would say, 'He can't do that.'

What a woman! Completely muddled. Ramkali wondered, with a sigh, if that was a result of the creator investing her with contrary qualities, or because her life had taken such a retrograde course.

Ramkali had been unable to understand her. At times, he had been dazzled by her dedication to her responsibilities, her immense skills and her infinite tolerance; at other times, her amazing indifference and unwarranted apathy would leave him speechless.

Sharada never feared to take on the entire responsibility of the Durga puja herself, and Ramkali would happily leave it to her. But this year, suddenly, Sharada had calmly declared that he should hand over the responsibility to someone else. She had offered no explanation. There are other people in the house, that's all!

Ramkali had summoned some brahmin women of the village and requested them to help with the puja because his daughter-in-law was unwell. And they had come and made the arrangements for the puja. But too many cooks had spoilt the broth. When the priest had sat down and could not find the puja item he needed, he had been livid.

Yet Ramkali could never remain angry with Sharada. Nor could he ignore her. He had realized that Sharada had substance to her character which inimical fate had shattered to pieces.

Inimical fate! The words were a goad to him. Ramkali had often thought that it had been nothing but fate, that humans were mere agents of the greater will, but he was finding it difficult to hold on to this belief.

But never mind that. Ramkali had made arrangements for everyone as best as he could, now it would depend on each one's luck. Even so, so many faces had looked at Ramkali in despair. As if to say, 'Are you abandoning us? Really! Why, you never ever told us that you would leave! We had all felt so very secure!'

Among those faces, Sharada's had been the most clearly etched; her eyes, the sharpest. Her gaze had held no dejection, but criticism.

Had it been the same when Ramkali had left many years ago? Had he looked back? No! How light-hearted and free that departure had been!

The reason for that renunciation had been rather crude, and it had its origins in his father's behaviour. Anger, sorrow, a sense of hurt and resentment had combined into a strong emotion and driven out that young lad whom Ramkali could now visualize.

The boy had sat inside a boat all day; nobody had noticed, and at one point the boat had set sail. The boy had hidden himself inside. He had been discovered after a long time. By then the boat had moved quite a distance.

Now Ramkali could almost see the boatmen questioning that boy. The boy had answered calmly—that he had nobody in the world, he was a poor brahmin boy, he could not pay for his passage, so if they could kindly take him wherever they were headed.

Maybe because they had sympathized with his circumstances, or perhaps because they had been struck by his loveliness, they had warmed to him and had taken him till Murshidabad. That was where he had found the shelter of Gobinda Gupta's home. As if blessed by a god.

That very young boy had thought how vast the world was! How kind god was! Or, had he thought that Gobinda Gupta was god himself? Had he appeared incognito to help Ramkali as the gods did in the Puranas? The boy had been sitting at the ghat. The doctor had come for a dip in the river.

He had stopped in his tracks and asked, 'I don't seem to know you? Whose son are you?'

Now Ramkali felt like laughing at the ease with which he had retorted, 'What business is it of yours?'

'Of course it is,' Gobinda Gupta had said with a smile. 'It won't do if I don't enquire about your family, or why you're roaming around on your own, or what kind of person you are.'

'Why?''

'How can I trust a person from another village?'

Later, Ramkali had learnt that that it had been a trick. A trick to irritate the person into revealing his true identity. But that day, the boy had been incapable of understanding that. So he had growled, 'Who is begging you to trust me? It pleases me to sit here. Is the ghat your property?'

No doubt, the dignified old man had been quite amused by the boy's words. He had deliberately continued the conversation just to entertain himself.

After that, a truce had ensued. Somehow the boy had found shelter at his home. And not just shelter, the boy had come to possess all the love that flowed from the hearts of that childless couple. Slowly his restless, loquacious nature had been tamed and he had become an intelligent student. He had been bequeathed not just with their affections, but their worldly possessions as well.

Amazing! Inspite of that, the doctor's wife had never cooked for him. She had arranged for him to have his meals at another brahmin house.

Suddenly all the scenes seemed to sparkle before Ramkali's eyes.

Ramkali had needled them, he had acted obstinate, he had argued, 'I have become one of your caste now.'

But the doctor's wife had replied with a smile on her lips and tears in her eyes, 'You mad boy! Can that ever happen?'

'You people wear the sacred thread too,' Ramkali had said.

Gobinda Gupta had laughed, 'That's true. But you know something? Everything has a rank. A cobra is never the same as a water-snake, so your sacred thread and mine are not the same. I wish I could adopt you, but I can't. Who knows what boundaries I'd overstep.'

A strange mixture of affection and respect.

At first, Ramkali had said, 'I don't have anybody, anywhere.' But slowly, everything had come to light. Gobinda Gupta used to say, 'Look, it is a sin for me not to get in touch with your parents. Don't stop me, let me send them word.'

Ramkali would respond, 'Why? Have I become an eyesore or what? All right, go and absolve yourself of all your sins! And you'll find that the bird has flown!'

The doctor's wife would shudder in horror, 'Why are you going on and on about your sins? They're his parents, let him decide. If a child doesn't cry for his mother, there must be a lack in the mother.'

'Can that ever be possible, Boro-bou?' the doctor would ask with a smile.

Ramkali would get further provoked and say, 'Yes, of course! My mother can't stand the sight of me. Or else why would she tattle to my aunt when my aunt scolds me?'

'May be she fears your aunt.'

'As if she does! Is fear greater than love?'

Later, Ramkali had thought at length about it. Really, he had never missed his mother. But when the doctor's wife fell ill, and when she died, he had secretly cried and given himself a headache. Why had that happened? Had Ramkali been so heartless? Or had his parents lacked in affection? Even if he could pass an easy judgement on his father, it would be difficult to say the same of his mother. Perhaps his conscience would not allow him.

But now as he stood on the brink, and saw his past life as clearly and wholly as the flowing river before him, Ramkali sighed and reflected on the fact that perhaps that was the only time he had received affection. From that old couple. All his life, Ramkali had received respect, awe, admiration, adoration—but never affection. Everyone had kept him at arm's length, they had worshipped him from a distance. It had been Ramkali's own fault. He had drawn a boundary around himself. Not deliberately perhaps, but on account of his personality.

Could he have ever picture himself sitting in a row with other brahmins at a common village meal? Or accepting a 'donation' made to a brahmin? Or chatting frivolously in somebody's temple courtyard? Or playing cards? He could never do that, not because it would be ridiculous to think that way, but because it would be wholly unimaginable. Yet so many kulins would spend their days in such pursuits. What then, were the qualities that made a kulin distinctive?

Now, when his moment to retire from the world had arrived, Ramkali was suddenly struck by a thought: all his life he had played the role of a victor, but had he really been victorious? If so, why did he feel that he had been carrying the burden of defeat all his life? What kind of defeat was that? Where did it originate? As Ramkali ruminated, he recalled something totally out of context. But perhaps not entirely.

Satya had said ruefully, 'I shall always regret that I couldn't cook for you even for a day.'

What harm would it have done if Ramkali had not left her with that regret? Would it have been a great loss if he had ignored the laws of custom?

Ramkali had placed a high value on certain things all his life. Could his be the last and final word on value? In that case, why would the image of Bhubaneswari smiling triumphantly appear before him time and again? Why would she declare to him, 'You've had a lot from life, and that exultation made you turn a blind eye to the world, but had you ever taken into account that your real home was empty? Had you ever thought of that? You'd always done your duty, but did you manage to love anybody?'

It appeared as though Ramkali had dived deep into his mind.

Love? For whom had he reserved that? No other face, except Satya's, floated up before him. All the rest appeared like creatures he had pitied. It was Satya who occupied a large amount of space in his heart. But had Ramkali ever expressed it to her? Hadn't he constantly buried it under sand because he believed that revealing it would be like admitting a weakness?

Suddenly Ramkali had cried out to the goddess—'Durga! Durga!'—as though he sought to anchor his straying mind. He called out, 'I say, when do we get to Munger?'

The boatman replied, 'We're nearly there.'

'Good. Let the boat weigh anchor at Kashtaharini ghat.'

FORTY

Though Sadhan and Saral kept their word, the matter did become public. It exposed Sadu's pettiness, and the duplicity of the boys.

The short, stout and sturdy gentleman with salt and pepper hair to whom they had delivered their aunt's letter after hunting out his house, turned up at their place the next Sunday. They had never dreamt of this possibility. Of course, that particular day, he had stopped the scared boys who were scampering away and had asked them their names, the name of their village and where they lived in Calcutta. They had interpreted that as mere curiosity. They had not suspected that in a couple of days the man himself would turn up calling out, 'Where are you, boys?'

It was a bolt from the blue! Their hearts stopped beating. The two brothers looked at each other apprehensively, and Saral had indicated with a gesture and a shrug, 'It isn't our fault, is it? We didn't ask him to come. Our aunt had asked us not to say ...'

And this too was communicated without words: 'We had lied that day. When Ma had asked why we were late, we'd said there was a football match at school.' But this exchange had taken just a few seconds because, in the meanwhile, the gentleman had crossed over into the courtyard and was repeating in a resounding voice, 'Are the boys not at home?'

Satyabati came out of the kitchen with her sari drawn over her head and asked clearly, 'Turu, see who's there. Ask him who he wants to meet.'

But Turu need not have asked, for he could hear clearly. And the gentleman walked up with a smile, 'I'm your brother-in-law. You must be my wife's brother's wife.'

Satyabati was flabbergasted. Nabakumar had just stepped out to the market, and here she was faced with a problem! Must be some wicked man, or someone who had made a mistake. So, she communicated through her son, 'Tell him he must have made a mistake.'

'Mistake!' The gentleman laughed, 'Mukunda Mukherji isn't so green that he'll enter someone's house without making enquiries first. I made thorough enquiries in the locality. Tell me, aren't you the wife of Nabakumar Banerji, the son of Nilambar Banerji from Baruipur? You can't deny that, can you?'

He laughed aloud at his own joke. His words, gestures and his speech were so crass that Satyabati began to smoulder in anger. This had to be someone wicked who had found out their name and address and would now start threatening her. Let him try. He had no idea what Satya was made of!

Satya responded irritably and sternly, 'Turu, tell him, it's not difficult to find out details from the neighbours. We don't know anyone by that name.'

But Mukunda Mukherji was not one to take umbrage easily. He kept smiling, 'It's true that you don't. There was no occasion to. Your sister-in-law seems happy to have disowned me. I just came to ask why her highness suddenly remembered what she had forgotten for so long. And why have you sealed your lips, boys? We chatted quite a bit that day when you brought the letter, and now you don't seem to recognize me! Didn't you tell your mother, then? That's probably why she thinks I'm a wicked person.'

Those were exactly Satyabati's thoughts. She looked at her boys, and saw that they obviously looked guilty. What could the matter be? Could this man be somebody from Baruipur? Somebody the boys had met at Baruipur and could no longer recognize? God alone knew! Satya already had a reputation of being a shrew at her in-laws, much else must have been added to that by now! From their pale faces it was obvious that something had happened. But Satya refused to yield. She said gently but firmly, 'Khoka, tell him that there's no man at home now. He should come back later and speak to him.'

Mukunda Mukherji looked grave, 'I have nothing to say. I only came to find out why your sister-in-law Saudamini Devi suddenly sent a letter to the husband she'd disowned.'

'Has she written a letter! To you? Are you ...'

Mukunda Mukherji failed to grasp what she meant, 'She's not written it herself, of course. Somebody must have written it for her. Your boys came and delivered it day before yesterday.'

'My boys? Day before?' Satyabati was upset and called out, 'Turu! Khoka!'

Both boys now stood with their heads lowered, their faces dark with guilt. Satya began to feel a little helpless and for the first time, felt distressed by Nabakumar's absence. Mukunda Mukherji soon discerned her distress. He had quickly guessed the matter— Saudamini must have said something to the boys about keeping the letter a secret. If he had known, he would have presented himself differently. The boys looked embarrassed, which was expected of course; after all, it was clear that they had a fire-breathing dragon for a mother! Goodness, this was like a police interrogation!

But Mukunda was one step ahead. He had come prepared, and had brought the letter with him. But there was one mistake he had made. He had assumed that Saudamini was visiting her brother in Calcutta and had sworn her nephews to secrecy. Or else, why should someone who had never kept in touch suddenly contact him? But now it was obvious that he had been mistaken. Saudamini was not here. But really, in that case, why...?

Setting aside the thought, Mukunda Mukherji took out the secret of the weak, creeper-like Saudamini and placed it on the floor of the verandah. And in a flash, Satya recognized the handwriting— it was that of her older boy. Which meant that Saudamini had got Turu to write it out for her.

It had not taken long for the facts to become clear as daylight. Only the inexplicable behaviour of her sons remained in darkness. How had they dared to do all this without telling Satyabati about it?

The contents of the letter became crystal clear as soon as Satya cast her eyes on it because she was familiar with the hand and every curl of alphabet. It wasn't a love letter; there was nothing in it that a nephew ought not write. Saudamini had written:

Most respected and worshipful,

I have not had news of you for a very long time. Nor have you ever enquired if this poor woman is alive or dead. But let that be. I wish to hear news about you. My brother, Nabakumar, now lives in Calcutta. If you would meet him, I would come to know how you are. These boys are Nabakumar's sons, Sadhankumar and Saralkumar.

Please forgive my audacity in writing to you. What else can I write? I pray to god for your welfare always.

> With millions of pranams,
> Your slave,
> Srimati Saudamini Devi

After reading it, Satya was dumbfounded. Who was Saudamini Devi? Their Sadudi? Did Sadudi pray for this man's welfare every day? For this short, stubby, aging man? Could it be possible?

When they sat down to eat, the only thing that was easily determined was that Saudamini certainly was not a widow. She would sit with her aunt and sister-in-law, sharing the rice and fish. That was all. Except for that, there was no other way of guessing that Saudamini had a husband. Strange! How very strange! Human beings were so peculiar. Not only did she remember him, but was also anxious to hear about him. So much so that she had thrown overboard all her dignity and signed her letter 'Your slave'!

How petty! How weak! After spending her youth placidly, had she become so restless in her middle age that she had lost all sense of pride and self-respect? Satya felt shamed by Saudamini's fall. Yes, it did seem like a fall to Satyabati. All of a sudden a rare thing happened to her—her eyes filled with tears. But she somehow controlled herself, and covering her head with the end of her sari she touched her brother-in-law's feet. And greeted him calmly, 'Please don't mind, I've never met you. Do sit down. He has gone to the market. He'll be back soon.'

Custom demanded that one used the honorific when referring to one's husband in front of elders and that was what Satyabati did. Mukunda Mukherji was, of course, sharp enough to catch that. At last he seemed pleased with the attitude of his sister-in-law and after politely asking her not to touch his feet, he walked up to the stool on the verandah and sat down with a lordly air.

Satyabati beckoned the boys and they too came and touched the feet of their new-found uncle. Saral even went out to make up a hookah for him. Even though Nabakumar never smoked, Satyabati would keep a hookah and tobacco at home for guests. After all, one had to be hospitable.

There were countless debts one accumulated in the world—debt to one's parents, to the gods, to the guru. Though people spoke about repaying them, they were merely words. In reality, it was obvious, that there was no debt equal to the one owed to relatives. How could Satya transgress the laws of hospitality just because the man was unworthy of being called a 'relative'?

She could not. Not at this moment, anyway. After all, she no longer was the young Satyabati who had refused to put together puja items for her father-in-law because she considered him fallen. This Satyabati was far more practical. The present Satya knew that even if one could not compromise with certain things deep down, on the surface one had to put on a facade. Otherwise, one would be accused of being antisocial, or uncivilized. Once you had chosen to be part of society, you would have to bear the burden of being social too.

Satya gave a short sigh as she entered the kitchen and took the pot off the fire. Then she summoned her older boy, and gave him money for rasagollas, and went and sat down by the door. From that point she could observe her brother-in-law without facing him directly. Until Nabakumar returned, she would have to put up with the pain of this contact.

After taking a blissful drag at the hookah, Mukunda Mukherji asked solemnly, 'How long have you been staying in Calcutta?'

Satya replied quietly, 'A long time now—nearly seven or eight years.'

'Is that so? My goodness, you must have been a green young thing! Did the old man and woman agree? Or have they died?'

Satya felt like banging the door on his face and sitting inside in silence. But she did not. Instead, she replied briefly, 'They're alive. How could they not agree? The boys needed to go to school ...'

'That's true. Nowadays, you can't afford to educate them in a village school. D'you have just the two? I don't see any crawling babies.'

Satya had no answer to that, so she was quiet. Something prevented her from saying, 'We didn't have more'—it pricked her like a thorn. For it seemed to her that the thorn was slowly taking shape in deep darkness.

But Mukunda did not stop there, 'Have they gone out with their father?'

Saral blurted out the answer to that, 'It is just the two of us.'

Who knew what virtue Mukunda saw in this, but he smiled and said, 'That's good! End of worries! It's like being free. Now you can go on a pilgrimage, turn pious, become a thug, or just run your house—do anything you like! Goodness! When I see the swarming babies in my house, my head turns. They aren't like human babies at all—more like chicks or ducklings.'

Satya stared in amazement, despite her irritation. She had no idea that a man could talk that way. She had seen many men in her father's village, 'effeminate' men too—like Nilambar, and

Nabakumar. Of course, she had not met any man who had matched her ideal of manliness—but this! Even rustics retained a modicum of decorousness, this city-bred lout seemed ugly and detestable.

And yet, if one looked closely enough, it was obvious that the man must have been considered handsome in the past. He was short, fair, with proportionate features, his salt and pepper hair was well dressed, and there were clear signs that every inch of his body was pampered. Even if his household was full of chicks, it was beyond doubt that he had managed to indulge himself. In her mind, Satya mockingly applauded Sadudi's co-wife.

There was silence for a while. While Mukunda dragged on his hookah, Satya anxiously watched the door, and poor Saral stood wooden and silent, waiting for the impending thunderbolt. He had no doubts at all that their trial would begin the moment the gentleman left. But it seemed like a long wait. To Satya it appeared as though Nabakumar had gone to the market ages ago. And Turu, too, was taking just as long. The sweet vendor was just round the corner.

Mukunda broke the silence again.

'I suppose your Sadu herself is taking care of your parents-in-law.'

There was veiled displeasure in his tone.

Satya replied softly, 'She's always lived there.'

'That she'd have to, especially when the son and his wife have grown wings. But she has a duty to her husband as well. My house is empty because it lacks a human soul. My second wife is an expert at entering the birthing chamber at any time at all—the children have a hard time. If my first wife came and stayed, it would save me so much trouble, and yet ...'

Perhaps because she was completely stunned by a discomforting disquiet Satya gave him the time to utter so many words. But soon her stupor passed. Forgetting that the man was a stranger and without doubt, an elder, she responded with a low-pitched intensity, 'Of course, that would save you trouble, but tell me, what would she gain from it?'

For a minute Mukunda Mukherji was thrown completely, he

had not imagined that he would have to face such vehemence; but it did not take him long to regain his composure. Adding a slight smile to his composed face, he said, 'I can see that my brother-in-law is fortunate to have such a wife. Beautiful and learned—you must be in the habit of reading novels and plays! Since you ask, let me tell you, even if she gained nothing now, she'd earn merit for her next life. After all, slaving at her husband's house isn't any less honourable than slaving at her uncle's.'

Satya stood up and tried to speak calmly, 'If you had any sense of what is honourable for a woman, you wouldn't be speaking like this. But I know for a fact that it wasn't my sister-in-law who disowned you—you disowned her. Now you need a maidservant for your house, and so you're bothered about what merit she'll earn in her next life.'

However calm Satya tried to be, her face was red with fury. And her rage was directed as much at the shamelessness of this crude man as at Sadu's unashamed behaviour. It was Sadu who had given the man a chance to say such things.

Because they were interrupted by the arrival of father and son, nobody shall ever know what Mukunda Mukherji might have said, or what Satya's retort might have been. Sadhan arrived with the rasagollas and Nabakumar came in with him. Since he had met his father on the way, Sadhan had already given him the news. He had been awfully relieved to have met his father, for his encounter with his mother could be deferred for a while.

Nabakumar, of course, knew immediately how he should greet an elder, and a rare relative at that! He promptly put down the shopping and touched his feet and said with a smile, 'How lucky I am that you're visiting after so long. How long have you been waiting?'

Meanwhile, Satya had taken the rasagollas into the kitchen. Mukunda had replied in a voice loud enough for Satya to hear, 'Quite a while. I was listening with bated breath to a lecture from your learned wife. She's from Calcutta, I suppose. Studied with a Memsahib, eh?'

Nabakumar lowered his head in shame, his ears were flaming.

And he felt speechless with rage. There were no limits to her audacity! Just because she knew how to use words, how could she say anything she pleased, to anybody at all? An elderly brother-in-law, that too one she had not met in all her life! Why, she was not even supposed to speak to him; she was expected to cover her head and withdraw inside the house. Instead, she had given him an earful, and now Nabakumar had to bear his sarcasm.

How awful! But he was supposed to contain his anger, swallow his pride and laugh at the brother-in-law's joke. So that was exactly what Nabakumar did. Satya quietly came out with a plate of rasagollas and a glass of water; she put them down and took the shopping basket in. After she had gone inside, Mukunda picked up the plate and sniggered, 'Making amends now, eh? Not bad at all! Never mind, a brahmin will rush even into a low-caste home for goodies ...' Nabakumar kept on laughing. Louder.

Satya did not come out after that. The boys slowly went inside and sat with their books. Mukunda chatted with Nabakumar for a long time.

Suhashini was not home, she usually spent Sunday mornings learning lace-making from a well-to-do housewife who lived nearby. The woman was childless and had a house full of servants. On Sundays, her husband would rush off in the morning to play cards with his friends, so on Sundays, as on other days, she had plenty of free time. The woman herself had peeped out through her window and made friends with Suhash.

'I'd be relieved if Suhash didn't come back while that man's here,' Satya thought to herself as she cooked. There would be no way of avoiding him. The man looked debauched! He was sure to demand a thousand explanations about Suhash. Human beings can be so coarse!

Slowly Satya's mind had turned to other thoughts. Human beings were not just coarse, they were greedy too. Or else, why would Sadu respect this wicked man as a husband? She had heard the story from Nabakumar. Sadu had left because she was abused. And Satya also knew that the abusive husband had married again. In spite of everything, how was it possible for Saudamini to think

of herself as his slave? Or had that been merely part of the
conventions of letter writing? Perhaps, she had done it because she
had temporarily felt impatient with the miseries at her aunt's. But
was that really the case? It looked as though it had involved quite
a bit of planning. Not something one did in a pique. If she had
asked a boy from their village, the news would have spread, perhaps
that was why she had waited and asked her nephews.

Of course, she must have forbidden them from mentioning this
to anyone. That was another reason why Satya felt upset with Sadu.
How could she initiate them into lying, being an elder, an aunt?
Because of her Satya could not scold them! For it would not be
fair! After all, an aunt is an elder. And they had promised her. Satya
herself had taught them how important it was to keep a promise.

But no matter what she taught them, Turu was turning out to
be just like his father. Spineless and spiritless. The only difference
was that unlike Turu, Nabakumar would usually lash out with his
words. Turu was a mild, harmless sort of boy. But was it really
desirable to become like that? All Satya had wanted was for her
children to be worthy human beings!

Perhaps, Saral would turn out to be different. But in what way?
Would he come anywhere close to the shape of the ideal human
that Satya had embossed in her mind?

Satya did not dare entertain such a hope. They would study
hard, earn well, people would praise them—that was all. Satya knew
it would not come to much more than that. If they had it in them,
the glow and the brightness would have been obvious by now.

It was in Suhashini that Satya saw possibilities, the hint of
radiance. Suhashini, who until her adolescence had stayed in a filthy
environment with only emptiness. May be that was the reason why
the difference between light and darkness had struck her so
intensely. The boys had not experienced such an intensity, so they
had remained out of focus. Although they were fourteen and fifteen,
it was not evident in the least that they thought about themselves
seriously, or if they had learnt to think at all. And if they had learnt
to distinguish good from bad.

It was strange that Satyabati's own flesh and blood should not come anywhere close to the ideal in her mind. God alone knew what new shape was forming inside her body after all these years. Satya had felt helpless at first, she thought of it as risky, but gradually, she had started to feel tender. So much so she had even started liking the idea of a change—it would not be a bad thing to have a girl!

Today it suddenly came home to her, that if indeed it was a girl, who could guarantee that she would not turn out to be like her father's mother in every way! Perhaps, that was how it would be. Satyabati's deep desire and regular prayers would be useless. Women suffer from such a curious kind of helplessness. Because no one can predict what the creature created out of her own flesh and blood, mind, sense and soul would be like!

Satya sighed as she thought of the shastras which proclaimed that men usually resembled their mother's brother. But what happened when the mother did not have a brother? The mother's father came a close second, perhaps. But the scriptures did not mention any such thing.

Her thoughts were interrupted by that stentorian voice thundering outside, 'Where is the mistress of the house? You've disappeared after lecturing me, have you? Allow your servant to take leave. I hope I'm permitted to come back?'

Satya came out and said with folded hands and bowed head, 'Of course.'

But her calm words had proved to be useless. No sooner had Mukunda left than Nabakumar came rushing in a rage.

'What's wrong with you? What nasty things did you tell him?'

Satya was irritated, 'Why should I say anything nasty?'

'Of course, you did! But he hadn't come on his own, had he? My sister had summoned him ...'

Satya stopped him with, 'That's what made me want to hang myself in disgust!'

'What do you mean?'

'Think that out for yourself after you've had your meal, and at leisure. Now go and have your bath.'

'Wait! You tell me, what did my sister do wrong? He's her husband after all.'

'That's for sure!'

'Of course.' Nabakumar carried on enthusiastically, 'From whatever he's told me, I could understand his pain. And whatever you might say, the man isn't a fraud. He confessed that he made mistakes, kept bad company, and used to drink; and he'd tormented my chaste sister. But later, he'd come to his senses.'

Satya asked innocuously, 'He did, did he?'

'Of course! Except for the hookah, he has no other bad habits. So he wants to apologize, fall at my father's feet and ask for her, but he's too embarrassed. But since my sister wrote to him herself, he could now take courage ...'

'That's wonderful! Absolutely joyful news! Send for your sister and give her away ceremonially for a second time! The two co-wives can live happily together.' But no sooner had she turned away with a bitter smile, a catastrophe took place.

Nabakumar repeated unthinkingly, something he had heard a moment ago, 'I believe she won't not have to suffer the co-wife for long. The other wife is suffering after childbirth. Who knows how long she'll last!'

It sounded as though a bomb had exploded that very instant! Satyabati hit her forehead with her fist and screamed insanely, 'Will you stop? Please stop! If you can't, then strike me dead forever!'

She managed the house single-handedly, and had not eaten anything because she was suffering from a loss of appetite; her weak body had been unable to take the strain. She collapsed in a heap.

The two boys rushed out to fetch water and a fan. Nabakumar brought a pillow from inside the house and placed it under Satya's limp head. At that moment, Suhashini stepped in and froze at the sight.

Suhash had walked back in a happy mood, because her lace-making teacher had told her, 'If you're willing, you could teach me to read. I hate being a rich housewife, sitting around and doing nothing. Looking at you, I wish I could read books like you. The days would pass nicely then. Going to school is out of the question, but if you were to teach me …'

She had offered to pay Suhash eight rupees a month. Suhash had protested, of course. She had said, 'Why the money? You have been teaching me something and I'll teach you something in return.'

But she would not listen, and she had pleaded saying, 'My husband is ever willing to spend money on my hobbies! He spends twenty-five to thirty rupees every time he takes me to the theatre—and this is a hobby too! Besides, one cannot learn without paying one's guru something.'

Finally, Suhash had had to yield. So she was back feeling cheerful and ready to announce to Satya, 'Look, Pishi! Not all wealthy people are mean. There are admirable people among them as well.'

Now Suhash immediately took charge of Satya. And that was when she heard the news for the first time. Nabakumar repeated it almost to himself, 'Her body is very weak. Women usually go to their parents or grandparents to give birth—but no point thinking about that. We'll send her off to Baruipur.'

Suhash stared helplessly for a while. Then she cursed herself for being so unsuspecting! A hulk of a girl! How could *she* have been so foolish? She spent so much time with her aunt—how had she not caught on? She was no different from the boys, then! She should have been the first to guess her aunt's state. She should have looked after her.

But she had not understood at all! Satya's boys were grown-ups now—may be that was why she had not been able to guess. Looking at her aunt's pale, unconscious face, Suhash felt bashful and scared of the unfamiliar. Suppose Suhash's bad fortune scuttled the only source of shelter she had? What if something happened to Satya?

She had heard it said that it could be dangerous for a woman to have children after a long gap. Her heart shuddered and froze with fear. For the first time, she realized how deeply she loved her aunt. Not only because she was her refuge, but also because Suhash had, through every moment of contact with Satya, given her a large place inside her heart.

Would there be nobody to look after Satya because her mother and grandmother had died? Of course not! Suhash was old enough to look after her!

FORTY ONE

Suhash's anxiety-ridden resolution to be of use to her aunt, finally came to nought. Satya refused to stay in bed beyond half a day. With utter disregard for Suhash's appeals and Nabakumar's nervous scoldings, she got up and said, 'Well, I feel fine now. Don't you go making a mountain out of a molehill!'

But the incident brought home to Satya her own vulnerability, and planted inside her a deep anxiety. Her sense of unease had practically nothing to do with her husband or sons, but was entirely focussed on the orphaned girl. Satya had been taking it easy so far, but what if something happened to Satya, what would the girl do? It was not as if Satya was going to die, but their were no guarantees. Here she was about to have one more 'go' at her age! Of course, there was a risk! She was not too worried about the boys, they were almost adults, and Nabakumar had his parents—something or other would work out for them. The girl would be left high and dry. Elokeshi would never accept such a beautiful woman. Besides, it was not merely a question of acceptance. Satya cursed herself for taking it easy for so long, and the next day she put forth a daring request to Nabakumar.

Nabakumar's head was buzzing from the moment Satya had collapsed. And ever since, he had been meekly trying to please her, but her request made his head spin again. So he reiterated in amazement, 'You shall go to Master-mashai's house! Why? What is the urgent need?'

'I need to.'

'But Nitai would be furious with me if he got to know.'

'Would he?' Satya smiled slightly, 'Really?'

'Yes. Besides, why do you need to go there?'

'I told you, I need to.'

Nabakumar forgot his meekness and said fiercely, 'Tell me, what do you need with a man who has lost his caste?'

Of course, he had become nervous as soon as he spoke. Who knew if Satya would faint again? But Satya had not fainted, instead she had stared woodenly at her husband and said, 'I wanted to ask for his advice.'

'Advice from a fraud? From a low-caste fellow with high-caste pretensions? Isn't there anyone from your own caste or status? Why do you need to go to that casteless so and so?'

Perhaps, Satya was determined not to lose her temper, in an even tone she said, 'There aren't people from my own caste and status here, are there? I can't be expected to consult the birds and beasts! But never mind, if you can't take me there, I'll have to make my own arrangements.'

'Your own arrangements!'

'Yes, of course.'

Nabakumar said even more fiercely, 'You're really the limit! You always do what you want to do! All right, if there is such an urgent need, I shall swallow my pride and ask him to come here.'

'No!'

'Why not?'

'Not when you yourself had told him not to come here again ...'

'Yes, I'd done that. Now I shall call him here and undo my crime.'

'Did you know that there are crimes which can never be undone? But never mind, I don't want to argue. I shall not ask him to step into this house. I shall go myself.'

'I shall be banished one day because of you.'

Nabakumar's expression was a study in extreme irritation. But Satya remained unperturbed, 'You won't be banished just because you say it, will you? Anyway, don't you worry about it. I shall make the arrangements. I'm just informing you.'

But how could Nabakumar abandon his responsibilities just because he was asked not to bother? He was troubled. But in the end, he had had to let go because he had been unsuccessful in finding a solution.

Meanwhile, Satya had ventured forth independently, on her own. With none other than Suhash for company. Yes, Satya took Suhash along. Suhash exclaimed when she heard the address, 'This is right next to our school!'

'All right then. You and I shall go together.'

Perhaps, Satya said this because in some corner of her heart she entertained a hope of showing the 'girl'. After all, if he was going to take charge of finding her a groom, he should be able to say what she looked like.

This time it had to be direct conversation, there would be no via media. Bhabatosh was dismayed. He knew, of course, that Satya had practically adopted an orphan girl, but he had no idea what she looked like or that she was such a grown-up girl! He had gazed at her in confusion and then lowering his eyes he had said, 'Such a girl wouldn't lack a groom, Bouma.'

'You're saying that out of affection. But you'd have to do something for this granddaughter. I've heard that your community has generous men who would agree to marry a widow.'

A widow! Bhabatosh floundered, 'A widow! But she is like Goddess Lakshmi herself. There's no sign of …'

Satya abruptly requested Suhash, 'Please go into the next room. I have some work here.'

Satya's audacity stunned Suhash as well. Firstly, it was a terrible aberration for two women to come visiting a man, and on top of that, she was asking to be left alone with him! Suhash left the room confused.

A baffled Bhabatosh stared speechlessly at this unfathomable intrepidity. And Satya remarked in an unwavering, mild voice, 'Now that I'm here, I shall tell you everything.'

Yes, Satya gave him an account of Suhash's birth. From the time before her birth to the story of her 'widowhood'—she left nothing out. She also mentioned Ramkali's clear, public disclosure after Shankari had eloped.

After he had heard Satya out, Bhabatosh sighed deeply, 'Now I know from where you have inherited such courage! From a father like that! But Bouma, our community is not as generous as you take it to be. There is a lot of rivalry, and ganging up. Besides, it would be hard to find a young man who would be strong enough to accept a girl who has no family name to speak of.'

Satya persisted doggedly, 'I don't know about that. But I've always known that you'll never ever turn me away. That's why I forced myself here. You must do something about this girl.'

Bhabatosh said nervously, 'How could you guess that I would never turn you away?'

Satya looked up at him and said clearly and calmly, 'It doesn't take much to guess that—I am a human being after all. But let that be. Promise me ...'

Bhabatosh said with a smile, 'I'll try, of course, but how can I say for sure? If I could pass off as a groom, I'd have broken my vows of celibacy and married her myself.'

Satya had burst out laughing as well. Then she had said naughtily, 'If only she were that lucky! But I am telling you, you have to take charge.'

Bhabatosh was distressed and perturbed and kept repeating, 'Why are you doing this to me? You're making me promise ...'

But Satya remained unruffled. She said firmly, 'I have come to the right place, Master-mashai. I know I can rely on you.'

So many thoughts rushed about at random in Bhabatosh's mind—where on earth could he find a groom to whom he could entrust such an embodiment of loveliness? Who would accept her after hearing of her origins? He found no answers.

He said with a sigh, 'There's nobody that comes to mind right away. But let's see. Tell me, does Nabakumar know that you've come here?'

Satya nodded, indicating, 'Yes.'

'That's good, then. But did he approve of you visiting a Brahmo house and with a marriage proposal for this girl?'

Satya shook her head, indicating 'No.'

Bhabatosh asked anxiously, 'So?'

'So what? We'll have to go ahead without his approval.'

'Would that be right?'

Satya raised her face and said, 'But it wouldn't do to sit calmly without sparing a thought for her future, would it? Of course, if we went ahead with it, there'd be a few quarrels in the family, the in-laws might boycott me. But that hardly compares to what we stand to lose if this girl's life is wasted!'

Bhabatosh looked unblinkingly at her for a moment, and said in an agitated, choked voice, 'It's getting dark, Bouma, you must head back home. I promise you that I shall take charge of her wedding.'

Satya turned to look at the sky, there was no sign of darkness approaching. She bowed her head slightly, 'I've always made unfair demands on you and you've always fulfilled them. So perhaps I've been too blatant today, please forgive me.'

'What do you mean? What should I forgive you for? If only I could forgive myself! But never mind, where has the girl disappeared?'

The girl! But of course! They had not heard a peep out of her all this while. Satya had come out briskly, and only then had it struck her that she had been sitting quite comfortably with a man in a house that did not have a second person in it and that she had conversed with him. Had Suhash found it detestable? Had she been offended at being asked to leave the room? Satya came out and wondered where the girl could be as she stood at the door of the adjoining room. Had she left on her own? Like a lightning flash, fear had shaken her, making her shiver. May be that was exactly what she had done.

'Where is she?' Bhabatosh asked.

Satya murmured, 'I can't see her! Hope she hasn't left on her own!'

Left on her own! Bhabatosh was incredulous, 'How could she do that? Must be in the room at the far end.'

'Why? What's in there?'

'Nothing. Just some—'

His words were left hanging. Suhash, her face radiant, came rushing out of that room and in a passionate outburst so contrary to her nature, said, 'Pishi-ma, come and see! There are so many books! My goodness! I don't feel like leaving!'

FORTY TWO

Time is the most skilled craftsman of all. One blow from his hands levels out every bit of unevenness; flattens out all irregularities.

The same game played itself out in Nitai's house as elsewhere. In the beginning, it appeared that Nitai was looking for any excuse to send his wife back to the village, or, that Bhabini would hang herself from the rafter that very night. But in actual fact, neither of those things ever happened.

Slowly, perhaps unbeknown to each other, Bhabini began to enjoy her independent household, and Nitai became addicted to another equally coarse habit and both of them became indispensable to each other. Therefore, after a while, that violent period faded into oblivion, and broad smiles dominated the market.

Now, Nitai's wife could make chapatis, and Nitai had begun to be scared of her. All his attempts to please her sprang out of fear. Gradually, Nitai had realized that belittling Satyabati was a worthy pastime for his wife—it was an excellent medicine for her mental perversions. That was the reason why Nitai always resorted to this worthy and excellent method. What else could he have done? A failure to see the world from one's wife's perspective could make it the most unendurable of places. At least, for absolutely domesticated souls such as Nitai. People like him had no other means at their disposal. After all, nobody could possibly run a house balancing a fuming pot on one's lap! One had to necessarily spray that pot with cold water!

No matter how helpless or soft women were as a species, they were like tigresses in their own territory. When threatened with the possibility of desires remaining unfulfilled, they would not hesitate to spread out their hoods and transform themselves into venomous snakes. Until and unless the peace-loving male of the species comprehended this crucial fact, conflict was unavoidable. The situation would continue to be beyond control as long as men insisted on disagreeing. And yet, once they made up their minds to give in, the problem was solved. Once the means of appeasement were discovered, peace reigned over the world.

So nowadays, whenever Bhabini lost her temper or stopped speaking to him, whatever the reason, Nitai would always somehow bring up Satyabati in the course of conversation. And never ever in praiseworthy terms. A couple of such attempts always brought him success, and the woman who had sworn to be silent would bellow out, 'Why bring all this up now? All my life I've only heard her praises! I've heard that lowly folks like us would be redeemed just by drinking the water in which she washes her feet!'

But Nitai would persist enthusiastically, 'You could say that, for I've certainly praised her myself. But it's no longer true. I know her well. What can I say, she's thick as thieves with that "Brahmo"—its so infuriating! But then ...' and Nitai would twist his mouth in derision, 'I've always suspected it, but never took it seriously. I'd say, "For shame! It's impossible! She's a brahmin." But now I know that she's shameless and desperate. She'd hired a coach on her own and visited him.'

'But then, is your friend deaf or dumb?' Bhabini would goad him on.

Nitai would smirk, 'A hen-pecked husband is not just that—he's deaf and dumb, stupid and daft, and sheepish—all of these things put together. Something that's slowly happening to me too!'

Bhabini's large black eyes would brim over in fond laughter. She would simper, 'Oh! Poor thing! If only this slave-woman here didn't have to tremble with fear twenty-four hours a day! I wish I could see what a sheepish man looks like.'

One day, Nitai had responded by saying, 'If that's what you wish, let's go and take a look. You hardly want to visit them.'

'What's the point in seeing that elsewhere?' Bhabini had narrowed her round eyes.

Nitai had responded, 'Is everything available at home? So if you want to feast your eyes, let's go. I just heard that Sadudi has arrived from the village to help with the childbirth. We can meet her ...'

'Sadudi's come?' Bhabini had looked amazed, 'Your Bou-than

will give birth here? Not in the village? She won't go to her mother-in-law even at this time?'

'That's what I've heard. She asks don't women in Calcutta give birth?'

'How wonderful!'

Nitai's wife's face had darkened. Ever since she had got Satyabati's 'news' she had nursed a faint hope that for a while at least the eyesore would be out of sight. And during her absence, Bhabini would invite her husband and sons home for meals and dupe them into complete submission and thus impress Nitai. Now this! She was planning to give birth in her Calcutta home.

Bhabini had fumed, 'I suppose the sheepish husband has agreed to that! His wife will act freely and produce her brood, shaming his parents.'

Nitai had winked, 'Even so. He is relieved that his wife won't be out of sight.'

Nitai had spoken from his own assumptions. But actually, the facts were different. Nabakumar had greeted Satya's proposal with a shudder and dismissed it as 'impossible'. It was beyond his imagination that an awesome thing like giving birth could happen in any place other than the village home. But in the end the usual thing happened. Nabakumar's hesitation, shame and fear were torn to shreds by Satya's piercing words. What was there to fear? People were born, and they also died in Calcutta. It was not as if there was nobody to cut the umbilical cords of babies born here! What was so shameful about it? How could giving birth in their Calcutta home be more shameful than having another child at this age? It was pointless hesitating.

Of course, Nabakumar was annoyed by this reference to 'age'. He said, 'Why go on about "age"? My youngest aunt had a baby girl after her grandson had had his thread ceremony.'

Satya had turned her blazing eyes on him for a moment and said briefly, 'Let that be. All I'm telling you is that you'll have to make arrangements here.'

Needless to say, even that had not been enough. Nabakumar had thrown up his arms and moaned for a long time, 'What do I know of such things? Do I know anybody here? You can't just tell me to make arrangements!'

Then a sharp retort from Satya had silenced him suddenly. After that, he had sensibly and quietly gone to Sadu's husband. He had heard that the man had a dozen children—all born in Calcutta. Therefore the man was experienced. This expert had abundantly reassured Nabakumar and at the same time advised him to summon Sadu. Nabakumar had taken three days leave and had gone to Baruipur and brought Sadu.

But it was easy enough to put it that way; in actual fact it had not been that easy. Only someone out of his mind would think that! As if Elokeshi would give up her cook, slave and sole companion of her lonely hours so easily. Hadn't she cursed and damned her odious, wicked daughter-in-law, and insisted that her shameless, wretched slave of a son leave by himself? Of course, she had. But Sadu had spoiled the fun. She had blurted out, 'I'll go.'

'You'll go?' Elokeshi had roared, 'You shameless, ungrateful nitwit, you wretch! You'll abandon us and go and grovel at the feet of that useless harridan, will you?'

But Sadu had remained unbending. Nobody knew that Sadu could be so stubborn! It was almost as though she had changed into a different person.

Sadu had packed the few clothes she had and stood ready at the door. All her life, she had faced humiliation, she had stuck to this place even though there was no hope of reprieve. But she was not going to pass up this chance to go and live near the Ganga. And her aunt's household? She had run it all her life. She also had the right to a holiday! If she were to die, they would not starve to death, would they?

How on earth had Sadu mustered the strength to rebel? Elokeshi had been speechless, Nabakumar flabbergasted. Nilambar Banerji had said in a huff, 'Go, if you want to, but don't you ever show your face here!'

Sadu had touched his feet and said humbly, 'All right.'

A bewildered Nabakumar had said, 'I'm so scared that my nerves will split, Sadudi! You don't have to come! If my wife is fortunate she will live, and if it is her fate not to ...'

Saudamini had smiled mildly, 'Do you think I'm going there to save your wife? Of course not! I want to try my own luck once again, so I'm going.'

Nabakumar had not understood the drift of her words. He had crept away like a thief from the presence of his parents.

Elokeshi had screamed aloud and commanded the gods, 'Judge her, you gods! Judge this wretch who set my soul on fire! Judge her for watching the fun as she drained me of all my strength in my old age! If you are a fair god, let the wretch not set her eyes on another day! May the doors of her teeming home be shut forever! May the food fall out of her mouth and turn to ashes! May she not have a place in hell!'

Elokeshi, of course, had called for harsher consequences for Satyabati, almost singing out her demands to her impartial god.

This was a fact. It would be a mistake to think of it as exaggeration. During Satyabati's time, women like Elokeshi were not at all uncommon. They exist even today, don't they? Except that the language of their cursing has become refined and polished. Their fierce shrieks have got transformed into sharp words.

Be that as it may, none of this reached Satyabati's ears. She was a bit disconcerted by Sadu's sudden arrival. But she soon regained her composure and said, 'That's good! There's somebody to take charge here. I can die in peace.'

Sadu frowned, 'Why should you die? Do all women die from childbirth?'

Satyabati smiled, 'Who knows? This time I get the feeling that I'll die. I can hear the knell, as it were.'

But no matter what knell she had heard, Satyabati had not died. But there had been a long struggle with death, her household had gone all topsy-turvy, and Satyabati's mind had reeled under many a crushing blow and emerged stronger.

In the midst of all that, Satyabati's newborn daughter had slipped away from a world of tears, and learned to peek into a world of laughter. Sadhan and Saral, her brothers, treated her as their beautiful doll of a sister, as their most precious possession; and Nabakumar, too, was swept away by a strong current of fatherly love. But even then he behaved like a coy bride.

Although a girl child was seen as quite useless, Nabakumar would often feel an urge to play with her out of curiosity. He would often be suffused with sweet feelings towards this object of love. Sadhan and Saral were the fruit of his unripe days, at an age when parental affection was not yet born in him. Indeed, during the ardent days of his youth he used to think of children as such a bother! But times had changed. Now Satyabati had gone beyond his reach. Yet, he harboured a hope that some feelings might grow out of this. And because life had triumphed over death, Nabakumar considered his daughter lucky. In other words, Nabakumar's life now ran smoothly.

But what about that girl called Suhash who used to live here? Where was she? Why was she not seen around? Had she died? Or had she followed in the footsteps of her fallen mother?

That was what Nabakumar believed. For that was the accusation he had made. He had not hesitated to articulate his derision harshly in front of the convalescing Satyabati, 'Let that thing not come anywhere near this house! Is there any difference between abandoning one's family and abandoning one's religion? She needn't have married him! A Hindu woman too! Couldn't she have spent the rest of her days in prayer? And the man's old enough to be her father, for shame! Listen! Mangoes never grow on a hog-plum tree, do they? You've watered the plant long enough— what did it yield? Like mother, like daughter!'

Satya had gestured to him to stop and turned her face away.

Satya was no longer bedridden now, but even then she spent most of the day in bed. Ever since Sadu had taken over the burden of running the house, Satya seemed to savour a strange taste of liberation. And if Sadu just remarked, 'Let it be, why are you bothering, you're still so weak.' Satya immediately went back to bed. She never argued as she used to. She would just go back into bed.

And if she stayed in bed too long, scenes from that day's drama would leap up before her eyes. Satya could recall the scene from the very beginning.

Sadu and Bhabini were chatting loudly at the door of the birthing chamber; they had assumed that Satya was unconscious. But even in that state of faint consciousness, the words had hammered themselves inside her head. But she had lacked the strength to stop them. She had been unable to move her limbs, or speak out. Bhabini had kept on talking and waving her hands about. Yes, Bhabini was the speaker, Sadu her audience. Back in her village, Bhabini had never dared to speak with elders. But it was different here, here she was a 'somebody'. So she never hesitated to wave her hands about when she spoke, 'Don't even mention it. We were all amazed. So much prancing around over a misbegotten, full-grown, unmarried hulk of a girl!'

'What was that you just said about her birth?' Sadu had shuddered. Or perhaps, her blood quivered, since it was nurtured by tradition. After all, Sadu had been eating the food the girl cooked! That was what Sadu brought up next.

'But who isn't eating that?' Bhabini had twisted her mouth, 'I suppose even if a meal had to be cooked for the gods, our mistress would send her niece ...'

'Niece!' Sadu had said, 'Wait, let me take this in. I'd heard that she was a widow, and you just said she wasn't ever married. You also mentioned her birth—it all sounds so absurd!'

Poisoned arrows had seemed to pierce the semi-conscious Satyabati, 'It isn't me, but Madam herself who has publicized that she is a niece. Beats me how a sister-in-law who was widowed at age twelve leaves behind a twenty-two year old! Her mother had disgraced the family and left, and the uncle-in-law, that is our Madam's father, had proclaimed it to all the respectable people in the village. And after all these years, Madam picked up this piece of trash from the garbage dump and made a goddess of her! What can I say? I was shocked at such goings-on in a brahmin household. As for being a widow, she's not even married. But who would marry a fraud, who's a bastard to top it all! Her hag of a mother claimed that she'd been married at five and widowed the same year—just to hide the shame of it! Our Madam too maintains the same lie. But now I hear that she's hunting for a Brahmo groom.'

After sitting in a daze for a while Sadu had said, 'She might do that. Especially because she's been sending her to a girls' school. Bou has many virtues, but she has more spunk than is good for her. Always too passionate, always too daring! Or which woman would have the guts to pick up something from the sewers and worship her! I'm shocked, I tell you. Even if you let her live here, why eat the food she prepares? And Naba too ...'

Even a dumb person would scream out if the limits of tolerance were surpassed. Suddenly, a furious cry had emanated from the semi-conscious Satyabati. Like the cry of an angry animal that had been muzzled!

Both women had jumped out of their skins. 'What was that?' they had shrieked at the maid in charge of the birthing chamber.

A few hours later, there was commotion in the house. Questions and puzzles! If she was not here, where had she gone? Who had seen her last? Nobody could remember that. Everyone saw her, all the time—how could a living person just disappear? Yet, that was exactly what had happened. Suhash was nowhere to be found.

Satya could still hear the words. The simple and utterly careless remarks of Sadu and Bhabini. After that the scene would change. Another scene would play out before her mind's eye. Satya had had to bear many a barbed comment for that. But Satya had no control over the scene. It would just unfold itself before her eyes.

Bhabatosh-master had appeared at the door of the birthing chamber. Holding on to a door, he had almost wailed out in a broken voice, 'Bouma!'

Satya had turned with a start. She had looked around in amazement. Why had he come? What kind of disaster was this! Why was he looking so frantic? What was he talking about?

It had taken her a while to comprehend, as was natural. Who would have thought that Suhash would find her refuge in no other place than Bhabatosh-master's house? She had visited him just once, and had never spoken to him! But she had spoken to him this time. And told him many things.

Bhabatosh had talked slowly in a voice that was choking, 'And she says, "You need a maid for your house! That's how I'll stay. I'll do all the work. Your faith is liberal, so you'd not find it disgusting to eat what I cook." Listen to that! A girl who looks like a goddess, why should I find her cooking disgusting!'

Satya had not had the strength to speak that day. So she had said softly, 'That's what you say. Others find it disgusting.'

'Disgusting?'

'Of course.' Satyabati had raised her head from the pillow and had smiled bitterly, 'And they would, of course! You know all about it, Master-mashai. The whole world would look down on her.'

'But how can they do that?' Bhabatosh had said in a voice choked with emotion, 'May be I don't belong to this world!'

Satya had looked unblinkingly at his face for a second and replied, 'I know that. And that wretched girl too had somehow found that out. That's why she fled from the blaze and sought you out as her shelter.'

'But what am I supposed to do now?' Bhabatosh had pleaded, bewildered and helpless, 'There is no other woman in my house ...'

'So what?' Satya had smiled, 'She'll manage.'

Manage!

Bhabatosh had said in despair, 'Have you gone mad too, like your niece? I could hardly make her see the point. I'd kept a horse-coach waiting and tried to make her come round, but she kept repeating, "I'll do all your work, just let me stay here in one corner. And let me read your books. I don't want anything else." Just listen to that!'

Satya had said gravely, 'Why dismiss it as madness? She wouldn't get a better shelter anywhere else. Who will respect her, or love her after hearing about her birth!'

Bhabatosh had said even more anxiously, 'I understand all that, that's why I can't seem to find a groom. Yet, you've instructed me to be honest about it. You don't understand one thing ...'

Bhabatosh had paused.

Satya had said calmly, 'Tell me what's bothering you.'

'All I wanted to say was,' Bhabatosh had coughed, 'I don't worry about myself—I have nobody in this whole wide world. I was thinking about her. No matter how old I am, it doesn't prevent tongues from wagging. How shall I introduce her?'

Satya had said with a smile, 'As your maid.'

'Are you joking?' Bhabatosh's lament dashed itself against the floor.

What a long drawn-out scene at the door of a birthing chamber! Sadu had been sitting with her chin cupped in her hands and Nabakumar had been pacing about like a caged tiger. He could no longer be patient. He had stepped forward and said, 'Master-mashai, is your horse-coach waiting outside or should I call one?'

Bhabatosh had focussed his bewildered gaze on his one-time favourite student and just at that moment he had heard Satyabati's faint but clear voice giving an order, 'Let that wait! No need to get anxious for a horse-coach either. I have a few things to discuss with Master-mashai; it would be good if everyone else moved away.'

If everyone else moved away! Why didn't Satya hit Nabakumar on the head with a stone instead? But there had been no other way out. The doctor had strictly instructed that the patient should not be disturbed in any way. So he had to suppress his anger.

Yes, a doctor had been summoned. To Nabakumar and Sadu's understanding, it was a new thing. But there was no other way. Sadu herself had insisted on it, 'Each age develops its own system of knowledge. Don't hesitate Naba! Now that you're living in Calcutta, do as they do here. She'd have died in that dark hole in Baruipur.'

And so, washing or bathing were forbidden following the doctor's instructions. The puja for the twenty-first day was shelved too. The confinement period stretched from twenty-one to thirty-one days. Besides this, there was no end to problems. Except for the low-caste Matangini-dai, there had been nobody to nurse her. How would she recover? In spite of all that, this episode was taking place right at the door of the birthing chamber!

'You want everyone to move away? Really!' Nabakumar had walked away briskly.

Bhabatosh had looked terribly embarrassed, 'I'll go too.'

'No!' Satya had said firmly, 'We haven't quite finished. How can you say that I'm joking?'

'What to do, I feel so helpless.'

'But you shouldn't,' Satya had answered calmly. 'There is help right round the corner. You joked that day and said that you'd dress like a groom too for your lovely granddaughter. Make the jest come true, then.'

'Bouma!'

'Don't fret, Master-mashai. I'm telling you, this will work out well.'

'Work out well!'

'Yes. Don't hesitate. A woman who has no social standing can't live with a man. Give her a proper position.'

'Why do you want to make me feel guilty for the rest of my life?' Bhabatosh's voice had sounded miserable and hurt.

But Satyabati's voice had appeared serene, affectionate and sympathetic, 'Why should you feel guilty? Accept this as my guru dakshina. I know you like girls to be educated and intelligent, and you'll find Suhash to your liking.'

Bhabatosh had given her a hurt smile, 'Liking isn't the monopoly of men alone! Will she like an old man, older than her father?'

'That hardly matters!' Satya had given an amused laugh, 'Shiva is old too, even so, girls fast and pray for a husband like him! If Suhash was unaware of that, she wouldn't have gone running to you.' Satya's voice had deepened, 'Suhash respects you, and I'm sure she knew what she was doing when she went to you. Can't you see? A woman can't be more open than that!'

'But, there's something I can't seem to fathom, Bouma. What could have happened to compel her to run away?'

'I'll tell you everything. But I can't speak any more today,' Satya had given him a tired smile.

But Bhabatosh had spoken. He had asked pathetically, 'So is this your final decision? And I just have to accept your punishment?'

Satya had again smiled in amusement, 'Now I shall really be cross. Is it a punishment to be my son-in-law?'

Bhabatosh had said after a moment, 'Even so, I don't think I shall be able to forgive myself, ever. I shall think ...'

'Don't torture yourself by thinking of it as a mistake. You know what I'd just been thinking?' Satya had continued almost to herself, 'I was thinking, that may be when I was moulding her to my heart's desires, I had you at the back of my mind. Only, I hadn't realized it until now.'

FORTY THREE

Perhaps, this was what an illicit affair felt like! Some cults take it to symbolize an uncomplicated way of worshipping god. And that was the path Mukherji-mashai had chosen. Though he had not been too concerned with god; he dealt with human beings. But the extraordinary thing was that the person he now hovered around, was the very person he had once kicked aside like a mere pebble.

Mukherji was now a regular visitor at Nabakumar's house. Usually he would arrive around evening when Sadu's chores were lighter. Yes, Sadu had voluntarily taken on every bit of work in Satyabati's household, perhaps out sympathy for Satya's shattered health, or out of sheer habit, or out of a desire to keep ever on display her usefulness to this family. Also because she had not wanted Nabakumar to think that she was no longer needed. If she were to let Satya shred the vegetables, Nabakumar would not have relied so readily on Sadu.

Only the mind can know its own secrets. All told, Sadu had stayed on in Calcutta till now and she would do each and every task in this household—from the most exalted to the lowliest. But she would still find the time to sit around when it was evening. For one thing, the work in a city house was a trifle for her, apart from which an intense sense of anticipation would prompt her to finish cooking dinner by evening. Mukherji-mashai would turn up every evening. Avoiding her nephews, Sadu would walk up towards him, blowing on the tobacco she had prepared, feeling as coy as a newly-wed, her face glowing like a bride.

There was a small room at the corner where Suhash used to stay. Suhash had left all her things behind. The new management of this household had not thought it fit to keep the room sacred to Suhash's memory and leave her things just as she had left them. Satya, however, never entered this room, ever.

Sadu had filled this room with junk, although there was a decent rug spread on the divan that Suhash had used as a bed. And bolsters! Mukherji-mashai would almost tip-toe into this room and sit down, leaning his elbows against the bolsters, and Sadu would hand him his hookah. Mukherji would take it with a mysterious smile and pull her hand close, 'Really! You're still such a blushing bride! Come, sit here.'

Needless to say, 'here' would indicate the tiniest sliver of space on that narrow divan. The hefty Mukherji would take up the rest of the space. Consequently there would be no other way except to sit extremely close. But Sadu would never oblige her almighty lord, 'No. I'm all right sitting here.' So saying, she would sit on the floor facing the divan.

Would she chatter away with the husband she had regained? No, she would not. What was there to say? It was not the age at which one chatted either.

Mukherji would noisily drag on the hookah and at one point ask, 'So, when are you going to step into my humble abode?'

Until this point, Sadu would be picking at her nails, or wrapping the end of her sari around her fingers; she would wake to the query and say, 'What's the use now of holding tight after having let go? Life has passed us by.'

Mukherji's portly bulk would quake with laughter for a while, and then he would say, 'Who would believe that Boro-bou? Your shape is sprightly and youthful still. Though the one at home looks older than the oldest of woman! The front of her head has gone bald, her teeth are ready to fall off, sores on her hands and feet, and her shape? What can I tell you ...' Mukherji would finish with an awful grimace. 'It's disgusting to look at her. I'm still generous enough to keep her; any other husband would have dragged her back to her father's home and dumped her there.'

Sadu disliked her husband's crass remarks about his other wife. She would look displeased and say, 'Of course, you'll say that now. It's just like you to talk about throwing out the gristle when you've devoured the pulp. No wonder they say that men and butterflies are of a kind!'

But such an accusation never embarrassed Mukherji. Instead, he would guffaw, 'God is responsible for that! He has given each group its qualities! But whatever you say, Boro-bou, I've fathered so many children, and married off two daughters as well, celebrated my grandson's rice ceremony with much fanfare—I've been doing so much and also looking after this herd of swine. Do I look run-down, tell me? One must know how to maintain one's looks!'

So saying, he would reach out and give her a tap on the cheek, 'But then one can't reproach you for not taking care of yourself. You know it too well, you too haven't had a wonderful and cushy life at your uncle's. You've slaved your life away, but look at the way you glow!'

Was Sadu supposed to be taken in by this flattery? Or was she supposed to reproach him with, 'At this age, you look at the glow of my body instead of looking at my soul? Aren't you ashamed?'

But she could not say that! Nobody in the whole wide world had ever looked at Sadu's slight body. This man had beaten her out of his house himself. Sadu had been in her prime then, really robust, and her charm was not to be scoffed at either. And what a sunny disposition she used to have!

Sadu had never understood at that point, that her robustness and her loveliness had actually harmed her. Her cheerfulness too. There were plenty of people living in the house then—her brother-in-law and nephews—it had never struck Sadu that she should conceal her vigour in front of them. Watching her, the blood in Sadu's savage husband's head would boil. Therefore, the thug would kick the very body that he desired to squash with his hands day and night, like a football, out of the room.

Nobody had ever told Sadu that she was robust and charming.

After that, much water had flowed under the bridge. Days, nights, and months passed, and the thing called Sadu's 'youth' had vanished without a word; but Sadu's chiselled shape had remained intact. And of late, a greedy old man was beginning to turn his lustful gaze that way!

This was hardly the gaze of a husband, but that of 'another' man. Mukherji now looked upon the wife he had thrown out in her youth as though she were the 'other' woman whom he had suddenly encountered.

Even so, Saudamini was overwhelmed. After all, she must experience this overpowering feeling at least once in her lifetime!

But unless and until he could take her home with him, what advantage had he? It would feel nice, of course, to take on the role of a young hero and come every evening for a chat, but that was hardly enough. Apart from that, it seemed clear that the younger wife was really dying.

His eldest daughter used to come from her in-laws and help with the cooking at times of crisis, but she was due to give birth soon. Although she was very young, Shashti, the goddess of children, had been very favourable to his second daughter. It was useless to rely on his daughters. Therefore, he pleaded with Sadu.

But Sadu was not one to agree easily. She had said, 'Why? This is nice. You visit, I get to see you.'

Mukherji had winked, 'That's not enough to fill my stomach!'

'No need to fill your stomach.'

'You can say that. I've been starving for a year now! I literally have to go without food almost five days a month. If the wretched dame takes to her bed with an "I can't manage", no one on earth can make her get up. I have to fetch puffed rice or parched rice from the shops to feed the populace.'

Sadu had asked with a frown, 'And what about you?'

'Me? There's a brahmin place nearby that serves meals—that's where I end up. I pay the price ...'

Had Sadu's heart swayed a bit? Had it dawned on her that she had cooked rice all her life, but when had it ever made her feel gratified? Had she ever served rice to her husband or son? What was the point of it if you could not serve your husband or son?

Son! Would the boys living in his house be like Sadu's sons? In a way they would be. They were, after all, her husband's sons. The bratas declared: 'Let kinsmen have more food and the co-wife, many sons.'

After a woman died, her co-wife's son also performed her last rites, and went through the rituals of mourning. Such thoughts would often spin about in Sadu's head, yet Sadu had not given in easily. She had said, 'I can't face forsaking Naba's household ...'

'Goodness, for what joy do you think like that? He has a skilled manager! Now that you're around, as they say, "she hobbles because she's seen a horse"! Once you leave, she'll manage fine.'

But that was something Sadu knew already. She had come to realize that Satya's subdued conduct sprang as much from her physical weakness as from mental exhaustion. That wretched Suhash used to be her beloved doll. And now she was gone. She could not even visit them because of Nabakumar's strongly worded oaths. For no matter how strong a woman is, she could never ignore an oath about looking on her 'husband's corpse' if she did what he forbade!

Her daughter was such a doll, yet she hardly expressed any desire to dress her up. Once Sadu was gone, the responsibility would fall on her and then she would do it all right.

And Sadu? She was really flustered. It was one thing to sit in one's own place and prepare his hookah and stroke his feet, and quite another to move into that unknown territory. Who knew what her co-wife and her children would be like? She had expressed her doubts in the course of a conversation the other day, but Mukherji had dismissed them in a flash.

He assured her vehemently, 'The children? They've been after me to bring their Boroma home. And your co-wife? She calls on death day and night! She says, "Bring your first wife just once, let me touch her feet and hand over these rascals to her. Then I can die in peace."'

Why had Sadu's eyes suddenly filled with tears? She had wiped her eyes and said in a choked voice, 'You men are so cruel! You've lived with her for so long; don't you have any compassion?'

'What nonsense! As if I don't or didn't! Till now she's given birth eleven times—who's made arrangements for those, hey? The joint family split up soon after she arrived. My mother moved in with my younger brother and died there. I'm condemned to deep misery. Or else, here you are—my married wife, but even so I can't demand, I have to beg like a beggar.'

'Please! You don't have to add to my sins.' Sadu had replied, 'I can understand the co-wife wanting to die in peace. But for what joy do the children want their stepmother?'

'Why else? Don't you see?' Mukherji's voice had been full of pathos, 'They long for a little bit of mother-love, so that they'd be fed on time.'

Tiny drops of water can slowly wear down a stone. And this was clay that had softened on its own.

Finally, one day, Sadu had said, with lowered head and tearful voice, 'All right, you talk to Naba, then. I'd find it hard to tell him myself.'

Naba too had found it difficult to tell Satya. He had stammered out somehow, 'I'm tired of Mukherji-mashai going on and on!'

Satya had raised her face to look at him. That itself was a question.

After that, Nabakumar had narrated in a rush the crisis in the Mukherji household and finished with a word about being considerate.

'It would be wrong not to send her under the circumstances, wouldn't it? We'd feel terribly selfish if we stopped her from going.'

Satya had replied calmly, 'There's no question of preventing her. She had come to Calcutta in order to go there.'

'To go there!' Nabakumar had been shocked. So he had sneered at Satya's lack of gratitude. To his thinking, Sadu had helped with the birth, and worked herself to the bone running this household. Was that nothing at all? Had Sadu known that she would meet Mukherji-mashai? That he would adulate her so much?

But Nabakumar had not been able to draw out the words that

were joggling about in his mind. Instead, he had said, 'All right.
I'll go and tell him, then. I know it will be hard on you ...'

'Hard on me!' Satya had retorted, 'If only you kept track of
what's hard on me, and what isn't! But never mind that. Ask
Mukherji-mashai to look up the almanac.'

FORTY FOUR

Jagannath's chariot rolls along; but sometimes its wheels get stuck
in sandy patches. And a million outstretched hands, regardless of
rank, tug at the rope and haul the chariot out. God's salvation lies
in human hands. That is the metaphor for the divine.

The chariot of Jagannath is a metaphor for the times. The wheels
of the present age spin swiftly at times, and slowly at others. And
relief from that slowness is also provided by human hands. An age
awakens when its people do.

Yet it must be said, that the god of our age is rather partial to
cities. The city advances at a rapid pace, the village dozes in the
shaded courtyard. By the time a city trend reaches the village, it has
already been abandoned by the city, which is busy chasing a new
one.

But are definitions of city and village dependent just on
geographical areas marked out in a map? Isn't it possible for the
city and village to reside together? One awake, the other asleep?
Aren't human beings as different from one another, especially in
their mental make-up?

Satya stayed home. Nabakumar roamed outside. He went out to
the market, to the shops, to play cards at Nitai's place, and to visit
Sadu to find out how she was. That was Nabakumar's world outside
the home.

But would Satya do anything unusual? She chopped vegetables,
ground the spices, cooked and fried snacks, made pickles. And
when she found the time she read books and magazines.

There was a tiny window—an open one, which brought her

news of the world outside. Her younger son, Saral, helped to keep it open. He shared with his mother all his stories and thoughts. Besides, he was tremendously enthusiastic about procuring books for her.

Nabakumar was clueless about this.

Sometimes Nabakumar would raise an excited hue and cry over a story he had heard while playing cards with his friends, 'Have you heard of the latest calamity? Women are going to England! To pass MA and BA! They want to climb to the very pinnacle of knowledge! What is this age coming to? And do you know, a woman from the Pirali Thakur family—'

Satya would exclaim, 'Stop it! Please don't talk!'

Nabakumar would get agitated, 'Goodness! I've grown old without ever being able to speak my mind.'

Satya would reply, 'Do go ahead then. But talk about things that are appropriate for you! The rising prices, what Kayet-thakur-po's wife fed you, about the head-clerk at your office ...'

Nabakumar would say huffily, 'Why? Am I forbidden to discuss the world at large?'

'Of course not! Why should you be? But speak only after you've grasped and fathomed it. That would make sense. You always seem to savour things second-hand!'

Nabakumar would feel crushed and hurt, 'I don't need to grasp or fathom anything! You can talk to your knowledgeable sons. Come, Subarna, we'll chat.'

Subarna? Yes! Of course, the name Subarnalata suited a golden doll like this child. She was about four, and her father's darling. She prattled like a parrot. And she loved playing at keeping house. She would call out, 'Come, Baba, have some rice. I can cook just like Ma, can't I?'

Nabakumar would reply within earshot of Satya, 'That's lovely, my dear! But don't you ever mimic your mother's temper.'

And so the days would pass at a leisurely pace. But one day, an upheaval ruptured that leisure. The disruption that came incarnated as Satya's absconding friend, Neru! Well, Neru had been more of a friend, she had rarely called him 'Dada' though he was supposed to be six months older than her. Satya had never accepted that. And she did not now.

She gave a shriek, 'Is that really you, Neru?'

Neru chuckled, 'Can't believe it, eh? Looks like Neru's ghost, eh? Just pinch yourself and rid yourself of doubts!'

'One could well say you're a ghost.' The sob in Satya's voice turned merry, 'You've become dark as a ghoul! Where has that milky complexion disappeared?'

Neru roared with laughter, 'What do you think I did with it? Do you think I sold it for food? But really, at times things would get so bad that I wished I could sell my hair, my nails, or my limbs. Just that nobody would have bought my complexion, or else I'd have sold it! I'm tanned by the sun now—that's what!'

Neru's raillery clearly indicated his plight, and that brought tears to Satya's eyes as soon as she caught on. But she checked her tears and reproached him as she used to in the past, 'What great explanations he offers now! But why did you suddenly get this urge to disappear, eh? What good did it do you to roam about in this wretched state, tell me!'

Neru's face hardened and marked by experience, instantly lit up as though by a sudden flash of lightning. And his face glowed as he answered, 'The good it did me can't be found among the things in your house, Satya! It's something invisible. But it's done me a great deal of good, I must say. I've tasted the world that god created!'

Did Neru's reply astound Satya? Did her face turn ashen and pale? As though someone had suddenly delivered her news of some tremendous loss? Was that why her face clouded over in confusion and agitation? Was that why Satya took a while to reply? May be she did want to conceal her sigh. After a while, she asked, 'But how far can your two legs take you?'

Neru gestured, turning his palms upwards, 'Listen to that! I don't have to tramp on every inch of earth in order to see the world, do I? There's a whole new world out there the minute you step out of your own familiar world, you know! It's a different kind of pleasure. Of course, those of you who belong to this world would call mine a wretched state, but I've really had a great time. I'd eat anywhere, sleep in temple yards or in some shop—it was such a rare joy! One day I'd get something to eat, and nothing the next day; one day I'd have a roof over my head, the next day, I'd be sleeping under a tree. There are times when people would look glum if I asked for a pot of water, and times when they'd invite me in for a meal and feed me with such fuss because I looked like a hungry brahmin. So many games the world plays! So many classes of people! A marketplace of charades!'

Satya listened to Neru's narrative, mesmerized. Amazing! Really stunning! The stupid boy whom Satya would always pity, had somehow moved beyond her. Satya quietly sighed. She asked softly, 'You like this very much, don't you, Neru?'

Neru clasped his unruly hair and tried to flatten it, 'I don't know about that, but it's a different way of life, that's all. Instead of being shaped in the conventional way, as pots shaped by the potter, it means creating your shape yourself—that's it! You may call me a wretch and a vagabond, or pity me. But I'll just laugh to myself and think—try living this way and you'll know my secret!'

Satya intervened again, 'All very well for you to say! But tell me, how can a woman become a vagabond? It's only because you're born a man that you have the joy of doing as you please. My father too had left his home ...'

Neru raised a finger, 'That's exactly what I'm trying to say! It's because he'd left home that he become a man among men. If he'd stayed on in the village he'd have become like my father.'

'Hey Neru, don't look down upon your own father.'

'I'm not, Satya, it's the truth! But never mind, tell me, how are you?'

Satya replied in a mildly resigned tone, 'Leave me out of it. I was born a woman ...'

Neru exclaimed, 'Goodness! You've learn to lament too! How you've changed! You'd be wild earlier if anyone said women aren't human.'

Satya replied in the same tone, 'I'd do that even now. But I've started lamenting now that I met you! How you've changed! I won't lie to you, but you know, I used to pity you for being so slow, but now I see that you had the sharpest brain of all. And I've so much respect and admiration. Never mind that, I'd better stop or you'll get a swollen head. But you know what? Had god made me a boy instead of a girl, I too would have left home like you. But that's not how it is. So I sit and pay the price for god's mistake. Enough of that, now tell me, how did you find my address?'

Yes, that was a question. How could the boy who had run away suddenly arrive at Satya's doorstep after all these years? It was almost like a boon of fate.

What emerged from questions and answers was this: Neru had arrived in Calcutta in the course of his wanderings a few days ago. And he had strayed into Kali tala, and that very morning as luck would have it, Satya had gone there to offer her puja to the goddess.

She regularly went there. Particularly on special occasions. Since it was ashtami, she had fasted and had gone there. That was when Neru saw her. But one could hardly accost a married woman on the streets and talk to her, so Neru had trailed Satya at a distance and identified the house. There had been a woman, a neighbour, with Satya. Neru had waited for her to leave before rattling the door-latch with great enthusiasm.

Satya had just shut the door after saying goodbye to her neighbour, she had not even climbed on to the verandah. She had thought it must be her neighbour who had forgotten something, or that Satya had brought in something that belonged to her by mistake. And so, she had opened the door confidently and almost at once she had faltered and taken two steps backwards.

But then, she had not shut the door quickly behind her as she should have done. It must be said that Satya had not done the right thing. She had stared in silence at the figure before her.

The thin, wiry shape looked dark as burnt copper, his face gaunt and rugged, with a headful of unkempt grayish hair. The figure had more length than width. Indeed, such was his height, that the dhoti that he was wearing appeared to be undersized. And his faded, high-collared coat seemed to have abruptly forsaken a substantial portion of his lower body.

Swinging a canvas portmanteau from his hand, the figure had smiled mildly. Satya stood and stared, oblivious of what people might say if they saw her like this. Finally, the man burst into laughter, 'Here, Satya! Can't you recognize me?'

And at that very moment, Satya recognized him. And suddenly choking on her words, she burst out, 'Neru! It's you!'

Neru came into the verandah and sat down, 'Thank goodness, you recognized me. Thank god, you didn't bang the door shut on my face thinking me to be a thief or a cheat!'

Satya scolded, 'Well, you couldn't really blame me, if I did, could you, Neru? Look at you—you look no better than a thief! I don't know if I should laugh or cry. Let me warn you right away, you're not leaving in a hurry. You'll have to stay here.'

Neru laughed, 'So that I grow fat on your cooking?'

'Of course!' Satya replied fervently, 'Eat, sleep and rest for a while and regain your health. If you carry on the way you do, you won't be around to see the world much longer.'

Neru could not ignore Satya's words. He stayed for a while. Quite happily too. At both meals, he would praise her cooking to the skies, and add, 'Oh no! From what I can gather, you won't ever let me leave my brother-in-law's house, Satya! You'll tie me down with your cooking.' And then he would say, 'Now I know why my brother-in-law looks so plump and contented …' He would summon the boys and tell them, 'Do you know that you have a gem of a mother—she's one in a million!'

Satya would look on, fascinated, moved. At times, she would even forget her sharp rejoinders.

Leaving his village and roaming around had changed Neru's speech in a strange way. The language and the tone did not belong to Nityanandapur. Satya had not heard this easy playful manner of speech in Baruipur either. Nor in Calcutta.

It brought up in Satya's mind's eye the entire throng of people she had ever known. Some restless, some serious, some busy, some impassive. Others fearsome, or ridiculous. But nobody among them had such a carefree laugh, or this easy cheerfulness, or seemed so free of burdens, and so unbiased!

Satya would finish all her work so that she could listen to Neru's stories, and her sons too would finish their school work quickly. Yes, her sons were as fascinated and charmed as she was. Neru would narrate stories about known and unknown places, about his various experiences. He would relish telling those stories ...

'Once I was totally broke, you know, I was really starving. And yet, I didn't want to admit defeat, you see! So I told the man at the dharamshala, "Stop bothering with me! What's it to you if I don't cook or eat? Do you have any rule in your dharamshala against it, hey?"'

'Well, the man just folded his hands like Garuda incarnate. He said to me, "Well, there are no such rules. But you are a brahmin's son—how can I see you go hungry? I've noticed that you don't cook or eat. Nor do you buy puris from the shops outside."'

'I told him, "I'm keeping a brata."'

'The fellow was really mulish, and he asked, "What brata?"'

'I said very solemnly, "You won't understand!"'

'He asked "What kind of brata is it that you can't even drink milk and holy Ganga water?"'

'I declared with some annoyance, "Why do I have to offer so many explanations to you, eh? All right, I'm off to another dharmashala." But you know, all the while, I was telling myself, instead of asking so many questions, why don't you get me a few bunches of bananas, a couple of sweet, juicy mangoes, a seer of malai, about eight mandas ...'

Sadhan and Saral would be rolling with laughter as he spoke. At times, Saral would add, 'About four dozen cham-chams, a basketful of hot jalebis ...'

'That's right!' Neru would say, 'I was so famished that I could finish off the whole universe! But I didn't want to look like a greedy brahmin. And then, you know what happened? The man really produced a large pot full of warm, thick, creamy milk and four huge bananas. He said, "It won't ruin your brata if you eat these." And I behaved like I was doing him a favour, and I polished off the lot. As I gobbled, I kept thinking, why didn't you bring a couple of more things to eat, eh?'

They would all explode with laughter.

Some days, Nabakumar would also join this gathering. He was growing quite fond of this vagabond brother-in-law. Privately, he would advise Satya, 'Trick him and detain him somehow, and find him a bride to marry. We'll see how this chap continues with his vagabond ways then!'

Satya would respond, 'Let him be. Let him roam about. What does it matter if one person doesn't marry? There's no rule that everybody must settle down, is there?'

'It would be different if he were a sanyasi. But he's neither an ascetic nor a householder!'

'So what?'

Nabakumar would say, 'There's nothing more to say then.' Then he would come to the gathering and ask, 'So, tell me, which pilgrim spots did you visit?'

Neru would say, 'None, I have hardly bothered with such things. Travelling itself is like going on a pilgrimage. Wherever there is a beautiful place, man has turned it into a pilgrim spot.'

Once Satya asked, 'Which was the last place you visited?'

'Kashi. I'd been there earlier too. In fact, the first place I'd ever visited was Kashi.'

'Kashi! Did you go there recently?' Satya asked choking on her words, 'Did you meet Baba?'

'Baba? You mean, Mejo-kaka?' Neru was puzzled, 'Has he gone there now?'

'He hasn't gone there on a pilgrimage, Neru. He's gone there forever. He's retired to Kashi.'

'My god! Really?'

'That's right.'

For once, Neru became serious. He sighed softly, 'I didn't know that. If I did, I would have tried to look for him. It's hard to imagine that Mejo-kaka isn't at Nityanandapur, isn't it Satya?'

Satya did not reply. Nor did she raise her eyes. She just sat there, holding Subarna on her lap.

Another time, the discussion had turned to Punyi.

Neru had visited Punyi's house in Srirampur for a day. He had not been able to stay longer. Punyi had become such a housewife that Neru had not been able to bear it. All the while that Neru was there, Punyi had given him advice and ridiculed him.

'How the world has changed!' Satya had said with a sigh, 'Do you remember our childhood, Neru?'

'Of course I do! But you know what, Satya? You were an only child—that too with parents like Mejo-kaka and Mejo-khuri. Your memories will naturally be different from mine. I was one among fourteen siblings.'

'Still, you were the youngest.'

'Forget it! Sounds more like a brood of chicken or ducks, not human beings!'

This kind of talk would embarrass Satya and she would promptly broach another topic. Perhaps bring up Punyi again. Was she still thin, or had she put on weight? Was her hair still thick and lustrous?

'Hair?' Neru had laughed aloud, 'She has a huge bald patch! And it's smeared with sindur. Just like Sejo-thakurma! I said, "Spare me, goddess! For I can't stand this any more!"'

Satya had laughed too, 'What a silly boy you used to be, Neru! Where did you learn to speak like this?'

Neru had responded, 'From the wind! The more people you meet, the sharper your brains grow.'

Neru seemed to be enjoying himself. And frankly speaking, in ten or twelve days, he was looking fit and fine. His appearance improved, his skin cleared. May be, if he stayed on for a month or two, the lanky Neru would have turned into a giant. But he did not stay. One day, he suddenly announced, 'Enough, Satya! I seem to be growing roots here—I must move.'

Satya was startled. She sat down suddenly, 'You'll go away?'

'Listen to that! But of course, I must be off. Do you think I've moved into my brother-in-law's house for good, with bag and baggage? I must leave right away!'

Ignoring Satya's pleas, Nabakumar's requests, and all the deals the boys attempted to strike up with him, Neru had packed his canvas bag and got ready. When it was time to leave, he had just said, 'All right, give me a packet of those coconut sweets you made. They won't rot. They'll last me a while. When I eat them, I'll think of you.'

Not just coconut sweets, Satya had made a whole range of sweets that day. Sweets of sesame seeds, milk candies, dal, fritters and sweet puffed-rice balls. She had insisted that he pack the whole lot inside his bag. And then, after making him swear that he would not refuse, she had pressed ten rupees into his hand.

Had the vagabond's eyes moistened with tears? Only he would know! But Satya had noticed that his voice had softened. He had put the money inside his frayed wallet and said tenderly, 'I'm taking it for your sake, Satya. Nobody else would have dared to force me.'

He had picked up Subarna and joggled her several times before saying goodbye.

Neru's arrival had created quite a ripple in Satya's unruffled and uneventful life. His stories echoed in the house for many days. And for a long time, Satya seemed distracted. Who knows if something akin to mother-love had been aroused in Satya for this brother of her's who was almost her age? And with it, a wonderful feeling of admiration combined with respect and awe.

Poor Neru. Stupid Neru. Yet now, Neru seemed to tower over Satya; he had moved beyond her ken. The vagabond's philosophy of life had transformed him in Satya's eyes into the noble hero of an inspiring fable.

FORTY FIVE

The days wore on, and the nights. There was less friction nowadays. Mainly because Satya now had the additional responsibility of looking after Subarna. And Satya, it appeared, sought to fulfill her life through her daughter. She was therefore keen on polishing and decorating with patterns whatever fragments she gathered.

But Subarna was Nabakumar's darling too. Thus, the girl now functioned like a harmonious bridge between the two.

Nabakumar would call out, 'Here, listen to what your daughter has to say.'

Satya would raise her eyebrows and say, 'Why don't you listen yourself?'

Nabakumar would tease her back, 'Me? All my life I've been scared to death of her mother's words, haven't I?'

Satya would laugh, 'Who knows what fate awaits your son-in-law.'

Nabakumar would joke, 'He's going to be a wee bit more unfortunate than his father-in-law. Because the mother's set on making a pundit of this girl!'

But all that was banter. Not dispute.

Subarna seemed to offer a bit of soothing shade in the midst of the blistering sands of life. Was it because she was a girl? Is that the reason a girl is referred to as 'Lakshmi' or 'Shree'? Well, such appellations could undeniably be bestowed on Subarna. She was the reason for the imperturbable serenity in Satya's life nowadays.

There had been some friction in between, centred around the higher education of their sons. But it had not lasted long. Nabakumar had mentioned, 'The Sahib sounded really pleased to hear that the boys have passed their Entrance Exam. He said, "Both of them! That's wonderful! Nabakumar-babu, I'd like to find them jobs here while I'm around."'

But Satya had interjected even before he had finished, 'What madness!'

'Madness! What do you mean?' Nabakumar had been dismayed. He had hoped to use this opportunity to hold forth on the Sahib's generosity, following which he could have joked about the way in which his colleagues at office would envy his good fortune. But Satya had swiped at his good news with her typically antagonistic attitude.

So Nabakumar had asked, 'What do you mean?'

'I mean that they're not going to work now. They shall study.'

'Study? How much will they study? After all, one studies in order to get a job, right? When that's available ...'

Satya had given him a cold stare and said, 'That's not true at all. One studies so that one can become a better human being. Besides, Sadhan's going to be a lawyer, Saral, a doctor.'

Sadhan's going to be a lawyer; Saral, a doctor! Craving nothing less than the moon!

Nabakumar had said fiercely, 'Instead of their earning a bit, you want to spend hard-earned money on turning them into pundits! Only the brains of a prodigal could think that up!'

'You wouldn't have to spend a paisa on their education.'

'Wouldn't I? Wonderful! Where will the money come from?'

Satyabati had replied confidently, 'They will tutor children and raise the money.'

Thus drawing the discussion to a close with her announcement, Satya had turned to leave, but Nabakumar had mocked, 'Tutor children! They're still wet behind the ears themselves—who'll take them on?'

Satya had laughed suddenly, 'Really! Weren't they being offered a job in an office?'

'That was as a favour for my sake!'

'Then regard this as a favour that people somewhere will do for me.'

'I wouldn't be surprised, of course!' Nabakumar had said angrily, 'You know best what you're up to! You're capable of embarrassing a dozen men!'

Despite his fury, he knew defeat was imminent. Once he had grasped that fact he had finally lamented, 'I don't know how I'll face the Sahib.'

'No need to worry,' Satya had assured him, 'Tell him that their mother wants them to study now.'

'Then it will appear that I'm hen-pecked.'

'It wouldn't really matter,' Satya had burst out laughing. 'In their society, their wives are listened to. All their commands are heeded.'

'As if you've gone there and observed their society!'

Satya had smiled some more, 'There are other ways of seeing too, other ways of learning.'

After that, the boys had started college and Subarna had begun to learn the alphabet from her mother. Sadu used to drop by off and on, and she had reacted with astonishment, 'Teaching the alphabet to this slip of a girl! Isn't it forbidden to touch books before age five?'

Satya had replied with a smile, 'That's a rule for boys. There are no such rules for girls. After all, she wouldn't even be allowed to do the hathe-khari ritual.'

'You can go ahead and have that ritual for this darling of your old age! You know you can always have your way.'

And Sadu had smiled. As always. Even now she had retained her smile though its shape had changed somewhat. Her body had grown plump and her face bore a sleek, contented look. Sadu would chatter away about her 'elder son', her 'third daughter'. She would go on about her 'second daughter' who would visit from her in-laws'.

Did that mean that Sadu's co-wife had died? Of course not! Sadu's co-wife was very much alive, and, if truth be told, in better health too. Her illness was gone, she looked healthier. She would tell Sadu, 'Didi, I've survived because you came!' She would say, 'All my life I've suffered at the hands of this butcher. Before you came, I never knew what it felt like to be cared for. My parents were poor, they just got rid of me by getting me married. May be you were my mother in another lifetime.'

Sadu would laugh, 'Rubbish! Don't you know our relationship? Can a co-wife ever be like a mother?'

But then, the attention Sadu lavished on her co-wife was more than what she would have spent on a daughter. After all, it was only natural for her to register her gratitude to the person who had granted her a share in this enormous family.

Mukunda had observed, 'I can see you've managed the impossible. You've revived that corpse!'

'Why should she be a corpse? Your neglect and contempt had shrivelled her up.' Sadu had retorted characteristically, 'But you know what? Even a wilted plant blooms if it's watered regularly.'

'I know that ...' Mukunda had attempted to sound enigmatic. 'Now that you brought your co-wife back to life, hope you won't feel the barb.'

'Saudamini has never feared such things! Don't forget that I've spent most of my life on a bed of thorns.'

Mukunda had said placatingly, 'I really regret that! When I had such a good wife ...'

For a second Sadu had looked distracted. She had said, 'You know, I feel a little bad for my uncle and aunt. My aunt would hardly lift a finger, now she must be slaving away in the kitchen.'

Mukunda had remarked furiously, 'That's sheer bad luck, especially when they have a son and a daughter-in-law. I'm not responsible for their hardship, am I?'

'I can't really agree about that! They'd given me shelter when I needed it most. If my aunt hadn't taken me in, who knows where I'd have gone?'

Her words had cut Mukunda to the quick. So his response had been sharper, 'They'd taken you in not for your sake, but for their own needs. Apart from that, custom says that nobody can snatch away the food that destiny has marked for you!'

The mention of the scriptures had silenced Sadu. Or perhaps, she had not responded because she feared losing her recently acquired shelter. Although she felt nostalgic whenever she thought of her aunt and uncle, the idea of going back always sent a shudder down her spine.

But that was a common reaction. Even a person like Nabakumar had become so accustomed to the comforts of the city, that he hardly thought of visiting the village.

But his untroubled existence did not last long. Suddenly, disaster struck. One day news arrived that Nilambar was dying. He had fallen unconscious on his way back from the ghat where he had gone for a wash after his meal.

Nabakumar began to sob as soon as he heard the news and started moaning and lamenting the fact that he had never ever done his duty as a son. Implying that his negligent and ungrateful behaviour had been induced by his wife's machinations.

On hearing the flow of his laments, Satya abandoned her packing and came in. She said harshly, 'Well, this is what hen-pecked men are like! It's best to compare them with sheep. What's the point in crying? Make arrangements to leave immediately. There'll be plenty of time to shed tears later.'

Nabakumar cleared his throat, 'I shall leave right away.'

'You're not going by yourself. I'm coming too.'

'You! You'll come with me?'

'Why are you so surprised? What is so strange about it?'

'I mean, why should you bother? The boys have their exams coming up.'

'They'll take care of their exams. How can that be a reason for my not going?'

'Who will cook for them?'

'They'll manage to cook some rice. I've explained everything.'

In other words, Satya had made all the arrangements in just a couple of hours.

Nabakumar gave a yell, 'What! By themselves? That's just inviting trouble. You think pushing them is the best way! Why don't they stay with Sadudi for a couple of days?'

'No.'

'Why not?'

'I don't have the time to explain the reasons now.'

'All right, if you disapprove of a relative, perhaps Nitai's wife could send some food. They could just cook the rice ...'

'Just stop it! Don't complicate a simple matter. They'll just boil vegetables with the rice till I come back. That's it!'

Once again, Nabakumar cried out loud, 'Who knows how long we'll have to stay? What if something should happen to Baba?'

'Whatever is fated will happen. Why fret about it?'

Sadu arrived a little later. Ashen-faced, she suggested, 'Bou, may be I should come.'

Satya took one look at that pale face. And wondered if the pallor was merely a sign of her anxiety. Or was it something else? Was Sadu afraid that she would be coerced into nursing the invalid? Or, was she alarmed that she would be unable to refuse even if no one pressed her? Out of some inner urge ...

Nobody would know what Satya figured out. She said, 'No. There's no need for you to go now. After all, we're going.'

'But I have a responsibility too.'

Satya said, 'Let it be. You've found refuge after crossing so many seas. Don't disturb that.'

Sadu was amazed. Coming from Satya, these were rare words! Sadu herself had figured out that Satya hardly approved of her going to live with her co-wife. So, what was this?

It was not something Satya understood herself. She could not fathom when the antipathy and repugnance she used to feel for Sadu had disappeared and given way to pity and compassion. Was it because she now perceived her as a nurturing mother that Satya realized how deprived Sadu had been in the past? Whatever her inner reasoning, Satya had begun to feel tender towards her nowadays. And she felt that way now.

Sadu's eyes filled with tears of gratitude when she saw that Satya did not want her to go to Baruipur. She wiped her eyes and said, 'Mami will think me ungrateful ...'

Satya said mildly, 'Even if you'd dedicated your life, you wouldn't manage to stop their thoughts and words. So don't lose heart over it. The boys will be here. Look after them.'

Sadu lamented, 'You've hardly left me that opportunity, Bou! They are to cook for themselves. Would they have lost caste if they'd dined at their aunt's?'

Satya was quiet for a while. Then, she said softly, 'It isn't a question of losing caste. I want to teach them to become self-sufficient. So that they don't become as hapless as their father.'

A few elderly neighbours were pacing up and down and the womenfolk were noisily bemoaning Elokeshi's bad luck in having such a son. Elokeshi too was convinced that her asinine son would be prevented from rushing home by his wife. Although the man was still alive, Elokeshi had begun lamenting the fact that despite fathering a son, he would not get his ritual last rites. And just at that moment, somebody came with the news, 'Look! Here they are!'

'Naba, is it?'

'Both of them. Naba and his wife.'

God alone knew if the news came as a disappointment for Elokeshi. However, she stepped out of the patient's room. And no sooner had the two figures stepped off the cart, she wailed out, 'O Naba! You worthless wretch! You've come at the very end to see your dead father, have you? Why couldn't you come alone? Why did you have to bring that demoness? Has she come to see the fun, or what? That she can see her proud mother-in-law humbled, eh? See her widowed, eh?'

Satya bent down and touched her feet respectfully. When she rose, she said calmly, 'It's better not to become restless during a crisis. Best to remain calm.'

On this occasion, however, Nilambar did not give up the ghost. But Yama, the god of death, withdrew only after leaving his mark. And the scar stayed. Nilambar remained paralyzed waist downwards. The doctor said, 'That's the pattern of this illness. If you push it, a stroke is inevitable.'

But the neighbours were stupefied. They praised Elokeshi for the strength of her wifely virtues. How else could anybody survive apoplexy? A few of course, were disappointed. They had been fantasizing about the grand funeral feast that his fat-salaried city son would throw, and about the ways in which the arrogant daughter-in-law would humiliate the widow. But that pleasure had been denied them now. Who knew how long the old man would live like this—paralyzed, his limp legs dangling like rags? The doctor had declared that such patients were known to live for a very long time.

When Nabakumar's sanctioned leave was over, he continued to stay on at the village, playing truant from work. But that could hardly go on forever. Therefore, Nabakumar decided to bring up the topic furtively. It had to be covert because he no longer met Satya at night. Satya shared a small room with Subarna, just next to her father-in-law's room. And she always left the door open! So they had to meet during the day. Nabakumar grabbed her hand when Satya was going to the ghat.

'What is this? Chi!' Satya snatched her hand away.

Nabakumar smiled sheepishly, 'You're as rare as a blue moon these days. I've some important work with you.'

Satya said, 'Tell me.'

'Well, it's time to wind up now, isn't it? My leave has got over for a long while now. I've dared to stay away because I'm in the Sahib's good books. But I mustn't overstep limits.'

Satya perused the hedges and the overgrown shrubs around the courtyard, and looked up once at the sunny sky, and then, turning to Nabakumar said, 'Why should you overstep the limits? Start out right away.'

'As if that's possible! One has to consult the almanac, find a maid to stay with my mother. We shall have to announce this tactfully to my mother.'

Satya responded calmly, 'You work at the Sahib's office and cannot stay away if your leave is over, right? Even a little boy can follow that, why shouldn't your mother?'

'Would she? She's misconstrued things all her life! Besides, it's true that no maid could work like you. So, you see …'

'Why should we get a maid to work? It isn't my leave we're talking about! I'm not going anywhere!'

Not going anywhere! What a cruel message! The sky fell on Nabakumar's head!

'You not coming?'

'How can I?'

'I know you are obliged to stay. But what about the boys? How long can they cook for themselves?'

'Till their grandfather gets better.'

'As if there is any chance of that!' Nabakumar almost wailed aloud, 'It is an incurable illness. It's a matter of counting the days now.'

Satya smiled slightly, 'Well, nobody is expected to count days by himself. They need the company of relatives, friends and children.'

'Does that mean you're going to stay?'

'I can't think of leaving now.'

Nabakumar was at his wit's end. He seemed to be in dire straits. He had not thought in his wildest dreams that Satya would take such a strange decision. Indeed, he had imagined the reverse—that

Satya would be ready to skip away to Calcutta—and she had been just waiting for the proposal. He could not understand it!

Initially, Nabakumar attempted to dismiss Satya's decision as being impractical, and impossible too; but soon, he began to plead with her. He begged her to think of her sons, brought up the matter of his office-meal that had to be served on time, and ultimately resorted to his final weapon, 'Hadn't you said that Subarna will start school from next month. What'll happen to that, eh?'

'That won't happen.' Satya said without flinching.

'Won't happen! You've got over the fad, have you?'

Satya said staunchly, 'If you must call it a fad, let me tell you, no fad can be more important than duty.'

Nabakumar began pleading once again. He kept begging her, 'Let's find a reliable maid, my mother will manage.'

Satya's response remained the same, 'That wouldn't be right.'

'And what if I say, I can't live without Subarna?'

'That's nonsense! You know it isn't true! After all, one might be forced to do that for umpteen number of reasons.'

Nabakumar looked helpless, 'Are you going to just abandon your husband and your sons? After all, my father is now ...'

'Don't be crazy! What if this had happened to me?'

Finally, Nabakumar gave up the straight and narrow path of logic in favour of random argument, 'Suppose one of the boys, or I should fall seriously ill?'

Satya smiled mildly, 'If that happened, if that is destined, could I help at all?'

'Well, at least you could nurse us. What about that?'

'How bizarre! Why are you thinking like that? You are fit and fine, and the three of you will manage fine. Why worry so much? Besides, Sadudi is there, in case anything happens.'

At this point Nabakumar became vicious. He gnashed his teeth, 'And why is Sadudi herself sitting so comfortably in Calcutta, may I ask? Can't she come and look after her uncle? She's spent all her life here.'

Satya was annoyed, 'Why place your burden unfairly on someone else's shoulders, eh? It isn't her duty at all, it's mine!'

A furious Nabakumar uttered, 'It's her duty as well. Her uncle has fed her and clothed her for so long ...'

'Stop it! Don't even utter such base thoughts. But since you mention the feeding and clothing, let me say that she's paid for every bit of that. Had she worked elsewhere, she'd at least have saved some money over and above the feeding and clothing!'

As always, the ever-forthright Satya did not hesitate to express her opinion clearly. But Nabakumar could hardly expose how angry he was. Because every time he tried imagining a makeshift existence all by himself in Calcutta, the whole world seemed dark and dismal.

Nevertheless, he could not stop himself from arguing. He asked scornfully why did Satya suddenly felt so dutiful towards her in-laws? Perhaps she had been finding it a bore to serve him his meal on time, and therefore, found relief in the irregularities of her village existence. He warned that her sons would go astray if they did not have their mother to keep an eye on them. And he said much else besides, jumbled and unbalanced. But Satyabati remained firm in her resolve.

She just frowned at his alarm over the boys going astray, 'If that's how I have brought up my sons, I shall poison them and hang myself afterwards.'

Finally, Nabakumar had to go back by himself. Subarna followed him up to the main road, and finally, came back home in tears.

On that day, however, as Nilambar was better, Elokeshi had come out of her room. In an attempt to eavesdrop on the heated dispute by the guava tree, she pretended to sweep away the dry leaves under the jackfruit tree. But the trouble with old age is that one's ears lose their sharpness and play false. It becomes hard to make exact sense.

Therefore, she felt compelled to ask, 'What was that row with Naba about?'

Instead of remaining silent, Satya answered, 'It was a private matter between your son and me; it wouldn't be of much use to you, Ma.'

Satya had used the honorific while addressing her mother-in-law! That was how she had been addressing her ever since she came back from Calcutta. Initially, Elokeshi had been amazed at this masculine brazenness! She had remarked, 'How can a woman speak the language men use in their drawing rooms, eh? Don't talk to me that way, my dear, I detest it.'

Satya had said, 'What's wrong with speaking in a civilized way? Should only men have the privilege of culture? It's good to use the honorific when speaking to elders.'

Firstly, the topic was so irritating, and Satya had used the honorific to top it! And Elokeshi lost control. Wrapping her sari around her waist, she screamed, 'Don't I know what you're like? You were squabbling so that you can abandon your half-dead father-in-law and go home! Don't I know it?'

Satya almost laughed in reply, 'Of course, you do! After all, you are older, and you have seen the world!'

'Yes, I have. But I haven't seen anyone like you! And I haven't seen a man as hen-pecked as my son either. He'll just carry you back!'

Satya replied mildly, 'No, he shall leave without me.'

A faint smile flickered on Elokeshi's face. Because, no matter how wicked her daughter-in-law was, she was a very skilled worker. Ever since she had arrived, Elokeshi had practically given up all responsibilities. In any case, nursing the patient, managing the household, the cows and all could be such a bother!

That apart, Elokeshi had grown attached to Subarna and the thought that the girl might leave agitated her terribly. The news that they would not leave pleased her no end. So, after declaring to Satya that her son had always been devoted to his father, she went to her friends and bragged, 'The wretched woman wanted to leave too. But Naba paid no attention. He said he'd kick her face in if he had to. And after that I can't describe the row they had! The birds fled in fear!'

Satya listened to her words without protest; she carried on with her work with a resolute patience.

Of course, there were women of Satya's age in the locality. Previously, they had regarded her with envy and malice but also respect. But watching Satya take on the daily grind after

Nabakumar had left without her, they took courage and came to befriend her. Most of them were no longer young, a few had married off their daughters, some had grandchildren. Satya had had children when she was much older. That too, the first had not survived, and the second and third were boys. Who knew when that tiny-tot daughter of hers would be married off! And so, they considered Satya still inexperienced.

With all their maturity, they would hold forth, 'Among the fiercest of women—even among those that kill their daughters-in-law—there couldn't be a specimen worse than your mother-in-law. Goodness! She really can give you an earful!'

Satya would respond, 'Everyone speaks whatever comes to mind when they get old. I'm sure we'll do it too. There is no point in getting annoyed.'

After a while, they stopped coming because she seemed too arrogant.

Slowly the months rolled by and a whole year passed. Nilambar's condition remained unchanged, suspended between life and death. And along with him, out of a sense of duty, dangled another person.

Nabakumar visited during the holidays along with the boys. But they all gave up hope of taking Satya to Calcutta as long as Nilambar was alive.

Nabakumar had declared, 'Some spirit has possessed her. It comes from roaming outside after dark, under the trees!'

Why else would Satya ruin her life in this way? It was like chopping off her own feet! Sadhan and Saral were astounded by their mother's resolve.

Perhaps, she was really possessed. Or, why would she suddenly lose interest in her daughter's schooling? After all, she had been literally counting the days for the girl to turn five!

But had she actually lost interest? Hadn't that been the one reason why she would sometimes feel the urge to run away?

Satya had thought she would have to adapt to the situation. She had resolved to tutor Subarna herself, so that Subarna would have two years of schooling at home. But Elokeshi seemed determined to disrupt even that. She would flare up whenever she noticed Satya sitting down to teach Subarna, and call the girl away at the slightest pretext. And she would confuse the poor girl by sharply demanding that she throw her pencil away whenever she sat down to write. Step by step, she had started playing various tricks. She would call out as soon as Subarna sat down with her books, 'Subarna, your grandfather is calling you!'

Subarna would look at Satya who would control her annoyance and say, 'Go, see what he has to say.'

But the girl would not come back for at least an hour or two. Elokeshi would not let her. Elokeshi would instruct her to gently stroke her grandfather's ailing body and hold forth on the heinousness of learning for women. If that failed, she would drag the girl with her to visit the neighbours.

Satya had tried saying, 'You go out leaving Thakur by himself. And here I get so busy with work ...'

Elokeshi would attempt to cover up her uneasiness with heightened irritation, 'What else can he do? As they say, "When you're forever needy, nobody spares alms, and if you're always sick, nobody has qualms." And the man can't even move any more! He can't speak, drools all the time, how can I talk to him? And look after him? I have no desire to do that either! All my life he's made me suffer and even now he tortures me. I ask you, why can't that strumpet who'd enthralled him all his life come and nurse him now?'

At times, Satya would feel embarrassed and keep quiet, at other times, she would ask mildly, 'Would you have let her enter the house if she had?'

Elokeshi would scornfully bellow, 'Enter the house! What do I have the broomstick and the cleaver for? Wouldn't I give her a thrashing in front of this old man? He might be a cripple now, but he has his eyes, doesn't he? He could just watch!'

Satya would not raise further questions. Nor would she retort.

However, behind the scenes, Satya would press Subarna to study. Sometimes, Subarna would burst into tears, at other times, she would retort vehemently, 'What can I do? Thakurma called me. She curses if I read. She has such a temper!'

Despite her protests, Satya had increasingly begun to feel that her daughter had started supporting her grandmother, and had got attached to her.

Eventually, Satya found the loss hard to bear. She could hardly blame Subarna. Her grandmother provided so many temptations at her fingertips! She could roam around the locality with her, sit at the temple, eat what she liked and hear so many stories. And not just fairytales, they also talked about other things.

Elokeshi would say, 'Do you know what your mother wants to do? She wants to make you work in an English school, or send you to work in an office! She won't get you married, won't buy you jewellery and saris. She'll just scold you and make you study. If you stayed with me I'd find you a handsome bridegroom, give you lots of jewellery, and a Benarasi sari. And your wedding will be such a grand affair!'

The child would move closer to her grandmother, thrilled and eager, 'What jewellery will you give me?'

Elokeshi would say enthusiastically, 'A tiara for your head, a choker round your neck, a heavy necklace, armlets, thick bangles, anklets round your feet …'

The girl would be pleased, 'And a gold flower-pin for my hair? Like the one the aunty next door has?'

'Yes, of course! Golden hairpins, dangling earrings. Now tell me, will you stay with me or go to Calcutta with your mother?'

Without any doubts in her mind, Subarna would say, 'I'll stay with you.'

'If your mother lets you! She'll give you a thrashing and drag you away!'

'Just let her try! I shall cry so loudly that the skies will burst!'

Elokeshi would reply with a smile, 'That you'd manage! You'd have the strength. You are your mother's daughter after all! The right whip for the right dog!'

And bit by bit, Elokeshi began to achieve her end. Slowly, the shadow spread over the full moon. That apart, Subarna had hardly had a chance to relate to her mother intimately. She had spent her infancy with Sadu, and later, on account of Satya's listlessness, had spent more time with Nabakumar. Moreover, Nabakumar had told her when he was leaving, 'Your mother wouldn't let me take you with me.'

Her mother was associated with studies—just what her grandmother detested. Besides, Subarna herself did not view it as a pleasant occupation. And so, she had developed a certain hostility towards her mother. Her friendship with her grandmother complemented that.

Satya witnessed the damage. And her pain was so intense that it left her sleepless at night. At times, she would question herself—had she made a mistake? Should she have heeded Nabakumar's suggestion? Who would have known that death could play such a cruel prank on Satya? Who would have known that an unfeeling piece of flesh would refuse to give up the ghost? Satya would check her thoughts and admonish herself. Thoughts such as these required penance.

But finally, Satya made up her mind. As a consequence, she wrote Nabakumar a letter. 'You should take a couple of days leave and come home. You must take Subarna with you and admit her to school. Let her stay with Sadudi until I can come. I cannot let the girl's future be spoiled this way. She'll be fine with Sadudi. In a certain sense, Subarna is hers.'

This was her first letter to Nabakumar. Prior to this she had written to the boys. This was her first letter, but it could hardly be called a love letter.

Nabakumar took the letter to Sadu and cursed and yelled about Satya's foolishness and stupidity. Sadu tried to restrain him, 'She hasn't said anything wrong, has she? Here is a patient, neither living nor dead, and a pile of domestic chores to boot! And on top of that, a mischievous girl! Besides, Mami has such a sharp tongue. How can she manage? It's been one and a half years. Just go and bring her here. I'll look after her. Poor Bou, she's obsessed with studies.'

Nabakumar almost said, 'Why don't you go for a couple of days—she can come back.'

But he could hardly bring himself to say that. Especially in the presence of her husband. After all, Sadu was no longer an unfortunate niece sheltered at her uncle's, she was the wife of this overbearing and imposing gentleman!

Therefore he drew back and agreed to go.

But perhaps the invisible almighty had been watching and was in the mood for a jest.

For what else could one call it but a jest of the gods?

Why else would that lifeless piece of flesh that waited for its days to end, accounting for every gasp of breath, suddenly relinquish the space it had occupied for so long? And at such a crucial moment too!

After much persuasion, and after she had earned a heap of disgrace and Elokeshi's curses, Satyabati had finally managed to coax Nabakumar into leaving with Subarna. Nabakumar had resolved, even as he was leaving, that he would make his daughter forget her mother forever. Just at that moment, the almighty had smiled in amusement. As a result of which Elokeshi's screams began to pierce the skies; she rushed out and threw herself down in the courtyard.

Her shrill screams made it difficult to comprehend what she was saying. But it would have been possible to make out that she was addressing the recently departed, 'They just killed you! With their own hands! Your son and his wife!'

That was it! In the end, Satya and Nabakumar were accused of murdering Nilambar. Elokeshi had shrieked out her elucidation, 'They conspired together and snatched away the darling of his heart—his granddaughter. How could he go on living after that! His life went out in a whiff the moment she left! How could his heart stand the blow after the main support had crumbled to dust!'

Whosoever heard it, condemned the heartless daughter-in-law from the city. Nobody stopped to ask if Nilambar had ever had a heart that could feel hurt. Or question the means by which Elokeshi had procured information about the inner state of that unfeeling piece of flesh waiting for its end. Especially since there had not been even a flicker of recognition when Nabakumar had called him repeatedly. Had his feelings, emotions and awareness flashed to life the instant Subarna left? No. No one had raised such questions. Satyabati's stone-heartedness had been the main issue.

Never mind that. Disgrace had always been Satyabati's constant companion; the problem started elsewhere. The question came up after a while. Nabakumar had spent more than he could afford on his father's last rites. And because of Satya's deep design, Nabakumar ended up spending more than he wanted to. Satya had invented many traditions—such as the freeing of four bulls, gifting away a hundred padukas to brahmins, etc. Sadu had come too, to participate in the grandeur of her uncle's last rites. And she had not come alone; she had brought her husband and two of 'her' boys. Everyone was dumbfounded at the display of Sadu's fortune that had been so long concealed. Nitai and his wife had taken the opportunity to visit the village too. Everything had worked out fine. The problem started when the time for departure drew near.

There was no further need for Satya to stay, so she would leave too. But leaving Elokeshi on her own had larger implications. So Satya had proposed, 'Why don't you come with us?'

When Sadu had come to know about this, she had taken Satya aside and scolded her, 'You stupid fool! That would be like taking her with you forever! And setting fire to your own house! You've worked yourself to the bone for so long and made your husband and sons suffer too. And there's nothing but disgrace to show for it. If you take her with you, she'll make your life miserable.'

That was what Sadu had said. Nabakumar though, had been thrilled about the proposition. What a fine arrangement—it would put all his worries to rest. Satya was clever and gutsy.

But Elokeshi paid no attention to such fine arrangements. Instead, she cursed her son for wishing to terminate the evening lamp ritual at his ancestral home. But would it not have been possible to request a cousin to undertake that task? Elokeshi refused to hear of it! She would rather hang herself! She could not imagine being beholden to those she could not stand! Why should she leave her familiar surroundings and suffocate in the prison of a city? And make life easier for that lady of leisure—her daughter-in-law? No, thank you! Nabakumar had better give up such depraved schemes!

What could be a possible solution? Nabakumar had to find a tough maid to stay with his mother at night, and leave his daughter behind to calm his mother's grieving soul. For, his mother would be sure to follow in her husband's steps if they tore the girl away from her!

Nabakumar was stumped; he asked, 'Did you hear that?'

Satya was packing and getting ready to leave. 'I did, indeed,' she answered.

'What shall we do now?'

'What else? No point in trying to choke your mother to death, is there? Better to find a maid.'

'And Subarna?'

'Subarna will come with us.'

That, in short, was Satya's mandate.

'Of course, you'll say that! But there's no end to the disgrace we've faced because of my father's death. And now should my mother ...'

'Should she what? You mean, should she die of a broken heart?' Satya tittered sharply. 'That would earn her the merit of dying with her husband, like a Sati! Seared by the same flames too!'

'Don't joke!'

'I'm not. It isn't something to joke about!'

'But I can't bring myself to tell her.'

'You don't have to. I'll say what I have to.'

A totally confounded Nabakumar could hardly comprehend what he ought to do, caught as he was between a mother lacking in reason and a wife neglectful of duty. There was, of course, one thing he could do. Something he had always done—he could start by refuting Satya's point. And that was exactly what he did. He said, 'I have sinned by killing my father. Do I have to be guilty of matricide too?'

But Satya remained unmoved, 'There is no other way. If that is what the gods have destined, you can hardly avoid it, can you?'

'Subarna isn't yours alone. Her grandmother has certain claims on her too.'

'Sure, she does. But one would have to drag them to court to find out what they amount to.'

'What? What did you say?'

'Nothing,' Satya replied, fiercely concentrating on the work at hand. 'You forced me to say that.'

'But then your sense of duty seemed to be overflowing for your father-in-law, and you treated me like a speck of dust then, didn't you? So why this aggression towards your mother-in-law, eh?'

'I don't have the patience to explain the reason. But this much I shall tell you, Subarna will come with me.'

That was Satya's final decision. And nothing could shake her. Besides, her two boys had grown up and now wielded some influence. They were utterly devoted to their mother and hardly got along with their father. Thereby, Satya commanded more support.

Though the boys had left because they could no longer be absent from college, they had asked that their mother's wishes be honoured. How disrespectful! How outrageous that their mother should matter more than their father!

Nabakumar had attempted to protest, but Satya had stopped him with a gibe, 'Why get so cross about this, I say! After all, they belong to a family of mother-worshippers. And they in turn will respect their mother, won't they? It isn't such a bad thing.'

Nabakumar was actually pleased about having his daughter and wife return with him; he protested more out of habit than anything else. And as always, Satya had her way. After nearly two years, she crossed the threshold of her in-laws' house, holding her daughter's hand, husband in tow.

They left behind an inconsolable Elokeshi, howling, thrashing about and beating her breasts.

This time round, the villagers did not support Elokeshi. 'You should've gone with them,' they chided. 'They'd offered to take you. It is a pilgrim spot, after all, with the Ganga and the Kali temple. What stopped you? You don't really expect your son to play truant from office, do you? Or expect that his wife will abandon her sons and her husband and stay here forever? Now who knows what problems you'll create for us! Especially if you were to die alone in this house? And besides, your son has just begun his year-long mourning for his father; this kind of crying would tempt the evil spirits, wouldn't it?'

Elokeshi's actions, which had always found approval, were thus criticized for the first time. What could be the reason for that? Could it be because the neighbours now perceived themselves as shouldering an undefined responsibility towards this solitary woman? Or had a subtle obstacle surfaced in their speculations about unoccupied land, orchards and ponds? Elokeshi had three orchards that were brimming with fruit, and two ponds teeming with fish. And much else besides.

But then, may be her friends were not really greedy. Perhaps this was a consequence of age-old convention. Widowhood always diminished a woman's worth. A woman is valued differently so long as her husband is breathing. After his death, her strength lies in her ability to shout others down. Well, whatever the reason, that was how matters stood.

On hearing about Elokeshi's hyperbolic wailing, even Nitai's wife started supporting Satya. May be also because she herself was already acutely upset. She had returned from the village in a happy frame of mind. But no sooner had she come back, the sky had collapsed on her head. It was an unimaginable event! Her youngest sister, her mother's last-born, who had been married just a few days ago, had died the previous day. She returned to find her brother wailing. He told her that she had been killed by her husband and her mother-in-law. Yes, they had killed her, and had spread a rumour that she had had a fall near the ghat at night and died.

Killed her! Nabakumar was astounded. Nabakumar and Satya had both come to see Bhabini on hearing of her bereavement. Nowadays, Bhabini would stand at a distance, and practically talk to Nabakumar. Her grief had made her bold.

'Killed her!' Nabakumar exclaimed fiercely, 'What kind of anarchy is this!'

'Exactly my question,' Bhabini replied, wiping her eyes. 'Every killer gets punished, but you go scot-free if you kill your wife! The old hag is sure to get her son married again. The loss is ours. She was just a child—nine going on ten—totally innocent. And such a lovely person too. How she'd sobbed and refused food and drink when she was sent to her in-laws! And this had to happen in less than a month. Can't imagine the state my mother's in!'

Bhabini moaned on. She had had no children of her own, and used to treat her mother's last-born like her daughter. And now she was gone! Satya had been sitting motionless and taking it all in. She had not tried to offer any consolation. After a long while, she asked softly, 'How do you know they killed her? It could well have happened as they claim.'

'Do you think such things can be hidden? The neighbours came and told my father.' Bhabini broke into sobs, 'I believe they said, "How barbaric!" They just smashed her head in with a grinding stone and finished her.'

Suddenly Satya's expression changed, her eyes took on a crazed look.

'Smashed her head in with a grinding stone!' she intoned.

Nabakumar was alarmed by Satya's transformation, though Bhabini hardly paid heed. She continued in the same manner, 'That's exactly what they did. The man had nearly finished her off anyway, and his mother didn't see it fit to leave her half-dead, so she killed her. That way she wouldn't speak again. And so another hard bash! Inhuman monsters! They pretend to be civilized, actually they're beasts.'

Once again Bhabini began to wipe her eyes.

Satya suddenly shrieked, 'And are you going to just sit and cry? Won't you do anything about it?'

Bhabini gave a start. She faltered before Satya's wild eyes, 'What can be done now? What was destined has happened.'

'Destined, was it?'

'What else can one call it? It was punishment fated for my mother, and at her age too ...'

'How wonderful! And don't they need to be punished? Don't you want to see them hanged by the neck?'

Bhabini hit her forehead with her palms, 'What would be the point? Our Puti won't come back, will she? Just a useless hassle with the police!'

Useless hassle!

Satya responded grimly, 'And aren't there a thousand Putis in our country? Aren't they tortured too?'

A thousand Putis! What could that mean? Bhabini was astonished. Why had Satya begun to look so maniacal? Bhabini had not understood her words, but she persisted nervously nevertheless, 'Of course, there is torture everywhere. After all, it is a woman's fate to suffer a battering in silence. But it's really sad that the child died. I think it's a good idea that nowadays they wait for girls to get a little older before marrying them off. A good thing too that you've started sending Subarna to school. It will increase her understanding and her strength. Our Puti was such a good girl ...'

Satya stood up abruptly and announced, 'I want to go home.'

Go home! Nabakumar was astounded by her complete disregard for propriety. And without a word of consolation too! He said agitatedly, 'Of course, you will go home. What's the hurry? Stay a while.'

'I can't. My head is throbbing. Don't mind my asking—but could you give me the name and address of your sister's husband?'

The name and address! Nabakumar was startled and he scolded, 'Why do you need that? It's none of your business.'

'I need it. Just give it to me.'

Bhabini limply intoned, 'His name is Ramcharan Ghosh, son of Taracharan ...'

'And where do they live?'

Nabakumar scolded again, 'Oh, what a bother! What do you

need their address for? Are you going to write them a harsh letter
or what?'

'Of course not!' Satya gave a grim smirk, 'What good would that
do? They wouldn't break down with remorse, would they?'

'Then why?'

'I need it for something. Just give me the address.'

'The address ...' Bhabini answered reluctantly, 'Panchanantala,
Howrah. There's a banyan tree at the crossing.'

'I don't need all that.' Satya then turned to Nabakumar, 'Why
don't you sit here for a while, if you want to. I'll be off.'

Nabakumar began to fuss, 'What will I do here? Nitai isn't home
either. Why don't you sit and talk for a while instead?'

With that Nabakumar fled from the scene in a rush. As though
he was scared. Of course, he had always been scared of Satya. But
earlier, he had trusted her. And the last two years of living apart
had created in Nabakumar an insecurity that overwhelmed him.
He could hardly look at Satya without feeling overawed. He no
longer felt confident enough to grasp her hand when no one was
looking.

The strange look on Satya's face stayed for a while after
Nabakumar had left. Then, she asked slowly, 'Did the neighbours
say why they did it? Which of her faults had made them thirst for
her blood?'

Bhabini no longer reacted sharply to any of Satya's words.
Perhaps because she was no longer able to. In answer to Satya's
query, she rubbed her eyes with the end of her sari and said, 'Her
fault? It's a shameful thing to talk about. I couldn't bring myself
to mention it in your husband's presence. It was her fault that she
was small and scrawny—you yourself saw how thin she was the last
time she'd visited. And she remained like that even after she was
wedded and bedded! Just a slip of a girl, and second wife to her
husband; a sturdy and strapping young man, full of lust ever since
his first wife died. She wouldn't dare go near him. She didn't want
to, she'd resist. And I believe, mother and son would yell and
scream, punch her, kick her and push her. And Puti too was such
an idiot! Really, when you can see they're stronger than you, better

to give in, no? Instead, she resisted—she'd refuse to enter the bedroom. What good did it come to? The monster became furious—and men do get provoked by such things—he just lost his senses. And his mother was there of course, to lend a hand! What a combination! It was destined.'

'Destined indeed!' Satya retorted roughly, 'In any case, it is ill-fated to be born a girl in this country. We wear blinkers and blame fate for everything.'

The tearful Bhabini frowned, 'What do you mean by blinkers?'

'Nothing! But let me ask you—didn't you have a grinding stone at home? And couldn't your parents have smashed the heads of that pair? After all, they did not have to fear for their daughter's widowhood or humiliation any longer!'

Bhabini felt a trifle irritated, 'What utter nonsense! Do you think we'd get away with it? We'd have been arrested for sure. After all, nothing can be said against beating, butchering or killing the woman one is married to!'

'Well, that's what I'd have done. I'd have ground his head to powder. And after that, they could hang me,' Satya retorted fiercely.

Once again, Bhabini burst into tears, 'That's what my mother's been saying too! And she's been weeping away. But that's impossible, isn't it? An aunt of mine was, in fact, blaming my mother for bringing her up to be so delicate. Or else, how could she refuse to go to her husband's bed after marriage? After all, she could hardly expect him to treat her like a doll, could she? And other such mean things. But this aunt herself has a strapping twelve-year-old girl.'

Before she had finished Satya rose to leave, 'I'm sorry, but I can't stay any longer; my head is aching.'

Bhabini noted that Satya had not offered a single word of consolation. In her mind she said, 'How stone-hearted she is! My own heart bursts when I see others suffer. How differently we are made!'

FORTY SIX

Satya had come away complaining of a headache, but nobody had imagined that her complaint would turn into a raging fever. Not even Satya herself, when she had lain down to rest. When Saral noticed that she had not got up to cook, he came and discovered that her body was burning. And she was delirious.

The poor boy panicked and called his father. Not that his father had much self-confidence in such matters—because he would slap his forehead like a woman at such times. And sure enough, after one look, he wailed out, 'Go immediately and call your aunt!'

Sadu arrived and took charge of preliminary treatment by placing a wet cloth on Satya's forehead and warming her feet. And after cooking a bit of rice for them, left late at night. She had not stayed the night. It appeared that the youngest son of her co-wife would refuse to sleep if Sadu was not there. And besides, Mukherji-mashai needed about ten refills for his hookah through the night. But she left with the assurance that she would be back at dawn.

Satya remained unconscious. Nabakumar kept on fanning her.

Deep into the night, Satya opened her eyes and said, 'Listen, come here and touch me.'

Nabakumar shuddered in dismay—was this delirium, or an indication that the end was near?

'Come here and touch me.'

Nabakumar nervously touched her.

Satya said fiercely, 'You know what happens if you touch someone and swear, don't you? Remember that! Listen, should I die, promise me that you won't get Subarna married early. Come, promise me that!'

It had to be the raving of a fevered brain! It would only get worse if one disagreed. So Nabakumar hurriedly said, 'Yes, I swear.'

'Say it then—I shall not get Subarna married before she is sixteen!'

Sixteen! Till the girl turned sixteen! Keep her unmarried till that age! Nabakumar wondered why Satya had this sudden fever that brought on delirium. Whatever the reason, she had to be calmed.

Nabakumar replied hastily, 'All right. Rest assured that's what'll happen.'

'No, that's not enough!' Satya pushed herself upright, 'Say it out aloud: I shall not get Subarna married before she turns sixteen.'

It never harms to cheat the mad. And there are very few differences between a raving patient and a lunatic! So promptly removing his hand from Satya's body, Nabakumar recited, 'Here, I swear that I shall not marry her off without your consent.'

'But you haven't said the most important thing!' Satya shrieked. 'Don't trick me! Don't kill Subarna! She must live. A thousand Subarnas must live, don't you see!'

With that, she fell back onto the bed.

Nabakumar began to fan her vigorously. A thousand Subarnas! God, this was deep delirium! Why did god do this? Goddess Kali, if you let the night pass in peace, I shall wash your cleaver and bring her the water to drink! Nabakumar also called on the goddess of his village. And vowed that he would make offerings to Hari as well. What else could he do?

He had heard that if the blood rushes to the brain in a delirious state, a patient raves on and dies of a hyperactive brain. It was clear from the symptoms that such an end would be inevitable if the fever did not let up by dawn.

Possibly, Kali took pity. The fever abated even without the antidote he had vowed. The temperature dropped just before dawn. And the fever withdrew, leaving the sheets sopping wet with sweat.

Yet nobody could guess how the intensity of delirium returned five days after the fever had passed, and how blood at normal temperature could boil over! Nor the way in which its force propelled the mind into a waywardness akin to raving. Otherwise, whoever had heard of such an outrageous thing? Was it ever possible for a girl from a Bengali household to take such a shocking step?

Even Satya's devoted, ever-supportive sons were stunned by their mother's unimaginable daring. Sadhan went out by the back door and summoned Sadu and her husband, and a jittery Nabakumar blurted out to Saral, 'The shastras say that one shouldn't care for seemliness in times of trouble. Please go and call Master-mashai right away!'

'Master-mashai!' Saral was dumbstruck. He could not believe that his father was asking for Master-mashai. He who was never mentioned or faced, and because of whom even Suhashdi had become a stranger to this household.

Nabakumar attempted to cover up his unease with briskness. 'Yes, yes, that's what I'm telling you. Didn't I say that the shastras discourage seemliness when danger strikes! Go and tell him that I have requested him to come. Tell him it's really serious, the police are here. Perhaps, they'll arrest your mother, and when they hear ...'

Saral hardly waited to question his father about the arrest or the shastras; he slipped on a short kurta and walked out of the kitchen door at the back of the house.

Thank god there was another exit. For a gigantic and terrifying Sahib-policeman was sitting at the front door. And he was interrogating Satya, sitting on the chair that the trembling Nabakumar had provided.

That is right. He was questioning Satya. In a Bengali that was ridiculously mixed, in vocabulary and pronunciation, with English. And the stout-hearted Satya was standing motionless and responding to his questions.

Even the confident Mukherji-mashai had refused to come at first; finally, he had agreed because of Sadu's pleading. He arrived holding on to his sacred thread, chanting the name of the goddess; and of course, avoiding the front door, he had followed Sadu into the house through the back.

No sooner had they entered than Subarna had come running to her aunt, sobbing, 'Look Pishi! The White man has come to take away my mother!'

'Of course not! Goddess protect us! Why should they do that?' Lifting the girl up, Sadu had asked under her breath, 'What is the matter, Turu?'

Sadhan's timorous description of events could be summarized thus: Satyabati had written a letter to the police on her own, without consulting a soul, and signed her name on it too! And the police had come for an enquiry.

The reason for the letter was as strange as it was inconceivable. It had to do with the untimely and tragic death of Bhabini's sister. Satyabati had described in vivid language the brutal murder and made a spirited appeal for justice against the monstrous act and that the pair of murderers be properly punished. For their inability to do that would prove that all their attempts at opening courts in the name of justice were worthless indeed! Satyabati had informed them about the name and address of the guilty too.

On hearing this, Sadu gave a sigh, 'All this is an outcome of that delirium, the blood rose to her head and totally wrecked her brains! Or, how could a girl from a Bengali household ever take such a shocking step? Your mother will die of apoplexy one of these days, that I'm sure of. She's always been this sturdy man in female shape! And over and above that, she's now got this dreadful ailment.'

Sadhan grew a shade paler, 'Of course, it is an ailment! She's always suffered from it; wherever there is injustice, she behaves as though the injury is hers! She takes on the pain and sufferings of others as if they're her own—that's what her ailment is! One day, she sacked a maid on the spot just because she'd cursed her son saying, "Why don't you just die?"'

'Weird! She's always been weird! God has given her beauty and brains, and she just failed to put it to good use! And I believe the other day, when she was raving with fever, she asked your father to swear that he wouldn't get Subarna married before she turned twenty-five or some such thing!'

The pledge was utterly ridiculous of course, so Sadhan hardly stopped to worry about it. People said anything when they were delirious. But he too believed that his mother had truly been blessed with brains, if only she was less stubborn!

'Will you step out that way, Pishe-mashai?'

Mukherji was agitated by Sadhan's request and said, 'I'm an old man, why pick on me? I've just had a bath and I've not finished my puja. I can't have contact with that mlechcha now, can I?'

'No, no, you don't have to have contact …'

'What a silly boy you are! Even speaking is a form of contact! It's no small matter to touch with words! And besides, you've studied in college, you have learnt English.'

Of course, he had learnt. But this had nothing to do with his curriculum! This was not his Sahib-teacher! This was extremely disconcerting. And in such cases, it was best to send an elder. But the elder refused out of fear of another bath. He just kept peeping from time to time to watch Satya looking at the Sahib as she talked.

Yes, Satya was in full flow, saying, 'Just tell me why have you opened your courts of justice? In our country we used to kill our women by burning them on their husband's funeral pyre; you stopped that practice and saved us from that sin. But that's nothing! There are heaps of sins that have collected over centuries. If you can rid us of those, only then would I say that you deserve to be lawmakers. Why have you taken on the guise of a ruler in another's land? Why can't you just huddle into your ships and leave?'

'Ma!' Sadhan advanced to restrain his mother. He could see that the Sahib had lost track of the little Bengali he knew and was repeating, 'What? What?' Realizing that his learning was totally inadequate before this veritable flood of words, and lacking the confidence to be an interpreter, Sadhan attempted to restrain his mother.

But Satya seemed to have lost sense of her surroundings and situation, so she ignored the hint and continued, 'I believe that in your country women are respected and honoured. Can't you open your eyes and see the way in which women are tormented and disgraced in this country? Can't you make laws to stop all that? You pass new laws everyday—'

'Boro-bou!' Nabakumar could no longer contain himself; he yelled out. And just at that moment, Bhabatosh-master arrived with Saral in tow.

He had probably heard the last bit of Satya's fiery speech. So he addressed Satya in a calm manner, 'Bouma, you shouldn't nurture the hope that foreigners will remove our social ills with their laws. That's a task for us.'

She was surprised to see Bhabatosh, but the riddle became clear to her when she saw Saral with him. Drawing her sari over her head, she did a little namaskar and went inside.

On seeing Bhabatosh, Nabakumar physically experienced the sensation of 'getting a load off his chest'. Now he could just let go! He could just go inside and sit on the bed and fan himself.

But he had to wait for the Sahib and Bhabatosh to leave. After that, he would really settle the issue once and for all. He had tolerated things long enough. And Mukherji-mashai had just passed a comment about how wives of hen-pecked husbands were invariably like this! The words had been stinging him.

The Sahib and Bhabatosh hardly talked, the Sahib showed Satya's letter to him and after a while left with a 'Goodbye'. Bhabatosh walked him out and returned once again to the courtyard. And he spoke very calmly to Sadhan, 'Tell your mother that the Sahib has promised that they will find the culprit and bring him to book. And ...' Bhabatosh added with a smile, 'he offered his congratulations to your mother.'

Mukherji-mashai found his voice at last. He climbed on to the courtyard with his hookah and asked, 'Namaskar, I should greet you that way because after all, you were Nabakumar's teacher. But what did you say that the Sahib offered Sadhan's mother?'

'Congratulations. I mean, praise.'

'I see. For what reason?'

Bhabatosh looked at this uncouth, self-important man and said with a sardonic and bantering chuckle, 'That shouldn't be difficult to understand at all! They praised her boldness. After all, how many have the guts to protest against injustice?'

Mukherji made a face, 'True, not everybody has the nerve to go and set fire to other people's homes or hit other people on the head—that is courage of sorts! But I don't think that kind of courage needs praise.'

'What you think hardly matters in this case.' With that Bhabatosh made to leave. But he was not able to. For Nabakumar rushed out and requested, 'You can't leave, you must eat something.'

Perhaps the reason behind such a proposal was his gratitude towards his teacher for saving him, just like a god! But his teacher was unprepared for such a proposal. So he gave a start and perhaps wondered too, about the extent of Nabakumar's insolence.

Bhabatosh was no longer the young man who had once written a spirited letter to Ramkali describing to him his daughter's sufferings at her in-laws. A lot of time had passed. He had gone though many conflicts, faced much pain and had become older and wiser; so he did not come up with some vicious rejoinder. Instead, he gave a mild smile and said, 'Are you mad?'

'Why should I be mad?' Perhaps Nabakumar's insistence stemmed from his refusal to remain indebted, 'You've come in the scorching sun! And over and above that you saved your Bouma from humiliation. You think she'll let you go without feeding you?'

Bhabatosh gave another start. Perhaps he felt powerless to solve the puzzle, and he asked helplessly, 'What was that? Who did you mention?'

'Your Bouma!' Meanwhile, Nabakumar had managed to send Sadhan to the sweet shop with just a gesture, and therefore, he felt confident. And continued loudly, 'She's making you a cool drink with sugar.'

Nabakumar had thought that this hint itself would ensure the making of the cool drink. But Satyabati walked out and said in a firm voice, 'Master-mashai, it's best not to waste your time standing in the sun listening to a madman. Please go home.'

Bhabatosh gave Satya one straight look and then left quietly.

At that moment, Nabakumar did something totally bizarre. He slapped himself on both cheeks and said, 'You might as well come and beat me with a slipper! That'll complete it! That'll be the ultimate punishment for a hen-pecked husband.'

Everyone was present—Sadu, Mukherji-mashai, Saral and also Sadhan, who had entered that moment with the sweets. Did Satya notice them? Probably not. She walked silently into the kitchen and resumed the work she had earlier discarded in a disorderly rush.

Sadu exchanged a knowing look with her husband. Then Sadu sat Nabakumar down and began to fan him and talk to him in an undertone, 'What's the point in losing your temper? It's all clear as crystal now! She was always a bit of a nut and it's become worse. I didn't think god would punish you like this!'

It appeared that Sadu had lost the sharpness that was so much in evidence at her aunt's. She was now transformed into a housewife; her speech went with her status.

Nabakumar requested, 'Bring me some water, Sadudi!'

Sadu promptly brought him water and said, 'Here. Now pull yourself together and go fetch a doctor to treat her. You'll have to see to it that she doesn't get arrested or something!'

Perhaps Nabakumar regained his strength with the water, so he boldly declared, 'Of course, she isn't mad! It's nothing but mischief! Don't I know it? Her only pleasure is to humiliate me in front of others.'

Well, that is what the boys had begun to note, as they had grown older. As children they used to treat their mother's words as sacrosanct and feel sorry that their father was such a simpleton. But over the years, even if the pity for their father remained intact, the sympathy for their mother was beginning to diminish. This was particularly true of her older boy, and he began to reflect.

What was this? A fight at any opportunity! Always inviting trouble to disrupt family peace! And forever insulting Baba! It was so unfair.

What a fuss she had created with Suhash! Even so, there was some logic there. She did need to work out something. But where was the need for such trouble for Bhabini's sister who had died and turned into a ghost now! Why did she have to punish her husband and sons in the bargain? Would the dead return to life or what? Of course not! But Nabakumar and his sons would now face humiliation worse than death. The whole locality had noticed the Sahib-policeman walk into their house. They would be speculating the reason for the visit. And nobody could explain anything to them. Even if anyone did, nobody would believe it. After this, they would surely have to move house, or they would have to stuff their ears with cotton wool to shut out the taunts whenever they stepped out!

Perhaps their aunt was right. Mother really was unbalanced. Odd that a person with such intelligence and so many abilities should have such a warped mind.

He recalled the mother he knew as a child. What a bright and cheerful memory it was! At least her sons cherished a dazzling and happy image of Satya.

And there used to be so much of scheming and planning behind Nabakumar's back. And painting a picture of the future with so many hues! Satya's two boys would become very distinguished; one would devote himself to uprooting every form of injustice and inequity from the country, and the other would dedicate himself towards freeing the country from the colonial masters.

But first of all, they would have to be educated.

'You won't be able to do a thing if you're not educated, Turu. Nobody will listen to you. Besides, that's how you'll derive your sense of right and wrong. You shall become a judge, a magistrate, a doctor or a teacher. And be so upright and strong that people will say that you've become a worthy human being.'

This glowing picture would have an enchanting effect on his infant mind. But as he had become older, he had noticed that his mother's radiance had grown into a blaze.

And after her two years at Baruipur, she had changed considerably. Now he feared her more than he loved her.

The younger boy always felt more inspired by his mother. But he hated the shouting and the disruption. After all, one had to guard against becoming disfigured oneself, when dealing with the deformities of society.

It was true that what his mother had done for Bhabini's sister was courageous, but it was outrageous as well. At least, she could have consulted her sons! Besides, if Indians wanted to get rid of the Sahibs, why ask for their assistance whenever there was trouble? He would have asked her that if she were in a normal frame of mind. But she was upset now.

However, both her sons were mistaken. Satya was not upset at all.

She was just silent and still. And preoccupied with one thought —her sons had cowered on seeing the Sahib; they had not come out to talk or explain and organize their mother's statement, or offer their support. The same boys whose college education she had pledged her life for; the boys she had pinned all her hopes on!

Perhaps, she had hoped for too much. May be, she had been focussing on their qualifications rather than their age. And perhaps, that was the reason why she could not understand why this incident did not have an impact on them.

She was unable to fathom it. But the thought that Saral could go and call Master-mashai froze her blood. Hadn't he felt ashamed, even one bit? Her sons knew about it. For they had seen him leave this very house after being humiliated. It was possible of course, that Nabakumar would not hesitate to call him during a sudden crisis, but how could her own flesh and blood do such a shameless thing without a thought? Her son had brought her down a notch or two! And at a place where she used to have so much esteem! What could she do now? Was the path she had walked all her life a false one? There was nobody from whom she could demand an answer.

The cooking had been done already. Even so, she sat in silence in the kitchen, as though she could not garner the energy to call them for the meal.

Since Sadu had left, she could not pass on that responsibility to her either. After a long while, Subarna abandoned her games and ran in.

'Are we going to eat, or are we just going to sit and think?'

Subarna was not old enough to talk this way, but had become quite an expert after spending so much time with Elokeshi; nobody could guess that she was all of six or seven. But it would be wrong to blame only Elokeshi. Precocious speech and an abundance of words were, after all, Subarna's inheritance and birthright.

How could Satya forget that? Glowering, she fiercely reprimanded her daughter with, 'Don't talk like that!'

Subarna took one look at her mother and was alarmed. She quickly responded with, 'Well, I feel hungry.'

The fire in Satya's eyes softened a bit. She immediately said, 'I'm coming. Go set the places for your father and brothers.'

Yes, Subarna had learnt to set places and pour out water. And much else besides—making the bed, and quite neatly too. She knew how to help her mother clean the greens.

Among other things, Satya had also taught her daughter poetry. And spellings.

Subarna left. And staring after her Satya wondered if she should finally pin her hopes on this girl. Would she turn out to be like Suhash? Suhash, whom she had nurtured but whose growth she had not managed to enjoy.

Nobody is supposed to derive joy out of the girl child. But then, had Suhash's life not taken such a turn, Satya would not have been obliged to cut off all ties with her. She could have met her. And the various stages of her growth would have unfolded before Satya's eyes. Now Satya had no opportunity of seeing how Suhash ran her house.

But Subarna would blossom before Satya's eyes!

The boys were turning out to be congenitally timid. They would probably be dominated by their women. Just like their grandfather and father.

Despite his dissoluteness, Nilambar used to be in awe of his wife. And Nabakumar was the same, of course.

Satya embarked on a self-analysis—would she have been happy if he had not been obedient at all? Would she? Satya attempted to explore every corner of her mind. Would it have satisfied her had her husband been a man who could demolish Satya's arguments with logic of his own?

Nabakumar was not like that at all. He found any excuse to protest against his wife. But that was about all. He never did manage to take a stand. And Satya always won in the end.

Was winning the only path to happiness? Were there no joys for the loser? Satya had never had the chance to savour the joys of voluntary surrender. Well, perhaps Subarna would become outstanding and distinguished. It would please Satya to submit to her daughter. And to be able to say, 'Goodness! How clever you are! Where did you learn so much!' And to say, 'Subarna, you're my prize!'

When Subarna informed her father and her brothers that the meal was ready, they were so pleased—as though they had been handed the moon! They were relieved that the household had returned to its usual rhythm. They had been wondering if Satya had cooked at all.

It was dreadful when there were disturbances at the centre.

They felt gratified as they sat down to eat.

Nabakumar hardly remembered that he had vowed to settle the issue once and for all. He had lost all his confidence after slapping himself. All he could recall at this moment were Sadu's words: 'She is mad!'

That had to be right! Why else would she behave in this way? It would be best to cure it to whatever extent it was possible. He and his sons felt gratified about the meal.

Subarna began to talk like a proper mistress of the house, 'Why don't you take a little more rice, Baba?'

Nabakumar attempted to please Satya by obliging. And when they had finished their meal, Satya announced her plan.

She put it casually, 'I haven't really recovered after my illness, so I was thinking of visiting my father in Kashi. A change of air might do me good.'

To Nabakumar it appeared as though Satya had granted him a boon. Perhaps, a similar tune was playing in his mind too—that Satya should go away somewhere for a while. She would recover, and Nabakumar would find relief as well.

But how could he just ask her to leave? So he reacted slowly and cautiously, 'Kashi? To your father? How is that possible? He lives all by himself. How can you stay there?'

Satya answered in brief, 'We'll see about that. Sadhan, you will take me there, won't you?'

Satya had appealed to Sadhan, because he was her first-born. But in lieu of an answer, Sadhan found himself between a rock and a hard place. He thought it was sheer madness on his mother's part to propose that he take her to Kashi on his own.

Seeing that her son was perplexed, a delicate smile played on Satya's lips, and she said mildly, 'You don't look confident. Let it be.'

Any other time, Satya would have severely reprimanded her son. But today, that was all she said and started putting away things.

Nabakumar was not supposed to notice that faint smile, but he did. And for some unknown reason he experienced a stab of insult and as a result blurted out, 'Why Sadhan? Why can't I do it?'

He did not announce that he would accompany her, he put it as a question. This time, Satya baffled them completely by bursting into a familiar laugh, 'How funny! Did I say you can't? But since they've grown up, I can, of course, expect them to do their duty by their mother.'

'Grown-up heroes they are!' Nabakumar drew the conversation to a close with his sarcasm.

And he began to scheme in his mind. He feared that another storm would start up, but nothing happened. He was relieved of course, and amazed as well.

Had Satya suddenly changed?

But a storm did start up elsewhere. The very next day.

Subarna returned from school, put away her books and put her arms around her mother, 'Ma, do I have a sister?'

Before she answered her daughter, Satya scolded her, 'I just changed my sari, how could you come and touch me before changing out of your school uniform, eh?'

'Never mind!' Subarna took her mother's hand in hers, 'School isn't a dirty place, is it?'

Now that her fresh clothes had been polluted, there was no remedy. So Satya hugged her daughter lovingly and said, 'I didn't say that, did I? But there's so much dust and dirt outdoors. Never mind now, what was that about a sister?'

'Yes!' Subarna replied excitedly, 'We have a new female instructor at school, she's my sister!'

'Really, Subarna! Why do you talk so crudely? Haven't I told you not to say "female instructor"?'

'That's what Baba says,' Subarna retorted stubbornly.

'Let him!' Satya responded firmly, 'Children shouldn't talk like that. Do you call them "female instructors"?'

'Of course not! We call them "Didi". And the new Didi says she really is my sister!'

Satya asked in surprise, 'Who's she? What's her name?'

'Her name? She's Suhash Datta.* She's married, but she doesn't wear sindur like the Hindus. She's Brahmo, you see.'

Subarna responded like a mail train rushing past. Perhaps she would have continued in that manner, but Satya stopped her. She asked intensely, 'Suhash Datta! Are you sure?'

'Of course, I am! Everyone says so! And she's so beautiful. She asked me, "Did you know that I'm your sister?"'

Satya asked with bated breath, 'And what did you tell her?'

'I said, "If you are my sister, why don't you come home?" She said she can hardly find the time. But tell me, is she really my sister? Is she really your own daughter?'

Satya said agitatedly, 'Don't be silly! How can I have a daughter that age! But she's like a daughter to me.'

'But then, why did she say, "Your mother is my mother too"?'

'Really! Did she really say that?' Satya was suddenly overwhelmed, 'And what did you say?'

'I said I'd ask you.'

'You silly girl! You should've said ...'

But Satya was at a loss for words. She did not know what could be said under the circumstances. Even then she persisted, 'You should've said, "In that case, come home with me!" You're really silly!'

Subarna looked disconcerted, 'Well, that's what I thought I'd say. But I felt scared that you'd be annoyed.'

Satya drew her daughter closer and asked gloomily, 'You felt scared? Do I always get annoyed?'

---

*Translator's note: If Suhash was married to Bhabatosh Biswas, how could she become a 'Datta'; or as a child had she adopted the surname of the Datta family? I have not been able to resolve this from internal evidence.

Subarna was hardly affected by her mother's change of tone; she responded readily, as if grateful to be given a chance, 'Why shouldn't I feel scared? I'm forever stiff with fear! Baba too—and everyone else! My heart just stops beating when I look at your face. And "Do I always get annoyed?" she asks! When she's the great goddess of wrath!'

The goddess of wrath! Did Satya laugh aloud at the charming appellation her daughter had found for her? Did she not exclaim, 'And you, my dear, are the goddess of words!' But she did not. Instead, she suddenly lost her voice. As though she beheld her own image in the words of the child.

Goddess! Well, if that's what she was, she was just a neglected idol, abandoned under a tree, scorched and withered by the sun; graceless, unsightly, terrifying!

Was that how her family saw her? Not with affection, but fear? Then in what way was she any different from Elokeshi?

Was that the level to which she had elevated herself? And had she become like a leafless tree in autumn, sapless, lacking in tenderness? And suddenly, quite inexplicably, the emptiness inside tugged at her heart, and tears rolled out of the depths of those dark eyes framed by thick brows. Subarna looked on with discomfort. She had no doubts in her mind that her mother was pining for her elder daughter.

But Satya controlled herself almost immediately. Smiling through her tears, she asked, 'How does this Suhash Datta teach?'

Subarna said shyly, 'She doesn't teach us. She teaches in the higher classes.'

So Suhash taught the higher classes! That was the height which Shankari's illegitimate child had reached! Was it her learning or her daring that had enabled her to get that far? Had Shankari the same strength, she would not have hanged herself!

Should Satya line her daughter's path of progress with the thorns of conflicts that were there in her mind? Should she go to Kashi to refresh herself, abandoning this child to the care of her father and brothers? Just to regain her own strength? Could that not be achieved by staying here? Did she not have that confidence in herself? Could she not regain her earlier form if she tried? Bring back the Satya who could laugh and tease, and cook new dishes for her husband and children. Even a few days ago, Satya had taught her daughter so many shlokas, and helped with her schoolwork.

It was as though Satya had neglected her home for days. And all this while she had looked outward, even though her eyes felt strained from the effort. Could it be that her younger son was right when he said, 'There are millions of wrongs in the world, just as there are millions of people. Your eyes will go blind if you try to look at all of them. Isn't it enough to see that you don't do wrong yourself?'

Had he been right, then?

Satya was lucky that Nabakumar did not share her idealism. But perhaps, it would be wrong to even expect that of him. For even one's own flesh and blood were hardly shaped by one's ideals. The older boy was turning out to be just like his father!

Supposing Satya's life had been extraordinary and different instead! Like Suhash's life or Shankari's! Satya shuddered at the thought and invoked the goddess.

All of a sudden, in her mind's eye, she saw Bhubaneswari's face. Her soft, timid face, framed by her sari, and a large red bindi on her forehead. Bhubaneswari had never bothered with the injustices of the world, nor fought against such things. She had held everyone in awe, and loved them all.

Yet, when Satya imagined her father's face, she felt a stab of hurt. As though he were connected in some unjust way with her mother's untimely death. She recalled how her mother had never had the courage to speak out against her husband, ever. Satya thought ruefully that she as Bhubaneswari's daughter was making up for all that now. Should Satya give her life a new turn? And burn brightly inside her domestic space? And try to be happy?

Drawing her daughter close to her, Satya buried her face in her hair and asked, 'Will you cry when I go off to Kashi?'

'When you go off!' Subarna sprang out of her mother's loving embrace and exclaimed, 'Am I not coming too?'

'You!' Satya was aghast, 'How can you come?'

'With you, of course! Or who else will come with you?'

'Listen to that! How can you come? You have school. I don't have to miss school, do I?'

Subarna said stubbornly, 'What does it matter if I miss school? Baba says that little girls are allowed to miss school.'

'Really? Wonderful! But I don't think it's a good thing to miss school. That won't do.'

'We'll see if it does or not!' Subarna said intensely, 'Just see what I do, if you leave me!'

Satya decided not to be annoyed by this. So she laughed and said, 'If I leave, how can I see what you do! Let me just cancel the trip instead, just to see what you do!'

'Oh, Ma!' Subarna said as she hugged her mother and rubbed her face on her shoulder, 'You're such a darling!'

Nabakumar arrived just at that moment of closeness, with a tall, north Indian man in tow. From his appearance it was not difficult to make out that he was a brahmin priest. This was Nabakumar's scheme. He had heard a few days ago, that about sixteen women relatives of a colleague at his office, had gone on pilgrimage to Gaya, Kashi and Mathura accompanied by this brahmin priest. Therefore, he had brought him home.

Satyabati covered her head with her sari, wrapped the end around her neck and did a namaskar from far. And Nabakumar announced in a high-pitched tone, 'Look! I brought him with me. He's really well-known—Ramesh Panda. He is going to accompany my friend's mother to Kashi, so I asked if you could go with them. He will take you to your father's address. He is willing. They'll leave the next full-moon night.'

The sari covering Satya's face did not move, but her voice rang out clearly, 'You just put him through trouble for nothing! I'm not going now.'

'What? You're not going now?'

'No.'

Nabakumar said a trifle heatedly, 'Well, we may not find him the next time you feel like going.'

'I know that,' Satya said mildly. 'You'll have to take the trouble then.'

'That's clever! You could have said that earlier. I wouldn't have bothered. I'm sorry I troubled you, she won't go.'

The priest, of course, was not one to give up easily; he spent a lot of energy in describing the glories of Kashi. But Satya said humbly, 'I can see that the lord of Kashi hasn't called me yet. When his summons comes, I shan't be able to ignore it.'

Nabakumar asked huffily, 'And why did you change your mind so suddenly?'

Satya again said calmly, 'Subarna won't let me go, she wants to come along and she'll miss school if she does.'

Nabakumar was the one who would always complain about separation, so nobody could figure out why he began on this contrary note. He should have been relieved that Satya was not going away, so why did he get into such a pique instead? Well, Nabakumar had a mind too, and there was a certain logic to its working. He had managed to get himself used to the idea that Satya was going to be away in Kashi, and he was going to bring his mother to Calcutta for that interim period.

The last thought was fairly recent and had consolidated itself as a consequence of the gibes of a colleague. His colleague had been amazed to hear that his mother had never visited Calcutta. He had sneered at Nabakumar and called him 'hen-pecked'. Since then, the thought had been tossing about inside his head. He had also realized that it would be best to invite his mother separately, not as a help for his wife. And besides, he had other plans too.

He intended to indulge in activities that Satya disapproved of and he, for his part, considered innocent. And those would remain out of bounds if Satya cancelled her trip. For instance, smoking a hookah. Everybody in this whole wide world smoked one, but Satya's husband was not allowed to. What a bother! It would be a good idea to get properly hooked on to it in her absence, and later, he could say that the doctor had advised him to continue or his stomach would start acting up. That would establish it permanently. Nabakumar craved deeply for this drug.

There was another thing too. To gamble at cards. So many had made a fortune that way, just sitting and resting their backs against bolsters. But there was a sword balanced right above Nabakumar's head in the form of his oath to Satya.

Naturally, anyone would feel smothered with so many obstacles and barriers.

When Satya was away at Baruipur, Nabakumar had lived an unfettered existence. But what stopped him from fulfilling his desires then? There was a psychological reason for that as well. His feelings were different then. The pain of separation would resonate within him and he felt reluctant to do anything that would displease Satya.

But his feelings had changed since then. Ever since that incident with the police, Nabakumar could see that Satya was becoming more difficult, day by day.

Now he could see that he had never had freedom although he was a man. He had always been yoked to the dread of Satya's likes and dislikes, her preferences, her displeasures. Nobody else seemed to be in bondage like him!

Take Mukherji-mashai, for instance. He made so many demands, and how he raved and ranted! And despite beginning her domestic life so late, Sadu would tolerate it all, and indulge him further! People thronged to his place to play cards. And Sadu would make stacks of paan for the gathering without a word of protest. Could Nabakumar ever envisage such a scenario? Not on his life!

That was the reason this desire to be free had raised its head. He had hoped to start such habits in her absence and thus register his protest, but Satya had dashed such hopes to the ground. And the reason being offered was that Subarna would miss school! Could there be a reason more aggravating than that?

Nabakumar gave vent to his resentment once more after the priest had left. He claimed that he could hardly hope to face his friend after this. And that he would be plagued with taunts. To which Satya smiled and said, 'If you know how to brush them off, it wouldn't matter!'

That was when Nabakumar had raised the real issue, 'And I ask you, what is the point in over-educating this girl, eh? She'll be ten times grander than you, isn't it? If the mother has such a temper after studying in a village, I can foretell how the daughter will turn out, educated at a fashionable city school and all!'

Satya smiled unprovoked, 'I didn't know you had the power of foretelling! What else can you see? Tell me, when will I die?'

'Don't dismiss everything as a joke!' With that Nabakumar left.

The animosity had persisted. If Satya had vowed that she would cease to be the goddess of wrath, her husband had resolved to the contrary. Perhaps this animosity would have continued indefinitely had not an unexpected event happened. In the evening, Sadu came with a match-maker. She almost came prancing in.

'Want to get your sons married?'

Satya was not too surprised. She had always dreaded such an attack. Who knows when this topic would come up for discussion! So she responded cautiously, 'Once they complete their education.'

Sadu said with some irritation, 'Who knows when that will be! I can't really trust them to finish their education, ever! They're well past the marriageable age. The older one has passed three exams, and before he could get his breath back you sent him off to study law. And who knows what you'll make the younger boy do after he passes the third exam! So will your boys marry when their hair turns gray or what?'

Satya gave a mild smile, 'I can see you're really cut up. But tell me, is it fair to marry them off before they start earning a living?'

Sadu was astonished. And she said scornfully, 'Would Nabakumar lack the means to feed his family if his sons married before they found work?' And she added, 'What kind of depraved talk is this, Satya? After all, you're a mother yourself!' Finally, she said forcefully, 'Give up your Memsahib ways now! Look, here is the match-maker, listen to her. She has details about two girls from good families—they'll bring good dowries. The girls are pretty. Get them married together. And think of your old mother-in-law! It'll be like a dream come true for her!'

Nabakumar could no longer bear to be inside the house. He came out to the courtyard and thundered, 'The world would come to a standstill if one had to ask consent from lunatics! Ask the match-maker to describe the girls. We shall consider.'

Satya had resolved that she would no longer be the goddess of wrath. So she smiled and drew her sari over her head and said in an undertone, 'That settles it then! The master of the house himself has taken charge!'

It would not be seemly to converse openly with each other in front of Sadu, therefore they both addressed Sadu.

Nabakumar retorted, 'This isn't a joke, Sadudi. I shall get the sons married soon. They're well past the marriageable age now. And Sadudi, ask her, when have her overgrown hulks earned any money? And whose fault was that, may I ask? It's their mother who stopped them from working! No matter how many times I brought news of jobs, she pushed it aside without a thought. Her sons are going to become lawyers, barristers and magistrates—don't you see?'

Sadu said in a tone of truce, 'And why shouldn't they, Naba? If they're lucky, they will! After all, such things happen through human effort—they don't drop from the skies! But where's the conflict with marriage? Shall I talk to the match-maker, then, Satya?'

Satya said with apathy, 'What can I say, when you've made up your minds.'

'You're the mother; of course you should have your say!'

Satya raised her face, 'In that case, I'd say let them finish their exams.'

The match-maker rasped, 'Why? Do you think your daughter-in-law will come and tear pages off your son's books or what? I don't recommend just any old family! I'm talking about the Mukherjis of Ghatal—they're real aristocrats. The women in their house have never stepped out of their house at all! The girl is related to this family.'

They never stepped out of their house!

Satya gave a laugh, 'Sadudi, tell the match-maker that in that case, we're not equal to them—I'm sure they'll find other boys for their girl. I really want a girl who has stepped out of the house.'

They were startled by this. 'What do you mean?' they asked.

'Let me put it clearly. I want a girl who can read and write. If you know of a girl who goes to school ...'

'What was that?' Nabakumar sprang up, 'It's not enough that you're making a pundit of your daughter. You want a learned daughter-in-law too! Do you want her to come and teach your son, eh?'

The match-maker gave an impish smile, 'That she would, of course! All men who are successful, learn from their wives these days! The wife is the tutor nowadays. And her teachings have to be honoured. But I don't have news of such a girl. What I have is an old aristocratic family going back to the time of the nawabs. They have a different kind of learning. Well, if there's nothing I can do, I'll be off!'

Sadu left with her too. She did not live far, but she had to be accompanied by someone after dark. And if she did not leave then, Nabakumar's sons would have to walk her home.

Nabakumar exploded as soon as they had left, 'What do you want to turn this house into, eh? The dwelling of learned millions! Isn't it enough that the sons are educated?'

Satya said softly, 'Why shout unnecessarily? The boys are studying, and your voice can be heard upstairs. But let me tell you—if you want to know my opinion—I don't want a blind daughter-in-law.'

'A blind daughter-in-law! What do you mean?' Nabakumar was stupefied.

Satya replied firmly, 'How else can I put it? When you can't read the alphabet, you're as good as blind. Because you have eyes, but cannot see.'

A tornado blew through the house following Satya's verdict. Fury as well as laughter! Nabakumar announced Satya's interpretation of blindness to everybody. Nitai and his wife, Mukherji-mashai and his younger wife, who had just recovered, and his elder daughter were totally engrossed in jokes and quips about this new interpretation.

Only Sadu felt numb. And at one point, she gave a sigh and

said, 'I don't think she's wrong, Naba. Had I learning enough to write a letter, I needn't have wasted my life away!'

And finally, Sadu reassured them that it would not be impossible to find a school-going girl. 'We'll find a different match-maker.' Indicating that she was taking charge of the matter. Because the ship could not set sail without a captain! Her reassurance reached Turu's ears too. And indeed, he began to dream and to hope. Because all his classmates were married; a few had children too. He had at times wondered why there had been no mention of his marriage.

But the younger boy said something very audacious. He said it to his aunt, 'Find a bride for my brother if you must, don't drag me into such matters. I'll have none it!'

'Why? Are you planning to turn into a sanyasi or what?' Sadu had blasted out.

The boy had replied with a laugh, 'I don't know what I'll turn into—a frog or a snake perhaps! But this much I've learnt from what I've seen, it's impossible to achieve anything if you have to drag around a burden on your shoulders.'

'And where did you see all that, I'd like to know? Your face is forever buried in your books.'

'But I managed to see it all the same!'

Anyway, Sadu decided to pay no heed. To her mind, there was no need to rush. There were just the two boys, and they could afford to splurge on both occasions. Once his brother had a pretty bride, all this desire to become an ascetic sanyasi would vanish.

Therefore, Sadu devoted herself to hunting out a pretty bride. But the boy was quite old—he was nearly twenty-three, and a suitable girl would have to be twelve at least. And it was almost impossible to find a pretty girl of that age! Because all the pretty girls were married off early. Nevertheless, Sadu worked hard.

Hard work can make the impossible happen; devotion, they say, moves the gods. After rejecting various girls, a bride was found for Turu. She was twelve, pretty, and knew how to read and write, having gone to school for three whole years.

Satya could no longer object. She agreed. Moreover, she had

guessed what her son wanted. The objection, however, came from elsewhere—from Elokeshi.

It is a well-known practice to get the first-born son married off from the ancestral home. So Nabakumar took ten days of leave from office and went to the village. He took Subarna along. In fact, Subarna demanded that he take her because her summer holidays had started.

Satya had been a little reluctant to let her daughter out of her sight for such a long period. Besides, if she was allowed to take off now, all that she had learnt would fly out the window. Ten days would rush past and the distraction of her brother's wedding would follow. But it was difficult to refuse.

Perhaps, Nabakumar would burst out, 'You're so possessive, you won't even let her see her grandmother!'

So she had said to her daughter with a smile, 'Go ahead. Feed yourself on the mangoes and grow fat. But remember, you'll have to work hard for your brother's wedding!'

Nabakumar had said, 'Listen, don't pack your daughter's ghagras for the trip. Pack just the saris she has.'

Satya had seen it as an appropriate suggestion. Elokeshi would create hell if she saw her granddaughter in a ghagra. So Subarna left enthusiastically, taking her saris with her, and wearing an old turquoise Jamdani sari that belonged to Satya. And that, I guess, spelt her 'ruin'!

Disaster started as soon as she entered the house. On beholding her sari-wrapped granddaughter, Elokeshi exclaimed excitedly, 'Here you are making arrangements for your son's wedding. Does anyone do that when there's a hulk of a girl at home?'

There was a woman who sat radiant in the midst of that gathering, and Nabakumar tried in vain to put a name to her face. She too voiced the same concern, 'How awful, and such an old girl too! And Naba is thinking of getting his son married!'

Elokeshi then held forth with some intensity on her daughter-in-law's whimsicality and her son's meekness, 'I tell you, Mukta, this family will suffer in hell because of his wife's lack of sense!'

Nabakumar tried to explain in a low voice, 'The girl isn't old at all, she is just eight. She's tall like her mother, that's all! The boys, have really grown up, though.'

His words, however, hardly stood to reason before the fierce assertions of the two women. They exclaimed, 'How can this girl be only eight! Are we fools or what?'

Strangely, Elokeshi seemed not to remember the date of birth of her own granddaughter! And she refused, at the same time, to believe that her grandson was twenty-three!

After a while, Nabakumar realized that the woman was none other than Elokeshi's friend's daughter, Muktakeshi. She was visiting her mother in the village, for a few days.

Poor Subarna had hoped to climb up the guava tree, run to the pond, roam about and pluck flowers. Instead, she was faced with this discussion! She stood there, bewildered.

Finally, Elokeshi declared, 'Go get your son married if you want to, but look around and quickly find a groom for your daughter. And get it over with at one go. So that people don't pass comments about this hulk of a girl being unmarried yet.'

Muktakeshi enthused, 'Don't worry at all! There'll be no scarcity of grooms for this beauty. You'll find a willing groom right away. I'll start looking.'

There was a sudden stroke of lightning.

Subarna abruptly exclaimed, 'As if you can marry me off like that! My mother will just kill my father. Just when I've gone on to the next class—'

Her words remained unfinished.

A fierce, shrill wail lashed at the girl like a tempest.

'What did you say? Your mother will kill your father! I say Naba, why didn't I die before such words entered my ears! Is this the learning she's acquired at school? Oh, Mukta, fetch some water and pour it on my head—for I feel it will burst! Just look! My one and only son is in the hands of some upcountry witch!'

Hearing his mother's lamentations, a helpless Nabakumar, finding himself incapable of any other response, gave his daughter a resounding slap.

FORTY SEVEN

Satya had not really been mentally prepared for her son's wedding, but once she had accepted the idea, she felt light and cheerful. It amused her to watch her son—his abashed attempts at concealing his joy. She would deliberately mention small details about the wedding and smile to herself as she watched his response.

She had suddenly shed the burden of age that she had gathered. Those dull and bitter days of her recent past lay buried, a sweet amusement animated her face during the day and filled her musings at night. As she went about making arrangements for the wedding, she wondered if on the wedding night she would find somebody to eavesdrop on the newly-weds. Such a task would be forbidden to her—given her relationship as mother. Even so, she did spend some time thinking about the possibility of drilling a hole on a door or window in the bedroom at the Baruipur house. Then surely somebody could use it appropriately! Folks from her father's side would come too—the thought excited and pleased her. If her first-born were a girl—which she had been, though she had not survived—she would have been married and Satya would have been a mother-in-law by now.

But things had not turned out that way. Satya had gotten on in years, and this was going to be the first significant ceremony of her life. And it was going to be a son's wedding too, a ceremony that had little to do with the disposal of a burdensome daughter! It was natural that Satya would want to invite every member of her father's household. She had decided not to pay heed to any objection.

And precisely at this point in time Nabakumar had chosen to be away. Otherwise Satya would have made him write to them right away. Long before the date and time of the ceremony was fixed, a letter had to be written, informing kith and kin about the family the boy was to be married to, so that they could make preparations to come and stay for a week at least.

Sharada would have to come, of course, but it would not be right to leave out the elder brother's second wife. Rashu's brothers had got married, so they would have to be invited as well. Natun-thakurma was still alive, and so was her husband. She could sit and itemize the ceremonies for the married women. Satya thought about her mother and let out a small sigh. She had been much younger than all the rest, and yet, they had lost her ages ago. If only she were alive now!

After a moment's silence, Satya resumed her list of tasks. She felt a trifle ashamed about not knowing the exact number of children each cousin on her father's side had. So she would have to compose her letter with a skill that would not give away her ignorance.

Finally, she discovered that there was just one person who could have a close, friendly relationship with her son, Turu—the wife of Rashu's son's friend! That was a wedding Rashu had begged her to attend. But she had been in such a sorry state then, right after Subarna's birth. She had been weak and could hardly move from her bed, she had not trusted herself to go to a wedding. She had not felt too eager either. Rashu and his wife had been understanding about it. They were both very fond of Satya.

Skipping from one thought to another, Satya suddenly laughed to herself as she recalled something quite unrelated. She thought about her prank of latching the door of Sharada's room. What a fool she used to be! And during her first pregnancy, when Satya had stayed at her father's for a long time, Sharada had brought it up and joked about it. At that point, Sharada had stopped taking the gap in their ages into account; she would treat her as an equal. Satya would listen to stories about life in the family, raise questions, and at times, protest. Sharada would say, 'All right then! Let's see how long this untamed, headstrong nature of yours survives. Life is a grindmill that crushes everything together.'

Satya often wondered if indeed life had managed to crush her.

At this moment, however, she was feeling light-hearted and such thoughts hardly weighed too heavily on her. She recalled her father's wonderful household at Nityanandapur, where her father no longer lived. What did it look like now? And she ruefully tried to guess at Neru's whereabouts. He who had appeared so fleetingly, had stolen their hearts and disappeared! Nobody could have supposed that the naive boy who used to play truant from school so often, had a heart so capricious and restless.

Satya would occasionally write to Rashu for news. Usually after long intervals, especially when she missed them. Rashu always wrote short responses, but he would give her all the news.

Ramkali would never reply to her letters. Just once, he had written, 'Don't feel hurt if you do not hear from me.' But he had not explained why that should be so. Satya had surmised that he had made up his mind to free himself of all ties and therefore did not to wish to respond.

Even so, she intended writing to him at some point to come and bless them. She would plead that the wedding would be a waste without his blessings.

The occasion of her son's wedding had brought to the surface, currents that lay deep down in the ocean of Satya's heart. Feelings that had been long buried under dusty layers, now intensified and resonated within her.

The most cherished and valuable fact of her close friendship with Punyi had slipped her mind entirely! It had been ages since they had met. Punyi lived close by, at her in-laws place in Srirampur. It would not take too long to get there by boat, even though it would have taken a while to get to the boat. But Satya had never considered visiting her, nor, for that matter had Punyi. For Satya, visiting Punyi at her in-laws' house would have been inappropriate without a formal invitation. But it would not have been inappropriate for Punyi to visit Satya's house in Calcutta! She could easily have done that using the excuse of visiting the Kali temple.

It was true that life pulverized each and everyone, especially women. It crushed out the sweetness, the tenderness, the inner core, blunting the edges, wearing it out and reducing it to dry dust. Or else, how could it be that Satya had not found the time to meet her even after Punyi had been widowed? But she decided now that she had to make arrangements, to bring Punyi to Turu's wedding.

That instant, her mind turned restless, and she took pen and paper and began a letter to Punyi. She addressed her respectfully, she was an aunt after all. Then, informing her of Turu's wedding, she begged her to make arrangements to come with her son, her daughter-in-law and daughters. Once Punyi confirmed, Satya would send somebody to fetch them. She would have to arrange that, of course, otherwise relatives who lived far away could not be expected to come. Social duties took precedence over friendship in such matters.

But she could not really post the letter even though she had completed it. It would not be right to act the boss and post it without showing it to Nabakumar. Despite all her daring, Satya never overstepped these domestic codes. It was only proper that the main invitation to the Nityanandapur family be written by Nabakumar, even if Satya wrote all the details separately. Though she would send a general letter inviting everyone, Satya also made a list of people who had to be specially requested. It was best to write such things down, for there would be no end to the embarrassment if someone were excluded!

Nabakumar's side of the family was not very large—a distant aunt and a few cousins. Satya had not heard of anyone else. And there was her mother-in-law's best friend, who Satya had seen a couple of times. During Durga puja and for other festivals they would send her a sari. Apart from that, Elokeshi would concentrate mainly on her neighbours.

Of late, there had been a largish addition—Sadu's family. Sadu's household could hardly be called small. But one could not let that become a stumbling block, because a son's wedding was no small matter either!

Satya thought back on her own childhood. Each and every ceremony used to be a massive festival. Not just weddings, or rice ceremonies or sacred-thread ceremonies—even her grandmother's anantachaturdashi brata, which was a vegetarian affair, would have puris and sweets on the menu. And such wonderful confectioners! There would be a mela of workers around the chullahs. Perhaps to compensate for the lack of fish in the fare, Ramkali would create a real flood of milk products; there would be a mountain of sweets!

Such were the scenes that floated up before Satya's eyes whenever she thought of a ceremony. And whenever she thought of festivals, she would always remember that time in her childhood. Therefore, she could hardly be satisfied with anything small.

She had once tried raising this issue with Nabakumar, but he had rolled his eyes and said, 'It isn't the money I'm worried about. God be thanked that I have no worries on that front. But who will take charge? We don't have enough people to help. As they say, you have to have strength on all three fronts—mind, money and people. We don't have that.'

Satya had been prepared for such discouragement and so she promptly retorted, 'The strength of money attracts people, and a strong mind controls them both. You may lack the last, but I have it.'

'You always talk big! How can you plan a huge affair and risk becoming a laughing stock?'

Satya had said firmly, 'Why should I become a laughing stock? I've learnt from what I've always seen.' Satya could hardly think negatively. She was determined not to mess things up.

Of course, the more convenient thing would be to have the wedding ceremony in Calcutta. After all, the most impossible items could be procured here if one had the means. But she had to firmly banish thoughts of convenience and contentment. Getting her eldest son married from a rented house would hardly be viewed as appropriate—the village home was the most suitable for such things. Other places hardly had the sanctity required for the rituals for dead ancestors that had to be performed before a marriage ceremony. Therefore, Satya had focussed all her thoughts and painted all her pictures around the village house. In such matters, her prime friend, philosopher and helper was her younger son, Saral.

It was convenient that the summer holidays had begun. Satya could call out at any time, 'Khoka, bring pen and paper. I've just thought of something, write it down now, or I'll forget.'

Saral would laugh, 'As if you ever forget! The refrain that your eldest boy is getting married is chugging like an engine inside your head!'

Satya would laugh too, 'Feeling jealous, are you? Don't worry, when you marry, there'll be a steamship inside my head!'

'Namaskar, Ma! One look at your face and all such desires fly away!'

That was how Saral talked. He was hardly the person to tremble fearfully before elders. He would quite freely joke behind Nabakumar's back and say, 'The head of the household has spoken! And his responsibilities are over!'

Satya would conceal a smile and say, 'You naughty boy! Isn't he an elder?'

Saral would feign alarm and say, 'How awesome! But when have I ever displayed any doubts about the fact? I just find it hard not to laugh at something funny.'

Saral would always find something or the other to chat with his mother. He would sit on a stool in the kitchen, drumming on any utensil that was at hand, and chatter away, 'You know, Ma, there's a strange car these days. It's looks just as bizarre as its name, it's called a tram-car. A pair of horses pull it along. And the other day, a huge crowd gathered around to see that. People were thronging on both sides of the road …'

Or he would say, 'You know, Ma, I had such a fight with a friend! We were chatting near Hedua. He said, "Bengalis won't get anywhere! They're a bunch of frauds and fads!" So I told him off!'

Satya would eagerly ask, 'What did you say?'

Saral would answer with an embarrassed laugh, 'What else? I said, "Aren't you ashamed of sniggering at your own people instead of trying to rid your race of its flaws? Go hang yourself or jump into the Hedua Lake!"'

Saral would usually sit with her when she cooked in the evenings. Those were happy moments for Satya.

Sadhan had always been different. Quiet, subdued and shy. Besides, he was scholarly. It would never strike him to come into the kitchen for a chat. And he was incapable of helping in the kitchen. But Saral would always help; in fact, he had made himself indispensable!

At this moment too the prelude sounded familiar, although the tone was very different.

Saral asked, 'I've heard it said when Baba married, he wore a velvet outfit and cap. What will Dada wear?'

Satya charged at him, 'Really, you cheeky boy! As if you went and saw what your father wore at his wedding!'

Saral replied, 'I said at the outset that "I've heard it said".'

'Heard? From whom may I ask?'

'Why, from Pishi, of course! I've heard all about your childhood and Baba's from Pishi!'

'I see!' Satya asked with a laugh, 'Tell me, what should Turu wear for his wedding—what do you think would suit him?'

'How do I know? And as if anyone would listen to me if I did! Even if you don't make him wear a choga, there's no escaping that piece of purple silk on the shoulder. It's awful how one has to dress like a clown in order to get married!'

'All right, we don't need your comments!' Satya said reproaching him. 'Instead, let's hear you read out the list of sweets. Hope you've made a separate estimate of the sweets that will be offered with the chyada?'

The confectioners who would make the sweets would be hired from Calcutta. Satya had sent Saral to finalize things with them. Saral kept track of everything, and so he had been sent on this errand. It hardly mattered whether Sadhan was home or not. And because Nabakumar and Subarna were both away, the emptiness of the afternoon suddenly affected Satya. So far she had coped with Subarna's absence by busying herself with the planning and listing of chores. Otherwise, she would find it difficult to cope with the void that the absence of that chatterbox had produced.

Nabakumar had stretched his ten-day visit to nearly a fortnight. And the wedding was fast approaching. As always, he was being irresponsible!

At the moment though, she was free of the small chores—Nitai's wife had volunteered to slice the betel-nuts, Sadu said she would make the lentil boris in small batches. Sadu's co-wife would make the wicks for the lamps. Everyone was excited. Besides, proper social etiquette also demanded that everyone be asked to help; to act in any other way would be considered objectionable. The bride's house was not too far away. They would often call on them about the details of the ceremony.

Of all times, Nabakumar had to choose such a time to be away! A feeling of desolation gripped Satya and a sense of lack and hurt suddenly reared its head.

She decided to organize her son's room without further delay. After the wedding at Baruipur, her daughter-in-law would live here in this house. Since the girl was old enough, Satya did not intend to wait a year to bring her home. Nowadays, there was a trend of bringing the bride home right after the main ceremonies were over—that was what she had noticed among her neighbours in Calcutta. The bride and groom were made to visit the bride's place within eight days of the wedding and after the visit, the bride was welcomed into the house with an arati. After that, there was no need to wait for the stipulated one-year period to bring the bride to live in the house. That was just what Satya intended to do. She had gathered that her son desired a wife! So the bride would have to be brought home as soon as possible. On that thought, she began to organize the rooms.

There were two rooms upstairs. Sadhan and Saral shared one, and the other was crammed with various household items. Downstairs, Satya shared her bed with Subarna, and Nabakumar slept on the other one. The single-storey house they used to share with Suhash had been far less spacious. It had fewer rooms and Nabakumar's needs could not be attended to. So Satya had arranged things differently here. Since he had gotten on in years, it would not do to let him sleep alone. The boys stayed up studying most nights, it would hardly suit Nabakumar to sleep in their room. Hence this had been her arrangement, which would have to change now.

Now, she would clear the spare room and move in there with Subarna. She would have to transfer Saral downstairs to share the room with Nabakumar. There was no other way. Etiquette demanded that she stop sharing a room with her husband once her daughter-in-law arrived. At least, that was how Satya saw it.

The room that the boys shared was well-organized already. The walls were adorned with pictures of gods and goddesses and great leaders, and the shelves were lined with books. There was a desk with pen, ink and paper in one corner, two stools, and a large bed.

As she rearranged things, Satya smiled to herself; the bachelor would now become a married man! The thought thrilled her. She tried to guess, with an almost childlike glee, the way in which her reserved boy would talk to his wife, or how he would display affection.

Truly, it was such a wonderful thing to marry after one had come of age! How strange it used to be in Satya's time! Any mention of the groom would bring on an attack of fever and nervousness! Of course, when Satya had arrived at her in-laws, she had not shared a room with her husband right away. And when she had, she was not very mature either. Indeed, she had no idea about marriage at all! How shameful! In her times, child marriages seemed to offer grown-ups the pleasure of playing with dolls.

And each ceremony held out a bait: 'gauri-daana', 'kanya-daana', 'prithvi-daana'. It was the same as readying the girl for a sacrifice much before she developed any understanding!

But how many girls were as self-willed as Satya? Most of them were timid and wracked by guilt.

Satya smiled again. Who knew what she would have done if her husband had been a different kind of man. But the mind can never beguile itself; she could hardly deny that deep inside she felt nothing but disdain for him. And yet, on this sizzling summer afternoon, her heart suddenly yearned inordinately for the husband she would scorn. Had Nabakumar been happy in his marriage? She felt a little guilty at the thought.

If only she were an 'ordinary' girl engrossed in domesticity, Nabakumar would, undoubtedly, have been contented.

At this moment, however, Satya was making arrangements to seize his only bliss! It was just a small pleasure—if they shared a room, they could have chatted at night. If Satya was in a good mood, Nabakumar could talk to her about his office and his colleagues. Now he would be denied that pleasure too.

She would be hard put to explain to him why it was bad etiquette to share a room with him after the daughter-in-law arrived. Elokeshi had shared the room with her husband till his dying day. Perhaps because she had felt the need to flaunt the treasure which had not been hers in the first place. Of course, there were many other examples. It would not be right to condemn only Elokeshi. It was not unusual for a nephew to be older than his uncle. It was not unusual for the youngest son of a family to grow up with hand-me-downs from a grandson! Satya knew that. But she looked on such things with deep disgust.

Inspite of that, the thought of moving her bed upstairs made her miss Nabakumar with a sudden intensity. Anyway, it was best to have the children around; such crazy thoughts never had a chance of churning up the mind then! But may be the emptiness she felt had to do with Subarna's absence.

Whatever the reason, she suddenly felt weary of dragging the boxes around. Leaving the work incomplete, she went and stood by the window.

The fierce sun was beating down. The sky seemed ready to explode, and the tree by the wayside and the houses lining the street all looked totally scorched. In the next street, a vendor was clanging a plate, trying to sell bell-metal utensils; the sound gradually receded.

Somewhere, far away, a bullock cart screeched, its bells ringing monotonously. Further away, the plaintive cry of cooing doves pierced the stillness of the landscape.

Had Satya never heard doves cooing? She had heard it all her life. But she could not fathom why she felt like sobbing at that sound. She could not understand why she suddenly felt bereft and desolate, and afflicted by a deep loneliness. The idea that nobody had ever felt any fondness, any affection or love for her, gripped her. She felt like she was walking alone on a road parched of tenderness.

Satya stood at the window as though drugged by the scene

outside, ignoring the blaze of the sun and the scorching breeze that touched her face. There was a hurting, gloomy ache mixed with her stupor. What pain was this? What was this emptiness? Would Satya succumb to the strange romantic desire of weeping without a cause?

Perhaps she would have done that, perhaps not. But she suddenly caught sight of Sadu coming, head covered with a wet gamcha, almost hopping in the heat.

Her heart stirred with an ill foreboding. What brought her here at this hour? And she came out of her trance with a start. She moved from the window and quickly came downstairs. As soon as she came down, Sadu's limp voice greeted her, 'Here you are, Bou! Are the boys not around?'

Satya shook her head, and forgot to ask her to sit.

After a moment's hesitation, Sadu sat herself down on a low stool and blurted out, 'There is some news. I'll tell you everything. Just get me some water first.'

After she had gulped down the water and regained her breath, the summary of what Sadu said, in a rather jumbled way, was that Satya would have to go to Baruipur.

Go to Baruipur? Of course, Satya knew she would have to go. And Sadu would go there too, in a few days. No, that was a different matter. Satya would have to leave right away. It would be best if they could go today itself, but it might take a while to organize transport. So, they would leave tomorrow, at dawn. Mukherji-mashai was making all the arrangements; Satya's elder boy would need to go along.

Sadu was trying to speak logically and lightly, but it all sounded so confused, her face looked foolish too. As though she was trying in vain to hide something.

Did she look pale because she had been walking in the sun? Was the tremor in her voice merely an attempt at reassurance? Because that was what she kept repeating, 'Don't be scared. There's nothing to fear.'

The act of reassurance itself seemed to stem from a nest of fear— at least that was what Satya thought. Her blood was beginning to freeze, and after shivering initially, her hands and feet were fast losing their capacity to tremble, and were turning numb.

Satya asked no questions, she just gazed at Sadu's face, bewildered. Should Sadu stop this beating about the bush and speak directly? Sadu hardly had the guts!

So, Sadu kept mouthing hollow assurances, 'Don't worry so much. Don't get flustered over it—you'll go and see that all is well. I shall come with you.'

Sadu would come too! Then there could be no room for further doubt. Satya could almost see the dark shadow of doom looming ahead.

At long last, a single word escaped from Satya's lips, 'Thakurji!'

Was that her voice? So utterly lacking in confidence! Had she reached the point of laying down the very oar with which she had steered her boat through so many seas? Would she give up her resolve of not losing out, ever, and now allow fate to overpower her? Was she suffering from some inner fatigue?

Sadu said, 'Just look at you! Don't lose heart! You've never done that! You're not the type to get perturbed. Then why are you so upset now?'

Satya gave a start. She was embarrassed that she had succumbed this way. But she could hardly prevent the limpness of tone, 'I don't know why, I've this sense of foreboding. I feel the end is near.'

'Goddess Durga protect us!' Sadu quickly consoled her, 'I assure you, nothing untoward has happened. What I can't figure out is why they summoned us so suddenly.'

Yes—they had been summoned. Someone had come from Baruipur to Sadu's house. Sadu was asked to bring Satya's family to Baruipur as soon as possible. They should preferably start today, and if that proved impossible, tomorrow, as early as possible.

Satya sighed, 'I can feel it in my bones, the end is near. I didn't feel this way, even when he'd fallen seriously ill.'

Yes, Satya's mind was stormy with anxiety about Nabakumar. As though her mind had established a link between this unexpected news and her intense sense of emptiness a moment ago. And perhaps, she had grasped her own vulnerability too. Or else, why did she suddenly recall the day she had called in the Sahib-doctor? The memory of her courage in the face of certain doom amazed her now as she thought about it.

So the drums of doom had really started up. Was this the time for Satya to recognize that the backbone of all her courage and daring had always been that spineless man? Now, when the man was ...

'Thakurji! Are you leaving?' Satya clasped Sadu's hand anxiously.

Sadu felt unsettled. Should she deliver this woman from her apprehensions? Should she say ... no, Sadu did not reveal much. She took her hand from Satya's grasp and uttered briskly, 'Don't fret, Bou! I'm telling you, Naba's all right. He is well.' Sadu climbed from the verandah into the courtyard as she spoke, 'Let me go. I have to pack for the journey. You pack too. And send Turu to my place when he gets back.'

Sadu then fled. Satya stood motionless, staring at her retreating figure for a long time. Another anxiety hacked at her heart. Sadu's last words were ringing in her ears, 'Naba is all right. He's well.' What could it be then? Was some other person unwell? Her mind shuddered to utter Subarna's name. But the mind never stops thinking.

The mind has a way of summoning up fears and apprehensions over and over again, no matter how many times one pushes them away.

The idea sunk in slowly. Something terrible must have happened to Subarna. Sadu had not elaborated. But what could have happened? Some terrible illness? Or had god sent the harshest of punishments? Was it possible that Subarna's name would be wiped out of Satya's life forever? The drums of doom began to beat in Satya's blood. Even so, she had to pack. She had to convey their aunt's message to her boys as soon as they got home.

And when the boys returned from their aunt's to say that a bullock cart and a horse-drawn coach had been fixed, and they would get there in a couple of hours, Satya hardly dared to look at their faces. It was not just Satya, who felt restless and low. Her sons too did not dare to look at their mother. They did not dare show their darkened faces to her.

The house would have to be locked up. As she locked each door, it seemed to her that she was closing all the doors of her life. That she would never open them again and embrace her domestic life once again.

But wasn't her elder son to be married in a couple of days? Would Satya not witness that? Would that wedding take place at all? Everything seemed to be fading away, and becoming unreal. Could anyone believe that just yesterday morning Satya had been thrilled to receive a basketful of neatly sliced betel-nuts from Nitai's wife? That she had marvelled at how finely sliced they were as she had poured out the lot? There had to be a reason. The mind usually had premonitions of future events. If there was no reason at all, why had the others who had boarded the coach with her, fallen silent? Sadhan and Saral? And Sadu?

On any other day, Satya would have broken this silence. She would have firmly announced, 'What's the point of hiding things. I can guess something's wrong, no point in torturing me to death. I'm prepared to hear it.'

But she was not able to do that; as though her mind had stopped functioning from the previous afternoon.

The coach was swapped for a cart at the appointed place. And Sadu broke the silence after she had settled down. She addressed the boys, not Satya, 'Your uncle had wanted to come too. But the cart put him off. He's got on in years now. And has lived in Calcutta all his life ...'

Satya could not catch the last bit. The words 'had wanted to come' kept ringing in her ear. Did it mean that it was not just his duty to come, but that he wished nevertheless that he could come?

What scene could that indolent, self-indulgent man desire to behold?

Silence breeds fear. Words, on the other hand, generate courage. So, having spoken once, Sadu found it easy to continue, 'Besides, he told me, Turu's getting married in a few days. I'll hire a palki then.'

So he would come to Turu's wedding. After a few days! So they were still holding on to that hope, were they? The wedding would take place as planned, and they would all come!

Satya felt a trifle embarrassed. She really had become unnecessarily perturbed. And she had made her feelings obvious to everybody. How terrible! Perhaps Subarna was slightly unwell. The messenger must have been a fool to have given a garbled message. So Satya spoke too.

She said, 'Now that you are away, it must be tough for him ...'

All of a sudden, Sadu's face lit up with a smile. Yes, Sadu managed to smile!

'Of course!' she said with a laugh. 'You're right you know. Now it's "Sadu this" and "Sadu that" at every step! So I told him, "Look how devoted you've become in just a few years. After all, you've spent all your life without me!" And the answer to that was, "It's an eternal bond, after all! Not something that will slacken because of early mistakes."'

Sadu's laugh made Satya feel stronger. She almost smiled and said, 'If it is an eternal bond, Thakurji, there's no escape from your co-wife even after death. You're tied to *her* eternally as well! And who knows if other co-wives from previous lives will come to make their claims in heaven!'

Satya nearly laughed aloud.

As if the phrase 'eternal bond' had amused her beyond belief.

FORTY EIGHT

The fiery afternoon heat stood defeated by a chorus of joyous female laughter. They had carried in the bride and placed her on the groom's lap. And the groom had fallen flat on the floor as a result. The rebellious bride had tripped in her attempt to escape. Hence the surge of gleeful giggling! They had both fallen on the wedding bed and were not hurt. So there was no harm done if one laughed, was there? Where else, except at weddings, could people laugh so freely? And in such a chorus it would be hard to tell apart the voice of a daughter from that of a daughter-in-law. Given a chance, those who acted bashful out of fear, would make the fullest use of the opportunity.

That was precisely what they were doing now. With complete freedom! Because it was conceivable!

Had they listened to the head of the groom's party, they would not have had so much time on their hands. They would have had to send off the newly-weds very early because the groom's party wanted to reach home before the inauspicious hour set in. But they had deferred their departure because of the plaintive pleas of the bride's father.

The father of the bride had implored with folded hands, 'There are so many hassles involved in the rituals, the women won't be able to cope. If you could just stay the morning ...'

The head of the groom's party had agreed, and earned for himself the merit of being cooperative. They had been put up at the Ghosh's place, some distance away, and there was no fear of the women's laughter reaching there. The women had passed the morning amusing themselves, the rituals could take place only after the inauspicious hour was over. Perhaps by that time, the most important person would have arrived.

The delay in departure was not a cause for too much worry because even though the groom was from Calcutta, he was staying in the village for the wedding. He had been temporarily put up at the house of the woman who had negotiated the marriage. Very convenient!

All the merrymakers were women from the locality. None of them too young, they were rather middle-aged. It might have been a steamy summer day but it was a wedding, after all. So the women were dressed in their heaviest saris and were sweating profusely. Of course, each one had brought with them an ordinary cotton sari to change into when they sat down to eat. But there was plenty of time yet, the groom's party had to finish eating first.

Well, it looked as though their limitless fun would be restrained somewhat by Khyanta-thakurun who appeared on the scene, irritated by the loud laughter. Instantly the silence of a cremation ground descended on the stage. Casting a sharp eye over the hushed figures, she said, 'Your laughter is bouncing around the marketplace! Can't you have fun on a slightly lower key?'

The silence thickened. Khyanta-thakurun's gaze passed over the key figures of the drama. One was staring at the ground, head bent guiltily like a thief caught in the act and the other was in tears. The body coiled up in a heavy sari was shaking with sobs. After observing the scene, Khyanta-thakurun said with a smile, 'The girl has shrunk to half her size with all that sobbing since yesterday! Can't you make her see sense? Here you are busy having fun!'

Finally, a sound became audible from the silent stage. An unmarried girl blabbered out, 'As if anyone can make her see sense through her tears! Apart from which her ...'

The older woman shrieked out her response, 'How very amusing! Now you fan the dying embers some more! Her face and her eyes are blooming red with all that sobbing! Nobody at her in-laws will call her a "pretty bride". Get her face washed, it's nearly time for the rituals. Start the arrangements. A girl is born to go to her in-laws.'

The young woman's face broke into a grin, 'It's easy for you to say that, Pishi. You hardly know what in-laws are about!'

'Me? Don't you bring me into it. Don't be crazy! I wouldn't curse my foe to suffer my fate. Now stop the racket, and get on with the arrangements.'

'Aren't we supposed to make them play with the cowrie-shells once more?'

'Of course! The inauspicious hour is over now. Let's see if the people from Calcutta arrive by then. Such a hasty wedding! Terrible! Bring the girl, she'll faint in that heavy sari.' With that, Khyanta-thakurun departed.

The women attempted to lift the bride to make her sit up, but without success. It was as if she had resolved to cry herself to death. It was practically impossible to regard her as a 'pretty bride'. But that was not unusual. All brides sobbed and no reveller could ever be expected to bother about such things! Nevertheless, they repeated their unsuccessful charade once again. If four of them bodily lifted the girl, they would manage. Though she flailed her arms and legs about, they were determined not to sacrifice their sense of fun.

The only difference this time was that their laughter was a little subdued, because of Khyanta-thakurun's scolding. From the far end, voices bustling with activity could be heard: Where're the curds? The curds for the ritual of departure? Everything is so disorganized! Goodness! Here's a pot, and now, where's the paan? No curds! I say ...

The interrogator kept on shooting away from her quiver of questions, 'The most important person hasn't appeared yet, who'll perform the "going away" rituals? I say, do you people do the arati with water first, or with paan? How bizarre—you actually use a new gamcha for this ritual? We use a bunch of dyed yellow yarn ...'

It was not difficult to identify the speakers, because all the neighbours had got involved. One could guess from the voice that the interrogator was Anna, Khyanta-thakurun's niece. Only unmarried girls had the freedom to raise their voices in this manner. The answer to Anna's question came in a resonant female voice, 'Yes, we use the corner of the gamcha. Each to their own! Ask your aunt which arati should come first, she'll tell us.'

Immediately, Khyanta-thakurun's voice rang out in displeasure, 'That's what I've done all my life. And yet, the rules don't allow me to touch anything! My job is to give instructions, isn't it? The married ones are the lucky ones; it's enough if they just shake their bangles.'

Somebody whispered, 'Just look! Now she's cast an evil eye on married ones. Goddess Durga help us. Her gaze is not only evil, it's poisonous too! Like Shani's eye, it destroys whatever it looks on. She's been shackled to widowhood all her life. No wonder she blisters with envy when a woman's fed and looked after well.'

A woman rose and left. One of those 'lucky ones' perhaps! Or one who had taken on that role, at any rate. Possibly, she would feel contented if she could start up a blaze by spreading the word while it was still hot. Not unusual in a house that was in the throes of a ceremony, when words were sown and harvested in the form of a war as dramatic as that between Rama and Ravana. And many a song of hurt pride was sung around questions of taking sides, separating friend from friend.

But such things usually remained confined to the women's sphere. They never reached the ears of the men, ever. If they did, they never paid any attention. Their sphere of work was different and wide-ranging. Men would fret about any conspiracy that could wreck the ceremony. Particularly a daughter's wedding.

Though not everyone would think that way. Some would work hard at preserving the dignity of the girl's father before kinsmen, and maintaining cordial ties with the groom's party. Of course, there were people in this world who would work themselves to the bone in order to help others. How else would the world go on? Perhaps such people have always been a majority, even though it often seemed otherwise. After all, just as fire always appears mightier than water, and poison seems more potent compared to a balm, malevolence appears stronger than benevolence. Its prominence, no doubt guaranteed by its dynamic quality.

But no matter how many supporters he had, the father of the bride was bound to feel dizzy with his responsibilities. And in this case too, his head was spinning. But then, was his queasiness caused by the anxiety about guests? Not really. In any case, the wedding, and the feeding of the guests had been taken care of. The going-away ceremony was to take place now. The women who had accompanied the sari-wrapped bride for a dip in the pond had just come back. For the present, everything was in order, just the parting rituals remained. But it was not unknown for vicious traitors to prattle to the groom's party and prevent a happy ending. Following which, the head of the groom's party could threaten to leave without the bride. So many things could happen.

But in this particular case, there was no such fear. Nor any fear of enemies.

So what could have driven the father of the bride to pace madly about since morning? From the house to the courtyard, then outside the house, and finally, to the crossing at Bakultala. It was a summer afternoon, and it appeared as though the blazing sun wished to devour everything. There was some shade here, at Bakultala. But a steaming hot breeze blew continually. There was no way of stopping it.

The man stood there, motionless as one in a stupor. From time to time, he would crane his neck and stand on tip-toe, in an attempt to see something in the distance.

There could be no doubt that he was waiting for something. What could it be? It did not look like something pleasant. For gradually the shadow of a fearful anxiety grew on his face. If any doctor were to check his pulse-rate at that moment, he would have panicked at its rapidity.

Did a criminal's pulse race like this when he was taken in for interrogation?

The wait seemed endless. Did this road that stretched far into the distance have an end at all? Whose arrival did he await?

A girl in a red-striped sari came running and called out, 'Thakurma's calling you!'

The man replied irritably, 'Why?'

'I don't know. She says that time is passing, soon it will become inauspicious or something.'

'Let it,' the bride's father responded, as he attempted to sharpen his gaze and throw it further into the distance. Was that a hint of the tiniest shadow becoming visible on the other side of the blazing green? Or were his eyes playing tricks?

There was no time to wait and disprove that delusion, for the girl spoke again, 'Come quickly. The priest is getting cross.' The girl went indoors. And who knows why, as he gazed after her, he felt his heart flaming as if it had been rubbed with chillies.

Why did he feel that way? Was it because she reminded him of his own daughter of about the same age, whom he had just given away? A moment or two later, he would have to say goodbye to her; exile her to the depths of strange inner quarters where her twitterings would be forever silenced. And perhaps, henceforth, she would cover her face in front of her father as she would before strangers?

But this was an age-old custom, nothing to get so agitated about.

Her mother and her grandmothers, before her, had all done the same. But this reasoning hardly eased the pain, his heart kept writhing.

Perhaps there was more to it than the ache of giving away a daughter. Perhaps a terrible guilt was gnawing at his heart. But why guilt when no crime had been committed? Why the fear if he had done what was right? There could be no doubt that this man was terribly faint-hearted.

The girl came running out once more and said in a scared, panicky voice, 'Look! Your mother is creating hell! She's asking if the kingdom should come to a standstill until her majesty arrives?'

After that he could no longer stand there. He had to run indoors as fast as he could.

And yet, had he waited a moment longer, the expected figure would have been visible. For over that dry, scorching field a hazy shadow was approaching and slowly taking definite shape. It seemed as though the pressure from the searing blaze was retarding the movement of the bullocks. No matter how hard the driver tugged at their tails and abused them, they seemed to be rolling backwards.

Frequently, Sadu craned her neck out of the thatch cover and anxiously asked, 'Here, boy! Your bullocks seem to be moving backwards. We're in a real hurry.'

The driver's retort was resentful, 'What can I do? I'm trying my best. They just refuse to run! The sun god too is shooting down fire, isn't he?'

The rancour in his voice was accompanied by a thrash and the bullocks scrambled forward a bit. Unable to endure this sudden jolt, Sadhan and Saral fell on their sides and Satya said in an exhausted voice, as she clutched the bamboo pole on the thatch, 'Let it be, no need to rush them. We might become guilty of cow-killing.'

Sadu called on the Goddess Durga. The cart speeded up a little, and, the road began to feel familiar.

But why were the doves cooing today? As if they wished to antagonize Satya for some reason. Or was that the sound of human weeping? It did sound like the collective cry of many female voices!

What was its source? The sound grew sharper as the cart drew closer. No, Satya would shut her ears, and her thoughts. She would deaden her senses, till she reached that cremation ground.

The continuous joyful ululations of the women attempted to compensate for the absence of pomp at the wedding. The rituals performed the day after the wedding occur in reverse order. The groom is made to play with the cowrie-shells before the bride, and the arati is done for the bride first. The woman who is in charge of the groom's side must also be a different one. So, a different woman had to occupy the stage. The search for a new female lead was on.

'Who will do it? Anna? Come here, Anna! Go wrap a nice sari around yourself. Don't you have an armlet? Or an ornate good-luck charm to wear on your arms? Borrow from someone then! It'll look attractive when you do the arati.'

Someone said, 'How sad that her mother missed all of it! Couldn't participate at all! How terrible! If she'd come now, she could have done the arati. She's ill-fated!'

Fate, of course! Where else could all the streams of lament flow into and lose themselves? All questions reached their final destination there. And so, dedicating events to the hands of fate, the grieving women proceeded to fasten the loops on Anna's armlet.

Once again, the ululations started, a little girl began to blow on a conch-shell like a proper matron, and the women started chattering all at once. Suddenly above that babble, a shout was heard, 'Here they are! Here!'

Delighted voices surrounded the cart that had taken so long to arrive! All eyes were feeling worn from staring at the road! Had they arrived just a little earlier, the groom could have been ritually blessed by his mother-in-law. Never mind, some good would come off it yet—at least she would be able to see them!

But who were these people? What were they saying? And to whom? And this piteous promise of pleasure for 'at least being able to see them'—was it in keeping with the riotousness of such festivities?

Why had Satya stiffened with intimations of something

inauspicious? After all, everything around her signalled to the contrary—the decorated puja pots, the alpana in the courtyard, the shamiana. Everything was bright and gleaming in the blazing sun. Each a symbol of auspiciousness.

But what were these preparations for? Sadhan, who was to be married was with Satya. Perhaps this family had an additional ceremony when a wedding was fixed! And everything here had been set up for that. Was that why Sadu had rushed her here? Just for fun?

What a hideous bit of fun!

But then, why did the ululation sound so jarring? Like doves cooing, like someone sobbing? Satya had heard women ululating all her life. She had never cared for it, but never before had she experienced such a hollowing of her heart!

Where was that sparkling face? And why hadn't two small plump arms come running to embrace her ecstatically, oblivious of all else, after hearing that she had arrived at last?

And that ever-familiar face? Which had made itself indispensable to Satya with its perpetually contrary pulls of affection and resentment.

With faint, unfocussed feelings, Satya entered Elokeshi's courtyard. Rather, she got there without using her feet. She was propelled there by the jostling women and children.

No sooner had she got there, her eyes turned to stone.

Who had painted this picture for Satya to see—this picture, so familiar to Bengali homes?

Who was that?

The scene was a familiar one—the ceremonial mandap decorated with young plantain trees, the married women greeting bride and groom with the arati. But who was that unknown woman? She, whose red silk sari has fallen off her face, oblivious of custom? Had Satya seen that face before? Had Satya ever seen those eyes before, wounded and helpless like an animal's? Never! Not in her life had she ever beheld them! The impact of unfamiliarity hardened her eyes to stone.

But had her ears turned to stone too? Why were so many unfamiliar voices dashing against her ears?

'Naba? Where did you disappear now? Weren't you restless so long for your wife? Now whom did you give the money to—the money for the leave-taking ritual? Wash your hands and your face, Bouma. Here, change your sari and come and bless your daughter and son-in-law! You've just the one daughter, and you couldn't see the wedding! But how could you come? You didn't get to hear of it on time. Your mother-in-law was in such a rush, as if the wedding would run away or something! But look! You now have a handsome son-in-law—with no effort at all! And don't they look good together? It's a good match, a fine family, close friends too.'

An engine seemed to chugging through Satya's head—the words spun mechanically, ringing like metal 'Thank goodness, you'd sent the girl with Naba. Your mother-in-law's bosom friend's daughter had come visiting just then, that's how it all started. Mukta's heart melted at the sight of your beautiful daughter. She claimed she couldn't rest till she had her as a daughter-in-law. The boy's birth month is Ashar, so it was best to marry him off in Jaishtha. Your mother-in-law was giving Naba hell for trying to get his son married before his daughter. And out of fear, Naba ... Oh my! Look at that! Here Sadu! Bouma is going out towards Bakultala. What for? Hey, hey Naba! Boys! Does your mother want to get on to the cart again, or what?'

Naba, who had been avoiding the scene, now made a public appearance. He asked Sadu tremulously, 'Didn't you tell her about the wedding?'

Nobody would ever find out why Sadu suddenly turned tough. She said adamantly, 'No, I didn't!'

'So that's why! Now I know! This is what happens when you bring her here without telling her.'

Nabakumar retorted huffily, 'How strange! If she were brought earlier, she'd have just put an end to the wedding, that's all! So what was the point of not telling her now that it is over? Why didn't you tell her?'

Why did the ever-patient Sadu suddenly turned impatient? She remained unrelenting, and responded in a hard and steely voice, 'I'd have told you why I didn't, had you been capable of understanding. I have repaid my debts to your family by bringing her here to you. But don't you glare at me for not being the hard-hearted butcher. I can see that she'll not even accept water from this place. She'll go back, and I shall leave with her.'

Sadu marched out briskly. Towards Bakultala.

And the bride created a bizarre scene. Suddenly she sat down in the courtyard and began to sob loudly in front of the groom, 'Why did you all do this to me? My mother will kill me!' But she had no way of following her mother—the end of her sari was tied to her husband's dhoti.

An absolute, inseparable bond. A bond that supposedly extended its power and its domain beyond eternity.

The entire western sky had amassed a red radiance that spread over the fields, the ponds and the trees.

The drooping bullocks had revived after some grass and water and were pulling the cart faster, soothed by a mild evening breeze. They had been ordered to cover the huge Bamunpara field by dusk. After that, if it really became impossible to proceed, they would rest near the market at Hat tala. Of course. it would be a relief if they found a horse-drawn coach there.

Many years ago, Ramkali had left this very village without pausing to refresh himself. Today, Ramkali's devoted daughter was emulating her father's action. Ramkali had had his palki with him. His daughter had none. So she had had to bribe the reluctant driver. She wore only two bangles on her left hand—an iron one and a conch shell one. She no longer wore the thick gold bangles with the shark-head design. That was the only thing she had with her, and she had given it away. How valuable was it? Surely, it could never be too high a price to pay to free herself from that 'eternal bond'!

Having released herself, Satya had left the village. But had it all happened as smoothly as that? That could hardly be expected! Nearly the whole village had milled around the cart trying to dissuade her. But Satya had not heeded their words. She had calmly said just one thing, 'Why are you wasting your time when I cannot agree.'

In the end, Elokeshi had arrived too. She had made the gesture of folding her hands and said, 'When you say you cannot agree, you mean you won't comply, right? So, here I am, your mother-in-law, pleading with you, please forgive me. I've done wrong, I admit it a hundred times. I hadn't realized that the girl was just yours, that she didn't belong to Naba at all! And without knowing that, I acted as a grandmother should, and tried doing good! Never mind, what has happened has happened, you can't undo a marriage. So, why create a scandal in front of the whole village, eh?'

Satya had sat motionless through it all, and controlled herself. She had just turned her face away. But what about Nabakumar, Elokeshi's son? Had he not swallowed his pride and come to make amends? Of course he had, as was inevitable. Ultimately, he too had almost folded his hands, 'Since there isn't a way out, why ...'

Although she had not talked to Elokeshi, Satya had spoken to her son, 'That's what I'll have to figure out for the rest of my life—if there is a way out or not.'

For the rest of her life!

'Is that what you'll think about for the rest of your life?'

For once, Satya had met his wounded, abject, imploring gaze with her stone eyes. And she had said in a voice bereft of emotions, 'Would that be too much? It wouldn't be enough even if I thought for several lifetimes! Would I ever find an answer?'

Nabakumar had responded gloomily, 'I've never ever understood your words, and I don't understand them now. But let me ask you, is Subarna the only one that matters to you? Don't Turu or Khoka matter at all?'

'I shall also need to think about who matters how much.'

'All my life I've noticed that love and affection mean very little to you. Your stubborness reigns supreme! Even so, I beg of you, at least for my sake, stop being headstrong, just this once.'

'Please forgive me.' Satya had drawn her sari over head, tighter.

Nabakumar had burst into tears. He had wiped his eyes with the end of his dhoti.

But Satya had always been cruel. Could she have ever changed just by resolving to stop being the 'goddess of wrath'? She had lowered her eyes and said, 'For thirty years, I'd done things for your sake. Now, at long last, I wish to take my own self into consideration.'

'Won't you bless your Subarna for once?'

Was Satya suddenly struck by lightning? Hadn't her mother, Bhubaneswari trembled once at such a question? On that last day of her life?

She avoided looking at Nabakumar's face, and said calmly, 'I'm going away forever; why do you want to force me to be rude now?'

The cart had started moving, but Nabakumar had followed it, 'Your father was such a judicious man and yet, he too performed the gauri-daana and gave you away when you were eight. How come you don't remember that at all?'

Satya's stony eyes had suddenly flashed, 'Who says that I don't? I have thought about it all my life! And now I shall go to my father and ask for an explanation.'

Even then, Nabakumar had held on to the flank of the cart. 'I promise you, I shall bring you back your Subarna by creating some misunderstanding with the in-laws ...'

Suddenly, Satya had done something unusual. In that open field, in front of everybody, she had reached out and clasped his hand. And had said in a voice half-crazed, 'Really? You'll bring her back? You'll wipe out this doll's marriage and bring me back my Subarna?'

Sadu was sitting inside the thatched cover of the cart. She had kept quiet all this while. She had softly said, 'Can one wipe it out just because one wants to? Is it something that can be wiped off? A ceremony which the gods themselves have witnessed?'

Satya had let go of Nabakumar's hand. She had smiled a strange smile, 'Those are the questions I shall take to my father. Do the gods really come and bless every marriage? Are all marriages bonds for this life and beyond? Those are the things I want to ask.'

Sadu had turned to Nabakumar and said calmly, 'One would never find the answers in one lifetime. Naba, now don't delay further. Go home, there's loads of work waiting to be done. No need to delay and start a fight with the in-laws.'

Nabakumar had made one last attempt. Even as he had turned to go, he said, 'I'm the culprit, punish me. What has Turu done? Why won't you be there for his wedding?'

'I don't have to be present. I can bless him from afar.'

It was becoming impossible to keep up. The cart was gathering speed and rendering all appeals useless. All the churned up emotions now burst forth, 'I knew it! You're not one to listen to requests. But let me warn you, nobody will carry you on his shoulders to Kashi.'

Had Satya finally felt relieved? Because here, at last, was her chance to leave with a laugh? Was that the reason her tone had eased and she had laughed in her familiar way?

'Goodness, why should I even demand that? Now that I'm climbing off your shoulders forever, I shall depend on my own feet and see if I can trust them to walk on Mother Earth. But that's also part of another question that I have.'

The driver could no longer restrain the bullocks which were raring to go. Nabakumar had done an about turn and jumped onto the cart.

'That's exactly why a woman shouldn't have any property. You dare to reject your husband because you have the power of your father's property! It's not good for a woman to be so daring. I tell you, you'll have a real hard time. That's my curse, as your husband!' He had raged.

Of course Satyabati knew that he was cursing out of anger, resentment, shame, frustration, and a sense of public insult, so she had remained unperturbed. She had almost laughed, 'That's what you've all done since time began—as husbands, fathers, brothers, or sons—it's nothing new! Our lives are cursed! But the property you mention, let me tell you that I had forgotten completely about that tattered piece of paper. Now that you've reminded me, it would be an insult to throw away what my father has given me. If Sadhan and Saral grow up to be worthy boys, let them use it to build a school for girls in Tribeni. And … and, tell them to name it "Bhubaneswari Vidyalaya". And wait—' Satya wrapped the end of her sari around her neck and touched her husband's feet, 'All my life I have said many wrong and hurtful things, and I've made you suffer a lot. Forgive me if you can.'

Then Sadu had scolded mildly, 'Naba, go home! There's no use running after your wife. You never had understood her, and you won't, even now. But let me say something—may be you lack sense, but how could you have no feelings at all? When you decided to listen to your mother and marry off your daughter, didn't you think of your wife even once? And you've lived with her for thirty years! How could you not have the tenderness one feels even for pets?'

Nabakumar had responded fiercely, 'How can you talk like that, Sadudi? Why would I think of her? I was really cornered …'

'Naba, you get off now! Your daughter and son-in-law are waiting, and the in-laws must be hopping mad. It won't do not to go there. Think of the girl.'

'Think of the girl! That's supposed to be *my* duty, is it?' Nabakumar had sounded like a madman, 'What about her loving mother who's leaving her all battered, eh? There she was standing stiff with fear and her mother just bolted out of the house without even sparing her a glance! Didn't that break her heart? What wrong had *she* done?'

Satyabati had stopped responding. She had shut her eyes and was resting her tired head against the thatch covering. Sadu had said firmly, 'Naba, will you get off?'

Nabakumar had done just that. And he had walked away, wiping his eyes, not turning to look back even once.

The cart moved on. It passed the field and approached the marketplace. A horse-coach would be available there. Saral would arrange for it. Sadhan had felt too annoyed with his mother to come along. His father might have done something unsanctioned, but the shameless commotion created by his mother was far worse, and, unbearable.

As the journey by bullock cart drew to a close, it was hard to ignore the sky. The whole of the western sky was awash with red-gold. Was there really a different world on the other side—where they had set fire to someone's funeral pyre? Was this the light of that blaze? Or was this the colour of a bride's red sari held out to the sun's last rays?

At one point, Sadu said with a sigh, 'But why give up hope just because she's married? How could you abandon Subarna forever? You yourself matured and grew up after you were married.'

Satya looked at Sadu. She could not resist a reply. She said softly, 'Well, now you've proof of how much good that has done!'

'But it's others who have let you down. You can't judge yourself from that. You really had such hopes for Subarna.'

Satya turned her gaze skywards. Was she looking for Subarna's face? Did she find it? Was that the reason why she responded in a trance, 'If Subarna innately possesses all that it takes to make a worthy human, she will become one. On her own strength. Then she will understand her mother. Otherwise, she'll think as her father does—that her mother is heartless! I can't stop her from thinking that way.'

'But your father has retired from the world and now lives in Kashi. Will it be right to disturb him and become a burden?'

Suddenly Satya seemed to regain her earlier firmness. She said in her characteristic manner, 'No, why should I disturb him or become a burden?'

She added with a smile, 'A long time ago, before Subarna was born, I'd opened a school and would play at teaching women—do you remember that? I'll find out if I still remember that game. It should earn a woman enough for her keep.'

'You'll earn your living! So that's what made you bold enough to leave home!' Sadu took a deep breath, 'I'm older than you and I'm not supposed to touch your feet, but that's just what I feel like doing. But didn't you say you want to go to Kashi?'

'Yes, of course. I'll go to Kashi, to my father. There are many questions I've stored up all my life. I shall go and seek out the answers first.'

Suddenly, a silence descended. The cart came to a halt at the marketplace. Hat tala. The journey by bullock cart was over.

GLOSSARY

Alpana	auspicious designs made on the floor with powdered rice paste for weddings and pujas
Alta	a lac-dye used by Bengali Hindu women to colour their feet, especially during pujas and weddings
Anantachaturdashi	the fourteenth day of the lunar fortnight in the month of Bhadra in the Bengali calendar when widows particularly observe certain rituals
Anhik	a ritual prayer offered twice a day, at dawn and desk
Arati	a part of a ritual during a puja when the sacred flame is waved in front of the idol
Ashar	the third month in the Bengali calendar, corresponding roughly to June–July
Ashtami	the eighth day of either fortnight of the lunar month
Ashwin	the sixth month in the Bengali calendar, corresponding roughly to September–October
Avatar	incarnation
Ayurveda	traditional Hindu medicine
Babu	a Bengali gentleman, usually Hindu; often prefixed to the first name as a mark of respect
Baisakh	the first month of the Bengali calendar, corresponding to April–May
Baksheesh	a tip
Bhadu	a woman worshipped in parts of the Manbhum region in Bengal (at present in the Purulia district)
Bonde	a sweet made by deep-frying tiny balls of gram flour and dipping in syrup
Bou-than	a term used to address the wife of one's elder brother or male cousin
Bagdini	a woman from the Bagdi caste
Badshah	the ruler of an empire
Bamun	brahmin

Basar	literally, the bridal bed. Here the reference is to the practice of relatives and other guests spending the night in the same room as the newly-wed couple right after the ceremony, and singing and teasing them.
Behai	formal way of addressing one's daughter's or son's father-in-law
Behula	legendary figure who danced before the gods in order to win back the life of her husband
Beyan	formal way of addressing a woman from one's daughter's or son's in-laws'
Bibi	a Bengali woman who imitates an European woman, especially the latter's leisurely lifestyle
Bigha	a measure of land equal to a quarter of a hectare
Bhadra	the fifth month in the Bengali calendar roughly corresponding to August–September
Bhadralok	educated Bengali gentleman
Bhagvati	another name for Durga
Bhori	a unit of weight used to measure gold and silver, equivalent to 180 grains
Bori	a small conical ball made from the paste of lentils mixed with other ingredients. This is usually sun-dried and fried, and added to curries.
Boro	eldest
Bou	wife; a woman would be addressed as 'bou' at her in-laws'
Brahmo	a member of the Hindu organization founded by Rammohun Roy in 1830. The members believed in one god, were opposed to caste practices and attempted to initiate the remarriage of widows.
Brata	rituals, usually for women
Catechu	Gambier or a similar vegetable extract, containing tannin, used in paan
Chanabora	a sweet made by deep-frying balls of cottage cheese and dipping in syrup
Chaitra	the last month of the Bengali calendar
Chhoto	youngest

Chaddar	a shawl
Cham-cham	a type of fried sweet which is soaked in sugar syrup
Chana-bora	fried sweets made of cottage cheese
Chandrakona	very fine cloth
Chaturdashi	the last day of the lunar fortnight
Choga	a loose outer garment worn by men
Chullah	a stove that uses that uses coal and wood as fuel
Chyada	ceremonial gift of dry food and ritual items made to brahmins and other guests during weddings and other ceremonies
Cubeb	a tropical shrub bearing pungent berries used in paan
Cutcherry	a magistrate's court
Dashami	the tenth day of the lunar fortnight
Dada	elder brother
Dasi	literally, female slave, a term commonly used as the last name by non-Brahmin women
Dhop kirtan	a popular form of kirtan started by Madhukon or Madhusudan Kinnor of Jessore district of Bengal, now in Bangladesh
Dhopi	a female singer of the dhop-kirtan
Dharamshala	a resthouse for pilgrims
Dharma	duty, religion
Durba	young grass used in rituals
Ekadashi	the eleventh phase of the moon when devout Hindus, especially widows, are supposed to fast
Gaja	a fried dry sweet made of flour
Gamcha	a piece of light cloth, often red in colour, used like a towel or a face-cloth
Gauri-daana	the ceremonial giving away of an eight-year-old daughter in marriage. The gauri-daana promised immense merit to the father of the bride.
Ghagra	a woman's long skirt gathered at the waist
Ghat	steps leading to the pond
Ginni	the mistress of the house

Guru dakshina	the ceremonial offering made to a teacher after one has completed training
Hathe-khari	the ceremony which initiates a child into reading and writing; traditionally, performed only for boys during Saraswati puja
Itu	a ritual of worshipping the sun god every Sunday, performed in the month of Agrahayana (the eight month of the Bengali calendar)
Jaishtha	the second month in the Bengali calendar, corresponding roughly to May–June
Jamdani	a type of fine cloth with woven floral motifs originating in Dhaka
Jatra	the traditional travelling theatre of Bengal and Orissa
Jethi	aunt, the wife of one's father's elder brother
Kaash	a type of cane with white fluffy flowers that usually sprout between September–October
Kaka	uncle, one's father's younger brother
Kaliyug	in Hindu tradition, the fourth and final age of human history characterized by corrupt and immoral people
Kanya-daana	the ceremonial giving away of a daughter in marriage. Unlike the gauri-daana where the girl child had to be eight years old, the kanya-daana is performed for any marriageable girl.
Karta	head of the house; a respectful form of address to upper class men by their subordinates
Kathak-thakur	a person who makes a living out of telling traditional stories
Kaviraj	a traditional doctor who practises Ayurveda
Khaja	a crispy sweet made from flour and sugar
Khas	land that is directly controlled by the landlord
Khichri	a cooked dish of rice, lentils and vegetables
Khuri	one's father's brother's wife
Khuro	father's brother
Kirtan	devotional songs usually about the love of Radha and Krishna, popularized in Bengal in the fifteenth and sixteenth centuries under the influence of Chaitanya

Kul	family; also name of a berry
Kulin	formerly in Bengal, a member of a high social class which enjoyed ritual status
Magh	the tenth month in the Bengali calendar
Malai	cream
Mama	one's mother's brother
Mami	one's mother's brother's wife
Manasa	the goddess of snakes
Manda-mithai	generic term for sweets
Mandap	a temporary platform used for wedding ceremonies and other rituals
Mashai	a respectful form of address; also used as a suffix with surnames
Maund	a unit of weight equivalent to 40 seers
Mejo	second, the one who comes after the eldest in a family
Mela	fair
Memsahib	European woman
Meye	girl
Mihidana	a sweet dish consisting of very small orange-coloured globules
Mlechcha	non-Hindu, in this context British
Muri-murki	a sweet snack made by mixing plain puffed-rice with sugar or jaggery coated puffed-rice
Napit-beyan	a term of address used for the barber women. Beyan is a respectful term for an older woman who belongs to the in-laws' family
Bath-bou	granddaughter-in-law
Notun-bou	new bride
Notun-thakurma	literally, 'new' grandmother, usually used in the context of the extended family
Paduka	wooden sandals
Palki	an earlier mode of transport signifying high social status. A palki had a covered seat inside a wooden structure with two poles, which four to six men would carry on their shoulders.

Pishi	aunt, one's father's sister
Pishe-mashai	uncle, the husband of one's father's sister
Pranam	a way of greeting a person older in age or status, usually by touching the person's feet
Prithvi-daana	the ritual gifting which is part of the last rites of a Hindu
Puri	a rolled out ball of flour, circular in shape and fried in oil. Puris are eaten with curries. In ritual terms it is less polluting to have puris when dining out. Puris were offered to brahmins when they were invited to a meal in a lower caste home during a ceremony.
Rabri	a dish of thickened milk to which sugar and flavouring agents have been added
Rasagolla	a ball of cottage cheese cooked in syrup
Sahib	European man
Sandesh	a dry sweet made from cottage cheese
Savitri	in Hindu mythology, the wife of Satyavan, who questioned Yama, the god of death, and won back her husband. Savitri is worshipped as a chaste woman.
Sejuti	a brata performed by unmarried girls in the evenings by lighting a lamp and chanting mantras, usually around November–December, i.e., corresponding to the Bengali month of Agrhayana
Shaad	a ritual performed for a pregnant woman, just before she gives birth
Shani	Saturn
Shakta	one who worships Shakti or the female principle of divine energy
Shastra	sacred texts of the Hindus
Sraddha	a Hindu ritual or ceremony performed for the dead
Sonar-Bene	a person of the goldsmith caste
Stotra	ceremonial chant
Taluka	a private estate acquired from the government and passed on to a younger family member after the death of the owner
Tandava	in Hindu mythology, Lord Shiva's dance of destruction

Thakurda	grandfather
Thakurji	sister-in-law
Thakur-po	brother-in-law
Thakurun	a term of address used for an older woman who is not a kin
Thali	a metal plate
Than	white or cream coloured cloth without a border, usually worn by widows
Tol	a traditional school
Trayadashi	the thirteenth day after the full moon
Tussar	a rough-textured silk, usually cream or beige in colour
Vaidya	a doctor who practices Ayurveda, usually belonging to a caste of the same name
Vaishnav	a Hindu sect that worships Vishnu
Vidyalaya	school
Yagna	ceremonial sacrifice performed to appease the gods; any large-scale celebration
Yuga	for Hindus, any of the four ages in the life of the world